SEPTOLOGY

JON FOSSE

SEPTOLOGY

TRANSLATED BY DAMION SEARLS

Published 2022
from the Writing and Society Research Centre
at Western Sydney University
by the Giramondo Publishing Company
PO Box 752
Artarmon NSW 1570 Australia
www.giramondopublishing.com

Designed by Jenny Grigg
Typeset by Andrew Davies
in Tiempos Regular 9/15pt

Printed and bound by Ligare Book Printers
Distributed in Australia by NewSouth Books

A catalogue record for this book is available from the National Library of Australia.

ISBN 978-1-922725-36-3

9 8 7 6 5 4 3 2 1

The Giramondo Publishing Company acknowledges the support of Western Sydney University in the implementation of its book publishing program.

This project has been assisted by the Commonwealth Government through the Australia Council, its arts funding and advisory body.

Contents

The Other Name

'And I will give him a white stone, and on the stone a new name written, which no one knows except him who receives it.'
Revelation

'Dona nobis pacem.'
Agnus Dei

I

And I see myself standing and looking at the picture with the two lines that cross in the middle, one purple line, one brown line, it's a painting wider than it is high and I see that I've painted the lines slowly, the paint is thick, two long wide lines, and they've dripped, where the brown line and purple line cross the colours blend beautifully and drip and I'm thinking this isn't a picture but suddenly the picture is the way it's supposed to be, it's done, there's nothing more to do on it, I think, it's time to put it away, I don't want to stand here at the easel any more, I don't want to look at it any more, I think, and I think today's Monday and I think I have to put this picture away with the other ones I'm working on but am not done with, the canvases on stretchers leaning against the wall between the bedroom door and the hall door under the hook with the brown leather shoulder bag on it, the bag where I keep my sketchpad and pencil, and then I look at the two stacks of finished paintings propped against the wall next to the kitchen door, I already have ten or so big paintings finished plus four or five small ones, something like that, fourteen paintings in all in two stacks next to each other by the kitchen door, since I'm about to have a show, most of the paintings are approximately square, as they put it, I think, but some-times I also paint long narrow ones and the one with the two lines crossing is noticeably oblong, as they put it, but I don't want to put this one into the show because I don't like it much, maybe all things considered it's not really a painting, just two lines, or maybe I want to keep it for myself and not sell it? I like to keep my best pictures, not sell them, and maybe this is one of them, even though I don't like it? yes, maybe I do want to hold onto it even if you might say it's a failed painting? I don't know why I'd want to keep it, with the bunch of other pictures I have up in the attic, in a storage room, instead of getting rid of it, or maybe, anyway, maybe Åsleik wants the picture? yes, to give

Sister as a Christmas present? because every year during Advent I give him a painting that he gives to Sister as a Christmas present and I get meat and fish and firewood and other things from him, yes, and I mustn't forget, as Åsleik always says, that he shovels the snow from my driveway in the winter too, yes, he says things like that too, and when I say what a painting like that can sell for in Bjørgvin Åsleik says he can't believe people would pay so much for a painting, anyway whoever does pay that much money must have a lot of it, he says, and I say I know what you mean about it being a lot of money, I think so too, and Åsleik says well in that case he's getting a really good deal, in that case it's a very expensive Christmas present he's giving Sister every year, he says, and I say yes, yes, and then we both fall silent, and then I say that I do give him a little money for the salt-cured lamb ribs for Christmas, dry-cured mutton, salt cod, firewood, and for shovelling the snow, maybe a bag with some groceries that I bought in Bjørgvin when I've gone there to run an errand, I say, and he says, a little embarrassed, yes I do do that, fair's fair, he says, and I think I shouldn't have said that, Åsleik doesn't want to accept money or anything else from me, but when I think about how I have enough money to get by and he has almost none, yes, well, I slip him a few more bills, quickly, furtively, as if neither of us knows it's happening, and when I go run errands in Bjørgvin I always buy something for Åsleik, I think, because I may not make much money but he makes almost nothing compared to me, I think, and I look at the stack of finished paintings with the homemade stretchers they're on facing out and every painting has a title painted in thick black oil paint on the top board of the stretcher, and the painting I'm looking at the back of, at the front of the stack, is called *And the Waves Beat Their Message,* titles are very important to me, they're part of the picture itself, and I always paint the title in black on the top of the stretcher, I make my stretchers myself, I always have and I always will as long as I paint pictures, I think, and I think that there may actually be too many paintings here for a show but I'll take them all to The Beyer Gallery anyway, Beyer can put some of them in the side room of the gallery, in The Bank, as he calls the room where he stores pictures that aren't in the show, I think, and then I take another look at the picture with the two lines crossing, both in impasto as they put it, and the paint has run a little and where the lines cross the colours have turned such a strange colour, a beautiful colour, with no name, they usually don't have names because obviously there can't be names for all the countless colours in the world, I think and I step a few feet back from the picture and stop and look at it and then turn off the light and stand there looking at the picture in the dark, because it's dark outside, at this time of year it's dark, or almost dark, all day long, I think and I look at the picture and my eyes get used to the darkness and I see the lines, see them cross, and I see that there's a soft light in the painting, yes, a soft invisible light, well then yes so it probably is a good painting, maybe, I think, and I don't want to look at the picture any more, I think, but still I'm standing and looking at it, I have to stop looking at it now, I think, and then I look at the round table over by the window, there are two chairs next to it and one of them, the one on the left, that's where I sat and sit, and the right-hand one was where Ales always sat, when she was still alive, but then she died, too young, and I don't want to think about that, and my sister Alida, she died too young too, and I don't want to think about that either, I think, and I see myself sitting there in my chair looking out at the fixed point in the waters of the Sygne Sea that I always look at, my landmark, with the tops of the pines that grow below my house in the middle of the centre pane in the bisected window, in the right-hand part, because the window is divided in two and both parts can be opened and each side is divided into three rows and the tops of the pines will be in the middle row of the right side and I can make out the pines and I've found the mark, right at the midline I can see waves out there in the darkness and I see myself sitting there looking at the waves and I see myself walking over to my car where it's parked in front of The Beyer Gallery, I'm there in my long black coat with my brown leather bag over my shoulder, I've just been to The Coffeehouse, I didn't have much of an appetite, I often don't, and just skip dinner, but today I've had a simple open-faced ground-beef sandwich with onions and now the day's over and I've bought everything I wanted to buy in Bjørgvin so now it's time for me to drive home to Dylgja, after all it's a long drive, I think, and I get into the car, I put the brown shoulder bag down on the passenger seat and start the car and then leave Bjørgvin the way Beyer taught me, one day he showed me the way, showed me how to drive into Bjørgvin and out of Bjørgvin, how to get to The Beyer Gallery and then leave The Beyer Gallery the same way going in the opposite direction, I think, and I'm driving out of Bjørgvin and I fall into the nice stupor you can get into while you're driving and I realise I'm driving right past the apartment building where Asle lives, in Sailor's Cove, right at the edge of the sea, there's a little wharf in front of it, I think, and I see Asle lying there on his sofa and he's shaking, his whole body's shivering, and Asle thinks can't this shaking stop? and he's thinking he slept on the couch last night because he couldn't get up and get undressed and go lie down in bed, and the dog, he couldn't even, Bragi, the dog, couldn't go outside, and he's still drunk, he thinks, really drunk, and he needs to stop shaking so badly, his whole body's shaking, not just his hands, Asle thinks and he thinks that now he really has to get up and go to the kitchen and get a little something to drink to stop the shaking, because last night he didn't get undressed and go to bed, no, he just stayed where he was and passed out on the sofa, he thinks, and now he's lying here staring into space while his body keeps shaking, he thinks, and everything is, yes, what is it? an emptiness? a nothingness? a distance? yes, maybe yes, yes maybe it's a distance, he thinks, and now he has to go pour himself a little drink so that the worst of the shaking will go away, Asle thinks, and then, then, he'll go outside and go out to sea, that's what he'll do, Asle thinks, that's the only thing he wants, the only thing he longs to do is go away, disappear, the way his sister Alida went away back when she was a child, she just lay there, dead in her bed, Sister, Asle thinks, and the way the neighbour boy went away, Bård was his name, he fell off his father's rowboat into the sea and he couldn't swim and he didn't make it back on board the boat or back to land, Asle thinks and he thinks now he'll make an effort and get up and then go to the kitchen and pour himself a stiff drink so the shaking stops a little and then he'll walk around the apartment and turn off the lights, walk around the whole apartment and make sure everything is neat and organised, and then leave, lock the door, go down to the sea and then go out to sea and just keep going out into the sea, Asle thinks, and he thinks that thought again and again, it's the only thought he can think, the thought that he's going to go out to sea, he thinks, that he's going to disappear into the sea, into the nothingness of the waves, Asle thinks and the thought goes around and around in his head, it won't stop, it just keeps on circling around, this one thought is all that's real, everything else is empty distance, empty closeness, no, nothing is empty, but it's something like empty, there in this darkness, and every other thought he tries to think he can't think, the other thoughts are too hard, even the idea that he should raise his arm seems too hard, and he realises he's shaking, even though he's not moving his whole body's shaking and why can't he manage the thought of getting up? of lifting his hand? why is the only thought he can think that he wants to go out to sea? that he wants to drink enough to make the shaking stop and then turn off the lights in the apartment, maybe straighten up the apartment if it needs it, because everything needs to be neat and tidy before he goes away, Asle thinks, and he thinks that maybe he should've written something to The Boy, but The Boy is a grown man now, isn't he, he hasn't been a child for a long time, he lives in Oslo, or maybe he could call him? but he doesn't like talking on the phone and neither does The Boy, Asle thinks, or maybe he should write to Liv? after all they were married for many years, but they were divorced so long ago that there are no hard feelings between them, because he can't go away just like that without saying goodbye to someone, that feels wrong, but the other woman he was married to, Siv, he can't even bear to think about her, she just left and took The Son and The Daughter away and moved far away from him, she'd left before he knew it, he hadn't thought about getting divorced at all and she told him she'd had enough and took The Son and The Daughter and left, she had already found a new place for herself and them, she said, and he never noticed anything, Asle thinks, and then for a while The Son and The Daughter came to spend every weekend with him, he thinks, but then Siv found a new husband and she took The Son and The Daughter and moved to a place somewhere in Trøndelag to be with this new man, she took the children and went away and then he was alone again and then Siv wrote and said he had to pay for this and that and as soon as she asked him he paid her, whenever he had money, he thinks, and why think about that? Asle thinks, it's just something that happened, now everything's been taken care of, everything's ready, all the painting supplies are in their proper place there on the table and the pictures are leaning against the wall, stretchers facing out, the brushes are in a neat row, all cleaned, big to small, all wiped clean with turpentine, and the tubes of paint are also arranged properly, next to each other, full to empty, every cap screwed on tight, and there's nothing on the easel, everything's clean and taken care of and in its proper place and he's just lying there shaking, not thinking anything, just shaking and then he again thinks he should get up and leave and lock the door and then go out and then go down to the sea and out into the sea, go out into the sea, go out until the waves crash over him and he disappears into the sea, he thinks it again and again, otherwise nothing, otherwise the darkness of nothingness, the way it sometimes sweeps through him in quick glimpses like an illumination and yes, yes, then he's filled with a kind of happiness and he thinks that there might be a place somewhere that's an empty nothingness, an empty light, and just think, what if everything could be like that? he thinks, could be empty light? imagine a place like that? in its emptiness, in its shining emptiness? in its nothingness? Asle thinks and while he thinks about a place like that, which is obviously no place, he thinks, he falls into a kind of sleep that isn't like sleep but more a bodily movement where he's not moving, despite all his shaking, yes, he's been shaking the whole time, everything's heavy and hard and there's a place in the big heaviness that's an unbelievably gentle shining light, like faith, yes, like a promise, Asle thinks and I see him lying there in the living room, or studio, whatever it's called, I think, he's lying on the sofa next to the window looking out over the sea and there's a table by the sofa and a couple of closed sketchpads on the table and some pencils, all in a neat row, it's his room, Asle's room, just that, I think, and everything in his room is neat and tidy and hanging on one wall is a large canvas with the stretcher facing out, the picture turned to the wall, and I see that Asle has painted *A Shining Darkness* on the stretcher in black paint, so that must be the title of the painting, I think, and there's a roll of canvas in a corner of the room, there are pieces of wood for making stretchers in another corner, I see, and I see Asle lying there on the sofa and his body is shaking and he's thinking that he has to go get a drink so he can stop shaking and he sits up and then he's sitting on the sofa and he's thinking that now he really needs a cigarette but he's shaking so much he can't even roll a cigarette so he takes one out of the pack lying on the coffee table, he gets a cigarette out of the pack and gets it into his mouth and gets his matches out of his pocket and strikes a match and manages to light the cigarette and he takes a good drag and thinks he won't take this cigarette out of his mouth, the ashes can just fall wherever they fall, and now he definitely needs a glass of something, Asle thinks, and he keeps shaking and he manages to put the matches back in his pocket and he bends over the ashtray on the coffee table and spits the cigarette down into the ashtray and I'm driving north and I think I should stop by and see Asle, I shouldn't just drive past his house here in Sailor's Cove, but I can't stop him from going out to sea and going out into the sea if he wants to, if that's what he really wants to do he'll do it, I think and I'm driving north and I see myself standing and looking at the picture with the two lines that cross and I see myself go to the kitchen in my old house, because it is an old house, and an old kitchen, and I see that everything's in its proper place and the sink and the kitchen table have been dried off, I see, everything is clean and nice, the way it should be, and I see myself go into the bathroom, turn on the light, and there too everything's neat and organised, the sink is clean, the toilet's clean, and I see myself stop in front of the mirror and I see my thin grey hair, my grey stubble, and I run my hands through my hair and then take off the black hairband holding my hair back and my hair falls long and thin and grey down over my shoulders, down onto my chest, and I push my fingers through my hair, pull my hair back behind my ears, then I take the black hairband and gather my hair and tie it back with it and then I go out into the hall and I see my black coat hanging there, how many years have I had that coat now? I think, no one could ever accuse me of buying lots of clothes I don't need, I think, and I see some scarves hanging on a hook and I think that I have a lot of scarves because Ales used to give me scarves for Christmas or as a birthday present, since that's what I wanted, she asked what I wanted and I usually said I wanted a scarf and then that's what I got, I think and I go into the living room, or studio, whatever it's called, really it's both, but I call it the main room or the living room and I see the brown leather shoulder bag hanging on the hook above the paintings I've put aside, the ones I'm not totally satisfied with, the ones leaning against the wall between the bedroom door and the hall door, and when I go out I always take the brown shoulder bag with me and I keep a sketchpad and pencil in it, I think, and I see the shoulder bag there on the passenger seat next to me and I'm driving north and I think how I'm looking forward to getting back home to my good old house in Dylgja and I see myself standing and looking at the round table by the window and the two empty chairs next to the table, there's a black velvet jacket hanging over the back of one of the chairs, yes, the jacket I'm wearing, there on the chair closest to the bench, the chair where I always used to sit, and Ales used to sit in the chair next to it, that was her chair, I think, and I see myself stand back up and look at the picture with the two lines that cross, I don't like looking at the picture but I sort of have to, I think, and I'm driving north in the dark and I see Asle sitting there on the sofa and he's looking at something and he's not looking at anything, he's shaking, trembling, he's shaking the whole time, he's trembling, and he's dressed just like I'm dressed, black pants and pullover, and over the back of the chair next to the coffee table is a black velvet jacket just like the one I have and usually hang on the back of the chair by the round table, and his hair is grey, it's pulled back to his neck in a black hairband the way my hair is, and his grey stubble, I have grey stubble too that I trim once a week or so, I think, and I see Asle sitting there on the sofa and his whole body's shaking and he lifts a hand slightly, in front of him, a bit to the side, and his hands shake and he thinks that it seems better now, easier, for some reason, and he thinks he needs to eat a little something but he's shaking so much that the first thing he needs to do is get up and go get something to drink, he thinks, sitting there on the sofa, and I think I can't just leave Asle alone when he's like that, I shouldn't have just driven past his building in Sailor's Cove, I should go see him, he needs me now, I think, but I've already driven a long way past the building where Asle lives, and I shouldn't have done that, and maybe I should turn around and drive back? but I'm so tired, I think, and I drive north and I see an old brown house at the side of the road and it's falling down, I see that a few roof tiles are missing, and that's where Ales and I used to live, I think, and it seems like such a long time ago, almost in a different life, I think and I drive past the house and after I've driven a bit farther I see a turn-off and steer into it and pull over and stop the car and then I'm sitting in the car, just sitting, not thinking anything, not doing anything, just sitting there, then I think why on earth did I stop at this turn-off? I've never stopped here before, even though I've driven past it so many times, no really I need to get home now, I should've gone to see Asle but now it's too late, I think, and I keep sitting in the car and I think that maybe I'll say a prayer and then I think about the people who call themselves Christians and who think, or in any case used to think, that a child needs to be baptised to be saved, and at the same time they think that God is all-powerful, and so why is baptism necessary for salvation? can't God do whatever he wants? if he's all-powerful then mustn't it be his will whether or not someone's baptised? no, it's crazy to believe that baptism is necessary for salvation, no it's too much, I think and I notice that the thought makes me happy, the thought of the folly of the Christians who think that salvation requires baptism, how could they ever have come to think that, the idea is so stupid, so obviously stupid that you can't even laugh, such obvious stupidity is nothing to laugh at, nor is the foolishness of the people who call themselves Christians, many of them, not all of them, obviously, I think and I think that people who think like that can't have big thoughts about God, and I think about Jesus, how much he loved children, how he said that children were of the kingdom of God, that they belonged to the kingdom of God, and that is a beautiful and true thought, I think, so why would they need baptism to become that? since they belong to the kingdom of God already? I think, and I think that baptism, child baptism, is all well and good but it's for mankind's sake, not for God, it's important for people or at least it can be important, or maybe it's just for the church, yes really it's mostly for the church, but it can't be for God, or for the children who are part of the kingdom of God already, and we must be as they are, we must become as little children to enter into the kingdom of Heaven, that's what the Bible says, I think and I think no, now I need to stop, now I'm thinking foolishly myself, thinking about other people's folly while my own thoughts don't make sense, they're never clear enough, they don't fit together, of course you don't need to be dipped in water to be baptised, you can also be baptised in yourself, by the spirit you have inside yourself, the other person you have and are, the other person you get when you're born as a human being, I think, and all of them, all the different people, both the ones who lived in earlier times and the ones who are still alive, are just baptised inside themselves, not with water in a church, not by a priest, they're baptised by the other person they've been given and have inside them, and maybe through their connection with other people, the connection of common understanding, of shared meaning, yes, what language also has and is, I think and I think that some people are baptised, as children or as adults, yes, some are washed clean with water, with holy water, I think, and that's all well and good in its own terms but no more than that, and every single baptism of this or that person is a baptism of everyone, that's what I think, a baptism for all mankind, because everyone's connected, the living and the dead, those who haven't been born yet, and what one person does can in a way not be separated from what another person does, I think, yes, just as Christ lived, died, and was resurrected and was one with God as a human being that's how all people are, just by virtue of being men and women in Christ, whether they want to be or not, bound to God in and through Jesus Christ, the Son of Man, whether they know it or not, whether they believe it or not, that's how it is, it's true either way, I think, Christianity knows a thing or two too, and sure enough I converted to the Catholic Church myself, something I probably never would've done if it hadn't been for Ales since I didn't even agree with the Catholic Church about child baptism, but I never regretted converting, I think, because the Catholic faith has given me a lot, and I consider myself a Christian, yes, a little like the way I consider myself a Communist or at least a Socialist, and I pray with my rosary every single day, yes, I pray several times a day and I go to mass as often as I can, for it too, yes, mass too has its truth, the way baptism has its truth, yes, baptism is also a part of the truth, it too can also lead to, yes, lead to God, I think, or at least to God insofar as I can imagine Him, but there are also other ways of thinking and believing that are true, other ways of honestly turning to God, maybe you use the word God or maybe you know too much to do that, or are too shy when confronted with the unknown divinity, but everything leads to God, so that all religions are one, I think, and that's how religion and art go together, because the Bible and the liturgy are fiction and poetry and painting, are literature and drama and visual art, and they all have truth in them, because of course the arts have their truth, I think, but now I can't just keep sitting and frittering away my time thinking confused thoughts like this, I think, I need to keep driving north and get back home to Dylgja, to my good old house, I have to stop sitting here freezing in my car, I have to start the engine and then drive to Dylgja, because I like driving, it gives me a certain peace, I fall into a kind of stupor, yes, to be honest it gives me a kind of happiness, and the thought of getting back home to Dylgja and back to my good old house makes me happy too, I think, even if I'm sorry I'm going back to an empty house now that Ales has died, no, that's not true, because even if Ales has been dead a long time she's still there in the house, I think, and I think that I should've found myself a dog because I've always liked dogs, and cats too, but I'd rather have a dog, there can be a greater friendship with a dog, I think and I've thought it so many times but I've never gone ahead and done it, got a dog, I don't really know why, maybe it's because I'd still rather be alone with Ales? because even though she's dead she's still there in a way, I think, or maybe I should just go ahead and get a dog? I think, but Asle has a dog, yes, he's had a dog for all these years, I think, and I think I shouldn't have just driven past Asle's building, someone like him the way he is now can't just be left alone, weighed down as he is now, so weighed down by his own stone, a trembling stone, a weight so heavy that it's pushing him down into the ground, I think, so I should turn around and drive back towards Bjørgvin, I think, and I should go see Asle, I think, I have to help pull him out of himself, I think and I see Asle sitting there on the sofa and he's shaking and shaking, I should have driven back, he needs me, but I'm tired and I want to get home, I want to keep driving north, driving home, because I've been to Bjørgvin and I've gone shopping for canvases at The Art Supply Shop and I bought wood for the stretchers at The Hardware Store, and I bought a lot of groceries, and now I want to drive back home to Dylgja right now, I think, and actually it did cross my mind to stay in Bjørgvin and go to evening mass at St Paul's Church but I was too tired, maybe I'll just drive back to Bjørgvin next Sunday to go to morning mass, I haven't been to mass in a long time so it'd be good to take communion, and then I can go see Asle, I think and I see him sitting there on the sofa and he's shaking and shaking, but doesn't he need to go walk his dog now? I think and I see Bragi lying there by the hall door waiting to be let out and I see Bragi get up and pad over to the sofa and then jump up on the sofa and lie in Asle's lap and then he's just lying there and the dog is shaking too and Asle can't move, he can't even lift his hand, can't say a word, just to say one single word feels like too much for him, it's as though he'd have to force himself to do it, he thinks, but now, yes, now for some reason his thoughts aren't so fixed any more, they're not going around and around in the same circle now, not any more, his thoughts have begun to calm down now that the dog has come and lay in his lap, he thinks

Good dog, Asle says

Good boy, Bragi, good boy, he says

and Asle strokes Bragi's fur with his shaking hand and kneads his fur and Asle thinks how can he have thought about going into the sea, because who would take care of the dog? there's no way he could decide to leave the dog, Asle thinks, and now he's shaking less, but he's still shaking, his body is trembling, I think and no I don't want to think about Asle any more, I don't want to see him before my eyes any more, his long grey hair, his grey stubble, I don't want to think about him any more, there's no point in thinking more about him because he's just one person among many like that, he's alone, he's one of the many solitary people, he's just one artist among many, one painter among many, just one of the many painters almost no one knows about except some close family members and a few friends from school days, and maybe a few fellow artists, he's one of thousands, no I don't want to think about him any more, I think, and then I think again that I should have dropped by to see him, alone as he is, falling apart as he is, I should have dropped by and asked him to come get a drink with me, yes, he could have a pint of beer with a glass of something stronger and I could have a cup of coffee with milk since I don't drink beer any more, no beer or wine or anything stronger since I stopped drinking, that's what I should've done, because if Asle had something to drink it would be easier for him, he'd stop shaking, then he'd calm back down, just getting something to drink would make things easier, the stone would get lighter, yes, his stone might shift off him a little bit so that he could get a little light and a little air, I should have taken him with me someplace where there are other people, where other people are having drinks, where people are together, comforting their souls, that's what I should have done, I shouldn't have just driven past his building,

I should've stopped and then taken him with me out into life, yes, so he could live a little, yes, but instead I kept driving north like I wasn't worried about him, like I was in such a hurry to get away from him, because I couldn't do it, I couldn't see Asle lying there, I think and so I just kept driving past the building in Sailor's Cove where his apartment is, as if Asle was too hard, as if his pain, or his suffering, maybe that's the better word, made me want to keep driving, not because I didn't want to see him or spend time with him but because, no, I don't know, but I wanted to get away, and maybe I thought I could drag his pain with me in a way, pull it behind me, that I could pull his suffering off of him and away from him if I kept driving? anyway that's an excuse I can think of now for not having stopped and visited his apartment but instead having just kept driving, because why didn't I go see him? was it because I was scared to? not prepared to share his pain with him? share his suffering, but what do I mean by that? that's just a manner of speaking, *share his pain, share his suffering,* it's a manner of speaking, as if you could share someone's pain, or suffering, I think and I see myself sitting there in the car and I'm looking out the window and looking at the playground down below the turn-off, there are no children in it, but there, yes, there's a young woman with long black hair sitting on the swing and there on a bench next to the swing is a young man, he has medium-length brown hair, he's in a black coat, wearing a scarf, it's late afternoon or early evening and he sits there and looks at the woman sitting on the swing, and there's a brown leather bag hanging over his shoulder, and she's staring straight ahead, it's autumn, some leaves have already started changing colour, this is the best time of year, the most beautiful, I think, and maybe most beautiful of all in the evening when the light is right at the point of disappearing, when some darkness has entered the light but it's still light enough to see clearly that some of the leaves have lost their green colour, I think, this is my time of year, it always has been, for as long as I can remember autumn has been my favourite, I think and I look at the young man sitting on the bench not moving and staring straight ahead as if not seeing anything and I look at the young woman sitting on the swing, she too is staring straight ahead, as if at nothing, and why are they sitting so still? why aren't they moving? I think, he on the bench, she on the swing, both just sitting there, why are they just sitting there? why aren't they talking to each other? why are they completely still, motionless, like a picture? I think, yes, yes, they're exactly like a picture, like a picture I might paint, I think and I know that precisely this moment, precisely this picture, has already lodged itself in my mind and will never go away, I have lots of pictures like that in my mind, thousands of them, and from just one thought, from seeing just one thing that it looks like, or for no reason at all, a picture can turn up, often at the strangest times and places, a picture, a motionless picture that still has something like a kind of motion in it, it's as if every picture like that, every last one of the thousands of pictures I have in my head or wherever I have them, is saying something, saying something almost unique and irreplaceable, but it's practically impossible to grasp what the picture is saying, of course I might think that the picture is saying this or that, obviously I can think that, and obviously I do think it, and I manage to think some of what the picture is saying but never what it's actually saying because you can't fully understand a picture, it's as if it's not entirely of this world, as they put it, and yes, it's strange, it's weird, he and she in that picture I see inside me that's so inexpressible, I'm really seeing them, he's sitting on the bench there, she's sitting on the swing there, they're sitting like they can't move, like something invisible is holding them in place, and like they've been sitting there a long time, that's how it seems, yes, it's as if they've been sitting there like that always, forever, for always, and she's wearing a skirt, a purple skirt, and the skirt has turned a bit dark in the early evening darkness, yes, the purple is moving towards black, and he's sitting in his long black coat, with the brown bag hanging over his shoulder, and his hair is brown and medium length, and I don't see any beard on his face, but I can't just sit here like this, I think and I think that they, he and she, are sitting without moving and that's what I'm doing too, just like them, I'm sitting without moving, and I can't very well just stay sitting in my car like this because anyone driving by will wonder why I'm just sitting in my car, why I'm not driving any farther, but there's no one driving by and if anyone did drive by they wouldn't find it unusual that I was spending a moment in the turn-off, and anyway so what if they did, the people in the playground would certainly think that if they noticed me but clearly they haven't noticed me, at least neither of them has looked up at me sitting in my car while it's slowly starting to get dark out, it's still light but darkness has come into the air, slowly, slowly the darkness comes into the air, I think, sitting there looking at the young man in the black coat on a bench with a brown leather bag on his shoulder and the young woman in a purple skirt on a swing, because they're still just sitting there, without moving, yes, like part of a painting, yes that too, but when I paint it's always as if I'm trying to paint away the pictures stuck inside me, yes, the ones like this picture, of him and her sitting there, to get rid of them in a way, be done with them, I've sometimes thought that that's why I became a painter, because I have all these pictures inside me, yes, so many pictures that they're a kind of agony, yes, it hurts me when they keep popping up again and again, like visions almost, and in all kinds of contexts, and I can't do anything about it, the only thing I can do is paint, yes, try to paint away these pictures that are lodged inside me, there's nothing to do but paint them away, one by one, not by painting exactly what I've seen or what's stuck inside me, no, I used to do that too much, paint just what I saw and nothing more, just duplicate the picture you might say, and that always turned out as a bad painting and I didn't get rid of the picture inside me either, the one I was trying to paint away, no, I have to paint a picture in a way that dissolves the picture lodged inside me and makes it go away, so that it becomes an invisible forgotten part of myself, of my own innermost picture, the picture I am and have, because there's one thing I know for sure, I have only one picture, one single picture, and all the other pictures, both the ones I see and the ones I can't forget that get stuck in me, have something about them that resembles the one picture I have inside me and that isn't something anyone can see but I do see some of what's in it, some of what's lodged inside me, yes, that's what it's like now in what I'm seeing while I sit in my car and look at a young man and a young woman just sitting and staring into space and not looking at each other, they're not saying anything to each other, but it's like they're listening together, like they're one, because it's like he can't be seen without her and she can't be seen without him, her black hair, his brown hair, her long hair, his medium-length hair, they are inseparable from each other as they sit there, and the fact that they're not moving is probably no odder than the fact that I'm not moving, I'm just sitting quietly in my car for no particular reason, just sitting, and why? I think and then I realise I could go down to them, get out of the car and just go right down to the two of them there in the playground, but it wouldn't be right to do that, would it? they should be left alone, the two of them are sitting there in such a big slow calm fragile peace that I can't go bother them, it would disturb them if I went down to them, they're so calm there, so peaceful, I think, but still, am I going to stay sitting in my car like this as if I can't do anything, can't manage anything any more, as if I'm exhausted from having seen Asle in his apartment by the sea in Sailor's Cove and seeing all the shaking in his body, as if I'm too tired after all the errands I ran in Bjørgvin, I think, now I need to get home, drive back home to my old house in Dylgja, my good old house, because enough is enough already, I think and I look at the young woman sitting on the swing and the young man sitting on the bench and he's thinking that when he was young they used to spend a few weeks every year in the summer with his grandparents, his mother's parents, and their house was next to a playground exactly like this one, a little playground with a swing, a bench, a seesaw, and a sandpit, it was a grey brick house, not too big, and the flagstone floor in the hall comes into his mind, and there was a little outbuilding half-hidden behind the grey brick house, surrounded by some bushes, and then, next to the house, a little beyond it, was a small playground, and he spent a lot of time in that playground, he thinks, and maybe he should tell her that, but she's probably not interested in hearing things like that and now they've been sitting there for such a long time without saying anything, he should break the silence by saying that when he was little he sometimes stayed in a grey brick house next to a playground like this one, he thinks, because they can't just stay sitting like this forever, can they, not even saying anything, he thinks

When I was young, he says

and he looks at her

Yes, she says

and she looks at him and it's like there's a lightness and expectation in her voice and yet he's still sitting there without saying anything else and she asks him what he was about to say

Yes? When you were young? she says

Yes, I sometimes stayed next to a playground just like this one, he says

You did, she says

It's almost like it's the exact same playground, he says

It's kind of strange, he says

It seems like it's the exact same playground, he says

But there's not a grey brick house here, is there? she says

No, no, it's not actually the same playground, of course, of course not, he says

It just seems that way? she says

Yes, he says

and then neither of them says anything, and again she stares straight ahead, and he stares straight ahead

It was a little house, a little grey brick house, he says

and she sits there on the swing, he sits there on the bench, they sit like that without moving and they're not saying anything and then she says that he grew up on a small farm, on a small farm on Horda Fjord, with fruit trees, she says, and he says yes, that's right, and he says that he stayed in the little brick house only sometimes, it was when they were staying with his mother's parents, his grandparents, that they lived in a brick house like that next to a playground like this, he says and I know that I need to paint this picture away, the next picture I start will be of these two people, I'll paint them away, I'll paint them in towards my innermost picture, because when I do that, if I can do that, then the picture will disappear and go away and the uneasiness inside me will stop and it'll bring me peace, I won't be haunted any more, and if I don't I'm sure that this picture will keep coming from inside me again and again, but I've probably always been painting this picture, or one like it, almost exactly like the one I'm seeing now, but in any case I need to paint it away yet again, I need to paint it away again and again, I think, but now I need to start the car again, I can't just sit here like this in my car watching two people who don't know I'm sitting here looking at them, I think and suddenly I feel miserable, I feel grief, yes, it's like grief is bursting from inside me, from nowhere, from everywhere, and it feels like this sorrow is about to choke me, like I'm breathing the sorrow in and I can't breathe it out and I fold my hands and I breathe in deeply and I say to myself inside myself Kyrie and I breathe out slowly and I say eleison and I breathe in deeply and say Christe and I breathe out slowly and say eleison and I say these words again and again and the breaths and the words make it so that I'm not filled with sorrow any more, with fear, with sudden fear, with this sorrow in the fear so strong that's suddenly come over me and that overpowers me and it's like it's made what's I in me very small, turned it into nothing, but a nothing that's nonetheless there, lodged firm, unshakable, even clearer in its motionless movement, and I breathe in deeply and I say to myself Kyrie and I breathe out slowly and say eleison, I breathe from the innermost part of me, I try to breathe from the thing that's most inside me, and I breathe in deeply and I say Christe inside myself and I breathe out slowly and I say eleison and I try to breathe from the thing that's there in my innermost place, from the picture that's there that I can't say anything about, I try to breathe from what I am inside, to keep the sorrow away, or in any case keep it under control so the fear doesn't take over, so the terrors don't overwhelm me, and I know that this sudden sorrow, these sudden terrors that have welled up inside me will get smaller and I will get bigger and I think that that's really ridiculous, if someone saw me now they'd laugh and laugh, if they saw me thinking I could sit in a parked car in a turn-off saying Kyrie eleison Christe eleison, it's absurd, they'd have to laugh, but let them laugh, let them, let them, because it helps! it helps! yes, now I feel calmer again and I look back down at the man and woman in the playground and I think that it's time to drive home to my wife and our child now, they're at home waiting for me, but I'm here on the road to Dylgja, this is the way to Dylgja, isn't it? yes now I need to keep driving to Dylgja, obviously, where else would I be driving to? and I'm driving back to my wife and our child, in a way, to wife and child, no, how could I think that? no, I have to drive back to the old house in Dylgja where I live, just me, alone, I live there alone, that's how it is, how could I think I was going home to my wife and our child, maybe it's because I wish I was? because I wish that that's what I was doing? going home to my wife and our child? not having to go home to an empty house, my cold and empty house? not having to go home to my own loneliness? and that's why I think I'm going to drive home to my wife and our child when actually I'm going to go home to an empty house, a cold house, although actually I left the heater on didn't I? and it'll be good to get home anyway, it will, to get home to my good old house, and really I can't stay sitting here like this, in my car, on this turn-off, I think and I look at the playground and it's already almost dark and I see that the young man has stood up and moved and is standing in his long black coat behind the young woman and he takes the ropes holding the grey wooden board she's sitting on and he gently pulls her back

No, she says

I don't want to swing, she says

I'm not a little kid, she says

and he lets go of the rope and she swings forwards

No stop it, she says

and she swings backwards

Stop it, stop it, she cries

and he goes on pulling her back towards him and then pushing her away, pushing harder each time, he makes her go faster and faster and she's swinging back and forth and he thinks that if she doesn't want to swing she can just put her foot on the ground and stop the movement of the swing, simple as that, she has shoes on, but she doesn't stop the swing

I don't want to swing, she says

Why are you pushing the swing when I don't want you to? she says

I didn't ask you to, she says

I didn't say I wanted to, she says

I don't want to, she says

You just started pushing me like it didn't matter whether I wanted to or not, she says

and he keeps pulling her back towards him and then pushing her away and he thinks now why is he doing this? also, why is he pushing her away from him harder and harder each time? and pulling harder each time, and she steadily soars ahead, away from him, and comes steadily back, towards him, and then he pushes her again, back and forth, away and back

It's just a game, he says

and he gives a push with all his strength and the swing flies away and she screams and her skirt flutters and her black hair is sticking straight out behind her, yes, that was a scream, she screams that he needs to stop, she doesn't like it, he really has to stop now, she's scared, she's really scared, she could fall off the swing, she cries, he needs to stop, enough, she doesn't want to any more

Stop, she cries

But you like it? he says

No stop, she says

You like it, he says

No, no, she says

You do too, he says

and she says no, she says what if she falls off when she's at the highest point, and he gives another push, pushing as hard as he can, and she flies away, her black hair sticks straight out behind her when she's on her way up, skirt flapping, and she screams, a kind of squealing shriek comes out of her when she's at the top of the swing, even louder than before, and on her way back down her dark hair flies to the side and forwards and she shrieks no, no, stop it, I don't like it, I'm scared, stop, I mean it, stop

You do too like it, he says

and when she comes back he makes her go faster again, he pulls the swing and gives her a good push and she flies forwards, up, and now she's not yelling, now she's starting to help, now when she's at the top she bends her knees back and as it were throws her upper body forwards and the swing comes back stronger and when she's come all the way back she raises her feet forward and at the moment he pushes on her back she as it were flings herself forward and amplifies the swings, she goes farther forward, higher up, every time it's farther forward, higher and higher

Faster, she cries

Push harder, she cries

As hard as you can, she cries

and she is out of breath and a little hoarse almost, and he pushes as hard as he can

Aahhh, she screams

Yeahhh, she screams

Like that, as hard as you can, she screams

and he thinks he can't push any harder, he's already using all his strength, he's already pushed the swing as hard as he can, he's starting to get tired, he thinks

Push harder, she cries

and he doesn't push as hard but he gives regular pushes, almost the same strength every time, even, regular, they are now in an even rhythm, up and down, she swings evenly back and forth and she shouts this is great, it's wonderful, she feels a tickling in her stomach, he can't stop, he needs to grab tight and pull her and push her away, perfect, so evenly back and forth, she says, a little faster now but still evenly, she says and now he has to pull as hard as he can once or twice, push her as hard as he can a few times, she shouts but she's shouting in a way softly, she keeps shouting softly that it's tickling, it's tickling so nicely in her stomach, all over her, but it's scary, awful, horribly scary, but good too, incredibly great, she shouts softly, breathlessly

Pull, push, as hard as you can, she cries

Do it, she cries

Do it a few more times and then we'll stop, she cries

and he thinks all right that's enough, you get tired of just standing and pushing a swing, and it's getting darker and darker, and at first she didn't want him to push her, now she doesn't want him to stop, that's the way it goes isn't it, he thinks and he steps back a little and the swing comes towards him

Push, push my back, she cries

and he backs slowly away

Can't you do any more? she says

and he pushes and she pumps her legs and swings by herself as well as she can, she pulls the ropes with all her strength and throws herself forward as hard as she can and when she's at the hightest point she shouts Aaahh, aaahh, aaahh, before she comes back down and back

This is great, she cries

More, she cries

and he looks at her and takes a running jump with the swing and hurls it forward with all his might

Yeahhhhh, she screams

and she draws it out, shrieks yeahh again, and then shouts yeahh more slowly

At first you didn't want to, he says

I was scared, she says

And now you don't want to stop, he says

No, no I like it, she says

But you've been swinging long enough now, he says

It's so good, it's great, she says

and the swing moves back and forth less and less, up and down, back and forth

It was scary in the beginning, but then I wasn't scared any more, she says

That's often how it is, he says

It was fun though, she says

and the swing has almost stopped moving, it's moving back and forth only a little and she says that when she was young she never dared swing, it was so scary, she felt, or else she did dare but only barely, a little bit forward and a little bit back, and he says maybe he shouldn't have pushed her so hard and she says it was great that he did, she liked it, even when she was saying she didn't like it she was actually liking it, she says and he says yes well that's how it often is, people often say one thing and mean something else, even the exact opposite, he says and she says she's not sure that it happens all that often but anyway it did just now with her on the swing, she says, and the swing is now moving back and forth by no more than its own width and he grabs the ropes and stops the swing and stops her and he stays behind the swing holding onto it until it stops moving altogether, and then he's just standing there and she's just sitting there and then she looks up at him

That was fun, she says

Yeah, even if we're grown-ups, he says

Or at least almost grown-up, she says

Kind of grown-up at least, he says

Kind of, yeah, she says

and he carefully pushes the swing again, pulls the rope

Kind of grown-up, she says

Kind of kind of, she says

and the swing is moving back and forth by itself, not very far each way now, but still up and down, gently now, gently back and forth

We'll be grown-up soon anyway, she says

Yeah, he says

and he takes the ropes again and the swing stops

But it's dark, he says

It's still a little light, she says

One last time? she says

and he grabs the ropes again and takes a step back pulling her with him, he goes as far back as he can go, he pulls her back as high as he can, and then lets go of the swing and she howls no, no, no more, not so hard, not so strong, I can't, no more, she shouts, aaahh, no, no, she shrieks and he moves away from the swing

Not so much, she cries

That's too much, she cries

Aaahh, she cries

and he stands and looks at her and he sees her swinging back and forth, up and down, but more and more gently, and then she pumps the swing herself a little, back and forth, up and down, and then it gets slower and the swing just drifts back and forth and he moves a bit farther away from the swing

Where are you going? she says

Nowhere, he says

But you're going to the gate, are you leaving? she says

No, no, he says

I'm not leaving you here, but it'll be dark soon, maybe we should go home? he says

Just wait till the swing stops, she says

and she puts her feet on the ground and stops the swing and she looks at him and smiles and says that was really fun, she hasn't been on a swing since she was a little kid, she says, and back then she didn't like it very much, she was such a scaredy-cat, she was scared of everything when she was little, when she was a little girl, she says

You were too scared to go on the swings? he says

To go that high, she says

Yes, he says

No, I really didn't dare, and when I did swing a little it was only to show I could do it, sort of, she says

and she says that that's what she was like as a child, yes, and then neither of them says anything, and then she asks if he was brave enough to go on the swings when he was little

Were you brave enough? she says

and he nods and she steps off the swing and she goes over to him and he looks at her long dark hair hanging straight down now and then she raises her face to his with half-open lips and he puts his mouth on her mouth and their mouths meet, open wide

That was a cautious kiss, she says

and he puts his hand over her hair, but off it, so to speak, without touching her hair, and then they put their arms around each other and hold each other tight and he puts his hand on her hair and starts to stroke her long dark hair, up and down, and she rests her head on his shoulder and I see them standing there, not moving, they're like a picture, like one of those pictures I'll never forget, a picture I'll paint, I need to paint them close to me and paint them away, I need to paint them close and paint them away just the way they're standing there now, I think, because now it's like a light is coming from them, standing there so close together, as if they were one, standing as if two people were one, yes they're so close as it gets dark and the darkness falls over them like snow, a darkness somehow like snowflake after snowflake yet also like one darkness, one undivided darkness, not bits of darkness but one snowing darkness, and the darker it gets the more light is coming from them, yes, a kind of light is coming off them, I can see it, even if the light is maybe invisible it's still visible, because light can come from people too, especially from eyes, mostly in glimmers, an invisible shining light, but from these two comes a silent even light always the same and never changing, it's like the two of them standing there are one light, yes, that's what the light coming from them is like, one light, I think and he realises that she's almost all light, at least that's how she seems to him right now, he thinks, standing there, but how stupid is that? he's standing here holding a flesh and blood woman and he's thinking that she's light, it's not a good idea to think things like that, he thinks, and sure he's never been all that smart but that's how it feels, like he's holding a light in his arms, that's strange, he thinks, and the fact that he's thinking something like that as they stand here with their arms around each other, she holding him, he holding her, no, it's too stupid, thinking that, he thinks, it's downright unmanly, he thinks, because she's not pure light, she's a flesh and blood woman and shaped like a flesh and blood woman, she's not light, no, she's a woman, she's his girlfriend, not made of light, he thinks and I see them let go of each other and then they move a little ways apart and I see the darkness move a little ways off from them and now they're standing there as if cut out of the darkness, they're standing a little apart from each other, and they look a bit tired and he thinks he can't think she's light, what a stupid thing to think, he thinks, thoughts like that are big and empty, he thinks and he takes her hand and then they go over to the seesaw and they let go of each other's hand and she sits on one side, sits almost all the way on the ground, the ground with its tufts of grass on the grey dirt, and then he goes and pulls the seesaw down a little and she helps with her feet and he raises one foot over the board and puts it down on the ground and then sits on the seesaw and then the seesaw starts to sink down to the ground on his side and she pulls in her feet and then she's up in the air

It was nice being up on that swing, it's been a long time, she says

I feel like we're children again, he says

We're making each other like children again, she says

I'm like a little girl again, either I'm soaring and moving on the swing, or hanging in the air, like now, she says

Every child likes being up in the air, she says

And every grown-up child, he says

Yes maybe, she says

We do anyway, he says

We do now, anyway, he says

But now we're saying such dumb things, she says

I'm almost embarrassed, she says

and then he kicks off and goes up in the air and she sinks to the ground and then she kicks off and goes up in the air and he sinks down to the ground

Everyone likes being up in the air, he says

and he reaches the ground and kicks off

Regular movements, he says

and she sinks to the ground and reaches the ground and then kicks off

Like breathing, he says

and he sinks to the ground and he kicks off

And like heartbeats, she says

and she sinks to the ground and she kicks off

Being in the same movement, he says

and he sinks to the ground and he kicks off

Being together in the movement, she says

and she sinks to the ground and she kicks off

Being the same movement, he says

and he sinks to the ground and he kicks off

Like waves, she says

and she sinks to the ground and she kicks off

Like waves in the same sea, she says

and he sinks to the ground and he kicks off

Like us together, she says

and she sinks to the ground and she kicks off

Like you and me, he says

and he sinks to the ground and he kicks off

Like us, she says

and she sinks to the ground and she kicks off and he lets it happen and lets his weight tilt the seesaw down and he's sitting astride the seat with his feet on the ground while she and her feet are hanging free in the air

That's how it'll be, she says

Like this, he says

and then he kicks off with his feet and she sinks down and her feet touch the ground

And like that too, she says

and she kicks off

Like that too, he says

and they stay like that, he on the ground, she up in the air

When you were little, she says

Yes, he says

When you lived there, over the summer, on summer holidays, in a little brick house, grey brick, she says

You just told me about that, she says

Yes, he says

But you grew up on the little farm, and you had a boathouse and a rowboat there? she says

Yes, he says

And your parents still live there? she says

Yes, he says

And an orchard? she says

Yes, yes I told you, he says

You did, she says

Yes, several times, he says

and then they're sitting and not saying anything

Why are you asking about that again? he says

I don't know, she says

No, he says

Couldn't we go there sometime soon? she says

and he doesn't say anything

Visit your parents? she says

Don't you want to? she says

Yeah, he says

and he hesitates as if he doesn't want to talk about it

You don't want to? she says

But we can go anyway, he says

It's nice there in Barmen, he says

And the farm is nice, it's on Horda Fjord, and it's nice being out on the boat in The Fjord, he says

Yes you've told me that, she says

That you really like being out on the water, she says

Yes, I've always liked that, he says

and then it's quiet, they're just sitting there

But we have to go there at least once, she says

And it'd be nice to see your parents, she says

I don't see them much any more, he says

No, you and your mother, she says

and she breaks off

We won't talk about that, he says

and again neither one says anything, and they sit like that for a long time and I think why are they just sitting there? it's like they're frozen in place, it looks like they're both looking away from each other, keeping their eyes fixed on something next to them, and for them to just sit quietly like that, for so long, yes, how can they do that, I think and then she looks at him

Do you think we should leave? she says

and he doesn't say anything and she asks if he's going to be painting again tomorrow and he says he probably will, yes, tomorrow the same as every other day, yes, since he was maybe twelve years old, somewhere around there anyway, there hasn't been a single day when he didn't either paint or draw, it just happens by itself, that's how it is, like it's him in a way, painting is like a continuation of himself, he says, and he stops himself and says no that's too much, way too much, really painting is just something he does, every day, true, it's an old habit you might say, he says, and she says well then that's how it is and she sounds a little sulky I think, her voice makes it seem like she doesn't entirely like what he's saying, and he says that the painting he's in the middle of at the moment might turn out to be really good but it's so hard to get it right, he has to be so careful, it only takes the tiniest thing to have done too much on it and then the whole picture can be ruined and it'll be impossible to find his way back to what was good in the picture, to what the picture was trying to say, or however you'd describe it, actually it can't be described, because a picture says something and doesn't say it at the same time, it speaks silently, yes, or more like it shows something that can't be said, he says and I think no, I've really got to be getting home now, it's late now and it's time to get moving, keep driving, I think and then she says it's even darker now, maybe they should go home soon? she says and he says yes they really should and he asks if she liked flying through the air and she says yes, she had a great view, even though it was so dark by then, a better view than the one she has sitting down anyway, she says, and that, the fact that she sees better than him, is an old story, let him paint as much as he wants yes she sees better than he does whether it's light out or dark out, she sees especially well, as for him he doesn't see anything but this or that picture, this or that thing right in front of his nose, she says, and then suddenly he pushes off, as if he's angry or something, I think, and she sinks down to the ground and she screams, a long low scream, and he lifts one foot off the ground and stands up and gets off the seesaw while slowly lowering the seesaw with his hand and then she's sitting safe on the ground and he walks around to her and holds out his hand to her and she takes his hand and she gets up and then they just stand there and I think now I've really got to be getting home, it'll be totally dark soon, and then I sit and look at the playground where a young woman and a young man are hanging around playing, like children, and by now it's so dark that I can only just make them out, or is all of this just me seeing things? this isn't all in my mind, is it? am I just imagining that they're there? no, of course not, I saw them, I'm seeing them now, I think, definitely, and maybe I should get out and stretch my legs? get a little fresh air? go down to the playground too? I think, but a person can't just do something like that, can he? if I do do it I have to do it before it gets too dark, I think, and it's probably not all that strange for a person to get out of his car and take a little walk? go down a little path to a playground and walk past it, leave the road and go down past a playground and up a hill on the other side, I see the hill, and obviously I don't need to go into the playground, just walk past it, yes, right now either I need to drive home or I need to get out of the car and stretch my legs, I think and I get out of the car and I look around, the mountain rises up gently on the other side of the road before getting steeper and rising up sharply, and there, up at the top, I see the sky, and the stars are out, shining weakly, and then there's the road, a narrow country road running along the base of the mountain, and then a hill leads gently down towards the playground and there's a little path down the hill from the turn-off to the playground and it goes past the playground and continues uphill to the top of another hill behind the playground and that's strange, I've never noticed that before, this path down to the playground and then continuing up a hill behind the playground, I think, and then I'm standing there looking down at the playground and I see him and her standing there in the darkness, they're barely visible, but I can see that they're standing without moving, holding hands, and it was a good idea to get out of the car and get a little fresh air, I think and I feel how nice the cool air is, I sort of revive a little and of course I'm as free as anyone else to take an ordinary little stroll, I think, yes, of course, but I always tend to think I'm not allowed to do things, that's why I always do the same things over and over, I think and I start walking towards the path and

I start down it past the playground and I look at the two people there in the playground and they must not have noticed me as they stand there holding each other, they're standing there like they are one, he holding her, she holding him, and neither can be separated from the other, and then they let go of each other and I walk carefully down the path

It's already dark, she says

Yes, it's autumn now, he says

Almost winter, she says

But not quite yet, he says

Yeah, she says

Now we've done everything but play in the sandpit, he says

Are you saying we should play in the sandpit? she says

and her voice sounds a little surprised almost

Yes, well, why not? she says

But we'll get sandy and dirty, he says

Maybe we shouldn't? she says

No, maybe not, he says

Our clothes'll get dirty, he says

and she says they could always take some clothes off and she takes off her jacket and pulls her pullover up over her head and now she's standing there in just a bra and her purple skirt, can you believe it, standing there almost naked like that, in this cold, I think and then she pulls him over to the sandpit and I walk slowly, step by step, down the path and I think this is unbelievable, I should quietly walk past the playground and up the hill over there, I should see what's on the other side of the hill, and then I should turn around, it's time to be getting back home, it won't be long before it's totally dark, I think and I try to stop looking at them but I see them bring each other over to the sandpit and then they're standing next to the sandpit and then she lays out her jacket and pullover on the sand

Now we're kids again, she says

Now we're doing whatever we want, she says

Yes, we're kids, he says

Naughty kids doing whatever they want, she says

and she lies down in the sand on her jacket and pullover, she's lying there in just her bra and purple skirt and her dark hair spreads out and then she says that he needs to take his clothes off too

No we can't do this, he says

Yes we can, she says

Someone might see us, he says

It's almost totally dark, she says

Come on, she says

and then she pulls up her purple skirt and tells him to come over, he needs to come over to her now, because it's cold and he needs to warm her up, she says and he says that's what he said, it's too cold to take off any of their clothes, and she says come on, come on, and he says no, no we can't do this, someone might see us, he says, she needs to put her clothes back on right away, he says and she says that it's almost totally dark, no one's coming, no one might see them, come on, come on, just come over here, she says and then he takes off his brown shoulder bag and puts it down next to the sandpit and takes off his long black coat and lays it over her and then he covers the both of them with the coat so that only his coat is visible and, and, no, I have no right to look, to watch this, I think, and is it really happening? or is it all just something I'm dreaming? or is it something that actually happened to me once? isn't that me, lying there in the sandpit on top of her with my long black coat covering us both? isn't that exactly what happened to me once? I think, but even so I have no right to watch what's happening, I think, and I keep walking, quietly, as quietly as I can, I continue slowly down the path and I don't want them to notice me, I don't want to bother them, I want them to stay alone in their own world, and now I can just barely see the coat there in the sandpit, or maybe I can't see the coat? maybe it's all just something I'm picturing in my mind? no, I think, and I can't watch, I have no desire to see this and now I need to turn around, now, I think, I need to turn around now and go back to my car, because all of this, is it even really happening? or do I just think it's happening? or remember it happening? is it something that happened to me once? it must have been a long long time ago because I can't remember it, but isn't that me lying there in the sandpit under my long black coat? and isn't that the same coat I wear all the time? my good old long black overcoat? and she, lying under me and under my long black coat that's covering us? isn't that me? isn't that us? I think, isn't that me sometime in the past? or is this happening now in reality, before my eyes, right there in the playground? I think and I stop and now it's dark, totally dark, and with a kind of clear-sightedness that lets me see in the darkness I see the two of them lying there in the sandpit and the clear sounds of breathing are coming from the sandpit and I hear them moving with the same regularity, like waves striking land, I hear the regular movements like waves, back and forth, again and again, and everything is one movement, one breath, out and in, hearts beating, two hearts beating against each other in the sandpit, and my own heart is beating, beating, and in a steady movement, like waves against the shore, I walk up to the road and my car, and I hear from the playground movements, waves against the shore, back and forth, and I'm walking in the same movement, step by step, and now I mustn't turn around and look at them, I think, and I keep going and then I don't hear the sound of any more movements coming from the sandpit and I look at the young man and now he's standing in the sandpit with his pants down below his knees but his black coat is still draped over her and he has a bucket in his hand and he fills it up with sand and then pours the sand out all over his coat, over her, he refills and empties the bucket, covering her and the coat with sand, no, impossible, incredible, he really is pouring sand over her as she lies under his coat with a little bucket some kid left behind in the sandpit and, no, I mustn't watch, now I need to get home to Dylgja because I can't walk in the dark like this and watch a young man stand next to a young woman lying under his long black coat and empty bucket after bucket of sand over the coat and her, I think, but I can't take my eyes off the two people in the sandpit and can't stop seeing him empty bucket after bucket of sand over her and then he finally pulls his pants up and buttons them and then he takes his coat off her and sand sprinkles off his coat and she stands up and tugs at her skirt, picks up her pullover and jacket, shakes out her skirt, brushes the sand off them and he shakes the sand off the long black coat and he puts it on and then drapes the brown leather bag over his shoulder and it looks like he's ready to leave

Come back here, she says

and she looks at him

Don't go, she says

Don't just leave like that, so suddenly, she says

Come to me, she says

and she holds out her hand to him and he goes over to her and takes her hand and they stand still for a moment

Time to go? he says

Yes, she says

and then she opens her arms and puts them around him and holds him close and I turn around and I keep walking, up to the road, and she says sweetheart, my darling boy, you, I, she says and he says sweetheart, my darling girl, my darling darling girl, my darling darling girl, you, he says and then she says it's pretty cold and he says yes it's really cold, he says he's freezing even though he has his coat on and I walk carefully and as quietly as I can and I look back at the playground and see her long dark hair, hanging straight down over her back, almost down to her hips, and he is just standing there, not doing anything, and his medium-length brown hair is tousled and sticking out in every direction like it's confused while her hair hangs straight down, and then she brings her face to his, her mouth to his, and she kisses him on the mouth and then she says that there's really a lot of sand on his coat

Yeah, he says

and he gives a little laugh

It's all over us, he says

It's 'cause you poured all those buckets of sand on me, she says

Yes, he says

You almost buried me, she says

Almost, not quite, he says

and they stand there and it's like they don't exactly know what to do or say

Now it's really dark, she says

And cold, too, she says

Like you said, she says

Yes, he says

We should go home, he says

and she nods, and then they move a little bit apart from each other and she looks at him, he looks at her

Because you're Asle, she says

And you're Ales, he says

and they smile at each other, they shyly smile at each other and she says can you believe we took our clothes off in the dark, when it's so cold out too, she says, we took our clothes off outside, so late in the autumn, when it's so dark, and so cold, and then to lie down in a sandpit, naked, she says and she laughs, but anyway it's somewhere to live, she says, yes even if the house is falling down, he says, practically a shack, she says, yes it's going to be almost impossible to heat that house, he says, but it's somewhere to live anyway, she says, and he says that when they get home he'll have to thoroughly brush all the sand out of their clothes and then they just stand there holding hands

And then we'll need to wash them, she says

Or at least brush and wipe all the sand off, she says

We're pretty wild, she says

No, what we did wasn't totally crazy, he says

Imagine what people would say, she says

Yeah, he says

I think there's a car up there in the turn-off, he says

No, she says

Yup, he says

It's cold and we need to get home, she says

To our new place, yes, he says

It'll be at least a little warmer there, she says

A little, maybe, he says

But anyway, that's the home we have, she says

And it's good we have somewhere to live, he says

And that we have each other, she says

We do, he says

and she turns her face towards him and they give each other a short
kiss

We have each other, she says

In deepest darkness we have each other, he says

And we stick together, she says

Through thick and thin, he says

There will always be us, she says

There will always be you and me, he says

Asle and Ales, she says

Ales and Asle, he says

The two of us forever, just us, you and me, she says

That's right, he says

and now it's completely dark and I've made it back to the car and I
get in and sit down and stay sitting there looking straight ahead and

I lean back in the seat and put my head on the headrest and look straight ahead and now I see nothing but darkness in front of me, just the black darkness, nothing but black, and I think that I'm parked in the turn-off by the brown house where Ales and I used to live, I stopped here to take a break because I was tired, I think, and because I wanted to pray, since I pray three times a day almost every day, I say a prayer that I've put together myself, in the morning and once in the middle of the day and then in the evening, yes, laudes or matins, as they call it, and then sextus, and then vespers, and I use a rosary with brown wooden beads to pray with, there's a loop with five decades, as they call them, five groups of ten beads each, with a gap between each group and then there's a string hanging off the loop with a gap and a bead and then a gap and then three beads and then a gap and then a bead and then a gap and then a cross at the end, and I always have my rosary with me, around my neck, it was Ales who gave it to me, it was she who taught me about rosaries, I had barely heard the word rosary before I met her, I think, yes, I remember that I heard the word once and wondered what it meant, I think, but now I always wear a rosary around my neck like a necklace and I always silently say to myself the Pater Noster or Our Father, two or three times, and I see every prayer before me, yes, like a picture, I've never learned any of the prayers by heart but I recall them by seeing them in front of me, since I can also easily see things written in front of me, but I try not to do that, so there are only a few things I see before my eyes in writing, and unlike with pictures I can decide whether or not I want to remember something written, I think and I think that I also like to pray three Ave Marias and one Gloria Patri each time, and I pray either in Latin or in my own translation into Norwegian, Nynorsk, and after that what I pray varies a little, it's often the creed, the short Apostolic Creed, that they say the apostles spoke, or anyway something like that, and in any case I say the whole thing silently, before the Pater Noster, the long creed, the Nicene

Creed, I see just pieces of that before my eyes, yes, light from light, Lumen de Lumine, visible and invisible things, visibilium omnium et invisibilium, and then I sometimes say something from Salve Regina right to the end and sometimes I try to stay silent, not think about anything while I'm praying and just let there be a silence inside me, and then I can pray for something, but I almost always pray for intercessions, I pray for other people, almost never for something I'm planning to do myself, and if it is then it has to be something I can do to help God's kingdom to come, for example paint pictures so that they might have something to do with God's kingdom, and I always make the sign of the cross, both before I start praying and after I'm done, and I say In the name of the Father and the Son and the Holy Ghost Amen or else In nomine Patris et Filii et Spiritus Sancti Amen, and in the mornings it's a short prayer, often just the sign of the cross, and in the middle of the day I pray the longest, and in the evening I usually pray myself to sleep with something from the Jesus prayer and saying to myself Lord Jesus Christ, and I say each syllable while either breathing deeply in or breathing slowly out, the same when I say Have mercy on me a sinner, again and again I say these words, or else I say to myself Domine Iesu Christe Fili Dei Miserere mei peccatoris again and again, breathing deeply in, breathing slowly out, but I almost always say this prayer in Norwegian, for whatever reason, and then I disappear into sleep, I think, I fall asleep either to that prayer or to the Ave Maria, I think, and what I'm looking for in all my prayers is silence and humility, I think, yes, God's peace, I think, and I take the rosary in both hands and lift it from under my pullover and pull it up over my head and then sit with the rosary in my hands and I hold the cross between my thumb and forefinger and I think that I must have fallen asleep and dreamed, but I wasn't asleep, and I wasn't dreaming, I think and it was all unreal and at the same time real, yes, all of that happened both in a dream and in reality and I sit there staring straight ahead into the darkness, now the darkness is blackness, it's not just dark any more, and I just look into the blackness and I think that now I have to start making my way home, but I've thought that so many times already and now as if it's the middle of a sunny day I see the two of them walking towards me, a young man with medium-length brown hair and a young woman with long dark hair, they stand out in the darkness, it's as if a light coming from them stands out in the darkness, yes, they're walking straight at me like they're illuminated, and their faces are peaceful and still, and they're holding hands, and they are like one, like one shape walking, and they might have noticed me or my car but they're much too involved with each other, they are in each other, they are present to each other, in their own world, and they walk past the car and I turn to follow them with my eyes in the darkness and I see his medium-length brown hair so clearly and I see her long dark hair hanging straight down her back and I see them slowly disappear into the darkness and go away and I let go of the cross and put the rosary back around my neck and tuck it under my pullover and then I make the sign of the cross and I say to myself In the name of the Father and the Son and the Holy Ghost Amen and then I start the car and I think no, that, that didn't happen, I think, and now I really need to get home, I think, now I need to drive home to my wife and our child, I think and I drive out of the turn-off and onto the country road and I think I should have gone to see Asle, he was so worn down, half-dead, I should have asked him to come out with me, I should have driven him into town to The Alehouse, like I've done so many times, and he could've had his beer and his something stronger and I could've had a cup of coffee with milk, and food, yes we could've bought dinner there, food and beer for him and food and water for me, yes I've totally stopped drinking, because I used to drink much too much and Ales didn't like it, she didn't like me when I was drunk or at least she liked me more when I was sober and that's why I totally stopped drinking, but I also stopped because by the end I was drinking way too much, yes, by the end I was never sober, to tell the truth, and I paint so badly when I'm drunk, and I've never missed it, not the beer, not the wine, not the stronger stuff, but that's because of her too, because of Ales, without her I never would have been able to stop needing to drink, I think, and now Ales is waiting for me, she and our child, and I need to get home to them, to my wife, to our child, but what am I thinking? I live alone there, I'm going home to my old house in Dylgja where I used to live with Ales but she's gone now, she's with God now, in a way I can feel so clearly inside me, because she's there inside me too, she isn't walking around on earth any more but I can still talk to her whenever I want to, yes, it's strange, there's no big difference or distance between life and death, between the living and the dead, even though the difference can seem insurmountable it isn't, because, it's true, I talk with Ales every single day, yes, most of the time that's what I'm doing, and we most often talk to each other without words, almost always, just wordlessly, and of course I miss her but since we're still so close and since it won't be long before the time comes when I myself will go over to where she is, yes, I manage just fine, but it's painful, yes, being without her was like being without everything in life, it almost finished me off, and we never had children, there were just the two of us, so why am I thinking that I'm driving home to my wife and child? it's probably just that I fall into a kind of stupor when I'm driving and when that happens thoughts can come to you, but I know perfectly well, I'm not crazy, that I'm going home to my old house, home to Dylgja, to my house in the little farming and fishing village of Dylgja, I think, the house where I've lived alone for all these years, yes, I wasn't such an old man when we moved there, and Ales was even younger, that was where we lived, first the years when I lived there with Ales and then afterwards all those years when I lived alone in the good old house, and it is good, it's good that I have my house, that I have a safe place to live, a house where I feel safe, because it's a well-built old house and I've taken good care of it, whenever any of it started falling apart I replaced the wood, I replaced all the windows, but I made the new ones as much like the old ones as I could, I put the windows into the same frames just with an extra pane of glass so that there'd be less of a draught, now there are two panes of glass instead of one in every window, one pane that opens out, one that opens in, and it was so much easier to keep the house warm after the new windows were put in, I ordered the windows from a carpenter who made them to measure, by hand, the same way they used to make windows, so that the new windows were just like the old ones, and then I put the windows in myself, but not alone, Åsleik helped me, without his help I'd never have been able to put them in, that's for sure, we had to work together, but together we could do it, even if the first window ended up being put in crooked and we had to redo it, take the window out and put it back in, but the other windows went in the way they were supposed to, the other windows were easy, I think, yes, Åsleik's helped me a lot, and I've helped him too for that matter, I think and now it'll be good to get home, light the stove, make some food, I'm really hungry, yes it'll definitely be nice to get back home to my good old house in the little village of Dylgja, where just a few people still live, good people, none of them lock their doors when they leave the house, or go on a trip, not that they do that very often, and most of the people who live there have lived there their whole life, and then I moved there, or we did, my wife and I, yes, Ales and I moved there and it was because Ales got her aunt's house when she died, her father's sister, old Alise, because her aunt was childless and there were no other heirs and since we didn't own a place to live anywhere and just lived in the rundown brown house that I just drove past we moved into the old house in Dylgja, yes, that was many years ago now, I think, and then we lived there, Ales and I, and then, no I don't want to think about that, not now, I think and I drive north and I think that I like driving, as long as

I don't have to drive in cities, I don't like that at all, I get anxious and confused and I avoid city driving as much as I can, in fact I never do it, but Beyer, my gallerist, he told me how to get to and from The Beyer Gallery which is in the middle of Bjørgvin, and outside the gallery there's a big car park and that's where I always park my car, so I can manage in the city of Bjørgvin, I think and I get to Instefjord and then I start driving out along Sygnefjord and I'm so tired but I'm almost home now, I think, it won't be long before I see Åsleik at the door, yes, Åsleik, actually I've never liked him much but in a strange way that's why I like him, I think, you can't always understand things like that, I think, and now it'll be good to get home, but I shouldn't have just driven past Asle's apartment in Bjørgvin, in Sailor's Cove, he's always shaking, before I drove home to Dylgja I should have driven him into town to The Alehouse like I've done so many times, of course he would've been fine there in The Alehouse alone, surely someone he knew would be there or would get there soon, I wouldn't have had to stay there with him, actually what I really should have done was drive him to The Clinic, but he'd never have gone along with that so we'd have ended up at The Alehouse anyway, he with his long grey hair and grey stubble, me with my long grey hair and grey stubble, in our long black coats, each with our hair tied back in a pony tail, I think

You look like a little girl, Åsleik says

Actually more like an old woman, he says

and I don't know what to say

I'm not an old woman, I say then

You almost are, Åsleik says

or maybe I am a little like an old woman, I don't know, I think, maybe a little? it's not entirely wrong to say that I am, I think, anyway Åsleik likes to say so, either that or he says I look like a Russian monk

You're like a Russian monk, he says

Why's that? I say

Because you are, you're like a Russian monk, he says

and how can he have come up with that? I think, and now I'm driving back to my house and the headlights light up the road and I can see the road in front of me and I see Asle sitting on the sofa with Bragi in his lap and he's thinking he wants to get up and go outside and then go out into the sea and he's thinking that all the paintings he's putting into his next show at The Beyer Gallery are bad paintings anyway, Asle thinks, and he thinks that he can't just stay sitting like this, he needs to go to the kitchen and get something to drink, to make this shaking stop, Asle thinks and he looks at Bragi lying on his lap and he thinks he needs to walk the dog, it's been a long time since the dog has been out, he thinks and I think I need to concentrate on my driving now, because the road to Dylgja is so narrow and winding, even though I've driven it countless times I still need to pay attention, I think, and it'll be good to get back to my house again, because it's my home, that's what it's become, and Ales lived there too for many years, yes, but then, yes, she died, with no warning, and now she's gone, that's all there is to say about that, I think, and now I need to just drive, slowly, just keep my eyes on the patch of light that the headlights make reaching forward on the road, they light up a bit of the landscape alongside the road too, and I'm driving carefully out along Sygnefjord, and I think that there's so many times one or more deer have been crossing the road or just suddenly standing in the middle of the road, or else bounding across the road, it's like the deer can't hear the noise of the engines or see the light from the headlights, like they just don't notice it, they've become used to the engine sounds and headlights and no longer pay any attention to them but at the same time they've never realised how bad it would be if a car hit them, I think and I turn off the country road onto the driveway leading up to my house, good, good, I think, now I'm home, that's good, and the driveway up to the house is one I had built myself, not so many years ago either, it was very expensive but it was certainly nice to have a driveway up to the house and no longer need to park the car a long way off down on the country road, I think, and even if the driveway is steep it's easy enough to drive on it, I think and I don't want to think about what it used to be like coming home when she was there, when Ales was there, when she was in the house with her long dark hair, it was so good to come home then, wasn't it, I think, but I don't want to think about that, and I can't complain, I think and I steer the car around the little hill and there, there in front of the house, is that Åsleik standing there? yes it's none other than Åsleik himself, my neighbour and friend, standing there in front of the house, as if waiting to welcome me home, and now that was a stroke of luck, that he should be looking in on me just when I got home, I think and I stop the car by the front door and I realise I'm happy to see Åsleik in front of the house but it wasn't exactly luck, because this isn't the first time he's been standing in front of the house when I get home from Bjørgvin, Åsleik must have been standing and waiting for me in front of the house for a long time, that's for sure, he sat down for a bit on the bench near the door, got up and stamped his feet a bit and then sat back down on the bench, because after all I bought a few things for him down in Bjørgvin the way I usually do and he's waiting for me to get back, keeping a lookout, even though he always acts like he never wants to accept what I've bought him but then he does anyway, as if without seeing it, I think, and since I always ask him before I go into Bjørgvin whether I should buy him anything there, since it's cheaper to buy things in Bjørgvin than at The Country Store in Vik, he says every time that it's not necessary, that what little he needed, as he liked to say, he could buy at The Country Store in Vik, in the little shop, if you can call it that, that we have closest to Dylgja, but it's certainly a good thing that we have the little shop at all or else we'd have to drive a long way just to buy the least little thing, and not everyone here has their own car either, or is able to drive it, some people are too old, some never got a driving licence, some don't want to drive because they're never sober enough to drive so they don't do it, but not everyone who drinks avoids driving, some drive no matter how much they've drunk, they just drive slowly and carefully, I think, and I think that Åsleik is about to say well that was a long trip to Bjørgvin, I spent a while there but when I got there, yes, there was probably so much to do that you'd have to expect it to take some time before I got back home, since if I didn't have anything special to do in Bjørgvin I could always just take the opportunity to hang around there, or go running around after the ladies for all he knew, that's what he's about to say, and then he'll give a good laugh I think and I open the car door

Welcome! Åsleik says

Glad you could drop by, he says

Isn't it me who should be saying that? I say

Or have you taken over my house too? I say

Sure did! Åsleik says

You did? I say

Yes, you said that it's mine now, he says

What are you talking about? I say

There's yours and there's mine, I say

Yes you have yours and I have mine, I say

That's how it needs to be, I say

I have my own place, even a farm, so there's nothing to argue about, he says

Yes that's what I meant, I say

But why did you say you're glad I could drop by? I say

Why not? Åsleik says

Is there something wrong with saying that? he says

Isn't that something you're supposed to say? he says

Something people always say? he says

It's something you say when it's your own place, that's when you thank someone for dropping by, I say

Especially when it's your own farm, he says

and in a way I probably have something like a farm too, even though it's just an old house with a few rocky hills and a little boggy soil and some heather and a couple of small pine trees around the edges

And it's not like this is a farm, Åsleik says

It's a house anyway, it's my house, I say

Your house, yes, Åsleik says

Of course it's your house, who would say it wasn't, he says

That's for sure, he says

In a way, yes, I say

and we fall silent and then Åsleik says of course it's my house, whose else could it be? even if I wasn't born and raised in this house it was still my house, no one can deny that, even if he does remember very well old Alise who used to live here, he says

Yes, I say

and we fall silent

She was a good woman, old Alise, Åsleik says then

Yes she sure was, he says

and we fall silent again and then I say that my wife, Ales, was named after her, and maybe that's why old Alise wanted Ales to inherit her house, I say

Yes, no, I know, Åsleik says

There weren't any closer relatives, after her husband died so long ago, and then her brother, Ales's father, was dead too, he says

and again we fall silent and then Åsleik says that he can just barely remember old Alise's parents, he's certainly getting on in years himself, he says, but they were truly old, as far as he remembers, yes, from an ancient time you might say, and it was a pretty bare house, but the father, old and bent, he sure was old, didn't he row to The Country Store in Vik to his dying day, he would go down to the water as long as he had the legs for it and then row to The Country Store, and that wasn't something for a frail old guy like him to do, no, Åsleik says

Yes, I say

They sure were made of strong stuff back then, Åsleik says

Of course it was hard work, a real chore for him, but how else could he get food into the house? he says

So he had to, he says

and then silence sort of spreads out and settles in

Yes, yes, I remember it well, Åsleik says then

Back then there were no cars around here, you know, it was a long way to walk, but just in the countryside, between the country farms, there weren't roads out of the country, no, he says

and he says he was quite old when they built a road out, yes, he remembers it well, and the old people in the country, isolated, religious folks, they thought it would've been just as well if that road never did get built because of all the evil and sinfulness that could come into the countryside now, and who wanted to drive out to the countryside anyway? some of them felt, so the best thing would have been if the road never got built at all but the road was built, and because of that Dylgja became part of the world too and because of that someone like me could move to the country, that's what it meant to have a road out, so actually maybe the pious old people had a point about what they said, despite everything? since now that a road had been built all kinds of people could come driving along and then before you know it one of them might want to move out here? Åsleik says and I think that Åsleik will always, always be like this, starting to talk about one thing and then ending up somewhere else, and he just keeps on talking, without stopping, maybe it's because he's alone so much and doesn't have anyone to talk to that he can sometimes just launch into talking nonstop, about this and that, past present and future all jumbled together, and it's all things I've heard before, many times over, I think

Yes now you've got a bad memory, he says

I have a bad memory? I say

and I don't understand why he'd say that all of a sudden, as if my memory was something we needed to start talking about of all things, Åsleik bringing up my supposedly bad memory just like that, out of nowhere, no, I don't know how I've been able to stand him all these years, how can I stay living here in this godforsaken place that time forgot, almost no one else lives here of their own free will do they? I think, and Åsleik says besides, maybe it's not really my house, in a way, don't I remember what I said, that time, yeah, that if he could move that boat I'd give him my house? he says

But that's just something people say, I say

Just something people say? Åsleik says

Did I manage to move that boat or didn't I? he says

I helped you move it, I say

You helped! he says

Yes, I helped! I say

I moved that boat by myself, he says

No, the boat was stuck until I grabbed it too and helped, I say

So you were lying, and now you'll break your promise, he says

I'm not lying about anything, I never lie, I always tell the truth, I say

You always tell the truth, he says

Nothing but the truth, he says

What I say is true, I say

and then it's suddenly quiet, we both stop talking and stand there a moment without saying anything

Nice weather we've had today, calm too, Åsleik says then

Yes, I say

It was dead calm all through the morning but then in the late afternoon yes then the wind picked up a little like always, he says

And what else would you expect, here we are in late autumn already, Advent's here, we should expect to see some storms, he says and then he says we won't have to wait long, the first storms of the year'll be here before you know it, it's strange that they haven't started already, he says, and then we stay standing there some more, not saying anything

And everything in Bjørgvin was the same as usual? he says

Yes, I say

and again it's quiet

It's nice to drive into town now and then, I say

Yes, I suppose so, Åsleik says

and I think now I should ask him about the last time he was in Bjørgvin, but I've done that so many times before and it always bothers him a little, he always squirms a little, shakes his head a little, because the truth is he's probably almost never been to Bjørgvin, maybe a few times long ago, that's it, so I shouldn't bring it up, not now, that wouldn't be nice, I think and again we're standing there not saying anything

I'm glad I can go fishing, have something to do during the day, Åsleik says then

Me too, I make the days go by in my own way, I say

Yes, you and those paintings of yours, he says

Yes, right, I say

You spend whole days painting, he says

and I think that Åsleik has said that so many times before, he's repeated it over and over, time after time, but then again I've said the same things over and over again myself, I've asked Åsleik again and again if he's caught anything today and again and again he'd say that his net came up empty, or else that it was so full he could barely heave it up on board The Boat, or else that there wasn't much, something like that, and if I showed him a picture I'd painted he'd say something, too, or else not say anything, but when he did say something what he said was always amazingly smart, he always saw something I hadn't seen myself, and then these stupid little arguments of ours, as if we always had to have a little fight over some tiny thing before we could really talk to each other, I think and I hear Åsleik ask me again, the same as he's done countless times before, why I paint, won't I ever stop painting these pictures of mine? I've spent almost my whole life painting these pictures and now I'm supposed to stop? no, he doesn't understand me, for him it's simply incomprehensible, he's never drawn even the simplest thing himself, not once, and he's always had someone else paint the house too, he's never even tried to paint the house, he can wax a boat no problem of course but that doesn't count, that's not like painting anything, no, he says and I say, the same as I say every time, that I don't know why I paint these pictures I just do it, it's a living, I say, and Åsleik says I've kept on painting since I was a little boy, and now I know he wants me to tell him about how I couldn't do maths when I went to school and so I sat there and drew in my maths books instead of doing maths, I drew The Schoolmaster and drew the boy sitting next to me, I drew my classmates one after the other, and why did I do that? I did it just to do it! simple as that! I did it so I wouldn't have to think about numbers, only about drawing, yes, I could add, and subtract, I could do that in my head if none of the numbers was too big or too hard, but when it came to multiplying or dividing or percents or anything like that, no, I just didn't understand it, pure and simple, I understood the difference between big and small numbers, and how to add more or take away, and that's all I needed to get through life, there was no need for more, but other than that I understood nothing, I couldn't do it in my head, and the poor Schoolmaster, he tried and tried, he was so patient, and he was confident too, again and again he tried to explain multiplication to me, and when I didn't understand he said surely I had to understand it, everyone had to learn how to multiply, he said, to get through life you needed to know how to multiply, and he said take two and multiply it by two and you'll have four, he said, two twos are four, he said, and I said I understood that, and he said so two plus two is four and two times two is four, he said, and if you take seven and multiply it by seven how much is that? The Schoolmaster said, and he said I could figure it out by adding seven plus seven and then seven more until I'd added seven plus seven seven times in all and I did it and got the wrong number every time, it was always wrong, but I should have just memorised what the number was, seven times seven, but I couldn't do it, no, I never ever saw the sevens before my eyes the way I could see pictures so easily, even that was practically impossible, and to this day I can't do the seven times tables, I can't, and I don't understand why it was always so hard for me, it was like the numbers shifted after I memorised them and turned a little too big or a little too small, there was just no way I could do it and that's why I'd draw, because I could do that, yes, I could draw anyone no matter who, either just their face or, preferably, someone in motion in some way or another, what I liked best was drawing the movement, drawing someone or something moving, drawing the line you might say, yes, it's hard to understand, and I didn't understand it either, I didn't understand why I liked it or how and why I could do it, but I thought about it a lot and I'll probably never figure it out, I think, but I know that Åsleik wants me to tell him the whole story again, he likes it when I tell it, when I talk about how I couldn't do maths but I did know how to draw, nobody in my class could draw like me, absolutely no one, but I don't feel like telling Åsleik that story again, not now, and the truth is I don't think he wants to hear it either, not now, he just wants us to be talking about something, anything, and it's been a long time since we've had anything especially new to say to each other, we've known each other so long and chatted together so many times, so I say just that I don't know why I paint and that I don't know why I've done it since I was young, and I think that at some point I'll tell him the whole story again, about drawing in my maths notebooks instead of doing maths in them, but not now, and then Åsleik will say that he wasn't good at much of anything in school, not maths, not reading, not writing, and definitely not drawing, but actually, he'll say, it wasn't because he couldn't have done it, done all those things well, it was because he was so scared of his teachers, he was so scared that he didn't do anything, whenever he saw a teacher it was like he was paralysed and not a single thought stirred inside him and he froze up and he couldn't do anything, that's what he'll say, the same as he always says, I think and then I say well I probably paint for the same reason he fishes

To pass the time, he says

Yes, and to bring in a little money, I say

Yes that too, he says

and there's another long silence

They're pretty much the same thing really, Åsleik says then

Yes, I say

and I ask Åsleik if he'd like to step inside and he says yes, maybe he'll do that, why not? he says and I go and open the door at the back of the car and Åsleik says, the same as he always does, that I have a big, practical car now don't I, you can fit a lot more into that back area than it looks like from the outside, he says, and I pull a roll of canvas out of the back of the car and he takes the roll under his arm and goes over to the front door of the house and opens it, since I never lock the door, it's never locked, no one in Dylgja leaves their door locked, that's how it's always been and that's how it'll always be, and I untie a thick bundle of pinewood boards ten feet long from the rack on the roof of the car, boards I'll use to make stretchers, and I take them inside and Åsleik has turned on the hall light and put the roll of canvas down in the corner by the door to The Parlour and I put the boards down next to the canvas, and later I'll carry the canvas and boards up to the attic, I think, because I have my storage space in a room upstairs, with all the stuff I need for painting, and I go into the main room and I turn on the light there and the cold hits me

It's cold in here, I say

and Åsleik comes into the room

It sure is, he says

Should I light the stove? he says

and I say yes, that'd be good, and I can bring in what I've bought, I say and I see Åsleik go over to the stove and crouch down and with wood chips in his fist he looks up and says do I know where these wood chips come from? and I say yes, yes, I know perfectly well, and I thank him very much for the wood chips and for all the wood he's brought me, I say and I see Åsleik put the chips and some kindling into the stove with the firewood, and yes, it's from Åsleik that I got all the wood chips, the firewood, all the wood, because he likes working with wood, as he says, gathering wood, and then I pay him for the wood, he always says that he doesn't want anything for the wood but he needs the kroner that I give him, I always have to give him the money kind of furtively, even though I'm doing well, as they say, strangely enough there are still plenty of people who want to buy the pictures I paint, I don't know why but that's how it is, ever since I was young I've made money from my paintings, the first pictures I painted were of the building next door in the farming village where I grew up, in Barmen, and in the pictures it was always a day of beautiful weather with the fruit trees in bloom and the sun shining over the house and the farm, the fjord blue, actually it was the light I was painting, not the buildings, they were pretty enough as far as that goes, it wasn't that, but painting the buildings as such was too boring, that was why I tried to paint the light, but in the sharp bright light of the sun what looks brightest are the shadows, in a way, yes, the darker they are the more light there is, and what I like painting the most is the autumn light but people always wanted to see their house painted in brilliant sunshine, and I wanted to sell my pictures, of course that's what I wanted, yes, after all that's why I painted them, so I had to paint them the way people wanted them, but none of them saw what I actually painted, nobody saw that, just me, and maybe a few other people, because what I painted were the shadows, what I painted was the darkness in all that light, I painted the real light, the invisible light, but did anyone see that? did they notice that? no, probably not, or maybe some people did? yes, well, I know there were some people who saw it, Åsleik too for that matter, he has a real understanding of pictures, I have to admit, but I painted buildings and houses, and people bought the pictures I painted, and that's how I could buy more canvas and tubes of oil paint, because oil paint on canvas has always been what I've liked, nothing else, oil on canvas, always, it was like that from the very first time I saw a picture painted in oil on canvas, and the first picture painted in oil on canvas I ever saw was in the local schoolhouse where a painting hanging crooked on the wall in one of the classrooms was meant to show Jesus walking on water, and to tell the truth it was a terrible painting but the colours, the individual colours in themselves, colours in certain places, colours the way they were on that canvas, yes, they were fixed on that canvas, they clung tight to it, went together with it, were one with it and at the same time different from it, yes, it was unbelievable and I looked and looked at that painting, not at the picture itself, it was so badly painted, but it was oil paint on canvas and that, oil paint on canvas, lodged inside me from the very first moment and stayed there to this day, yes, that's the truth, yes it somehow lodged itself in me for life, the same way oil paint fuses with the canvas I was fused with oil on canvas, I don't know why but I guess I needed something or another to cling to? get attached to? and The Schoolmaster noticed, he noticed that I was always staring at that painting, and he told my parents that I had a gift for drawing, and probably for painting too, if I could just try it, and that way if I couldn't do maths I could at least paint pictures, yes, that's how it was, and then my parents got hold of some kind of kit with tubes of paint and brushes and a palette, and a tool for mixing colours and scraping the paint off if the paint was wrong, a palette knife they call it, one of those was included too, and I was astounded, I was beside myself, I knew what I wanted to paint because at home there was a picture hanging in the living room that Mother and Father had been given as a gift, I think it was Father who'd been given it when he turned forty, and the picture was called *Bridal Procession on the Hardangerfjord*, by Tidemand and Gude, it was what they called a reproduction, a word I liked a lot, what I didn't like as much was that both the paint and the canvas were missing, the picture was flat with no oil paint stuck to any canvas, but anyway I decided to paint a copy of this picture, none other, as well as I could, yes, I'd told my parents that this was the first picture I wanted to paint and both my mother and my father said I'd never be able to, and I told The Schoolmaster too and he too was sure I'd never be able to do it, but I'd decided to do it, I wouldn't touch a brush until I got a canvas in a frame exactly the same size as *Bridal Procession on the Hardangerfjord* so my father bought me a canvas and frame in that size, I was given that too, I remember, it was a Christmas present, I think I must have been about twelve, yes, somewhere around there, yes, and then they took down the picture and I put both *Bridal Procession on the Hardangerfjord* and the empty white canvas on the floor, up in the attic at home, and I started to paint, carefully, slowly, because the colours had to be exactly right and had to go in exactly the right places, I painted carefully, almost point by point but at the same time they were supposed to turn into brushstrokes somehow, it went slowly and took days, the whole week between Christmas and New Year's I was up in the attic busy with my painting and my parents were more and more beside themselves with amazement because miracle of miracles my picture looked like it, yes, to a T! it was almost better than the picture I was copying! they had to admit that they would never have believed it, they said it was exceptional, unbelievable, and Father couldn't restrain himself and he went and told The Schoolmaster and then The Schoolmaster came by to see the picture for himself and then he asked if he could buy the picture from me, and Father hummed and hawed, he'd probably be willing to let go of the picture I'd copied, how about that, Father said, but The Schoolmaster wasn't interested in buying that, and I said I needed money, both for tubes of oil paint and more canvas, so I wanted to sell the picture, and since after all it was me who'd painted it Father had to go along with what I wanted and The Schoolmaster bought the painting from me and paid good money and I can still see The Schoolmaster before my eyes, one Sunday not far into the new year, walking down the driveway away from the house with my painting under his arm and I stood there with the notes in my hand, I can't remember how much it was but I can remember that one day I took the bus from Barmen to Stranda, because that's where the shops were, most of the shops were there, and at The Paint Shop in Stranda they sold both house paint and art paint, and that's where I went and I bought tubes of oil paint, and a roll of canvas, and wood for stretchers, and ever since then it's been oil on canvas, I have lived on nothing but oil paint on canvas, I've never made money doing anything else, yes, since I was a boy, because already as a boy I made enough money from my paintings and that is what Åsleik likes me to talk about most of all, yes, how I could paint pictures of houses on the neighbouring farms and sell them to the neighbours and use the money to buy tubes of oil paint and more canvas, but I don't feel like talking about that now

You've sure got it good, spending your whole life painting, Åsleik says

That's true, I do, I say

Really good, I say

You get by anyway, Åsleik says

Yes, I get by, I say

You could always get by, he says

and I don't want to talk yet again about when I was young and painted pictures that I sold, because actually they were terrible pictures, beautiful lies, about as bad as pictures can be, only the shadows were painted well, and the copy I painted of *Bridal Procession on the Hardangerfjord* was even worse, that's why I don't want to talk about it, not now, it can wait, some time later I'll tell Åsleik about it again, I think, and I think that I'm ashamed of those pictures I painted in my youth, but why? well, the fact is I was violating something, degrading something, those sunny pictures I painted back then were pure lies, except in the shadows, the darkness, the light, yes, sometimes I was close to something but then I tried to sort of hide it in the picture, I would paint over it, yes, I painted over the best things in the picture! and it's awful to think about, but the picture looked real, it looked so real, and the fruit trees were in bloom and the sun was shining on the pretty white house and the water in the fjord was blue, and the only thing I needed to paint a painting like that was a photograph of a house, or farm, or whatever they wanted me to paint, and then I'd find out roughly how big they wanted the picture to be, and once they'd told me that I got started, and oh they looked so real and oh how ashamed I was of those pictures I painted, but really it wasn't anything to be ashamed of, I should've been proud of myself, actually, it's not the worst thing in the world for a kid to be able to paint like that, it looks so real! they said, and they paid me and I painted and that's still true today, it wasn't the worst thing in the world for a kid to paint pictures like that, and yet I'm so ashamed of them, it was like I was disrespecting, yes, desecrating something by painting them, and I wish all those paintings would just disappear! let them vanish for all time! if I could've burnt every last one of them I would have, and that's what I thought even well before I started at The Academic

High School, and I really didn't like painting pictures like that, and luckily I never wrote my name on those pictures, sometimes someone would ask me to and when they did I wrote my first name in the right corner but just my first name, no more than that, and however upset they got about that I didn't write any more than that, it would have to do, but sometimes people would write on the back of the picture that I'd painted it, and in what year, and those ugly portraits I painted of my parents! I really wish they would just disappear from the face of the earth! they were total lies, they looked so realistic, just like my parents, and they looked so nice and pretty, it was all disrespecting, yes, desecrating art, pure and simple, to tell the truth, and those pictures, those pictures were what Åsleik liked to hear me talk about, and he just couldn't understand why I was so ashamed of those pictures, he'd seen some of them himself, he had relatives in Barmen, his mother was from Barmen and he'd been there a few times and he'd seen those pictures of mine, they were the best and finest pictures I'd ever painted, that's what he thinks, there was nothing I painted later that he liked as much as what I painted back then, he said and I thought he didn't know what made a good painting any more than a horse's arse, that's who I was dealing with here, a fool, yes, this person I constantly saw was just an idiot, I think and I look at Åsleik making the stove burn well and he puts a birchwood log in and I go outside and get two shopping bags out of the back of the car and I go back inside and into the hall and open the kitchen door and turn on the light and then go in with the bags and put them down on the kitchen table and then go into the main room and I see Åsleik standing in front of the stove with the hatch open and he says that it's burning nicely now so he can help me bring the rest in and then he shuts the stove door and we go outside together and I hand him two bags and he takes them and I say he can put them on the kitchen table and then I take out the last two shopping bags and put them down and I take the door to the back of the car and shut it and it clicks shut and I see Åsleik go up to the door of my house and I say it's good we live somewhere where no one needs to lock the door

That's for sure, Åsleik says

There's never been talk of locking front doors here in Dylgja, he says

Never, he says

and he emphasises the word as if he's now said something that really means a lot, and he has, too, he really has, there aren't too many places left where people can leave their front doors unlocked when they aren't home

It's good we can count on each other here in Dylgja, I say

Everyone in Dylgja can count on everyone else, yes, Åsleik says

and I see Åsleik from behind, standing in the doorway with the two bags and I know deep inside that I will never forget this exact moment, this exact flash, yes, a flash is what it is, because there's a light in it, coming to it, or coming from it, there where I see Åsleik in the doorway with his back to me, his bent shoulders, that almost bald head with a ring of long grey hair below the bald spot, and I can see his long grey beard, I think he's hardly ever cut his beard since he started growing one as a teenager, I think, and then those two plastic shopping bags weighing him down, one on each side, making his shoulders round, it's like he's framed by the doorway, and even though it's dark and there's no outside light on and there's just a little light coming out from the light in the hall I can see him as a shape, as a shape with its own light, that's how I see him, and it's probably the light of his angel, I think, but if I were ever dumb enough to say something like that to him he'd have a good laugh and say I was like those old wandering fiddlers who learned to play from the Devil, that's what I was like, but in a Christian way, something like that is what he'd say, and it's always been this way, these glimpses of this or that thing that lodge inside me and never leave my head again, never, they lodge there as pictures and stay there and I can never get rid of them, so they have to be painted away, yes, that's how it is, that's how I am, I think, but this light, this flash is part of Åsleik the person too, I think, but why isn't he going into the house? why is he just standing there in the doorway? or is it only for me that time has stopped? I think

You need to take those to the kitchen, I say

I am, Åsleik says

But I don't understand, why did you stop in the doorway? I say

I didn't stop in the doorway, he says

You need to go inside, I say

Yes that's what I'm doing, Åsleik says

and he goes inside and I pick up the two bags next to me and I go inside and I see Åsleik walk through the open door into the kitchen and I go in after him and he puts his bags down on the kitchen table and then I go and put my bags down there

You sure bought a lot, Åsleik says

Six bags, he says

Yes, that's a lot, it always turns out to be more than you think it'll be, I say

and I go out into the hall and shut the front door and then go back into the kitchen and shut the kitchen door behind me

Do you need all that, a man living alone? Åsleik says

Not really, I say

You did buy a lot, Åsleik says

Anything to drink in there? he says

and he winks at me

No, I say

and I knew he was going to say that, it's like he always wants to remind me that I don't drink any more, I've stopped drinking, yes, it's been many years, since, no I don't want to think about that

No beer, nothing stronger either, he says

And Christmas coming soon and all, you know it's a common custom, right, people usually have some beer in the house, or something stronger, Åsleik says

But you didn't buy anything? he says

No, no, let's not talk about it, I say

With Christmas coming? he says

No, I say

Don't you like Christmas? Åsleik says

No, or, how should I put it, I say

You don't like being alone on Christmas? he says

No I can't say that I do, I say

I can imagine, Åsleik says

and we stand there in the kitchen not saying anything

And on Christmas you're going to your sister's house in Instefjord, same as usual, I say

Yes, Åsleik says

and then he says, the same as always, the same as he's done for years, that ever since Sister, yes well of course her name's Guro but he always calls her Sister, has lived alone, ever since her man ran off and never came back, that loser, yes, she's always asked him, Åsleik, to come over for Christmas, she's practically begged him, she has, and he has no reason not to, nothing against going to Sister's house for Christmas, because she serves the best Christmas lamb ribs you can find anywhere, how does she get them to taste like that, you know he has no idea how she always manages to give those lamb ribs of hers that exact special flavour, and she, Sister, won't tell him, but he can guess, he says, and anyway Sister is just joking around, or maybe more like trying to annoy him, when she refuses to tell him how she gets that flavour, it must have to do with how the lamb is smoked, but it can't be that because she has a smoking room in the cellar not a special smokehouse like he has, Åsleik says, so that means it must be about what she uses to smoke the lamb with, yes, he's figured out that much, he says

She gets the lamb from you? I say

Yes, Åsleik says

I kill and clean and carve it myself, you know that, he says

Sure, he says

Every year she gets a ewe lamb from me, he says

and he says that every autumn he takes a newly slaughtered and carved lamb with him and takes The Boat up through Sygnefjord to Øygna, where Sister lives, there by Instefjord, and I've seen her house lots of times, every time I drive to or from Bjørgvin I drive right by it, he says, a little grey house, it could use some repainting, anyway a lot of the paint has flaked off, he says, but yes, well, she salts and smokes the lamb herself, the old way, no one knows how old, Åsleik says, I know how he does it of course, I get lamb from him every single year, and if you ask him he makes a pretty good smoked Christmas lamb himself, good dry-cured lamb too, or mutton, they call it, but Sister always insists on salting and smoking hers on her own, he could easily do it for her but she's right to want to do it herself because it gives her lamb a totally special and exceptionally good flavour and whether or not he wants to admit it Sister's Christmas lamb ribs taste better than his, it's not easy to accept that, not easy to admit it, but that's the truth, and what's true is true, Åsleik says, yes, Sister's lamb ribs taste incredible, you've never tasted anything like it, he says, and anyway now that the man she used to live with, The Fiddler, skipped out, he, Åsleik, has taken The Boat and rowed across Sygnefjord to Sister's every Christmas, because Sygnefjord never ices up, the currents are too strong for that, so even though she lives way up in Sygnefjord, by Instefjord, in Øygna, where there's the inlet, and he lives as far out as you can, where Sygnefjord opens out into the Sygne Sea, out into the ocean, yes, it's not without good reason that the place a bit farther in at the end of

Sygnefjord where Sister lives is called 'Inste' Fjord, it's the farthest in, yes of course I know that already, he's just saying whatever comes into his head, Åsleik says, but still, well, every year during Christmas week he takes The Boat over to Sister's, and the crossing takes some time, most of the whole short day, right, and up to now it's always been good or at least pretty good weather but still, the weather can be rough at this time of year, the sea can get so choppy that only a fool would set out on it, only someone not used to the water, a landlubber, but he was no landlubber, not him, he knew when he should stay ashore and when he should set out, but, there's no way around it, the weather does sometimes change all of a sudden and it's practically impossible to predict even with all his long experience, no one can ever be completely sure about it, still if the wind picks up he just needs to reach land as quick as he can, and if he's far from shore then it can be a hard job, it can, but up until now he's always made it safe back to harbour, and that isn't true of everyone now, there's many a fisherman who never made it back to land, many a boat lying on the bottom of the Sygne Sea, yes, in Sygnefjord too, that's for sure, everyone knows that, many a man's found his grave there, yes, when all is said and done the sea is the biggest graveyard there is in these parts, that's a fact, but it's better nowadays, now people have motors on their boats, but before, when people rowed, or sailed, well that wasn't the same at all, nowadays as long as your motor doesn't stall, and that didn't happen as long as you remembered to change the filter every so often, ideally once a year, and personally he always keeps a spare filter on board, in case the engine goes out, yes, truth be told he always has two filters with him in case there's a problem with the first one or he damages it while putting it in, you never know when that might happen, because isn't that always the way, filters almost always get clogged just when the water's bad, yes, when it's at its worst in fact, plus it's not always so easy to get down there on all fours and take out the old filter, even if you've got needlenose pliers, which of course you do, and even if he's changed the filters lots of times he's had to do it in bad weather only once, yes, the motor stopped and a medium-strong gale was blowing, if not a storm, and the weather'd turned bad all of a sudden, the way it can sometimes do you know, and bam the motor cut out and he couldn't get it started again and then he realised that the filter was clogged and he cursed himself for having been lazy and not having changed the filter, how long had it been since he'd changed it, no, he didn't even know, but however long it'd been there it was and now while The Boat rocked from side to side and bobbed up and down and the water crashed over the sides he had to open the engine hatch and keep it open and, no, Åsleik says and he shakes his head, but it turned out all right, yes, the fact that he's standing here chatting and complaining right now is proof of that, he says, but he'd had a tough time of it, he can't remember exactly how he got through it but luckily he did, the motor started back up and he steered The Boat well in the choppy water, he could do that, whenever the motor was working he could always manage that, well, almost always, he says, but just almost, and Åsleik falls silent for a moment, yes, well, he says then, but there's one thing he knows for sure and that's that it's not too fun being out on the water in rough weather, in a strong wind, in a storm, no, that's for sure, he definitely avoids that whenever he can, of course he doesn't go out when the weather is bad, he's not that big a fool, but, yes, well, as he said before, you can never be sure, the sea changes so suddenly, it's fickle, you never entirely know what you're going to get, but there's one thing you can know, if the weather's good and the sky's clear then you can assume the sea won't get too rough, Åsleik says, and I say in English, Red sky at morning Sailor's warning Red sky at night Sailor's delight and Åsleik says let's have none of that now, stop it, he remembers hardly any of the English they taught him in school, and his teachers weren't good at English either, Åsleik says, and that's why, since it's so hard to know in advance how the water's going to be, it's really not a totally good idea that he waits until Christmas Eve every year before taking The Boat in to see Sister, the way he's always done, Åsleik says, what he really ought to do of course is sail in during Advent on a day with good weather, then the weather most likely won't turn around and get too bad, yes, when Christmas is approaching and the Sygne Sea is more or less calm or at least calm enough that it's not too bad to go there, and there's no hint that it'll suddenly get rough, yes, that's when he should go, even if it's several days before Christmas, but he'd rather get to Sister's house as close to Christmas as he can, then go home again as soon as Christmas Eve is done with, on Christmas Day, yes, that's what he's always done and strangely enough the sea has always stayed calm even on the first day of Christmas, yes, it's almost enough to make you superstitious, those exact days, Christmas Eve and Christmas Day, have had good weather every single year for as long as he can remember, but to tell the truth he likes it best at home, yes, this is where he belongs, where he's comfortable, he says, but these visits to see Sister in Øygna have turned into a kind of habit by now, and if he's going to be totally honest about it he doesn't really like being all alone on Christmas, there are so many memories, about when he was a boy, when he and Sister lived at home, and about their parents, about Father and Mother, now long since passed, but they were good people, Father and Mother, and at Father's funeral the pastor said he's gone to a good place, and at Mother's funeral he said the same thing, she's gone to a good place, he said, and that's the kind of thing he sits around thinking about when he's alone on Christmas Eve, about Father's funeral, Mother's funeral, and the food doesn't taste as good, however good the lamb ribs are they don't taste good to him then, plus he just likes it at Sister's, she doesn't like being alone on Christmas Eve either, but when Sister was living with The Fiddler, well that's what he calls him, never called him anything else, yes, then it wasn't so festive being there with them for Christmas, the fact is he didn't like it one bit, of course Sister still asked him to come spend it with her then too, with them, and one year he did go but it wasn't an especially merry Christmas that year, yes, the fight they had that night, he's never told me about what happened has he, he will at some point, yes, someday he'll tell me about it but it's got to wait, he'll tell me that another time, because it's not a secret or anything, far from it, still it's not so nice to think about, The Fiddler sure liked his drink, yes, well, yes, well, as long as Sister lived with The Fiddler he preferred to spend Christmas alone, but every year since The Fiddler skipped out, and couldn't she have found a better man? he did like to hit the bottle, The Fiddler, that's for sure, to tell the truth, whenever he had one drink he couldn't stop, he never really understood why she hadn't found a better man, she wasn't bad looking, Sister, she wore her years well, she'd had her hair in the same style for as long as he could remember, medium-length blonde hair with not a grey hair in it while the little he had left had turned all grey, not to mention his beard, that was all grey, no one would think they were brother and sister to look at them, and there wasn't even much of an age difference between them, him and Sister, even though he was older, but yes, as long as Sister was living with The Fiddler, except once, he spent Christmas Eve alone, since their parents had died of course, and no, that's probably not something he should think about, or talk about, it's terrible how he talks, just talks and talks, Åsleik says, he spends too much time alone and that's why he always talks so much whenever we see each other, he says, but anyway in any case he's going to spend Christmas with Sister again this year, same as usual, he adds, she got the house in Øygna from her uncle and his wife, who died childless, while he, as the oldest son, got the farm in Dylgja, he says, she got the house cheap, practically free, yes, for little or nothing, to tell the truth, but then he didn't have to pay too much to buy out Sister when he got the farm either, he says, and it's not like she had money to pay him with, she doesn't earn much sitting there sewing her Hardanger embroidery, tablecloth after tablecloth, big and small, table runner after table runner, short and long, and then the colourful embroidered bodices for folk costumes, there's a little money in that but not much, just barely enough to live on, and some years, like after she finished school, she worked at a shop in Bjørgvin, called Hardanger Regional Products or something like that, but then the shop went under and she came back home and the house in Øygna was standing empty so she ended up there, and she did her best to take care of the house, when it needed a new coat of paint she painted it, once anyway, and then it was The Fiddler who painted the house, you have to give him that, before he skipped out, and actually it was Sister who got tired of him and sort of said he should go, she hinted at it and said she was sorry but he should go away and proud as he was that's what he did, he left on the spot, but as long as he was living with Sister he did look after the house, and he made a little money from his music gigs, he'd come home with a few kroner, not drink it all up before he got home, plus he almost always had a few bottles of booze with him, Sister had told him, but anyway he painted the house, once, he did do that, Åsleik says, and he doesn't drop by to check in on Sister too often, he says, except on Christmas Eve, since Sister's been alone, it's better to spend it at her house than to be alone anyway, and Sister's lamb ribs, as he's said, are unbelievably good, Åsleik says, and he stops for a second as if thinking something over and then he looks right at me and asks me couldn't I come with him this year, just once, he says, and spend Christmas with him and Sister, it's always been nice with just him and Sister together, it goes well, but it wouldn't hurt to have someone else sitting around the table, there are always so many memories, about Mother and Father, and for Sister about her man The Fiddler, who skipped out and settled down somewhere in East Norway with another woman, people say, so why can't you come along? Åsleik says, but he doesn't have high hopes, he says, because he's asked me about this plenty of times before, he might as well give up, he says, because I've never ever come with him, he says, and hasn't he given Sister one of my paintings every single Christmas? a small one, always one of the little paintings, and every single Christmas since she's been alone Sister has said that he needs to ask me to come spend Christmas with them next year, in fact he has to admit he wonders why she hasn't given up asking him because I've never come, and Åsleik says he tells Sister he's asked me to come lots of times, he says, and yes, yes he's sometimes thought that Sister might have ulterior motives, because she and I are the same age more or less, and we're both single, and some people, well, especially women, well, no, there's no difference between men and women when it comes to that, some people don't like to live alone, and after The Fiddler ran off, yes, he just left and never came back, that loser, he never even said goodbye to Sister, and now he's probably, people say, gone off to East Norway or some other place, with some woman or another too, yes, it's probably way out east in Telemark he's gone, but he was a really good fiddle player, no one could deny that, and if he's being honest he'd have to say that he thinks that's why Sister wanted to be with him, because he played so well, he really was a virtuoso, you have to say, Åsleik says

Yes you've told me that before, I say

Yes well is there anything I haven't told you before? he says

Good point, I say

and it's quiet and we both stand there looking down

Won't you come this year either? Åsleik says

No I'd rather stay home, I say

You're going to paint on Christmas this year too? Åsleik says

Yes, I say

and it's quiet again

Even on Christmas Eve? Åsleik says

Yes, I say

But you'll at least eat some Christmas lamb ribs on Christmas Eve? Åsleik says

and I say no and hum and haw a bit and Åsleik says yes well since you get lamb ribs and lutefisk and wood and other things in exchange for the painting I get to give Sister, mutton too, now Sister has a whole collection, almost a whole wall of her living room is covered with pictures you've painted, yes, and then there're the three pictures hanging above the sofa, and more in the hall, they're everywhere, so actually it's a good thing that you've always given me small pictures in exchange for everything, Åsleik says, even if it's just out of stinginess that you've only given me small pictures, he says

You can have one of the big ones this year, I say

Well thank you, Åsleik says

and then he says that what makes it better is if, after I've eaten all the mutton from the lamb bones he's given me, I add potato dumplings and cook them with the bones and then have him over for dinner, he says, yes, he always looks forward to these meals, he has to admit, yes, and add a little Voss smoked sausage, some bacon, carrots, turnips, it makes him hungry just thinking about it, Åsleik says and I say yes I eat lamb ribs and lutefisk too over Christmas but not on Christmas Eve itself, you know that Åsleik, I've told you that before, I say, and of course I'll have him over for the potato dumplings that you cook when there's not enough meat left on the bones to have on its own and you cut the bones into pieces and cook them, I say, and Åsleik says yes of course he knows that, and besides he comes over every Advent to have some lamb ribs or lutefisk, we take turns, this year I'll serve the lamb ribs and he'll serve lutefisk at his place, and the food I serve him is always really good, because food always tastes so much better when you're not eating alone, he says, that's probably why the two of us always have no less than three meals together around Christmastime, two of them during Advent and then we always spend New Year's Eve together too, either over at his place or here at my place, one year at one place, the next at the other, and we always have lamb ribs, Åsleik says, but he, Åsleik, has provided both the lamb ribs and the lutefisk, of course, Åsleik says, he's caught the fish and cleaned it and dried it and soaked it in lye and raised the ewe and slaughtered it and skinned it and salted and smoked the lamb, he says, and I say I never liked Christmas, it's a bad time, the worst part of the year, and Christmas Eve day is the very worst day, I say, and I go into the main room and Åsleik follows me and then we're standing in the middle of the room and I think that the only thing I want to do on Christmas Eve is make the day disappear, paint it away, and that's what I do, and I'd rather not eat anything on Christmas Eve either, I just fast, as they call it, and paint, I paint from early in the morning through the whole time I'm awake until night, except for when I nap for an hour in the middle of the day, and fortunately I get tired early, I usually go to bed early, by nine o'clock, and yes, however stupid it is to think so, and whether or not it's true, but there's some truth in it too, the one thing that makes Christmas bearable, other than going to mass on Christmas Day at St Paul's Church in Bjørgvin, and other than painting of course, yes, the one thing that makes Christmas bearable is thinking about a young man and a young woman in love, yes, a little like Ales and I once were, it's just that we never had children, it just never worked out, no, I can't think about Ales, I think, it's too terrible, I'd rather think about a young woman with child and a young man in love with her even though he's not the father of her child, the two of them are the only ones in the world, and he, the young man, is thinking that the young woman makes him so happy that even though he isn't the father of the child she's carrying he has to help her, they have to find a place where she can give birth, the young man thinks, and then the two of them, the man and the woman, go off to find a place somewhere and someone who can help, but as they're walking it starts to rip and tear inside the young woman's body and then they're at a farm, they go up and knock on the door but no one opens up, so either there's no one home or else no one wants to open the door for them, but the house is dark so probably there's no one there, so they go into the hay barn, there are some cows in the stalls, some sheep walking around in the main part of the barn, and it's probably the heat that the animals are giving off that makes it less cold in the barn than it is outside, so the girl lies down in the straw and there she gives birth to a baby and she says that an angel has told her she would give birth to a baby boy so it must be a boy, she says, and she says that the angel told her not to be scared because God was with her and the young man sees that a light is coming from the child, an incomprehensibly beautiful light, and then the young woman takes her breast and she gives it to the baby and the boy falls silent, and he sucks, he sucks, the young man thinks, and everything about it is unbelievable because there's such a strange light shining from the baby lying there at the young woman's breast, then she looks up at the young man and she smiles at him and the young man thinks that this, this light, no, he can't understand it, because this light from the child in the darkness, in the dark barn, no, it's impossible to understand, he thinks, and he goes outside, because even though it's cold at this time of year he's covered in sweat now, so he stands out there in the wind, in the cooling wind, and he lets the cool air brush his face and he looks up and sees a star shining bright in the sky, yes, so much brighter and stronger than all the other stars, and it's shining straight down at the barn, the light from the star is just like the light that's coming from the child, he thinks, and he sees the star send a beam of light right into the barn, such a sharp clear line of light, and the light coming from the star is precisely the same light as the light coming from the child, he can't understand what's happening, the young man thinks as he stands there looking at the beam of light, following with his eyes the line of clear strong light down from the star through the sky until it goes straight into the barn, no, he can't understand it, he thinks and now he has to go back inside and help the young woman, he thinks and then he hears footsteps and then he sees three strange men, three men he's never seen before, three men unlike anyone he's ever seen, come walking up, they have long hair, and long beards, and are wearing very colourful dishevelled clothing and they come walking up to him and he sees that their hands are full of beautiful blankets and clothes and food and jewellery and wine and who knows what else they're carrying and when they see the young man they say that every night they sit and look at the stars and try to figure out what meaning the stars might have and tonight they saw something they'd never seen before and something they're never going to see again, they saw a star start to shine so much clearer and brighter than any other star and then they saw a beam of light come down from the star, a mysterious, incomprehensible light, it was beautiful and warm and there to look at and disappear into, they say, and the beam of light was pointing somewhere, and then they knew, they said, that this light meant that God had now sent his Human Son to earth, they were sure of it, it had finally happened, so they followed the light from the star and set out and then miraculously arrived at the place the star was shining at, and now here they were, outside a barn, and the light from the star is shining straight into the barn, they say and now they want to go give their gifts to the newborn child, they say and I think that it's this light, yes, this exact light, yes, that this light is what I think about to get through Christmas Eve day and to stop thinking about all the other things that it's so awful to think about, I think, and also I paint, on Christmas Eve day the same as every other day, and there has to be a light in everything I paint, an invisible light, I think, and maybe the light I try to paint has something to do with the light coming from the child in the barn? and from the star? I think, but no, it's not like that, and what's strange is that the easiest way to get pictures to shine is if they're dark, yes, black, the darker and blacker the colours are the more they shine and the best way I can tell if a picture is shining, and how strong or weak the light is in it, and where, is to turn out all the other lights, when it's dark as blackest night, of course it's easiest to tell when it's as dark as possible outside, like now, during Advent season, but in summer too I try to cover the windows and make it as dark as possible before looking at where and how much a picture is shining, yes, to tell the truth I always wait until after I've seen a picture in pitch blackness to be sure I'm done with it, because the eyes get used to the dark in a way and I can see the picture as light and darkness, and see if there's a light shining from the picture, and where, and how much, and it's always, always the darkest part of the picture that shines the most, and I think that that might be because it's in the hopelessness and despair, in the darkness, that God is closest to us, but how it happens, how the light I get clearly into the picture gets there, that I don't know, and how it comes to be at all, that I don't understand, but I do think that it's nice to think that maybe it came about like this, that it came to be when an illegitimate child, as they put it, was born in a barn on a winter's day, on Christmas in fact, and a star up above sent its strong clear light down to earth, a light from God, yes, it's a beautiful thought, I think, because the very word God says that God is real, I think, the mere fact that we have the word and idea *God* means that God is real, I think, whatever the truth of it is it's at least a thought that it's possible to think, it's that too, even if it's no more than that, but it's definitely true that it's just when things are darkest, blackest, that you see the light, that's when this light can be seen, when the darkness is shining, yes, and it has always been like that in my life at least, when it's darkest is when the light appears, when the darkness starts to shine, and maybe it's the same way in the pictures I paint, anyway I hope it is and I've tried to tell Åsleik that but I've never been able to make Åsleik understand anything about that, that's why I don't say anything about it to him any more, because he'd just say that he, Åsleik, is not a believer, someone lives and then he dies and that's that, no more no less, and he doesn't want to hear anything about any invisible light, that's exactly what Åsleik would say and that's why I don't want to say anything to him about it, someone lives and then he dies and that's that, no more no less, Åsleik says and he's probably right about that too, but then again maybe it isn't so simple, because life isn't something you can understand, and death isn't either, actually to put it in other words it's like in a weird way both life and death are things you can understand but not with thoughts, this light understands it in a way, and life, and paintings, I think, get their meaning from their connection to this light, yes, when I'm painting it's actually about an invisible light, even if no one else can see it, and they definitely can't, or don't, I don't think anyone does, I think, they think it's about something else, it's about if a painting is good or bad, something like that, and that's why I can't stand thinking about the pictures I painted to make money when I was young, they were just pictures, they didn't have any light in them, they were just pretty and that's why they were bad, they looked so real and the sun was shining and there was light everywhere in the picture and that's why there was none of this light, because this light is only in the shadows, maybe, I think and suddenly I hear Åsleik say that even if he's just a fisherman he knows a thing or two about how everything goes together, everything fits into a big unbreakable whole, people catch fish, for food, and for the fish to be caught this and that has to happen and for someone to successfully catch the fish this and that has to happen and so everything goes together in a mysterious way, everything is one big whole, but you believe in God and I don't, he says, and I say what I always say, that no one can really say anything about God and that's why it's meaningless to say that someone does or doesn't believe in God, because God just is, he doesn't exist the way Åsleik imagines, I say and I think that Åsleik and I have talked about this so many times, it's something that's nice to talk about again and again, and also boring to talk about again and again

Yes, well, I say

You won't come to Sister's for Christmas this year either? Åsleik says

No, I'll just stay home, I say

Yes, well, Åsleik says

But you believe in God and I don't, he says

and I say what I always say, that no one can say anything about God, but it is possible to think that without God nothing would exist, but because God isn't anything He is separate from the world of created things, where everything has a limit, He is outside time and space, He is something we can't think, He doesn't exist, He's not a thing, in other words He's nothing, I say, and I say that no thing, no person, creates itself because it's God who makes it possible for things to exist at all, without God there's nothing, I say and Åsleik says what's the point of thinking like that? that's not something a person can believe in, is it? there's no point in believing in nothing, is there? and I say that he's right about that, we agree on that point, we do, but it's also wrong to say that God is nothing because at the same time He is all, everything all together, because what I think, I say, is that since nothing can exist without God sustaining it, without God having made it exist, given it being, as they put it, then it's He who is, it's He that everything has in common, yes, God says about Himself, about what we should call Him, that His name is I AM, I say

Now that I don't understand, Åsleik says

No, I don't really understand it either, I say

It's just something you think? Åsleik says

Yes, I say

and then neither of us says anything and we stand there and look at the floor

You and this faith of yours, Åsleik says

I don't always understand you, he says

But no one can think their way to God, I say

Because either they can feel that God is near or they can't, I say

Because God is both a very faraway absence, yes well, being itself, yes, and a very close presence, I say

Maybe it's like that for you, Åsleik says

But it doesn't really make sense, he says

and I say no it doesn't, that's for sure, it's a paradox, as they call it, but then again aren't both he and I paradoxes too just standing here, because how do the soul and the body go together, I say, and Åsleik says yes who can say and then we stand there and neither of us says anything and then I say that the cross is already a paradox, with those two lines that cross, the vertical and the horizontal, as they say, and that Christ, yes, God himself, died and then rose again to conquer death, he who came down to earth when people were separate from God because of what they call original sin, when evil, yes, devils took control of this world, as it says in the Bible, yes, it's impossible to understand that, I say, and I say that evil, sin, death, all of it came into the world, yes, into the universe, it all exists because God said yes but there was also someone who said no, if you can put it that way, I say, because otherwise there would be neither time nor space, yes, everything that exists in time and space has its opposite, like good and evil, I say, and everything that's in time and space will someday pass away, in fact most things, almost everything that there's ever been in time and space is already gone, almost every last thing is outside of time and space, it isn't anywhere, it just is, the way God isn't anywhere but just is, so it's not at all strange that someone can want to leave this earth, get away from what can be found and rest in what just is, in

God, as Paul said, yes, something like that, I say and Åsleik says that we've talked about this a lot before and we'll probably talk about it a lot more and I say you're right and I see Åsleik go over to the picture I have standing on the easel, which is set up in the middle of the room, and unusually for me it's a rather big canvas and rectangular, and first I painted one line diagonally across almost the whole surface of the picture, a brown line, in very thick drippy oil paint, and then I painted a matching line in purple from the other corner and it crossed the first line in the middle, forming a kind of cross, a St Andrew's Cross, I think they call it, and I see Åsleik stand there and look at the picture and I go over to it too and look at it and I see Asle sitting there on his sofa, and he's shaking and shaking, he's thinking he can't even lift his hands, he feels too heavy even to say a word, Asle thinks, and he thinks that the only thought he can think is that he should disappear, go away, he'll leave and go out and then go out to sea and then he thinks it's been a long time since he's walked the dog and I see that the thick oil paint has dripped a bit more, and where the lines cross a totally new colour has formed, more shining than it was when I looked at the picture earlier today, I think and I stand there and look at the painting and I think that really it was because of Asle that I decided so suddenly to drive into Bjørgvin today, I just didn't realise it, I realised it only when I drove past the building where his apartment is, in Sailor's Cove, but then I didn't stop to see him even so, didn't stop to help him, not when I was driving into Bjørgvin and not when I was driving back out of Bjørgvin either, I think and I think that all my pictures are like that and I think I don't know what I mean by that, all my pictures are like that? like what? what do I mean by that? because this isn't a picture yet, it's just a picture I've started on, but in all the pictures I paint there is something this picture reminds me of, however different this one is from all the others I've painted, this is what I'm always trying to paint, and when I get a light into the picture, when I get a light to come from the picture, it's by doing this, I have to go into myself, as deep in as I can, so that I can come back out and go into the picture, I think and I hear Åsleik say now this here looks like something real, I've painted a picture that looks like something for once, it looks like some kind of cross, he says and I say that this is something I just started painting today, before I drove into Bjørgvin, and he says why did I start a picture and just paint two lines and then rinse the brushes and put them away and drive into Bjørgvin instead of painting more? he says and I say that it just felt like the right thing to do and Åsleik doesn't say anything and then he says it just felt right, yes well then it probably was, he says, and I think that now Åsleik's probably thinking that I'm talking nonsense, I think, but he probably always thinks that about me anyway, I think and then Åsleik says again that he doesn't understand why I would paint just two lines and then stop, why didn't I paint anything except those two lines? he says and I say that it's not so easy to explain and Åsleik says no of course it isn't, the truth is he's never really totally understood me, or my pictures, he says and I think that Åsleik has said this so many times and well it's something nice to talk about over and over, and it's also boring to talk about it over and over, the same as talking about how God, or in any case some divine force, came down to humankind to give them help in all their despair and need when Jesus Christ came to earth and died and rose again, yes, this unbelievable story, this foolishness that there's really no way to believe, and I think what I really believe in is the force of this foolishness, the power of thinking this way, I think, and I believe in this and Åsleik doesn't, but what's the difference really whether someone believes it or not? there's no difference, in the strict sense, I think, and I don't always believe in Jesus Christ as a saviour either, just in God, in God's presence, yes, in his absence too, yes, I can never doubt that, because it's reality, not belief

So, you won't come to Sister's for Christmas this year either then? Åsleik says

No, I'll stay home, I say

and I think he keeps asking this over and over, can't he just stop already, I think

Yes, well, he says

and Åsleik stands there, it's like he doesn't want to leave, and he looks at the picture where I've painted two lines that cross

You don't get sick of all this painting? he says

And you, you're always fishing, you don't get sick of all that fishing? I say

That's different, he says

Yes, you're right, painting and fishing aren't the same, I say

How stupid do you think I am, Åsleik says

and we look at each other

No, you're not stupid, I say

Well then, he says

Fishing a lot doesn't make a person stupid, I say

It looks like it's upside down, he says

Painting a lot is what makes a person stupid, more like, he says

and I can't argue with that, fishing gives a person a lot more wisdom and understanding than painting does, yes, fishing contains a beautiful truth, I say, because you never know what's going to happen, whether you'll catch a fish or not, I say, it all comes down to luck, just like life, I say and Åsleik says I may be right about that but the important thing you need to do to catch fish is go fishing and it's not blind luck that decides whether or not you go fishing, it's something you decide to do, fishing is, it's something you do, a task, a mission, see he can use big words like that too, he says, and when someone undertakes this mission, namely fishing, when he does it for the first time, because one of those times is going to be the first time, there's always a first time, and later if he does it again and again, yes, you have to admit that too, he'll end up really knowing how to fish, and where the fish are, and if they're biting, and he'll learn the various landmarks and seamarks for various fishing grounds, each has its own qualities, some grounds are good when the tide is rising and some when the tide is falling, not to mention the currents! and how much it depends on the season, the month, the moon, even the week! how much fish you'll catch, yes, of course that's not something you can talk about, because it's obvious, it's self-evident, Åsleik says, but he emphasises the word self-evident, and then repeats it, *self-evident,* yes, it's *self-evident,* he says and I say yes it certainly is

So no it's not all just blind luck, it isn't, he says

No but in life it's not all just blind luck either, that's obvious too, I say

Of course, Åsleik says

and then he looks down at the floor in that way he has and when Åsleik looks down in that way it's like he isn't looking down, it's like he's looking up, like he's looking at everything all together, like he's seeing a big context without being clear about it and then something comes over his face, yes, it's like he is suddenly falling out of this evil world and into a still and peaceful clearing or clarity, an area of stillness, of light, yes, of shining darkness, because it's like he's fallen out of himself, out of where he usually is, like he no longer knows himself, like he's gone, away from himself, as he stands there looking down with a light that's like what the sky can give off, together with the clouds, when that's what the light wants to do, yes, a light like that comes from him, the kind of light that can come from a dog too, from a dog's eyes, yes, that happens a lot, when I think about it I've often seen that strange light coming from a dog's eyes

So that's why you drove down to Bjørgvin today? he says

To check in on that friend of yours, the one with your Name? he says

It just suddenly came over you that you should do that? he says

and Åsleik looks down again and I think I didn't tell him anything about Asle and also I didn't drive to Bjørgvin to see Asle, it was just something I decided to do, I wasn't thinking about Asle at all until I drove past the building where his apartment is, but then again maybe I was thinking about him in a way, without realising it? and I say that that happens sometimes, a picture makes me suddenly decide to do something, but that's rare, very rare, while most of the time, in fact every time, a picture has something to do with something I've seen, something that's stuck inside me in a way, and that I suddenly see again, yes, it's like a vision, it's like I have a huge collection of pictures stored in my head, of pictures I can't forget, and like I'm trying to get rid of them by painting them, I say and Åsleik says that makes sense and he stays there looking down at the floor and I too bend my head, look down, and we stay standing like that for quite a long time

No, I've never amounted to anything, Åsleik says

and he's saying it as if to himself

Nothing, he says

I was born in Dylgja and I lived in Dylgja and I'm going to die in Dylgja and be buried in the ground and turn into the ground myself, he says

I've never made anything of myself, he says

I was baptised in Vik Church and confirmed there and that's where my funeral will be, I'll be buried in the churchyard of Vik Church and that's where I'll rot away, Åsleik says

and I think now he's about to start saying what he usually says about how he's remained a bachelor and Åsleik says that there's no woman in the world who'd want someone like him, that's easy enough to understand, why would anyone want a ridiculous guy like him? and so, getting married like a respectable man, he gave up on that when he was young, yes, he wasn't yet old when he knew he'd be spending his life alone, in solitude, there wasn't going to be any wedding in Vik Church for him, or any baptism of a child of his either, he said, and then there's the farm, or piece of land really, it was more like a steep hill with stones as big as boathouses scattered across the fields, if you can call them fields, beneath steep cliffsides, and it happened pretty often that a stone came loose and tumbled down the rock face and came to a stop in the fields, almost every night he'd lie there before he fell asleep in fear and think now, now, soon, it's coming, the big stone, or the big avalanche, that'll take his house and farm and field and sweep it all together into Sygnefjord, yes, he's seen it in his head so many times, he's seen in his mind's eye how a stone as big as a house would come loose, or maybe the whole rock face would come loose and turn into stones hurtling down faster and faster and picking up grass and dirt and smashing houses into boards and splinters and sweeping away everything he owned and the sheep, and him in the middle of it all, inexorably sliding down the mountain until it was all gone, until it disappeared into the water, he along with his whole farm, he along with everything he had, all disappeared into the water, yes, he would lie there like that and see it all in his mind before he fell asleep, it was like these thoughts were never satisfied, and lots of times this or that small avalanche had woken him up, and he'd inherited this fear of avalanches from his parents, especially Mother, but also Father, they used to talk constantly about the avalanche that was going to come one day, yes, it wasn't just maybe going to come, it had to come, it was only a question of time, today, this morning, in a year, in twenty years, in a hundred years, or even longer, but eventually the avalanche would come, that was certain, they knew that, they just didn't know when it would come, that's the kind of thing Father and Mother would say to each other, while he and Sister were still little kids too, and listening, they'd talk like that, because did grown-ups ever think about how such talk would enter into a child? no, not back then, never once in all that time did they think that, and he and Sister, who were nearly the same age, he was two years older, and the heir, that word was always spoken as if there was something especially splendid about it, yes, the word *heir* was always given its own special emphasis, spoken with special respect, *son and heir,* he was the *son and heir,* it was he who would one day take over the whole small farm along with everything on it, the same way Father had taken it over from his father one day, and he from his own father, yes, no one knew how long people from his line had lived on this farm but it was a long time, yes, that much was known for certain, a very long time, yes, the farm had passed from father to son and obviously all the men before him had found a wife, since the farm had passed from father to son all the way down to him, which meant he was the first one to stay unmarried, a bachelor, yes, well, he'd tried, more than once, put himself forward a few times, but no, he'd had no luck, not a single old spinster wanted to have him, so he never got a wife, he stayed a bachelor and looked after things and puttered around, now he had these sheep, they brought in a few kroner, for the meat, and a little for the wool, not much, but then again he didn't need much, and when he had a good catch fishing he'd dock at The Wharf in Vik, go from The Wharf to The Country Store in Vik, and that's how he'd sell a little fish, yes, there were lots of people who didn't fish themselves who bought fresh fish from him, and dried fish from him too, because he hung up pretty much all the cod he caught to dry, either in the attic of his house in the winters, or, in the summers, outside under the eaves, and it was always easy to sell the dried fish, and then there were crabs and lobsters, they were usually pretty easy to sell too, that's for sure, he'd made quite a few kroner from those, it had added up to a tidy little sum over the years, that's the truth, yes, and then there's the woods, it was quite a number of cords of wood he'd cleared and sold over the years, at first to country people but after the country road got built it was mainly people from Bjørgvin who wanted to buy wood from him, there were knocks on his door so often, on weekends and holidays, that to tell the truth he'd started locking his front door, no, he'd never done that before, but recently he'd actually started locking his front door and not opening it when people knocked, so he'd always managed to get by, and other than that? yes well he'd always liked to read, and he went into The Library in Vik almost every time he was in Vik, it wasn't so far away from The Wharf, it was in The Town Hall, yes, I knew that perfectly well, I'd been there many a time myself, now why would he tell me where it is? so almost every single time when he was there doing business at The Country Store he went into The Library and he's read almost everything they have, on any and every topic, or else poetry, yes, he even liked reading poetry, he enjoyed it, especially poems by the younger poets, what wouldn't they think of next? those poems rarely meant much or had much connection with anything but there were sudden turns of phrase, quick bursts of wind, that were said in a new way, put in a new way, often in ways impossible to predict beforehand, and he liked most of them, but when one of them was too much like the others, when there was one you could hardly tell apart from the others, then it was hard to read it, a poem had to have some kind of quality of its own in it to be worthwhile, yes, that's what he thought about that, it was just his opinion, nothing more than that now, yes, well, Åsleik said and then he fell silent

And so there's a lot to do on a farm, the buildings need a lot of work, Åsleik says

and he says that he's tried to the best of his ability to take good care of the buildings, the house, the barn, the outbuilding, the smokehouse, the boathouse, but in recent years he'd let things go a bit, so the house needed painting, well in fact all the buildings did, yes, they've needed it for a while, but the avalanche might still come, he was sure about that, and the time was approaching, the time was always coming closer and closer, and so that's why he'd let things go a bit, since there wasn't much reason to paint the house, or the other buildings, yes, or maintain them in other ways either, when the avalanche was going to come any day now, that's how he saw it, but now thoughts like that weren't exactly pearls of wisdom, no, really they were more like an excuse not to do anything, a kind of cover for his own laziness, it was crazy really, everyone before him had done so much to keep up the farm, and the buildings had stood there all that time and they were still there, the same as they'd always been, yes, the house, the barn, the shed, the smokehouse, the boathouse, and a lot of work had gone into all of them, done by both of his parents, his grandparents, his great-grandparents, his great-great-grandparents, however far back in time you wanted to go, but there wasn't much point in going back too much farther than the grandparents, that's what he thought, the rest was part of the great silence, he said, that's more or less how he thought of it, and there's not really anything that you can think about what's part of the great silence, there's no point, it's just there, it just is what it is, yes, he says

Yes, I say

The great silence, he says

and I think I should say that God is in the great silence, and that it's in the silence that you can hear God, but then I think that it's probably better if I don't say that, and we stand there and I think that this too, like everything else, is something I've heard Åsleik say so many times before, because once he gets started he can go on and on about stuff like this, and it's probably because he spends so much time alone, I think, and I think that even if he's said it before it's in a way new every time he tells me, I think, something about it is new, something's different in how he tells it, how he looks at it, every time, I think and Åsleik says that the only thing that bothers him, yes, the only thing is, no, not that he never got married, not that, a female would've been a nuisance and a burden, when you came right down to it he was a born recluse, a hermit, as they say, but, he says and then he says nothing for a long time

Yes? I say

Yes, that, he says

Yes that what, I say

That there's no one to take over the farm after I'm gone, Åsleik says

and again he looks down at the floor and then he looks up and looks at the stove and he says that it probably needs another log, a good dry birchwood log, he says and I see Åsleik go over to the stove and open the hatch and put a log in and he closes the hatch and I think I really should have gone to get a glass of something with Asle at The Alehouse in Bjørgvin, and even if where he really should've been taken was The Clinic he'd never have gone along with that, he wasn't doing well these days, Asle, when he wasn't drinking he was thinking all the time about putting an end to himself, it just felt like he couldn't go on, so I should have dropped by, and so why did I just keep driving? I think, was it because I dreaded seeing him? because I didn't feel like going to The Alehouse? I think and now Asle is just sitting there on the sofa, with his long grey hair pulled back behind his ears and tied in the back with a black hairband, and his grey beard too, and he's shaking and shaking, I think and I see Åsleik go over to the easel and stop and look at the picture I'm in the middle of painting and I go over to the stove and I open the hatch and even though Åsleik has just put a log in I put another log in anyway and I stand there with the hatch open and I look at the firewood and I see Asle sitting there on the sofa and he's thinking that food no longer tastes good to him, he knows he needs to eat but he doesn't want any food, it disgusts him, to tell the truth, he tries to eat but it makes him want to throw up and he spits out the food and goes looking for something to drink, but he can't drink without eating, that is one rule he's always stuck to, and it's already long since daylight and he needs to stand up, no matter how hard it is to get to his feet, no matter how hard it is to put one foot on the floor in front of the other he has to do it, yes, even while he's shaking all over, and his hands are shaking most of all, but even so he needs to get himself something to drink, a little glass of something, Asle thinks and he gets up and puts one foot down on the floor and then the other and he feels himself shaking all over and he thinks he has to get to the kitchen and pour himself a drink, and he leaves the main room and goes to the kitchen and unscrews the cap from a bottle that's on the kitchen table next to a glass and he holds the round bottle in both hands and sticks the opening into the glass and manages to pour a glassful without spilling any and with both his shaking hands he holds the glass tight and raises it to his mouth and empties it in one gulp and he puts it back down on the table with trembling hands and then supports himself on the edge of the table and shuts his eyes and he breathes in deeply and then breathes out slowly, he does that many times, and then he puts both his shaking hands around the bottle again and even though he's shaking all over he fills his glass and he feels a gentle warmth spread through him, and he feels his hands shaking less, and immediately he feels the warm gentleness inside, Asle thinks, and then he thinks he should roll himself a proper cigarette now, and he takes the tobacco pouch out of his pocket and now he can roll a cigarette and then he lights it and it's so good to feel the smoke spread through his body, he thinks, there is such a big difference between hand-rolled cigarettes and packaged cigarettes, Asle thinks, and he thinks he should drop by The Alehouse and he sees himself sitting there in The Alehouse alone and reading a newspaper, and there aren't many people at The Alehouse, and then the street door opens and a woman about his age, somewhere around forty or fifty, something like that, walks in and she has medium-length blonde hair and Asle sees her as it were come to life when she sees him and she comes over to his table and he looks up and he too as it were comes to life, his eyes sparkle

No, is it really you, Asle says

Yes, she says

and she's a little shy

Are you waiting for someone? she says

No, no, he says

and it's quiet for a brief moment and then Asle says she should just sit down, if she wants to, if she's not doing anything, he's here alone, as she can see, yes, just with his glass, he says and he raises the shot glass and she says it's sure been a long time and that it's great, really great, to see him again, she says

Have a seat, if you want, he says

You and me, we're old friends, he says

You and me, Guro and Asle, he says

and she doesn't say anything and they're quiet and Asle thinks that Guro's hair is the same medium-length blonde hair it's always been and she's still standing there and she turns a little, slowly, and Asle looks at her and he feels like they're right back where they've always been, they're exactly the same as they used to be, they're in the same place, they are the same place, their place, they are still each other's secret, they are still each other's own beautiful world

It's so great to see you again, she says

You too, he says

And things are still the same with you? she says

Yes, not much new with me, he says

But I'm so happy to see you here, she says

It's great for me too, that you saw me, he says

and I see her sit down at his table and I see Asle standing there next to his kitchen table pouring himself another glass of something strong and I think he's going to make it, he's about to stop shaking now, I think and then I see the dog come walking up to him

Here you are, Asle says

Good boy, good Bragi, he says

and he says the dog must be hungry and thirsty too and he fills the dog's water dish and takes a handful of pellets of dog food from a bag on the floor next to the kitchen table and puts them down in the dish on the floor and Bragi goes over to the dishes at once and starts eating and then there's a knock on his front door and he just stands there, he stands with his glass in his hand, there's another knock, and he puts his glass down and puts the cigarette in the ashtray on the kitchen table and goes and opens the door with Bragi at his heels and two little girls are standing there and looking at him with their eyes wide in surprise and one of them asks him if he'll give them some money for this or that cause and he says he'll see what he has and then he goes back into the main room and over to the black velvet jacket that's on the chair by the coffee table and he finds his wallet in the inner pocket and finds a few coins there and with the coins clutched in one hand and the wallet in the other he goes back to the two girls and one girl holds out a box with a slot in the lid and he puts the coins in, one by one, and the girls say thank you at almost the same time and then he sees them turn around and go to the door across the hall, to the neighbour's apartment, and Asle shuts the door, locks it, checks to see that the door is locked, and then thinks about Bård, the neighbour boy who drowned, he and Bård were the same age, they hadn't even started school yet, he thinks and then he goes back to the kitchen and he thinks he'll just drop by The Alehouse, or maybe he'll go knock at Guro's door? or maybe she's even at The Alehouse? Asle thinks and he sits down at the kitchen table and stares emptily into space and he picks up his glass and drinks and looks, yes, what is he looking at? he's looking at something or other, but it doesn't matter what because it's like he doesn't see anything, he just feels the warm intoxication fill him up and he pours himself another glass, and drinks it all down, but not as fast as before, more gently, sip by sip, and with more time between the sips, then he pours himself another glass and watches the level of liquid in the bottle go down and he needs to save a little for tomorrow, he thinks, because how else will he be able to stop the shaking? he thinks, so maybe he really should go out for a bit, to The Alehouse, buy himself something to drink there, since he has to leave some of what he has here until tomorrow, and maybe he'll drop by Guro's in The Lane and knock on her door on the way to The Alehouse? or maybe it'd be better on the way back? he thinks, it's been a long time now, he thinks, and maybe he can spend the night at Guro's at her apartment in The Lane? yes, like so many times before, the first time he did it was many years ago when he was living with Liv, but then a man moved in with her, a fiddler, in any case Guro always called him The Fiddler, and then of course he had to stay away, and Guro and The Fiddler lived together for many years, but then The Fiddler just disappeared one day, just went away, he moved to somewhere or other in East Norway, it was certainly somewhere a long way east of Telemark, Asle thinks, and since then he's often thought he should go drop by Guro's place, but it's never happened, he thinks, and he thinks that he needs to go buy some more to drink tomorrow, the quarter bottle he has left will be enough to last him till tomorrow morning, he thinks, so he'll just put on his warm clothes, because it's cold out, it's snowing, and go to The Alehouse, or maybe he should stop by Guro's place in The Lane? like he used to do so often, no, she probably doesn't want him to come by so he'd better just go to The Alehouse and then he'll need to buy himself more to drink tomorrow morning, because sitting in his kitchen drinking beer until the shaking goes away, no, he can't do that, his hands'll be shaking so much that it'll be all he can do to get a shot glass up to his mouth, but now that he's managed to get a couple of glasses down yes he's calmed down little by little, the shaking's gone away, it took a little while but he's stopped shaking, and now he won't need that much to drink for the next several hours, just a little beer, yes, there were lots of times, before he needed to drink something strong to get the shaking to stop, Asle thinks, and he thinks that he's alone, and that it's good to be alone, if only he were better, if only he didn't have to drink all the time, he thinks, this horrible shaking, he thinks, and aside from those two girls in the hall he probably hasn't talked to anyone in a week, for sure, barely a word or two when he went to buy something to drink or a little food when it wasn't like it was today, before, when he wasn't lying there heavy and unable to move and shaking all day, yes, on days when there wasn't that weight and things were easy and one day disappeared into the next and neither day existed on its own then everything was good, floating along, then it was good to be alone, yes, everything was a floating picture then, in a way, Asle thinks, and then he painted, and when he started on a picture he could totally disappear into the picture, but that was before, now he can't paint any more, he can't do anything, it's all too big and heavy for him, and he shakes all the time, and he's tried to call The Boy, who lives in Oslo, but The Boy didn't answer, and The Son and The Daughter live somewhere in Trøndelag, and he hasn't seen Liv even once in many years, or Siv either, and these weights inside him, his stone, and these shakes, because if he doesn't get something strong to drink he shakes, and sometimes he shakes even if he has drunk quite a bit, he thinks, the only thing he can do now is have a little drink when he wakes up, and then a few more times throughout the day, but he often can't get rid of the shakes even then, or else he needs a lot to drink before he can stop shaking, which means he'll need more to drink by tomorrow morning, Asle thinks, so he'll go buy some more tomorrow morning and by evening he might feel so much lighter that he can think about going out, the same as today, yes, drop by The Alehouse, the same as now, because it's like he's feeling a little stronger again, yes, and if he doesn't have the strength for anything else then at least he has the strength to pour himself another drink, at least he feels that, he thinks, and that's something, he thinks, but thinking things like that, yes, drinking's helped him a lot, he thinks, but now the drinking is taking over, after it got to the point when he was so heavy that everything felt too heavy, even speaking a single word, drinking was the only thing that could make things a little lighter, so that he could move his hands, get up, say anything, and he takes another big sip, and again he feels the warmth spread through his body, because on these days when there's nothing moving inside him, when he's just heavy, yes, he has always been heavy, heavy of spirit as they say, melancholy, as they put it, but never before has he been so heavy that it was hard to say a single word and the only thing he wanted to do was go outside and down to the water and go out to sea and disappear into the sea and do it in the light that shines now and then from the darkness, when the darkness is most impenetrable in a way, he thinks, but now he doesn't want to be alone, he wants to go out, and he wants to go to The Alehouse, and maybe he'll run into someone he knows there, someone or other, someone he can talk to? maybe Guro's there? it's been so long since she's gone there, but maybe he could meet someone he's never talked to before? someone he didn't know before today? and tomorrow he has to go buy more to drink and since he has to save what he still has at home to drink in the morning he needs to go out, go drop by The Alehouse, or The Last Boat as it's called, Asle thinks and I see him put his wallet back in his inside pocket and put on the black velvet jacket that's hanging on the back of a chair by the coffee table and then he goes out into the hall and puts his long black overcoat on, then he puts on a scarf that's hanging on a hook there, then he feels his coat to make sure he has his wallet in his jacket pocket, and it's where it should be, and he has money in it, he knows that, and he's been carrying in his wallet for all these years a little reproduction of *Bridal Procession on the Hardangerfjord,* of all things, he saw the painting in a schoolbook back when he was a boy, in a school textbook, and he thought it was so beautiful, so beautiful, he knows some people look down on this painting but he still thinks it's wonderfully fine, yes, people can say whatever they want, it's an exceptionally good painting, he's never painted anything like it himself, far from it, yes, what he's painted himself can't compare to that painting in the least, but ever since he was a boy he has always kept the little picture he tore out of the school textbook in his wallet, yes, he tore out the page with the picture from the textbook they used in his school and then cut out the picture and then put it in the wallet he had at the time, because he already had a wallet then, even if he rarely or never had any money in it, anyway he had this little reproduction of *Bridal Procession on the Hardangerfjord* in his wallet, and since then he has always kept this picture in his wallet, yes, he's changed wallets many times of course but he always transferred the picture of *Bridal Procession on the Hardangerfjord* from the old one to the new one, and now the picture was so worn that you could barely see that it used to be *Bridal Procession on the Hardangerfjord* but in a way that just made the picture even more beautiful, not that he looked at it very often, but still he did take it out sometimes and to make more room in his wallet he'd folded it in quarters, folded it once and then again, and so over time the picture had obviously come apart into four pieces, the folds had torn of course, but he'd taped them back together on the back once a long time ago and the tape had lasted well so that's why the picture was still in one piece, more or less anyway, and so he went around with this picture in his wallet, the same as before, and even if it was basically impossible to see what the picture showed any more he still sometimes took it out and looked at it, never at home, but sometimes when he was sitting alone at The Alehouse or somewhere else and had nothing else to do, it wasn't all that often that he looked at the picture but sometimes he'd look at this old photograph of *Bridal Procession on the Hardangerfjord,* torn out of the textbook from his schooldays, yes, cut out on one side and torn out on the other, Asle thinks and then he thinks that now he needs to pick up his keys from the bureau in the hall and then go out to the front door, and now he just has to not run into anyone, any of the neighbours, as long as no one comes up to him on the stairs, Asle thinks and he sees Bragi standing there looking at him and Asle thinks that he needs to take the dog out but he can't do it now, he'd rather do it when he gets back home, it won't be too many hours till he's back and then he says to Bragi now be a good boy and watch the apartment and the dog just looks at him and then Asle unlocks the apartment door and then he goes down the stairs and he walks past the bicycles and pushchairs down in the hall and he thinks that as long as he doesn't run into some neighbour or another, he thinks, and he goes to the street door and he opens it and he sees someone walking towards him

Good evening, the man walking towards him says

and Asle stands there and holds the door open for the man and he says Good evening and the man Asle is holding the door open for asks if he's going out for a walk

Yes you have to every now and then, Asle says

Some fresh air, that's a good thing, the man says

Yes, Asle says

and the man walking up to him says that it's so nice out now that the new snow is falling and Asle says yes, yes, it's so white, it's like it's shining, he says and Asle sees the man go into the lobby and he shuts the door behind him and it slams shut and I stand there and look at the firewood in the stove and I hear Åsleik say it's burning nicely in the stove now isn't it? should I shut the hatch? he says and I say I'll do it and I shut the hatch and I think I should have gone to see Asle, I shouldn't have just kept driving, going right past, because his drinking is going to finish him off before long if someone doesn't do something, if someone doesn't help him, I think, but I, I, I just looked at the building in Sailor's Cove where his apartment is and drove right past it and then I think I need to drive back into Bjørgvin, because I need to go see Asle, I just have to, I think, yes, a mute voice inside me tells me I have to drive back into Bjørgvin and go see him, and that must be the voice people call conscience, I think, yes, even though it'll take a couple of hours to drive to Bjørgvin I'll just make that drive, I'm not too tired, I think, and then I'll just spend the night at The Country Inn where I like to spend the night, in Room 407, the smallest room they have, as long as it's empty I'll stay there and not just because it's one of the least expensive rooms, I also like it best, the room has windows looking out onto the back yard, although something, I think it must be the lift shaft, blocks half the view from the room where I stay if it's available, and I usually book the room well in advance but even if I haven't booked it ahead of time I've never once had it happen that there wasn't room for me somewhere at The Country Inn, true there was one time when it was full and I had to sleep on a spare bed in the attic, they put up an extra bed for me there, I think, anyway now it's decided, I'm going to drive into Bjørgvin and look in on Asle, I think and I hear Åsleik say well it's time to get going home and I look at him and I say that I stupidly forgot the most important thing I needed to do in Bjørgvin so I need to drive back there right away, I say

Now, tonight? Åsleik says

and he seems both surprised and a little alarmed, as if I've gone a little crazy, as if he's suddenly become a little nervous about me, I think

Yes, right now, I say

You've already done a lot of driving today, Åsleik says

and he says do I really want to do this? now, so late? and it might snow too, he says, yes, a few snowflakes started coming down this afternoon and the weather seems like it might well start snowing and I say I've already put the snow tyres on and Åsleik says well that's good, yes, if there was one thing he regretted in life it was that he never got a driving licence, he said, even though it would've been nice to have a car, especially given where he lives, instead he has to either walk or drive the tractor, it's a good thing he has that, and he's had the same tractor for probably thirty years now, yes, must be that long at least, he says, yes if he needs to drive somewhere he has to either take the tractor or ride with someone else or else take The Boat, no, mustn't forget that, it's good he has that as a means of transportation, yes indeed, he says and I say yes, well, I have to go to Bjørgvin, I can tell him about why some other time, I say and I say that I can give Åsleik a ride, and he says thanks for the offer but he'd rather walk, it's fine, it's not far, just a mile or two, of course he'd have nothing against getting a ride, he says and then he asks me again if I really need to drive back to Bjørgvin, I just got home, and right after coming back into the house after being in Bjørgvin I'm going to drive back again, dark as it is, and night is falling, and it might start snowing, as he said, and I say I just have to, I'll tell him why later, I say and Åsleik says all right then that's how it is, I'm going to just do what I want to do, he says and then he says well I guess I'll just go out front then and Åsleik goes outside and I see that the wood's still burning in the stove and I turn off the light in the main room and go to the kitchen and turn the light off there and go out to the hall and turn the light off and then I go outside and shut the front door behind me and I see Åsleik standing out front and I tell him he can have a ride, since I'm going in his direction, but I could have driven him home anyway, the way I've done so many times before, I say and Åsleik says well thanks for that, since I'm driving in that direction he could always ride with me but he's used to walking, walking's fine with him, he does it all the time, it's no problem for him to get home, not at all, but well he could also ride with me since I'm driving down the same road, he says, since it is pretty cold out, yes, now that it's late autumn, well, more than that, we're already in Advent, it won't be long before it's Christmas, and winter, yes, Åsleik says and it's going to start snowing tonight too, Åsleik says and he gets into the car and I get in and start the engine

Yes it's definitely going to start snowing, I say

The first snow of the year, it is, Åsleik says

But it won't stick, I say

No, but still a lot might come down, Åsleik says

Yes, I say

And I'll clear your driveway while you're down in Bjørgvin, yes, that'll need to be done, Åsleik says

So that you can come back to a cleared road, he says

Thank you, thanks very much, I say

'Cause I can drive a tractor anyway, even if I can't drive a car, Åsleik says

It sure comes in handy, I say

And it's old but it works great, I can get it to start every time, after a minute or two anyway, he says

Anyway you've had that tractor for as long as I can remember, I say

It was my father who bought it, old as he was, Åsleik says

But it's still running, I say

and I drive down the driveway and turn right, onto the country road, because Åsleik's farm is a mile or so farther in along Sygnefjord and Åsleik says that that was an odd picture, yes, a strange picture, the one I'd started painting, with the two lines, one purple and one brown, he says and I feel myself not wanting to talk about it, I've never liked talking about a picture I'm working on, or about any picture I've finished either for that matter, never, once a picture is finished the picture says whatever it can say, no more no less, the picture says in its silent way whatever can be said, and if it's not finished yet then how it's going to turn out and what it's going to say isn't something that can be said in words, I think, and after all these years Åsleik must have realised that I don't like talking about my pictures, about what they represent, about what they mean, I can't stand any of that kind of talk, not in the slightest, and now Åsleik's going to start going on and on about those two lines as if they were just two lines and then he says that it's a St Andrew's Cross I painted and he says the words with such emphasis that I almost jump and I notice how proud he is of having those words at his disposal, St Andrew's Cross he says again, very proud of himself, *St Andrew's Cross,* he is genuinely proud of knowing such a term and what it means, and now, after Åsleik has said this term that way, sort of haughty and proud about knowing it, I think that I simply don't get how I can stand him, year after year, day after day, he's such a fool, and probably the only reason I put up with him is that I don't have anyone else to talk to, or be with, no that's not true, he's no fool, he's not stupid, Åsleik, he's pretty wise in his way, I think, so it was bad to think that, disgraceful really, I think and then we're at the bottom of the driveway to Åsleik's house and I stop and Åsleik asks when I'll be back and I say I'll be back tomorrow and maybe he can come by again then, tomorrow evening, I say and Åsleik says that he'll do that because then maybe he can pick out a picture that he can give Sister for Christmas, he says, and I say sure we can do that and then Åsleik says thanks for the ride and he gets out of the car and I raise my right hand and wave goodbye and Åsleik raises his hand and waves too and then I keep driving slowly in along Sygnefjord and I think this is madness, I think, sheer madness, driving back into Bjørgvin now after I've already driven both there and back earlier today, and I'm tired, I realise, so maybe I should turn back? I think, no, no, I have to go and see Asle now, I think, I should never have driven by his building in the first place, that was practically cowardly, I think, so now I need to drive back into Bjørgvin, I think, and why did Åsleik have to start talking about the picture I started painting earlier today, haven't I told him time and time again that I don't like talking about a picture I'm in the middle of working on, and don't like talking about pictures I've finished either, done is done, painted is painted, it turns out however it turns out, both pictures and life too, I think, and then his bringing up the St Andrew's Cross over and over, I think, and I think that Asle is just lying on the sofa in his apartment almost all the time now, under the window that looks out onto the snow, and that's why I painted those two lines that cross in the middle, it's probably in some strange way a picture of Asle lying there that I've painted, I think, and in another way it's not him and of course I shouldn't have driven home without looking in on Asle, because he's in such despair, but it is a long way to drive to Bjørgvin, I'm tired after being out all day, after driving to Bjørgvin and back, and now I'm driving to Bjørgvin a second time today since I feel such uneasiness inside me that I just have to drive back again, I think and I drive and I fall into a kind of peaceful unthinking stupor and I see a few snowflakes land on the windshield and I drive farther in along Sygnefjord and I see more and more snowflakes land on the windshield and I turn on the wipers and they make semicircles for me to see through, and it's white around them from the snow, and I think that Asle probably isn't home, he's probably gone out, to The Alehouse, I think, so I shouldn't go ring his doorbell, I should drive into Bjørgvin and park the car in front of The Beyer Gallery and then go to The Country Inn and get a room for the night and then go to The Alehouse, because Asle's probably sitting there alone at a table, I think, and if he's not there I can drive back to his place and ring the bell, but maybe I should go by his place first, probably? maybe he is home? but anyway he probably won't answer even if he is? I think and it's snowing and it stops snowing and I drive south and I get closer to the turn-off I stopped at earlier today, by the playground, and I think that this time I should just keep driving, and I'm really not sure whether what I saw in the playground today was something I really saw or something I just imagined, yes, dreamt, in a way, I think, but it was real, I'd be lying if I said otherwise, I think, and I think that anyway it wouldn't hurt to take a little break from driving, I did drive for a long time today and I'm probably more tired than I realise, so maybe I should stop in the turn-off I'm coming up to and take a little break there again, yes, get out, stretch my legs, get a little fresh air, yes, I'll do that, I think, and I keep driving south and I'm at the bend that the turn-off is just past and I drive around the bend and I see the turn-off and I pull into it and stop the car and now it's so dark out and the snow is falling so thick that I can't see the playground, I think, and there's no one here now, I think, and I think that I'll just rest here for a minute, get out of the car and get a little fresh air, and stretch my legs a little, I think, and I stop the engine and step out into the snow, there's already a good layer of it on the ground, everything is white, the benches, there's snow on the trees and I stand there and look at the snow coming down and then there are just isolated snowflakes falling and then it stops, and goodness it's so much brighter when the landscape is white, yes, the white snow gives light to the night, and there, on the path down to the playground that's covered in new snow, I see a couple walking hand in hand, and it's the same two people I saw earlier today, yes, definitely, so it wasn't something I just imagined then, was it, I think, because now I see a young man with medium-length brown hair almost covered in snow walking next to a young woman with her own long dark thick hair, and her hair too is almost totally covered in snow, and I hear her say it's so unbelievably beautiful here with all the new snow

Yes, it's beautiful, he says

Beautiful and white, he says

Everything's turning white, the trees, the benches, everything, he says

And we're turning white, she says

We're turning white too, he says

and then they let go of each other's hands and he puts his arm around her shoulders and she puts her arm around his back

It just so sad when the snow turns to slush, he says

We have to enjoy it while we can, she says

Yes, while it's bright and white and lovely, she says

Since it'll probably rain tomorrow, like usual, he says

and they look at each other and they give each other a kiss

But let's not think about that, he says

What shouldn't we think about? she says

About the snow being washed away by the rain tomorrow, he says

And that it'll turn to slush, she says

That's how it goes, he says

Yes, she says

and then they go into the playground and he picks up a bit of snow and makes a soft snowball and throws it at her, but misses, and then she picks up some snow and makes a snowball and packs it tight between her mittens and she throws it at him as hard as she can and he ducks and the snowball flies over his head and I stand there in the snow looking at them but they don't notice me, and I feel how good it is to have stepped out of the car into the fresh air, and then I just stand there and then I see their footprints in the snow, how clear they are in the snow, going along the country road and then turning and going down the path to the playground, and then I start walking the same way and I follow their footprints when they turn and go down the path, the same path I went down earlier today, and I look at the playground and I see the two of them holding each other and it's like they're totally swallowed up by each other and I carefully follow their footprints and I see that they've let go of each other and she lies down in the snow with her arms at her sides and her legs pointing straight down and then she brings her arms and her feet up, and then she moves her arms and legs down, and then again, several times, and then she's lying with her feet sticking out and her arms straight at her sides, like she's frozen stiff, with an open mouth and wide-open eyes, and then I hear him say with fear in his voice that she mustn't lie there like that, it almost looks like she's lying there dead, she needs to stand up, he says and she stands up and she says she didn't mean to look dead and then he says she didn't really and she says yes well, and she goes over to him and takes his hand

Look how beautiful snow angels are, she says

Yes, he says

Can't you lie down and make one too? she says

I could, he says

and I walk past the playground and start up the hill on the other side, carefully, step by step, up to the hilltop, and there are no footprints on the path there, I am leaving my own new footprints in the new snow, and then I stop, turn around, and look at them still standing there holding hands and I think it's strange that they're so occupied with each other that they don't notice me, they only have eyes for each other, but if they did see me, did notice me, wouldn't they be scared, or maybe they'd feel embarrassed? or maybe they wouldn't care about me being here at all? I think and I see them let go of each other's hand and he lies down in the snow and does what she did, just faster, with sharper movements, like he's rushing to get it done almost, and she says no not like that and he stops and she says now it's her turn, she wants to make a third snow angel, because it's better with three angels than two, she says, and then he too lies stiff in his snow angel, with feet together, arms at his sides, with wide-open eyes and an open mouth, and she says he mustn't lie like that, she doesn't like it, it looks like he's dead, she says, and just like he didn't like how she was lying she doesn't like how he's doing it, lying there so that he looks dead, she says, so he needs to get up, she says and he stands up and then she again says she wants to make another snow angel, she says, and he goes over to her and they are standing there looking at the two snow angels lying there so pretty, next to each other, one of the angels practically touching the other with one of its wings, but just practically, just almost, or maybe not just almost, yes, the wings are touching each other and she says the snow angels are so beautiful like that that they should just leave them the way they are, she doesn't want to make a third angel after all, she says and he says that's what he thinks too, that the two snow angels are so nice that it's better just to stop with two, that feels right, sort of, he says

Until they get covered in more snow, he says

Or rained away, she says

Yeah, or both, he says

and they take each other's hands again and walk out of the play-ground and up the path to the road and I stand there and look at them and he says look, there's a car there, in the turn-off, it wasn't there when we walked by earlier, was it, he says and she says she can't remember if there was a car there before or not, in any case she didn't particularly notice a car, she says and I stop and stand stock-still for a moment because I don't want them to notice me, I'm not sure why but for whatever reason I don't want them to, I think, and then I start down the path again, carefully, taking short steps since it might be slippery, and I go down in my own footsteps that I left there when I went up and I'm looking down and I stop and look up and I see them, she and he are crossing the country road and I see them walk past the turn-off where my car is parked and then I look at the two beautiful snow angels in the playground and then I go into the playground and stop and stand there and look at the snow angels and they are so beautiful, so beautiful that if I tried to paint them it would turn out to be a bad painting, compared to the sight of the snow angels, I think, because that's how it is, that's how it almost always is, what's beautiful in life turns out bad in a painting because it's like there's too much beauty, a good picture needs something bad in it in order to shine the way it should, it needs darkness in it, but maybe, can I maybe paint a picture of two snow angels dissolving as they melt away? could I make a picture like that shine? I think and I know at the same moment, at this very instant, right now, that another picture has lodged inside me, it will be there forever, another picture has entered into me that I'll have to try to paint away, I think, and I notice at the same time that it's extremely cold now, I really need to get back into my car and then make it to Bjørgvin before it gets too late, so I really ought to get driving now, I think and I see the footprints in the snow, four of them going down, right next to one another, two bigger and two smaller, and four of them going up, right next to one another, two bigger and two smaller, and then mine going down after the four, and my footprints look so lonely, so alone, and so uneven, so erratic, as if I wasn't entirely steady on my feet, as if I was drunk, or staggering a little, I think, but I'm not drunk, it's been many years since the last time I had anything to drink, so maybe it's just my gait that's become a little unsteady, I think, but anyway it feels like I'm walking steadily and evenly like I used to, or maybe I didn't use to, I think and I go straight to the car, stamp the snow off my feet, brush snow off my trouser legs, sit down in the car and start it and pull out onto the road and in a kind of stupor I start driving south towards Bjørgvin, but I need to be sharper, because there are no tyre tracks on the road, everything's white, and I need to stay on the road and not drive into the ditch, I think, and then I see in the light from the headlights the two people I saw making snow angels walking hand in hand and he says it'll sure be nice to get home now and she says they'll be home soon

Ales and Asle, he says

Asle and Ales, she says

and I drive carefully past them and I drive farther south and I think that it was so beautiful seeing those two snow angels in the playground, and I'm absolutely sure that I saw what I just saw, it's not just something I saw in a dream or imagined, what I saw earlier today wasn't and the two of them lying under the black overcoat wasn't because that was the same long black coat he was wearing just now, I think and it's a coat like the one I'm sitting in now, I think and I fall back into a kind of stupor without any thoughts, I just drive south and a little farther along I catch up to a car that leaves tyre tracks on the road and then it gets easier to drive, I can follow its tracks, I think and it's really something, what I'm doing, I think, driving from Dylgja to Bjørgvin and back home and then back to Bjørgvin again on the same day, late, in snowy weather, but, yes, it feels like the only answer, I think, and I fall into that stupor again and I think that the reason I like driving so much is that my thoughts go away, I'm just concentrating on driving and so no thoughts bother me, no sorrows come over me, I'm just driving, no more no less, and time passes and I drive south and I get closer to Bjørgvin and not far up ahead I can take a right and drive down a road and then get to the block where Asle's building is, in Sailor's Cove, and I think it hasn't snowed any more since it stopped snowing at the playground but it was snowing in Bjørgvin too, everything is white and beautiful in Bjørgvin too, even if there are tracks, of both tyres and footsteps, and I think I should ring Asle's doorbell just in case, even though he's probably not home, or in any case won't open the door for anyone, and I turn off the main road and drive down to the building where Asle lives and park on that block and then go over to the front door of the building and press the doorbell button next to his name, and I stand there and wait, but of course no one comes to open the door, and I ring Asle's bell again and this time I hold the button down for a long time, and then I let go, I stand there, wait, but no one comes, and of course Asle's not home, I didn't think he was, he's probably at The Alehouse, at The Last Boat as it's called, he's probably sitting alone at a table there, I think, because he always goes to The Alehouse with all the retired old sailors, everything's cheap there, and sometimes he buys dinner there too, dinners are cheap and the beer is cheap plus you can get a shot of something stronger for a reasonable price, I think, yes, I don't believe he ever goes to any other restaurants or bars, not any more, he always goes to The Alehouse, to The Last Boat, so that's where

I'll go and look for him, I think, and I have my regular parking place not far from there, the car park at The Beyer Gallery, and I get back into my car and start it and think now I'll drive straight to The Beyer Gallery and it's almost unbelievable how much Beyer has helped me, I think, not only did he give me my first show in The Beyer Gallery back when I was still going to The Art School, and it rarely or ever happened that anyone debuted there while they were still at The Art School, yes, to tell the truth I was the first artist he ever showed before that artist had graduated from The Art School, yes, that's what Beyer said, and even more unbelievable was that all the paintings in my debut show sold, and since then it's been Beyer who's sold my pictures, yes, I don't know what I would have done without Beyer, and I remember very well the first time I saw him, it was the first time I set foot in The Beyer Gallery too, it was Ales who brought me there, she'd been in The Beyer Gallery many times, ever since she was a girl, even when she was little her parents used to take her along to exhibitions, and the first exhibition I saw in The Beyer Gallery was of paintings by Eiliv Pedersen, who would later be my painting teacher at The Art School, I think, and ever since my first show at The Beyer Gallery it was Beyer who's sold my paintings, I think, and he always manages to sell almost all of them, but sometimes, in the first couple of years, I have to admit, they sold for a terrible price, to tell the truth, but most of the pictures sell for a good price now, and there are always a few that don't sell, the best pictures too a lot of the time, and Beyer doesn't sell those ones cheap any more, he stopped doing that a long time ago, he'd rather put them in what he calls The Bank, the side room of the same gallery, where he keeps in storage the pictures that aren't in the show, and Beyer has the idea that the pictures that don't sell in Bjørgvin might sell in Oslo, because his good friend Kleinheinrich, who runs The Kleinheinrich Gallery in Oslo, likes having a show of my pictures as soon as there are enough of them, so when Beyer has enough unsold pictures sitting in The Bank The Kleinheinrich Gallery shows them in Oslo, eventually there's enough for a show in Oslo, about every four years, and since then I've sold almost all of my paintings, and then Beyer puts aside the paintings that didn't sell in Olso either because sooner or later he'll show them in Nidaros, at The Huysmann Gallery, because Beyer knew Huysmann well, he said, Huysmann ran the best gallery in Nidaros, Beyer said, yes, that's what he thought, Beyer said, and sooner or later there'll be a show in Nidaros too, I think, and Beyer himself also owns a large collection of my pictures, he's bought a picture for his collection from every one of my shows, and a few years ago when it was hard to sell my pictures for a good price he bought lots of them himself, and then other people copied him and bought pictures too, Beyer said, no I truly have no idea where I'd be without Beyer, I think, and now I'm going to have another new show at The Beyer Gallery soon, every year I have a show there before Christmas, a kind of Christmas show, yes, that sounds bad but the annual show I have there is just before Christmas, during Advent, because that's the best time to sell pictures, or in any case my pictures, Beyer says, and by now I have enough pictures waiting in Dylgja for the show this year, because I paint and paint, day in and day out, so now I just have to drive my paintings to Bjørgvin and if I'd thought about it I could have brought them with me earlier today, of course, but that would have been too much, I think and I drive to The Beyer Gallery where I always park my car when I'm in Bjørgvin

You can park in front of the gallery whenever you want, Beyer told me

and I said thank you and then Beyer taught me how to drive out of Bjørgvin from The Beyer Gallery and into Bjørgvin to park in front of The Beyer Gallery, which is located more or less in the centre of Bjørgvin, so that's where I've parked my car all these years, and other than that I never drive into Bjørgvin or any other city, I like driving but not in cities, in cities I get confused and anxious and feel lost and can never find where I'm going and sometimes I've gone down one-way streets the wrong way and everything's a mess, but I did learn how to drive to The Beyer Gallery and how to drive away from it, Beyer met me in Sailor's Cove once and sat in my car next to me and he told me everything I needed to do to drive in and then we drove into Bjørgvin, to The Beyer Gallery, and then we turned around and drove out of Bjørgvin, and at Sailor's Cove we turned around and drove back in to The Beyer Gallery again, and then we drove out of Bjørgvin again, to Sailor's Cove, and then in to The Beyer Gallery again, we took many trips in and out and eventually Beyer said now I should be able to remember the way, and I said that I thought I could, and I could, I think, and having learned how to drive to and from The Beyer Gallery has come in very handy, that's for sure, and without Beyer's help I'd probably never have dared to drive into the centre of Bjørgvin, most likely not, but now I simply drive straight to The Beyer Gallery at 1 High Street and park in front of the Gallery, as long as there's an empty space there, and there almost always is, if not I just sit and wait a little in the car and then a space always opens up, I think, and if it takes too long then I drive out to Sailor's Cove and turn around and then drive back, and it's never happened that there wasn't a space in front of The Beyer Gallery then, I think, and I know the quickest way to walk from The Beyer Gallery to The Alehouse, you just go down High Street for a bit and then down one of the little narrow passages, The Lane, which at its narrowest is honestly no more than three or four feet wide, and when you go down The Lane and out onto the street you see The Fishmarket just a few yards to the left, and then you cross that and take the street to the right along The Bay to get to The Alehouse, and next to The Fishmarket there's also The Prison, but if you take a street to the right after you get to The Lane and go to the first crossing, then go down the side street a little way, you'll get to The Country Inn, it's on The Wharf itself, with The Coffeehouse on the ground floor, yes, and I've taken these streets so many times that on the whole I have no trouble finding my way even when it's totally dark, I think, now, at night, all the snow that's fallen is shining, and the streets are partly lit by the light coming from the windows of all the buildings, I think, and I park my car in front of The Beyer Gallery and then go down High Street and then the snow starts falling and it's not just a flurry, the snow's really coming down, big wet snowflakes, and I stop, I squint, I run my hands through my hair and brush some snow from my eyes with the back of my hand and it's unbelievable how hard the snow is falling, now I just want to get indoors, and well it's not that far a walk to The Alehouse, to The Last Boat as it's called, and Asle will probably be sitting there, I think and I feel how tired I am, so tired, so if Asle isn't there I'll go straight to The Country Inn and ask if they have a room for me, I think and I brush snow off of my hair and eyes again and I walk on and I think that I'm tired, I'm truly exhausted, so maybe I should go to The Country Inn first and reserve a room right away and then go look for Asle in The Alehouse, and if he's not there I'll go straight to The Country Inn and lie down, in a warm room, on clean sheets, I think and I keep walking and I start down The Lane and that's not someone lying in the snow up there, is it? yes it definitely is, it's a person, that's what it looks like, I think, yes someone's there in the snow, covered with snow, with his head up on a little step, facing a building's front door, a person is lying in the snow that's falling and coming down on the person lying there and I hurry over to him and it's him! it's Asle! yes, Asle's lying there in the snow! how is that possible? Asle is just lying there in the snow and he seems lifeless, it's like he's lying there asleep, it's like he just fell, toppled forward, and he's lying there and the snow is falling and covering him and I hurry over and grab his shoulder and shake him from side to side and he says hello, well then, how lucky, yes he's alive but he wasn't conscious when I got here and I think what, what happened?

Did you slip? I say

I must have, Asle says

and Asle thinks he must have slipped, he's slipped for some reason, he thinks

But I don't remember slipping, he says

No, I say

and then I stand there and look at Asle and hold his shoulder

I don't understand what's happening, Asle says

and I keep my hand on his shoulder and then I put my hand under his arm and I try to lift him up off of the ground and he stays kneeling and his whole body is shaking and I say he must be freezing and he says no, no it's not that, and he breaks off, but you don't happen to have anything to drink on you? he says, yes, that's why I'm shaking, I need a drink, he says, you need to get me a little something to drink, something strong, he says and I say we need to catch a taxi and go to The Clinic

No, Asle says

and he's thinking he's not going to any damn Clinic, all he needs is a little something to drink and then everything'll be fine, everything'll be all right again, he thinks

I don't want to go to any Clinic, Asle says

I don't need to, he says

and again Asle says that all he needs is a little drink, he says and he kneels up and I stand back up and then take him under both his arms and pull and he helps as best he can and then Asle is standing and it's stopped snowing now and Asle shakes himself off, brushes the snow off himself

Well I'll be damned, I must have slipped, he says

and he says that now we need to get over to The Alehouse, to The Last Boat, yes, it's not far, it's just over there, he says, we just have to go the rest of the way down The Lane, he says and I see that we're standing in front of building number 5 in The Lane and he says yes and then we just need to take a left and we'll see The Fishmarket and there, on the other side of The Bay, there's The Alehouse, with a view onto The Bay, Asle says, and it was really great to run into me again after all this time, he says and I think well then we'll go over to The Alehouse and I'll buy him a little something to drink so he stops shaking and then I'll drive him home, I think

It's really been too long since we've seen each other, I say

Yes, Asle says

But now we'll have a glass of something and talk, he says

Yes, I say

and I think that this was an act of God, it was God's doing that I drove into Bjørgvin again, just think if I hadn't done that, think if Asle had stayed lying there in front of 5, The Lane, he'd have frozen to death, if no one had found him in time he'd have frozen to death right there in the snow, I think, so I absolutely did the right thing by driving into Bjørgvin, but why did I do it? when I was so tired? it turned out to be the right thing to do but what made me do it at all? I think and I hold Asle's arm and we walk down The Lane and now he's walking steadily, I think

I'm not drunk, Asle says

You don't need to hold my arm, he says

and I let go of his arm and Asle thinks that things are all right now, he's almost not shaking any more, but what a damn shame that he passed out, yes, he must have thought that he should ring the bell at Guro's house, and now why would he do that? what kind of a notion was that? he thinks, and then he passed out in front of the door and why was he lying on the steps of the building where Guro's apartment is, he thinks

I never get drunk any more, Asle says

I wish I did, he says

and I ask him in that case why does he drink, and he says that he drinks to get back to normal, to not shake, yes, to be normal the way other people are, he says and I say yes, yes, if that's how it is then that's how it is and by now we've come out from The Lane and we take a left and walk down the pavement and I see Asle start shaking again and I think that the way Asle's shaking now he needs something to drink in a hurry, to be normal again, I think

I only need a shot or two to be all right again, Asle says

and I think he mustn't drink so much, he needs to cut down on his drinking, he needs to get rid of this horrible shaking of his, I think, but can he do it? does he want to do it? I think and I say now we'll go to The Alehouse, to The Last Boat, and he can get a shot there and warm himself up a little, I say, and I say that after that I can drive him home

I'll buy you a shot or two and a glass of beer, I say

This round's on me, I say

No I can get this one, Asle says

I'm positive it's my turn, I say

Yes all right thanks, he says

No way are you buying, I say

and Asle says thanks, thanks, that's nice of you, he says and now we've reached The Fishmarket and I see Asle stagger a little and I grab his arm and he says thank you and then I hold Asle's arm and I say we'll be there soon, it's not far, no, I say

Yes, yes, he says

and it seems like he's shaking a little less, but now and then I notice that it seems to come in waves, the shaking moves through him like a wave and then he's still again

We can already see the sign from here, The Alehouse, he says

and then suddenly, totally unexpectedly, he crumples next to me, and I grab him and try to hold him up but I can't do it, Asle just collapses and stays lying on his side and I bend down and I shake him and he doesn't wake up and I hold my hand in front of his mouth and he's breathing, no, impossible, I can't take him to The Alehouse, we need to go to The Clinic, I think, and Asle sort of wakes up and he thinks damn it, he must have passed out again, he thinks and he looks up at me

I seem to have slipped again, he says

and I think it's good that I'm here, it's good that Asle isn't alone because what would happen to him then? he's totally weak and helpless now, isn't he? he's not exactly in good shape, I think, and anyway he couldn't be, I think, and I say again that we really ought to go to The Clinic and Asle says no, we're almost at The Alehouse and if he just gets a little something to drink he'll feel better, he says

I haven't had much to eat in a while, he says

I've hardly eaten in the past couple of days, that's why I'm so weak, he says

and he says that first he'll just have a drink, then he'll get himself a little food, they have good food at The Alehouse, first something to drink and then something to eat

All right, I say

But you just collapsed, I say

You're not okay, something's wrong, I say

and Asle thinks he's okay, it's just this shaking, and he does need to start drinking less, cut down, wean his body off drinking, he thinks

It's just that I need a drink, he says

We need to go to The Clinic, I say

No we'll go to The Last Boat, Asle says

and he tries to sit up and I grab him under his arms and help him get to his knees

No, you're not well, I say

and Asle says that he doesn't want to go to any Clinic, he'll be fine if he just has a drink, he says and I hold out my hand to him and he gathers his strength and I pull and he pushes off from the snow with his other hand and struggles up and gets up and then he's standing steady on his feet and I hold his arm and I think yes, well, then we'll just go to The Alehouse, but Asle isn't well and I should have taken him to The Clinic, I think, but I won't refuse him anything, he has to do for himself whatever he thinks is best, I think and then we walk carefully onward, step by step, and now he's steady on his feet, I can see that, and it's stopped snowing now, and I think that we'll make it, it's just up ahead, he'll get something to drink soon, and then something to eat, I think and I open the door to The Alehouse and Asle goes in and he says thanks and now he's perfectly steady, except that he's shaking, his whole body's shaking, especially his hands, and he stops right inside the door and brushes the snow off himself with shaking hands and I say he should sit down and I'll go buy him a drink, I say, and Asle walks over to the nearest table and sits down with his black overcoat still on and he puts his brown leather shoulder bag down on the chair next to him

It must feel good to sit down, I say

Yes, Asle says

and he's thinking that it's nice and warm in The Alehouse and if he just gets a drink then the shaking will stop and he sits nice and straight on the chair and I see that his whole body is shaking, and he needs some food, I think, but he probably can't manage to eat anything, I think

I'm having trouble getting food down, Asle says

As soon as a bite comes near my mouth I feel like I want to throw up, he says

Have you eaten anything today? I say

No, he says

Yesterday? I say

I don't think so, he says

and he looks at me and I say then I'll just go buy some beer and a shot for him, as for me I just want a cup of coffee, with a little milk, nothing else, I say and Asle nods and I go over to the counter and say what I want and the bartender goes to fetch it and I pay and then go over to the table where Asle's sitting and put a pint of beer and a shot glass down in front of him and then I go back and get the mug of coffee, which I add a little milk to, and then the second shot glass, and I go put it down next to Asle and I put the mug of coffee down on the table by the chair across from Asle and he puts his hands around the first shot glass and tries to pick it up but his hands are shaking too much and a little splashes out and I take his glass

I'll help you, I say

Thanks, he says

and I raise the glass to his mouth and Asle swallows it all in one gulp and then he breathes deeply in and out and he says now he'll feel better soon, everything'll be better in a minute, he says and he's thinking that if he just has that second drink then he'll be fine again, he thinks

I'll just have that too, Asle says

and he points at the full second glass and I ask him if I should help and Asle says he'll try to do it on his own

Yes, you do what you want, I say

and Asle raises the glass to his mouth with both hands and empties half of it and he thinks that was sure good, he already feels himself starting to calm down, he feels himself shaking less

That went well, I say

Yes, um, he says

and there's silence

You're not drinking any more? he says

and I say that I stopped drinking many years ago, I drank way too much, to tell the truth I was always drunk, and I needed to be sober in order to paint, I say, and Ales, my wife, well, of course she didn't like that I drank so much so I decided to stop, and it was hard at the beginning and I had to change a lot of what I was used to but I managed it, I finally managed to stop drinking, but I needed help, I say, and I think that I've already told Asle this so many times and still he always asks me if I've stopped drinking, I think

That's good, Asle says

That you were able to stop, he says

No, well, I say

It wasn't that hard, I say

and I think that I shouldn't say how I was able to do it, the fact is that I prayed and prayed to God every time the great thirst came over me, and also that if it hadn't been for Ales, and for my faith, I never would've been able to do it, I think, but since Asle's alone, and isn't a believer, I can't tell him that

I need to stop too, Asle says

But I can't, he says

It's impossible, he says

You need to get help, I say

Yes, he says

and then he puts his hands around the pint glass and tries to pick it up and he's shaking but not as much as before and with both hands he manages to bring the pint to his lips and he takes a good gulp of beer

That went all right, then, he says

I'm fine and dandy if I just have a drink, Asle says

and he thinks that he wants to live, so he needs to stop drinking, but often, yes, most of the time, he doesn't want to live any more, he's always thinking he should go out to sea, disappear under the waves, Asle thinks and he says as soon as he has a little something to drink he stops shaking, yes, it's like he gets all his strength back, he says and then there's a long silence

But you were lying there, in the snow, I say

Yeah, Asle says

Do you remember falling down? I say

No, he says

I just remember that you were there, that you woke me up, he says

and I sit down on the chair across from Asle and I see that there aren't many customers in The Last Boat at night, there are a few men scattered around the place sitting alone, each one by himself, each at his own table, one here and one there, with a pint of beer in front of him and a tobacco pouch on his side of the table, they roll themselves a cigarette, light it, take a good long drag of it, exhale the smoke, pick up the pint and take a sip of beer, sitting there alone, one here and one there, they sit there all alone in the world, each one at a different table, and it's like they never notice that anyone else is even there, I think and Asle takes out his tobacco pouch and box of matches and then rolls himself a cigarette and he says he often shakes so badly that he's had to start buying packs of cigarettes, but nothing tastes as good as a hand-rolled cigarette and beer and he's left the pack of cigarettes at home, Asle says and he lights his cigarette

You stopped smoking a long time ago too, right? he says

Yes, I say

and there's a pause

It's been years and years, I say

I switched to snuff and that's enough for me, I say

and I take out my snuffbox and take a good pinch

Maybe snuff would work for me too? Asle says

and again there's a pause

But the most important thing is to start drinking less, he says

Yes, I say

and I think that it's good he wants to drink less, but he won't be able to do it without help, I think

It was hard to break the habit of drinking, the thirst was still there, but after the beginning the thirst did go away and then it was easy to leave it alone, I say and I say that I didn't actually want to stop smoking, but I was smoking so much that I'd wake up in the middle of the night to have a cigarette or two, and I was so tired of that that I started taking a pinch of snuff and then I would sleep through the night, and before that I always had to get out of bed to smoke as soon as I woke up, but when I started taking a pinch of snuff the need for a morning cigarette went away and I could lie in bed and relax without needing to get up to smoke, I say, and there's a pause and I take off my shoulder bag too and put in down on the chair next to me and I look around at the other people in The Alehouse, sitting with their beer and tobacco in front of them like a fragile line of defence against the world, clinging to their cigarettes, their pints, as they sit there, and the sea inside them is large, whether stormy or calm, as they sit there and wait for the next and last crossing they'll set out on, the one that will never end, that they'll never come back from, and they don't feel fear, it'll be how it is and how it has to be, it must have a meaning, yes, Our Lord must have given it meaning, they think, he writes straight on crooked lines, they think, or anyway the good Lord is part of it all somehow, and it's the devil who made the lines crooked, they think and they hold onto their cigarettes and pints and then they pray a silent prayer, a prayer more like a look out over the sea inside them, wordless, but as far as the eye can reach over that sea the prayer extends, entirely wordless, because the words will be left behind, definitely, but there must be a port for people like them too, they're probably thinking, and then they feel a prick of something like fear so they raise their pint and have a taste of beer, the good old taste, it gives them a sense of security, I think and I see Asle raise his pint and take a gulp of beer

Delicious, he says

and I raise my mug of coffee and milk and clink his pint with it

Cheers, I say

Yes, cheers, he says

You're allowed to toast with this too, I say

Now we'll have some more to drink and then we'll take a taxi to The Clinic, I say

No, Asle says

and there's silence

You should just drive me home like you said, he says

and I think that whatever happens I can't leave him, because he's not well, just think if I hadn't driven back to Bjørgvin tonight, if I'd let myself think that I was too tired to drive, that a tired driver is a dangerous driver, if I hadn't made myself drive back to Bjørgvin or had been afraid to, I think and I don't understand why it felt so important that I do it, I think

That would be best, Asle says

Okay, I say

and I think that if Asle had fallen in The Lane, on the little steps outside number 5, and had lain there, covered in snow, had just stayed there under the snow, who knows how it would have ended? because people rarely walk by there, not in weather like this at any rate, he could have frozen to death, he definitely would have frozen to death in the snow, I think and I raise my coffee and milk again and Asle raises his pint

We've known each other a long time, you and me, I say

Almost our whole lives, he says

That's what it feels like anyway, he says

and he takes a sip of beer and puts the pint back down and he says he needs to piss and now that he's recovered it'll be fine, Asle says, and he gets up and I stay in my seat, looking straight ahead, at his pint, at the golden yellow beer, and then I hear a crash and I look up and I see Asle lying on the floor in his black overcoat and I get up and go over to him and The Bartender comes over to us and stands there with his hands hanging down and I look at Asle and the men sitting alone each at his own table get up and come over to us and one of them bends down and takes Asle's hands and holds it for a long moment, then looks diagonally up at us

His pulse is weak, he says

and he looks at me and I just nod and I hear Asle softly say help me up then, he says, and the men who came over are just standing there and I say it's no good, you're not well, this is the third time you've collapsed, I say and the man standing there says yes that happens sometimes, that happened to him too, I've probably heard of the shakes? he says, or delirium tremens, as they call it, the DT's, he says and he says that twice he's been on boats where people died of it, but that was a long time ago, he's not a young man any more, not by a long shot, no, he says, and he says that they took both of the men who died and wrapped them up real well and tied a weight to their feet and then they were carefully lifted overboard and then when the captain said rest in peace they dropped the body into the sea while one of the religious people onboard, because there are always one or two believers onboard a boat, said the Our Father and then anyone who knew a little of the psalm tried to sing Nearer My God To Thee and then it was over and everyone felt relieved and then, especially then, you felt better after a drink or three and someone else says yes, you sure did, and a third says yes that used to happen a lot before, that someone would die far from shore and be dropped into the sea, he says, what else were you supposed to do with the body? so far from shore? in the heat? in the boiling hot sun? the only thing you could do was wrap the dead man up well and tie a weight to his feet and then drop the body into the sea as soon as you could, he says, and the sea took him in, he says, and someone else says yes, yes, that's true, for the sea has God in it, he says and a third person says that the sea is the biggest graveyard in the world, and maybe the best one too, someone says, yes, there's more of God in the sea than in the earth on land, someone says and then it's quiet and then someone says

Sea and sky, he says

Sea and sky, yes, someone else says

and two other people say that they'd also been there when people had the DT's and died from it and were buried at sea, but that was a long time ago, it's not like that any more, that's just how it used to be, before, a long time ago, now boats have freezer rooms of course, and they've had them for a long time, someone says, and thank goodness for that says the third man, and someone says that he used to have the DT's himself, he says, yes, well, who hasn't, someone else says, but he's shaking so badly, I say, yes the best thing would be for you to take him to The Clinic, The Bartender says and someone else says that's right, someone there'll probably admit him, and he'll get medicine that'll maybe make him stop shaking, he says and Asle says they need to help him up and he thinks dammit what happened? what's wrong with him? he's fallen down again, and he's on a boat? yes, he is, and since he's so wobbly on his feet they must be on some some really rough seas, he thinks and his drink, where's his drink? he thinks, because if he just has a little more of something strong, and a little more beer, he'll be fine again, Asle thinks and I hold him by the arm and The Bartender takes his other arm and then we pull and Asle helps as much as he can and we get him to his feet and then Asle is standing and I'm holding his arm

Little to drink and I'll be fine, Asle says

No I don't think so, The Bartender says

You need to go to The Clinic, I say

and Asle says what the hell, he doesn't need to go to any Clinic, he's not sick, he just needs a drink, a lot to drink, he says and I say it's time for us to go to The Clinic now and the men standng around us say yes he's right, and one says he knows too many people who died from the shakes and The Bartender says he can call a taxi and I say yes and Asle says what the hell, but what can he do? there's no place for him here on this boat, Asle says and I see that The Bartender has gone over to the bar and picked up a phone and he's saying something into it and then he comes back and says he's called a taxi and it'll be here in a couple of minutes and he says maybe I need a drink for strength and I'm about to tell him that I don't drink, I had to stop, but The Bartender has already gone and he comes back with a generous pour in a glass and he holds it out to me and I say I don't drink any more, I've had my share and that's enough, I say and The Bartender says he understands and he lifts the glass to his own mouth and empties it in one go and then he says we can go outside now, the taxi'll be here any minute, he says and I see Asle standing there in his black coat and I go and put on my shoulder bag and pick up Asle's and put it on him and then I take Asle by the arm and steer him across the room and one of the other men takes Asle's other arm and a third goes to open the door for us and we go out and then one of the men who's come outside with us gives Asle's shoulder a shake and says it'll be fine, he'll get through this, he himself has been through what Asle is going through now, even if it was a long time ago, and he got through it, just barely, he says, but he was on a boat, far out to sea, and Asle is on land, and there's good medicine you can take now, medicine that reduces the shaking and helps you get to sleep, he says and the taxi comes and The Taxi Driver gets out and opens the rear door and Asle gets in and I go around the car, open the door, and get in next to Asle and I say we're going to The Clinic and The Taxi Driver starts driving without saying anything and I don't say anything either and when we're in front of The Clinic I pay for the ride and I say no when The Taxi Driver asks me if I want a receipt and then I open the door and get out and The Taxi Driver gets out too and opens the door on Asle's side and I take Asle's arm and get him out of the taxi and The Taxi Driver asks if I can handle the rest on my own and I say yes it'll be fine, I say and then Asle says where the hell is he? wasn't he just on a boat? in rough weather, the weather was bad as hell! he says and I hold Asle's arm tight

I can walk fine by myself, he says

But you kept collapsing, I say

Yes I know that, he says

That's just because the weather's so rotten today, he says

and then Asle says he just needs a little more to drink and everything'll be fine, a drink is all he needs, he says and I say yes yes and I open the door to The Clinic with one hand and we go inside and I see that no one else is there and Asle says I need a drink, he says that several times, and then he asks where he is, and I say we're in The Clinic, because he's not well, I say and while I keep hold of Asle's arm we go over to the reception desk and the woman sitting behind the desk slides open the window she's sitting behind and I say he's not doing too well and I nod at Asle and she asks me his name and date of birth and I've never been able to remember birthdays and I ask Asle when he was born and he answers who do I think he is, do I really think he's someone who goes around remembering things like that? he says and she asks for his relations, yes, that's what she says, and I say I'm just a friend but I know that his parents are dead, and he also had a sister but she's dead too, Alida was her name, and now why am I saying that? I think, and then I say that he was married twice and he has three children, one grown son and two younger children, a boy and a girl, and she asks if I have their names and addresses and I say I don't even know their first names, he always just talks about The Boy, who's grown-up now and lives in Oslo, and The Son and The Daughter, who live with their mother somewhere in Trøndelag, and I say that the only thing I know is that his first wife was named Liv and the second was Siv, I don't know their last names or addresses or anything like that, I say and then I say where he lives and I give her my name and my address and phone number and she says that a nurse will come get us in a moment and then a doctor will examine Asle and I thank her and then Asle and I go sit down on a sofa and I say now we'll just wait a little and then a doctor will examine him and he says he doesn't want anyone to examine him, not a doctor and not anyone else, he doesn't need any doctor, that's the first thing, he says, and the second thing is that there isn't any doctor here on this boat, so the only thing he needs is a drink, and this boat? why is he on board this boat? and where is he? and what's the name of this boat he's on? is he on The Last Boat? Asle asks and he says he doesn't think we're in Bjørgvin, this is some other city, so where are we now? Asle says and I say that we're in Bjørgvin and Asle says no, no goddamn way, he's been in Bjørgvin long enough to know what it's like there so where are we? we're not on a boat, have we landed on Sartor? he says, are we in Flora? where are we? he says, now, yes, now he's got it, we're on Sartor, no doubt about it, he says, yes, that's where we are, Asle says and then I see a nurse holding a door open and I take Asle over to the door and The Nurse says welcome and then we go through the door and The Nurse points across a corridor and she opens the door to an office and we go in and a man is sitting behind a desk inside and that must be a doctor and The Doctor says yes and I say he's shaking like this and he collapsed a few times, he was unconscious for a bit, and he's started saying things that don't make sense, and well he doesn't entirely know where he is and stuff like that, I say and Asle again says can't I find him anything to drink, he needs a drink, if he could just get a little drink everything would be fine again, he says, and why are we on Sartor? what are we doing on Sartor? he says, when did he get here? he says and I look at The Doctor and I look at Asle and The Doctor says Asle needs rest and The Nurse says I can leave now, they'll take care of him now, Asle needs his rest now, just rest, he needs to sleep and rest as much as he can, she says, but I can call tomorrow and then maybe I can come see him, or maybe the best thing would be to let him rest more and I won't be able to see him, she says and I say Asle might need some things and I can come by and bring him whatever he wants at least, I say and she says I can call tomorrow and they'll know more, she says and I say thank you for all your help and then I tell Asle take care

You're leaving? he says

You don't have to go, he says

I do have to go, I say

But you can't, we're too far out to sea, he says

I have to go, I say

And you need to take good care of yourself, I say

and then I leave and cross the corridor and go out to the reception area and I see that some more people have come to The Clinic now, they're sitting and waiting their turn, and then I leave The Clinic and stop outside the door and I breathe in deeply and breathe out slowly and I see that it's started snowing again, big white snowflakes are falling and falling and I think now I'll go to The Country Inn and get a room there and then maybe I'll see Asle tomorrow morning, and then I'll drive back to Dylgja, as early as I can, I think and it's snowing, not heavily, not lightly, but evenly, quietly, the snow is coming down in big snowflakes evenly and quietly over Bjørgvin and I think now I really need something warm to drink, yes, a cup of coffee, a cup of coffee with milk would hit the spot, I think and I walk away from The Clinic and I think that I was only able to take a couple of sips of coffee back at The Alehouse before we had to go to The Clinic, and it would have been nice with something to eat too, just something light, I think, so now I need to go somewhere you can get food and drink, anywhere's fine, I'll get a cup of coffee with milk, definitely, I think and I think that if only I had a phone number for one of Asle's children I could have called them, the best would be The Boy, the eldest, who lives in Oslo now, but I don't even know his name, and I've heard about The Son and The Daughter and I know that Asle's first wife was named Liv and the second wife was Siv but I don't know where they live or anything like that, I think and then I see the lights from a sign above a door and the glowing sign says Food and Drink in a blue swoop of letters, that's where I'll go, I think, and then I'll go to The Country Inn, and I'm sure I'll be able to get a room there even though I haven't reserved one, sure, there are lots of times I've just showed up at The Country Inn and asked for a room and they've always had space for me, even if I had to sleep on a spare bed in some kind of store room in the attic that one time, so I'm sure it'll be fine, they're so helpful and nice at The Country Inn, I think and I open the door beneath the shining blue sign that has Food and Drink on it and I go in and right inside the door I stop and look around and I see that there's a bar in the middle of the place, it's not an especially big place, there's some kind of rectangle in the middle of the room and then some tables by the walls, but no customers, yes actually there's one woman sitting alone at one of the tables, with medium-length blonde hair, she's sitting and rolling herself a cigarette and there's a glass of red wine on the table in front of her, and she looks familiar, doesn't she? no, I've never seen her before, that's just something I'm imagining, since people look like other people, I think and I wait and I watch for a bit to see if I can just go sit down or if I'm supposed to go over to the counter and then The Bartender nods towards me and I go over to the bar and The Bartender looks at me and holds out his open hand towards me

A glass of beer for the gentleman? he says

No thanks, I say

What can I get for the gentleman? he says

Just a cup of coffee, I say

I can do that, he says

and then The Bartender is already filling a white mug with coffee from the percolator and Food and Drink is printed on the mug and then he asks if I'd like a little something to eat with that and I say yes, maybe, a bite to eat with that would be nice, I think and The Bartender hands me a menu and I glance at it quickly and I see that I can get an open-faced ground-beef sandwich with onions and I say I'd like an open-faced sandwich, ground beef, anyway I always get that, I think, and The Bartender says he can take care of that, I can just take my coffee and sit down and he'll bring me the sandwich, he says, and I say thanks very much, and then I ask him if he has any milk for my coffee and he apologises and says he should have asked me about that himself of course, he says, and yes of course he has milk, he says and then he puts a little pitcher of milk down on the kitchen table next to the mug and he hands me a little coffee spoon and I take the spoon and pour a little milk into the coffee and stir it and then I look for an empty table, and I see the woman with the medium-length blonde hair sitting alone and there's an empty table behind her and I go over to the table and put the mug down and at the exact moment I sit down the thought comes to me, Asle's dog! Bragi, his dog, he's alone in Asle's apartment! and it may be a while before Asle gets out of The Clinic in the worst case, yes, it might take a long time before he gets back home to his apartment and his dog, so I need to get into the apartment and get his dog, Bragi, and walk him, and then it'd probably be best to take him with me back to Dylgja, I think, because I need to take care of the dog until Asle is better, until he's back home, I think and I take a sip of the coffee and it's very hot but good, coffee really warms you up, and I take another sip, yes, that's good, I haven't had anything to eat or drink for most of the day, I think, almost nothing, so this'll be good with a little food, and at the same moment a feeling of happiness comes over me, I'm glad I can just be sitting here together with other people, so to speak, even if it's just the woman with the blonde hair sitting in front of me drinking red wine and smoking, and people should drink as much as they want, I mean except for people who can't stop when they need to, no that's not what I want to think about any more right now, I think and I wonder if I've seen her before, the woman sitting in front of me with her back to me, some time or another? maybe we've even spoken to each other? or met somehow? it's definitely possible, and anyway it's good that there's somebody else at this café too and I didn't end up sitting alone, it's always a little sad to sit all by yourself in a café, it's like something that should be there is missing, not like when I'm at home, then it feels like something's wrong if I'm not alone, but not when Åsleik's there, but anyway there's no one who ever comes to see me besides him, I think, so how can I even think about it? about how I get sort of uncomfortable when people come visit me, I think, and I think that Asle's dog can't be left by himself, so I need to go get the keys to his apartment and then get the dog, I need to go back to The Clinic and get the apartment keys and then I need to drive and get the dog, yes, Bragi, yes, and then I'll need to look after him until Asle is better again, I think and I see The Bartender coming towards me carrying a white plate with a ground-beef sandwich on it in one hand and a knife and fork in a white napkin in the other hand and he puts the plate down in front of me and he puts the knife and fork in the napkin next to the plate and then he says he hopes the food tastes good and I think it looks absolutely great, I'm so hungry, and I start eating right away and I eat the food and drink my coffee and it tastes incredible, I was really hungry, I think and I see the woman with the medium-length blonde hair sitting at the table in front of me stub out her cigarette and stand up, and I see that she's pretty drunk and I think now she's going to come talk to me, and I look down and I take another mouthful of ground beef, onions, and bread

It's you, it can't be, she says

and I look up and see the woman with the medium-length blonde hair standing in front of me holding the edge of the table and I know that I've seen her before, but I can't quite remember when it was, where it was

Don't you remember me? she says

and I try as hard as I can to recall who she is

Silje, she says

and she laughs

You really don't remember me? she says

Not even my name? she says

and the woman who says her name is Silje looks at me almost amazed, and then she says that she thinks about me a lot, she's often hoped we'd run into each other, it's been so long, but I was married then, wasn't I? and she didn't know where I lived, all she knew was that my name was Asle, she says

And now here you are, sitting right in front of me, she says

At last, she says

I almost can't believe it, she says

It's been so long since I've seen you, she says

You remember me, right? she says

You weren't that drunk, were you? she says

And you came to my place a bunch of times, she says

and I start to see before my eyes a small apartment, a sofa, a bookshelf, some photos on the walls, and, no I don't want to think about that

You must remember me, don't you remember? she says

My place in The Lane? she says

Ground floor, she says

and I don't say anything and I see that I've finished eating my open-faced sandwich, I sure was hungry, that went down quick, I think and I put the knife and fork down on the plate next to each other

Anyway it's great to see you again, she says

and I nod, I drink my coffee, empty the mug, and then I say I'm afraid I have to go, there's something I need to do, I say and I wave to The Bartender and scribble in the air with my hand and he nods to me and then she says I really should come and see her, she still lives where she did before, number 5, The Lane, ground floor, she says, and she says surely I remember her? I can't have been that drunk all the time? and I must remember that she was with me at The Country Inn too? she, Silje, or whatever her name was, maybe it was something else? was it maybe Guro? yes, she'd even slept in the same bed with me at The Country Inn, she says, and she remembers it, yes, even though it was a long time ago, even though I had medium-length brown hair back then worn loose and not the grey hair tied back with a hairband I have now, she says and she laughs and she says she even remembers my birthday, because I told her my birthday so she could calculate my lucky number, she says and she asks if I remember what my number was and I say I need to go and she says it was eight, or four times two, and then she says she'd be happy to see me if I came by sometime and The Bartender comes over and I take the bill he's handing me and I take out my wallet and take a note out and hand it to him and I say that's fine and he says thank you and I get up and then I push my chair in and she lets go of the edge of the table and I see that she's not too steady on her feet and I say I need to go, I'm actually in a real hurry, I say and she says she knows my name is Asle and that I'm an artist, and she knows more than that, she says, because every single year during Advent she goes to the show I have up at The Beyer Gallery, she says and she falls silent and suddenly she gets a kind of dreamy look in her face and then she says that it was so long ago but ever since the first time we met she's seen all of my shows in Bjørgvin, and she's often wanted to buy a picture, but she couldn't afford it, yes, she thinks my pictures are really great, she says and I say have a good night and she says she'd be happy if I dropped by sometime, number 5, The Lane, that's where she lives, surely I remember? I was never that drunk, she says

Silje, she says

and she laughs and puts a hand on my back

Or maybe it was Guro? she says

But The Lane, number 5, you remember that much? she says

And so my name is Guro, she says

and I say I have to go now but it was nice to see her and I hear her say something but I can't quite catch what it is and then she says good night and I say thanks same to you and then I leave and I think now I need to go back to The Clinic and get the keys to Asle's apartment, because his dog can't be left there by himself, and I can take care of the dog while Asle's sick, I need to tell Asle that, I think, and I think I'll find my way to The Clinic, it'll be fine, I wasn't walking for long before I came to Food and Drink so it'll be easy to just go the same way in the opposite direction, I think, standing there in the snow on the pavement outside Food and Drink and I think I should go straight, in one direction or another, so now it's only a matter of picking the right direction, I think, and when I was coming here I was on the other side of the street, and when I saw the sign saying Food and Drink I crossed the street, that's what happened, I think, so now I obviously just need to cross the street and go straight, that must be right? I think and I think that it's good it's stopped snowing, it's easier to find your way when you can see where you're going, obviously, I think and I cross the street and I go straight and it's not snowing now but for some reason or another I almost always go the wrong way, I think, I don't know why, even if I know the way very well I somehow always manage to get it wrong, it's like with numbers, whatever I'm supposed to do with them goes wrong, I don't know why, I always add wrong and I always walk the wrong way, so the best thing to do would be to take a taxi, if one comes, I think, because I need to go to The Clinic and get the keys to Asle's apartment because his dog is still there, and he, Bragi, can't stay there alone so I need to go get the dog, I think and once they give me Asle's keys I need to get back to my car in front of The Beyer Gallery and then drive out to the building in Sailor's Cove where Asle's apartment is and get the dog, Bragi, and then I need to drive back and park the car in front of The Beyer Gallery and then I need to go to The

Country Inn and check into a room, I think, so first things first I need to get back to The Clinic, I think and the moment I think it I see a taxi and I stick out my hand and it stops and I open the door and get in and I say I'm going to The Clinic and The Taxi Driver says yes, that'll be no problem, it's not far, he can get me there no problem, he says and I say don't know my way around Bjørgvin too well and The Taxi Driver says that's all right, if I don't he does, he says and then neither of us says anything and he drives and practically as soon as he starts driving I see the sign that says Clinic and The Taxi Driver stops by the entrance and I pay and I say that wasn't a long way and he says well a ride is a ride, he says and I get out of the taxi and I'm a little embarrassed, I didn't think we were that close to The Clinic, it was maybe a block away and I took a taxi, which is almost crazy, I think, and I go into The Clinic and now the entrance is empty again and I go over to the reception and the woman there is the same woman as before and I go straight to the window and the woman sitting there recognises me and she slides the window open and I ask about him, yes, Asle, yes, and she says they transferred him to The Hospital almost immediately, she says, so if I want to see him I have to go to The Hospital, she says and I ask, I don't know quite why, if she's been on duty a long time and she looks at me and smiles a slightly tired smile and says it's been a long shift, yes, because the woman who was supposed to relieve her couldn't come because of a sick child and they didn't find anyone else to substitute and so she said she could stay on duty until they found someone else and the woman who's supposed to relieve her is on her way now, she says, and gosh it'll be good to get some sleep, she needs to go to sleep, and sleep well, when she gets home she's going to sleep, just sleep, she says and I look outside and I see the taxi I came in still parked by the entrance to The Clinic and I say if I hurry I can maybe take the taxi that's there to The Hospital and she says yes it's still there, the taxi, and I say goodbye and she says thank you at the same time and then I hurry outside and open the rear door of the taxi and I ask if it's still available

Yes, sure, The Taxi Driver says

That was a quick visit, he says

Everything's quick with you isn't it, he says

and I ask him to take me to The Hospital, because the man I wanted to see has been transferred there, I say

It must be serious then, The Taxi Driver says

Serious? I say

Yes, the only people who get transferred to The Hospital are the ones in really bad shape, he says

and then I get into the taxi and I think yes, he truly was in bad shape, yes, Asle collapsed several times and I found him lying in the snow, covered in snow, there in The Lane, there in front of number 5, and wasn't that where Silje or Guro or whatever her name was said she lived? or was that number 3, The Lane? yes I think it probably was, and what a strange coincidence, I think, and Asle was shaking so badly, his whole body was shivering, I think and it was so lucky, so lucky that I drove back to Bjørgvin, and actually it's a total mystery why I did it, I think, since I'd already driven to Bjørgvin and back earlier, but this uneasiness or whatever you want to call it just came over me, and if I hadn't found Asle he might still be lying under the snow and shaking, no, no, that's not true, someone else would probably have found him, there are plenty of people in Bjørgvin, someone or another is always out and about, I think and I hear The Taxi Driver say he hopes there's no more snow tonight, but at least the people who're supposed to keep the streets clean have done their job for once, both the main roads and the side streets have been ploughed well, he says, they don't usually get it done so fast, he says and I don't say anything and then The Taxi Driver stops talking too and we start driving and there's not much traffic and the taxi pulls over in front of The Hospital and stops by the entrance and I pay and say thanks for the ride and I go into The Hospital and

I see the reception desk and I go over to it and the woman sitting there looks up at me drowsily and I tell her my name and say that I'm here to see Asle and she says we have the same name and she says yes well she'll see where he is and she flips through her papers a little and then she looks me, she looks long and hard at me, and she asks what I said his name was and then she says ah yes Asle yes and then she pages through the pile of papers sitting in front of her

Asle, yes, I say

Asle, that's right, she says

and she turns more pages

Yes your Namesake was admitted, tonight in fact, she says

Can I see him? I say

No, not now, she says

and she looks down and I felt something give a little start inside me, because his dog, Bragi, his dog can't be left alone, I have to go get his dog

Is he seriously ill? I say

Yes I should say so, she says

and then she says he was admitted tonight, not long ago, and that he's seriously ill, yes, she says, and she says that I'm listed as a relative and I say we're old friends but I'm just a friend, but it was me who brought him to The Clinic, I say

But does he have a family? she says

Yes but he lives alone, I say

and I say that he's divorced, he was married twice, and that neither of his ex-wives and none of his children live in Bjørgvin any more, but he has a dog, and his dog is alone in his apartment, and the dog can't be left alone there and she nods and says so he's divorced and he has three children

Divorced twice, I say

Three children, I say

and I say that I know he doesn't have much contact with either ex-wife or any of the children, but still, it's his dog I'm thinking of, he, the dog, Bragi's his name, can't be left alone in the apartment, someone has to go get him and take care of him

Someone needs to look after his dog, I say

Of course, she says

Can I have the keys so I can get the dog, walk him, and take care of him until Asle's able to do it himself? I say

I can't give you the keys to his apartment, she says

and then she says that he has children, and I'm just a friend

But the children don't live in Bjørgvin, I say

The oldest son lives in Oslo and the two others live somewhere in Trøndelag, I say

and I say that he's not in contact with either of his ex-wives and he's barely in contact with his children, just a little with the oldest son, The Boy he calls him, but The Boy lives in Oslo, I say and I think there's no way she's going to give me the apartment keys and I think what in the world am I going to do then? will I have to break into his apartment? because the dog, Bragi, can't stay there alone, I think, and now she doesn't want to give me the keys, I think and I see her pick up a telephone and she dials a number and then she says something about seriously ill and someone who's asking about him and he says there's a dog alone in the apartment of the man who was admitted and then she looks at me and asks if there isn't some super or custodian there and I say that there isn't, not that I know of, I say and she nods and then she says into the phone that there isn't a custodian where he lives and that I really want to go look after the dog, and there aren't any close relatives in Bjørgvin who could do it, she says

The dog can't just be left alone, I say

and she listens more and then says thank you, good, yes, she says and then she says that they've taken all his clothes, his sketchpad, his keys, everything he had with him, and put them in a closet in the room where he is now but someone will go get the keys and then that person will drive me to the apartment and go in with me so I can get the dog, since she can't give me the keys, because the rules are that she can only give the keys to a family member and I'm just a friend

Yes, I'm just a friend, I say

Right, she says

and she sighs and she says I can sit and wait for as long as it takes but it shouldn't take too long, because someone'll get the keys and then take me to the apartment to get the dog, yes, this isn't the first time something like this has happened of course, she says, in fact they have a strict procedure for what to do, she says, and look, here he is already, she says and I see an older man come walking towards me and he says he'll take me to pick up the dog, he says

Thanks, I say

and then I say thank you for your help to the woman sitting at the reception desk and then I go over to the older man and he doesn't say anything and then we go out and get into a car and then the older man says that there's been a lot of snow but he's already brushed the snow off the car, he says, and I can hear that he's from Bjørgvin and I say yes it certainly was coming down earlier and he says that this happens sometimes, someone's admitted and they have a pet at home that someone needs to look after, but they're usually not in a position to tell anyone about it themselves so then it's some neighbour or another who calls and complains about a dog yapping and says it's been yapping for days, that happens a lot, he says, and then a lot of the time it's him who goes to get the pet, that's part of his job, and he takes the pet to The Animal Rescue, or sometimes it's a relative or neighbour or friend or someone who takes care of the pet, like I'm planning to do, the older man says and he says well, he's a kind of handyman at The Hospital, he says, and I explain to The Handyman where Asle lives and he says he knows where that is, and that it's not far, he says and then we sit there in silence and drive on and The Handyman stops and parks the car in front of the building where Asle's apartment is, almost exactly where I parked earlier, and then we get out of the car and he unlocks the front door of the building and I say Asle's apartment is on the second floor on the left and we go there and we hear the dog yapping and I say the dog is waiting by the door yapping and yapping and The Handyman says that's quite a voice on that dog and I say that little dogs, and this is a little dog, I say, often have the loudest voices

Yes and of course they often bite people too, The Handyman says

Are you scared of dogs? I say

No, he says

and then he turns and then he says that he's a little scared of dogs

It must be, well, it must be because a dog bit me once when I had to go get him, The Handyman says

And they often act very threatening, dogs, when I come to get them, he says

And when I'm alone I wear thick protective gloves, he says

and he holds out his hands

I can go in first, I say

If you wouldn't mind, he says

I'll unlock the door and then you open it and go in, he says

and then The Handyman stands there and fumbles with the keys and then unlocks the door and I open the door and go in and as soon as I'm in the hall the dog starts jumping up and down at my feet and he's yapping and yapping and I feel around on the wall with my hand and find a switch and I turn on the hall light and I look down at the dog yapping and jumping around at my feet and then I bend down and pick up the dog and I hold him in my arms and I pet him on the back, I pet him and pet him and say good boy, good boy, Bragi, good boy Bragi, I say and the dog calms down and The Handyman comes into the hall behind me and I say I think I know where the leash is and The Handyman says we can't stay in the apartment, we're not allowed to, it's not permitted, we have to just pick up the dog and leave, he says and I say I'll just look for the leash and I know that it's usually on the bureau a little way down the hall and I see the leash sitting there and I see that all the doors are shut, the one to the kitchen, the one to the living room, or the studio, and I say I should have used the bathroom earlier and The Handyman says well I can go ahead and do that, surely there's nothing wrong with that, he says and I go into the bathroom and I find the light switch and I turn on the light and I see that everything is clean, everything smells clean and fresh, so Asle must have washed the floor and scrubbed the toilet and the sink, I think and I think no, if he's cleaned everything so nicely maybe I should hold it in until I get to the room in The Country Inn, but the dog? I can't just take the dog to The Country Inn with me? are people allowed to bring dogs to The Country Inn? I think, and no, I hadn't thought of that, but, yes, well, the dog can probably sleep in my car, simple as that, and then tomorrow I'll drive to Dylgja and I'll bring the dog home with me of course, I think, and it'll be nice to have a dog, actually I've always wanted a dog, but when I was little Mother didn't want me to get one, and Ales didn't want a dog either, and after Ales was gone, well, I sort of stopped thinking about how it might be nice to have a dog, but anyway now I'm going to have a dog for a while at least, I think, yes, when I wake up tomorrow morning I'll have a little breakfast, I think, and as I think that I realise I'm hungry and I see in my mind the generous breakfast buffet at The Country Inn, fresh bread, scrambled eggs, bacon, some of the bacon is crispy and some of it's still soft, and I have to admit I'm really looking forward to breakfast because that ground-beef open-faced sandwich, it was good, but it wasn't exactly filling

You need to come out now, The Handyman says

Yes, right, I say

The rules are that we have to just pick up the house pet and not stay any longer in the home than we need to, he says

and I say I'm coming, and I turn out the bathroom light and go out into the hall and I see The Handyman standing in the front doorway and he's holding the door handle and I think now I want to look in the main room and I open the door to that room

No, we need to leave now, The Handyman says

I just thought I should make sure everything's all right, I say

Yes, okay, he says

and I turn on the light and I see that everything's where it belongs, everything's in its place, and pictures are stacked in neat piles, all with their homemade stretchers facing out so that you can't see a single painting, and the brushes and tubes of paint and everything are in their proper places on the table, and a roll of canvas is propped in a corner and there's wood for stretchers in another corner and I hear The Handyman ask if everything's all right in there and I say yes everything's fine, everything's where it should be and he says in that case we need to leave and I say yes all right and turn out the light and shut the door to the living room or studio or whatever it should be called and The Handyman says all right come on then and I think it's horrible how he's fussing about all this and I say I need to just look in the kitchen too, and he says yes, yes, that's probably fine, yes the rules allow for that too now that he comes to think of it, they say a person can look around to make sure everything's in order, that the lights are off, that the burners aren't on, things like that, yes, but he usually doesn't do all that because the most important thing is just to do what you need to do and get out, do it and leave right away, for example get the dog, or the cat, if necessary, and other than that, yes, well, it's the family, the relatives, who should take care of the rest, he says and I say yes yes

But hurry up, The Handyman says

Yes yes, I say

and I open the door to the kitchen and feel my way over to the light switch and turn on the light and of course, yes I think of course, yes, obviously everything here too is as it should be, everything's where it belongs, there's a glass in the sink and a bottle with a little still water in it on the table, there's not a crumb anywhere, and it's almost creepy how neat Asle kept everything, I think, and I don't know why that should be sort of creepy

Now we need to go, The Handyman says

Yes yes, I say

and I turn off the kitchen light and I shut the door and then I pick the leash up off the bureau with one hand while I hold the dog with the other and then I go towards the doorway where The Handyman is standing and he steps aside and I turn off the hall light and he shuts the door and then I stand there with the dog in my arms and I see The Handyman lock the door and then I start down the stairs and I hear The Handyman checking to feel if the door is locked and checking it again and I go to the front door of the building and once we're outside I put the dog down and the second I put him down in the snow he jumps a little to the side and raises his leg and I see him make a yellow hole of piss in the white snow, it's not so nice to look at, and then the dog starts hopping and dancing around in the fine white loose snow and I kick some snow over the yellow piss and everything's white and pretty again and the dog jumps around and around in the snow, burows his muzzle into the snow, rolls around, yes, it's like the dog is taking a bath in the snow and then I hear The Handyman say well then that takes care of that, he says, and he asks me where he should take me now and I say I'm staying at The Country Inn and he asks if guests are allowed to bring dogs into the rooms there and I say I don't know and he asks what I plan to do with the dog if I can't bring him up to the room and I say in that case he can sleep in my car

Yes I suppose he could always do that, The Handyman says

and then we stand there and look at the dog skipping and jumping around in the snow

Did you know him well? The Handyman says then

Did I? I say

Yes, right, do you, he says

Yes, I say

He's a good friend? he says

Yes, I say

Just a friend? he says

Yes, just a friend, I say

Just a friend, okay, he repeats

and then The Handyman says we should go and I say I'm sure the dog needs to go, and I watch the dog hunch up, with his rear end sort of sticking up over the snow and his tail in the air, and he takes a good long shit

That wasn't nothing, The Handyman says

He really needed to go, didn't he, I say

and The Handyman nods and the dog is finished and then The Handyman asks shouldn't I pick up the shit and I ask him if he has a bag to pick it up with and he says he doesn't and I say I don't either and so I kick some snow, powdery white snow, over the dogshit

Yes it's sure been snowing, The Handyman says

It's not often it snows in Bjørgvin, he says

No, I say

Pretty unusual actually, he says

But it's nice with the new snow, he says

Nice and white, he says

Yes, I say

and then we stand there and look blankly at all the whiteness and neither of us says anything

Even when it's dark out, it glows when there's new white snow, The Handyman says

It's a little like daytime even though it's night, he says

Yes it is nice, I say

But in Bjørgvin the snow never stays long, he says

No, it'll get rained away soon, I say

and The Handyman asks where I live and I say I live in Dylgja

Is it the same there? he says

Yes, yes, one day it snows and the next day it rains, I say

It turns into dirty snow and slush, I say

Right, The Handyman says

Not to mention when it turns icy, he says

Right, the first thing that happens is it ices over, I say

and then we start walking towards his car and I call Bragi and then the dog comes jumping towards me

So the dog's name is Bragi, The Handyman says

Yes, I say

Bragi, right, he says

Yes, Bragi's his name, I say

Tomorrow it'll rain again, The Handyman says

Yes, yes, it will, I say

That's how it always is, he says

There's never a real winter in Bjørgvin, there's maybe two days a year when it's really winter and that's it, he says

That's how it is, he says

Have you ever lived in Bjørgvin? he says

Yes, well, I say

Many years ago, I say

Did you work in Bjørgvin? he says

I went to school here, I say

and I think that The Handyman is so inquisitive he's probably going to ask what kind of school I went to, but if he does I'll just say something to make him think it was just a normal school, I think, but he doesn't ask me anything else and we get to his car and he unlocks it and the dog shakes, shakes the snow off, and I stamp my feet and kick my shoes against each other, to get the snow off, and then I pick up the dog and brush snow off him

You like dogs? The Handyman says

Yes, don't you? I say

No, he says

Because one of them bit you? I say

Probably, he says

But I never did like them really, he says

I like cats though, he says

Me too, I say

I like dogs and cats both, I say

But you like dogs the best? he asks

Well I think more about getting a dog, at least, I say

You want a dog? The Handyman says

Yes, I say

and there's silence

But it's a big responsibility too, having a dog, I say

and it's silent again and we get into the car, and I sit with the dog on my lap and The Handyman asks me where I want him to take me, to The Country Inn, right? he says and I say he can take me to a place near The Lane and he asks if that's near where I parked my car and I say yes it is, so he can drop me off there, but I don't want to tell him where I parked my car because then he'll start asking me if I know Beyer, if I know rich people in Bjørgvin, the high society, or maybe I'm an artist, or maybe an art collector, he'll start asking things like that and he says yes all right and I don't say anything, but no way will I tell him where I parked my car, but I'm lucky to have a regular place to park, it can be really hard to find somewhere to park in Bjørgvin, lots of times the parking space is too small and too narrow for a large car to fit, people always say the spots are itsy-bitsy, I wonder why, you never hear anything called itsy, whatever that is, or bitsy either, whatever that is

I can do that, The Handyman says

Do what? I ask

Drop you near The Lane, he says

Great, I say

and then he starts the car and drives and we sit there in silence and then it starts snowing again a little, one snowflake after another falls down through the air and The Handyman turns on the windshield wipers and then he turns them off again, and again snowflakes land on the windshield one by one and he turns the wipers on again

It's pretty with the new snow, The Handyman says

and then we sit there not saying anything, me with the dog in my lap, and Bragi is lying there totally peacefully and it's nice to feel his warmth, I think and I pet his back again and again and the warmth from the dog does me good, it's good to feel his fur, I think and it snows and snows and the windshield wipers go back and forth, back and forth, and I see The Beyer Gallery and The Handyman says maybe he can stop here and I say that's fine and he stops and he asks a little uncertainly if this is where I wanted to be dropped off and I say yes great thanks and then I ask if I should pay for the ride and The Handyman says I shouldn't and then he says good night and I say yes good night and then I get out and I shut the car door behind me and then I stand there with the dog in my arms and it's snowing and snowing and I see The Handyman turn the car and drive away down the same street he drove here on, and I think now I should just go over to my car and put the dog in the car and then go on foot to The Country Inn, I'm sure I know the way from The Beyer Gallery to The Country Inn, I've learned how to get there, of course I can do that, that was where I was going when I found Asle lying in The Lane, covered with snow, I think, yes, if I can't even manage this then I shouldn't be living alone, I think and I see my car parked outside The Beyer Gallery, covered in snow, and as more snow keeps coming down I go over to it and I think I can't leave the dog in the car, it's suddenly turned wintry, and maybe he's never slept alone in a car before? maybe he'll be scared and spend the whole night yapping or howling and the neighbours will come complain to Beyer and then maybe he won't want anything more to do with me because of it? and what'll I do then? where will I show my paintings then? how will I make enough money to live on? I think, and it's cold out, the dog might be cold, so no, it was not a good idea to think the dog could sleep in the car, but then what can I do with him? I could always drive back to Dylgja now, but I'm so tired, so tired, so it wouldn't be safe to drive back there tonight, but maybe I can keep the dog with me at The Country Inn? maybe he can sleep in my room? I've never had a dog with me there before, and never seen anyone else with one, so bringing your dog probably isn't allowed, but maybe you can? I can ask in any case, I think, and I tie the leash on him and put him down on the ground and then we start walking across High Street and there's so much snow on the ground that the dog's head just barely sticks out above the snow on the pavement, it's a small dog, but he easily pushes his way through the loose powdery snow, with his snout in the air, and I march ahead, and then we start walking down The Lane and I think that's lucky, it may be snowing hard but it's not far to The Country Inn, I think, and now I need to go straight to The Country Inn because I'm tired, so tired I feel like I might collapse too, I think, and it's snowing and snowing, it's not a flurry any more it's really snowing, with a wind too, you might say it's practically a snowstorm, I think and I think that with all the snow coming down being blown by the wind it's hard to see where you are, but I've walked from The Lane to The Country Inn so many times that I could find my way to The

Country Inn even if it were pitch black and impossible to see anything, I think, so if it's snowing too hard to see anything that doesn't matter, because it's not far now, we're almost there, I think and I walk and I look at the dog ploughing through the snow and it looks like he's getting a bit tired too, he's puffing and panting hard, since he is just a small dog, and getting on in years, so I stop and pick the dog up and then keep walking with the dog in my arms and I'm not thinking anything and it's snowing and snowing and there's no one in sight and it's snowing and snowing, but it's not far to The Country Inn, you just take the first right at the end of The Lane, and I've done that, then you get to an intersection and go down that street, and I've done that, but I don't see it anywhere, The Country Inn with The Coffeehouse on the ground floor, so did I go too far? maybe I walked past the first intersection, which I should've gone down? I think, it feels like I went too far since it's really not far from The Lane to The Country Inn, but I can't have gone the wrong way, can I? it's impossible, it's unbelievable! I've walked from The Lane to The Country Inn so many times, I don't even know how many times, you just walk down The Lane and take a right and go down the first street you get to and you can see The Country Inn down on The Wharf, and I took a left and crossed and went down a street but I can't see The Country Inn, and I've never had to walk this far, I don't think, so I must have gone the wrong way somehow, since I couldn't see where I was going because it was snowing so much, I think and I stop and I try to figure out where I am, but damned if I know, I can't remember ever being on this street before, there is nothing about it I recognise, to the extent that I can see anything at all in this blizzard, but it's just unbelievable that I couldn't manage to get from The Lane to The Country Inn, I did the same thing I've always done, walked the same way I've always walked, or did I do something different? I haven't seen The Country Inn today since it started snowing, have I? but, no, I must have gone the wrong way, so I just need to turn around and go back the same way I came, I think, and I start going back along the same street, and now I'll be at The Country Inn any minute, I think, and I keep walking with Bragi in my arms and it's snowing and snowing and the wind is blowing, that too, yes, it's a real snowstorm now, I think and I think now I better run into someone soon so I can ask them the way to The Country Inn, I think, or else if a taxi drives by I can hail it and take the taxi to The Country Inn, yes, it doesn't matter how short the ride is, I think and I keep walking and I think anyway I'm sure to run across someone soon, I think, or else a taxi is sure to come driving by, but there's no one in sight, no people and no cars, it's snowing so much that people are probably staying indoors and that's why there are no taxis either, I think, but I just have to run across someone or other soon, or a taxi, because I need to get to The Country Inn, on foot or by car, and get a room there, because there's surely a room free at The Country Inn, and some of the people working at the reception there have worked there for so many years and they'll recognise me, and that's also partly why I always stay at The Country Inn, yes, it feels a little bit like coming home when I arrive there, a little like that, I think and I should have gone straight to The Country Inn, but I seem to have gone the wrong way somehow, I think and I'm really tired, anyway I'm definitely too tired to drive home to Dylgja, because even if I like driving it would be totally reckless to drive now, and I'm a careful driver, at least I try to be, and driving while I'm exhausted is not a good idea, after having driven a car for many years I know that you have to be alert, to pay attention, that might be the most important thing, you have to realise that something unexpected can happen at any moment, and be prepared for it, yes, you need to be able to see the future so to speak, since deer can suddenly appear in front of your car, in a flash a deer leaps out onto the road, and in the dark too usually, or at dusk, or dawn, something unexpected can always happen, yes, and often does happen too,

I think, you have to know if a car is coming around a bend and know if it's going to stay on its side of the road, and if it doesn't you need to be prepared for that, maybe even slow down to almost a stop and wait for the car to come around the turn, and the roads that go from Instefjord and to Dylgja, or from in on Sygnefjord out towards Sygne Sea, I bet one of them is the most narrow and winding road in all of Norway, because I've driven a lot in Norway, yes, when Ales was alive we drove all over the Nordic countries, Sweden and Denmark too, and Iceland, and the Faroe Islands, and Finland, but I don't think I've ever driven roads like these anywhere, so narrow, with so many sharp turns, and when the weather's bad too, as it often is of course, yes, after a heavy rain that leads to flooding, rain that comes off the cliffsides and steep hills and floods the roads, yes, then there're holes in the road it can be real trouble to drive over, otherwise I like driving, to tell the truth there's not much that makes me happy any more but driving makes me happy, I think as I push ahead through the snow on the pavement, with Asle's dog Bragi in my arms, at my breast, and I think about how lots of times while driving the roads between Instefjord and Dylgja just for the fun of it I've thought that a car is just about to come around a bend or else that there's no car, like I was seeing the future, and every single time my prediction was right, when I thought a car was coming a car came and when I thought no car was coming no car came, I've tested it so many times that it got kind of boring since I was right every single time, or maybe I was wrong once or twice but I was right so often that eventually testing my predictions was no fun and I stopped doing it, but obviously I know that being able to predict things is very important for driving safely, and I'm good at driving safely, but not at finding my way, especially in cities, but in general, finding the right way to walk or drive when I'm somewhere unfamiliar is something I'm terrible at, I always walk or drive the wrong way, it's just as inevitable as my being able to predict whether or not a car is going to come around a bend, and now isn't that strange? mysterious? I think, and I think that even after living in Bjørgvin for several years I didn't know the city any better, and still couldn't find my way around, no, I'm almost always wrong but not quite always, I think and that's why I always go down the same streets and alleys again and again, I've found my paths through the city so to speak, for example from where I park my car in front of The Beyer Gallery, across High Street, down The Lane, and from there to The Alehouse, or The Country Inn, I think, so I can't have walked completely the wrong way, I must have made a little mistake, and if only someone would walk by I could ask them the way, there has to be someone or another out walking, even at night, that I could ask? but I don't see anyone and anyway it's a good thing I'm in a city at least and not out in the middle of the mountains, not to mention at sea, I think, yes, yes, I think, today I need to figure it out myself since there's no one anywhere in sight and no taxi either, because what usually happens is that I run into someone who shows me the way or I hail a taxi and it takes me where I'm going, that's how it usually works, I get lost, go in the totally wrong direction, away from where I'm trying to go, I stop people on the street and ask them to tell me how to get where I'm going, and people are nice and helpful and they point and tell me where I should go, go there and then there, but then I get lost again anyway, so I have to ask the next person I meet, it's pretty much the same as it was with numbers when I was going to school, it turned out wrong no matter what I did or didn't do, it came out wrong anyway, and I'm still like that with numbers, it's almost like not being able to do maths and not being able to find my way are related, but they can't be, can they? because a sense of direction and mathematical aptitude are very different, aren't they? but the one thing I know for sure is that I have neither, I have no sense of direction and no mathematical aptitude, yes I think that's the term the The Schoolmaster used, you have no mathematical aptitude, he said, something like that, mathematical aptitude, it was probably a term that The Schoolmaster had come up with himself, mathematical aptitude, but sense of direction is a normal term and I don't have that either, obviously, because now I've already been walking for a long time, much longer than it should take to get from where the car is parked in front of The Beyer Gallery to The Country Inn, that's for sure, for all I know I've been walking in circles and I'm about to be right back at The Beyer Gallery, that would be the best case, actually, and it must be because it's snowing so hard, yes, it's a real blizzard, and it's hard to see, and I walked the wrong way, there can't be any other explanation since I've walked this way so many times before, but I've really managed to get lost today, I've been walking so long now, much longer than it usually takes to walk from The Beyer Gallery to The Country Inn, but maybe I can put the dog down and he'll go back to The Beyer Gallery and I can follow him? he might, maybe he can smell the way we took? I think and I put Bragi down and he just stands there and looks up at me with his dog eyes and then I shake the leash a little and I say go Bragi, walk, and then the dog starts walking and he goes the opposite way from how we were walking, he goes back and I follow him, because I can't think of any other way to find out where we're supposed to go, I think, so I just trust that the dog will go back to The Beyer Gallery, I think, because anyway we're nowhere near The Country Inn, that's for sure, I think, but that doesn't mean, as far as I can tell, that we're getting closer to The Beyer Gallery, there's nothing I recognise about the buildings I can glimpse through the snow coming down so hard, but at least the wind has let up a little so now it's just a heavy snowfall, not a blizzard, I think, and even though I've been walking for a long time, at least that's how it feels, I haven't passed a single other person and I've only seen a couple of cars drive by, no taxis, and if only a taxi would drive by I could hail it, I think, and what a fool I was not to have The Handyman drive me to The Country Inn, why did I ask him to drive me to The Lane? what kind of idea was that? was it because I didn't want him to know that I was going to stay at The Country Inn? I think, but I'd already told him I was going to stay there, I think, yes, I had, but for some reason or another I asked The Handyman to take me to The Lane, I think, following the dog, and if the dog is heading somewhere then it must probably be back to The Beyer Gallery, right? I think, because he probably can't smell a path anywhere else? I think, but it's terrible to watch the dog pushing his way through the snow on the pavement, with his snout up, he's puffing and wheezing, and I walk along behind him and he's going uphill and it's pretty steep and I think now surely someone has to turn up soon and I can ask them the way? or a taxi I can hail will turn up? I'm in Bjørgvin after all, despite everything, Norway's second biggest city, I think, but it's not an easy city to find your way around, that must be said, and now where am I? no, I have no sense at all of where we are, but anyway I don't think we're heading towards The Beyer Gallery, I think, and then I think that if I just go downhill towards the sea I'll be able to find The Country Inn, because it's on the water, along The Bay, I think, it's even on The Wharf, yes, but now what direction should I go in to get to the water? I think, because now I'm following the dog uphill, but that was a bad idea, I think, because to get to the sea we need to go downhill, so now I'll turn around and go back downhill, despite everything, that must be better than wandering around after a dog uselessly hoping that he's heading back to The Beyer Gallery, I think, because we have to go in one direction or another and if we go downhill we'll eventually get to the water somewhere, I think, and I shake the leash and the dog stops and then I start walking in the opposite direction, downhill, and now I'm walking in the footprints the dog and I have made in the snow, and with the dog at my heels, but it's still snowing and it must be tiring for the dog walking there with his snout in in the cold winter air to keep it above the snow, and I look at the dog and then Bragi walks past me and he keeps going, you have to give him that, Bragi, yes, and now the snow isn't falling so hard and there, there's someone walking towards me, thank goodness, there is finally someone here and I go over to the person walking a little to one side and I say excuse me, excuse me, but I'm from the country and I think I've managed to get lost in the city and a woman looks back at me from under a thick white knit cap covered with snow and she asks me where I'm trying to get to and there's something familiar about her voice and I say I'm going to The Country Inn, the hotel, The Country Inn, yes, I say and she says yes well in that case I'm going in the exact wrong direction, she says and she laughs and then I see that it's the woman who was sitting alone at a table at Food and Drink, who recognised me, and I sort of recognised her too in a way, yes, it's definitely her, the woman called Guro, or maybe Silje? and she was sitting drinking wine at Food and Drink the whole time until now, yes, she must be really drunk by now, I think and I say I thought I should go downhill because The Country Inn is on the water, and if I just get to the water I'd find my way to The Country Inn, I say and she says yes, I might think that, sure, but it's really not the right way, for all she knows I could have ended up in Denmark Square as easily as The Country Inn, she says and it's not easy to go along the water either, it's not so simple, there are too many places where you can't follow the edge of the water, she says, well anyway, she says, it wasn't so easy for her to find her way around Bjørgvin either when she first lived here, it took quite a long time before she was sure she knew where she was going, but now, after so many years in Bjørgvin, yes, now it's easy, she can't claim to know every last nook and cranny, every last itsy-bitsy lane and alley, but still she at least knows what direction to go in to get to this or that place, and I, yes, I ought to know better, because I used to lived in Bjørgvin for many years myself, even if it was a long time ago, she says, but anyway I'm not heading towards The Country Inn now, that's for sure, it's down on The Wharf and I'm walking in the exact opposite direction, so I should go with her, she's going the same way, she says, because she's going home, and as I know perfectly well she lives at 5, The Lane, near The Country Inn, she says and I think now that's strange, running into Guro or whatever her name is now, the same woman as was sitting at Food and Drink when I was there, and I thank her, I say thank you very much and then I start walking downhill again, walking next to her

You do remember that my name is Guro? she says

and she gives a little laugh and I say yes and we walk downhill and the woman named Guro says it sure came down suddenly, and so much snow, now we're slogging through it and no one's shovelled and no one's ploughed a path through the snow, and what about the dog, it must be really hard for him to walk? she says, and I pick Bragi up again at once and brush the snow off him and she says I didn't have a dog with me at Food and Drink and she asks if I had him tied up outside Food and Drink, and now is that something to ask a person? I think, and I won't answer, why would she ask something like that? I think and then she asks me why I've come to Bjørgvin and I say that a friend was sick so I wanted to check up on him, and it was a good thing I drove down because he was in really bad shape, so I took him to The Clinic and they admitted him, transferred him to The Hospital in fact, I say, and she says that in that case I definitely did a good deed, she says, and I have nothing to say to that and she says so I still live in Dylgja? and I nod and she says she actually knows that already, since she knows me, she says and then she says that she can hear in my voice that I'm originally from Hardanger, yes, even if she didn't already know I'm from Hardanger she could hear it, she says and I say yes, she's right about that, I grew up there, in Hardanger, I say, in Barmen, on a small farm there, an orchard, I say and she says yes she knows that, I've told her all that, don't I remember anything? she says, but I was probably too drunk to remember anything, one time, long ago, I told her that I was from that region, that I grew up on an orchard in Hardanger, she says and I say yes that's true that was where I grew up, but then I lived in Bjørgvin and now I've lived for many years in Dylgja, I say and she says if I lived in Bjørgvin so long I should know my way around the city, and I say she's right, she's totally right, but it's been many years since I lived in Bjørgvin, and when I did live here I didn't walk around the city much, I went to The Art School, in a course of study they called Painting, but I never graduated from The Art School, I say, and she says no then I wasn't here all that long, she says and she says that she knows all that, I've told her that already, I'm an artist, yes, she says and I say yes I guess I am in a way and she says that even if she wouldn't call herself an artist she's good with her hands, she likes doing crafts, in fact that's what she lives on, she's sewn countless tablecloths, big and small, and table runners, short and long, in Hardanger embroidery, she says, and she learned how to make Hardanger embroidery from her grandmother, so she works firmly in the tradition, she says, and she makes bodices for the national folk costume too, decorative bodices, and she learned that from her grandmother too, yes, she's lost count of how many bodices she's sewn, but it's a lot, because it seems like everyone wants national folk costumes nowadays, and there can't be many people left who still do Hardanger embroidery and decorative bodices, she says, and so she supplies The Craft Centre and that's how she makes a living, she says, and she ended up in Bjørgvin by chance more than anything, but once she finished school she worked in a shop called Hardanger Regional Products and she worked there until it went out of business and then she just stayed on in Bjørgvin, she'd lived in other places but she's been here for years now, yes, she's lost count of how many, she rents an apartment not far from The Country Inn, at 5, The Lane, on the ground floor, she says, as I know perfectly well, she adds, and today she went to Food and Drink to get a glass of wine before going to a girlfriend's house, but if she'd known winter was coming so suddenly, that the snow would come so suddenly, she would have just stayed home, she says and I think that she likes to talk and talk and I can't take in any more, I think and I think that she wasn't at any friend's house, she just sat at Food and Drink drinking more red wine, because she's very drunk, I think, but maybe she drank red wine at her girlfriend's house? I think, and she says again that she was going to a girlfriend's house and she thought she should have a glass of red wine before she went to her friend's place, she says, so she went into Food and Drink, and I was tempted to drop in there too, while she was there, she says and I think yes, yes, she could have stopped in Food and Drink first and then gone to her girlfriend's house and kept drinking red wine there, I think, yes, and whether it's true or not she does know how to get to The Country Inn, I think and then I say I hope there's a room free at The Country Inn, and she asks didn't I reserve a room already and I say no, I usually do but this trip came up kind of suddenly and I say I often stay at The Country Inn and some of the people who work at the reception have been there for ages and I know them and they know me, some of them, not all, because in the past few years there've been a lot of new people working at the reception, it seems like people have only just started when they're gone again, I say and she says yes, I know, there are so many hotels and other places to spend the night in Bjørgvin, and new ones keep opening up, so whatever happens I'll be able to find a roof over my head, she says, and if for some crazy reason it's full everywhere then I can always spend the night at her place, she says, she'd never refuse to put up someone from the country who's in Bjørgvin and needs a roof over his head for the night, and especially someone who's even slept in her apartment several times before, yes, in her bed even, she says and I don't understand what she's talking about, she must just be chattering away, I've supposedly slept in her bed? I think and I say thank you, thank you, thanks very much, but I don't like intruding on people, I'm shy that way, I say, and I'd rather just stay at The Country Inn as long as there's room there, I say and she says I can do whatever I want, but if The Country Inn is full then, yes, I can always spend the night at her apartment, because she's even slept with me in the same bed at The Country Inn, after all, she says, yes she remembers it well, even if it was a long time ago back when I had medium-length brown hair worn loose not like my grey hair now tied back with a black hairband, she says and I don't understand what she's talking about and she says in this weather it'll be a real pain to go from hotel to hotel looking for a room, even if there are lots of hotels next door to one another on The Wharf, she says and I say again that there's usually always room for me at The Country Inn and she says yes there are rooms free there most of the time but sometimes there are various events in Bjørgvin, classes, conferences, conventions, even gatherings of fiddlers, she doesn't know, but she does know that it might be full at The Country Inn, she says and she starts going on about a confirmation or was it a wedding or maybe a funeral or whatever it was when she tried to reserve a room at The Country Inn for some people who were coming to Bjørgvin and there were no rooms to be had at The Country Inn and I don't answer and then we start walking uphill and before long we've reached The Hill, where The University is in Bjørgvin, I think, and that place, even the name, has always, well, not intimidated me but filled me with a kind of respect, yes, even awe, and I don't know why, but a university, a place where people read and think and write day and night, and have conversations, and know all about all kinds of different subjects, yes, I'd have to say I admire a place like that, and the people who work there, I think and my Ales studied there too, she studied art history and specialised in icons, I think and when I was going to The Art School it was someone from The University in Bjørgvin who gave art history lectures, Christie was his name, a professor from The University, and those lectures might have been what I got the most out of during the years I went to The Art School, yes, more than anything else, to be told about the history of painting from the earliest times to the present, because Professor Christie talked and explained and showed slides, he had slides of drawings and paintings and sculptures from every country and every period, and he talked and talked, and it was absolutely overwhelming all the things he showed us and told us, every work of art was a masterpiece, one after another, to tell the truth, and if I hadn't understood it before I learned then how little I myself had to work with, but not nothing, I had something too, something all my own, because there was something in my pictures that wasn't in any other picture I was shown, I saw that, and even if it wasn't all that much it was something, I could do something, I knew something, I saw something that you couldn't see in anything Professor Christie showed us, something different, with its own light in it, but was that good enough? could someone be an artist and consider himself an artist just because he had something all his own in the pictures he painted? doesn't a person need more than that? yes, that's how I used to think and I started doubting I could paint pictures that were worth anything, maybe I should just give it up, I was just barely what you could call an artist, I knew that, and I had something that no one else had but it was probably too little, so maybe I should just, yes, well, what else should I do? was there anything else I was good at? was there anything else I had a talent for? anything else I had a gift for, as they say? no, what would happen? and was there anything I wanted to do besides paint pictures? I thought, walking along next to this woman apparently named Guro who I've apparently slept with, yes, even slept with at The Country Inn, no, there's no end to what she's making me listen to, I think and I pet the dog's back over and over and he's nice and warm against my chest and then the woman who I think is named Guro says it's not far now, we're getting close, even if it's slow, since it's hard to walk in all this snow, more like trudge really, she says and I think that I gradually came to understand more and more clearly that the pictures that meant the most to me, and the artists I felt closest to, were the ones who most clearly had their own pictures, or however you'd say it, the pictures they'd paint again and again, but their pictures were never similar, no, not that, never, they were always different, but every picture resembled one another too, and they were like a picture that's never been painted, that no one could paint, that was always invisible behind or in the picture that had been painted, and that's why the picture that had been painted was always like the invisible picture, and this picture was in every single one of the individual paintings, I think, and for me there was never any doubt about which paintings mattered, it was oil on canvas, no more no less, nothing else, because sculpture and drawing and prints of various kinds in various techniques can be as beautiful as they want, sure, but for me only oil on canvas matters, and I truly cannot stand acrylic paint, and of course I could draw, and I drew a lot in the years when I was at The Art School, they said it was important to be able to draw, but after I was set free from The Art School, yes, I have to admit that's how I think about it sometimes, so after I was released I rarely or never drew, in the strict sense, but now and then I do scribble a sketch, scribble down a design for a picture, even if it most often looks nothing like the picture I paint later, it's more like it points towards it, or just suggests it, gives you an idea of it, and maybe that's why I always keep a sketchpad and pencil with me in the shoulder bag I always have with me, I think and I hear the woman who I think is named Guro ask me, just like everyone else, if I can live off my art, off my pictures, my paintings, and I've been asked this question so many times by now that I don't want to answer it any more and I don't understand how she, of all people, someone who makes a living sewing tablecloths and table runners in Hardanger embroidery and decorative bodices, can ask that and I just say yes well

Yes well you know, she says

That's not the worst thing, she says

You need to be a good painter to do that, she says

Well anyway I already know you are, she says

and she gives a little laugh and she's about to say more but I sort of quickly say painting pictures is what I can do in life, more than anything else at least, I say

Still, she says

And there are people who want to buy your pictures too? she says

Yes, there are, I say

and she says she knows that of course, that people buy my pictures, because she, yes, I didn't know that, but she goes to my shows, and she herself has often wanted to buy a picture, she really admires my pictures, but of course there are some pictures she likes more than others, she says

It's like pictures talk, the same as people, she says

A kind of silent language comes out of a good picture, she says

Yes, it's hard to explain, but a really good picture says something all its own, something you can understand but that can never be said in words, she says

and I say she's exactly right, that's how I think about it too, I say, and she says she's never been able to afford to buy a picture I've painted, and besides, yes, well, now that she thinks about it, she says, the way I support myself is probably not all that different from how she supports herself, not really, she just sits and sews this Hardanger embroidery of hers, these decorative bodices, and that's how she makes a living, well a kind of living at least, more or less, yes, she's been doing it since she was a girl, yes, since she was sitting in her grandmother's lap, she says, yes, because even back when she was sitting in her grandmother's lap she was watching how she was doing what she was doing, how she was sewing, yes, following along with her eyes while her grandmother did it, and when she was older her grandmother taught her everything she knew about Hardanger embroidery, and how to sew bodices, and then she started doing it herself, yes, when she was still a girl, and she's kept doing it ever since, to this day, and during all those years she's sold what she made to The Craft Centre, when she felt she had sewn enough she went to The Craft Centre with what she had, and she was paid well, cash on delivery, so that was nice, but especially after her husband left, yes well she calls him that even though they weren't actually married, and she says that he left, yes, he just disappeared even though it was actually more like she threw him out, and she's really regretted that

It was so stupid to do that, she says

and she says it's painful to talk about it, because he was a good man, or had been one, she doesn't like big words and doesn't use them much but still she can say that they loved each other, but, yes, she says and she stops and we keep walking in the snow, trudging ahead, because it's still snowing, but less now, it's more like individual snowflakes, and I keep petting and petting the dog's back and I'm holding him pressed to my chest and then she says she's never heard anyone play the fiddle like he did, never, and when they lived together she always called him The Fiddler, just that, are you coming, Fiddler? it's time to eat, is The Fiddler hungry? and he was such a talented Hardanger fiddler, and he won lots of national contests, first place, yes he sure could play, but, but, she says, but then there was all that drinking, she says and she stops and then she says that in the end she couldn't take it any more, his drinking, his over-doing it, she threw him out, because it was her apartment, the apartment on The Lane that she'd rented for all these years, and she said she'd been supporting him for a long time, and he should at least pay for his booze himself, even though he actually did she said it anyway, she says, yes, she said one nasty thing after another to him, that she'd had enough, that she wanted him to leave, and then he did leave, The Fiddler, and he wasn't slow to do it either, he just took his fiddle and headed out over the mountains to the east, and there, yes, no, she shouldn't talk about it, but he was from East Norway, so then, well, I probably know what she means, the fiddle had disappeared and the rest too, yes, and he was sleeping away from home a lot, she'd heard it not from him but from other people, yes, I know what she means, she says, and so it was probably some woman or another somewhere in the east, in Telemark, who took pity on him and took him in, let him stay with her, she probably owned a house or some other place to live, and then she's sure he stayed living there for some years and then he died, and he surely drank to the very end, but he was a good man, he was, and she missed him, yes, she really did, every day she missed him, not a day went by without her missing him, she said, and she's often thought it was so stupid to do that, to tell him to leave, she's so often regretted it, yes, she's so often sat and cried over her own stupidity, she says, because he'd never just taken his fiddle and left before so she started to miss him, and that was how she'd felt every day since that terrible day when he skipped out, she says, because she hadn't meant what she said, even though it was true, but she did ask him to leave and then he just looked at her and as drunk as he was he didn't say anything, because in some ways he was never drunk, not in the usual way, just in his own way, he played the fiddle the way only he could play, even when he was totally drunk in his own way, at least he didn't get drunk the way other people did, he was sober from drinking in a way, yes, he wasn't like anyone else, and she had no idea how he got his booze, and how he paid for it, no, but somehow or another he always managed to, and it's probably always like that with people who need to drink, with real drinkers, she says

Will you still be with me when I'm dead? she says

and she looks at me and I feel something give a little start inside me

That's what he used to say to me, she says

Imagine saying that to someone, she says

and she says that he said that exact thing to her so many times, yes, when he'd been drinking, or at least in the last few years he'd said it a lot, because then he was almost never totally sober, she says and she laughs and she says that he played best when he'd drunk a little, but not too much, when he drank too much it was ruined and got confused, yes, one time he was so drunk that he got up and left the stage in the middle of his set and said no, it's no good, and then walked off the stage, or more like staggered off, she was there, she saw it with her own eyes, she says

Right in the middle of a tune he got up and left the stage, she says

It's no good, he said, and then he left, she says

and she says that it's probably partly, at least before he was, well, an alcoholic, you'd probably have to call him that, it's probably partly because he was shy that he drank, yes, it was from shyness, and then also his moodiness and sadness, but it worked out fine for many years, yes, that's the truth, believe it or not, everything was balanced in its way, he earned some money from his playing, gradually more and more, he played at weddings the way fiddlers have always done, and then it got to where he would play almost every week at dances in Gimle, one gig or another would always turn up, but he drank, he was drinking the whole time, and it wasn't too much, at least not until the drinking totally took over and there were lots of times when he wasn't in any shape to actually play and his playing was nothing but a big mess of notes and screeches, yes, you know how people always say the Hardanger fiddle sounds like a cat screeching, now how can people who consider themselves fine upstanding Bjørgvin women bring themselves to say things like that, they know so little, these fine women, they understand so little, she says, yes to tell the truth she regrets with all her heart that she told him to leave, how stupid was that, she says again, because as long as he drank she never had that much trouble with him, he was always nice, and they used to have a drop or two together too, lots of times, because she liked a little something to drink too, it wasn't that, she was no tee-totaller, I knew that, I saw her with a glass of red wine in her hands today, she says, and the best moments she can remember, yes, the best moments in her whole life were while she was sitting and drinking red wine and he was playing, it was the most beautiful thing she's ever heard in her life, it almost makes her cry just thinking about it, just hearing his tunes in her mind, she can't think about it any more, she says, because in the end the drinking totally took over, but he was a good man, yes, even then, truly, and we shouldn't speak ill of the dead, she says, anyway, yes, the first time she saw him it was at a competition, it was the first music contest she'd ever been to and he was sitting at the front of the stage and playing like an ordinary fiddler but then he played his way farther and farther into the music and sort of moved away from himself and from the others and it was like both he and the music and everyone listening rose up into the air and then he turned around on his stool and played with his back to the concert hall, his back to everyone listening, and everything kept swinging through the air, it was exactly as if the music he was playing just flew up and sort of disappeared into the air and into nothing and then he stopped and then he got up and walked right off the stage without turning around and the audience was clapping and clapping, yes, the applause wouldn't stop, it was like the people in the concert hall had witnessed something like a miracle, she had never heard anyone play that well before or since, not him or anyone else, and that was, well, since she's told me this much she might as well say the rest, that was the night when they became he and she, became a couple, she says, and then we walk silently on, step by step through snow no one has walked in before us

Yes, alcohol is both good and bad, I say

He used to say that too, she says

and then she asks if I drink and I say yes I used to, quite a bit too, but, well it's a long and difficult story, I say, and in the end it came down to either drinking or painting, yes, drinking or staying alive you might say, and yes, well, somehow I got free of the alcohol's hold on me, but it wasn't easy, I say, and of course Ales, my wife, didn't like that I drank, and if it wasn't for her then no I don't know what would have happened to me, I say

You don't drink any more? she says

No, I say

and there's silence

And Ales, your wife? she says

She died, she's gone, I say

and there's a long silence and then I say that I haven't drunk at all since I stopped drinking and she says good for me that I could do that and I say no, no, it wasn't about me, I just did what had to be done and I had help, and without help from both earthly and heavenly forces, yes, why not say it, it's true, from heaven too, I'd never have been able to do it, but most of all it was thanks to Ales that I could do it and once I'd managed to stop drinking it wasn't hard at all to not start again, but stopping in the first place, weaning myself off drinking, well that was hard, yes, that was a struggle, I say and she says that her husband, yes well as she mentioned she calls him her husband anyway, yes, The Fiddler was never able to stop drinking, and he didn't really try either, she knows that, and then that woman in Telemark took him in to live with her, but she was a big drinker too, yes, she almost had to be, or else she wouldn't have been able to stand him, and so it happened the way it had to happen, he wasn't an old man, no, she doesn't want to think about this sad and unpleasant situation any more right now, she says and she raises her face and look, she says, and she raises her arm, look there, there, on the, on the other side of The Bay, you can see The Country Inn, there it is, you're saved, she says and she chuckles a little and I say thank you so so much for helping me, and she says it's no problem when you know the way, she says, but if you don't know the way that's a different story, she says and she says she didn't mean it in a bad way when she laughed just then, if there was any reason at all for her to laugh it was just that she recognised herself, country folk in Bjørgvin, she says, but yes, well, as she said, if they don't have a room for me at The Country Inn I can always spend the night at her place, she says, anyway there's more than enough room in her apartment, all too much room, she says and I think that I've never really liked going into other people's homes, I've always been shy about that, yes it was like I was doing something I had no right to do, like I was intruding, forcing myself into other people's lives, like I was getting to know more about their life than I had a right to know, like I was disturbing their life, or at least I felt disturbed by their life, their life intruding on mine, yes, like another life was sort of filling me up, I think, and for someone to come into my house, well that's one of the worst things I know of, yes, I get so nervous and uneasy then that I don't know what to do with myself, no, it doesn't happen when people I know well come over, like Åsleik, nothing happens then, it's just normal, yes, everything's the way it should be, that's how it is with friends, they sort of belong there in a way, and I also don't think it's hard to go into the houses of people I know well, friends' houses, but there aren't many of those people, I think, strictly speaking there's just Åsleik now, I think, yes, Åsleik and no one else, not many, and when he comes over it's almost not like someone else is coming over, and when I go to his house it's not like going to someone else's house, because Åsleik and I have known each other for so long and it's like you no longer have much of anything to hide from a person like that, well of course we have some things, but it's like we both know what we're hiding or like we know it but don't want to know it, and don't dwell on it, don't think about it, it's like we just leave it alone, leave it in peace, let it lie, without waking it up or shaking it, without disturbing it, but it's not like that with people I don't know, and visiting people? earlier in my life? yes, strictly speaking it was only when Ales and I were living in Bjørgvin that we had people come over, after we ran off to Dylgja it was just Ales and me, and then, while she was still alive, yes, the only person who came and visited us in Dylgja, aside from her mother Judit, and Åsleik of course, was Beyer, but only once, no, I can't think about that, about Ales, it's too much, I'd just sink and sink into it and disappear, I think, but the day Beyer came to see us Ales didn't want to stay home, she wanted to be at her mother Judit's house in Bjørgvin instead, so the day before Beyer came I drove her to Bjørgvin, yes, to The Beyer Gallery, and the day after I went to get her from The Beyer Gallery, because if I didn't like getting visits from anyone Ales liked it even less, I think

I think I know you better than you realise, Guro says then

and I don't understand what she means, she knows me better than I realise, what's that supposed to mean? it's true I've been interviewed a few times by *The Bjørgvin Times*, I'm afraid so, but that can't be what she's talking about

My name is Guro, she says then

and she says it emphasising the name like she's sort of trying to remind me of something and then she says now at least I know her name, in case I'd forgotten it, she says, so if my memory's so bad that I can't remember much more about her at least I'll have to remember her name now, she says, and she says it's about time we said hello properly, she says, and she shakes my hand

So, my name's Guro, she says

and I shake her hand and hold Bragi with just one hand

And my name's Asle, I say

Okay, now we know at least that much about each other, she says

and there's something like mockery in her voice

Our names, she says

Yes, I say

and it's silent for a moment and then she says she'll go to the next show I have at The Beyer Gallery, and that it'll probably be during

Advent this year the same as every year, that's always when they have it, she says and she's gone to all my shows, she says, and we get to The Country Inn and I say I'll go in and ask if there's a room free for me, and she says she can wait outside, in case it's full, you never know, and if it is I can always, as she's already told me, spend the night at her place, she says and I thank her and she says she might as well go inside with me and then I open the front door and the woman named Guro goes in ahead of me and I go in after her with the dog in my arms and I see that it's the old guy from Bjørgvin, The Bjørgvin Man, sitting at the reception desk, where he's been for all these years, he's one of the people I know, one of the people who's checked me in and checked me out of The Country Inn before, he's a polite older man from Bjørgvin, and I see that there are a lot of keys hanging on the wall in the reception area behind The Bjørgvin Man, so there must be rooms available, I think

Good afternoon, or good evening I should say, The Bjørgvin Man says

So this is the fellow who's out and about tonight, he says

and he looks at me and then at the woman standing behind me

Or rather the two people, he says

and it seems like he recognises the person I'm with and he stands up and bows

Ye, yes, I say

You don't have a room for me, do you? I say

You mean for the two of you? he says

No, just for me, I say

and at that same moment I think that maybe he didn't mean me and the woman apparently named Guro but me and the dog

I see, The Bjørgvin Man says

Well for me and my dog, I say

You've got a dog with you? he says

Yes, I say

and I think that I don't want to get into the whole business of why I have a dog with me

It's not actually allowed, having a dog in the room, The Bjørgvin Man says

And you've never had a dog with you before, he says

No, I say

Well, I don't know, The Bjørgvin Man says

and Guro says that she can take the dog with her, and I can get him back tomorrow, she's always liked dogs, and she used to have a dog herself, but that was back when she was a girl, she says

I'm sure we can work something out, The Bjørgvin Man says

Because, he says

and suddenly there's a long silence

Because, well, yes, since it's you, one of our regular guests, yes well I think I can make an exception, I'll hardly lose my job over it, he says

and I stand there and I don't know what to say, because I've never brought a dog to The Country Inn before

As long as the dog doesn't bark, The Bjørgvin Man says

No, he won't as long as I'm with him, I say

That's good to hear, he says

Because even if there aren't that many guests at the hotel tonight, I'm sure they won't exactly want to be woken up by a yapping dog, he says

Of course, I understand, I say

But I can take the dog with me, Guro says

and I think that she said she was called something else when we were talking at Food and Drink, Silje or something like that, I think, but now she's said many times that her name is Guro and now I think of her simply as Guro, I think

Your usual room is free, The Bjørgvin Man says

Room 407, I say

and I say that this trip into Bjørgvin came about a bit unexpectedly, I usually reserve a room in advance and The Bjørgvin Man says yes he knows

Yes, great, that room, same as always, I say

Your room is free and since it's you we'll take the risk and assume everything'll be fine with your dog, he says

and I say thank you, thanks very much, and I say that as long as the dog is with me he won't start barking

That'll be fine, your room is ready and waiting for you, The Bjørgvin Man says

and he takes a key off the hook on the wall behind him and he hands me the key and he says have a nice stay and he's sure I can find my own way and that I know when breakfast is served and all that as well as he does, he says and I say thank you, thanks, everything'll be fine, I say and I turn around and Guro is standing there and I say thank you so much for your help and she says it was no problem, and then she says she hopes we run into each other again, and I say that yes I'm sure we will and then we shake hands and say goodbye and then I walk towards the lift and she walks towards the front door and then she stops and then she says

But what about breakfast? she says

and I turn around and look at her

You'll have to leave the dog alone then, won't you? she says

You have a point there, The Bjørgvin Man says

You can't bring the dog to breakfast with you? she says

and I say I hadn't thought of that and The Bjørgvin Man says he wouldn't recommend it, and why did she have to bring up breakfast? hasn't today been long enough? aren't I exhausted? can't I get a little peace and quiet? I need to go to sleep, and I suddenly realise how totally exhausted I am, I'm so tired I might collapse right here

You have a point, The Bjørgvin Man says

and I don't know what to say and Guro says that she can take the dog with her and I can get him back tomorrow morning, she says and I realise I can't talk about it any more, I'm done, the dog'll sleep wherever it'll sleep, I think and I look at her

I'll come back here at ten o'clock with the dog, she says

Or you can come by and ring the bell around then, or earlier if you want, she says

and I nod and then Guro says that if I want to get the dog then, or earlier, or later, well I know where she lives, it's on The Lane, number 5 The Lane, she says, as she's said before, she says, so she lives right near The Country Inn, you just take a right and then take the first right after that and the first narrow street you get to is The Lane, uphill to the left, she says and she smiles and The Bjørgvin Man looks at me and Guro walks up to me and I hand her the dog and I say his name is Bragi and she takes the dog and the leash and The Bjørgvin Man says that it's probably for the best, all things considered, yes, even for the dog, maybe, he says and I turn around and walk towards the lift and push the button with an up arrow and the lift comes and I turn around

Goodnight, I say

and both the woman apparently named Guro and The Bjørgvin Man say goodnight and I open the lift door and I hear the front door close and I go into the lift and I press the button with 4 on it and then I stand there in the lift and it jolts into motion and I feel so tired, so tired, so unbelievably tired, I think and I think that it was a good thing I drove back to Bjørgvin, because imagine what might have happened to Asle if I hadn't? he was lying there covered in snow, he was sick, he was shaking constantly and kept collapsing, falling down and just lying there, and what would have happened if I hadn't come back to Bjørgvin? I think and the lift moves slowly upwards, it's an old lift and it rises slowly, and with little jolts, and I think that now I don't want to think about Asle any more, or about anything else, now I'm tired, so unbelievably tired, so now I'll just go straight to bed, I think and the lift gets to the fourth floor and it stops with a jolt, and bobs up and down a little, and I look at the lift door and it feels like forever before I can open it and I go out into the hall and suddenly I don't know if I'm supposed to take a right and go down that corridor, or if I'm supposed to take a left and go down that one, even after having stayed in Room 407 so many times I'm still not sure, dammit I'll just go either left or right and then see where I am, I think, and I feel really angry, as I should, I'm angry at myself, I seriously curse myself and I take a right and I see 400 on a door and I go down that corridor and the numbers on the doors get higher and higher so I am going the right way and there, there at last, is 407 on a door and I use the key and I unlock the door on the first try and then I go into the room, turn on the light and then take off my brown leather shoulder bag and put it down on a chair and then I take off my black coat and I hang it on the chair and then I go right to the bed and lie down without taking any of my clothes off, even the black velvet jacket I'm wearing, and my shoes are still on, and then I breathe deeply in and breathe slowly out several times and then I fold my hands and I make the sign of the cross and I say to myself Pater noster Qui es in cælis Sanctificetur nomen tuum Adveniat regnum tuum and I stay lying down and I say to myself Our Father Who art in heaven Hallowed be thy name Thy kingdom come and I think God's kingdom does need to come, but it already has come, I feel it, whenever I feel or realise how close God is, yes, he is all around me like a field, or maybe it's his angel, my angel, that I feel? I think and may God protect him, may God protect Asle, let Asle get better again, I think and then I think that it won't be long now before I too come to God, to God's kingdom, I think and then I breathe in deeply and I say inside myself Kyrie and then I breathe out slowly and I say eleison and then I breathe in deeply and I say Christe and then I breathe out slowly and I say eleison and I say that over and over and then I just lie there quietly and stare straight ahead into empty space and at first I don't see anything and I just feel how tired I am and then I see a canvas there on an easel and I see two lines there that cross each other and then I hear Åsleik say St Andrew's Cross, he says it with his provincial pride, St Andrew's Cross, and suddenly I feel an aversion to the whole picture, there's nothing more to do with that picture, just get rid of it, be done with it, because it's done, despite it being so unfinished it's done, it's finished, the way it's painted is just the way it is and the way it's going to stay, it doesn't need any more, the big white canvas and then those two lines crossing, the lines forming a cross, and that's it, obviously what I was painting was Asle but I don't like to think like that, not now, because now I'm at peace, and I say to myself Pacem relinquo vobis Pacem meam do vobis and I say Peace I leave with you My peace I give unto you and I don't know what more I can do with the picture, it's stiff, it's dead, it's just two lines, two thick lines that cross in the middle, it doesn't have the light in it that a good picture needs to have, it's really not a picture at all, it's a St Andrew's Cross, Åsleik says, and he's right, and then he says it again, St Andrew's Cross, he says and he puts a heavy stress on the words like he's proud of knowing them, proud that he, Åsleik, knows a term like that, something like that is what he's saying in the way he says the words, and things like that just make him look stupid, putting on that provincial pride makes him worse than he is, I think and I lie there and think that I just need to forget that picture, or try to forget it, but the picture is firmly in my mind, because some of the pictures I paint get lodged inside me but most of the other pictures I have lodged in my mind are pictures from life, not my own paintings, yes, these glimpses of something I've seen that stayed with me and that torment me, actually, because I can never get rid of them, and that I try to paint away, and in a way I do manage to paint them away, or in any case paint them into being something that doesn't just exist in my mind, something that isn't stuck in there, in a way, I think and I think that all the paintings for the show I'm having soon at The Beyer Gallery are already finished, so if I had thought of it I could've brought them with me and delivered them to Beyer today, or maybe tomorrow morning, I think, but I don't always think in such reasonable ways, or plan well, for example this morning I just decided to drive to Bjørgvin to go shopping and then I did, and I think that tomorrow when I get back home I'll put aside that picture with the two lines, the St Andrew's Cross, as Åsleik says, yes the picture should be called *St Andrew's Cross,* and I'll paint the name, the title, in black oil paint on the top edge of the stretcher, the way I always do, and then I'll paint a big A on the picture itself, in the lower right-hand corner, the way I also always do, unless I've already done that? haven't I already added the picture's title and signed it with a big A and taken it off the easel and put it aside with the other paintings that also aren't done stacked together with the stretchers out between the bedroom door and the hall door? haven't I done that already? I think, but if I haven't then I'll put it aside as soon as I get home tomorrow, I think and then I'll take out another painting I have stacked in that pile of unfinished pictures, of pictures I've almost managed to finish as good pictures but not quite, pictures that are missing something, that I can't figure out what to do with and have to let sit for a while, when I get back home to Dylgja, finally get back home to Dylgja, I'll take out one of the paintings deep in the stack, which means one of the unfinished paintings that I set aside a long time ago because I wasn't entirely happy with it, I wasn't satisfied it was the picture it needed to be, I think, and then I think that I need to put the paintings stacked in two piles next to the kitchen door with the stretchers facing out from the wall into the back of my car and drive to Bjørgvin and deliver them to Beyer, because those are the pictures I'm done with, there's a stack of big ones and a stack of smaller ones, and it's those pictures that I set aside and decided I was done with after I realised I couldn't do any more with them, I made those pictures as well as I could make them, I don't know how good they are but I know that I can't make them any better, so they're ready for the next show, yes, there are always either too many pictures or not enough, I think, but if Beyer feels there are too many he just puts the ones he doesn't want to include in the show in the side room, The Bank, as he calls it, and I do need to drive the pictures to The Beyer Gallery soon, it's getting kind of urgent, so I need to get it done, because Beyer hangs the pictures up himself, and he puts a lot of thought into the installation, I think, and it was thanks to Beyer that I could make it as a painter, because for someone to live off painting pictures he's really got to stick it out, I think, yes well more or less the same thing is true of probably every profession or craft, even if being an artist is supposed to be different, not a job like ordinary house painting but one that's out of the ordinary, noble and special, there's something affected about the whole thing, to tell the truth, actually I'm ashamed to be an artist, an art painter, but what else could I have been? and now, anyway, now that I'm so old? no, unfortunately I'm not much use for anything else now, besides painting pictures, because I've always been clumsy, in everything, yes, even when I draw or paint, yes, it's hard to believe it, it can't be because I'm physically unable to do something well that I can't do it, no, it must be something else that prevents me, and I don't know what it is, so I would have been a bad tradesman, that's been true ever since I was a kid, and as for anything to do with maths I can't do it, that's for sure, and nothing with writing either, or, well, actually to tell the truth it's pretty easy for me to write, there was nothing wrong with my style in school and I was pretty good at English, yes, I even used to be able to write in English well enough, and German too, and I enjoyed reading books in both English and German back in the day, there were quite a lot of words and idioms I didn't understand but I got the meaning one way or another, and then I read Swedish and Danish books too, of course, it was back when I was going to The Art School that I started reading foreign books in the original languages, because a lot of the literature Professor Christie referred to was written in either English or German, especially German, and occasionally in Swedish or Danish, rarely in Norwegian, and then always written in Bokmål, never in Nynorsk, and for a lot of the books I wanted to read I had to venture into the stately University Library and ask to borrow them, and since I was going to The Art School I was allowed to borrow books from there, and not many of the books Professor Christie mentioned were available at The Public Library, and I read and read and didn't understand even half of what I read, probably much less than that, but it sort of didn't matter much, I understood some of it, and what I did understand gradually helped me learn more and more of the language I was reading, because even though I had dictionaries I didn't like looking things up in them so I'd either guess what a word meant or, most often, I could figure it out from the context, the word had a clear meaning when it was in context with other words, so yes, I was pretty good at languages, it was mathematical aptitude that I always had a problem with, and what I totally don't have is a sense of direction, a sense of place, plus I'm so clumsy, so it's true probably the only thing I could have ended up doing was painting pictures, and if I wanted to make a living I needed to paint, and that's both good and also wrong, but that's what I did and kept doing, I painted picture after picture, I did that at least, and when I wasn't painting I often spent hour after hour just sitting and staring into space, yes, I can sit for a long time and just stare into empty space, at nothing, and it's sort of like something can come from the empty nothingness, like something real can come out of the nothingness, something that says a lot, and what it says can turn into a picture, either that or I can stay sitting there staring into empty space and become completely empty myself, completely still, and it's in that empty stillness that I like to say my deepest truest prayers, yes, that's when God is closest, because it's in the silence that God can be heard, and it's in the invisible that He can be seen, of course I know my Pater Noster and I pray with it every day, to tell the truth, at least three times a day, and often even more in fact, and I've learned it by heart in Latin, and learned it by seeing it before my eyes, I never memorise mechanically because I can remember written things by seeing them, a bit like pictures, yes, but I try to only remember the written things I think are important to remember, and unlike with pictures I'm able to turn off the memory of written things, and then I made my own translation of the Our Father into Nynorsk, and of course I know that by heart, yes, I can see it in my mind, but still it's probably these moments when I'm sitting and staring into empty nothingness, and becoming empty, becoming still, that are my deepest truest prayers, and once I get into the empty stillness I can stay there for a long time, sit like that for a long time, and I don't even realise I'm sitting there, I just sit and stare into the empty nothingness, and probably in a way I am the empty nothingness I'm looking at, I can sit like that for I don't know how long but it's a long, long time, and I believe these silent moments enter into the light in my paintings, the light that is clearest in darkness, yes, the shining darkness, I don't know for sure but that's what I think, or hope, that it might be like that, I think and I lie there and I think now I need to go to sleep soon and I'll pray one of the quick prayers with my rosary, my usual kind, because it's not that often that I pray in my own words, and when I do it's for intercession, I'm embarrassed when it comes to that, if I pray for something that has to do with me then it has to be to let me be good for someone else, and if it specifically has to do with me then I pray that it should be God's will that it happen, yes, Thy will be done Fiat voluntas tua On earth as it is in heaven Sicut in cælo et in terra and I am so tired so tired I need to sleep but I'm probably too agitated to get to sleep, I think and then I sit up on the edge of the bed and stand up and I take my black velvet jacket off and hang it on the back of the chair with the brown shoulder bag lying under the black overcoat and then I push my heels against the floor and kick off my shoes and I take off my trousers and I leave them on the floor and then I take off my black pullover and drop it on top of the trousers and the room feels cold and then I turn off the light and get into the bed and I tuck the duvet tight around me and I gather my thoughts and then I think may God be good and help my friend, Asle, to get better, he's too young to die, he paints pictures that are too good for him to have to die now, yes, I don't presume to know what's best for Asle better than God but that's what I want, and I think that I can hope that in all humility, and as meekly as I can I pray to God to please let Asle live, let him regain his health, yes, yes, I pray to you, dear God, that you will make Asle better, I think and then I stay lying there and looking into the emptiness before me, into the dark nothingness, and I must be tired, tired, so tired, but maybe I'm too worked up to get to sleep? I think and I think that maybe I paint better when I'm under pressure, when I need to finish a few more paintings for my show? because even though I like painting, yes, there's often a lot of pain in what I paint, and in me too in a way, because these pictures lodged inside me, yes, they're almost all connected to something bad that I remember, the light is linked to the darkness, yes, that's how it is, and there are painters who don't like getting rid of their pictures, who'd rather keep them, not sell them, but I'm happy every single time I sell a picture, happy to be free of it, almost, and maybe that goes back to when I was a boy and made a few kroner by painting pictures of neighbours' houses and farms, back when I was still a kid, but it made me happy to do that, yes, to paint pictures and then get rid of them and get money for them, and it still makes me happy to this day when I sell a picture, yes, selling the picture in itself makes me happy but then also, yes, I have to admit that I think this way too, when I sell a picture I'm also giving away, almost like a gift, the light that the picture has to have in it, yes, it's like I'm passing on to someone else a gift that I myself have been given, I think I've been paid for the picture itself but not for the light that's in the picture, because that's something I was given and as a result I have to give it away again, and that light, yes, it's most often connected to something bad, to pain, and suffering, I might say, if that's not too big a word, and I'm paid for the painting itself, for the picture, but not for the light, and the person who buys the painting is also given some of the light, and the suffering too, the despair, the pain that's in the light, I think, and if there isn't any light in the picture well then I keep it, a picture's not done until there's light in it, even if that light is invisible, I think, yes, even if no one else can see the light, just me, it has to be there, see the light, yes that's what they say, he's seen the light, they say, and if they only knew how right they were, even if they always say it about someone they consider more or less lacking in wisdom and intelligence, someone not entirely of this world, as they also say, with a certain mockery, but what difference does it make? because I see what I see, I've seen what I've seen, I've lived what I've lived and I paint what I paint, so they can say whatever they want, I think, yes actually that's another reason I'm happy to sell pictures, because I'm passing along the light, I think, and since I also make my living from the pictures I paint, since I've never made my living from anything else, I obviously need to sell the pictures! how could I live off my painting if I didn't sell my pictures? no, I'd have been in a bad way, destitute, there are plenty of painters who live in the most dire poverty, even if most of them try to hide it and peacock around and scatter money to the winds once they manage to make a few kroner, but I've never been someone like that, I've never spent more money than I needed to, I think, usually less in fact, if you want to put it that way, yes, I've lived modestly, they say, and I've always managed to get by, I think, and one of the reasons was my being so modest, even thrifty, probably to the point of stinginess, even penny-pinching as the old folks say, the fact is I just don't like to spend money, and I've never liked to spend money, but I need it just like everyone else, even if all I like buying is canvas and tubes of oil paint, yes, all kinds of painting supplies, but I like buying those things so much that I have so much canvas and turpentine and so many tubes of oil paint and boards for stretchers and brushes and rags and whatever else that I basically don't need to buy any more of any of it for the rest of my life, almost, and I've stored most of it up in a room in the attic, it's all up there, well organised, everything where it belongs, I think, and still I keep buying more new supplies rather than using what I have up in the attic, like how I bought a roll of canvas at The Art Store today and a good amount of boards for stretchers at The Hardware Store, but it feels like that was so long ago, yes, like it was ages ago that I was in The Art Store and The Hardware Store, even though it was earlier today, but yes well when it comes to buying what I need to paint with I never think about saving money, and that probably goes back to my childhood too when I sold a picture and with the money I made I bought canvas and tubes of oil paint and turpentine, I think, lying in bed at The Country Inn, in Room 407, in the bed I've slept in so many times before, and I am so tired so tired and I can't sleep, because how is Asle doing? what's happening to him at The Hospital? because Asle needs rest, they said he needs to get his rest now and that's why I couldn't go see him, and of course I didn't argue, I just left, and it's only to stop thinking about Asle that I'm thinking about all these other things, all the things I usually think about, because Asle needs to get some rest, that's the best thing for him, The Nurse said, and that's why it was best that I come back again tomorrow and ask if I can see him then, she said and I said I could do that, but if he's asleep when I come by he'll need to keep sleeping, because he needs to rest now, what's important now is that he sleep as much as possible, she said and I said I'd come back tomorrow and ask if I can get anything for him, if he isn't asleep then, and if he is asleep then that's great, I won't get him anything, I'll just come back another day, because I live a long way north of Bjørgvin, in Dylgja, if she knows where that is, I said and The Nurse said that she didn't know and I said well no it's such a small place that almost no one has heard of it, I said and she said well then that's what we'll do, I should come back tomorrow or some other day, and I can call first to see if I can come and we'll tell you how it's going, she said, that's how it went, or is that just something I'm imagining? that it went like that? that The Nurse and I had a conversation like that? I think and anyway now I'm lying in bed at The Country Inn, in my regular room, Room 407, and I can't get to sleep and I think that a lot of the people who are supposed to know what's good and what's bad, what's good art and what's bad art, don't think much of my pictures, yes, for several years now painting pictures wasn't something you should do if you wanted to be a real artist, paintings as such weren't real art, and during that time the people who painted pictures were obviously said to be less worthwhile, they weren't considered artists at all, just illustrators past their expiration date or something like that, and the worst of all were the people who painted pictures and then sold them, who put pictures they'd painted on sale, yes, the people who painted pictures someone actually wanted to buy were the worst, because where was the art in that? weren't such pictures mere entertainment? purely commercial? nothing but something to put on a wall? something to hang above the sofa since after all something has to hang there? maybe yes maybe no, but in any case it's not art, they would say or think, but I know what I'm doing, I know the difference between a good picture and a bad picture, and I know I can paint pictures that only I can paint, because I have my very own inner picture that all the other pictures come from, so to speak, or that they all try to get to, or get close to, but that one innermost picture can't be painted, and the closer I am to that inner picture when I paint the better I paint, and the more light there is in the picture, yes, that's how it is, I think, and what I've seen and lived, and know deep inside, in my innermost picture, is also something I want to tell the world, something I want other people to know, or to have hanging over their sofa for that matter, because I want to, yes, share what I know, show it, yes of course it can't be said but maybe it can be shown? at least a little of it? and insofar as it can be shown I want to show it to someone else, since it's true, I'm sure of it and I know it's good, it's good for me and it's good for other people too, and what I want to show to other people has to do with light, or with darkness, it has to do with the shining darkness full as it is of nothingness, yes, it's possible to think that way, to use such words, and it's also something that comes from the picture I have inside me that I see when I see something that lodges itself inside me and that I can never get rid of again, these flashes of pictures, clear pictures, that I have in my mind and that torment me, yes, it's true, and it's been like that since I was a boy, there are so many pictures like that, there are countless such pictures, like those black boots of Grandfather's on the road in the rain, one dark night, or Grandfather's hands, shining, glowing, in a flash, and some pictures come to me again and again while others just lay there in a group sort of resting, and emerge only rarely, but one that comes to me again and again is Ales's face in the rain, in the darkness, the rain running down over her despairing face, but in all the pain, all the suffering, there's her light, that black light, yes, I should be ashamed of myself but my eyes are starting to get teary as I lie here, the light, the black light in her despairing face, the invisible light, those desperate eyes, twisted, her mouth half-open, and the rain running down her face in the dark night, or the opposite, yes, glittering on Ales's thoughtful peaceful face when she disappears into herself and in this movement becomes like part of an incomprehensible light that streams invisibly from her face, yes, there are so many faces in my mind, some in pain, some resting, and most of all faces that are just there, unconscious in a way, just full of, yes, what exactly, yes there are so many faces that they're about to merge together into a single face, I think, and then from Ales's face spreading out all over shines the light of care and tenderness on all that she's looking at, I think and now I need to sleep, I am so tired so tired and I'm just lying here thinking thoughts that I've thought so many times before, I think, but I can't sleep, lying here in my bed at The Country Inn, Room 407, the room I always stay in, as long as it's free, and if it isn't I rent an adjacent room, I stay in Room 409, or Room 405, and all those rooms are small and look out on the backyard, I think and I lie there and I can't sleep and tomorrow I'll take a taxi to The Hospital and look in on Asle and tell him that I went to get his dog, and ask him if I can bring him anything, buy him anything, I think and then I'll take a taxi to The Lane and then I'll pick up his dog and then I'll walk to my car parked in front of The Beyer Gallery and it's probably totally covered in snow by now, but obviously I have a good snow brush and a good scraper with me so I'll manage, I'll get the car ready to drive so that I can drive to Dylgja and get back home, because I so wish I was back home and lying in my own bed and not at The Country Inn, yes, even though I've spent so many nights here in this bed too, it just isn't my own bed, it's a bed where lots of other people have slept too, and where lots more people will sleep in the future, that's how it is, yes, in fact it's so obvious that why think about it? why think these thoughts? because sometimes I really like being at The Country Inn, after all that's why I've stayed here so many times, that's why I always stay here whenever I need to spend the night in Bjørgvin, and I can't count the number of times I've spent the night at The Country Inn, so obviously I'm comfortable here, but I just can't get to sleep tonight, it's impossible, I don't know why, but I'm too restless, I can't sleep, everything is like it's crumbling and falling apart and I see Asle lying in bed with The Nurse and The Doctor standing next to the bed and they're saying something about him needing an IV, something like that, and then The Doctor takes his pulse and I see Asle lying there asleep, his long grey hair hanging down past his shoulders and then his whole body jerks and shakes, while he's sleeping his whole body is shaking and The Doctor says they should give him even more of some kind of medicine or another that he says the name of and The Nurse says they've already given him as much as they can and The Doctor says yes well in that case they should probably just wait a little and then give him more later, he says, and Asle's long grey hair, the shaking, the jerking and then I see The Nurse and The Doctor leave the room and then Asle is lying there and he's asleep and his body is trembling the whole time, and it's wrong to be looking at this, I don't want to see it, and it was good that I found him, when he was lying outside the door of number 5, The Lane, covered in snow, I think and I can't sleep and I think it was good that I drove back to Bjørgvin, and now why did I do that? it makes sense that I would think of it but why did I actually do it? I don't totally understand, it was like something was forcing me to, or guiding me to do it, I think and I see Asle on Father's shoulder and he's sobbing and sobbing and the crying has taken on a kind of life of its own, and he's twisting and writhing, because it hurts, his stomach hurts and Father is walking back and forth carrying him and rocking him back and forth in his arms and Father has left the upstairs bedroom and Father said he'd take Asle out into the hall so that at least Mother and Sister could sleep, he said, and Father walks and carries Asle, holds him against his shoulder, rubs his back, and Asle cries and cries and his crying gets louder and sharper, he's gasping, he's crying in bursts, he's crying so loud that it almost sounds like shrieks and Father rubs and rubs his back and then Asle's body gradually relaxes and the crying gets weaker, it turns into breathing, and Father walks back and forth with him, and Father and Asle and the breathing and the stroking of Father's hand on Asle's back are like one and the same movement and then Asle goes away, he disappears from the pain, from the stabbing in his stomach, and Father walks back and forth with him across the upstairs hall and then Father opens the door to the bedroom with his free hand as carefully and quietly as he can and Father and Asle go into the darkness and he hears Father from far away whisper he's sleeping now, he's finally asleep and he hears Mother say that's good, he's been crying for such a long time, she says and he realises that Father has put him down in his bed and spread the blanket over him and then Father has lightly stroked his hair and then Asle has disappeared from there into his calm breathing, and into his calm sleep, and with his face turned aside he lies there breathing evenly and Father goes and lies down next to Mother and she says softly that Father must be so tired, first a long day of work, from early in the morning until late at night he's been out gathering pears, and then now, at night, all the way up until now, late at night, Asle's been screaming and Father was walking back and forth carrying him, she says and Father says that he is tired and that he'll try to get to sleep and I see Asle lying there and his body is shaking, jerking up and down, he's trembling, and then I see Asle being held against someone's breast, he's a little boy, it's not Mother's breast, it's another breast, but he feels warmth from a breast against his cheek, he is almost pressing his cheek against the breast, yes, he's leaning all the weight of his little head against the woman's chest and I see that most of her chest is covered by a dress, a flower-patterned dress, it's green and there are white flowers on it and it goes down in a V at the neck and behind the V are two big breasts, like two O's pressed against each other and Asle puts his little little hands on one breast and the woman holding him in her arms laughs and smiles and she rocks him back and forth against her chest and he looks at her and he looks at her chest, and at the crack between her breasts, and he thinks it looks like a butt, is she holding him against her butt? he thinks, she can't be, can she? there's no butt up top is there? and he doesn't understand, so he needs to ask, Asle thinks and he asks if she has her bud up here, because he can't say his "t"s, and then he hears a sudden laugh burst against his ears and laughter fills the room and the woman holding him against her chest bends forward and laughs so hard that Asle is moved up and down and she holds him tight to her chest and he feels her movements, and he's sort of hanging in mid-air, but she's holding him tight, she's holding him even tighter to her chest than before, yes, she's sort of clutching him to her chest and she laughs and laughs and Asle sees Mother standing there and she's bent over with laughter and he sees Grandmother standing there and she too is laughing and laughing and he understands that he's said something strange, and he doesn't totally understand what was so strange about what he said, and then the woman holding him to her chest starts to walk across the room and he hears her say can you believe the things he says, really, she says, and just two years old too, Grandmother says, yes that was really something, what he just said, Mother says and then the three women laugh again, but less wildly now, not as loud and sharp, more slow and kind, and Mother says well they should go sit down at the table, the coffee's ready, she says and Asle twists free and the woman who was holding him at her breast puts him down on the floor and then Asle stands there and he looks at his Grandmother who has sat down at a table and then he goes over to Grandmother and he hears the woman who'd held him against her chest and put him down say he's a good walker even though he's so little, and Mother says yes he's a toddler now, she says, and he goes to Grandmother and she says now come to Grandma my boy yes, she says and Grandmother holds her arms out towards him and he goes towards Grandmother's arms and he reaches them and she takes him under his arms and picks him up and puts him on her thigh and then she hugs him to her and all at once he is in her good warmth and she rocks him a little in her warmth and I see

Asle lying there with his hands down by his sides and his whole body's jerking up and down and there are several tubes attached to his body running up to a metal stand and I see The Nurse standing next to him put her hand on his forehead and then The Doctor opens the door and walks in and The Nurse says it's bad, the spasms need to stop soon, she says and The Doctor nods and he says that they've given him what they can give him now, they can't give him any more, he says and they stand there without saying anything and then The Doctor says he doesn't know how this'll end, if he'll make it, and The Nurse says yes, yes it's bad, she says, and the question is whether he should be kept under constant observation now, she says, if he needs to be moved to a room where he can be kept under constant observation, she says and The Doctor says that would be best and I lie in bed at The Country Inn, in Room 407, and I can't get to sleep and I see Asle lying there, shaking, trembling, jerking, his long grey hair moving up and down and I hear The Doctor say no it doesn't look good and The Nurse says the question is whether he'll make it, she says and The Doctor says it sure looks bad, but maybe these spasms will stop soon, or at least get weaker, he says and Asle needs somebody with him at all times, The Doctor says, maybe he's strong enough to pull through, he says, yes The Nurse says and I see someone come in and they wheel his bed and the metal stand with all the tubes attached to his body out to the hall and into a lift and they take the lift one floor up and then Asle is wheeled down a corridor and then he's wheeled into a room where there's already a man lying in a bed and a man in a white uniform sitting on a chair and I see that Asle's face is almost totally grey and the man sitting there stands up and goes over to the bed Asle's in and helps wheel that bed over to the wall opposite from where the other bed is and then Asle lies there and his whole body's shaking, trembling, the jerking is going through him the whole time and then Asle just lies there and he wakes up and he looks at the man sitting on a chair in the room and the man sitting there says Asle should just sleep, he needs to rest now, what you need now is rest, sleep, he says and Asle shuts his eyes and then he just lies there in his shaking and I lie in bed at The Country Inn, Room 407, and I see Asle standing next to Father and he's looking down at a hole in the ground and he knows that the box with the wreaths and flowers on it is going to be put down into the hole and his Grandfather is lying there in the box and he was big, tall, broad-shouldered, enormous, and then Asle feels tears coming into his eyes and people are standing around the open hole in the ground, lots of people, and they're all standing far enough away from the hole in the ground so that there'll be room for the people carrying the white box with his Grandfather inside and they'll be able to walk next to the hole in the ground and there's a mound of dirt past the end of the hole and Asle stands there and he sees the pastor, in his black pastor's robe, with his white pastor's collar around his neck, come walking in the lead and behind him are the men carrying the white box with his Grandfather inside and Asle looks at the box and he feels a fear take hold of him and he sees the pastor step aside a little and take his place and then he's standing there in his black pastor's robe with the white pastor's collar and the men with the box come closer and closer and Father steps back a little and Asle steps back with him and everyone else steps back a little too and then the men carrying the box with all the wreaths and flowers walk past Asle and he sees that they're walking bent to one side, because it's heavy, carrying Grandfather, big as he was, Asle thinks, and they put something like a frame with straps across it over the black hole in the ground and the men lift the box over the hole in the dirt and they carefully put the box down on the straps across the top of the hole that are attached to a frame and then the pastor speaks and he throws earth onto the box and he says from dust you come and to dust you shall return and then the people standing around the box start singing Nearer My God To Thee and then one or the other of them starts lowering the box down into the hole, down, down, and Asle puts his hand into Father's hand and then they stand there, Asle and Father, and watch the box with Grandfather in it being lowered farther and farther down into the dirt and then the box is out of sight and now Asle can't hold back his tears any more and the tears start running down his cheeks and he holds Father's hand and all he feels now is Father's hand and people start walking away from the hole in the ground where the box with his Grandfather in it is now down in the earth, surrounded by dirt, and it's a long way down to the box, and to his Grandfather, and Father goes almost all the way up to the edge of the hole in the dirt and then Asle looks up at Father and he sees Father standing and looking down at the box and then he too looks down at the box and while everyone else walks away he and Father stay standing and looking at the box where his Grandfather is lying and eventually it's just Asle and Father there and Mother and Sister and Grandmother are behind them and then he hears Mother say

Should we go? she says

and Father nods and quietly says yes and then Father stays where he is

All right, let's go, Mother says

and he sees Mother and his sister Alida start walking behind the others but a long way behind them while Grandmother stays where she is, and then Father shakes his head and I'm lying in my bed at The Country Inn, Room 407, and I can't get to sleep I see Asle lying there and his body is trembling, shaking, jerking up and down, he's shaking all over and The Doctor says it's bad but they can't do anything more for him now, they've given him as much medicine as they can, they can't give him any more, The Doctor says, and then both The Doctor and The Nurse leave the room and I'm lying in bed at The Country Inn and I can't sleep and I see Father and Asle go over to Mother and Sister who are standing waiting for them and Asle thinks his sister's name is

Alida, there aren't many other people named that, he tries to just think about that, his not knowing anyone else named Alida besides his sister, he thinks, his sister Alida, yes, Asle thinks and then his Grandmother puts her hand under Father's arm and then Father and Asle and Grandmother and Sister and Mother walk away together after the others and I think that I need to get to sleep now, I can't lie awake in bed at The Country Inn all night, I think and I see Asle sitting in an upstairs room in an outbuilding and he's reading a book, and he's sitting in a rowboat with Father and he's sitting on a bus and he's thinking that a friend of his is dead, he has just then heard the news, he's sitting there and reading a book, and he's lying in a bed and reading a book, he's drawing, he's painting, he's walking down a street, he's drinking beer and she's naked and she's lying there in bed and he doesn't know what to do he puts his hands on her and he realises he wants to lie down on her and he does it and he doesn't dare enter her something is holding him back he doesn't dare because just when he's about to a fear comes over him and he pulls back and she just lies there and her name is Liv and he's lying on top of her and then he's sitting at a schooldesk and he's standing there smoking rolling a cigarette books a teacher is saying something he asks the class drawing painting the other eleven students painting class girls boys smoking beer painting drinking beer talking and then just going there and waiting and then, finally, finally, he was born, finally he came out into this world into the light and Asle has become a father he is young very young but he's become a father and his long brown hair and everyone else is so much better than him he's worthless she just wants to be with the others with all of them all of the others and it's over and he wants to lie down and sleep in the snow because it's so far to walk and he's so tired and so drunk he sees the stars shining clearly one star and then he and Father are in a rowboat his son they're fishing books drawings paintings reading painting just painting just that and beer vodka that good rush the best nothing much at first and then better and better and he drinks and she says he mustn't drink every night a little rush every night and he drinks paintings money no money sells pictures for money has no money exhibition exhibitions critics selling pictures tubes of oil paint canvas always oil paint and always canvas oil on canvas stretchers boards stretchers nails canvas her and the woman who comes and sits down at his table and they start talking and she's seen his exhibitions home to her place lying next to each other kissing the woman one of his sons kissing her they take off their clothes he holds her tight they lie next to each other they talk go home she's lying there his son is asleep go home she's lying there she's lying there on the floor she's almost not breathing ambulance boy crying and crying howling ambulance he and his son she writes him a letter they meet kiss eat together he's sitting and drinking and she comes and sits down exhibitions oil paint canvas stretchers need to find a place to live boards nowhere to stay pictures the others vodka feeling warm beer another pint talk about this and that laugh she comes and it's Christmas lamb ribs summer her parents' house the white house the silence and painting never stopping always continuing they can say whatever they want just continuing the dark eyes children several children paintings house he sits and drinks children paintings their house needs repainting pictures days nights can't get to sleep and he lies there and he shakes up and down jerks trembling shaking and the man sitting there gets up and I sit there and I look at the picture, those two lines that cross and I see Åsleik standing there looking at the picture and he says St Andrew's Cross, it's a St Andrew's Cross, Åsleik says, and that heavy stress he puts on the words, he's so proud of knowing the term that he stresses it, a provincial pride, St Andrew's Cross, this pride in knowing the term and there's nothing more to do with the picture so I'll just put it aside, but not yet, maybe I should paint over those two lines, maybe it can turn into a good picture if the cross disappears from the picture, if it becomes invisible, or almost invisible, if it's turned into something way back behind the rest and I get up and I go over to the picture and then I pick it up off the easel and I put it back down on the easel and I think that I probably don't actually want to put it in the stack of paintings leaning against the wall between the bedroom door and the hall door, the stack of pictures I'm still working on and am not yet done with, the one that my brown leather shoulder bag is hanging above, and I step a little bit away from the picture and I look at it, and it's not totally terrible, but some paintings just aren't there yet, but maybe this one can still get there? because it can take a long time for me to finish a painting sometimes, if I can ever finish it, because there's something missing, but what? and that's how it almost always is, I think, or if not always then very often, the picture is almost what it's supposed to be, I'm almost there, but not quite, I'm close, so close, I think, but it's too early to put the picture in the stack leaning against the wall with the stretchers facing out and I see the man sitting between the two beds stand up and he goes over to the bed where the other man is lying and he presses his fingers against his shoulder and the man is just lying there and he holds his hand in front of the man's mouth and he feels for his pulse and he leaves the room and now I need to get to sleep soon, I don't want to know what time it is, but I'm so restless, I don't know what's wrong, and anyway it's a good thing I drove back into Bjørgvin and found Asle, he's never sober now, actually for several years now he's never been sober, not once, not really, in all these years, even if he says he only starts drinking in the evening or maybe late afternoon it's been a long time since he wasn't drunk, I'm sure of that, I think and I think that I'm going to get up soon and take a taxi to The Hospital and see Asle, tell him I'll take care of his dog, Bragi, and then maybe I'll buy something for him, or bring him something from his apartment, anything he needs or wants, maybe a book, and then I need to get his dog from Guro's apartment, that was her name right? the woman who lives on The Lane, and she told me what number it was and I can't think of it at the moment but I'm sure it'll come to me, yes, Bragi, his dog, is there at the apartment of the woman I ran into, who makes a living doing Hardanger embroidery, she took the dog with her and so I need to go get the dog from her, and she lived at number 3, The Lane, or was it number 5? it was on The Lane anyway, and it's probably morning now, I think, anyway I'm awake, and it was around ten o'clock that I was supposed to go pick up the dog but I could also go by earlier, or I could go by later, however it works out, yes, that's what we arranged, something like that, I don't remember it too clearly, but she did live in The Lane, I remember that much for sure, and first I need to take a taxi to The Hospital and see Asle and I need to tell him that I'm looking after his dog, Bragi, while he's in The Hospital, so he doesn't need to worry about the dog, I have to tell him that, I think, and I can bring him anything he might want, from his apartment, or go buy what he wants, because there, in The Hospital, he probably can't paint but he could sketch or draw, but he doesn't like to draw, he's always said that, drawing was never for him, he said, always that, he's always said that he's a painter, not a draughtsman, for him what matters is oil paint on canvas, nothing else, and he doesn't know why but that's how it has to be, oil on canvas, still he always keeps a sketchpad and pencil with him in the brown leather shoulder bag he always carries with him, so he can sketch down something that might turn into a painting later, yes, I know that, I think, but I don't understand why I'm so restless, I can't get to sleep and I can't get up either, but why? what should I do? or is it tomorrow already? did I sleep at all? or just doze off in a kind of half-sleep and dream or half-dream? I think, and since this trip happened so suddenly I didn't bring anything with me, not even a toothbrush and toothpaste, no change of clothes of course, and even if I have a sketchpad and pencil in my shoulder bag I don't feel like sketching anything now, because what would it be? I think, and I didn't bring a book, I read a lot, and recently I most often read around in The Bible, a little of one part and then a little of another part, yes, I used to read through the whole Bible but now I jump around at random and read a little from whatever page I happen to open to, but I don't feel like reading in the Bible that's sitting on the nightstand there, if I'm going to read in The Bible I want to read in my own Bible, for whatever reason, and I consider myself a believer, yes, a Christian, yes, I've even converted to Catholicism, but I can't believe in a God as vengeful as the God of the Old Testament, who had children put to death and wiped out whole peoples, no, I can't understand that, but that's exactly why Jesus Christ came to earth, as the New Testament tells us, isn't it? he came to earth to proclaim that God is no longer a vengeful God, but a God of love, a merciful God, yes, to proclaim that God is now a benevolent God and not one of vengeance and punishment and destruction, that now he is a God of love for all people, and not just Israel's God, yes, that's how it had to be, that the old vengeful God took his own life in and with and through Jesus Christ's death on the cross? I think, even if it's the same God, because it's only we human beings who have long misunderstood his will, what his kingdom really is, I think, because there's also a lot that's beautiful and wise in the Old Testament, it's not that, and things in the Old Testament point ahead to what happens in the New Testament, or at least it can be read that way, if you want to, but, as they always say, what stands written in the Old Testament has to be understood in the light of Jesus Christ, of God become man, who gave himself to mankind and let himself be crucified and killed, yes, changing the human condition and re-establishing the connection, the oneness between God and humanity that had existed before the Fall, which separated human beings from God, brought them into sin and death, yes, before the devil, Satan, came to rule over this world, as stands written, yes, before the great breaking point when humanity, or Adam, tempted by Eve, as stands written, abandoned their oneness with God and gave themselves over to sin which spread through the world more and more, yes, God still understands people who sin, he was human too and he took his own life, or let people take it, and then he was the good God he'd always been when he rose up from the dead as Jesus Christ and left this earth, as God and man, undivided and whole, so that it would be possible for all people to do the same thing, since sin and death rule this world, it's like it's in the devil's power, God became human and died and rose again so that everyone who died, or who had died, could afterwards live in God, because he, the Son of Man, made it so that humanity and God were joined together as one again, in God's kingdom, which already exists, God's kingdom exists in every moment, in the eternity that's in every now, but do I believe that? do I actually believe in its reality? is it even possible to believe something like this? in this foolishness we're proclaiming, as Paul wrote, yes, that stands written, no, I probably don't, no one can believe something like that, it goes against all wisdom and understanding, because either God is all-powerful and then there's no free will, or God isn't all-powerful and there is free will, within limits, but in that case God is not all-powerful, so ever since God gave humanity free will he gave up his omnipotence, something like that must be true, because without a will that's free there can't be love, and God is love, that's the only thing that is said of God in the New Testament, and that's why God lacks divine omnipotence, he has God's weakness, impotence even, but there's a lot of strength in weakness, yes, maybe the weakness is itself a strength? and it's possible that God is all-powerful in his weakness and that there is free will, even if it's impossible to think that, because there are so many things that a person can't think, for instance that space goes on forever, and the strange thing is that it's possible to believe in the Christian message anyway, in the gospels, strangely enough you can because as soon as you start to believe it you believe it, the belief comes by itself, yes, it's like God's wordless nearness, or maybe like your angel, I think, and I am one of the people who believe, or rather one of the people who know, without knowing why, no, I can't say why, not about the whole thing and not even partly, because belief, or insight, knowledge, yes knowing is what I'd prefer to call it, is something that a person suddenly and mysteriously understands is the truth, and this truth has never been said the way it is, and it can never be said because it isn't words, it's The Word, it's what's behind all words and what makes words, makes language, makes meaning possible, and maybe it can be shown but it can't be said, yes, that's how it is, and a faith like that, an insight, a knowing like that is a grace that some people receive, but the grace, the knowledge, that these people are given can extend to cover even the people who haven't themselves been given it, yes, or don't even know it exists, the mercy embraces all of humanity, I think and I think that even just that isn't a very clear thought, if you can even call it a thought at all, I think, it's like a thought in a dream, I think, and I don't want to go to mass any more, because it's all just lies, I think, and I don't want to read from the Bible any more, I've done it enough, and especially not the Bible sitting on the nightstand, it annoys me, it's sitting there like it's staring at me, like it wants something from me, and plus it's so ugly to look at, that cover with a bouquet of flowers, it's a totally undignified Bible, I've never understood why almost every single hotel has to have a Bible sitting on the nightstand in every room, I think and now I want to sleep, just sleep, I am so tired so tired and maybe I'm dozing off a little, maybe I'm not, and I think that the first thing I'll do in the morning is eat a nice big breakfast, because they always have such good breakfast at The Country Inn, fresh-baked bread, the most wonderful scrambled eggs in a big bowl, and thin slices of bacon in a big tray with a curved metal lid, and you slide the lid back and out comes the most wonderful bacon, some pieces are crispy, some are just warm and soft, it all tastes amazing and I always take a lot of bacon and a lot of scrambled eggs and then I cut one or two thick soft fresh slices of bread for myself and find a table by a window, as long as there's one free, because I like to sit by the window and look out at The Wharf and down to The Bay, at the boats lying moored there, and then I get two glasses of water and then a big mug of coffee with milk and then I sit there and enjoy the best meal of the day, and maybe I get a newspaper, I often do, but not always, because more often than not reading what's in the paper only annoys me, and that's why I don't subscribe to any newspapers because I disagree with almost everything they say, yes, almost always, and especially what they say about art, for instance the man who writes about art for *The Bjørgvin Times* doesn't understand a thing about art, it's hardly possible to have any less understanding for art than he has, and yet a newspaper for some incomprehensible reason has him write about art, it's a mystery, he has hardly a single nice word to say about my shows, that is if they're discussed or mentioned at all, usually they're not even given a single word and now breakfast might be starting already, I think and I look at the clock and I see that it's almost six and that's when breakfast starts and I lie there in the bed and I've hardly slept a wink all night, or I guess I have been kind of asleep, as much as I'm going to be, and I probably might as well just get up and have breakfast, I think, and if Asle is better then maybe I can get him from The Hospital and then we can walk together to my car that's parked in front of The Beyer Gallery, because Asle knows the way so we can go there, and then pick up the dog, Bragi, from The Lane, before I drive Asle and the dog back home to his apartment, yes, it was quite a coincidence wasn't it, that the woman who makes her living sewing Hardanger embroidery and decorative bodices for folk costumes took Asle's dog home with her and she lives on The Lane, at number 5

The Lane, or was it number 3? and it was outside number 3, The Lane, that I found Asle lying on a step covered in snow, wasn't it? yes it was, and why just there? maybe he was going to see the woman who lives there? yes, Guro as she's apparently called, yes, that might well be, because Asle was lying sort of up on the step and turned to face a front door, so maybe it was her, Guro, that he was going to see? no he was just on his way to The Alehouse, and then he just happened to slip and fall there, because anyway that's where I was going, I think, but it's probably better if I get his dog from The Lane first before heading to The Hospital, I think and I can't get to sleep so I might as well get up, I think and did I sleep at all or just doze off? just lie there in a half-sleep? but I was gone a little, off in a sleep a little, a little in a dream, I think and then I realise that Ales is lying next to me and she's lying there with her arms around me and I take the brown wooden cross that's hanging at the bottom of the rosary, that I got from Ales once, I hold the cross between my thumb and index finger, and I think that maybe God doesn't exist, no, obviously He doesn't exist, He is, and if I were not then God wouldn't exist, I think and I see before me what Meister Eckhart has written, that if humanity didn't exist so wäre auch "Gott" nicht, daß Gott "Gott" ist, dafür bin ich die Ursache and wäre ich nicht, so wäre Gott nicht "Gott" and of course it's like that, I think, and I see in my mind Pater noster Qui es in cælis Sanctificetur nomen tuum Adveniat regnum tuum Fiat voluntas tua sicut in cælo et in terra Panem nostrum cotidianum da nobis hodie et dimitte nobis debita nostra sicut et nos dimittimus debitoribus nostris Et ne nos inducas in tentationem sed libera nos a malo and I move my thumb and index finger up to the first bead which is between the cross and the set of three beads on the rosary and I say to myself Our Father Who art in heaven Hallowed be thy name Thy kingdom come Thy will be done on earth as it is in heaven Give us this day our daily bread and forgive us our trespasses as we forgive those who trespass against us

And lead us not into temptation but deliver us from evil and I move my thumb and finger up to the first bead in the set and I think I usually sleep if I either say the Jesus prayer or Ave Maria and then I see the words before me and I say I say inside me Ave Maria Gratia plena Dominus tecum Benedicta tu in mulieribus et benedictus fructus ventris tui Iesus Sancta Maria Mater Dei Ora pro nobis peccatoribus nunc et in hora mortis nostræ and I move my thumb and finger up to the second bead and I say inside myself Hail Mary Full of grace The Lord is with thee Blessed art thou among women and blessed is the fruit of thy womb Jesus Holy Mary Mother of God Pray for us sinners now and in the hour of our death and I move my thumb and finger up to the third bead and I say inside myself Ave Maria Gratia plena Dominus tecum Benedicta tu in mulieribus et benedictus fructus ventris tui Iesus Sancta Maria Mater Dei ora pro nobis peccatoribus nunc et in hora mortis nostræ

II

And I see myself standing and looking at two lines that cross, one brown, one purple, and I see how I've painted the lines slowly, with a lot of paint, thick paint, two long wide lines, and they've dripped, and where the lines cross the colours blend beautifully and drip and I'm thinking that this isn't a picture but suddenly the picture is the way it's supposed to be, it's done, and then I step a little way back from the picture and I stand and look at it and then I see myself lying in the bed at The Country Inn and I think it's Tuesday today, only Tuesday, and I might as well get up, or in any case get dressed, I think and I sit up on the edge of the bed and I think well now, that was quite a night, I think and I get up and go get my trousers from where they're lying on the floor and I put them on and I pull my black pullover over my head and I put on my black velvet jacket and then I sit down on the edge of the bed and untie my shoelaces, pull my shoes on, tie the laces again, and I see my black overcoat hung on the chair and I think that I hardly slept at all even though I was so tired when I lay down, or actually, I must have slept, but maybe I just didn't realise it? I think, and strangely enough I'm not as tired as I was before, I think and I get up and go into the bathroom and splash cold water on my face, once, several times, and I take off the hairband and run my fingers through my long grey hair and and gather up my hair again and tie it in the black hairband and then I rinse out my mouth with cold water, gurgle, spit it out, I do that several times and now I'm ready to go get breakfast, as ready as I'll ever be, I think, they start serving breakfast at six o'clock, I remember that, yes, I haven't started forgetting everything even if my hair has turned grey, I usually go to bed early and get up early, around nine o'clock I go to bed and I usually fall asleep right away and I wake up at around four and get up and I'm usually painting by five, that's how it goes, I think, and I think that breakfast'll be good and then I drape the long black coat over my arm and I put the brown shoulder bag on and then I unlock the door and turn off the light and I shut the door and I put the key in the pocket of my velvet jacket and I walk over to the lift and I make the sign of the cross while I'm in the lift, I do that every morning, either I just make the sign of the cross or I both make the sign of the cross and say a Pater Noster or Our Father and make another sign of the cross after the prayer, I think and the lift stops with a shudder or two and I go out into the dining room, into The Coffeehouse, because in the morning The Coffeehouse is the breakfast room for the guests at The Country Inn who are eating there, and it's good to have left the room, I always sleep so well there, in Room 407, but last night I had an uneasy sleep, if I slept at all, but it's strange, I don't feel tired, I think, and there's no one else in the breakfast room, it's probably too early, I think and I take a big portion of food and go to a table by a window with a view of The Bay and The Wharf and I sit down and then I eat but the food doesn't taste as good as it usually does because the whole time I'm thinking about Asle, how he's doing, has he recovered? or is he doing a little bit better at least? will he be discharged today? and if not, then maybe The Handyman can get his apartment keys and then he and I can go get Asle anything he might want, because I can't take the keys myself, no, to get into his apartment I need to go with The Handyman so he can let me in and then lock up behind me, that's how it was when I went to get the dog last night, I think, yes, I was so confused by everything going on that I don't remember some things, I think and I look around and I'm still the only one in the breakfast room and I think that there must not be many guests at The Country Inn at this time of year, plus I'm up early, they've just started serving breakfast, and I haven't seen a single person out walking on The Wharf, I think, and there are no boats moored in The Bay, and everything's covered in snow, everything's white, and it's pretty, I think, but the food doesn't taste as good as usual and I only manage to eat a little scrambled eggs and a little bacon and a little coffee and even though it's a shame to leave so much good food behind I get up and go over to the reception and say good morning and the night attendant, someone I've never seen before, looks sleepily up at me and I say I'd like to pay for one night and she draws up a bill and I pay it and I hand her the key and I leave and it's not that dark out, because the moon, it's a full moon, is shining and the snow is shining white and it's cold and clear, yes, pretty, definitely, and the stars are shining and the snow has already been shovelled outside the entrance to The Country Inn, yes, the whole pavement's been shovelled, and now? what should I do now? I think, it's early, it's probably too early to go get the dog, because the woman who took him is probably still asleep, the woman who'd lived with a fiddler who eventually just drank all the time and she told him to leave and he did which she's really regretted since then, but now what was her name? and where was it that she lived? oh, I remember, her name's Guro and she lives in The Lane, number 3, yes of course, but I'm sure she's not up yet, or maybe she's also someone who wakes up early? anyway I can just go to my car first, it must be totally covered in snow but I have a snow brush and scraper in the car, of course, so I'll go to the car and get the snow off it, I think, and now, yes, now I feel confident about the way, I think and I almost have to laugh at myself, because the way from The Country Inn to the space where I always park my car when I'm in Bjørgvin, in front of The Beyer Gallery, yes, in the place to park that Beyer so to speak assigned me at one point, yes, I know the way backwards and forwards, even if I somehow, unbelievably, managed to get lost on it last night, but that was because I couldn't see because the snow was so thick, it was practically a blizzard, I think, but now I'll just walk away from The Country Inn up the street and then take a right and walk a little bit and take a left and take The Lane up to High Street, and go down the pavement a little more, and then The Beyer Gallery will be right there in all its glory, The Beyer Gallery's address is 1 High Street, and there's plenty of space to park in front of the gallery, so I'll just go there first and brush the snow off the car and scrape the ice off the windows and then maybe I can take a walk, or, darn it, yes, after I've brushed and scraped the car and maybe started the engine to warm the car up, then I'll go and ring her doorbell, the woman who lives in The Lane, named Guro, yes, Guro, in The Lane, at number 3 The Lane, and since I've got that right I'll ring the right door at least, I think and I walk down the pavement and then I walk up The Lane and there's just a narrow opening, no more than six feet wide or so, and then it gets even narrower until it's just about three or four feet wide, and then it gets a little wider, I think, and now I should look for number 3, and I stop, and I see in the half-darkness, it would have been so dark if it hadn't been for the full moon, that the number 3 is above my head by the nearest door, and I go to the door and I look at the nameplates next to the doorbells and they say Hansen and Nilsen and Berge and Nikolausen, but there's no Guro on any label, but since she lives in number 3 her name must be Berge, probably, that must be it maybe, since Hansen is a more common name but not for people from the country, I think, and I look up, and all the windows are dark, and then I turn around and I look at the other side of The Lane and there's the step that Asle was lying on covered in snow, I'm almost sure of that anyway, and there's a sign with the number 5 there on the wall next to the door and I go over and look at the nameplates there and they say Hansen, Olsen, and Pedersen and then, thank god, one of the doorbells actually says Guro, but didn't the woman apparently named Guro say that she actually lived in number 3, The Lane? but I guess I misremembered that too? I must have gone around thinking of the wrong number, I guess the surprising thing would've been if I'd actually got it right, and it's dark in all the windows of number 5 The Lane too, but this must be where she lives? because she's exactly the kind of person who would write just her first name on the doorbell, I think, so now I know where she lives at least, and I know that she wrote her first name and not her last name, and that I've once again messed up some numbers, I think, and it really was a stroke of luck that she wrote Guro on the door, I think, since I don't know her last name, but it's about time I had a little good luck, I think and I say out loud to myself that she's still asleep, Guro's still asleep, and I think that I can't ring the bell and wake her up now, maybe a little later, I think, so first I'll go brush and scrape the car, start the engine, warm up the car, the whole car, and then I can wake her up, I think and then I think that it was on those steps outside the front door of number 5 The Lane that I found Asle last night, with his body on the little steps in front of the door, outside the front door of number 5 The Lane, so maybe he was going to see the woman named Guro? maybe, because he did have girlfriends he liked to go see, maybe Guro was one of them? and now she has his dog, if there's not another Guro who lives in the building across The Lane? since I thought the woman who took the dog with her said she lived in number 3 The Lane, because that is what she told me, isn't it? that she lived in number 3 The Lane? so maybe it really is the woman whose last name is Berge who has the dog? and she's not named Guro? because at first she did say her name was something else, didn't she? now what was it? it was Silje or something, so maybe Guro isn't really her name? I think, but what was that other name? the one she said at first that she was called? back at Food and Drink? I think, yes, Silje, that was it, I think and I keep walking up to High Street and when I get there I see The Beyer Gallery up the street, the building containing The Beyer Gallery is there in all its white glory, the gallery is downstairs, Beyer's apartment is up on the second floor, and I see my car, it's parked next to Beyer's car, totally covered in snow, and it's still a little dark out but the light of the full moon and the streetlamps and the white snow make it bright enough to see pretty well, so now let's see, I think, and I think that when I saw my car again something like a little flash of joy went through me, that's how childish I am, I think and I go over to the car and unlock it and get in, so now let's see if the car starts the way it should, and it will, because it's a well-maintained car and the battery's in good shape, I think and I put the key in and turn it and the car starts right away and I turn the heater all the way up because it's cold in the car, then I get out and go around to the back and open the door and I take out the brush and shut the door and then I start brushing the snow off the car, and it's snowed a lot, there's about a foot of snow on the roof of the car, about a foot, yes, I think and I sweep off the snow and I think that when I've got most of the snow off the car and scraped the windows I'll go ring the bell where it says Guro, yes, definitely, and I'll probably wake her up, but that's not so bad, she can just give me the dog and then go back to bed and sleep some more, but, yes, I was thinking this whole time that she lived in number 3 The Lane, not number 5, so maybe I should ring the bell where it says Berge instead? because she did say at first that her name was something other than Guro, back at Food and Drink, yes, Silje, or maybe Silja or something else like that? and she said that we knew each other, very well, yes, didn't she even say that we knew each other in the biblical sense? can she have said that? or maybe something like that? yes, it could be, it's not totally unthinkable, no, I think and I brush and brush and the car gradually starts to look more or less good, I won't get all the snow off it obviously but I'll get most of it off, I think, and now I need to scrape the windows, I think and I open the door to the back of the car and put the brush back in and take the scraper out and shut the door and then I start scraping the windows and both the front windshield and the back windshield have already warmed up a little so it's pretty easy to scrape the ice off them, then I scrape off the side windows as best I can and then I say to myself okay enough scraping and I put the scraper back in the back of the car and then I get into the car and it's a little bit warm inside and I sit there and I look straight ahead and I'm both wide awake and very tired, I realise, and now I need to go get the dog, Bragi, yes, that's the first thing I need to do, I think and I look at the clock and it's after seven, yes well then I can just go ring the bell at the woman named Guro's building, she still has the dog, because that's what the woman who took the dog was called, yes, she was kind of just playing around with that other name back at Food and Drink, I think, and if I'm wrong then that'll just be one more person mad at me, I think and I turn off the engine and I get out of the car and I lock it and now, I think, I should go straight down to number 3 The Lane and ring the doorbell next to the name Berge, I think, because she said she lived in number 3 The Lane, I'm sure of that, whereas she said both different names were her name, so I'll ring the bell there, at Berge's apartment, I think and I walk down the pavement, down High Street, and then yes, yes, I take a left and I'm already in The Lane and I walk down The Lane and then I see the sign saying 3 and I see that all the windows in the building are dark and I go over to the front door and I push the button for the doorbell next to the name Berge and I hear a bell ringing inside, not loud, it's soft, a faraway ringing sound and so now I just need to wait, I think, because maybe she's still asleep? maybe nothing's happening? maybe I need to ring the bell again? after all, I gave a short ring just then, I pushed the button as little as I could since I didn't want to make too much noise, so now maybe I should ring the bell again? I think and I push the button again and hold it down for longer this time and then I see a light come on in the window right next to me, so she does live on the ground floor, unless I've woken up somebody else, but she said she lived on the ground floor, didn't she? yes, I believe she did, I think and then I stand there and I think that I don't like this, I'm waking up Guro or whatever her name is now, or maybe even someone else, whoever that might be, and it's too early, I think, but I can't just walk up and down the street either, or sit waiting in my car forever, I think and then I see a face appear in the window and it's a middle-aged woman, no, the face I see is the face of a women well on in years and she comes and opens the window

Yes what do you want? she says

and she peers at me, either angry or crabby somehow, or else just indifferent, and no oh no, I think, so I did get the number wrong, I screwed up yet again

I was sleeping you know, she says

and I think I probably need to say something, but what should I say?

Well? she says

and I say I'm so sorry, she should please forgive me, I am so very sorry, because I made a mistake, I rang the wrong doorbell, which is bad in any case, I say, but especially bad so early in the morning, that doesn't make it any better, going around waking people up

You didn't wake me up, the old woman says

I'm glad to hear that at least, I say

I almost never sleep any more, she says

and I don't know what to say

I almost never sleep any more, I'm just waiting until I fall asleep forever, for eternity, she says

and I just stand there and again I say that I'm very very sorry and I say that I was trying to ring the bell of a woman who I think is named Guro

You think? the old woman says

Yes, ha, her, she says

Yes there are men coming round and ringing her doorbell at all hours, she says

So you go right ahead and ring there, she says

She should be ashamed of herself, she says

But she doesn't know the meaning of the word shame, she says

And she had a good husband too, then she kicked him out, she says

and she shakes her head and she says it doesn't make any sense, she herself never kicked her husband out even though she had every reason to, he went around with other women, yes, it wouldn't surprise her if he was going around with that Guro woman too, even though she's so much younger, but she stuck it out with her husband, she did, she didn't go running around after men, and after he died she really missed him, she did, he was a good man despite everything, he did the best he could, he worked and toiled and supported himself and his family the way a man should, he did, but then, and I see her wipe her eyes with the back of her hand, yes one morning he was just lying there, he was dead and stiff, it was some years ago but it still brings tears to her eyes just thinking about it, she says and I say yes I truly am sorry I bothered her and she says I should just hurry on down the street and ring that hussy's doorbell in that case, since that's what I want to do so badly, the old woman says and I say no and sorry and she shuts her window and then I see the light go out and I think so I got the number wrong again, same as always, it wasn't number 3 The Lane where she lives after all, I guess, and so I really hope she's at number 5 The Lane, where it says Guro next to the doorbell, if she isn't there I have no idea where to go get the dog, Bragi, and if Asle doesn't get his dog back, no, what'll that do to him? I think, but the woman who took the dog with her did say The Lane, I'm sure of that, because words I remember, yes, I'm good with words, that's why I can read and reread books, too, several times even, I think and then I turn and cross The Lane and I see the sign saying 5 and I see that it's dark in all the windows there too and then I push the doorbell next to where it says Guro and I see a window open in front of me on the right and the woman named Guro, yes, it's her, thank god it's her, sticks her head out and says in a sleepy voice yes who's there?

It's me, I say

Aha, she says

and her voice doesn't sound exactly nice and then I hear a dog start yapping and I go over to stand under the window

Oh it's you, she says

I, I thought it was somebody else, she says

Ah, I say

Just someone, she says

and she laughs a little and it seems like she's awake now

Yes, you know, she says

I was asleep, I, she says

Ah, I say

Yes well, you know how it is for a single girl, she says

and I just stand there and can't get a single word out

But won't you come in? she says

and I don't say anything

You can't just stay out there in the cold, it's nice and warm inside,
she says

and she says I need to come in, she'll come open the door for me,
she says and I realise that I don't want to go into her house, I've never
liked going into people's houses, it's like I'm getting too close to them
or something

You've been here before, after all, she says

Lots of times, she says

and she laughs

But I guess you don't remember? she says

You didn't even recognise me last night, she says

I would've thought you would, she says

and she says she's thought about me a lot, because I did used to
come looking for her, yes she says come looking for her, lots of times,
but I must've been too drunk to remember anything, yes, clearly, she
says, clearly I was too drunk, she says, and anyway she's definitely
wide awake now, I think and I say yes I was just, the dog, I

You woke up early? she says

Yes, I say

You couldn't sleep? she says

No, I say

You were lying in bed thinking about him? she says

and I say yes that's true I was lying in bed thinking about how Asle was doing, yes, and now I want to go home, drive home, and take his dog, Bragi, well she knows that's his name, I say, with me, of course, yes, as I'd planned, I say

Yes, yes, she says

And I know, I remember you live in Dylgja, she says

and she gives a short laugh and I nod and she says that as she's already told me she's gone to see every one of the shows I've had in Bjørgvin, at The Beyer Gallery, up on High Street, she says and she nods in that direction and she emphasises the words *The Beyer Gallery*, as if it was something big and special, and she emphasises *High Street*, just like how Åsleik emphasises the words St Andrew's Cross, yes, exactly the same way, identically, with the same provincial pride, I think and she asks yet again if I won't come in and I say no and then she says well now I know where she lives anyway, because I'd probably forgotten? so the next time I'm in Bjørgvin I should drop by and see her, she says, but it would probably be a good idea if I called beforehand, she says, since, she says and she stops and she gives another short laugh and I ask if I can have the dog and she says yes of course of course and her voice sounds a little annoyed and then she's gone and then I hear footsteps and the front door opens and there she is in a yellow bathrobe holding the dog against her chest and she hands me the dog and I take him and hold him against my chest and I rub his back and I say thank you thank you so much for your help, I say and she says it was nothing, of course she had to help in a situation like that, she says and I start to put the dog down and I realise that the leash isn't there and I ask about the leash and she says wait, wait here, she'll go get it, she says and she shuts the front door and goes back inside and I stand there rubbing and rubbing Bragi's back and I think it's good to have you back, Bragi, it's good I got you back, I think, and I wait and wait and isn't she coming back? what's happened to her? she was standing there in the doorway and then she was just gone, I think, because it shouldn't take that long to find a leash, should it? I think and then the window to the right opens again and she sticks her head out and she says she can't find the leash, of course, isn't that always the way, she must have put it somewhere or another, she says, but if I come back a little later I'll get it back, because it has to be somewhere, she'll find it, it'll turn up, she says, and it'd be nice if I came by again anyway, she says and I say thank you, thank you, and I apologise for waking her up, but now she can just go back to sleep, I say and she says well then she'll expect me later, to come back to get the leash, and she'll make me a cup of coffee and a bite to eat, she says, yes, maybe she could even make me dinner? she says and I say thank you, thank you, but I need to get going back to Dylgja right away, it's a long drive, I say and she says to have a nice day anyway and it was nice to see me again and I say thank you, same to you, and then she shuts the window and she turns out the light and I start walking up The Lane with the dog held tight against my chest and it does me good to feel the warmth from the dog against my chest, it feels comforting and good and I walk up The Lane and I tell Bragi how nice it is to see him again and that we're going to my car now, I say, and then we get up to High Street and I go straight to my car and I unlock it and I see myself putting Bragi into the backseat and then I sit down properly in the front seat, take off my shoulder bag and lay it on the passenger seat, start the engine, and it's already cold again in the car but the heater is on full strength so it'll be warm again soon, I think and I pull out onto High Street and I think there's probably no reason to drop by The Hospital first, I probably won't be able to talk to Asle, it's too early, or else he'll be too sick to see me, I can feel it, I know that, I think, Asle needs to just rest, he needs to sleep, I think and I'm afraid, what if Asle just sleeps and sleeps and never wakes up? I think, and I think now, now I should drive back home to my house in Dylgja and then I'll rest too, get back to normal, and then I should paint, I think and I think that when I get home I can call The Hospital and ask if I can see Asle and if I can stop by today then there's no reason I can't drive back into Bjørgvin, at least if there's anything I can do to help him, I think and I drive confidently up High Street and I quickly turn around and see Bragi lying there on the back seat sleeping and I look forwards again and I see Åsleik standing and looking at the picture with those two lines crossing each other and then he says St Andrew's Cross, and it's like he's proud of knowing the term, and I think that I'm sure he teaches himself new words every now and then, studies them, yes, and once he's learned a term he has to say it whenever he can, like St Andrew's Cross for example, it's like he needs to show that he's someone who can do something too, the way he emphasises the word shows that yes, he can use it, him too, even though he has just a middle-school education, he only did what was mandatory, nothing more, but that doesn't mean he's stupid, oh no, not Åsleik, even if he says for instance St Andrew's Cross with provincial pride, I think, no, he's a sharp one, Åsleik, he can say the smartest most insightful things and make someone understand something in a way they hadn't understood it before, see something in a way they hadn't seen it before, and that's exactly what you're trying to do when you paint too, yes, see something you've seen before in a new way, see something as if for the first time, no, not just that, but both see it afresh and understand it, and that's the same thing in a way, I think and I see that the two lines are Asle lying on his sofa unable to think anything except one single thought, the only thing he can think is that now he needs to get up and then he'll go down to the sea and then out into the water and then he'll wade out into the sea and the waves will wash over him and he'll just be gone, gone forever, because the pain now is unbearable, the suffering, yes, the despair, whatever you'd call it, yes, the pain was so unbearable and heavy that he couldn't even lift a hand, and plus he was shaking so much, his hands, his whole body was shaking, so he had to stand up, had to get himself something to drink, at least that, first I'll have a little drink and then I'll go down to the sea, wade out into the sea, Asle thinks, lying there on his sofa, thinking, and at the same time I was standing there in my living room or studio or whatever you'd call it and painting him as two lines of paint, one purple, one brown, I think, and I look at the road ahead and I feel happy, I'm so happy, so happy, and I don't understand how I can feel such joy just from driving away from Bjørgvin, I think and I think that maybe it's because I have a dog with me now, Bragi's with me, I think and when I get home I'll call The Hospital and ask when I can come see Asle and if I can bring him anything and I'll ask them to tell him that his dog, Bragi, is all right, I have him at home with me now, so he doesn't need to worry about that at all, I think and now I'm already out of Bjørgvin, I think and I'm driving north and I turn around and see the dog, Bragi, lying asleep on the backseat there and I feel both great joy and also worried, I realise, I have such a strong feeling of being worried that it's like something's breaking inside me, and I keep driving steadily north and I think that I just drove past Sailor's Cove, I didn't even look down at the building where Asle's apartment is, I think and I'm driving north and I'll be home soon, I think, and the first thing I'll do is go to sleep, because I feel so tired, so tired, and I fall into a kind of stupor and time just passes and I approach the turn-off and the playground and I think that even though I feel so tired I shouldn't stop at the turn-off and I shouldn't look at the playground and I shouldn't look at the old brown house where Ales and I used to live, because it's so hard to look at that house, when I do the loss of Ales overwhelms me and I drive past the brown house and I see a young man with medium-length brown hair, and he's wearing a long black coat, and a girl with long dark hair, I see them go up towards the brown house, hand in hand they walk up to the brown house and I look straight ahead and I keep driving north and I see Asle standing holding Sister's hand, his sister Alida, the two of them are standing by the side of the road, and it looks like maybe they were thinking about crossing the country road but they're so little, and why are they there alone? where are their parents? and do they live in one of the two white houses visible behind them, two houses next to each other on a not so steep hill? I think and I see Sister turn around and she says look, look at the houses behind us, she says

That's where we live, she says

Yes, says Asle

What about the houses? he says

That's where we live, Sister says

We live in one of those houses, and Grandmother and Grandfather live in the other, she says

I know, Asle says

Yes yes but I just realised something, Sister says

That we live there, in the taller house, she says

The house we live in is called The New House, and the house Grandmother and Grandfather live in is called The Old House, Asle says

It looks like the houses are holding hands, Sister says

Sort of, he says

The same way you and me are holding hands, the houses are holding hands like that, Sister says

You're right it does look like that, Asle says

and then they look at the houses and there are no grown-ups in sight, neither Mother nor Father, and not Grandma or Grandpa, just the houses, both white, one old and long and the other newer and taller, and both stand out so clearly against the green, the green fields with all the fruit trees, and the green leaves on the trees, and against the black hill rising steeply up that looks so massive like a black wall behind the meadows that slope up the hillside, and then the red barn behind the white houses

And that black hill, Sister says

Yes, Asle says

I think the houses are holding hands because they're scared of that big black hill, she says

and Asle says he's never thought that before, but that's exactly how it is, now he can see it too, the two houses are holding hands because they're scared of the black hill, yes, that's really how it is, Asle says and Sister says that the black hill is really scary, because it's so steep, and because it's always wet, water comes out from springs in the hillside, she says and she asks if Asle has heard of the princesses in the mountain blue, and he says yes he has

The mountain blue, Asle says

and Sister says that this one really ought to be called the mountain black because it's so black and Asle says that it is more of a black mountain yes and then they turn around again and stand looking at the road and I drive north and I think why are those children there alone? why aren't there any grown-ups with them? why isn't anyone watching them? I think and I see the children standing by the side of the road, along a small country road, and on the other, downhill side of the road directly above The Beach, a little ways off from the children, there's a little blue house, and a little farther down the road, a little ways past the blue house, there's a bend in the road, around Old Mound, and cars come driving fast around that bend in the road, I think, and those two kids aren't walking out onto the road are they? I think and I see that there's a mud puddle in the middle of the road and then Sister lets go of Asle's hand and runs out onto the road, into the mud puddle, and then she starts stomping her feet and the muddy water splashes up her legs, and onto her dress, and it's a good thing they have boots on, Asle thinks, and he says she can't do that and Sister says it's so fun, he should come splash around too, she says and Asle says she's getting all dirty, she mustn't do that, what is Mother going to say? she'll be so mad, she'll start yelling, Asle says but Sister acts like she doesn't hear him and just splashes away and now her dress is almost entirely muddy, almost covered in grey splotches, Asle sees and he just stands there watching and then he says she needs to stop now, it's not just that Sister's getting all dirty but it's dangerous to be in the middle of the road, a car might come, cars come driving by all the time, and the person driving the car might not see Sister and as soon as he thinks that he runs out onto the road and grabs Sister's arm and she shrieks and he drags her over to the other side of the road and she's screaming and saying she wants to splash some more and Asle says she can't, just look at that dress, how filthy it is, he says and Sister looks at her dress

Yeah, she says

and it's like she's about to start crying

It was so nice, so nice and blue, she says

And look at it now, Asle says

and he sees Sister start crying and he says she mustn't cry, a dress getting dirty isn't so bad, it can be washed, and Mother won't be that mad, and he'll say it was his fault, he'll say he asked her to go out into the mud puddle and then she'll yell at him not her, he says, because Mother always yells at him anyway, whatever he says and whatever he does, he says and Sister wipes her tears away and Asle says no, he doesn't care if he gets yelled at, not him, and he thinks that he's showing off a bit now isn't he, he thinks

But my dress is all dirty, Sister says

and she starts crying again

Well if you're going to be so stupid about it, Asle says

and when he says that Sister really starts crying hard

I'm sorry, I shouldn't have said that, Asle says

I didn't mean it, he says

You're not stupid, really you're not, you're nice and sweet and bright and clever, he says

and then Sister's just sniffling a little and Asle says it'll all work out, it'll be fine, he says, but, he says, now she knows she shouldn't do things like that, not with a nice dress on, he says and Sister doesn't say anything and they just stand there and then he takes Sister's hand and they stand there not sure what to do and Asle thinks that they are going to get yelled at, he's going to get yelled at, Mother's going to get really angry when she sees how Sister got her dress all dirty, and on purpose too, Asle thinks, and he's promised Sister that he'll say it was him who told her to do it, told her to stand in the mud and stomp and jump, he's promised her that, yes, so now he has to keep his promise, Asle thinks, and even though he doesn't care that much if he gets yelled at he still doesn't exactly like it, he thinks, but anyway they shouldn't go straight home, he thinks, maybe they can come up with some other idea

Maybe we should go over to Old Mound, maybe the blueberries are ripe there? he says

and Sister just stands there, still not sure, saying nothing

Don't you want to? Asle says

and Sister is still just standing there and she doesn't say anything and Asle realises he's getting impatient, getting bored almost, he thinks, they can't just stay here on the side of the road like this, it'd be better to keep going to Old Mound, but if they want to do that they'll have to cross the road again, and if they do that they'll need to look carefully first, to make sure no cars are coming around the bend there before Old Mound, he thinks

You don't want to keep going to Old Mound? Asle says

and Sister just shakes her head and Asle asks what do you want to do then and she doesn't answer, and then he asks her if they should go to the smaller blue house, on the downhill side of the road, they've never done that before, and he's often thought about how he wanted to go see that house, Asle says and Sister shakes her head again and then he asks if they should go down to The Beach, down to The Boathouse, out onto The Dock, down to look at The Rowboat, as Father so often says, well I better go down and take a look at The Rowboat, Father says, either he says I better go down and bail out The Rowboat, and Mother tells him he needs to be careful and Father says he always is, he's always careful, he says, or else he says he'll go out on the water for a bit and try to catch a few fish and then Mother says the same thing, that he needs to be careful, Asle thinks, and both Mother and Father have said that they, he and Sister, must never ever go down to the water alone, it's dangerous, if they fell in the water they might drown, she said, and then she would tell them about the boy she went to school with, in the same class as her, who fell in the water, he was alone in a fishing boat and he tried to climb up out of the water and the water was cold and it's hard to get back on board a boat out of the water, it's almost impossible, Mother says, and he couldn't do it, and they found the boat empty in the water, it was just floating there, and the boy, the one she'd gone to school with, they couldn't find him anywhere, until a week later, maybe even longer, some men were out in a boat and saw something floating down in the water that looked like a person and they hooked the body and pulled it on board and it was him, yes, the boy she used to go to school with, and he didn't look too good, the men said, no, she can't think about it, it's too horrible, Mother says, and then they brought him back to land and then there was a funeral and she and all the other kids who went to the school were at the funeral and she remembers how sad it was, how the boy's parents and siblings cried and cried, it was like the tears would never stop running down their faces, and the pastor had said something about God's inscrutable ways, incomprehensible, yes, but there is meaning in everything that happens, the pastor said, and he said that God writes straight on crooked lines, or maybe it was the other way around, or maybe it was slanted lines, she can't remember exactly but she remembers it, Mother says, and she couldn't understand what meaning it could possibly have for a boy to get drowned, and the pastor said that too, that it was impossible to understand, it lay beyond human comprehension, he said, but even if he couldn't understand what the meaning was and no one else could either it still had meaning, that was certain, the pastor said, Mother said, because ever since Jesus Christ, who was God, part of the Trinity of God, had died and risen up again, yes, ever since God had become human and lived as people are fated to live, birth and then life and then death, ever since then death has been turned into life for us, the pastor had said, for all humankind, yes, for those who lived before Christ and those who lived at the same time as him and those who lived after him, death, yes, death had been turned into life, into eternity, the pastor had said, Mother said, and now the boy was with God, yes, he had come home, come home to where he had set out from, the pastor had said, and God had been with him when he drowned, and had taken as good care of him as he could, he was certain of that, the pastor had said, and Mother said she couldn't understand how that was any consolation because the boy was gone, he would never come back home, he was gone forever now, the sea had taken him, taken his life, and his body had been laid in the ground, Mother said, so they never, Mother said, they must never ever ever go down to the water, The Beach, The Fjord, alone, Mother said, only when she or Father or another grown-up was with them, only then could they go down to The Beach, to The Fjord, and they must absolutely never go out onto The Dock, because out past The Dock the water was very deep, she said, so they must never, never go out onto The Dock, she said and Asle stands there holding Sister's hand and he thinks that now they'll go down onto The Beach, yes, then they'll be able to wash all the dirt off Sister's dress, so it'll be clean and nice again, and then, once they'd washed her dress, yes, Mother couldn't be mad at them, she'd have to be happy, yes, because she wouldn't have to wash the dress herself if they'd already done it, Asle thinks, and plus there's probably nowhere he likes being more than down by the water, there's so much to see there, little crabs scuttling around between the stones on the beach, and there's seaweed, with bubbles you can squeeze or step on and then they crack, and tiny little fish swimming back and forth near the land, and then there are all the seashells, blue and white, some almost yellow, and it's so nice to sit on the rocks and just look at the water, at The Dock, at The Rowboat floating there nice and brown, moored with a buoy and floating on the water, and then there are all sorts of things that can wash up on The Beach, branches, broken oars, buoys, yes, maybe there'll even be a message, a scrap of paper in a bottle with something written on it, but he's never found a message in a bottle, not yet, even when he walked slowly along The Beach, he's walked all the way in to The Dairy and back again and seen so many things lying on The Beach but never a message in a bottle, although he's seen lots of bottles washed ashore, that's normal, so now if they walk slowly along The Beach in towards The Dairy they'll definitely find a bottle somewhere or other, and anyway down below The Bakery there's a huge pile of bottles, there must be hundreds, but that, he knows, is because they drink, both The Baker and his wife, The Baker's Wife, they live there and after they've drunk a whole bottle they take it down to The Beach and put it in a pile, not quite on The Beach, but the hill down from The Bakery goes down to The Beach, yes, it's really unbelievable how many bottles there are there, Asle thinks, and he's often found bottles on The Beach, and he always finds driftwood, and twice he's found balls on The Beach and he still has them both, there was hardly any air in either one but then Father inflated them so they were good to use, and they've played with those balls a lot, him and Sister, Asle thinks, and he's gone down to The Beach so many times, even though Mother said he's not allowed to, but Father never said that, and of course that's because he went to The Beach so much when he was little, when he was a boy like Asle is now, yes, because Father has always lived on the farm where they live now, he was born in the long white old house where Grandmother and Grandfather live, and Grandmother is Father's mother, and Grandfather is his father, yes, Father was born in that house and he's lived there ever since, and maybe he will too, Asle thinks, or maybe he won't, there are so many other places a person can live, he knows that because Mother was born in a town called Haugaland and grew up on the island there, Hisøy, and he's visited there lots of times, and he was born in the hospital in Haugaland, so that, yes, that's somewhere he could live too, he thinks, there or lots of other places, they don't need to live on the farm where they live now, the way Father always has

What should we do now? Sister says

It's so boring just standing here, she says

We need to think of something to do, she says

Maybe we can finally go to the blue house? Asle says

I've always wanted to go there but I've never done it, he says

But what if the people who live there come outside, I'm so dirty, my dress is all dirty, Sister says

and Asle says that her dress isn't totally clean but it's not that bad, they should just go over to the house, and no one will see them, or see that her dress is dirty, he says, and since she was stupid enough to go splash around in a mud puddle then of course her dress'll be dirty, even she must understand that, he says, but maybe they can go to the blue house anyway, Asle says and then Sister says well all right and they go down the side of the road and when they get to the blue house they stop and stand there looking down at the house

It's a nice old house, Asle says

Yes, Sister says

It's a really pretty blue, he says

and Sister nods

I'm sure it wasn't that pretty when it was new, but now it's prettier, the rain and the wind and the snow made it pretty, Asle says

and he says that the paint is flaking off in some places and that just makes the blue even prettier and Sister says she can't see it, that the colour is prettier, but she does see that the house is blue anyway, she says

You know the names of the colours? Asle says

Yes, Sister says

Because there aren't so many, he says

There are lots more colours than there are names for, or at least that I know any names for, he says

Yes, you're right, Sister says

Yellow, blue, white, Asle says

Red, brown, black, she says

And purple, he says

Yeah and a lot more, Sister says

and Asle says that's right, the colour of the blue house is totally different from the blue of the sky or the blue of the water or the blue of her dress, he says, she can just look

Yes, look how different the house blue is from your dress's blue, he says

and he says that colours are never exactly the same as one another and plus they're always changing, it has to do with the light, he says, so it's impossible to have names for all the colours there are, there'd be so many names that no one could ever learn them all, he says and Sister says still, blue is blue, she says, and yellow is yellow, she says

Yes, yes, you're right, Asle says

Of course that's right, he says

and then they stand there, holding hands, and Sister says that they've done something they're not allowed to do, hasn't Mother said over and over that they mustn't walk down the country road, she says, and Asle says yes well and he says if they listened to everything Mother says then they'd never be able to do anything at all practically, he says and then they just stand there and then they see the front door of the blue house open and someone comes out and it's a man and he has a big belly and a hat on and he turns around and shuts the door and then he walks on the gravel path to the road and there's a crunching sound when he walks and Sister whispers they need to leave, her dress is so dirty, she says and the man looks at them and stops and bends down

Well now, look who we have here, he says

What a long journey you two have been on, he says

You've walked all the way to The Knoll, he says

I didn't think your mother let you go such a long way by yourselves, he says

and both Sister and Asle look down

But it's nice to see you, the man says

And now what are your names? he says

My name's Asle, Asle says

And my name's Alida, Sister says

Asle and Alida, the man says

My name is Gudleiv, he says

And I knew your names already, but still I had to ask you, he says

and then Gudleiv holds his hand out to Asle, and then Gudleiv and Asle say Asle, and then Gudleiv holds his hand out to Sister and Gudleiv and Alida say Alida, and Gudleiv says well now they've finally been properly introduced, the way good neighbours should be, and it's about time, such close neighbours as they are, and now wouldn't they like to come inside their house? because his wife, her name's Gunvor, yes, she'd certainly like to be introduced too, actually he needs to go to The Co-op Store to buy a few things but there's no rush, now that he and his wife have received such fine visitors the shopping can always wait, neither The Co-op Store nor the things for sale there are going anywhere, he says, so why don't they just come inside for a bit? Gudleiv says and Sister looks at Asle and whispers in his ear that they really need to go home, Mother doesn't know where they are, and she's told them so many times that they're not allowed to go down the country road, she says and Asle looks at the man, at Gudleiv

Just step inside and say hello to Gunvor, she'll be so glad to see you two, he says

and Gudleiv turns around and starts up the gravel path and it crunches as he walks and Asle holds Sister's hand tight and almost drags her with him up the path after Gudleiv who's walking ahead of them with his hat

Yes, it's so nice to see you, he says

It's certainly a surprise, he says

But it's always nice to get unexpected visitors, he says

and he opens the front door and he says

Yes, welcome, he says

Welcome to our home, he says

and then he calls inside to Gunvor, come here, we have some surprise guests, he calls and he says that Asle and Sister should come inside and Asle goes in and he's holding Sister's hand and he almost drags her in after him and then he sees Gunvor walking over to them, and she's leaning on a cane

No, how nice, she says

If it isn't Asle and Alida come to visit, she says

You two have never been to The Knoll before, she says

But do come in, she says

and Gunvor turns and goes into the living room and Gudleiv shuts the front door and says they should go in and Asle says that Sister's dress isn't entirely clean and Gudleiv says yes he can see that, yes, even if his sight is pretty bad he can still see that well enough, he says and Asle says Sister just had to go stand in a mud puddle on the country road and splash around even though he said she shouldn't because her dress would get dirty, but still she kept doing it, he says

Little kids are like that, Gunvor says

But I can wipe off the worst of it, she says

and Sister looks down and she tugs a little at Asle's hand, as if she wanted them to leave, and he squeezes her hand and she says ow and Gudleiv asks if something is wrong? and both Asle and Sister shake their heads and she says no no nothing's wrong

It's nothing, Asle says

and Gudleiv says they should take their boots off and come in and Asle lets go of Sister's hand and they pull off their boots and put the two pairs of boots down next to each other

It's always a good idea to wear boots in weather like this, Gudleiv says

and Asle sees Gudleiv take his shoes off and then he puts on a pair of slippers

Come here little girl, Gunvor says

and Sister goes over to Gunvor and Gunvor holds her hand out to Sister and says her name is Gunvor and Sister says her name is Alida

Nice to meet you, Gunvor says

You too, Sister says

and Asle goes over to Sister and he sees that Gunvor is holding her cane with one hand and Sister's hand with her other hand, and she pushes open a door with the cane and then Gunvor and Sister walk through it and Asle sees Gunvor run some water into the sink and pick up a washcloth and wet it and then she starts wiping the dirt off Sister's dress and Gunvor says it's not so easy, is it, she says, but she should be able to clean off the worst of it, down by the hem, Gunvor says and Gudleiv tells Asle they should go into the living room and then Gudleiv opens the living room door and says come in come in and Asle goes in and Gudleiv says he should have a seat on the sofa and Asle goes and sits down on one end of the sofa, and then he sees Gunvor come in with Sister and Gunvor is holding her hand and she says Sister should have a seat on the sofa, next to Asle, and now they'll go see if they have something to offer their guests, Gunvor says and she looks at Gudleiv

Yes, maybe you two would like something to drink? Gudleiv says

Do you like soft drinks? he says

and both Sister and Asle nod

Yes, that'd be great, Asle says

and Sister nods and she says yes and Gudleiv says he didn't think they'd like soft drinks

Really, are you sure you like soft drinks? Gunvor says

Yes, Asle says

Yes, Sister says

Well I'll go see what we have, Gudleiv says

and then he opens a door and disappears from the living room

He's checking to see if we have any in the kitchen, Gunvor says

I think we have a bottle, she says

and Gunvor sits down in an easy chair and leans her cane against the chair and Asle sees that there's a huge loom in the living room, it takes up almost half the room, and it looks like a double loom, like two looms facing opposite directions pushed together

Yes, there are our looms, Gunvor says

We sit there and weave, one on each side, Gudleiv and me, she says

We weave the ribbons on folk costumes, the ones that hang down from the belt in the front of the apron, they're called lap bands, Gunvor says

Yes, Asle says

Lap bands, Sister says

You two have probably never really noticed those bands, have you? she says and both Asle and Sister shake their heads

Folk costumes, Sister says

Yes, the kind women wear when they're really trying to look nice, Gunvor says

and then they don't say anything and then Gudleiv comes in and he's shaking his head and he says he was so sure there was some soda in the kitchen, two bottles at least, but no, there wasn't even one, he says and Gunvor says that's strange and then Gudleiv says he'll go down to the cellar and look there, maybe there's some soda there, he's almost sure there is, he says

There must be some soda in the cellar, Gunvor says

and then Gudleiv opens a door and leaves the room and Gunvor points at the door and says that behind that door there are stairs going down to the cellar and she says yes, she and Gudleiv weave those ribbons for the folk costumes, she says, and that's how they make the money they need, she says, and when Gudleiv comes back upstairs he can look for a finished lap band so that they can see how it looks, Gunvor says and Asle says that would be great and then Gudleiv is standing in the door holding a bottle of fizzy lemonade in his hand and he goes and puts the bottle down on the coffee table in front of Asle and Sister, right between them, and then he goes and shuts the door they use to get to the cellar and then he goes out to the kitchen and comes back in with two glasses and he puts one in front of each of them and then takes a bottle opener and takes the cap off and Asle thinks where did that bottle opener come from? the man named Gudleiv must have been holding it in his fist? he thinks and then Gudleiv pours a little soda into each glass and says enjoy and both Asle and Sister say thank you and then Gunvor says she hopes they like it and then Asle and Sister raise their glasses and drink and Asle thinks it tastes unbelievably good, he must have been really thirsty, and he drinks up all the soda in the glass and he puts the glass down and Gunvor tells

Gudleiv that she told them they could see a lap band and then Gudleiv goes and gets one and hands it to Gunvor and she lays it out on the coffee table and Gudleiv smooths it down on the table and Gunvor says so that's what it looks like, a lap band for folk costumes, she says and Asle looks at the colours and the pattern and he has no words for what he is seeing and the colours and pattern lodge in his mind at once and no, he never knew, he never would have believed it possible that a piece of weaving could be so beautiful, he'd seen Mother or Grandmother in folk costumes probably lots of times and he never really thought the costume was especially nice but now that he's seen the lap band laid out in front of him, now that he's seen the colours, and seen the pattern, yes, he's seeing something he's never seen before, one of the most beautiful things he's ever seen, Asle thinks and Gunvor asks if he thinks it looks nice and Asle says it's one of the most beautiful things he's ever seen, yes, and he can't believe they made it, it must be really hard to make that, Asle says and Sister says she thinks it's beautiful too and she's also drunk her whole glass of soda and she puts her glass down on the table and then Gudleiv asks if they want a little more soda and both of them nod and then he pours the rest of the soda into the glasses, first Sister's, then Asle's

And that's the end of the soda, Gudleiv says

But it was good while it lasted, right? Gunvor says

It tasted really good, Asle says

Yes, Sister says

and she picks up the glass right away and drinks

I guess you do like soft drinks, don't you, Gudleiv says

and Sister drinks the whole glass and then she says yes quietly and puts the glass down on the table

You can have more the next time you come see us, Gudleiv says

and Asle drinks a little soda too and then he looks at Gunvor and he says again that the lap band is really beautiful and Gunvor says it made her swell up inside when he said it was the most beautiful thing he's seen in his whole life, she says and Gudleiv says you have a good eye, Asle my boy, a good sense of things, he says and then there's a knock at the door and Gudleiv says he'll go open it

Your mother must have seen that you'd come down here and now she wants to fetch you, Gunvor says then

and both Asle and Sister look down at the ground

She doesn't know you're here? Gunvor says

No, Asle says

But she must be worried about you? Gunvor says

and neither Asle nor Sister say anything

You just came? Gunvor says

Without permission? she says

and there's no answer

Then you need to go home right away, she says

Your mother must be wondering where you are, she says

I bet she's worried about you, Gunvor says

Maybe, Asle says

Yes, Gunvor says

But it was nice of you to come, and you'll have to come see us again soon, and when you do you need to tell your mother or father where you're going, she says

Yes, Asle says

and Asle sees Gudleiv come in and next to him is a big tall man with a giant belly and he's totally bald and Asle thinks he's The Bald Man that children need to watch out for, both Mother and Father have said that, and they've said that Asle must never go with him, either in his car or into his house, Asle thinks and Gunvor tells Gudleiv that their mother doesn't know where they are, they just came here, so it would be best if they went home right away, Gunvor says and Gudleiv says no, no, that's not what he thought

In that case they need to go home right away, Gudleiv says

Promise me you will, Gunvor says

and Asle and Sister get up and The Bald Man sits down on the sofa

And I also have to thank you for dropping by to see us and I hope I'll see you again soon, Gunvor says

Thank you for the soda, Asle says

Yes, thank you, Sister says

It was nothing, Gunvor says

and then Gudleiv says yes, they must come by again, it was so nice to have such nice children over for a visit, but when they do they must must promise to tell their mother where they're going, he says and then Gudleiv takes them out into the hall and they put their boots on

Thank you for the soda, Asle says

There's no need to thank us, it was nothing, Gudleiv says

Thank you for the soda, Sister says

There'll be more for you the next time you drop by, Gudleiv says

and then Sister puts her hand in Asle's hand

We hope to see you again soon, Gudleiv says

Yes, please do come and visit us, he says

But only if you've told your parents first, Mother or Father, he says

and he opens the front door and Asle and Sister go outside

Bye, Asle says

Bye, Sister says

Goodbye, Gudleiv says

and then he shuts the door and then Asle and Sister stand there outside the little blue house and Asle says that the tall fat bald man who came over is the one they call The Bald Man, yes, he's heard that many times

The Bald Man? Sister says

and both Mother and Father said that children have to watch out for him, he says

Watch out for him? Sister says

Yes, Asle says

Never get into a car with him, or go home with him if he asks you to, he says

and Sister doesn't say anything and then she and Asle go up the path with the gravel and they get to the country road

I want to go home now, Sister says

and they start walking along the side of the road and then they hear a car and they turn around and then they see a car coming up from Old Mound and they stop and stay perfectly still and the car drives past them

Or maybe we could go down to The Beach? Asle says

But we're not allowed to, Sister says

I know, Asle says

We need to go home, Sister says

No we'll go down to the water, Asle says

Why should we go right home? he says

There's nothing to do there, he says

I can play with my dolls, Sister says

and then they stay there standing at the side of the road

No let's go down to The Beach, he says

and Asle thinks that he's done it so many times but Sister's never once been to The Beach with him ever, she's never stood right at the edge of The Fjord and looked out at the water, and she's never seen The Boathouse, or The Rowboat, he thinks, and it'll be nice for Sister to see those things, he thinks, he himself has seen them so many times because he's constantly going down to the water, even if Mother tells him he's not allowed to, yes, maybe he doesn't go down to The Beach every day but he does go pretty often, and Mother doesn't notice, she probably thinks he's playing somewhere or other around the farm, maybe in The Barn, and that's why Mother hasn't yelled at him, but

Sister has probably never been down to the water with him? no, it's never happened, and she's too little, Sister, and plus he knows she won't like being on The Beach, but maybe she would like it? maybe she would think it's beautiful to stand by The Fjord and look out at the water? and maybe they can go out onto The Dock and look at The Rowboat? he thinks

But Mother says we can't, Sister says

I know, Asle says

So we can't go down to The Beach? she says

But I go down to the water all the time, Asle says

and then they just stand there and then Sister says she wants to go home and then Asle says no they're going down to The Beach, no matter what Mother says, because Sister's never once been there, has she? he says and Sister says can they really just do that? and Asle says they can do whatever they want and then they go over to the path leading down the hill to The Boathouse

It's exciting inside The Boathouse, Asle says

Do you want to go inside it? he says

It's scary, Sister says

No it's not, Asle says

and he holds Sister's hand tight and they start down the path to The Boathouse and Asle thinks he really hopes Mother doesn't see them now, because then she'd come running after them and then they'd be yelled at double, both for Sister getting her dress dirty and for doing something they're absolutely not allowed to do, going down to the water, to The Boathouse, The Beach, The Fjord, The Dock, The Rowboat, they're going to see everything they're not allowed to go see, Asle thinks and Sister says no she doesn't want to she doesn't dare and she stops and Asle tugs at her hand and she says he needs to stop

Let go, let go of my hand, Sister says

and Asle lets go of her hand and then they stand there on the path leading down to The Boathouse and Asle looks at the roof of The Boathouse with the grey stones and he knows they're called slate, Father told him, slate, and one stone is laid on the roof against another with a little of each one on top of another one, and the roof of The Boathouse is a play of grey colours, he thinks, it's almost unbelievable that there are so many different greys, Asle thinks, and plus they look so different depending on what the weather's like, when the sun is shining it almost looks like there are just two grey colours but the shadows are lots of different grey tones, because the colours are always sort of moving and at the same time it's like they're resting, yes, the colours are moving at rest and resting in motion, Asle thinks and that's not to mention the walls of The Boathouse, the siding has turned totally grey and the cracks in the wood give it so many different grey colours, Asle thinks and he says that The Boathouse is grey but it's also so many different colours of grey that don't have names and Sister says yes and he holds her hand tight because it's almost enough to scare you that there are so many different kinds of grey, and so many kinds of the other colours, like the ones called blue, just blue, but there must be thousands of different blue colours, thousands, at least, no there are so many that you can't even count them, Asle thinks

And blue, you know, there are so many blues that you can't even count them, he says

Yes, Sister says

Blue, she says

The sky is blue, she says

Sometimes, Asle says

But today it's grey too, he says

And it almost always is, he says

Yes grey, Sister says

The sky is grey and The Boathouse is grey, the stones on the roof are grey and the walls of The Boathouse are grey, but you see how they're such different greys? he says

and Sister nods

You see that? he says

Yes, Sister says

But it doesn't bother you, he says

No, she says

We can go into The Boathouse if you want? he says

But isn't it scary? Sister says

It must be so dark in there? she says

and Asle says does she see the hatch there in the side of The Boathouse? the side right in front of them? and does she see that rusty hook there? it's so they can open the hatch and go into The Boathouse, he says and Sister says she doesn't want to go into The Boathouse

No, all right, Asle says

and then they go around the corner of The Boathouse and they go down the path around The Boathouse to the front corner of the building and then Sister says it's scary, she doesn't know if she's brave enough to do it and Asle says that if they just go a little farther then Mother won't be able to see them from home but then they can see The Beach and The Fjord and The Dock and The Rowboat and Sister stops, and then Asle stops too, so now they're both standing there, he and Sister, and she's in her dress all covered with mud

They were nice, Gunvor and Gudleiv, Sister says

Yeah, Asle says

They gave us soda and everything, she says

But Gunvor didn't get much dirt off your dress, Asle says

We need to wash it or else Mother'll be mad, he says

Yeah, Sister says

We can wash it in the seawater, he says

That works? she says

Yes, it works fine, Asle says

And then Mother won't be mad? Sister says

No, no, not if the dress is clean, he says

Well okay, she says

and then they start moving again, going to the corner of The Boathouse and now they're far enough that Mother can't see them from home, not from the living room window and not from out front, Asle thinks, so now they're safe, he thinks and then Sister stops and she stands still and she says look, the path in front of them is, yes, it's full of tall burning nettle plants, doesn't he see them? she says and Asle doesn't answer and he sees that some of the burning nettle is taller than he is, and the leaves are jagged and pointing their teeth at them, and Asle tells Sister to walk as close to the wall as she can, behind him, and then he walks towards the burning nettle and pulls the plants down and Sister says she doesn't like this, it's scary, she says

Can we go back? Sister says

But it'll be fine as soon as we get around the corner, then we'll see the water, Asle says

I don't think I want to, Sister says

And anyway Mother said we can't ever go down to the water, she says

And now we're doing it anyway, Sister says

and then Asle starts walking again, slowly, and he moves ahead and Sister follows him holding onto his pullover and Asle looks ahead and he sees that lots of burning nettle plants are reaching their big jagged leaves across the path, big green jagged leaves, there are some farther downhill and others uphill, some of the leaves reach high above his head and are swaying a little, even when there's almost no wind the leaves are swaying, and now he sees a burning nettle leaf coming right at his face and he stops and lifts his leg and pushes the nettle down with his foot and then they go farther and Asle sees a burning nettle leaf sticking out like it's poking his legs and he lifts his foot and pushes that one down and then he sees a nettle with its leaves sticking almost halfway across the path, lots of leaves, so many leaves, and he needs to push those down too, Asle thinks and he lifts his foot up and pushes the nettle down and Sister says it's so scary, she's so scared, she says and she holds Asle's pullover tight and he walks carefully and as close to the wall as he can and Sister says don't go so fast and Asle starts to go slower and then he lifts a foot and pushes another nettle down and now there aren't many burning nettles reaching across the path and the corner is just up ahead and they go towards it, him first, then Sister, and Asle goes around the corner and Sister comes after him and then they're around the corner and Asle takes Sister's hand and he can't understand why it feels so good to see the water but it does, he thinks

I see the water, Asle says

Me too, Sister says

It's so nice looking at the water, he says

Yes, she says

and they are out on the big rocks and up ahead is The Dock, the beautiful stone Dock, and there's The Rowboat and The Fjord and everything, Asle thinks and Sister stops

But, she says

Yes, he says

Mother says, she says

and Asle interrupts her and he says that Mother says that they can't ever go down to the water but now they've done it anyway, he says

Right, Sister says

and she grips his hand tight

We did what we wanted and not what Mother wanted, she says

and she says it with something that sounds a bit like pride in her voice, Asle thinks, as if now they've really done something big, they must be pretty grown-up to do what they did, they did what they wanted to do and not what Mother wanted and told them to do, Asle thinks and he lets go of Sister's hand and then he walks up ahead on the rocks and he sits down and then he sits there looking out at The Dock and at The Rowboat while Sister stays standing, and then she's standing there, Sister, and he's sitting there, Asle, and he thinks that it's so beautiful seeing The Rowboat floating out there almost totally motionless in the water, moored to the buoy by The Dock, and then The Fjord, it's almost totally still today, the wind is making just a few small waves, and The Rowboat is just barely moving, a little up, a little down, a little to one side, a little back, and The Rowboat is brown and beautiful and there are so many brown colours to look at on The Rowboat that it can be totally bewildering to look at them but it's beautiful to see how the brown Rowboat is brown in so many ways, that it has so many different hues of brown even if it's just brown, and Asle sees before his eyes like in a vision all these brown colours as exactly what they are, brown colours, not as brown colours on a boat but as separate colours, just colours, and he sees how the different hues slip into one another and how each brown colour changes the next, in fact all of the others, and makes them something different from what they were before, and it's unbelievable that they're all called brown, just brown, because The Rowboat is brown, no doubt about that, and caramelised cheese, brown cheese, is brown, and Mother's handbag is brown, he thinks, even though they're colours that are almost completely different

Isn't it weird that people just say The Rowboat's brown? Asle says

What else should they say? Sister says

I mean, The Rowboat is brown, she says

Yes, Asle says

But there are so many brown colours and they just say The Rowboat's brown, he says

The Rowboat is brown, Sister says

I know it's brown, Asle says

But so is brown cheese, and Mother's handbag, he says

and Asle hears in his voice that he's a little angry, and he doesn't know why

Is that anything to get mad about? Sister says

A brown boat is a brown boat, she says

Yes, Asle says

But, he says

and he falls silent

I don't know what you're talking about, Sister says

If we had to say that The Rowboat is this brown and the cheese is that brown and that other thing's this other brown then we'd never stop talking, she says

Yes, Asle says

But you do see that The Rowboat is a lot of different browns? he says

Yes, in a way, Sister says

But it doesn't matter, she says

and she says that even if The Rowboat's brown colour isn't the same all over it's still brown and so The Rowboat is brown, she says

Yes, Asle says

And you don't feel how beautiful it is to see all the different browns? he says

They're not different, Sister says

They're the same really, she says

And I don't think brown's a very pretty colour anyway, she says

and Asle doesn't say anything and then Sister sits down next to him and then they sit there for a while and Asle looks at what's in front of his eyes, the browns of The Rowboat pulling away from The Rowboat, he sees the brown colours as if they're all gathered on a single surface and he sees how everything changes if he moves any of them slightly, how all the other browns turn different

Aren't we going to do anything? Sister says

All right, Asle says

Maybe we can pull The Rowboat in towards The Dock, I know how to do that, he says

and Sister says no, they, no they can't do that, because then not just Mother will get mad but Father too, she says and Asle says that maybe they should just leave The Rowboat there but they can go out onto The Dock anyway and Sister says Mother says they mustn't ever do that, go out onto The Dock, never ever, Mother said that too, Sister says and Asle says he doesn't remember her saying that, she just said that they must never go down to the water, to The Beach, he says and then Sister says yes she did, she did say it, she's definitely said it lots of times and now they've done exactly what Mother said they must never do and Asle says yes, exactly, yes, now they've done what they wanted to do and Sister says she didn't want to do it, it was he who wanted to, she says and Asle says yes yes and he says that that's true enough but he wanted to go down to the water, at least he did, and isn't it beautiful here? he says, it's so beautiful with The Dock and The Rowboat and The Fjord and all the rest of it, he says and Sister says well it's not bad but that burning nettle was horrible, and if she'd known that it was growing across the path then she would never have come down to the water, she says and Asle says he doesn't remember the burning nettle from before, it was there of course but the plants had never been so big before

Burning nettles, Sister says

They were giant burning nettles, Asle says

and he spreads his arms as wide as he can and Sister says they were so big, that big, she says, and then she says that it's boring just sitting here like this and Asle says they could go down onto The Beach, because there's always something to see there, crabs, tiny fish, and plus there's always stuff that's drifted onto land, flotsam and jetsam, he says

Flotsam and jetsam, Sister says

Yes it's called flotsam and jetsam, Asle says

Flotsam and jetsam, okay, Sister says

and Asle stands up and Sister stays sitting and then he goes out onto The Dock and he says come on and he unties the mooring and Sister says what are you doing? and Asle says he just wants to pull The Rowboat in and then get on board and be on The Rowboat for a little bit, he says, and he pulls The Rowboat in towards The Dock and he climbs on board The Rowboat

Be careful, Sister shouts

Okay, Asle says

and then he's on board The Rowboat and then he starts to pull the rope to the buoy and The Rowboat moves out onto the water

You can't do that, Sister shouts

It's dangerous, she shouts

No it's not, Asle says

and he thinks he'll show Sister how safe it is, and he climbs up onto the middle seat and stands on the plank

Sit down! Sister shouts

and Asle sits down on the plank and starts rocking from side to side and The Rowboat rocks from side to side with him and he calls to Sister look how beautifully The Rowboat's rocking, what beautiful waves it's leaving in the water, and Sister doesn't answer and Asle thinks he should probably get back onto land and he stands up and walks forward in The Rowboat and he pulls The Rowboat in towards The Dock, climbs out onto The Dock, and then pulls the rope to move The Rowboat out again and it floats there so beautifully bobbing up and down in The Fjord and he moors The Rowboat and then he walks over to Sister who's still sitting where she was sitting before and she says can't they go home now? she doesn't like being disobedient, and they're not allowed to go down to the country road, or to the water, she says and Asle says now they have to go down onto The Beach

Come on, he says

and Sister just stays sitting on the shore rocks

I don't know if I want to, she says

Don't be stupid, he says

I'm not stupid, she says

Why're you telling me I'm stupid? she says

You're the one who's stupid, she says

I didn't mean it like that, Asle says

You're stupid, I'm not stupid, Sister says

I didn't mean it like that, Asle says

and Sister says well then, if you didn't mean it, that's all right, she says and Asle says she's not stupid and she says he's not stupid and then he holds out his hand to her and she takes his hand and then he pulls her up onto her feet and then they walk on the shore rocks down The Beach, and it's high tide so there's almost nothing to see on The Beach, and the waves are coming up over the rocks with little splashes and Asle says the tide's so high now that there's almost nothing to look at on The Beach itself, but he always finds something or another that the sea has washed up onto land, far up onto the shore, somewhere between The Beach and where the hill starts, he says and she asks what and he says maybe a bottle, like he said before, and maybe there'll be a letter in one of the bottles, and that's called a message in a bottle, like he said before, he says, and Sister says okay and he says that even he has never found a bottle with a letter, a message, but he's found lots of bottles, and outside The Bakery there's a pile of bottles, yes, like he said, he says, yeah she won't believe how big the pile is, it's like a mountain, he says, and they can go down The Beach past The Bakery, till they get to The Dairy, but no farther than that, he says

Should we go all the way to The Dairy? Sister says

We can, why not, Asle says

and they start walking hand in hand across the strip between the water and where the grass starts growing and back again and they don't say anything for a while and then Asle says look, look there, look, the sea has washed a whole log up onto land, he says and Sister doesn't say anything and they keep walking and then there's a screeching sound and they walk farther without saying anything

What do you think that noise was? Sister says

I don't know, Asle says

and they keep walking

It was a really loud screeching noise, Sister says

Yeah, and like something's grinding, Asle says

A grinding noise, Sister says

It's kind of strange, but the sound seems to be coming from the country road, so it's probably an old tractor, Asle says

and they've walked as far as Boathouse Hill and they keep walking and past Boathouse Hill they get to The Headland and then they see the beautiful rowboat that the people who live at The Headland Farm have moored to a pier there in Hardangerfjord, and up there, in the white house, that's where Bård lives, Asle thinks, and from there, from The Headland, they can see all the way to The Dairy at the end of The Beach, below The Bakery and before The Co-op Store, but they can't see The Co-op Store because The Dairy blocks it so that they can't see it, and next to The Dairy is the big yellow house where The Bald Man lives, but they can't see that either, Asle thinks and Sister says it looks really far to walk, all the way to The Dairy, and Asle says it looks like a long walk but it isn't as far as it looks, he says

It's a lot closer than it looks, he says

Yeah, it's a long way, she says

and Asle grips Sister's hand harder and then he looks up at The Headland Farm and now he sees Bård standing there in front of the house looking down at them and he doesn't like talking to Bård because he's always so rude, he's always saying that their farm is bigger, their rowboat is nicer, his father is stronger than Asle's father, stupid things like that, Asle thinks and they start walking to The Dairy

That noise must be coming from an old tractor, Asle says

But it's really loud, like it's coming from right next to us, or somewhere near us, Sister says

Yeah, Asle says

Can a tractor really make a noise like that? she says

A screeching grinding noise? she says

I think it can, an old one can, Asle says

and they walk on and they aren't saying anything but it's like an uncertainty has come over them, and they think without thinking it in words that they shouldn't have done this, now they're doing something they're not allowed to do, something Mother has said again and again that they shouldn't do, they're doing something forbidden, and maybe that's why they heard that screeching grinding sound? maybe it didn't come from a tractor but just because they were doing something wrong? that's why they suddenly heard that sound? Asle thinks, because the truth is an old tractor can't make a sound like that, he thinks and he doesn't like the sound, he thinks and they walk farther and then they stop and Asle turns around and he says now Bård is standing in the rowboat they just walked past, he's standing up on a seat, he says and Sister turns around

That looks dangerous, she says

He's just doing it because he saw us walk by, Asle says

That Bård's just trying to act tough, he says

and he says Bård's a big scaredy-cat and he must be scared to death standing on the seat there and he's doing it just to act tough for them, there's no other reason, so they shouldn't look at him any more, they should just keep walking, Asle says and he and Sister turn around to face forward and they walk carefully on and Asle says that when they get past where The Beach kind of bends away they won't be able to see Bård any more, and that's good, he says and they keep walking and they're holding each other's hand and they go past the bend in The Beach and now they can't see The Headland any more and they walk towards The Dairy and Asle lets go of Sister's hand and points

Look, there's an oar there, he says

and Asle runs over to where the hill meets the beach and Sister stops and then Asle lifts up the oar

Look, he shouts

What's that, Sister says

It's an oar, Asle says

Yeah, Sister says

I found an oar, Asle says

A whole oar, perfect for using, he says

and Asle swings the oar back and forth in the air and he says maybe there's another oar farther up The Beach, closer to The Dairy, oars come in pairs, he says and Sister says she wants to go home

I don't like that noise, she says

No, Asle says

But we can just go to The Dairy can't we, he says

I don't like that noise, Sister says

We'll go as far as The Dairy and then turn around and go home, Asle says

Well all right, Sister says

and then they stay standing there and Asle puts the oar back down on the hill and then he gives Sister a big hug and then he says well they can just go to The Dairy, and then go look at all the bottles out behind The Bakery, and then, yes, then maybe they can go to The Co-op Store, because there's lots to see in the shop windows there, Asle says and Sister says they can't do that, because Mother's told them they mustn't go on the country road, it's dangerous, the road's so narrow that there's hardly enough room for both a car and people, so they can never walk there by themselves, only with grown-ups, only with Mother or Father, she said, Sister says and Asle doesn't answer and they walk carefully down The Beach and Sister says she's tired of walking and Asle says in that case they can sit down and rest for a bit and then they sit down, each on their own round stone, and they sit there and don't say anything and Asle thinks that it's boring just sitting like that, and it feels like they've been sitting there a long time, he thinks

Can't we keep going? he says

Okay, Sister says

You're not tired any more, he says

No, my feet are a little less tired, Sister says

and then they get up and Sister takes Asle's hand and they walk on and they see The Bakery up ahead and then The Dairy, Asle thinks, and they'll have to go up the path to The Bakery to get to The Co-op Store, past all the bottles, past the pile, yes, mountain of bottles, and then up to the country road, and once they're up there they'll be able to see The Co-op Store, and it's not so far to walk from The Bakery to The Co-op Store

Can't we turn around and go back now? Sister says

No, Asle says

I'm scared, she says

There's nothing to be scared of, Asle says

Yes there is, Sister says

What? Asle says

If we go to The Co-op Store we'll have to walk past the big yellow house, the one next to The Dairy, Sister says

And that's where The Bald Man lives, without a single hair on his head, in the big yellow house, she says

He looks so scary, she says

Yeah, Asle says

And he's the one children have to watch out for, you said so yourself, Sister says

Yeah, Asle says

and they walk carefully, step by step, up the path towards The Bakery

That bad noise is gone now, Asle says

and Sister nods

And there's the mountain of bottles, Asle says

and he points

Yeah, Sister says

and then she says that it's really not worth looking at, a mountain of empty bottles, she says and Asle says maybe not but they're empty bottles of alcohol, he says, because The Baker and The Baker's Wife both drink, and when they drink they don't stop, and then they bake lopsided bread but they bake even when they've been drinking and are drunk, because when people drink alcohol they get drunk, and then they're not always steady on their feet when they walk and sometimes they shake and anyway the bread that The Baker and The Baker's Wife bake then always comes out lopsided but what they bake when they haven't been drinking is straight and nice, he says and Sister nods and then she says that she wants to go home, now they're almost at the country road where Mother has said so many times that they can't walk by themselves and the hill is so steep and she's so tired, she says, and she sits down on the grass and then Asle sits down too next to her and they just sit there and they don't say anything and then Sister says that she can hear a voice and Asle says he can't hear anything and Sister says okay I guess not and Asle thinks that they need to keep going, it's boring just sitting like this, he thinks and he gets up and then he holds his hand out to Sister and she takes his hand and he almost yanks her onto her feet and then she stands there and she says she can hear voices, but they're far away, and Asle says he can't hear anything and then he almost drags Sister after him up to The Bakery and up to the country road and Sister says they're not allowed to walk on the country road here, both Mother and Father have told them that over and over again, she says and Asle says that's true and then someone behind them says look at that, two kids out for a walk and they turn around

Look who's here, The Baker says

Maybe your mother sent you to buy some bread? he says

Maybe you're big enough now to run errands for your mother and buy some bread? he says

What clever children, The Baker says

and they just stand there

Or maybe you've just gone out for a walk? he says

and the door to The Bakery opens and The Baker's Wife comes out

Well I never, look who's here, she says

They're probably out for a walk, The Baker says

But their mother doesn't let them walk here, The Baker's Wife says

No, The Baker says

Probably not, he says

and he goes over to them and then he puts one hand on Asle's shoulder and one on Sister's shoulder and then he says that the two of them need to go straight home to their mother right now, she must be worried about them by now, she must be scared, The Baker says

I'm sure she is, The Baker's Wife says

and then she says wait a second and she goes inside and comes back out almost right away and she comes walking up to them and she holds out her hands to them with a roll in each hand

Nice children like you deserve a roll, The Baker's Wife says

But only if you go right home to your mother, she says

Thank you, thank you very much, Asle says

Yes, thank you, thank you, Sister says

Don't mention it, nice children like you, The Baker's Wife says

Nice children, yes, The Baker says

But now you need to go home to your mother, really, The Baker's Wife says

I'm sure she's scared and worried about you, she says

And maybe she's already gone looking for you, she says

Because I'm sure you're not allowed to walk on the road alone, The Baker's Wife says

We went along The Shore, Sister says

And you definitely aren't allowed to do that, The Baker's Wife says

To go down to the water, she says

I'm sure you're not, she says

and Asle and Sister both start eating their rolls and they must have been hungry because they bite and chew and The Baker's Wife asks if the rolls taste good and Asle and Sister say yes at the same time and with their mouths full and The Baker says he's glad they taste good and Asle thinks that as long as The Baker and The Baker's Wife are there they can't go to The Co-op Store, because both of them, The Baker and The Baker's Wife, said they have to go back home to Mother, that she's worried about them, and that she doesn't let them walk alone like this, and that's true, but they haven't done anything wrong, it's just Mother who thinks they have, and it's only because she's always so scared about them, she gets scared and worried about everything in the world, they're not allowed to do anything, not walk down to the country road, down to The Boathouse or The Shore, nothing, they're not allowed to do anything, all they can do is stay home, inside or out in front of the house, nowhere else, ever, Asle thinks, and it's only because Mother's always so worried about everything, he thinks, and then he hears a voice inside himself, it's Mother telling Father that that's not true and then he says that it is true, they're not allowed to walk down to the road, or to the water, that's how it is, he says and Mother says you hear that, you hear that, Father is saying the same thing she is, Mother says, Asle thinks and there, over there, that can't be Mother running up to them, no, no, now they'll get caught and once they get home they'll be yelled at and he's the one who'll be yelled at and Mother comes running up towards them and she looks scared and it looks like she's been crying and she comes towards them and Asle doesn't understand, was she really that scared about them, he thinks, no, in that case they never should have done what they did, he thinks and then Mother puts her arms around him and Sister and hugs them both against her and then out of breath she says to The Baker and The Baker's Wife that, that, that, have they heard yet? have they heard that he drowned? that the boy from The Headland Farm, Bård, the boy the same age as Asle, was just found drowned, just now, she was going up The Beach, because she didn't know where Sister and Asle were and then she got scared that they'd gone down to the water and she went down to The Beach to look for them but they weren't there, then she went up along The Beach and when she got past Boathouse Hill and out by The Headland she saw a crowd of people on The Beach below The Headland Farm and she saw that The Doctor's car was parked up there in front of The Headland Farm and she went over to the people there and then she saw Bård lying on The Beach, no, she can see it now, it's too horrible, Mother says and she lets go of Asle and Sister and covers her eyes and then hugs them to her body again and then Mother says that a woman, she can't think of her name right now, it doesn't matter anyway, this woman, yes, said, said, this woman told her that as she was walking past The Headland Farm, on the road, over there, Mother says and she points, she looked down at The Fjord and saw something floating in the water next to the rowboat that belongs to The Headland Farm people and it looked like a little person, and then she ran and knocked at the door and the mother was home and then the two of them ran down to The Beach and when they got to The Beach the mother saw that it was her son Bård lying there floating in the water

It's Bård, she'd said

and then Bård's mother waded out into the cold water and started swimming until she got to Bård and somehow she got him onto land

and then she picked him up and held him to her breast and she carried him onto the hill of The Beach and he wasn't breathing and he was lifeless and she, yes, she, when she saw the lifeless boy she thought she should go call The Doctor and she ran up to the house at The Headland Farm and looked up The Doctor's phone number and dialed it and he said he'd come right away and that they had to try to blow air into the boy, put your mouth against his mouth and blow air in, and when he's breathed it out blow more in, The Doctor had said, something like that, and she'd run back down to The Beach and then she'd taken a deep breath and blown it into Bård's mouth, again and again, she'd, she couldn't remember her name, she'd kept doing that with the breathing until The Doctor came and then The Doctor had done the same thing and pushed hard, both on Bård's stomach and on his heart, and he kept doing that for a long time but Bård was still lying there lifeless and eventually The Doctor looked up, yes, up at the sky, and he'd said Bård was dead, he'd drowned, that woman told Mother, and Mother saw Bård lying dead on the hill and she can see it now and it's too horrible, she says and Mother squeezes her eyes shut and then Mother says she'd started thinking where were her own two children? could they have drowned too? it'd been a while since she'd seen them and then she'd run towards home and out onto The Dock but nobody was there and she'd looked in the water around The Rowboat and she couldn't see anyone in the water and then she'd run back down along The Beach and then then she'd run up to the country road and she was running faster than she'd ever thought she could, Mother says, and now after running all over here they were, here were Asle and Alida, yes, both of them, and they were alive, they were alive, and she couldn't believe it, they were alive, they were alive, Mother says and she starts crying again and then she presses Asle and Sister hard against her, so hard that it hurts, Asle thinks, and he tries to get loose but then Mother just holds them even tighter, yes, she's holding them so tight, so hard, that they almost can't breathe, Asle thinks and he hears The Baker's Wife say she can't believe it, so young, just six or so and now he's drowned, he hadn't started school yet anyway, and now drowned, no, it's too terrible, The Baker's Wife says and Asle looks at The Baker just standing there staring and staring at nothing

Little Bård from The Headland Farm is drowned, he says

No, impossible, I don't believe it, he says

It's unbelievable, Mother says

He probably just wanted to go on their boat, The Baker says

and Mother says he'd pulled the rowboat in and got on board and then pulled the rowboat out and then he'd fallen into the water somehow, into the cold water, and he couldn't swim, and then he hadn't been able to get back on board the boat, that's how it must have happened, Mother says and she says that when she was a girl the same thing happened to a boy in her class, he was out fishing and he fell into the water and then they found him drowned, and after he'd been in the water so long, Mother says, and The Baker says it's too horrible he can't believe this has happened

It's unbelievable, The Baker's Wife says

There are no words for it, The Baker says

No, there aren't, Mother says

No, no, no, she says

and she hugs and hugs Asle and Sister to her and Mother says that when she couldn't find Asle or Sister she got so scared, more scared than she'd ever been in her life, because by that point she was sure they'd been out in the rowboat with Bård from The Headland Farm and they'd fallen into the water too and were lying on the bottom, on the shelf underwater, Mother says, and then here they both were, Asle and Alida, outside The Bakery, large as life, and never, no, nothing she had ever seen had made her happier than seeing her two children standing there large as life, each eating a roll, Mother says and the tears are pouring down her cheeks and she lets go of them and wipes the tears off her cheeks with her hands and away from her eyes with the backs of her hands

Yes, I gave them rolls, The Baker's Wife says

And then I said that they had to go home, because their mother doesn't let them go for walks alone like this, she says

and Mother says no of course not

These children don't do what they're told, she says

and then she laughs with pure joy between her tears and then she says it was probably Asle who decided to do it, but now, no, now she's so happy, so relieved, that she can't be angry, and anyway now, yes, now she just wants to go home, get her children back into the house, she says and The Baker's Wife says she can have a few more rolls to take with her and then The Baker's Wife goes into The Bakery

No, it's beyond belief, The Baker says

No, Mother says

It's just too terrible, The Baker says

Yes, Mother says

and then they just stand there and then The Baker's Wife comes out with a brown bag

Have some rolls, she says

and she hands the bag to Mother

Okay thanks thank you, she says

and then Mother takes the brown bag and Asle thinks that this bag is yet another brown colour and then Mother grabs Asle's hand with one hand, the one she's holding the brown bag of rolls with, and she grabs Sister's hand with her other hand and then Mother says now they're going to go home and get back inside safe and sound and they stand there not moving

What horrible news, The Baker's Wife says

Unbelievable, I can't believe it, The Baker says

I don't understand it, he says

I can't believe it, The Baker's Wife says

How can God let something like that happen? The Baker says

How can a good God let something like that happen? he says

There is no God, The Baker's Wife says

Not a good God anyway, she says

Or not a God who's all-powerful anyway, The Baker says

I believe that the little boy is with God now, he's resting with God, Mother says

Yes, he is, The Baker says

He's at peace with God now, the boy is, he says

Bård, yes, The Baker's Wife says

and then they just stand there and Asle feels Mother gripping his hand so hard that it hurts and he shakes his hand a little and Mother loosens her grip a little

We have to believe that he's at peace with God now, Mother says

and then she turns around and they start to go up to the country road and after they get to the road they start walking up the road and they can see their house and Asle thinks that Bård, from The Headland Farm, is drowned, he's dead, he's gone forever, he'll never talk to him again, and he can't understand it, because it's only old people who die and are gone forever, not children, children don't die, Asle thinks, he didn't think they could, and dying, being gone forever, was something so far in the future that you couldn't even see it, Asle thinks and he hears Mother say that she has never been as happy as she was when she saw them, never ever in her whole life has she felt that happy, felt such joy, she says

I was so happy I could've jumped for joy, Mother says

and then she jumps and she starts laughing

When we get home I'm going to make hot chocolate for you two and then we'll eat these rolls and drink chocolate, she says and Asle thinks that sure he can eat the rolls and drink the hot chocolate but he doesn't really like them, no, but he can't say something like that, he couldn't tell The Baker's Wife when she was trying to be nice and giving him and Sister a roll, all he could do was take it and eat it and say it tasted good, and now he'll probably have to do the same thing when they get home, even if Mother knows full well that he doesn't like hot chocolate, or rolls, but she's probably not remembering anything like that now, he thinks, because anyway she likes rolls and hot chocolate, Asle thinks and I sit here in my car and I look straight ahead and I'm already at Instefjord and I start driving slowly up Sygnefjord and I drive carefully and I think that actually I didn't want a driving licence or a car and now I like driving, I think, and Father was the same way, he didn't want a car, but Mother kept bringing it up, again and again, she said how great it would be to have a car and then Father says yes and Mother says in that case they should do it soon and actually buy a car and Father nods

Can't you get a driving licence? Mother says

and Father says he supposes he could, but he doesn't know if he can afford to buy a car, he's just about getting by with his orchard and his boatbuilding out in The Shed, and it'll be expensive to get a driving licence, and even more expensive to buy a car, and however good the fruit harvest is, however many kroner it brings in, and however many boats he builds and however good and beautiful they are, no, it doesn't add up to all that many kroner, he said, they managed, yes, they got by, but was there really any way to lay out all that money and buy a car? no, he really doesn't know, Father said and Mother said they had to be able to manage it the same as everybody else, they weren't any worse off than other folks, she said and Father said that he wasn't sure he could afford to buy a car, he just wasn't, and Mother said she was sure he could do it and Father said yes well and then he'd have to find the time, he was so busy, he had so much to do, he'd have to build quite a lot of boats that winter for them to manage it and then in the spring the fruit trees'd have to be tended to and trimmed and fertilised, and sprayed, and the summer is when it's easiest to sell boats, because everyone with a cabin by the water needs a boat, and then comes fall and all the fruit needs to be picked and sorted and packed and sold, Father says, and he doesn't know how he's been able to do it, he says and Mother says yes, it's a lot to do, you work hard, but it would really be great to have a car, and more and more people in Barmen have cars now, yes, half the families their age in Barmen have bought cars, or almost half anyway, yes, she says

Soon there'll be more people driving to The Co-op Store to do their shopping than walking, Father says

Just about, Mother says

Plus we could take car trips, she says

We could drive out to Haugaland, and Vika on Hisøy, to visit my parents, she says

And my brothers and sisters, and nieces and nephews, she says

Yes, Father says

and then he doesn't say anything else

A car's expensive, he says then

You work all the time, you must make some money, and if other people can buy a car why can't we? she says

But people are paying less and less for boats, most people want plastic boats now, and there's less work to do on a plastic boat, so it's harder and harder to sell wooden boats, for a good price anyway, and I don't get paid as much for the fruit either, that gets lower prices too now that there's so much imported fruit, Father says

But you work so hard, you're always busy doing something, Mother says

and then she says that other people, other people who work a lot less than he does, they have driving licences and cars, she says

A driving licence isn't free either, Father says

and then they don't say anything else

But yes, we'll get a car sooner or later, Father says

Well I'm really looking forward to it, Mother says

It would be nice, Father says

and I've driven past Åsleik's farm, and the roads are well cleared, like always, because as soon as any snow falls there's Åsleik with his tractor, I think, and it'll sure be nice to get back home, I think and I turn off of the country road and I drive up my driveway, and Åsleik has cleared that too, I think, as soon as it snows up comes Åsleik clearing the snow with his old tractor, I think and I stop in front of the door and I stay sitting in the car and I breathe slowly out and I think that it feels so good to be back home, back home in Dylgja, back to my good old house, I think and I get out of the car and then open the passenger door and pick up Bragi and then put him down in the snow and he runs around in the snow and jumps here and there and then he lifts his leg and lets out a yellow stream and he makes what looks like a black hole in the snow but there's yellow and when he's done he starts running around and around in the powdery snow and I call him and Bragi stops and he stands there and looks stubbornly at me and I think so I finally got myself a dog, I think and then I say come on Bragi and then he comes trotting over to me and I go into my house with Bragi at my heels, and then I go into the main room and then out to the kitchen, still with Bragi at my heels, and I run some water into a bowl and I put the bowl down in the corner behind the hall door and Bragi is there in a flash and he drinks and drinks and then I get another bowl and I slice a piece of bread and tear it into pieces and then I put the bowl of bread pieces down next to the other bowl and Bragi is there in a flash and he eats and eats, so he must have been really thirsty and hungry too, yes, I think, standing there looking at the water bowl and I see that Bragi has drunk up all the water and I refill the bowl and I put it back down and then I see that the food bowl is empty too and I slice another piece of bread and tear it into pieces and put them in the bowl, but now Bragi just sniffs at the bread and water a bit, he doesn't touch it and then I go back into the main room with Bragi at my heels and I go and stand where I can look at the painting with the two lines crossing and even now, well into the daytime hours, it's only half-light, or half-darkness, whatever you'd call it, I think and I see that the picture is shining, yes, even in the half-dark it's now like there's a light shining from almost the whole picture, and it's impossible to understand, and yet I do understand, at the same time, that with these two lines I've made something, I've actually painted a good picture, in its way, in its own way, and I know that I won't do anything more with this picture, and I think that I can sell this picture, but for a low price, for much too low a price, even though this might be one of the best paintings I've ever managed to paint, I think, one of the paintings with the most light in it, I think and I think I should keep this painting for myself, because if I sell it it'll go away somewhere and then it'll be gone, and then maybe it'll be sold or given to someone else in turn, and I know I wouldn't get much for this picture anyway, no one wants to pay much for a picture like this, not one painted by me anyway, I know that, so I should keep this picture for myself, because really, yes, even if this picture may be a failure in others' eyes, and for all I know may actually be a bad picture, still it's one where I've truly painted some of what I try to get into all of my pictures, I think, that something, that, that, yes, it can't be said but maybe it can be shown, or almost shown, yes, whatever it is that can be captured in a picture somehow and shown rather than said, but not only in a painting, it can be shown at least as well in writing, in literature, I think, and this picture isn't like the others I've painted, you can tell just from the canvas, because I usually like to paint the whole canvas white first instead of letting the canvas show through, that's why I use so much white oil paint, I think and I think that I'm so tired now that the only thing to do, the only thing I want to do, is get a little sleep, I think and I hang up my brown shoulder bag on its hook between the bedroom door and the hall door and then I go out into the hall and hang up my black coat and I take off my shoes and then I go back into the main room and I take off my black velvet jacket and I hang it on the back of the chair to the left of the round table and then I go over to the bench that I have in a corner and I lie down, and even though it's cold in the room, despite the electric heater that's been on full-strength while I was gone, and even though I should light the stove I just lie on the bench and drape the grey wool blanket over me, the one Grandmother had when she was lying sick at home in The Old House and that she handed to me when they came to get her and drive her to The Hospice and that I took with me when I left home to go to The Academic High School and that's stayed with me ever since, wherever I lived the blanket came with me, I think and I see Bragi come padding over and he hops up onto the bench with me and he lies down next to me and I spread the blanket over him too and then I stroke and stroke his fur, up and down, and Bragi presses against me and he's good and warm and then I think well then I've got myself a dog and it really was good that Åsleik cleared the roads, yes, the main road and the driveway too, yes, how would I ever get by without Åsleik? without him and his old tractor? who else would clear the road up to my house? yes, I'd probably have to do what I did before, before I had the driveway built, park my car down on the main road and walk up, but it's steep and it feels like a long walk especially when I'm carrying something so it was a real slog to carry everything up to the house, yes, a real slog, but it was all right, I managed that too, one way or another, before I had the driveway built, I think, but now as soon as any snow falls there's Åsleik with his tractor, and he's always home, except for the two days a year when he goes to see Sister in Øygna, right by Instefjord, for Christmas, I think and I tuck the blanket around me better and I lie there on the bench with Bragi tucked against me and I close my eyes and suddenly I start in fright, because I can clearly hear a screeching sound, the same sound, I think, and it sounds like it's coming from somewhere right near me, right next to me, a screeching grinding sound, and it has to be coming from an old tractor, I think and I think that I don't feel so tired any more, so I must have nodded off, I think, and now I need to get up and get some things done, I think, and now the screeching grinding noise is very near me, I think and I get up and Bragi gets up and he stands on the bench and looks at me, so, I have a dog now, yes, I think, and I've thought so many times about getting a dog but never done it, I think and I look at the chair I always sit in, on the left next to the round table, and I go and sit down in the chair and Bragi comes and jumps up and lies in my lap and I take my bearings, the top of the pine trees outside my house have to be exactly in the middle of the middle right pane of glass in the window, and then I look at the landmark I always look at, near the middle of the Sygne Sea, and I see waves and it makes me feel calm in a way to look at the same place, at my landmark, at the waves there, every time I fall into a kind of light doze that's a bit like sleep but isn't, maybe, I think, and then I notice that the room is cold, so I need to light a fire in the stove, but it's always so sad and painful to do that, I usually put it off as long as I can until it's so cold that I absolutely have to light the stove, I think, and now, yes, now the room's cold enough that I really do have to light the stove, I think and then I pet and pet Bragi's fur and I think now I'll go light the stove, I think, and then there's that noise, that screeching sound, that grinding, I think, but how can I just sit here like this so sluggish that I can't even light the stove no matter how cold it gets in the room, I think and then I listen to that screeching grinding noise, and now it's very close, and it's unmistakable, that screeching grinding noise must be coming from Åsleik's old tractor, I think, so now Åsleik'll probably be standing outside the door any minute and knocking, I think, and that means it must have snowed more, I think and I look at the waves and I see Asle and Sister walking over to The Dairy, they're walking hand in hand, and they've started walking so fast that they seem to want to get to The Dairy quickly and then right back home, I think and now I really need to stand up and light the stove, I think and then I hear that it's fallen quiet, so Åsleik's probably standing in front of the house now, I think and I hear Sister say that now that screeching grinding noise has disappeared and Asle says yes and Sister says that it was a terrible noise and I hear a knock at the door and I get up and I'd forgotten I had Bragi on my lap and he falls onto the floor when I stand up and he starts yelping loudly

Hush, I say

and Bragi just keeps yelping

Hush, I say

and now he's barking in a loud and strong voice and so I pick Bragi up and I hold him in my arms and Bragi stops barking and I think that it was probably Åsleik at the door, my neighbour and friend, I think and I go out into the hall and I open the front door and I see that it's snowed a lot since I got home and I see Åsleik standing there in his brown snowsuit with the brown fur hat with flaps over the ears down to his long grey beard

Did you get a dog? Åsleik says

That's a surprise, he says

Is it a puppy? he says

and I say that I'm just watching the dog for someone I know in Bjørgvin, and he's not a puppy, just a small dog, I say and Åsleik asks if I'm watching the dog for my Namesake and I say yes and Åsleik says that I've talked about getting a dog so many times that he thought I'd finally gone and done it

No, I say

and I put Bragi down and he barks a couple times at Åsleik who is holding out his fist to him and then the dog sniffs his hand and then he relaxes

His name's Bragi, I say

That's a good name for a dog, Åsleik says

and I see Bragi run out across the snow and he lifts his leg and then he stands there and pees

I cleared your driveway earlier today, Åsleik says

But then it started snowing again, he says

We don't usually get so much snow in Dylgja, I say

Sometimes it's years between snowfalls, he says

and then we stand there and I feel tired but I can tell that Åsleik's in the mood to talk and I can't very well not ask him in

You should come inside, I say

You don't mind? he says

No, come in, I say

You waited a long time before inviting me in, he says

Please, you're always welcome, I say

Well, he says

It's cold standing in the door, I say

All right, Åsleik says

and then he says he has something for me and then he goes over to his tractor and he takes two shopping bags out of the driver's cabin and he comes walking over to me holding up the bags

I have something here for you, he says

And I bet you can guess what it is, he says

and he hands me the bags and they give off a powerful smell of the best smoked lamb ribs and I see that one bag is almost full of sliced Christmas lamb ribs and in the other are lots of big pieces of lutefisk packed up well in their own plastic bags

Thank you, I say

Just the way it should be, Åsleik says

Glad to help, he says

Yes, thank you, I say

and then I stand there with a bag in each hand, and the weight feels heavy on both arms so Åsleik really must have filled the bags up, I think

I brought a lot this year, Åsleik says

Can you tell? he says

More than usual, he says

Yes, I can tell, I say

And I did it for a reason, Åsleik says

Yes, I say

and then there's silence

And that is, Åsleik says

Yes, I say

It's because this year I want a bigger picture to give Sister as a Christmas present, he says

She has enough small ones, he says

You've always given me one of the small ones, he says

I was almost starting to think you'd paint a bunch of small pictures just to make sure you could give me one, Åsleik says

and I hear what he's saying and now that I think about it maybe he's right? could I maybe have been doing that? but I've painted hardly any small pictures recently, I have just a few, four or five maybe, so it's fine to give Åsleik one of the bigger pictures, but the newest one, the one with the St Andrew's Cross, no, he can't have that one, that's for sure, I'd rather he just take all his lamb and fish and go right back home, but no, that's a bad idea, because Åsleik makes exceptionally good Christmas lamb ribs every year and his lutefisk tastes exceptionally good too, not to mention the dry-cured mutton he makes, but we still need to come to an agreement about which picture he'll get, it's just that Åsleik really understands pictures, he can see pretty much right away if it's a good picture or a bad one, and he's always picked out the best one, yes, the best of the small pictures he's been choosing up until now, I think and then Åsleik says Sister has pictures of mine all over the house by now, in the hall, in the living room, in the stairwell, yes, he can't think of anywhere she doesn't have pictures I've painted, and she has three small pictures hanging over her sofa, but it would look nicer there with one big one, he says, so this year he would really like one of my bigger pictures, and I say that's, that's fine, because it's true what he says, he's always taken one of the smaller pictures, but I'd never thought about it before, even if what he's saying is totally right, I say

Yes you can pick one of the big pictures this year, I say

and Åsleik says that he doesn't want to be pushy, or rude, but he'd be grateful if he could take the picture with him today, because Christmas is coming soon and he has to wrap the painting in proper wrapping paper with pixies and angels and such, and he needs to put the nicest red ribbon he can around the package, and a little card that says For my dear sister Guro, he says, and, yes, well, he knows he's asked me about this every year recently but it really would be great if I'd come with him to Sister's to celebrate Christmas, it's just the two of them so it would be nice for them if I came along, and of course it's also always much nicer and safer to have two people in a boat than just one, he says, so it would be a great help to him as well as making him very happy if I'd come with and celebrate Christmas with Sister, way up in Sygnefjord, yes, it takes a whole short day to go to Øygna in The Boat, he says, but that's what he's done every year now for quite a few years, rowed there and rowed back, he says

You call her just Sister? I say

and I think why am I asking him that now

I guess I do, Åsleik says

Yes, I guess I've always called her just Sister, it's true, Åsleik says

Yes, I say

But her name's Guro, Åsleik says

Yes, I say

Guro, yes, he says

and then we stay standing silently

But, please, come in, I say

and Åsleik says thank you and he comes into the hall and I call Bragi and he comes running right into the hall and then he stands there on the floor and shakes the snow off himself and snow flies in all directions and I shut the front door and Åsleik says he can't go tracking snow into my living room, or studio, as it's called, or whatever it is, in his boots, so if it's all right he'll just take off his boots and pick out a picture today, yes, that would be great and I say yes, yes of course, he should just come right in, he's always welcome, I say and Åsleik says then in that case he should probably take off his snowsuit too, even though it's a bit of a hassle, he says and then he takes off his boots and fur hat and then unzips the front of his snowsuit and starts twisting and turning and he says this coat is a real pain but it always keeps you warm, it really does, he says

My sister's name is Guro, yes, Åsleik says

Yes, I say

and I think that that's strange too, because the woman I ran into in Bjørgvin who kept Bragi for the night at her place was named Guro as well, and it's not such a common name, but maybe it was a common name in the countryside at one point, I think

And the dog's name is Bragi, yes, I say

What a nice little scamp, Åsleik says

and again he holds out his hand to Bragi, who goes over to Åsleik and licks his hand a couple of times and then Åsleik clutches Bragi's fur and tugs a little and now they're good friends, I think

Bragi, yes you are, Åsleik says

and he says if I need someone to watch the dog for me I should just call him, he says and I think that actually it's kind of strange that in all these years Åsleik has only ever talked about Sister and almost never called her Guro, I think and we go into the main room and Åsleik says

I keep it so cold in the room that he should probably go back out to the hall and put his snowsuit back on, he says, don't I have a fire in the stove? I have plenty of wood in The Shed, last summer he drove a giant load of wood to my house and we stacked it all in The Shed, good dry birchwood, and a generous amount of kindling, and wood chips, he says, and now here I was without a fire in the stove, and not only do I have more than enough wood in The Shed, there's also lots of wood in the woodbox, he can see that, and kindling, and wood chips, yes, so now things with me have reached the point that I'd rather sit there freezing instead of lighting a good fire in the stove, he just doesn't know, Åsleik says and I don't know quite what to say, because I do probably need to defend myself or explain myself somehow but what should I say? and why haven't I lit the stove? yes well it's probably just that I was too tired or something, I think, and that's something I can say

I was so tired that I just lay right down, I say

Yes, well, that makes sense, Åsleik says

Back and forth to Bjørgvin three times in the same day and then again the next day to get back home, that'd tire you out, he says

Yes, I say

When I got home I lay down on the bench with the blanket over me and the dog was lying next to me, so I wasn't cold, I say

If you're wrapped in a good blanket it's true you don't get cold so easily, Åsleik says

and he says that your body heat stays trapped in the blanket somehow, and that's how it keeps you so warm, but since I'm tired he can light the stove for me, that's easy enough, he says and I see Åsleik go over to the stove and open the hatch and he starts putting wood in it and I go out to the kitchen and I see the six shopping bags I bought yesterday on the kitchen table, yes, I drove right back to Bjørgvin without even taking everything out of the bags, I think and I need to put the food away soon, there are already so many bags on the kitchen table that I need to put the lamb and fish Åsleik brought me in the pantry under the stairs to the attic right away, the same as I usually do, but it can wait, because both the lamb ribs and the lutefisk will be fine in the cold kitchen, I think and then I put the two shopping bags Åsleik brought me up on the table with the other bags that are already there and now there are no fewer than eight shopping bags there, I think, and I go back into the main room and I see the stove hatch standing open and Åsleik is there looking at the logs in the stove

It'll catch in a second, Åsleik says

So we'll be warmer soon, he says

and he holds out his hands to the stove and he says that the stove is already nice and warm

You're probably freezing, you should come over here and warm up, he says

and to tell the truth I do feel a little cold and I go over to Åsleik and I stand next to him by the stove and I hold my hands above the stove and it's good to feel the warmth coming up towards my hands, they really were quite cold, I feel

It'll start to warm up in your stove soon, Åsleik says

and then Bragi comes slinking in and he lies down in front of the stove and then I just stand there not saying anything

And now I can take a look at the pictures, and pick out one for Sister? Åsleik says

Yes, I say

and Åsleik turns around and he says that the stack of finished big paintings is big now, but the stack of smaller pictures isn't that big, he says, so I must not have been painting as many smaller pictures as I usually do, he says and I say that's right, and I don't know why, that's just how it is, I say and Åsleik says well that's usually how it goes, things turn out however they're going to turn out, he says and then we just stand there by the stove and I feel warmth spreading through my body and it feels good and Åsleik again says that this year he wants a big picture, I've always, for whatever reason, given him one of the small pictures every other year and that's fine, of course I need to be thrifty to get by, tubes of oil paint and canvases aren't free now are they, no, and of course I get more money for a big painting than I do for a smaller one, he understands all that, but he's been thinking for some years now that he really wanted to give Sister one of the bigger paintings, but I'd always taken him over to the stack of small paintings and shown him those and he'd decided among them and chosen a small picture, and if he hadn't been able to decide on one of those then I'd found some more pictures and put them on the living-room table, but always small ones, yes well what do I mean living-room table, it's been years since you could call it a living-room table strictly speaking, a table you could sit around, could eat at, because there've been tubes of paint and brushes and a hammer and nails and a saw and cloths and rags and other junk and he doesn't know how I can find what I need in that mess, but then again I do have that good long kitchen table, yes, it's been there all these years, since long before when Ales and I moved into the house, yes, it was there when old Alise lived in the house, Åsleik says, yes, and that goes for the living-room table too, of course, all the furniture, yes, we didn't change that much, because there's also the round table with the two chairs that's still in front of the window the same as it was when old Alise lived in the house, and the same bench in the same corner it used to be in, Åsleik says and then there's silence

Yes, you and Ales, he says

Ales and Asle, yes, he says

Yes, I say

It's so sad she got sick and passed away when she was so young, so young, and it was so sudden too, Åsleik says

and then we just stand there and we don't say anything, it's like we're frozen in place and I see Ales the first time we walked into the kitchen together and she says she'd always thought they were so beautiful, old Alise's old kitchen table with the old chairs, she said, and then when we went into the living room she said the same thing about the furniture there, and she especially liked the round table with the two chairs in front of the window so that you could sit and look out at Sygne Sea, that in particular she'd always liked so much, she said and then she'd sat down in the chair on the right and I'd sat down in the chair on the left, and that's the way we always sat from then on, me in the chair on the left, where I still sit, and Ales in the chair on the right, I think and I turn around and I see Ales sitting in the chair on the right looking out at Sygne Sea, she's sitting there at the window without moving and her long dark hair is hanging loose down over her back and I don't want to see her and I don't want to think about her, because it's too terrible, the pain is too great, so I don't want to do it, I think and Åsleik says he's sorry, he shouldn't have mentioned Ales, and I don't say anything and then we just stand there by the stove and then Åsleik says the best thing would be, yes well, as he's already said, if he could pick out a picture today, or at least look through them today so he can think it over, think about which picture Sister would like best, if he didn't see it right away, he says and I say that's fine, of course he can look at the pictures today, and I think that actually there's no one besides Åsleik that I show my pictures to, before they're shown at The Beyer Gallery in Bjørgvin, and that it won't be long before I have a new exhibition there, but I have enough pictures for the show, so now I just need to, actually as soon as I can, drive the pictures to Bjørgvin, yes, the thirteen pictures I'm going to show, or at least it's going to be thirteen once Åsleik has taken one for himself, no more and no less, though that's fewer than usual, usually I have thirteen big pictures and six small pictures, nineteen all in all, I really believe in the number nine and I always want it to be in there one way or another, or else it can be a number where the digits add up to make nine, or something, I think, but the woman supposedly named Guro told me that the number that brings me luck, yes, my lucky number, is eight, or four times two, as she also said, because that was the number she got to by adding up the digits of my birthday, she said, but I've stuck with nine, and also three, I think, and so now I'm not sure about the number thirteen, because I think that thirteen can be both a good number and a bad number, the same with eight maybe, I think, no, anyway, eight is a good number, I think, but usually I've always had it be nineteen pictures, some of them small, because The Beyer Gallery isn't that big and Beyer told me that he doesn't want any more pictures than that so I've never had more than nineteen, but one time I brought nine pictures and Beyer said it wasn't enough, or barely enough, it couldn't be any fewer than that in future, he said, it didn't really matter much how big the pictures were of course, though the pictures I paint are never that big, they're just bigger or smaller, and almost no pictures are long and thin like the picture with the two lines crossing each other, which, obviously, there's no way around it, I think, I'll call it *St Andrew's Cross,* and I'll paint the title in thick black oil paint on the top of the stretcher today and then sign it with a large A in the right-hand corner of the picture itself, like I always do, and if I was alone I'd do it right now, but I'll sign the picture as soon as Åsleik leaves, I think, and then I'll need to drive the pictures down to Bjørgvin soon, just get it over with, I think, but now I've driven to Bjørgvin twice without bringing the paintings with me and I guess the reason why I haven't taken them to Bjørgvin yet is that Åsleik hasn't chosen the picture he wants yet, even though I didn't realise it, without thinking about it that way that's what it was, I think, it's after Åsleik chooses his picture that I'll drive the paintings down to Bjørgvin, because Beyer always wants to hang the pictures himself, he says that it's so important to hang them right, the whole exhibition is like a painting of its own, he says, and that, yes, that's the painting that he paints, or assembles or however you'd put it, Beyer says, and really I have no opinions about how the pictures should be hung, which ones next to which other ones or anything like that, and before Beyer sees the pictures the truth is and has been ever since Ales has been gone that Åsleik is the only one who sees them, and he has an amazingly good eye for pictures, more often than not he sees the same thing that I see, and he almost always has the same opinion about a picture as I do, so he almost always picks one of the pictures that I would have picked myself if I had to choose one, so from one point of view Sister, this Guro woman, probably has the best collection of my pictures anywhere, limited to the small pictures, but truth be told I'm doing something different in the bigger ones, and she's only been given smaller ones, that's true

And you can take one of the big ones, of course, I say

Obviously, I say

I shouldn't have said that about always being given one of the small ones, Åsleik says

and I think that it's true, I've always offered him one of the small pictures, but it wasn't on purpose and I feel a bit ashamed about it now, it's not that I think he doesn't deserve a bigger picture, or Sister for that matter, but for some reason I've acted like Åsleik would always prefer to give Sister a smaller picture and Sister would always prefer to get a smaller picture, yes, in a way I'd have felt like I was forcing it on her if he tried to take a big one, since she'd come to own a lot of paintings over the years, a new one every year, so I probably thought a big one would be too much, she wouldn't have enough space on the wall for them all

Sister's whole house is almost full of your paintings now, Åsleik says

And that's all well and good, it's not that, he says

and Åsleik says that Sister is still just as happy and just as grateful every year for the picture she gets, he says and then he goes over to the stack of the bigger paintings and I see him start to look through the stack and he looks closely at each picture, one by one, and I'm standing by the stove and looking in at the flames and I think that up in the attic, in one of the storage spaces, I have some pictures stored that I didn't want to sell, and two of them are among the first ones I painted when I started painting the way I wanted to paint and not just pictures of people's houses from photographs, and those two pictures are still two of the best I've ever painted, they're pictures where I felt like I'd really accomplished something, yes, more than I'm capable of actually, more of something that's bigger than life is, maybe you could put it that way? yes, even if that's kind of a grand way to put it and it feels too big and grand, still, yes, but, in some of the pictures I've done what I wanted to do, I can see that, I know that, and obviously the picture can say what can't be said in any other way except precisely how that picture is saying it, and I don't want to sell these pictures, my very best ones, because I know that most likely no one else wants to see what's in these pictures, but I almost always have one on display up in the attic room I don't use for storage, and for a long time now it's been a portrait I painted of Ales, I think, because there are two rooms up in the attic, with two storage areas, and I use one room for storage too, I keep a lot of wood I can make stretchers from up there and a lot of canvas and more than a few tubes of oil paint and a whole lot of turpentine, but in the other attic room, on the left, I have only a chair in the middle of the room between the two small windows in the gable and I always have one of the paintings I don't want to sell sitting on that chair, and I don't want to sell it because the ones I sell just go away to someone else and then they're gone, like the two stacks of pictures leaning against the wall by the kitchen door are about to do, because even if Beyer carefully notes down the name and the address of the buyer of this or that picture, yes, he's photographed every single picture since the very first exhibition and numbered them and written down the buyer's name, even then no one knows what happened to the painting after that, if the buyer gave it away or sold it to someone else, yes, strictly speaking the picture vanishes into the unknown and there's no way to find it again, yes, there are pictures I've sold and regretted selling, especially the ones I painted when I was going to The Art School before I realised that there are some pictures I'm just not willing to sell, and those are the ones up in the attic, I keep the pictures I don't want to sell in the storage space in the room on the left, and then I put a new one out, in place of the one I have sitting on the chair, and sometimes, especially when I sort of haven't been painting for a while, when it's stopped, I've gone up to the attic to look at the picture I have on display on the chair or else taken one of the other pictures out of the storage space and put it on the chair and then I also have a chair a few paces back from the chair with the picture on it and I sit down on it and then sit and look and look at the picture, yes, I can stay there for a long time, I don't know how long, and I try to see why I actually keep painting pictures, and I sit and silently fall deeper and deeper into what I'm seeing, into what's bigger than life, maybe, but that's not the right way to say it, because what it is is, yes, a kind of light, a kind of shining darkness, an invisible light in these pictures that speak in silence, and that speak the truth, and then, once I've entered into this vision, or way of seeing, so that it's not me who's seeing but something else seeing through me, sort of, then I always find a way I can get farther with the picture I'm struggling with, and that's how it also is with all the paintings by other people that mean anything to me, it's like it's not the painter who sees, it's something else seeing through the painter, and it's like this something is trapped in the picture and speaks silently from it, and it might be one single brushstroke that makes the picture able to speak like that, and it's impossible to understand, I think, and, I think, it's the same with the writing I like to read, what matters isn't what it literally says about this or that, it's something else, something that silently speaks in and behind the lines and sentences, but, yes, this is what happened, the pictures I keep in the attic are only some of the bigger pictures because Åsleik chose all of the truly good smaller pictures and took them to give to Sister, yes, it's a bit ridiculous, but he must see the same way I do, or pretty close, anyway there are lots of pictures Åsleik picked out and gave to Sister that I really wish I had in my own collection up in the attic, not all the ones he's bought, or rather traded for lamb and fish and wood and clearing the snow, there aren't many of the ones he took that I wish I still had, but all the small pictures I might have imagined keeping in my collection up in the attic are ones Åsleik took and gave to Sister for Christmas, yes, it's almost unbelievable but it's true, her collection of my smaller paintings is a collection of the best smaller paintings I've ever painted, or even the best pictures I've ever painted altogether, that's how I see it, not counting the paintings I have up in the attic, and the one I've had out on the chair up there for quite some time, I don't remember exactly how long, is the portrait I painted of Ales, and I can't bring myself to put it away, to swap it out for one of the other pictures in the storage spaces there, I think, and it would be nice to see the best smaller paintings I've ever painted again, just once, and anyway it's a good thing that I know where they are, because it doesn't matter so much whether I have them here in my house as long as I know where I could go see them, I think, but I've never gone with Åsleik to visit Sister, the truth is I've never even met her, even though I've driven past her house every single time I drove to or back from Bjørgvin, and it's a pretty, old, small house, even if it does need a little paint, a grey house, but a bit rundown, it's true, and obviously it's never occurred to me to go knock at that woman named Guro's door and ask if I could take a look at the pictures, but still, it really is a bit strange that I've never met Åsleik's sister, because she drops by to see Åsleik now and then, to come see her childhood home, as they say, but she's never spent the night there, Åsleik has said, she takes the bus round-trip the same day, yes, because there's a bus connection once a day between Dylgja and Bjørgvin, to Dylgja in the morning, from Dylgja in the afternoon, it's a small bus, because there aren't many people who take it, I think, it's basically empty past Dylgja more often than not, but some people do travel to or from Bjørgvin, I think and I think that Åsleik said that Sister doesn't want to spend the night in her childhood home, he says, and he doesn't understand why she doesn't want to but anyway it's high time we met, what with all the paintings of mine she has hanging in her house, I think, so maybe I will go with Åsleik for Christmas at Sister's house this year? after all, Åsleik asks me every year if I can't go with him to celebrate Christmas with her, and he says why can't I come? because it would have to be much nicer for me than spending Christmas alone in Dylgja? he says and I always say no, I'd rather be alone, I say, but now, this year, maybe this year I can go with Åsleik and celebrate Christmas at Sister's? because then I'd get to see all the good smaller paintings I've painted, if nothing else? and Åsleik said it'd be easier for him, too, if I came along, because then he wouldn't have to go to Øygna alone in The Boat, and it's always so much safer in a boat when there are two of you on board, but he's always alone, Åsleik said, and I see that he's pulled a picture out of the stack and now he's looking at it and he's not saying anything

Maybe I can come for Christmas with you and Sister this year, I say

and I look at Åsleik and there's silence for a moment

You think you might come to Sister's for Christmas? Åsleik says

and it's like he can't believe his ears

Yes, maybe, I say

That's a surprise, Åsleik says

Well there are a lot of paintings Sister has that I'd like to see again, I say

Yes I suppose there are, Åsleik says

and we stand there silently

I'm having a new show at The Beyer Gallery soon, I say

Yes, Åsleik says

But I have enough pictures, more than enough, of the big ones too, so you should take whichever one you want to give Sister today, I say

Since I need to drive the paintings down to Bjørgvin soon, I say

Is that why you didn't take them with you when you kept driving to Bjørgvin, because I still had to pick out a picture? Åsleik says

and I say maybe, yes, maybe that's part of the reason, but it was probably mostly that I wasn't paying attention to the date and I realised only recently that the show is coming up soon

So it's fine if you pick out a picture today, I say

Thanks, Åsleik says

I just realised, I say

Realised what? Åsleik says

That I have a show soon, I say

So I need to drive the paintings down to Bjørgvin in the next few days, I say

and I think that then I can also check on Asle in The Hospital, because there's no way I'll be able to visit him today, but maybe I can tomorrow? or the day after? I think and I say yes I'll probably drive down as soon as tomorrow, or the day after, down to Bjørgvin with the picture, even if that means a lot of driving, I don't think I've ever driven to Bjørgvin so many times so close together before, I say

You could have taken the pictures with you yesterday, Åsleik says

Yes, I say

But you didn't think of it? he says

No, to tell you the truth I didn't, I say

and there's silence

Because I could have chosen the painting I want yesterday, or a few days ago, Åsleik says

Yes, I say

You've probably never driven to Bjørgvin twice in the same day before, you're right, he says

No, I say

and we stand there not saying anything

You usually never drive to Bjørgvin to go shopping more than once a month, do you? Åsleik says

and I say he's probably right, anyway it's no more than that, I say

And then you do go almost every Sunday, papist that you are, to mass at St Paul's Church, he says

and I nod and I think will he never stop using that word? it's like with St Andrew's Cross, it's like he's proud that he can say this word too, can say papist, I think

It takes you all day, he says

Yes I often do, I say

No, I really don't understand you, Åsleik says

Plus you're practically a Communist, he says

No, I don't get it, Åsleik says

A Catholic and a Communist at the same time, he says

and Åsleik shakes his head and then we just stand there and then I say that Christmas is coming up soon and I need to drive the pictures down to Bjørgvin this year same as every year, because every year I have an exhibition at The Beyer Gallery before Christmas, as he knows of course, I say

During Advent, yes, he says

But you should pick out a painting first, I say

and then I say that it's good he wants to do it today

I'll pick out a painting today and just take it with me, Åsleik says

and I realise that I'm kind of hungry, after all I haven't eaten anything since breakfast at The Country Inn this morning, and I didn't eat much then either, I think, but I don't feel like cooking a big meal, I'm too tired, but I can always fry an egg with some bacon and onions, I have good fresh bread, yesterday I bought bacon and onions I can fry up, and I ask Åsleik if he'd like some fried eggs with bacon and onions and he says he wouldn't say no to that, it sounds delicious, Åsleik says, and I see him looking at one of the big paintings and then Åsleik says he'll just look at the pictures a little more so maybe he can choose one while I'm frying the bacon and eggs and onions and I say that's fine and I see that there's a good fire in the stove and then I put a log in the stove and I shut the hatch and then I go out to the kitchen and I see all the shopping bags on the kitchen table, yes, I didn't even unpack what I bought before I drove back to Bjørgvin yesterday, I think, and now, yes, now I'll unpack them and put all the food away because there's eggs and bacon and onions and bread somewhere in one of the bags, I bought a lot of bacon, and lots of bread, and I need to wrap them in plastic bags and put them in the freezer out in the hall, because there are two main rooms in the house, and the one next to the kitchen is where I paint, and where I read, it's where I spend my time, and then there's a little room off the side of the main room with a double bed where I sleep, and that was where Ales and I slept too in the years we shared, the years we were together, and then there's the hall, and off the hall there's one more room, yes, The Parlour as old Alise used to call it, and that's what Ales always called it too and so that's what I still call it, The Parlour, because the room was thought to be especially nice somehow, it had the ugliest wallpaper I've ever seen, yes, red and white roses twined together from floor to ceiling, and old Alise was so proud of the room that she practically never used it, and the first thing Ales and I did when we moved into the house was paint over the wallpaper, we painted the room white, but other than that we didn't change too much in the house, I think, we took it over just the way it was, plates and bowls, knives and forks, I think, but we did paint The Parlour white over that wallpaper with roses on it and after a while it was there, in The Parlour, that Ales painted her paintings, and it comes back to me that it was then, while we were painting The Parlour, that I stopped smoking, yes, Ales thought that when we were moving to Dylgja was a good opportunity to stop smoking, the same way I'd stopped drinking when we moved into the brown house, yes, she said, and that's what I did, yes, I stopped smoking and started taking snuff and even though Ales didn't exactly love that I took snuff she accepted it, I who had smoked almost constantly, rolling a cigarette and lighting it while I was still smoking the last one, I had stopped, but I did start taking snuff at the same time, and now why am I starting to think about that? I think, and I think that at first after Ales was gone, after she'd gone to her rest with God, I'd left everything how it was, but it was too sad to keep the room the way she'd left it so after a while I moved the tubes of oil paint and brushes and such out of The Parlour, yes, everything she'd used for her painting I took and used myself, except what she'd used to paint icons, because in the last few years she'd painted nothing but icons, and everything that had to do with icon painting was still where it was when she'd died, on the big bookshelf I made myself to cover the whole long wall there are her books, but also my books, and I've put the ones I've bought more recently on the bookshelf there in The Parlour too, it's turned into a real library, not least because of the many books Ales bought about icons and icon painting, and when Ales was gone I hung all her icons up in The Parlour, including the ones that weren't totally finished, and then I hung up the few paintings she'd left behind, because she'd painted over almost all her paintings with white and some of the best paintings I ever managed to paint were on canvases where Ales had painted over her own pictures in white, I think and I think I can't just keep standing here like this not doing anything and so I go over to the kitchen table and I start to unpack a bag of groceries, I put the groceries on the table and I take the groceries out of all the other bags and then the table is covered with all kinds of things, meat, bacon, potatoes and vegetables, butter and margarine, flour, soap and shampoo and I don't know what else, and then the two bags I got from Åsleik are left, one with lamb ribs and one with lutefisk, and I think I'll carry them out right now to the pantry under the stairs up to the attic, and I take the bags and leave the kitchen and I put them in the pantry and I think now I need to get everything that needs freezing into the freezer, I think, I have a large freezer in the hall, yes, so big that when I bought it and had it delivered it barely fit through the front door, because I wanted a big freezer since I can sometimes go quite a while between shopping trips, and since I really go shopping only when I go to Bjørgvin, because I don't like spending money, I think, and I think another reason it's good to have a big freezer is that I can get more fish from Åsleik now, I don't only get lamb ribs and lutefisk from him, no, I get dried fish and smoked herring and dry-cured herring and fresh cod and I don't know what else, I think, and now I need to fit all the food into the freezer, I think and then after that I need to make some fried eggs and bacon and onions, I think and I go into the kitchen and I put the bread and the packages of pork cutlets and the ground beef and frozen vegetables into two bags and the frozen things have thawed but I'm sure they'll be all right to eat even if they've thawed once, I obviously should have put them in the freezer yesterday, and I can't believe I was so forgetful that I didn't, I think and I go out into the hall and I hear Åsleik call what are you doing? and I say I just need to get the groceries into the freezer and I hear him answer yes it's certainly time you did that, if I was in such a hurry to get back to Bjørgvin that I didn't even unpack the groceries and put them in the freezer, no, I'm really something, I hear Åsleik say, and I put the two bags in the freezer and I think I should have put the groceries in the freezer properly, item by item, because I keep the freezer neat and organised, everything in its proper place, in the freezer like everywhere else, and what Åsleik calls the mess on the table in the main room is actually very organised, I think, but I'll have to organise the food in the freezer some other time, because now I'm really hungry, I think and I go back into the kitchen and there's Åsleik

Yes you sure did some shopping, he says

Yes, I say

and I know Åsleik is thinking about whether I've bought anything for him, because I usually do since it's cheaper to buy things in Bjørgvin than at The Country Store in Vik, everything's expensive there, which makes sense, The Shopkeeper has to mark it up more to make enough to live on, and there isn't much choice there, because there aren't that many customers in Vik or Dylgja, so I always tend to buy something for Åsleik when I go shopping in Bjørgvin, I think and I don't want to take any money from Åsleik for the things, because he has so little money, he's just barely getting by, I think, and when I try to give him what I've bought he never wants to take it at first, because he gets by just fine on his own, he doesn't need help from anyone, he doesn't need anything from the city, no, he doesn't need charity, no he always says something like that and I always say yes yes I know and then I say that it's payment for everything he's done for me and eventually he takes the bags of groceries kind of like he doesn't realise it, but he absolutely refuses to take any money, even if I sometimes do slip him a few kroner when I notice that he's in bad shape, and then we both pretend that neither of us notices what we're doing, kind of

Did you decide on a picture? I say

Yes well, Åsleik says

and then he goes back into the main room and I start putting various things into one of the bags and I go out into the hall with the bag and I put it under the hook all my scarves are hanging on and Åsleik will get it from there, I think and then I go back into the kitchen and then I start putting the fresh vegetables and other things into the big refrigerator, because I have a big refrigerator too, and both the fridge and the freezer were bought when Ales was still alive, I think and I can't start thinking about Ales again now, I think and then I start putting the dry goods away in the cupboard in the corner and I put the cans and soup and bags of flour and sugar and salt and various bags of pepper and whatever else away and then I take the one piece of bacon I have out, I've put the rest in the freezer except for two pieces in the bag for Åsleik, and the egg carton and an onion and a chunk of bread, and I put it on the kitchen counter and then Åsleik comes back into the kitchen

Yes you sure did buy a lot of groceries, he says

You know I don't really like going shopping, so I buy a lot when I do go, I say

I know, Åsleik says

and I look at the frying pan sitting on the stove where it usually is, and it's an old stove, it was there in the kitchen when we moved in, we inherited both the range and the frying pan from old Alise, but every burner on the stove works, and the oven too, so I imagine I'll be able to keep this range as long as I live, I think and I turn on the burner with the frying pan on it all the way and I cut a thick slice of bacon, enough to fill the whole pan, and I lay it in the pan and it starts sizzling right away and I turn down the heat and then I cut some slices of bread, two for Åsleik, two for me

You're such a good cook, really, Åsleik says

Well now, I don't know about that, I say

and the good smell of bacon starts filling the kitchen and I go turn the meat, because one side is all cooked, and then I get two plates and knives and forks and Åsleik says those are old plates, he remembers them from when he was a boy, from old Alise's time, he says

That smells great, Åsleik says

and I stand by the stove, and I look at the bacon sizzling in the old pan and the pan is so heavy that Ales said it was too heavy for her, she complained about the pan constantly, and she also thought it smoked too much, so that's why we bought a new frying pan that Ales always used while I always used the old cast-iron pan, and the one Ales used was in the pots and pans cupboard next to the stove and it's almost like I can feel the tears coming just from thinking about the other frying pan, I put that pan way back in the back of the cupboard so that it would be hard to see, because that pan always reminds me of Ales and it hurts so much every time I see that pan, yes, tears come to my eyes, to tell the truth, but I don't want to think about that now, about when Ales and I bought a new frying pan, that's another thing I can go around remembering, I can remember it like it was yesterday and go around in circles remembering it, I who have such a bad memory about other things, yes, except for the store of pictures in my head, all the pictures that fill my head, yes, those I remember all the time, but other things, like when Ales and I bought a frying pan, things like that, yes, well, I remember those things too, as clearly as anyone can remember anything

Don't forget about the bacon, Åsleik says

and I give a little start and realise right away that it's starting to smell burnt and in one movement I take the pan off the stove and turn off the burner and I turn over the bacon and it has burned a little but there's such a smell of burnt bacon in the kitchen that most people would think the bacon was totally burnt black but it isn't, it's just cooked well on one side, you might say

I came here a lot to see old Alise, Åsleik says

And she cooked for me a lot, he says

and he says that he has a feeling she used to think that they were practically starving back at their house and then he says well it's certainly true they were in a bad way when he was growing up, but it was just him and Sister, there wasn't a big flock of kids with mouths to feed, the way it was in a lot of families in those days, for whatever reason there was just him and Sister, yes, but, well, after his father never came back from the sea, yes, well, Åsleik says and he breaks off and I put the bacon on the two plates, and I'll put the bacon that's less burnt on the plate for Åsleik, I think and then I put the four slices of bread in the pan and fry them in the bacon fat a little before putting them on the plates and then I take a big onion out of the cupboard and I peel it and slice it and chop the slices into smaller pieces and then put it in the pan and then stand there stirring the onions and I see that they quickly turn slightly yellow, and I like onions best when they're only lightly fried, yes, just soft and barely cooked, and then I get four eggs from the cupboard and I crack one after another against the side of the frying pan and empty them over the onions and then I stand there looking at the pan and not thinking anything and Åsleik doesn't say anything

Food'll be ready soon, I say then

and I say it kind of to break the silence and I think that I almost never do that usually

And I sure am hungry, Åsleik says

Those onions are going to make it taste really good, he says

Onions kind of make everything taste different, he says

and Åsleik says that bacon and fried eggs are always good but they're especially good when you make them with onions, he says

and I think it'll be good to have something to eat because it's night-time and I've had almost nothing to eat all day, I think, yes, my stomach's grumbling, so it'll be good to have something to eat, yes, I think and Åsleik says that this is a real meal fit for a king, he says, and he says it again, a meal fit for a king, yes, fit for a king, he says and again it's like Åsleik is proud that he knows the idiom, because that's how he is, there are words he has to emphasise, give weight to, and sometimes that's fine, with a term like St Andrew's Cross, because there aren't actually that many people who know what that means, but fit for a king, such an ordinary phrase, old-fashioned even, yes, why would anyone be proud of knowing that? I think, and I say that the eggs are done and then I put them and the onions on the two plates and then I take one plate, the one with the bacon that's less burnt, and put it down in front of Åsleik and then I get a knife and fork and give those to him

Looks good, Åsleik says

and then I go get the other plate and knife and fork and I put them down at the end of the table where I've always sat, right here at the head of the table, is where I sit, and Ales always sat to my left, that's where the two chairs are, and when Åsleik ate with us he always sat on the right side, on a bench that's along the wall so a person sitting there could lean his back against the wall, and that's where Åsleik is sitting now, where he's always sat, I think and I sit down and I say bless this food and then we start eating and we eat without saying a word, and it tastes good, yes, it's unbelievable how good simple food can taste, the eggs are just eggs, the onions are just onions, and the bread I buy is just bread I pick out at random, whatever's cheapest, so the bread usually tastes the same but sometimes a little different, while that's not true of the bacon, there can be a big difference there, sometimes it shrivels up into almost nothing and sometimes the fully cooked slices are practically as big as they were raw, and the taste is different too, yes, I think, but today, today everything tastes unbelievably good, and maybe it's because I'm so hungry, I think and then Åsleik says it tastes good, yes, I always cook bacon and eggs and onions in the best way but even so today it tastes even better than usual, he says and I want to say something to him but I agree so I don't say anything and then Åsleik puts the knife and fork down next to each other on the plate and says yeah that tasted great and I finish and then put my knife and fork down on my plate too and Åsleik says thank you so much for the food, but now he really should be getting home, because I must be tired after all that driving, two round trips to Bjørgvin, one after the other, he says and I say yes you really start to feel it after you've eaten and Åsleik says yes well he's looked at the pictures but he isn't totally sure which one he wants, so maybe he can come back tomorrow and take a painting then? he says

But if you still want to drive the paintings to Bjørgvin tomorrow maybe it's better if I just pick one now, he says

You can if you want, sure, I say

But I'll have to drop by tomorrow anyway, because it's supposed to snow so much tonight that I'll have to clear your driveway tomorrow too, he says

and then Åsleik says that he'll stop by tomorrow, early tomorrow, both he and I get up early, so he can probably pick out a picture for Sister tomorrow, that way he'll have time to sleep on it too, because he's deciding between two pictures, he says, so if it's all right with me he'll come over tomorrow morning, and then he can help me load the pictures I'm taking to The Beyer Gallery into the car too, he says

Yes, you usually do that, I say

Well it needs doing, Åsleik says

Yes, I say

You need to be careful handling pictures, he says

And every one of them needs to get wrapped in a blanket, he says

Yes, I say

That's how I do it, yes, I say

I use a whole blanket for each big picture, and half a blanket for the smaller ones, as you know, I say

That's right, Åsleik says

Yes, I've often wondered where you got so many blankets, he says

and I knew he was going to say that, because he says it every time, and I've sworn to myself that I'm never going to tell him, he will never know, I need to keep some things to myself, I think, even though it's nothing, the answer is totally normal and boring, I just bought the blankets at The Thrift Shop in Sailor's Cove, a little north of the centre of Bjørgvin, in fact on the block where Asle lives, and obviously I didn't buy them all at once but I've been to The Thrift Shop lots of times and sometimes there'd be a blanket or two there and I'd buy them, and that's how after a while I got to have so many blankets

So, see you tomorrow morning, Åsleik says

See you then, I say

and Åsleik gets up and picks up his plate and knife and fork and Bragi is already at the ready next to the table wagging his tail and Åsleik puts the plate down on the floor and Bragi licks it and then Åsleik puts the plate and knife and fork into the sink and I fill Bragi's bowl with water and put it where it goes in the corner behind the hall door and Bragi runs over to the bowl and slurps up the water and I pick up my plate and put it in the sink and I see Åsleik standing in the door to the hall and he says yes Bragi needs his too, he says and then he says see you tomorrow morning and he'll pick out a painting for Sister then and I can think some more about whether I want to come with him this year to celebrate Christmas in Øygna, since I think maybe I can this year, because then, well, then we could probably just drive there together? he says, since I have a car, and a driver's licence? but no, that wouldn't be right, in all these years he's always gone to Øygna in The Boat for Christmas, there's a good landing there in a small bay, so that's how he'll go this year too, he says, but no one's getting any younger, so if I start coming regularly to celebrate Christmas with Sister, with Guro, then maybe some other year, when it gets too rough to go in The Boat, maybe we can take my car to Øygna? he says, well I should think about it, he says, because Sister's hardly some kind of a monster, maybe I'll even be glad I met her, and talked to her, yes, there's aren't that many people I talk to during the year, no, there can't be many, there's him, Åsleik, and then Beyer, the gallerist, and then I probably talk every now and then to the man with my Name, Åsleik says

But there's something I wanted to ask you about, Åsleik says

and I look straight at him standing in the doorway

Yes, I say

Yes, I've thought about asking you lots of times, but I've never done it, he says

But now, well, now that you're maybe thinking about coming to spend Christmas with me and Sister, since this might be happening for the first time, yes, well, I feel like I can ask you, he says

Go ahead, I say

Why is your hair so long? Åsleik asks

and I realise I'm about to start laughing but I manage not to

Beats me, I don't know, I say

Yeah? Åsleik says

I've had long hair almost since I was a kid, I say

Yeah, Åsleik says

and I say that one time when I was young I decided I wanted long hair, and so I grew my hair out, and then my mother dragged me to a hairdresser's, because even in Barmen where I grew up there were places where ladies would cut your hair, and now that she was getting her first chance to cut my hair she really went at it, I was left almost bald, it was a disaster, and since then I've never let any lady at a hairdresser's touch my hair, any barber either, and all my mother had to do was mention that I needed a haircut and I'd almost go after her with my fists, I say, even though I'm not a violent person, I've never hit anyone, but Mother eventually realised she had to give up on getting me to cut my hair and she let it just grow, and when it did get too long I would cut it myself, the way I still do, I just need two mirrors and a pair of scissors, I say

But now, well, now that it's gone all grey? Åsleik says

And so thin too, he says

That doesn't matter, I say

And with that bald spot you've got, too, it's pretty big, he says

and there's silence

When my hair started thinning out, I started tying it back with a black hairband, I say

Yes, a ponytail they call it, Åsleik says

The name says it all, he says

and I say I don't know how many years I've been doing it, wearing my hair in a ponytail, but yes, it's been a long time, because my hair turned grey early, I say, and I think I should have asked Åsleik why he has such a long grey beard, but I know what he'll answer if I do, I think

So it's because your mother made you get a horrible haircut once that you still have long hair? Åsleik says

If you want to put it that way, he says

Yes it's partly that, I say

I also just like having long hair, it's like it helps me in a way, it gives me a kind of protection, I say

Protection? Åsleik says

Helps you? he says

Yes, it helps me, helps me paint well, kind of, I say

and Åsleik says that he can't understand a thing like that and he says I look tired and I say that I am tired

I'm going to go right to bed, I say

When you're tired that's the best thing, Åsleik says

Even if it's early, he says

Yes, I say

So then it's probably time for me to go, he says

and Åsleik goes out into the hall and I follow him with Bragi at my heels and I open the front door and Bragi runs out and I see Åsleik standing there pulling his brown snowsuit on

He was sure in a hurry, Åsleik says

and I see him put on his boots and the brown fur cap with the earflaps

He must've needed some fresh air, I say

Yes, probably had to get some fresh air too before he lay down, Åsleik says

No big difference between dogs and people there, I say

Good point, Åsleik says

and he goes outside and I think now he's going to start talking about why he doesn't have a dog and I can certainly listen to all that, I've heard it so many times already, but I'm too tired now and I say goodnight to him and he says see you tomorrow, because he wants to come pick out a picture for Sister, yes, before I take the pictures to Bjørgvin, of course, yes, he says and I think that he's already said that and I say yes yes see you tomorrow and then I call Bragi and he comes running over and into the hall covered with snow and then he stands there and shakes off the snow and I see Åsleik climb up to the cabin of his tractor and I remember the bags of groceries I bought in Bjørgvin to give to Åsleik, they're still under the hook with the scarves, and I pick up the bags and I step into my boots and I hurry over to the tractor with Bragi at my heels

Wait a second, I shout

What is it now? Åsleik says

and I know perfectly well that he knows why I'm asking him to wait

Just wait, I say

I was just leaving, Åsleik says

and I hear Åsleik start the tractor, with a grinding sound from the engine, and I hold up the bags of groceries

Here, I say

You know I don't need anything, Åsleik says

I don't need any charity, he says

It's payment, for clearing the roads, I say

I don't need to get paid for that, he says

and I put the bags down at his feet and he just barely audibly mumbles thank you and then he starts carefully driving off and I go back to the front door with Bragi at my heels and I see him run into the hall and then I shut the front door behind me and then I go and make sure the burners on the stove are off and then I turn off the light in the kitchen and go into the main room and I stop in the middle of the room and I think that before I lie down I want to take a little look at the picture I'm working on, the one with the two lines that cross in the middle, and I think that maybe I should shut the curtains, I usually do, but now it's so dark out that I can look at the picture in the dark just fine without closing the curtains like I usually do, maybe it's a strange habit, always wanting to look at my paintings in the dark, yes, I can even paint in the dark, because something happens to a picture in the dark, yes, the colours disappear in a way but in another way they become clearer, the shining darkness that I'm always trying to paint is visible in the darkness, yes, the darker it is the clearer whatever invisibly shines in a picture is, and it can shine from so many kinds of colour but it's usually from the dark colours, yes, especially from black, I think and I think that when I went to The Art School they said you should never paint with black because it's not a colour, they said, but black, yes, how could I ever have painted my pictures without black? no, I don't understand it, because it's in the darkness that God lives, yes, God is darkness, and that darkness, God's darkness, yes, that nothingness, yes, it shines, yes, it's from God's darkness that the light comes, the invisible light, I think and I think that this is all just something I've thought up, yes, obviously, I think and I think that at the same time this light is like a fog, because a fog can shine too, yes, if it's a good picture then there's something like a shining darkness or a shining fog either in it, in the picture, or coming from the picture, yes, that's what it's like, I think, and without this light, yes, then it's a bad picture, but actually there's no light you can see, maybe, or is it that only I can see it, no one else can? or maybe some other people can too? but most other people don't see it, or even if they do sort of see it it's without knowing it, yes, I'm completely sure about that, they see it but they don't realise that it's a shining darkness they're seeing and they think that it's something else, that's how it is, and even though I don't understand why it's at night, in the darkness, that God shows himself, yes well maybe it's not so strange, not when you think about it, but there are people who see God better in the daylight, in flowers and trees, in clouds, in wind and rain, yes, in animals, in birds, in insects, in ants, in mice, in rats, in everything that exists, in everything that is, yes, there's something of God in everything, that's how they think, yes, they think God is the reason why anything exists at all, and that's true, yes, there are skies so beautiful that no painter can match them, and clouds, yes, in their endless movements, always the same and always different, and the sun and the moon and the stars, yes, but there are also corpses, decay, stenches, things that are withered and rotten and foul, and everything visible is just visible, whether it's good or bad, whether it's beautiful or ugly, but whatever is worth anything, what shines, the shining darkness, yes, is the invisible in the visible, whether it's in the most beautiful clouds in the sky or in what dies and rots, because the invisible is present in both what dies and what doesn't die, the invisible is present in both what rots and what doesn't rot, yes, the world is both good and evil, beautiful and ugly, but in everything, yes, even in the worst evil, there is also the opposite, goodness, love, yes, God is invisibly present there too, because God does not exist, He is, and God is in everything that exists, not like something that exists but as something that exists, that has being, they say, I think, even if good and evil, beauty and ugliness are in conflict, the good is always there and the evil is just trying to be there, sort of, I think and I can't think clearly and I understand so little and these thoughts don't go anywhere, I think and I look at Bragi and I see life shining in his eyes and I think I understand so little while it's like these dog eyes looking at me understand everything, but they will rot too, will pass away, the same as all human eyes, they'll rot, they'll pass away, or else flames will consume them, once it would have been on a bonfire and now it's in an oven, for an hour or two or however long it takes now in an oven and then the whole visible human being, the body, is gone, but the invisible human being is still there, because that is never born and so it can never die, I think, yes, the invisible eye is still there after the visible one is gone, because what's inside the eye, inside the person, doesn't go away, because there's God inside the person, it's the kingdom of God there, yes, as stands written, and yes, yes, that's how it is, in there, there inside the person is what will pass away and become one with what is invisible in everything, and it's like it's tied to the visible but it isn't the visible, yes, it's like the invisible inside the visible, and it's what makes the visible exist, but out of everything that exists it's only people in whom the invisible in the visible is so closely related to what's invisibly visible in everything else, but different from everything that exists because it belongs to everything that exists, even though it doesn't exist itself, not in space, not in time, it is not a thing, it's nothing, yes a nothing, I think, and only while the person is alive does it exist in space, in time, and then it leaves time, goes out of space, and then it's united with, yes, with what I call God, and that, yes, invisible thing in the visible, which acts within it, which sustains it, yes, it shows itself in time and space as shining darkness, I think, and it's that and nothing else that my pictures have always tried to show and once my eyes get used to the darkness so that I can see a little, yes, then I can see if there's any of the shining darkness in the picture, and if there isn't then I'll usually always paint a thin coat of white or black, either one coat or a few thin coats of white or black, in some place or another, a glaze, they call it, and then I keep doing it, sometimes with just white, sometimes with just black, but always with a thin coat of oil paint, I keep doing it until the picture shines darkly, I paint with white or black in the darkness and then the darkness starts to shine, yes always, yes, yes, sooner or later the darkness starts to shine, I think, but now I'm so tired that I just want to go lie down, I think, but first I have to look at the picture with the two lines crossing in the middle in the dark, because maybe there's the shining darkness in the picture and maybe there isn't, and I have to see if it's there before I lie down, I think, and I turn off the light and I can't see anything in the room and then I stay standing up to get used to the darkness, until I can see a little, because I do need to be able to see a little even if I'm painting in the dark, of course, and it doesn't take long before my eyes get used to the dark so that I can see a little and then I go stand a few steps back from the easel and I look at the picture, step closer, step back a little, and I see that the black darkness is shining from the picture, from almost the whole picture, the black darkness is shining, yes, I've hardly ever seen the black darkness shine like that from any other picture, I think and I stand there looking at the picture and I think that this picture is done, I won't do anything else to this painting, and I won't sell this painting, I'll put it up in the attic with the other pictures I want to keep for myself and not sell, the pictures I go look at every now and then when it sort of stops for me, when I sort of can't start painting any more, my best pictures, and the ones I think no one else would get anything from anyway and wouldn't want to pay anything for, like this picture with the two lines crossing, and I stand there and I look at the picture, I step a little to one side, I look at the picture from that side, then from the other side, from below, from above, and it's the same however I look at it, yes, the picture has its shining darkness and I think that tomorrow the first thing I'll do when I wake up is take this painting up to the attic and put it in the stack in the storage space with the other pictures I don't want to sell, because this picture, yes, it's finished, and I don't want to sell it, and if someone did want to buy it I'd get paid barely enough money to cover the cost of the stretcher, the canvas, and the oil paint, at least after Beyer takes his cut, because he takes half of whatever a picture sells for, I think and I am so tired so tired, I think and now I'll lie down, I think, but first I have to sign the picture and I turn on the light and I

298 Jon Fosse

pick up a tube of black oil paint and a brush and then I paint *St Andrew's Cross* on the back, on the top of the stretcher, and then in the lower right-hand corner on the painting itself I paint a large A and then I wipe the brush off with turpentine and put it back where it goes and then I open the door to the side room where I sleep and I feel a rush of cold hit me, because I've always slept in cold rooms, but now the open door will let a little warmth into the side room and I turn on the light in there and go back into the main room and turn off the light there and go back into the side room and I get undressed and hang my clothes on a chair and then I'm standing there naked and shivering a lot and then I turn off the light and lie down in the bed and I tuck the duvet around me and I think I'm too tired to go brush my teeth and then I call Bragi and he comes right away and he jumps up onto the bed and crawls in under the duvet and I tuck the duvet well around both of us and Bragi lies down against my side, all the way under the duvet, and I press the duvet against his body and I feel so tired so tired and then I feel Ales lying there next to me in bed and we're holding each other tight and giving each other warmth and I can't think about Ales, not now, and then I say I'm so tired and I want to sleep now and so she should have a good rest and it won't be long before we see each other again, I say, and I feel how close Ales is, because even if it's been many years since she died she is lying next to me in bed and I say I don't want to talk any more now, I can't talk with you tonight, Ales, I say, because then I'll start just missing you so much, so terribly much, I say, and I have my arms around Ales and I hold her and she holds me then I say that it won't be long before we're together again, she and I, and actually we are always together, now too, I think, but now I want to sleep, there's been too much today, and yesterday, I say, and then Ales strokes my hair and then I take the cross on my brown rosary that I got from Ales once and I place the cross down on my belly, and I'm lying there, and I realise I'm so tired, so tired, and I think even so I need to say a Pater Noster before I go to sleep and so I make the sign of the cross and then I take the cross between my thumb and index finger and hold it tight and I say to myself Pater noster Qui es in cælis and I pause after those words and already I'm starting to drift off into the fog of sleep and I say Sanctificetur nomen tuum Adveniat regnum tuum and I think yes Hallowed be thy name Thy kingdom come, yes, God's kingdom must come, your kingdom, come, I think and I breathe deeply in and I say to myself Kyrie and I breathe slowly out and I say eleison and I breathe deeply in and I say to myself Christe and I breathe slowly out and I say eleison and I breathe deeply in and slowly out and then I see Asle standing at the side of the road, with a tin milk canister in his hand, and he sees a white car come driving up, and it's The Bald Man's white car, the man who lives in the big yellow house, on the downhill side of the road by The Dairy, and it's a big car, a wide car, taking up the whole road, and so Asle is standing a good ways back on the hill with a tin milk canister in his hand, because Mother has asked him to go shopping by himself, so he's going to go to The Bakery to buy bread and then to The Dairy to buy milk, and then he'll go to The Co-op Store to buy what Mother has written down in a shopping list, and the person at the cash register in The Co-op Store will write down what it costs in a little notebook, and Asle thought he would go to The Co-op Store first, since it's farthest, and then to The Dairy, and then up the hill to The Bakery, and then he'll go home to Mother with the things, he thought, and Asle sees the white car stop and The Bald Man rolls down his car window and asks Asle if he wants to come with him and take a drive with him and why not, Asle thinks, he could do that, even though both Mother and Father have told both him and Sister that they must never get into a car with The Bald Man and never go into his house if he asks them to, Asle thinks, but he's never entirely understood what's so dangerous about sitting in The Bald Man's car, and it might be nice to take a little drive, Asle thinks and The Bald Man looks at Asle and he's obviously waiting for an answer and it might really be nice to take a drive, Asle thinks as he stands there at the side of the road with the tin milk canister in his hand and he asks where they'd drive to and The Bald Man says he needs to go see a man at Innstranda to discuss something with him and Asle thinks yes sure he could always go for a little drive with The Bald Man, yes, as long as his parents don't find out, he thinks, because he's not that busy, after all, there's no big hurry to buy what Mother said to buy for her, and he thought he'd go to The Co-op Store first so this way The Bald Man can drop him off at The Co-op Store after they come back, Asle thinks

I'm going shopping for my mother, he says

At The Co-op Store? The Bald Man says

Yes, Asle says

And then at The Dairy and The Bakery too, he says

and Asle holds up the tin milk canister and The Bald Man says he can see that Asle is carrying a tin milk canister, isn't he, and it must be his mother who asked him to go shopping for her, he says and Asle says yes it was and The Bald Man says he can get in and sit with him if he feels like coming along on a drive, and then they'll drive on over to Innstranda, because he needs to talk to a man there, The Bald Man says and then he asks Asle to get into the car and The Bald Man rolls up the window and then opens the front door and Asle gets in and sits in the passenger seat with the tin milk canister between his legs and he slams the door shut and then The Bald Man starts driving and he doesn't say anything he just sits there and grips the wheel and looks straight ahead and then Asle sits there in the front of the car and they drive past The Bakery and past The Dairy and past the big yellow house where The Bald Man lives and then they drive past The Co-op Store and around a bend and once they've taken that turn they can see a long way up The Fjord, up Hardangerfjord, all the way to where The Fjord ends, they can see to The Bottom Of The Fjord and then they

drive in along Hardangerfjord towards Innstranda and The Bald Man
says he needs to have a little talk with a man at Innstranda, yes, and
Asle hears that The Bald Man's voice is a little shaky and he thinks it
must be lonely living by yourself in such a big house like The Bald Man
does and then The Bald Man puts a hand on Asle's leg and Asle pushes
his hand away and he thinks why did The Bald Man put his hand on
his leg? and then they drive farther and neither of them says anything
and then The Bald Man puts a hand on his leg again, and he runs his
hand up and down Asle's leg and Asle pushes his hand away and then
he asks The Bald Man why he's doing that and he doesn't answer

You mustn't tell anyone, The Bald Man says

and his voice is shaky and he's looking straight ahead and he keeps
driving

It would be best if you didn't tell anyone that you came for a drive
with me at all, The Bald Man says

Especially don't tell your parents, he says

and The Bald Man says that if Asle comes home with him he has both
soft drinks and hot chocolate, if not today then maybe some other day,
he says and Asle doesn't say anything and then The Bald Man turns
off the country road and drives up a driveway and he stops the car and
turns off the engine and then he gets out and knocks on a door and a
man comes out and he and The Bald Man stand in front of the house
and the man looks at Asle and The Bald Man talks to the man who's
come out of the house and who's looking at Asle, and why did The Bald
Man put his hand on his leg? Asle thinks and then The Bald Man comes
back and gets into the car and he starts the car and he puts his left hand
on the wheel and drives down the driveway and Asle looks a little off
to the side and then The Bald Man puts his hand on Asle's leg and then
puts his hand on his fly and unzips his fly and takes his penis in his
hand and moves his hand up and down on Asle's penis and it tickles
and Asle pushes his hand away and he hears The Bald Man breathing

as if he's out of breath and Asle turns and turns and looks at The Bald Man and sees that he's pulling up and down on his own penis, and The Bald Man's penis is big and long like a stick and Asle looks straight ahead again and he hears The Bald Man groan and then The Bald Man puts his right hand on the steering wheel too and he looks straight ahead and again The Bald Man says that Asle mustn't tell anyone that he's been on a drive with him, he says and Asle sits there with the tin milk canister between his legs and he says he won't tell anyone and he thinks that he'll never tell anyone, never, because this, he knows, is something you don't talk about, you can't tell anyone about something like this, and especially not Mother or Father, Asle thinks and The Bald Man asks shouldn't he do his shopping at The Co-op Store now and Asle says yes he should and The Bald Man says he can give him a few kroner so that he can buy something nice for himself and then Asle can come over to his house someday and get ice cream and hot chocolate, he says, but yes the best thing to do would be to drop Asle off a little before The Co-op Store, he says and Asle says that's fine with him and then they drive out along Hardangerfjord without saying anything

You musn't tell anyone, The Bald Man says

I'll give you a few kroner if you promise not to tell anyone, he says

and Asle says he won't tell anyone and The Bald Man pulls over and stops and then he takes out his wallet and gets three kroner out and he gives them to Asle and he puts them right into his trouser pocket and at the same time he zips up his fly and then The Bald Man says that it would be best if he stops here, because it's not far to The Co-op Store, he says and Asle says yes and he puts his hand down into his pocket and he feels the three kroner he's been given, that's money for three ice creams right there, he thinks and The Bald Man bends down over Asle and his belly is covering Asle's whole body and then The Bald Man opens the door on Asle's side and he gets out of the car and then Asle is standing here holding the tin milk canister and then

The Bald Man drives on and Asle goes to The Co-op Store and I lie
there in bed, and did I doze off? or maybe I've been awake the whole
time? I, Asle, I think and I'm probably too tired to fall asleep, overtired
they call it, I think and then I stroke Bragi's fur as he lies stretched
out next to me, and a dog gives off a good warmth, I think and now
I can't start thinking about how I found Asle there in the snow, almost
covered with snow, I think, because then there'll be no way I can get
to sleep tonight, and I'm so tired, so tired and I see Asle lying there
and his whole body's shaking, jerking up and down and The Doctor is
standing there looking at Asle and he says it's bad and I hold between
my thumb and index finger the brown wooden cross on the rosary I
got from Ales once and I say inside myself Pater noster Qui es in cælis
Sanctificetur nomen tuum Adveniat regnum tuum Fiat voluntas tua
sicut in cælo et in terra Panem nostrum quotidianum da nobis hodie et
dimitte nobis debita nostra sicut et nos dimittimus debitoribus nostris
Et ne nos inducas in tentationem sed libera nos a malo and I move my
thumb and finger to the first bead and I say inside myself Our Father
Who art in heaven Hallowed be thy name Thy kingdom come Thy will
be done on earth as it is in heaven Give us this day our daily bread and
forgive us our trespasses, as we forgive those who trespass against us
And lead us not into temptation, but deliver us from evil and I think
that I want to say a Salve Regina but I haven't managed to make a good
enough Norwegian version of that so I can only say it in Latin, I think
and I move my thumb and finger down again and I hold the cross and
I say inside myself Salve Regina Mater misericordiæ Vita dulcedo et
spes nostra salve Ad te clamamus Exsules filii Hevæ Ad te suspiramus
Gementes et flentes In hac lacrimarum valle Eia ergo Advocata nostra
Illos tuos misericordes oculos ad nos converte Et Iesum benedictum
fructum ventris tui Nobis post hoc exsilium ostende O clemens O pia
O dulcis Virgo Maria and I hold the brown wooden cross between my
thumb and my finger and then I say, again and again, inside myself,

as I breathe in deeply Lord and as I breathe out slowly Jesus and as I breathe in deeply Christ and as I breathe out slowly Have mercy and as I breathe in deeply On me

I Is Another

'Je est un autre.'
Arthur Rimbaud

III

And I see myself standing and looking at the picture with the two lines, a purple line and a brown line, that cross in the middle and I think that it's cold in the main room, and that it's too early to get up, it doesn't matter what time it is, so why did I get up then? I think and I turn off the light in the main room and I go back to the little bedroom and I turn off the light there and I lie back down in bed and I tuck the duvet tight around me and Bragi lies down against me and I think well I got a little sleep last night, even if not that much, and today is Wednesday and it's still early in the morning, or maybe it's still night-time? I think and it was so cold in the main room that I didn't want to get up, I think and I pet Bragi, rub his back, and then I look into the darkness and I see Asle sitting on the swing outside his front door and he's not swinging, he's just sitting there, and he's thinking he can't figure out anything to do and he swings carefully, slowly back and forth a little and then Mother comes out onto the porch and she's angry and Asle doesn't know why she's so angry

Come here! she says

What's the matter, he says

Get over here, Mother says

Okay, Asle says

and he gets off the swing and goes over to Mother who's standing on the porch and she's looking right at him and he walks up the stairs

Yes, he says

There you are, she says

and he doesn't understand why Mother's voice is so angry, what's wrong with her? what has he done now to make her so mad at him? he thinks

Look at this, Mother says

and she opens her hand and Asle sees three one-krone coins lying in the palm of Mother's hand and she stands there holding out her hand with the three krone coins in it and she doesn't say anything and Asle thinks how did Mother find the three kroner? and he'd meant to hide them somewhere clever, yes, he'd meant to put them under one of the flagstones outside the front door but then he forgot, it just disappeared from his mind and now Mother is standing here holding the three coins out to him, and how did she find them anyway? Asle thinks, and then he thinks of course she found them in his pocket because he forgot to take them out of his trousers and hide them

Where did you get these? Mother says

and Asle thinks that he can't say he got them from The Bald Man, that he got them after sitting with him in his car, and he definitely can't say why he got them, no

Answer me, Mother says

and Asle thinks that he definitely can't tell her the truth, that he got them from The Bald Man, and that's because he mustn't tell anyone that he went for a car ride with The Bald Man, and that The Bald Man put his hand on his leg and then took his hand away, at least twice, that The Bald Man did that, he thinks

Where did you get these coins? Mother says

Well, answer me, she says

Don't just stand there with your mouth hanging open, she says

and then she grabs his shoulder and she shakes him and she says he needs to answer her when she asks him something and she's almost shouting

Answer me, Mother says

and he has to say something, anything, Asle thinks

I found them, he says

You found them? Mother says

Where did you find them? she says

Answer me, tell me where you found them, she says

and Asle just stands there and Mother lets go of his shoulder

On the road, he says

On the road you say, Mother says

Yes, on the road, Asle says

Where exactly, she says

Outside The Bakery, he says

You found them outside The Bakery? Mother says

and she says does he expect her to believe that, that he found them, outside The Bakery

You stole them, Mother says

I didn't steal anything, Asle says

Yes you did, you stole them, she says

I did not, he says

You did, she says

and Mother says she checked her own purse because she had a few krone coins in there, yes, she doesn't have that much money but she did have a few krone coins in there, and she didn't remember how many, but it was several, and for all she knows he stole the krone coins from her, she says, but she's not sure, because she has five one-krone coins in her purse now but she can't remember anymore if she'd had more in there, she might well have had more, yes, she could have had eight not just five

Did you steal this money from me? Mother says

and Asle says that he didn't steal the money, he found it, like he said, yes, outside The Bakery

You're lying, Mother says

I'm not lying, Asle says

and then they stand there and neither of them says anything and then Mother says that she was about to do the laundry and she checked in his pockets like usual, what hasn't she found in there, she always finds something, a stone, pine cones, nails, marbles, rope ends, she doesn't even know what all she's found, but never, ever before has she found three shiny new krone coins, and she doesn't know how Asle could have gotten them but it can't have been honestly

I found them, he says

Yes you said that, Mother says

and then they just stand there and then they see Father coming around the corner of The Old House where Grandma and Grandpa live and Mother calls Father and tells him he needs to come here and Father comes up to them just walking slowly

What's going on? he says

and he looks at Mother

Yes, she says

You don't look like everything's all right, Father says

No, Mother says

and it's silent for a moment

So what's wrong? Father says

Look, Mother says

and she holds out her hand with the three krone coins

Three kroner, yes, Father says

Yes, exactly, Mother says

And I need to drop everything for that? he says

But, Mother says

and she breaks off

But? Father says

But I found them in his pocket, Mother says

and she looks at Asle and then Father doesn't say anything and they just stand there

Where did you get them? Father says

and Asle says that he found the coins

He says he found them outside The Bakery, Mother says

Yes well that could happen, Father says

You believe that? Mother says

and Father doesn't say anything

Look in your wallet, see if anything's missing, Mother says

and Father takes out his wallet and he looks inside it and he says he can't remember exactly how many coins he had in there, so there's no way for him to know if someone took any coins out of his wallet, but why would Asle have done that? he doesn't steal, does he? Father says and he looks at Asle

I don't steal, Asle says

I've never stolen anything, he says

No, Father says

and then Father says that he might have found the coins outside The Bakery, but in that case there's someone who lost them, and maybe they've noticed they're gone, Father says, and maybe they'll think that they might have lost the money outside The Bakery, after they'd bought their bread, or maybe they'll think they forgot to get their change at the counter once they'd paid with a five and they were going to get three back, yes, and so maybe they're going to go back to The Baker or The Baker's Wife and ask if maybe they forgot their three kroner or dropped them outside The Bakery and The Baker or The Baker's Wife found them, Father says, and he says that the best thing to do would be for Asle to go to The Baker or The Baker's Wife and give them the coins, in case anyone lost them and dropped by to ask about it, Father says and Mother says she was sure that Asle had stolen the coins and Father says we can't know that for sure can we? he says

I'm glad to hear you say that, Mother says

It's a good thing, that you think like that, she says

and she looks at Asle and she says that if he really found the coins then she owes him an apology, for thinking he must have stolen them, but he might have found them, she hadn't thought of that, she says

You might have found the coins, sure, Mother says

Anyway I owe you an apology, she says

I shouldn't have suspected you of stealing, of being a thief, she says

and Father says they don't need to say anything more about it and Asle you'll go to The Bakery and give the krone coins to whoever comes out when you ring the bell, either The Baker or The Baker's Wife, and you'll say you found them outside The Bakery and then, if no one's come to ask The Baker or The Baker's Wife about some money, well then you can keep them, right? Father says

And that would mean you sure were lucky, finding three krone coins, he says

Yes I should think so, Mother says

I'll run over there right now, Asle says

and then he runs down the driveway and up the country road to The Bakery and he walks in the front door and goes to the counter and picks up the bell sitting there and he shakes it and it rings and The Baker comes out and stands behind the counter and Asle says that he found these three krone coins outside The Bakery, and now, now he really is lying, it's bad and he's ashamed, Asle thinks and he's really stammering and The Baker looks at him and he says yes, yes, he says

Yes, yes, The Baker says

and he looks at Asle

If you found some kroner then you found some kroner, you were lucky, Asle, yes, The Baker says

But maybe someone lost them, maybe they came to buy bread and then lost them? Asle says

I didn't give three kroner in change to anyone recently, at least not that I can remember, The Baker says

So they're yours Asle, he says

You found three kroner and now it's your money, he says

and Asle looks at The Baker

That's what I think, he says

and even if there's a smell of drink coming from The Baker and he's holding onto the counter as he stands there, still he's right when he says that, Asle thinks

and The Baker says that he has a custard roll around, one last one from the ones he baked, and since it'll be time to close up the shop soon, yes, he should have closed up already, Asle should just take the custard roll, since he's such a nice honest boy, The Baker says and he picks up a custard roll, the only one left, and wraps it in grey paper and hands it to Asle and he thinks that this is really really wrong, he is standing here lying and now he's getting a custard roll on top of everything, and it's a good thing he never liked custard rolls with vanilla custard and confectioners' sugar and coconut on top, it's a disgusting combination, that disgusting confectioners' sugar or whatever you call it, and the coconut, that's what that's called, but Sister likes custard rolls, so she can have it, she'll be really happy to get a custard roll, Asle thinks

Thank you, thank you, he says

and The Baker hands Asle the custard roll and he stays there for a moment watching The Baker raise a cup of coffee to his mouth and take a sip and he says today was really your lucky day Asle, finding three krone coins, no, not bad, he says

And then getting a custard roll too, Asle says

Yes well that's nothing, The Baker says

and he goes back through the door behind him, and Asle knows that the door leads to The Baker's and The Baker's Wife's main room, and Asle runs home and he tells them what The Baker said, that he'd found the money so now it was his, and he, The Baker, didn't remember giving anyone three krone coins in change to anyone recently, and definitely not today, Asle says, and The Baker said that Asle found the coins so they were his, that he'd really been very lucky, The Baker said, Asle says and Mother says well then maybe that's how it was and Father says yes The Baker's right about that, now that he thinks about it the coins are his all right, Father says and Mother asks him if he bought a custard roll now that he's come into all this money, she says, and Asle says The Baker gave him the custard roll, it was the last one left and since he'd been honest enough to try to give back the money and since The Baker was about to close up for the day anyway he should just take the one custard roll that was left, that's what The Baker said, Asle says and Mother says that was really nice of The Baker, but Asle never liked custard rolls did he, or rolls at all, not cake either, nothing like that, she says

No he never did, Father says

No, Mother says

and Mother laughs and Father says well he doesn't take after her, she likes custard rolls, if anyone does then she does, he says

And Sister, Asle says

Yes custard rolls are really good, Sister says

and suddenly Asle sees that Sister is standing next to Mother, he hadn't even noticed her, he thinks

But I don't really care too much for them, Father says

and then Mother says that they should eat that custard roll while it's fresh, shouldn't they? she says and Father nods and says he doesn't feel like a custard roll and Asle says he doesn't feel like a custard roll either and then Mother goes to the kitchen and she comes back in with two little plates with half a custard roll on each plate and she gives one plate to Sister who's sitting on the sofa and then Mother sits down next to Sister and then they sit there on the sofa eating the custard roll and Asle stands there and looks at them and he thinks what's the matter with The Bald Man? why did he touch his leg like that? and he tried to move his hand so far up on his leg, and Asle pushed it away, he thinks and Mother called him a thief, and he isn't that, but he did lie, he thinks, today he lied to Mother and to Father and to The Baker and then he got a custard roll from The Baker for being so honest, Asle thinks and he thinks he wants to go outside

I'm going to go out for a bit, Asle says

Don't go away from the house, Mother says

I thought I could maybe go to Per Olav's, Asle says

Yes, you're building a truck together aren't you, Father says

That's what you told us, he says

Yes, Asle says

But don't be late, Mother says

and then Asle goes outside and he thinks that it was nasty of The Bald Man to touch his leg, and eventually he pushed his hand away, several times too, or at least two, he thinks, and he can't tell anyone, because it's embarrassing, it's shameful, and if anyone finds out it'll be even worse so he can't tell anyone, not any grown-ups anyway, because that would be totally wrong, he thinks, now it's just a little wrong and also yes also a little exciting in a way, yes, that too, even if he hadn't liked when The Bald Man touched his leg, Asle thinks and he's never going to take another car ride with The Bald Man again, that's for sure, and he'll never go into his house, that's for sure too, Asle thinks and he goes out to the road and then he sees a tractor coming towards him from far away and it's an old tractor and it's driving slowly and the engine is making an unbelievable noise and Asle keeps walking, and the tractor is far away but coming closer to him, slowly, and now he's about to cross the country road and then soon he'll go up the other driveway and the hill to where Per Olav and his family live and he'll ask if Per Olav is home and then, if Per Olav is home and he feels like it, maybe they can start working on the truck they were building, or something, Asle thinks and he crosses the road and wow that noise from the tractor driving towards him from far away, it's a horrible screeching noise, Asle thinks and he walks up the driveway to where Per Olav and his family live and he knocks and Per Olav opens the door and Asle says hi and asks him if he wants to do something together and Per Olav says yes yes, sure, he has something he wants to show him, he says in a quiet voice and then Per Olav puts on his shoes and a jacket

We need to go somewhere where no one can see us, he says

and Asle nods

And then we can do something we've never done, he says

Maybe we should go down to The Boathouse? Asle says

Your family's Boathouse? Per Olav says

Yes, Asle says

and Per Olav says that's a good idea and then they go down to The Shore, below the country road, and they walk along The Shore and they get to The Boathouse and then they go behind The Boathouse because the back door there, or really it's more like a kind of hatch, is kept shut with just a rusty hook and Asle opens the door and Per Olav goes in and then Asle goes in after him and it's almost totally dark in The Boathouse itself and Asle keeps the hatch half-open and Per Olav takes out a matchbox and strikes a match

You've got a match? Asle says

Yeah, Per Olav says

And more than that, he says

and then Per Olav takes out a pack of cigarettes

Where did you get those? Asle asks

I took them from Grandpa, Per Olav says

He left some on a shelf in his room, he says

and Per Olav lights another match

Have you ever smoked? he says

No, Asle says

You? he says

No, Per Olav says

and then the matches burn out and Per Olav says now he'll open the pack of cigarettes and they'll each have a smoke, but it's strong and Asle needs to not inhale the smoke into his belly because then he'll throw up, he says, yes, someone told him that, that he'd had a cigarette and when he sucked the smoke down into his belly he threw up right away, but it was probably also because he'd sucked all the smoke into his belly, Per Olav says and now their eyes are used to the darkness in The Boathouse so they can see fine and Asle sees Per Olav open the pack of cigarettes and he hands a cigarette to Asle and then Per Olav puts a cigarette in his own mouth and then he says that Asle has to breathe in just when he puts the match to the cigarette and Per Olav lights a match and he puts it to the white cigarette and Asle breathes in and the cigarette lights and Asle holds it away from his mouth between his index finger and middle finger and he sees the glow and he sees smoke rising from the glow and it's beautiful to watch and then he puts the cigarette back between his lips and he sucks in a breath and a little smoke comes into his mouth and he breathes the smoke out and it smells good

The smoke smells good, Asle says

and he takes another drag, and slowly breathes the smoke out, and he sees the smoke vanish into the darkness, and then he takes another drag and he holds the smoke in his mouth a little longer before he breathes it out and Asle realises that he likes smoking, so he's going to be a smoker, Asle thinks, and he takes another drag and he sucks the smoke a little way down into his throat and he hears Per Olav start coughing

Ugh that was horrible, he says

and Per Olav throws the cigarette down on the floor of The Boathouse and steps on it

I felt sick right away, he says

and Asle sucks smoke even farther into his throat and he feels something like a nice tingling in his whole body, yes, it's like he feels calmer and somehow better, he thinks

You like it, you like smoking? Per Olav says

Yeah, Asle says

Really? Per Olav says

Yeah, Asle says

and he says that when he gets older he's definitely for sure going to start smoking and Per Olav says well not him, and then he says Asle can keep the cigarette pack and the matchbox and Asle asks doesn't he want them himself and Per Olav says no way and then Asle says thanks and he puts the cigarette pack and the matchbox in his pocket and then he thinks that the best place to hide the cigarette pack and matches is probably in The Boathouse, there are some beams running crosswise near the roof with various nets hanging on them and some of the nets are so rotted through that they fall apart as soon as you touch them and Asle thinks he can put the pack of cigarettes and matchbox up on one of those beams, one with a junky old net on it, he thinks and then he climbs up on a couple of fish crates and puts the pack of cigarettes and matchbox up on a beam

I think I'll go home, I feel kind of sick, Per Olav says

and Asle nods and then Per Olav leaves and Asle leaves and he puts the hook back in place and then they go up the path and when they get up to the road they say see you and then Per Olav goes farther up the way and Asle crosses the road and then walks up his driveway and he goes inside and hangs up his jacket in the hall and takes off his shoes and then Mother comes over to him and she says you smell like smoke

Have you been smoking? she says

Are you big enough to smoke now? she says

Breathe on me, she says

and he breathes on her and she asks how Asle got cigarettes? and who did he get them from? and he just says he got them from someone, and she asks who he got them from? and Asle says that he'll never tell her, never in his whole life, not even if she kills him, he says and then he sees Mother go up the stairs and I lie there in bed and isn't that the sound from an engine I hear, and a grinding noise? a screeching noise? yes it is,

I can hear a tractor engine far away making a loud noise and I hear a plough scraping and it's cold where I am in bed under the duvet, so I probably need to just get up, I have to get up now, I think and I stand up and I turn on the light in the bedroom and I see my clothes lying there on the chair and I get dressed fast and the clothes are cold and I go into the main room and I turn on the light there and it's cold in the main room and I think that I should have started a fire in the stove and not just stood there peering into the nothingness, but I'd rather go back into the bedroom and lie down in bed again for a bit, yes, the way Bragi's smart enough to be doing, I think, because it's still early in the morning, I think, but I don't want to know what time it is, I think and wow is that tractor making a racket, I think and I look at the picture where the two lines cross, there on the easel in front of me, and I see that I've signed the picture with a big A in the lower right-hand corner which means that I think the picture is done whether it is or not, I think and I look at those two lines crossing, one purple and one brown and I see Asle running downstairs into his basement at home, they were having potato dumplings for dinner and Mother asked him to go get a bottle of juice and Asle pitter-pattered on his little feet down to the basement and went into the pantry where the glass jars of preserved plums and apples and pears were, and lots of bottles of juice, because in the autumn Mother makes juice from all the gooseberries and redcurrants they have, and there's a bin full of potatoes, and Asle takes a juice bottle and runs outside, and no, no, I can't think about that, I think and suddenly Ales is right next to me and she puts a hand on my back and she just stands there next to me and it's so good to feel her hand on my back, I think and I see Asle sitting in a car and a man is holding a towel around his wrist and they're driving to see The Doctor and Asle is somewhere outside himself and he looks back at where he lives, at The New House and The Old House, and he thinks that this is the last time he's ever going to see the house and everything is shimmering slightly, in a mysterious light that he's part of and that's much bigger than him, yes, it's everything that exists, and from this light, yes, that's like it's put together out of tiny dots of flickering yellow, yes it's like a cloud of yellow dust and from that cloud of shimmering yellow he sees himself sitting there in the car with his bleeding hand because Asle slipped on the ice and smashed the juice bottle and a piece of glass cut the artery in his wrist, and Asle feels very weak, and he is in the shimmering cloud of glinting shining transparent yellow dust and he's not scared, he feels something like happiness, like a great peace, no, there's no word for what and how he feels, how he's seeing, Asle thinks and I look at the picture there in front of me and Ales is stroking my back, up and down, and I see Asle sitting there in the car with his bleeding hand and Ales rubs and rubs my back and it's so soothing and good to feel her hands, I think and I see Asle sitting there with a bleeding hand and I don't want to think about that any more, it's better to put it in my pictures as best I can, I think, and it's in the painting with the two crossing lines too, I think and then I realise that Ales has taken her hand off me and she's gone and I just stand there and look at the picture even though it's cold in the room and I should light a fire in the stove and I see Asle standing outside the front door at home and looking at Father who is looking almost without believing it at a brand new car, it's grey, and it looks like Father can hardly dare to touch the car, much less sit in it, and Mother is standing there and she says it's amazing, now they have their own car too, she says, yes it's hard to believe, but it's true, she says and Father says that it's not exactly their car yet, it's the bank that owns the car, he says and Mother says well still it's their car, and Father says yes yes and then he says look, look down at the bus stop, there's The Bald Man, he doesn't take buses very often, just when he needs to go to Bjørgvin, Father says and Asle looks down at The Bald Man and it's so cold in the room, I need to light a fire in the stove, I think, but what I really want most to do is go lie down and tuck myself nice and tight under the covers with Bragi, I think, and it would be fine for me to go lie back down in bed, warm up a little, why not, I think, and I go back into the bedroom and lie down on the bed fully clothed and Bragi is lying there and he lies down right next to me and I spread the covers around us well and I feel Ales lying down right next to me, there's Bragi on one side and Ales on the other side, and she's warm and comforting, and I think it was good to come back to bed and warm up under the covers instead of standing there in the cold main room, I think and Ales asks me if I'm doing all right and I say everything's fine, everything's the same as usual with me, yes, as she already knows, I say and Ales doesn't say anything and then I just lie there and I think that I should have turned off the lights, in the main room and in the bedroom, but that's all right, I think and I hear Ales say that we are always together, the two of us, and I stare straight ahead and I see Asle and some other kids sitting under an overhanging rock, in a kind of shallow mountain cave, there's alpine blue sow-thistle there, it's still raining out, and there are three boys and three girls and they've climbed a little way up from the country road, it's not so far up to the overhanging rock, and then they went under it and there are tallow candles they've left there and a box of matches and they light the candles and it's pretty cold so they sit close together and Asle puts his arms around the waist of the girl sitting next to him and she leans against him and she puts a hand on his leg and then Asle feels her mouth on his cheek and then she finds his mouth and they kiss and she opens her mouth and he opens his and then they touch the tips of their tongues together and their mouths kind of suck together and Asle feels his dick getting hard and he puts a hand on one of her breasts and it's small, but it is a breast, and her breathing starts to get faster and he strokes her breast, over her pullover, and then she takes his hand and puts it under her pullover and brings it up to her breast and then Asle holds her breast in his hand and it fits into his grip and then he feels that her nipple is hard and he takes the nipple between his thumb and finger and she's breathing even faster and then she moves her hand from his leg and puts it on his trousers where his stiff dick is and she keeps her hand there and then she gently moves the palm of her Hand back and forth and the whole time their mouths are stuck fast to each other and then Per Olav says no look at those two and they let go of each other and Per Olav says he didn't know they were a couple but he knows it now, Per Olav says and I look straight ahead and I realise that Ales is gone now and I think is it still early in the morning? or maybe it's still night even? but I don't want to look what time it is, I think, and I should have slept more, I feel sleepy, I think, and I retuck the covers around me and Bragi but it is morning already because I hear the racket from the engine in the old tractor, and a scraping noise, like from a plough, or is that just something I'm imagining? no I hear it, a screeching noise, I think and I think that it was a good thing I drove back to Bjørgvin and that I found Asle there in the snow, because it's so cold now he really could have frozen to death, I think, but how is he doing? they took him straight from The Clinic to The Hospital and I need to drive to The Hospital to see him today, I think, and I need to drive the paintings down to Bjørgvin today and bring them to The Beyer Gallery, I haven't made any plans with Beyer about that but even if he isn't there I can take the pictures in and put them in the room Beyer calls The Bank, because the gallery is open and there's always some girl or another there, if Beyer isn't there himself, and it's always a new girl, a student, Beyer says, it's a student who wants to make a little money, he says, but they never stay long, there's always a new face to see there, so he probably pays them badly, he must, and so he always has to get a new girl, I think, because Beyer, well, he doesn't throw money around, and that's why he's become the well-off man that he is, I think and then I hear the racket from the old tractor disappear and I think that in that case Åsleik must be here already, he's parked the tractor out in front on the stoop, because he was supposed to come over today, but I didn't think he'd come so early,

I think, and then I hear a knock at the door and I think that if I don't open the door Åsleik will just come inside and I get to my feet and it's so cold in the bedroom that I wish I could just stay lying in bed all day, I think and I'm so cold I start to shake my arms to warm up and Bragi is lying there in the bed, under the covers, and he looks at me with surprised eyes

You just stay right there, I say

Just stay where it's nice and warm, I say

and I hear footsteps and I hear a door open and I go into the main room and there's Åsleik standing and looking at the painting of the two lines crossing, in warm clothes and a fur hat and boots, he's standing and looking at the picture and he says boy I certainly get up late, it's been light out for a long time, he says

You didn't get up? he says

Yes I did, I say

And then you just lay back down, he says

Yeah, I say

Anyway it's ten o'clock, he says

Yeah, I say

and I think that I never would have guessed it was so late

You're usually up at five or six, he says

Is something wrong? he says

No, I say

You must have just been especially tired, he says

Yes, that's to be expected, he says

and he says that driving down to Bjørgvin and back the same day and then driving there again the same day, and in such conditions, snow and blizzards and slick roads, the way I did the day before yesterday, and then driving from Bjørgvin back to Dylgja again yesterday, yes, that would take a lot out of anyone, he himself would barely come out alive, Åsleik says and then he says that it's so cold in my living room that it's warmer outside and he'll just light another fire in the stove then, like he had to do yesterday, and the day before too, it really seems to have turned into his job now hasn't it, pretty much, he says, but maybe I could at least make some coffee? Åsleik says and I say yes

No, I shouldn't have stayed in bed all morning, I say

I don't think I've done that for years, I say

No well I can't remember the last time I did anyway, Åsleik says

and then he goes over to the stove and he puts the wood chips and kindling and a log in and he lights the kindling and then Åsleik stands there and looks in at the wood and says that's good dry kindling so it'll catch in a second, he says, and who do I have to thank for that kindling? and wood? yes, for being about to have a nice warm room? it's him, yes, sure is, Åsleik says and I don't say anything because I've heard this so many times before, so many, I think and Åsleik says he's here to get something in return for the wood chips, kindling, and logs, the driest birchwood, he says, and that, that, as I know he wants a painting to give to Sister for Christmas, and every year before he's always chosen one of the small paintings but yesterday we agreed that this year he should pick one of the big paintings, or bigger ones, none of the pictures I paint are really all that big, Åsleik says and he says now he wants to choose one before I drive to Bjørgvin and deliver the pictures to The Beyer Gallery, and that's why he dropped by so early, or earlyish, because if he didn't misunderstand me I was planing to drive back to Bjørgvin again today with the paintings and take them to Beyer, who I had such trust in, such faith in, even though he, like a lot of other Bjørgvinners, was just out for money, to make money, money money money, buying low and selling high, that was the only thing people in Bjørgvin cared about, whether they bought and sold fish or paintings, yes, that's how they'd always been and that's how they still were, Åsleik says and I've heard him say this so many times before, obviously, because neither Åsleik nor I ever have that much new to say to each other and that's why we always talk about the same things, because you have to say something

Yes it's burning well in the stove now, Åsleik says

and he stands there and looks at the logs

I'll let it burn a little with the hatch open, then I'll put another log in, he says

Because damn it was cold in your room, he says

But it won't be long now before it's nice and warm, he says

At least warm enough to be in the room without a coat and hat and boots on, he says

and I go over to the stove and stand there and stretch my arms out above the stove and it's nice to feel the warmth coming up to my hands, my arms, my whole body, I think and Åsleik stands next to me

Now it's warming up the room, he says

Yes, I say

But what did you do with the dog? Åsleik says

He's sleeping, I say

In the bed in your bedroom? he says

Yes, I say

and then we stand there silent

Bragi, that was his name, right? Åsleik says

Yes, I say

and again it's quiet

You've talked about getting a dog so many times, now you've finally done it, he says

and I don't answer and then Åsleik goes over to the easel where the picture with the two intersecting lines is and he says St Andrew's Cross, yes, of course he says that, I think, St Andrew's Cross he says again and he emphasises the term, like the words are so important, it's like he's saying he can do more than just fish and clear roads you know, like that, wait don't go over there, I think and then Åsleik says that that's the picture he wants even if it's isn't finished, he says and I freeze for a second, because I want to keep that picture myself, I don't want to sell it, so I don't want to give it to Åsleik either no

But it's not done, I say

Doesn't matter, he says

It's good the way it is, he says

But don't you want to look at the other pictures first, the ones in the stack there, the big ones? I say

and I point at the stack leaning solidly against the wall next to the kitchen door

I've found the one I want, Åsleik says

But I'm not done with that picture, I say

Doesn't matter, he says

But I want to finish it, I say

Yes yes, but it's finished in a way the way it is, he says

And you signed it, he says

And it wasn't signed the last time I saw it, he says

Doesn't that mean you've decided you're done with it? he says

and I don't say anything and I think you can't pull a fast one on him so easily can you, on Åsleik, he always picks the best picture to give to Sister, often, yes, well, usually, it's been a painting I've wondered if I wanted to keep for myself, in the collection I have upstairs in the crates, but that would be just the painting that Åsleik would say and think and feel the same way about, the one I wanted to keep

But at least take a look at the other finished paintings, I say

Yes, at the big ones, I say

and I stand there and point at the stack of big paintings leaning against the wall next to the kitchen door and Åsleik says he will, yes, he'll do that if I come and bring him a steaming hot cup of coffee soon, yes, if I put the pot of coffee on while he looks through the pictures, he says and then Åsleik goes over to the stack of pictures and I go out to the kitchen and I turn on the light and I put the coffeepot on and then I look outside and wow it snowed a lot last night, my car is totally snowed in, so it certainly is good that Åsleik cleared the road, I think, and do I really need to drive the pictures into Bjørgvin today? after it's snowed so much, and with the roads so slippery? and why in the world didn't I just take them with me the day before yesterday? I can't understand why I didn't think of it the day before yesterday, I think, but the first time I drove to Bjørgvin was to go shopping, and the second time was because I wanted to check in on Asle, and actually that's really why I want to drive to Bjørgvin today too, because I want to go see Asle in The Hospital, and maybe buy him something or bring him whatever he needs from home, that's mostly why, I think and I look out at the white snow and I see Asle lying there in bed and there are all kinds of tubes and things attached to his body that are hanging down from a metal stand and he's lying there asleep and his body is shaking up and down, his body is constantly quivering and Asle wakes up and he opens his eyes and he looks to the side and he sees that three other people are lying in three other beds in the room he's in

So, you're awake, one of them says

and Asle doesn't answer

You're awake now, you've been asleep a long time, I don't know how you could sleep through that noise from the street, a tractor or something, he says

and Asle doesn't answer, he just closes his eyes again, and then he's shaking even harder and then a doctor and a male nurse come in and The Doctor says someone needs to be watching him at all times, so he needs to be transferred, and Asle just lies there and he doesn't know quite where he is or isn't and everything's confusing and he's shaking and then two men come and take the bed and the metal stand and they wheel Asle out into the hall and he closes his eyes and his whole body's shaking, jolting up and down, and then they wheel him into a lift and I stand there in the kitchen and look out at the snow and I see them wheel Asle down a corridor and then they open a door to a room and there's a bed in there and a man is lying in the bed and his hair is all grey and his face is all grey and a man is sitting next to the bed half-asleep and he's watching over the people lying there because they're so sick, I think and I watch them wheel Asle's bed in and put it against the wall across from the other bed and the man sitting in the chair stands up and looks at something hanging on Asle's bed and then he sits back down and after a moment he gets up and goes over to the bed and prods Asle on the shoulder

Asle, he says

Yes, Asle says

and then I see the man who prodded Asle's shoulder, who's keeping watch in a way, sit back down on his chair and I look and look at the snow and I think I have to drive the paintings into Bjørgvin today and then go see Asle in The Hospital, because he's really sick, I think and I turn around and see that the coffee is ready and I pour out two mugs of coffee and then go back into the main room and I see that Åsleik has set up four or five of the big paintings along the wall where the kitchen door is and now he's standing there looking at each one and I go over and hand him a mug and he says thanks

You've been painting a lot of good paintings recently, haven't you, he says

Thank you, I say

and then we both stand there, sipping our coffee, and then I go and stand and look at the picture with the two lines crossing and Åsleik says that that's the picture he wants, the one I'm looking at, but if I really want to keep it then there are several other very good paintings too, Åsleik says, and he's already picked out one, he says and he asks me if I can guess which one it is and I say I can try and I walk over to a picture of something that might be a kind of boat gliding on the sky, and the picture is brown and purple, a little like heather, the same as a lot of my paintings, but what really makes the picture shine is the thin layer of white paint I painted in a few places after I looked at the picture in the dark, it's these clear movements, it's this white and a couple of black movements that make the picture shine, yes, or give off a stronger light at least, yes, in its own way, and now that I look at this painting again I think that this is another one I'd like to keep for myself actually, but if I had to choose I'd rather keep the one of the two lines crossing and Åsleik asks if I remember what I called that picture

Because you're good at titling your pictures, he says

A picture needs a good name, I say

Yes I can see that, Åsleik says

and then we stand there silent and I think that I've always given my pictures names, and not every painter does that but I always do, because after I've decided I'm done with a picture the last thing I paint is a big A in thick black oil paint in the lower right corner of the picture itself, so that it's easy to see that there's an A there, and on the top edge of the stretcher I paint the picture's title, also in thick black oil paint, and now Åsleik asks me what the painting he wants is called and I think I remember, I'm not totally sure but I think it's called *Silent Boat*, that's something you might call a picture, I think, actually it's an awful title, I don't know what I could have been thinking calling it that, I think, and I say that I think the picture is called *Silent Boat* but he can just look for himself, I say and Åsleik says that he's already done that of course and then he goes and picks up the painting and turns it around and on the top edge of the stretcher, in the middle, it says *Silent Boat* in thick black oil paint

You always remember, Åsleik says

I'll take this picture, he says

Sure, I say

and then Åsleik puts the picture back down on the floor but leaning against the easel now and then he steps back a little to look at it and

I go with him and I too can see that it's a good picture, maybe one of the best ones I've painted in a long time, but if Åsleik wants it to give to Sister then he can have it, that's perfectly fine, I think, but the picture on the easel itself that's been given the title St Andrew's Cross I absolutely won't let him have, I want to keep it myself, and Åsleik must have realised that, that he couldn't have it, I think and then I go over to the picture and I see that I've already signed it with an A in the lower right corner and then I turn the picture around and I see that I've painted St Andrew's Cross on the top part of the stretcher and I think that I must have done that yesterday, no, my memory is just terrible, I can't remember things from midnight till noon, as they say, I think

St Andrew's Cross, I say

Yes that was really the only thing you could call that picture, Åsleik says

and then luckily he doesn't say St Andrew's Cross several times

You've finished that picture? Åsleik says

So you were trying to trick me? he says

Yes, I probably was, actually, to tell you the truth, I say

and Åsleik says that he can tell that that painting is finished, even if it looks unfinished it's still finished, of course it is, he says and then we drink our coffee and Åsleik says now do I really want to drive down to Bjørgvin again today, with all the snow we've had? and he says that he doesn't understand me, two days ago I drove to and from Bjørgvin, and then I even drove back again the same day, all without bringing my pictures to The Beyer Gallery, and now I want to drive back to Bjørgvin again today, it's almost too much, he says and I think I need to go and see Asle in The Hospital but I don't want to say anything to Åsleik about that

I'll take the paintings in today, get it out of the way, I say

It's not only because of the pictures that you want to drive to Bjørgvin, is it? Åsleik says

No maybe not, I say

You probably want to go to mass, he says

and I can hear scoffing in his voice, because it's true that I drive to Bjørgvin every now and then, and in the summertime usually every Sunday, to go to mass at St Paul's Church

You Papist, Åsleik says

and I think that he'll never stop with this word, never stop saying that, it's probably another word that he taught himself and that he's proud of knowing, Papist, St Andrew's Cross, he kind of shows off and puffs himself up with words like that

Papist, yes, he says

and I think that it would be a good idea to go to mass, but I hadn't thought of that, really I was only thinking I should go and see Asle in The Hospital and at the same time take these paintings in as soon as I can, the paintings I kind of have to deliver to Beyer

Or is it because of a woman? Åsleik says

and he says how dumb he was not to think of that right off, he says

and I think that I don't really like Åsleik, he can be so annoying, but I don't let it show and I let all the foolishness just vanish into thin air in a way, I think

No, I say

No no, he says

and we stand there without saying anything

But you probably were thinking of going to mass again soon? he says

and I say yes maybe and Åsleik says didn't I go to mass yesterday when I was in Bjørgvin shopping? and I say I didn't go to mass yesterday and Åsleik says well that's strange, I usually always go to mass, every time I'm in Bjørgvin, he says and I have to say something and then I say I'll just start getting the paintings ready then and put them in the back of the car

You wrap them in blankets, Åsleik says

Yes, always, I say

Those blankets have seen a lot of use, he says

Yes, I've had them for many years, I say

and then I stand there and hope that Åsleik doesn't ask me where I got the blankets, and that I don't have to tell him yet again that I got them at The Second-Hand Shop in Sailor's Cove, I didn't get them all at once, but one this time, one another time, whenever I was in The Second-Hand Shop I would look for blankets and if I didn't see any I'd ask if they had any blankets and then they'd always ask what I meant and I'd say wool blankets and sometimes they'd have one or two blankets in the back, sometimes not, but after a while I'd bought quite a collection and now there was a big pile of blankets on the floor in a corner of the attic room where I keep everything I need for painting, tubes of oil paint, canvas, and of course the boards for making stretchers from, getting nice and dry, I think and Åsleik says he can help me pack up the pictures and carry them out to the car and I say thanks and then he hands me his mug and he says thanks for the coffee and I see that I've only drunk a little of my coffee, and that's how it is every morning, I fill up a mug of coffee and then only drink a little, I think and then I go to the kitchen and put the mugs in the sink and then I go up to the attic and I put my arms in a kind of hug around the whole heap of blankets lying tossed in a corner and I go downstairs and dump the pile on the floor in front of the paintings and I see that Åsleik is standing and looking at the picture he chose as a Christmas present for Sister that's now standing on the floor leaning against the easel and then he looks at me

Yes so that's the picture I want, he says

It's a deal, I say

and then I take a blanket and one picture from the stack of finished big pictures and I wrap it up well in the blanket and I put in on the floor and then Åsleik takes a blanket and a picture and wraps it up and puts it on top of the one I put on the floor and we keep going like that wrapping up painting after painting and it's Åsleik who takes the last painting and then all the big paintings are on the floor in a neat stack and then I take a blanket and wrap up one of the small paintings and Åsleik does the same thing and there are only four small paintings in all

There were thirteen paintings in all, Åsleik says

Yes, I say

That's an unlucky number, he says

It can be either lucky or unlucky, at least for me, I say

and Åsleik says he's never heard that before and I say that that's how it is for me anyway

Yes I guess it might be, he says

and then Åsleik says he can't understand why I want to drive back to Bjørgvin again today, and I say I've already told him, I'm going to take the pictures to The Beyer Gallery, get it over with, I say and Åsleik says there must be some other reason and I say there might be and Åsleik says that I should dress warm, yes, I should put on my coat, and then we'll need to carry the pictures out to my car, he says and I nod and then it's silent

You've always gone and done whatever you wanted to do, Asle, Åsleik says

and he wraps the picture he chose up in a blanket and puts it back down leaning against the easel

You'll get the blanket back after I've given the picture to Sister, same as always, he says

and I say yes it'll be the same as usual and I say I want to go start the car and turn on the heat and brush off all the snow of course and Åsleik says he can help me with that and then I put on my black velvet jacket and I go out into the hall and put on my black coat and a scarf and then I slip into my shoes and then I go out and start the car, and it starts at the first try like always, and then I open the back and find the snow brush and then I brush off the car and then we start carrying the pictures I'm going to drive down to The Beyer Gallery out to the car and we put them down carefully in the back and after we've done that Åsleik says well then he'll get the picture he's planning to give Sister for Christmas and I see Åsleik go into the house and I shut the back of the car and I see Åsleik come out onto the stoop and he stands there with the picture under his arm and I go back inside my good old house and go into the main room and I see my brown leather bag hanging on its hook, between the pile of small paintings and the pile of big paintings, the pictures I'm not done with yet, and I put the shoulder bag on and then I stop and I look at the picture with the two lines crossing, yes, St Andrew's Cross as it's called, and there's a lot in that picture, I think and I think that now I need to go, because Åsleik is waiting, and I go into the little side room and I turn out the light and I go into the main room and I turn off the light there and I go out to the kitchen and I see that there's still a little water in Bragi's bowl so I fill it and then I cut a slice of bread and break it into chunks and put them down in the other bowl even though there's still a lot of bread there from before and I think that Bragi is still lying asleep in my bed so I guess he can stay here at home, I think and I turn off the light in the kitchen and I go out to the hall and I turn off the light there and then I open the front door and go outside and I see Åsleik still standing where he was before on the stoop with the picture wrapped in a blanket under his arm

That took a while, he says

Yes, I say

What were you doing in there? he says

and I don't answer

I almost got tired of waiting, he says

I guess you had to go to the bathroom and had trouble getting it out? he says

Yes that's right, I say

But here you are at last, Åsleik says

No, I know you, I know what you were doing, he says

All right, what? I say

You were looking at the picture with the two lines, St Andrew's Cross, he says

and I nod and Åsleik says that he's always been able to take the picture he wanted to give as a present to Sister, every time before, but then again he's never asked for a big painting before, Åsleik says and then he says that this isn't exactly weather to stand around outside in, so he'll go sit in the tractor, he says, and we'll get driving, him first, so that at least the driveway will be all clear, and the country road until the turn-off to his farm, and I'll drive after him and he hopes I have a good drive to Bjørgvin and drive carefully since the roads might still be slippery in some places, because there might be ice under the new snow, he says and I say that I always do drive carefully and Åsleik says he knows that, of course I drive carefully, he says and we'll see each other soon, he says and I say it's just a day trip, I'll drive home after I've dropped off the paintings, I say

You always have a show not long before Christmas, he says

Yes, I say

Because it's easier to sell paintings then, of course, yes, during Advent, he says

and I say that's true, at least Beyer says so, and my pictures especially are easiest to sell then, maybe Beyer means that they're good to give as Christmas presents but he also thinks that it's best to open an exhibition not too long before Christmas, I say and Åsleik says that that's what he thought and then he climbs up into the cabin of the tractor and starts the engine and it makes a horrible noise, that screeching, it's hard to believe an engine can make a sound that bad, I think and I go sit in my car and I put the brown leather bag on the passenger seat and the car has warmed up nicely and I turn the heat down a little and then

Åsleik looks back at me and then forward again and then the tractor goes around the corner of the house and I drive after him and Åsleik drives the tractor out onto the country road and I follow him and it certainly has snowed a lot, there must be four inches on the ground, but it's not snowing now, I think and I drive ten or twenty feet behind Åsleik, he's driving slowly and steadily towards his farm, and it always takes a while to get there, and the road twists and turns a lot too, I think and I drive a good distance behind him and then Åsleik turns off and he stops the tractor and gets out and I stop the car and roll down the window

You drive carefully, now, he says

Yes, I will, slow and safe, I say

and I add that once I get to Instefjord there'll be good roads all the way to Bjørgvin, because they always clear those roads, I say and Åsleik says that I have good tires on now, newish studded tires, plus I had enough money to buy a car with four-wheel drive and so that's what I did, and with good studded tires and four-wheel drive my car or van is practically a tractor, he says and I answer that I've had enough problems driving in winter conditions in my life, experience eventually taught me something, I say and Åsleik says that's all right then and then we each raise a hand to say goodbye and then I drive slowly on, and now it's my car that's leaving tracks in the snow, in front of me I see nothing but white snow, and then luckily there are all these snow poles with reflectors on them set up to mark where the edge of the road is, without them it would be easy to end up off the road, yes, it would be impossible not to, I think and I drive slowly, the way I always do, first I'll be on the small roads along Sygne Fjord to Instefjord, and they're not cleared, but then, after I get to Instefjord and get on the main road to Bjørgvin, it'll be easier, because those roads will have been cleared, I think and I look at the white road and I see Asle standing in front of Mother and he's thinking that he can't stand going to that damn school anymore, the teachers are unbearable, why on earth should he keep going? and luckily he's almost done with school, he thinks, and if he didn't have so little mandatory schooling left he'd have just quit today, Asle thinks, but as it is he has to just try to stick it out, and he thinks that he still wants to drop out, even if he'll be done soon, he thinks and he tells Mother he wants to stop going to school

Are you out of your mind? she says

Drop out of school? she says

Children have to stay in school, she says

If you drop out they'll come and take you away to a school for delinquent boys, and it's strict there, and the school's on an island so no one can run away, she says

And anyway you're almost done, she says

and Asle thinks can that really be true, that he might get sent to an island just because he doesn't like going to school? no, he didn't know that, Asle thinks, but he doesn't really believe it, no more than he believes the other things Mother says, neither the stuff about Jesus and God nor that you can get sent to an island for dropping out of school, but he doesn't give a damn, if he wants to stop going to school he'll stop going, Asle thinks, but there's one thing, he's heard that to get into The Art School in Bjørgvin, and he's gradually started thinking that maybe he could go there, if he gets in, anyway to get into The Art School in Bjørgvin you need to have gone to The Academic High School, and if it wasn't for that he'd have stopped going to school already, then and there, no doubt about it, Asle thinks, but he's not going to do that, he's not going to drop out of school, it was just something he said because Mother gets so angry when he says it, no, it's not that he has any desire to go to The Academic High School but it's something he has to do, and he's so clumsy that there's hardly anything he can do, so what's going to become of him? as Father always says, Asle thinks and I look at the white road in front of me and I drive slowly out along Sygne Fjord and

I see Father standing in front of Asle and he says you're a good kid Asle but what's going to become of you? he says

I don't know, Asle says

But you need to get an education, you have to be something when you grow up, Father says

and Asle says that the only thing he's good at is drawing and painting and then Mother says well then he's probably going to become an artist, even if there are hardly any jobs for artists, still there must be some work for people who know how to draw, at the newspapers for instance, newspapers have a lot of drawings, and there are a lot of drawings in advertisements, someone has to draw them, so it must be possible to make a living by drawing and painting, Mother says, but you can't get into The Art School unless you go to The Academic High School, she says and Father says that true, to get into The Art School you need to have graduated from The Academic High School and Asle thinks that he doesn't understand why someone has to learn not just adding and multiplying but also what they call mathematics to be a painter

Drawing and painting aren't the same thing as doing maths, Asle says

No, no, Father says

and Mother says she doesn't understand why it's like that either, but the people in charge have decided that you have to go to The Academic High School and then you can go to The Art School, if you get admitted, she says and Asle says that he's no good at anything but drawing and painting, okay well he can read, obviously, and he likes to read sometimes, and he even thinks he can write pretty well too, well enough, but the Norwegian teachers at his school don't think so, so he has bad marks in writing, yes, same as in all the other subjects, he says

You never do your homework, Mother says

That's true, Asle says

And now you're sorry, she says

Yes, yes, Father says

and Mother says that he'll need to do something in the future, he can't just sit at home and paint, she says and Asle doesn't say anything

And if you start at The Academic High School you'll need to move into an apartment, Mother says

and Asle thinks that it sounds like Mother's glad he'll be moving out, and that makes sense, he thinks, he is sure looking forward to getting out, leaving home, getting away from Mother and her constant nagging and whining about how he needs to cut his hair or needs to paint pictures that people can understand, where you can see what it's a picture of, or about how he needs to do his homework, she nags him about absolutely everything

I want to go to The Art School, Asle says

But then you need to paint like you used to, so that it looks like something, Mother says

Yes, Father says

Not those pictures that don't look like anything at all, she says

If you keep painting those you'll never get into The Art School, no matter how much high school you've had, she says

Yes, Father says

and I look at the white road and I think that I still haven't driven that far along Sygne Fjord so it's still a long way to Instefjord, I think and I see Father standing there and he says he can call The Academic High School right now and find out what Asle's chances are for getting in and Father goes out to the hall and Asle can hear him talking on the phone and then Father comes back in

It'll be fine, he says

There's a spot for you at The Academic High School, he says

On what they call the Modern Languages track, he says

and Asle hears what Father's saying and he thinks that's good isn't it? because what else could he have tried to do when he grows up? he thinks

And so you'll need to get a room in Aga, Mother says

Yes, Father says

But there are lots of people from Barmen who've gone to The Academic High School in Aga and rented a room there, so I'm sure it'll work out, he says

I'll put an ad seeking a room in *The Hardanger Times*, Father says

and Asle says he'd be grateful if Father did that and I look at the white road and I drive toward Instefjord, and it'll be good to get there, because then I'll be on the main road that's been cleared already and then I can start driving south to Bjørgvin, I think, and I don't think that I've ever, in all the years I've lived in Dylgja, driven to Bjørgvin so many times so close together, I think, and I look at the white road and I see Father standing there and he's saying that an older woman has called and said that she has a room I can rent, it sounds like it's a hayloft that used to be a shoemaker's workshop, a room up in the attic, and the shower and toilet are downstairs, on the ground floor, she said, Father says and he says that it sounded good, all things considered, and the rent wasn't so bad, he says, so he agreed on the spot, he says and they arranged for Asle to move in when The Academic High School starts, Father says and Asle says that's great, all things considered, and he thinks it's good he'll be living in a house by himself, not in a room in a house where other people live, Asle thinks and he sees Mother stand there looking at him

But you've painted pictures of so many people's houses and you've never painted your own, she says

Don't you think you should do that before you move out? she says

That's true you haven't, Father says

and Asle thinks that now he'll have to paint The New House and The Old House too, and The Barn and The Shed and all the fruit trees and

The Boathouse and The Dock and The Rowboat and The Shore and The Fjord and everything, can he really bring himself to do all that? he thinks

No you haven't, she says

You've painted pictures of almost every single house in the whole town, and some in Stranda too, but never your own, she says

Yes well then I guess I should paint the farm then, Asle says

With everything, he says

Yes, The Old House, The New House, The Barn and The Shed and The Boathouse and The Dock and The Rowboat, The Fjord too, not leave anything out, he says

I'm really looking forward to seeing that picture, Mother says

and she says that she's been thinking about it for a long time but she hasn't brought herself to ask him about it, because he'd been having a hard time since, Mother says and she breaks off and then there's a long silence and Asle thinks why did Mother have to remind him about Sister again, about how she was gone so suddenly, how she just died, was just lying there dead in her bed one morning, yes, the thought of his sister Alida just lying there and dead he can't take it

Anyway, Mother says

and Asle notices that Mother is about to start crying

I have a good photo of the farm you can paint from, she says

and Asle thinks that it's too much, that Sister was gone so suddenly, and then Mother goes and gets a photo and hands it to Asle and it's a good photo, it looks very nice, Asle thinks and Father says that he's thought the same thing, that it's really too bad that almost every home in Barmen, practically all of Stranda too before long, has a painting that Asle's painted of their house hanging in the main room, while they, his parents, don't, he says, because Asle still hasn't painted a picture of his own childhood home, he says

Yes yes, Asle says

You really haven't, Mother says

So before you move out you need to paint one, she says

and then they stand there silently and then Mother says yet again that his hair has grown so long now that it's high time he gets it cut, it's shameful, for him and for her and for Father, that he's going around with that long hair, hanging straight down his back, it's too awful, she says

I don't know how many times I've told you you need a haircut, she says

And you don't do it, she says

But now that you're starting at The Academic High School you'll have to cut your hair, she says

and she looks at Father and she says can't he say something too

Yes you need to cut your hair, Father says

I've never seen a man or boy with such long hair, he says

Me neither, Mother says

and after that it's silent and then Mother says that he doesn't want to get confirmed and he doesn't do his homework and he gets such bad marks that she's sure he'll end up on the waiting list to get into The Academic High School and on top of all that to run around with long hair hanging down his back, she says, yes, that shaggy brown mess, she says and again she says that Father should say something

Yes you need to cut your hair, Father says

and Asle thinks that he's had enough of all this nagging, ever since he started growing his hair out and refusing to cut it Mother has been harping on at him, you have to cut it, you can't go around looking like that, they'll talk about you in town, no man in Barmen has ever had hair as long as yours, she said and Asle answered that he'll wear his hair however he wants to, it's his hair, and those curls Mother does her hair in look totally awful, that's what he thinks, if you want to know the truth, but still he doesn't go around saying over and over again that she has to get a new haircut, what if almost every single time he talked to Mother he said that she should go get a new haircut, he said, Asle thinks, but still he had to listen to her constant, never-ending nagging, she hardly ever talked to him without telling him he had to get a haircut, didn't she ever think about anything else? was there not one single other thought in her head besides his needing to cut his hair? he thinks

I don't want to paint that picture, he says

You don't want to paint your very own childhood home, Mother says

and then Asle just leaves the room and he thinks about the time when he was in primary school and Mother took him with her to a hair salon and when he went he had nice hair, a little long, and then The Hairdresser Lady cut almost all his hair off, she practically shaved him bald it was so short, and it was like both Mother and The Hairdresser Lady were glad they'd done it, yes, it was like cutting off all his hair gave them both a kind of evil pleasure, Asle thinks and the next day he didn't want to go to school, he looked so horrible and humiliated that he was ashamed to go to school, it was totally awful how he looked, Asle thinks and he said he was sick and that he didn't want to go to school but he went anyway, but he wore a hat pulled down over his ears, he thinks and no he doesn't want to think about that anymore, Asle thinks, and no one was going to give him such a short haircut ever, ever again, that's for sure, fucking never again, he thinks, and it was so horrible going to school the next day, Asle thinks and I look at the white road and then I see some snowflakes hit the windshield, one by one, snowflakes, then it starts snowing more and more and it gets even harder to see where the road is, and I have to drive even slower, but it'll be much better after I get to Instefjord, or Øygna, where the woman Åsleik calls Sister but who's actually named Guro lives, I think, because then I'll be on the cleared main road that runs south to Bjørgvin, I think and I look at the falling snowflakes, and now they're falling so thickly that you can't tell one flake from the others, and I look at the white road and I see Asle sitting there on the floor of the main room in his house and he's looking at a white canvas and he's thinking that today they found Sister dead in bed and just now they've left and taken her away in an ambulance to get an autopsy, they say, because they need to cut Sister up to try to find out why she died so unexpectedly and suddenly and since it isn't every day that someone dies all of a sudden so young they have to try to find the cause of death, they said and Asle sits and looks at the white canvas and he thinks that now, no, it can't go on, he can't anymore, he thinks, now it's just, he thinks, now he doesn't want to paint from photos anymore, he doesn't want to paint any more rooms and barns in the sun with a flagpole flying the Norwegian flag, and birch trees in blossom, and a still blue Fjord, now he doesn't want to paint house and home anymore, now he wants to paint just his own pictures, because his head is full of pictures, it's a real torment, yes, pictures get lodged in his head all the time, not as things that have happened but like a kind of photograph, taken right there, right then, and he can kind of flip from one of the pictures in his head to another, it's like he has a photo album in his head and the strangest things are there as pictures, like Grandpa's black boots in the rain one time, one day, or Father stroking him on the head, just there, just then, or the light coming down from the sky over the Fjord, just there, just then, and now a whole bunch of pictures of Sister dead have lodged in there and it's like they follow one another like a series of magic lantern slides in Asle's head, one after the other, and he raises his hands to his eyes and pushes on his eyes but the pictures don't go away, they just get stronger, and he takes his hands away from his eyes and now, he thinks, instead of painting pictures from photographs of house and home, yes, now he'll paint away the pictures he has in his head, but he doesn't want to paint them exactly how he sees them in his head before his eyes, because there's something like a sorrow, a pain, tied to every one of those pictures, he thinks, but also a kind of peace, yes, that too, yes he'll paint away all the pictures he has collected in his head, if he can, so that only the peace stays behind, Asle thinks and he looks and sees his sister Alida's white face just there, just then, and he sees the stretcher halfway inside the ambulance, with Sister's face covered, just there, just then and he looks at the white canvas and he thinks he'll start painting the pictures he has in his head soon, he'll paint them away, but he can't manage to paint the worst of them, it's too painful, it's like they're tearing him apart, everything he is, that's how bad it is, but even the pictures that aren't so hard have something about them, something sad, yes, a kind of grief, he thinks, but also a kind of peace, yes, that too, in addition to the pain, anyway there's a kind of peace in the pictures he has lodged in his head of his sister Alida, Asle thinks and then he suddenly thinks that now, no, now he doesn't want to see pictures anymore, he simply can't deal with all these pictures, not the ones in his head and not the ones there on canvas, now he wants to be done with pictures, so now he doesn't want to paint any more pictures, he wants to listen instead of seeing, yes, now he wants to listen to music, Asle thinks and he gets up and now it's decided, he wants to play music, and he wants to play guitar, a guitar makes a lot of noise, he wants to play electric guitar, loud, with distortion, he wants to play loud loud loud, Asle thinks and I look at the white road there in front of me and now it's stopped snowing, so it's much easier to see where the road is, I think and I feel white and empty, and now I've driven all the way down along Sygne Fjord and I'm about halfway from Dylgja to Instefjord, I think, and I'm driving slow and steady, I think and I look at the white road and I see Asle there on his knees and the white canvas is on the floor in front of him and he's thinking that he doesn't want to see anymore, see all these pictures, he wants to hear now, he wants to hear the pictures away now, and for that to happen he has to make a lot of sound so he wants to buy an electric guitar, Asle thinks and I look at the white road and then I see a herd of deer standing in the middle of the road and I start driving even slower and the deer look at me and then they hop off, away from the road, but one is still standing there looking at me, and I think that I've seen a lot of deer, they've leaped right across the road many times, so it's pure luck that I've never hit a deer in my car, I think, but I usually see deer after it's dark or around sunrise or sunset, never during the day, but then again at this time of year it's never really light out, not even during the day, I think and then I drive carefully closer to the deer that's still there and then he too bounds away and I drive on and I look at the white road and I see Asle standing there on stage in The Youth Centre, his brown hair is hanging down in front of his face and hiding him, he is standing there bent over a black guitar that's hanging on him and he's playing all kinds of chords and Terje is on the drums playing everything he can play without any rhythm at all, it's just noise, and Geir is thumping the bass strings totally at random and Olve's standing there screaming and then he starts playing something kind of like a solo on his guitar and they all stop for a bit and then Olve calls out now they need to pull themselves together and play a real song, because what we just stopped playing was nothing but noise, he shouts, it's no good just making noise like that, you need to be able to play one decent song, Olve says and then Geir says that we can't play even one decent song but we'll be a band anyway, he says and Terje says that we all play terribly, not one of us knows how to play, or actually Olve can play a little but no one else can, he says, so we might as well give up on the whole band, he says and Asle just stands there with his guitar on and says nothing

And there's Asle not saying anything, same as always, Terje says

No, his hair's too long for him to talk, Olve says

And his name's not Asle anymore, it's Ales, he says

Nope, quiet as usual, Geir says

He doesn't know how to talk, Olve says

That must be why he never says anything, because he doesn't know how, he says

and Asle just stands there and he thinks it's no good, he has tried as hard as he can to learn how to play the guitar but no matter how much he practises, no matter how much he tries, he's never any good, and Olve had been nice to him, it was he who'd taught him the little he can play on the guitar, he drew little pictures of the chords and then Asle learned them, one by one, that was easy enough, but even just tuning the guitar was hard for him, and figuring out on his own which chord should come next in a song, no, he never managed to do that, so Olve always wrote it down for him, and when he tried to play a solo it was just a mess, he never managed to learn to play the guitar, Asle thinks, and actually Asle couldn't stand Olve but to tell the truth Olve was the only reason they could do anything at all, without Olve they couldn't play a single song, Asle thinks, and ever since he started playing guitar and joined this band he hadn't painted a single painting, or drawn a single drawing, and the pictures in his head that he wanted to drive out with the loud noise hadn't gone away, they just got stronger, so it's not working, Asle thinks, because even if he's just fourteen and, sure, has a lot of time ahead of him he'll never be a good guitarist and it doesn't make sense to keep trying something you can't do, something you'll never be able to do even sort of well, it's not like with pictures, those he makes easily, like there's nothing hard about it, but as for guitar playing, well, he's just never going be able to do it, and if the pictures in his head are sort of stuck there and loud noise doesn't make them go away then, yes, well, he'll just have to try to paint them away, Asle thinks, because drawing and painting are things he can do, but he can't play guitar, Asle thinks and then he takes off his guitar and puts it down leaning against the amp and Olve looks at him and asks him what he's doing

Why are you taking your guitar off in the middle of practice, Olve says

I'll never be able to play it, Asle says

You've only just started, Olve says

Yes, Asle says

and then they just stand there and Terje and Geir don't say anything

You'll get better, Olve says

You've already gotten a lot better since we started our band, he says

Maybe, Asle says

Come on, try again, Olve says

Pick up your guitar, he says

and Asle just stands there and then Olve says that maybe they'll take a break, if that's all right with everybody, he says and both Terje and Geir say it's fine with them and Olve says he has four bottles of beer with him, so now they can take a break and have a little beer, everyone always plays better after a little drink, he says and Geir asks where he got the beer from and Olve says his dad bought it for him

You've got a nice dad, Terje says

Yeah, Geir says

Yes, he is nice, Olve says

and then he says that his father is usually nice, after he's been drinking too, but sometimes he gets so confused, yes, angry too in a way, he says and then he always talks about how he never should've started a family, that's the kind of thing he says, you know, because he misses playing, travelling around and playing at dances, yeah, he really misses it, mostly the music, the playing itself, yes, but also the travelling, he says and then his mother always falls totally silent and she leaves the room, Olve says, and then he always tends to say that father can just start playing again, Olve says, and then his father says that he's too old, he can't bring himself to do it, there were several times he just couldn't pick up his guitar even though he wanted to play, he says, and that's why he gave Olve his guitar, and all the other equipment he has, and he taught Olve most of what Olve can do, and now Olve is already better than he ever was, both at singing and at playing guitar, his father says, Olve says, and then his father drinks more, first beer, and then he switches over to spirits and then his mother comes back in and says he mustn't drink so much, and his father says he'll have had enough soon and then he drinks even more and then he starts singing, and he sings beautifully, his father, and then his mother says he needs to come with her now, they need to go lie down, he has to go to work in the morning, she says and then his father usually goes with his mother, it's only on Sundays and holidays that he keeps on drinking but then he can drink all day, yes, he starts in the morning and drinks till he goes to bed, and he drives to Stranda to buy beer even if he's had a lot to drink, and if they're out of spirits he drives to Bjørgvin to buy some, he buys as many bottles as he has money for, almost, Olve says, and today, yes, today he'd asked his father if he would buy a few bottles of beer for him to bring to practice and his father had said that both Olve and the other band members were too young, they were still going to middle school, so he couldn't buy beer for them, no, it wasn't allowed, Olve says his father said, but then, after a while, he said he was going to drive to Stranda and buy a few bottles for himself and he could buy four bottles that Olve could bring to practice, one for each of us, no more than that, because playing music without having had a drink was never the same, that's what he said, so it was kind of good for them to learn that right away, but it was important not to drink too much, because then you played terribly, and that's why it was dangerous, there've been a lot of musicians both in the past and today who drank themselves to death, so you had to be careful, his father said, Olve says and then before he had to leave for the bus to practice his father gave him a shopping bag with four bottles of beer, he says, and now, yes, now they'll sit backstage and drink one bottle each and then everything'll feel better, for you too, he says to Asle

Maybe, Asle says

and he sees Terje get up and stand next to his drum set and Geir has put the bass down against his amp and Olve is already walking to the back of the stage

Come on, Geir says

and Asle goes over to Geir and then they and Terje go sit down on some chairs backstage, and then Olve comes and hands them each a bottle and then he opens his own and passes the opener and they all open their bottles in turn and then Olve raises his bottle and says cheers and Terje and Geir and Asle raise theirs and say cheers and Olve says that now, yes, now they're real musicians, now they should drink and then they'll try to play through the songs they know, there are five songs they sort of know anyway, and three songs they know really well, Olve says, but up till today it's all been a total mess, he says and they drink and Asle has had beer before but not too many times, and he doesn't think it tastes bad but it's not exactly good either, he thinks, and then they just sit there and don't say anything, just sip their beer, sip by sip, and then Olve says that beer really doesn't taste so good but it works, he says and then he takes out a tobacco pouch and he rolls himself a cigarette and he passes the tobacco pouch around to everyone else and they each roll a cigarette and Asle thinks that he's already smoked lots of times, and he likes that, yes, from the very first time he smoked a cigarette in The Boathouse at home with Per Olav he liked smoking, and he smoked the whole pack of cigarettes Per Olav had given him and he'd hidden in The Boathouse, he'd gone down there to smoke, Asle thinks and he thinks that someday he'll be old enough to go buy a packet of tobacco and cigarette papers and matches for himself at The Co-op Store, and then he'll hide them on a beam in The Boathouse, and he thinks that he's looking forward to being old enough to buy cigarettes, he thinks and he knows that some people get sick and throw up and stuff like that the first time they smoke but it wasn't like that with him, it just tingled a little in his body, in a good way, and he felt calmer, so he's going to be a smoker, as soon as he's old enough to buy tobacco for himself that's what he's going to do, Asle thinks and Olve passes around a cigarette lighter and Asle lights his cigarette and he sucks the smoke into his mouth and then he takes a real pull and he feels a sense of wellbeing spread through his body and then he sits there and smokes and there's a mug that they use as an ashtray sitting on the floor between them and Asle smokes and takes a sip of beer now and then and Olve says it'll be fine, they can't give up now, Asle is turning into a good rhythm guitarist, or good enough anyway, he just needs to practise more, Olve says and the others say they all think so too, and Terje says that he plays the drums even worse than Asle plays guitar and Geir says that his bass playing isn't anything to write home about either, no, he says and Olve says that it'll be fine, and actually he's already talked to the guy in charge of The Barmen Youth Group and he'd said that they might be interested in having them play at the dance, so once they learn enough songs they should just tell him, the guy in charge said, Olve says, and then, once they get some gigs, they'll start to make a little money too, but pretty much the first money they make they'll have to use to pay his father for the mikes and speakers, because his father hadn't given them the equipment for good, he'd only said they could borrow it and then pay for it after they'd brought in a few kroner playing, his father had said, Olve says, and Terje says of course, obviously they need to pay for the sound system as soon as they can, but then, after a while, they can split the money they make playing at dances among themselves, it'll be a few kroner each, he says, and then they'll be getting girls too, Olve says, because girls are always crazy about musicians, that's how it's always been, he says, they used to go crazy for Hardanger fiddle players and then it was accordion players and now it's for guys in a band, Olve says and in fact that's how his father and mother met, yes, his father was playing at a dance once, and they're still in love with each other even after all these years, Olve says

Everything'll be fine, he says

and Asle thinks that maybe it won't be so bad, and maybe he isn't such a terrible player, not much worse than the others anyway, and of course he can get better, even if he never gets really good, but he doesn't really need to, he just needs to get good enough that his playing is passable, he thinks, and it is good when he smokes, he likes smoking, and it's good with beer too, yes, he thinks, beer doesn't taste great but it does good things to you, he thinks and Olve says it'll be fine and they each smoke their rolled cigarette to the end and finish their bottle of beer and then Olve says that now they'll try to get through the songs they know, more or less, he says, and it won't be long before they'll be playing their first dance, he says and then they get up and go over to their instruments and Asle drapes the guitar over his shoulder and then Olve says one two three and then they start and it doesn't sound so bad and then they play through the other two songs they've more or less learned how to play, and those don't sound so bad either, and Olve says that a little beer sure helped and then Terje starts pounding away like wild on the drums and cymbals and Geir thumps like wild on the bass and Asle thinks no, this isn't right, he doesn't want to play guitar anymore, it's the wrong thing, the noise won't get rid of the pictures he has in his head, it only makes them worse, he thinks, so he wants to stop, he can't do it anymore, he should paint now, he should be where it's quiet now, in the silence, where he'll paint away the pictures he has lodged in his head and he'll neither make noise playing the guitar nor paint from photographs of houses and barns, people's homes, he'll paint his own pictures, Asle thinks and then he takes his guitar off and puts it down leaning it against the amp and he turns off the amp and then he gets down off the stage in The Youth Centre in Barmen, and it was he who'd gone to the guy in charge of The Barmen Youth Group and asked if they could practise in The Youth Centre, and they'd been given permission to, Asle thinks and then he stops in the middle of the room and stands there and looks at the other three still standing on stage and behind them someone has painted a set, a scene of a farming village with a high cliff and a blue fjord and blossoming birch trees, it's still there from a play that was put on in The Youth Centre in Barmen sometime or another, a long time ago, Asle thinks, and then he hears Olve yell into the microphone and ask where he's going? and Asle just stands there in the middle of the room and looks at the stage set

Are you leaving? Terje says

and Asle doesn't answer

What are you doing? Geir says

and Asle doesn't answer

Answer goddammit, Olve yells

and he yells it into the microphone so that it booms throughout the whole auditorium and Asle turns around and starts walking towards the door to the hall and Terje shouts after him and says he can't leave, they've just started practice, where's he going? what's wrong with him? Terje calls and then Asle turns around and he sees Terje walking up to him and Asle stops and he stands there waiting for Terje

You're not leaving, are you? Terje says

I am, Asle says

and then Geir takes his bass off and he too comes down off the stage and over to Asle

You're just leaving, Geir says

Yes, I can't play, Asle says

I'm not going to play guitar anymore, he says

and Olve yells into the mike you can't fucking quit, I won't fucking let you, he yells

You're at least as good as the rest of us, Geir says

No I'm not, Asle says

We need you, Terje says

We need two guitars, he says

and then Olve yells into the mike that it's just fucking wrong to act like that, now that they've started a band, found bandmates, and they talked during every single break-time at school about how they should start a band as soon as they got instruments and the other equipment they needed and found a place to practise, and now they have everything all set up and Asle is going to bail just like that, and it's extra shitty since he was the one who started talking about starting a band in the first place, yes, extra shitty, Olve yells into the microphone and it booms and echoes through the auditorium and then Olve bangs the pick as hard as he can across the open strings of his guitar and screams no fuck no into the mike so that it booms and resounds through the auditorium, yes, it echoes through the whole Barmen Youth Centre, and then Olve takes his guitar off and then he gets down off the stage and comes walking over and he stops right in front of Asle

You can't fucking do this, he says

You got us to start this band and now you're just leaving? he says

and he grabs Asle's shoulder and shakes it hard

It was you who wanted us to start a band, he says

and he holds Asle's shoulder tight as Asle just stands there and doesn't know what to say, he just knows that he doesn't want to play guitar anymore, he thinks

We can't play without a rhythm guitarist, Olve says

and Asle doesn't say anything

Say something for fuck's sake, Olve says

and Asle still doesn't say anything

You're not serious? Geir says

You'll ruin the whole band, he says

and Asle says that he doesn't want to play guitar anymore and again Olve shakes him back and forth

You can't just ruin the whole band like that, Geir says

and then they stand there, all four of them, and they don't say anything and then Terje asks what he's going to do instead of playing guitar and Asle says he's going to start painting pictures again, because that's something he can do, he says

Yeah just fucking go home and paint more of those goddamn barns, Terje says

Just keep on doing your paintings, he says

Pictures of goddamn houses, pictures of goddamn barns, he says

Or maybe you're going to go suck The Bald Man's dick? Olve says

and then it's suddenly quiet for a moment and then Geir says Asle can't just leave, they've been talking about starting a band for so long, every single break-time for a long time they'd talk about it, and it was Asle who came up with the idea, and then the others went along with it, and now they'd gotten all the equipment, everything they needed, and gotten permission to practise in The Barmen Youth Centre, yes, everything had worked out and now he was just going to leave? Terje says

And it was me who did almost everything else, Olve says

Sound system, mikes, microphone stands, yeah, who was the one who got all of that together? he says, it was him wasn't it, Olve, and that was because it was all sitting up in the attic at home since his father had played in a band once upon a time, he'd been a guitarist and singer in a band before he got married and since then his father always said that girls had broken up a lot of bands, and he'd thought about that a lot, Olve says, but for a band, a whole band, to be destroyed just because one person didn't feel like being in it anymore and just left, no, no way, he says

So get back up here on this stage, he says

and Asle just stands there and again Olve shakes him by the shoulder

Someone else can borrow my guitar and equipment for now and then pay for it whenever he has the money, Asle says and Olve shakes Asle's shoulders and then he lets go of the shoulder in his right hand and he raises that hand and he stands there with his fist in Asle's face

You hear what I'm saying, now are you going to do it or not? Olve says

You hear me, huh? he says

Do you get what I'm saying? Olve says

and Asle just stands there and then Geir says can't he just come back up onto the stage? and they can practise a little more? it's going so well with their three songs, he says

You can't just leave, you can't just quit, Geir says

I quit, Asle says

You quit? Geir says

Yes, Asle says

and it's silent for a moment

I can't play, he says

and no one says anything

And I'll never be able to play, he says

The only one here who can sort of play is you, Olve, Asle says

Shut up, Olve says

and his fist is still in Asle's face

And Asle, you lent me the money for the drums, Terje says

The whole band is thanks to you, he says

It's because you didn't have anything yourself, Olve says

And your parents didn't want to help you out either, he says

They couldn't, Terje says

Because your father doesn't have a job, Olve says

The bum, he says

He's barely worked a day in his whole life, Olve says

Apart from getting women knocked up, he says

Other men's wives, he says

Fuck that fucker, he says

All right, shut up now, Terje says

and then they all just stand there and Asle says that there are lots of bands with just three people, drum and bass and guitar and Geir says that those bands are good too but the best bands have two guitarists, a lead guitarist and a rhythm guitarist, he says

Someone plays rhythm and someone else plays lead, he says

And sometimes they both play rhythm, Terje says

And I'm the lead guitarist in this band because I'm the only one who can play a solo, or can learn how to play a solo, Olve says

and he says that he's the singer because he's the only one who can learn songs, both the words and the tune, so without him there'd be no band at all, Olve says and then no one says anything

I'm trying my best to play the drums, Terje says

Yes, yes, Olve says

and he just stands and holds his fist pointing right at Asle's face

Me too on the bass, Geir says

Yes, yes, Olve says

and he says that we haven't been at it very long, we've barely started, he says

I don't want to anymore, Asle says

and Olve's hand making the fist comes closer to Asle's face and then Terje grabs Olve's arm and pulls it back and Olve yells what the fuck are you doing and he jumps at Terje to shove him away and then beats at Terje with his fists but Terje is much bigger and stronger and he grips Olve's hand and then Terje hits Olve hard in the face and knocks Olve down and it's quiet and Asle sees blood coming out of Olve's mouth and Olve wipes his mouth off and then raises a hand and feels around his mouth and he says you fucker you've fucking knocked two of my teeth out, he says and Olve gets up and he opens his bloody mouth wide and both of his top front teeth in the middle are half-gone and then Olve puts a hand inside his mouth and takes out the two bits of broken teeth and Terje says he didn't mean to, he's really sorry, he shouldn't have done that, he was just so mad because Olve was talking shit about his father, Terje says and I look at the white road, and now it's probably as light out as it ever gets this time of year, and I drive slowly and carefully on the narrow winding road to Instefjord and I look at the white road and I see Asle standing in the auditorium of The Barmen Youth Centre and on stage there's Olve and Terje and Geir and also Amund, who bought Asle's guitar and joined the band, Asle thinks, and this is the first time they're playing at a dance, he thinks, and Olve has gotten new front teeth and Amund bought the guitar and the mike and amp from Asle and started playing rhythm guitar instead of him, and with a little of the money he got from Amund he bought himself a brown leather shoulder bag to keep his sketchpad and pencil in, Asle thinks as he stands there and Sigve is standing next to him and Asle thinks that Sigve is the only person he knows of who lives in a boathouse, he is a few years older than Asle and he lives with his parents upstairs in a boathouse, a little ways before The Co-op Store, and then Sigve asks if maybe they should go outside and have some beer, he's put his bag behind a rock outside a little ways off from The Youth Centre and it's full of beer, he says and Asle says a little beer would be good and Sigve and Asle go outside and Asle rolls a cigarette and lights it and he and Sigve go over to the rocks where there's a black bag of beer bottles and Sigve opens a bottle and passes it to Asle and he takes it and drinks some and then Sigve opens another bottle for himself and then he raises the bottle and he says cheers and Sigve and Asle drink and Asle notices that Sigve has already drunk a lot and then he says that Asle needs to be careful with alcohol, that's something he needed to learn himself, yes, Asle's probably heard that he's spent some time in prison, yes, The Prison in Bjørgvin, by The Fishmarket, Sigve says and Asle doesn't respond and he thinks that the night he went home after the last time he played with the band it was darkest autumn, and he'd run into Sigve on the road and Sigve was carrying a black bag in one hand and had a bottle in the other and it was the same bag he has with him tonight, Asle thinks and Sigve was on the cup of being drunk and he'd said you have to go see your parents sometime and then he'd handed Asle a bottle and Asle had taken a little sip from it and it had burned in his mouth and then Sigve had slapped himself on the cheek and said again that you have to go see your parents sometime and then Asle gave him back the bottle and then Sigve walked on carrying the black bag and the bottle, Asle thinks and now he and Sigve are sitting and drinking beer by a rock above the Youth Centre and Sigve says that Asle probably remembers the night when he was going home after being in prison, he took the bus home from Bjørgvin, because he was in The Prison by The Fishmarket, and that night he got out the bus a long way before he needed to, and then he'd walked so slowly that Asle had caught up to him, and everything he owned was in that bag, Sigve says and he points at the black bag, and to tell you the truth it was three half-bottles of spirits and a chessboard with pieces, because he'd learned to play chess in prison and the first thing he did when he got out was buy a bag, yes, the one he had the beer in now, and then three half-bottles of spirits and then a chessboard with pieces, Sigve says and he says that he was so dreading going back home to his parents but he didn't have anywhere else to go, he says and then Asle and Sigve sit there by the rock a bit above The Youth Centre and Asle smokes and takes a sip of beer and he notices how much he likes beer and cigarettes together

You've probably heard? Sigve says

Heard what? Asle says

Who my real father is? Sigve says

and Asle says he heard it was a German soldier, he says

There's nothing more shameful, Sigve says

and he says that it brought shame on both his mother and him, and he didn't understand his stepfather who married his mother, it was probably because no one else wanted to marry him, the stepfather, Sigve says and then he says that he, the stepfather, was always nice to both him and his mother, it's not that, but why did they have to live like that, there was no one except him and his parents who lived in a boathouse, in a loft in a boathouse, and there was a steep flight of steps, practically a ladder, leading up to the loft, and there they had a room with a kind of kitchen, and two small bedrooms, that was it, Sigve says, and he understood perfectly well that neither his teachers nor anyone else had liked him, the German kid, he says and he drinks his beer and then he says that Asle doesn't like him either, but that doesn't matter, he's good to drink with anyway, and that was why he'd ended up in prison, because of his drinking, but now he had no money again, like so often, and so he couldn't drink either, he says, but he'd made a few kroner during the fruit harvest and that's how he could buy a few bottles of beer, he says, and now The Labour Office had found him work at The Furniture Factory in Aga, he was due to start in a week, and they'd also found him a little old house right in the centre of Aga where he could live, and the rent was low, Sigve says and Asle looks at the three blue dots Sigve has tattooed between the thumb and index finger of his right hand and he has a heart, a cross, and an anchor tattooed in the same place on his left hand and Sigve says that Asle despises him as much as everyone else does and Asle says he doesn't despise him, how can anyone choose who their father is? and as for living in a boathouse, in a loft in a boathouse, what's wrong with that? Asle says and Sigve says that there's no one else in the village who lives in such a hovel and then Asle says cheers and raises his bottle and Sigve raises his bottle and they drink and I look at the white road and I think it'll be good to drop off my paintings for the next show, because almost every time it feels in a way like I can start painting again only after I've delivered my pictures, I think and now I've reached Øygna and up on the hill I can see the house where Åsleik's sister lives, Sister, as he calls her, whose name is actually Guro, and where Åsleik always celebrates Christmas, it's a little grey house, and you can see all the way from the road that the paint is flaking off, and it looks like the house is on the verge of collapsing, and then there's a barn next to the house, it's about to fall down too, a lot of tiles have already fallen off the roof, I see, but inside that house, that dilapidated grey house, is a whole collection of pictures I've painted, of small pictures, yes, almost all of the best small pictures I've ever painted, I think, and I think now I've never even met this Sister Åsleik talks so much about and whose name is Guro and who, every single year since the man she used to live with left her, The Fiddler, Åsleik invites me to go visit with him for Christmas, I think, and every year I've said no, but maybe this year I will go with Åsleik to spend Christmas at Sister's house? I think, and I told Åsleik I would, or maybe would, and why shouldn't I, really? I think, or maybe not, because ever since Ales died and went away I don't really want to do anything for Christmas and maybe it's because I like driving to Bjørgvin on Christmas Eve to go to Christmas Mass at St Paul's Church and I couldn't do that if I was in The Boat with Åsleik sailing to see Sister, this Guro, no I don't know, but maybe this year I'll go with him anyway, spend Christmas at Sister's? that way at least I'd be able to see all the pictures again that Åsleik has bought and given to Sister as Christmas presents, and since they're some of the best small pictures I've ever painted it would be nice to see them again, I think, so I can just think about that, because Åsleik keeps asking and asking me to go with him and maybe I should go and I think Åsleik was really surprised, I think, yes, almost shocked that I would go with him to spend Christmas with Sister, with Guro, as her name is, and that was what the woman I ran into the day before yesterday was called too, the woman sitting in Food and Drink, who I saw later that night, when I was managing to get lost in the snowstorm in Bjørgvin when I was just supposed to go the short way from The Beyer Gallery to The Country Inn, it's hard to believe but whether I believe it or not it's just as bad, I think, and I must not have been entirely myself, I think, not since earlier that evening when I'd found Asle lying covered in snow in The Lane, and I really thought at first that he was dead, but I got him up and then there was everything else that happened at The Alehouse, at The Last Boat, as it's called, and then at The Clinic and everything, I think, and so I ended up getting lost in the snowstorm and luckily I ran into the woman who's also named Guro and she brought me to The Country Inn, I think, and she said that I'd been to her apartment many times, yes, that I'd spent the night there sometimes, but that I'd been so drunk that I couldn't remember it, she said and I think that I've driven past the house where Guro, Åsleik's sister, lives and I'd never noticed before how much the paint was flaking off that grey house of hers, I think and then I think about my sister Alida, who died so suddenly, no, I can't think about that, not now, it's still, even now, still, still, I think and I'm at Instefjord and I turn onto the bigger country road that runs north and runs south down to Bjørgvin, and the road is well cleared and there are lots of tracks of cars that have driven on it after it snowed and I drive south and I look at the white road and I see Asle standing outside his house looking at Father who is standing there looking at a brand new car, it's grey, and it looks like Father can barely bring himself to touch the car and Mother is standing there and she says no it's unbelievable, now they have a car too, and it's about time, everyone their age she knows has a car already, she says and both Mother and Father stand there like they're almost too scared to touch the car, much less get in it, much less drive it, and The Car Salesman, a guy from Stranda, is standing there, it was he who drove the car up to the farm and a friend is now waiting for him in another car to drive him back to Stranda and The Car Salesman holds out his hand to Father and says pleasure doing business with you and Father says thanks you too and then Father and The Car Salesman just stay standing there in silence and then The Car Salesman says, because someone has to say something, that well Father's a car owner now and Father says well it's the bank who owns it, not him, and The Car Salesman says there aren't many people these days who have enough cash to buy a brand new car outright without taking out a loan, he says, and Father says he's probably right and then The Car Salesman says that they should get into the car and he'll explain the car to Father, he says, and he wouldn't believe how many people wanted to buy a new car these days, so many, he says, yes, he can't get enough cars to sell them, he says, so Father too had to wait a little while before it was his turn, The Car Salesman says and Father nods and Mother says it certainly took a while and The Car Salesman says that people are so impatient nowadays, they can't wait to get their own car so they can drive for themselves, drive around wherever they want, he says, every day he gets calls from people waiting to get their new car, isn't it ready yet? soon? they ask, The Car Salesman says and Mother says anyway they got their car eventually, she says

   This is a great day for us, she says

   Yes, it truly is, The Car Salesman says

   and then he tells Father that he should get into the car, in the front seat, and he'll show him how the car works, he says and Father goes hesitantly over to the car door and opens it and then Asle sees him get in and sit stiffly upright in the driver's seat and he grips the steering wheel and twists and turns in the seat and Mother says that it won't be many years now until he too can get a driver's licence and she says well it'll be a couple of years anyway and Asle says that he doesn't want a car and Mother says she knew he'd say that and then The Car Salesman sits down in the other front seat

   Just think, you'll be fifteen so soon, she says

   Yes, yes, Asle says

and then she says that anything she says is wrong, that he always blurts out an answer as soon as she opens her mouth, she says and Asle doesn't answer and then he hears the car start and he sees Father sitting behind the wheel doing this and that and The Car Salesman is gesturing and a nice sound is coming from the engine and then the car jerks suddenly forward, yes, almost makes a hop, and both Mother and Asle are startled and then luckily the car stops and Father is sitting looking straight ahead and he looks totally scared out of his wits, Asle sees

No, what was that all about? Mother says

I don't know, Asle says

and then the engine starts again and The Car Salesman says something and his arms and hands aren't moving and then the car just barely starts moving slowly across the gravel in front of the house, and then it stops, and then it sits there and the engine is running smoothly and then The Car Salesman waves an arm and then Father looks back and the car starts barely moving backwards and then it stops again and then the indicators come on and turn off and the headlights come on and turn off, and then Father drives slowly forwards again and he turns off towards The Barn and then the car reverses again, slowly, and then it stops for a good little while before Father turns the wheel and the car creeps forward and then the car stops and Father turns the engine off and then The Car Salesman opens the door and gets out and he tells Mother that wasn't so bad now and Father gets out and he looks pale and Asle sees that his hands are shaking and The Car Salesman says again that wasn't bad at all no, and then he says that practice makes perfect and that Father just has to take it easy and drive slowly and carefully especially the first time and that he has to get going now, on to the next buyer, because he's supposed to deliver no less than two more cars today, The Car Salesman says and then he shakes Mother's hand and says congratulations and then he shakes Father's hand and says good luck and both Mother and Father say thank you thank you and then The Car Salesman goes over to the man sitting in the other car waiting for him and then Mother and Father stand there and look at the car and neither of them says a word, it's as if they don't dare say a word and Father seems nervous and then Mother says that this summer they'll be driving their own car and they'll go visit her parents and brothers and sisters on Hisøy, and then, while they're there, they can drive to Haugaland to go shopping, she says and Asle sees Father stand there writhing not really knowing what to say

Isn't it beautiful? Mother says

Yeah, Father says

and he nods and he sort of can't stop nodding, he nods and nods, and then he stops his nodding

Well it was sure expensive enough, Father says

Let's not talk about that now, Mother says

and then they stand there and neither one says anything

Should we go on our first drive? Mother says

Guess we have to, Father says

Yes, we really do have to, Mother says

and she asks if Asle wants to come along and he shakes his head and says that the two of them can go for a drive on their own and then Father goes and gets behind the wheel and Mother goes around the other side and gets in and then Father starts the car and then they just sit there and then the car gives a sudden jolt forwards and then stops and Mother looks at Asle and she shakes her head and Father looks utterly desperate and then he starts the car again and it doesn't move and then it slowly slowly starts to move forwards and then Father turns the wheel and Asle sees the car slowly disappear around the corner of The Old House and Asle walks after the car and he sees Grandma standing in the window and Asle sees the car drive slowly slowly down the driveway and Grandma opens the window and she shakes her head

Foolishness, she says

Spending all that good money to buy a car, she says

and Asle says he doesn't understand it either and he sees the car barely creeping down the driveway and he runs after the car and then walks behind the car and it pulls out onto the country road and drives slowly slowly down the road and then Father drives a little faster and Asle starts to jog slowly behind the car and then he runs past the car and he turns around and he waves at Father sitting and staring stiffly straight ahead and he waves at Mother and she waves back with a stiff smile and Asle runs some more and then he stops and the car gets closer to him again and then he starts walking next to the car and Mother is tensely looking straight ahead and then a couple of boys come biking up behind them and they swerve aside and bike past the car without stopping and Asle feels embarrassed and looks away and he turns around and walks home and he turns back and he sees the car creeping slowly, slowly down the road along The Shore and it's embarrassing, never in his life has Asle seen anyone drive a car that slowly, he thinks and I drive south on the country road that runs north and south down to Bjørgvin, and it's much easier driving now because the roads are cleared, and besides it's almost as light out now as it ever gets this time of year, and I'm driving slowly south and soon I'll be at The Playground where I saw a young man with medium-length brown hair and a young woman with long black hair playing the day before yesterday, I think, and when I drive past The Playground I won't look down at it, I think and I won't stop at the turn-off either, by the path down to The Playground, I think and I drive past The Playground and I drive past the turn-off, and I don't want to stop, because I don't feel tired, I think and I get to the old brown house where Ales and I used to live once, and the paint is flaking off that house too and I look at the house and I see a young man with medium-length brown hair standing and looking out the window of the brown house and he thinks that despite everything they were lucky to find this house to rent, even if it's old and run-down, the old kitchen is good enough, and everything they needed was already there when they moved in, an old stove and a fridge that was almost as old, and all the frying pans and table linens and knives and forks they needed, yes, everything you need in a kitchen, and there was furniture in the main room and a double bed in the bedroom, yes, it was like moving into a fully furnished house, and in fact that's what it was, because the man they'd rented it from had taken only his mother's most personal belongings with him, his mother had lived in that house until she died, and she died in her bed, in the double bed where he and Ales were now sleeping, Asle thinks, so all of the furniture was already there in the house, and a good thing too because he and Ales had practically nothing, just a couple of pans and some mugs, and some sheets and blankets, that was it, so it was great for them that the house they were moving into was like a newly furnished home, it was as if the woman who'd lived there had stepped out and not come back, and then her son, the one who'd rented them the house, came by and took her clothes and gave them to The Second-Hand Shop in Sailor's Cove, and threw out her toiletries and everything like that, and then he took two or three things he wanted for himself, and then he rented out the house, and Ales's mother Judit knew him, they worked together at The Hospital, and so Ales heard through her mother Judit that the house was for rent and she'd mentioned that they should rent it and so they did, because they wanted to get out of Bjørgvin and have a little more space than they had in the flat they were renting there on The Hillside in Bjørgvin, and so they rented the house and moved in, but of course they didn't want to keep the house exactly the way the woman who used to live there had had it, living there her whole life with her husband and child, and then later alone, so they'd packed up a lot of the stuff there and put it down in the cellar or in a room up in the attic, and there were bracket lamps everywhere when they moved in and they unscrewed every last one, that was the first thing they did, and then they got rid of a couple of armchairs and then they moved all their painting supplies into the main room and they put up a bookshelf that Asle had made himself, yes, they'd really been lucky, Asle thinks standing there at the window, being able to rent this old house, and the brown paint on the outside of the house was still in good shape, actually, he thinks, and when he and Ales first lived together, he thinks, they'd lived in a two-room basement flat, but they wanted to live in a house, and they wanted to live outside of Bjørgvin, and then they got this house and now they've lived here for a while and things are good, before they left Bjørgvin they bought a car and before that he got a driver's licence, something he never thought he'd do, he didn't want a driver's licence but he realised that if they were going to live on their own so far from other people they needed a car and so one of them needed to get a driver's licence and since Ales didn't want to any more than he did, well, he was the one who did it, and then they bought an old used car, mother Judit simply gave them the money to buy the car as a wedding present, because she still worked at The Hospital and made money, she was from Austria, and Ales's father was from Dylgja, and his unmarried sister, old Alise, still lived there, in their childhood home, hers and Ales's father's, she lived in a pretty white house with two main rooms and an adjoining bedroom, and with two rooms and two crawlspaces up in the attic, Asle thinks, yes, mother Judit was from Austria but it was hard to tell that she wasn't Norwegian, she had learned to speak Norwegian so well, to the point where it was hard to say where in the country she came from, there was something universal about the way she spoke Norwegian, yes, it was actually kind of strange, her language, Asle thinks, but he met Ales and they moved in together and they got married, it was like it was already settled that they'd do that, it kind of happened by itself, they were together ever since the first time they met and they got married in St Paul's Church and only they and the best man and maid of honour were there, mother Judit and Beyer, and then, before they got married, Ales got Asle to convert to The Catholic Church, he'd been confirmed, with two witnesses there, not that long before the wedding, and one of the witnesses was Catholic, Ales's mother Judit, and the other witness was Beyer, and it was also in St Paul's Church that he'd been confirmed, only the priest was there plus the two witnesses, and Ales too of course, because her mother Judit was Catholic, and that was why Ales had been baptised Catholic and went to her first communion and was confirmed in St Paul's Church, whereas he had been baptised in The National Church and confirmed there in a Protestant way, and the baptism was valid but the confirmation wasn't, which was why Asle didn't have to be baptised, and the Catholic confirmation felt good, and he can still feel the priest drawing a cross on his forehead with the consecrated oil, and afterwards he and Ales got married, also in St Paul's Church, and then they lived for a while in the little apartment on The Hillside and then they moved into this old house, Asle thinks, standing there looking out the window and he thinks he just saw someone drive by on the road, and he's seen that vehicle several times already, a large car like a small van, he thinks, so whoever owns it must live in somewhere north of here, he thinks, but now, yes, now there were rumours that the man who'd rented them the house needed it back, Asle thinks, probably one of the man's children needed a place to live, and so, yes, he didn't come right out and say it but he was talking as if they couldn't keep renting the house where they lived for much longer, he said they should move out as soon as they could, that was what he'd said without saying it outright, Asle thinks, and Ales had thought they could move in with her aunt in Dylgja, old Alise, she lived there alone and could certainly use a little help around the house, but Asle didn't want to do that, yes well Dylgja was fine and the house, yes, he couldn't imagine a nicer house to live in, but he didn't want to live with anyone else in the house, he wanted to live there with just Ales, and Ales had said she was sure they could live upstairs in the old house in Dylgja, and just keep their food downstairs, and then they could go shopping for her aunt and help her, she was old now, old Alise, and she could use some help with the shopping, with keeping the house clean, with everything really, Ales had said, and maybe they should move there, because Ales had already spoken to her old aunt Alise about it and Alise had felt it was a good solution, yes, if Ales and Asle wanted to she would be glad and grateful to have them move into her house, she'd said, but Asle hadn't wanted to, he couldn't stand living so close to other people, anyone, the only person he could stand having nearby was Ales, he'd said, Asle thinks, and Ales had said she understood and then they'd just acted like nothing was happening and stayed living in the house they were renting, Asle thinks, standing there in the window looking out and then he hears Ales coming and he turns around to face her and he holds out his hand and she takes his hand and then they give each other a hug and Asle says that he's seen a little delivery van drive by several times and Ales says the owner is probably someone who lives nearby and I look at the white road and I'm driving south and now I'm getting close to Bjørgvin, and what a relief it'll be to drop off these pictures, I think and I look at the white road and I see Asle standing outside the house in Barmen in his black velvet jacket and with the brown leather shoulder bag hanging over his shoulder and he takes out a packet of tobacco and rolls a cigarette that he puts between his lips, and then he takes out a matchbox and takes a match out, he lights it, and Asle thinks that the day Father got his new car The Bald Man was standing down at the bus stop waiting for the bus to Bjørgvin, and that was the last time he ever saw The Bald Man, he thinks, because The Bald Man never came back from Bjørgvin alive, he came home in a coffin, Asle thinks and then he stands there and sees that the boot of the car is open and there's a hotplate in the boot, a hotplate for a studio apartment, with one burner, and a box of clothes, underwear, socks, a warm pullover, shirts, trousers, shoes, and a box with kitchen utensils, a bread knife and plates and knives and forks and spoons, and he's put all his painting supplies in the boot, and they're in a single box, and everything he owns is here, and some canvas and wood for stretchers, Asle thinks and he stands there and takes a good long pull of his cigarette and he thinks that now he's been smoking for more than a year already, almost, and he sees Mother come up with a duvet and a pillow and a burlap sack

Here's your duvet and pillow, she says

and Mother puts the rolled-up duvet and the pillow into the bag and puts the bag into the boot of the car and she says that, as he saw, the duvet cover and pillowcase were on the duvet and pillow, Mother says

Thank you, Asle says

Yes so we've probably got just about everything, Father says

Not the raincoat and boots, Mother says

and then she goes back inside and she comes out with a raincoat and boots and she puts them in the boot

So that's about it now? Father says

And something to eat for the road, we need that, Mother says

And a little food for the new place too, she says

and Mother goes back inside and Father says it wouldn't hurt if Asle brought a little food with him, but now that he was going to start at The Academic High School in Aga and live by himself he was going to have to learn how to go shopping for himself, and the old studio stove with the one burner he had had the year he went to Agriculture School and lived in a rented room was already in the boot of the car, Father said, and the pots and pans are packed, so now Asle can try to cook for himself now and then, Father says, because it can get expensive to buy dinner every day, even if there is a café in Aga and a cafeteria at The

Academic High School, and even if it doesn't exactly cost an arm and a leg to buy dinner either at the café or the cafeteria, he says

And every month I'll send you the money you need, he says

And plus you'll get a little stipend since you have to live in an apartment and can't live at home, he says

Yes, Asle says

You won't have much to spare but it'll definitely be enough to live on, he says

and Father says well he also has the kroner he made selling paintings over the summer, yes, it was a good idea to have an exhibition in The Barmen Youth Centre, because sure enough he sold all the pictures, he says and he says that the agreement is that Asle will pay rent for the room once a month, the first day of the month, unless it's a holiday and he's home of course, he says

Okay, Asle says

and then they stay standing there in front of the house and they don't say anything

You were lucky to get a room for such a good price, Father says

In its own building, too, he says

Yes, Asle says

We just needed to put an ad in *The Hardanger Times* and it all worked out, Father says

and he says that the woman who called them said she was a widow and that her husband had been a shoemaker and The Shoemaker's Workshop belonging to the deceased husband was next to the house where she lived and there was a room in the attic there with a bed and a table and a little pantry too with a window, where you could prepare your food if you wanted to, and downstairs, on the ground floor, well that's where there was a toilet and shower, it was laid out like that because her husband had always had an apprentice who lived in the attic in The Shoemaker's Workshop, yes, that's why there was a toilet and shower on the ground floor, she'd said, Father says

It sounds great, Asle says

Let's take a look, Father says

Okay, Asle says

and he rolls another cigarette and lights it and then they stand there silently in front of the house and Father says it's a strange day, because Asle, their only son, yes, their only living child, is leaving home, moving out and moving away and going to live by himself, yes, it's a memorable day, Asle is leaving his childhood home while he's still so young, so that's the end of his adolescence, the end of childhood, but that's how it is out in the country, if you want to go to school you need to move away, Father says and Asle doesn't say anything and he thinks finally, finally, he's leaving home, he can't wait, he's going to live by himself, alone, and not have to listen to Mother constantly nagging about him needing a haircut, about how it's just not acceptable to go around looking like he does, about how he needs to paint proper paintings, like he did before, when he was younger, not these messes that don't look like anything, and nagging him about how he needs to be like other people his age, he's really no better and no worse than anybody else, he's just pretends like he's so different, she's said that and again she says that he needs to cut his hair, a boy just can't go around with such long hair, she's said and she nags him like that day in and day out, Asle thinks and then Father says again that this is a big day

You're leaving home today, Father says

and Asle doesn't say anything

You're only sixteen and you're moving out to live by yourself, he says

and Father says that he never did that himself, never moved away to go to school, and he regrets that, yes, except for the year at Agriculture School he's lived his whole life on this farm, he stayed here and tried as best he could to grow fruit and build boats, traditional Barmen pointed boats, yes, the way he'd learned to from his father, Asle's Grandfather, and now it must be something like ten years since he died, Father says, yes, it's a fine kind of boat, traditional Barmen boats, and he likes being a boatbuilder, it's not that, he says, but Asle had never seemed interested in building boats and he'd never wanted to put pressure on him to learn, he says and they stay standing there silently for a moment, and so, Father says, he kept on, growing and cultivating fruit, yes, he spent all his time building boats or growing fruit, he says

I should have gone to school too, Father says

So I'm glad you have the chance to do it, he says

and he says that after Asle goes to the high school, and gets good enough marks, he'll be able to do whatever he wants

You can become a doctor, or a minister, Father says

and he laughs

A minister, are you kidding, Asle says

You be a minister, he says

Well then a doctor, Father says

A doctor, me? Asle says

Yes, well, a doctor, a teacher, Father says

I don't even like school, Asle says

and then Father says that The Academic High School is totally different from the schools Asle's been to up until now so maybe he'll be happy at The Academic High School at least sometimes, he says

Maybe, Asle says

Yes who knows, Father says

But you need to go to class in any case, do as well as you can, he says

Yes, Asle says

Because you're a clever one, you're smart, he says

You must realise I know that, he says

and Father says that both he and Mother knew that his bad marks in school weren't because he lacked the ability, he says and he says that as long as Asle listens to his teachers and does his homework he'll graduate from The Academic High School just fine, he's sure of it, he says and Asle sees Mother come out with two shopping bags and she says it's the food she wants to give him to bring along and she puts the shopping bags in the boot

The boot's almost full now, Father says

Yeah, Asle says

Get in the back, Father says

and he points at the back seat and Asle suddenly remembers that he's packed all his other painting supplies but forgot the easel

I need to get the easel, he says

But we don't have any room for it, Father says

Well I need it, Asle says

and he says it can be folded up and he can hold it in his lap

And I need to bring my finished paintings too, he says

and he suddenly thinks he can put them in the old suitcase at his grandparents', up in the attic of The Old House, and Asle tells Father that and then Father unlocks the door to The Old House and Asle runs up the stairs to the attic and gets the suitcase sitting on a box there and then he thinks that he wants to bring the grey blanket Grandmother had covered herself with when she was sick, the grey blanket that she gave him and said he should have on the day they came to get her and drive her to The Hospice, and he goes into the main room and the blanket is sitting there nicely folded on the bench and he opens the suitcase and puts the blanket in and then he hurries outside and into the room that was his in The New House and he opens the suitcase and puts all the finished paintings in the suitcase and he tries to put layers of the blanket between the different paintings, and then he goes outside and puts the suitcase on top of everything else in the boot of the car

Well now it's full, that's for sure, Father says

and he pushes the lid of the boot closed and then Mother gets into the car, in the front seat

I can't forget my easel, Asle says

and he hurries into the room he used to have and he goes back out and while he's folding up the easel Father locks the front doors, both The New House's and The Old House's, and then Asle gets into the car, in the back seat, with the easel on his lap, and there's plenty of room for the easel if he holds it crossways on his lap and then he puts his shoulder bag on the seat next to him and then Father starts the car and it doesn't start right away but then it does with a little jolt forwards

Oof, Father says

What's wrong with you now, he says

and then the car stays still for a second before Father starts driving slowly forwards and turns the corner of The Old House, where Grandmother and Grandfather lived, and it's been many years since Grandfather died, Asle thinks and he thinks that he woke up and saw Grandmother lying in Sister's bed, since Asle and Sister shared a room, and Grandmother looks at Asle with tears in her eyes and he sees tears running down her cheeks and she says Grandfather's dead

Grandfather died last night, Grandmother says

and Father drives slowly down the driveway and Asle sees Grandmother lying there on the bench in her main room, there in The Old House, with the grey blanket spread out over her, and she can hardly move, her arms are all she can use the same as before, and she can talk a little, but not like before, and Asle sits there next to her a lot and talks to her a little and maybe she asks him to get her something or help her move a little or something like that and he does it and then one day an ambulance comes and when the men pick up the stretcher with Grandmother on it she hands Asle the grey blanket and he's a little surprised and then he says thank you and Grandmother tries to say that he should have it, Asle thinks and then they carry Grandmother out the door and into an ambulance and then they drive her to The Hospice, and The Hospice is in Aga too, not too far from The Academic

High School, on a hill behind The Hotel, so they'll go visit Grandmother at The Hospice today, that's the first thing they'll do, Father said, Asle thinks, and then they'll drive to the house of the woman who's renting the room out to Asle, he said, he thinks, and Father drives out onto the country road and Asle looks at his home and he thinks it's good to be driving away, it's a deeply good feeling, he thinks

Yes so first we'll look in on my mother? Father says

Yes, Mother says

and it's like there's a kind of bad feeling in her voice

Yes, that's what we'll do, Mother says

And then drive to the apartment, she says

Yes, Father says

You know where it is, right? Mother says

Yes, she explained it all, the woman who's renting it, there are two green houses by the road before you get to the centre of Aga, on the downhill side of the road, just before a little river, and he could just turn in and park between the buildings, is what she said, Father says

Right, Mother says

And then ring the bell at her house, of course, Father says

And if we can't find it we have her phone number and there's a phone booth in the centre of Aga, next to The Co-op Store, he says

Yes, I remember, Mother says

and then they drive on and no one says anything

But first we'll go look in on my mother at The Hospice, Father says again

Right, Mother says gruffly

and they drive on and no one says anything and Asle thinks that he can't wait until they've left and until he has his things in the room he'll be renting and living in now and he can't wait to be alone there, and in the morning he'll start at The Academic High School, tomorrow morning is when he'll start at The Academic High School and from then on he'll be a high-school student, he thinks, but not until eleven o'clock, he thinks, and it's a bit of a walk from where his rented room is to The Academic High School, so he needs to leave in plenty of time, Asle thinks, and he looks at his watch, which Grandmother gave him as a confirmation gift, and Asle should never have gotten confirmed, he thinks, because it's hard to imagine anything more idiotic than all that Christian nonsense, he thinks, but he got confirmed anyway for some mysterious reason and the reason was probably the simple one that everyone else was doing it and had always done it in the village, but he doesn't want to think about that, not now anyway, no, it was just awful but he did get some presents and a little money, Asle thinks and as soon as he turns sixteen he'll officially withdraw from The National Church, he thinks, he's sure of that, because he saw it when he almost bled to death, he saw it then, yes, he saw that no National Church and no Minister knows anything about it, and The Minister just babbled on and on, Asle thinks, because reality, facts, that's something no Minister knows anything about, Asle thinks and it won't be long before he turns sixteen and the day he does he's going to write to The Minister and say straight out that he doesn't want to be a member of The National Church anymore, Asle thinks and he wants to say that out loud but he lets it go, because if he says it Mother will just start in with her nagging again, and then he says it anyway

When I'm sixteen I'm officially leaving The National Church, Asle says

Yes, you've already told us that, Mother says

You've said that lots of times already, she says

The day will come when you need God, you too, she says

I'm sure it will, Asle says

But God and The National Church have nothing to do with each other, he says

Yes, yes, Mother says

What they're doing there is an abuse of God's name, Asle says

and then it's quiet and Father doesn't say anything and Asle sees himself sitting on the swing outside the house and Grandfather is dead and Grandmother is standing in the door to The Old House and she's holding at arm's length a bundle of dead Grandfather's clothes and Asle sits on the swing and looks at her and Grandmother asks him if he could carry Grandfather's clothes down to the cellar and Asle can't say no, no matter how much he doesn't want to do it, no matter how creepy the thought is, he thinks, and then he goes over and takes the clothes and it's a whole armful and he goes down to the cellar and he opens the cellar door and he drops dead Grandfather's clothes right on the floor and he goes back up to the area in front of the house and sits back down on the swing and he sees that there's a grey wool sock right in the middle of the area in front of the house that must have fallen out of the bundle of clothes and he sees Grandmother come out to the door and she points at the sock and she's sobbing and she says can't he take the sock down to the cellar too and Asle goes over to the sock and picks it up between his thumb and one finger and holds it as far away from himself as he can and he carries the sock down into the cellar and drops it on Grandfather's other clothes, Asle thinks, and then he hears Mother say you need to let them pass and Asle turns around and the easel twists a little and he sees a long row of cars behind them

Yes as soon as I can, Father says

Yes, Mother says

There's a long row of cars behind us, she says

Yes I can see that, Father says

sitting there bent forward, his chest almost leaning on the steering wheel, and he's staring straight ahead and he's driving so slowly so slowly, and man how embarrassed Asle's always been about Father's driving, he always drives so, so slowly, he thinks, but now he's not embarrassed about it anymore, now he no longer has to care about it, he's not embarrassed anymore the way he was when he was young, Asle thinks and Father signals and pulls over and the car stops and the first car behind them speeds past with an angry blast of the horn and then a long row of cars drives past them

Yes, yes, Mother says

It's good you finally pulled over and let them pass, she says

and Father doesn't say anything and he just drives on and Asle dozes off and maybe falls asleep and then they're in Aga

So we'll go see my mother first? Father says

Yes, Mother says

and they drive up to The Hospice on the hill above The Hotel and Father parks the car and then they go in through a double glass door and Father goes over to the reception desk and the woman there tells him what room Grandmother is in, and on what floor, and then they go up some stairs and down a corridor and Father stops in front of a door and he knocks on it and there's no answer and then he opens the door and goes in and Asle goes in and he sees Grandmother lying in a bed and her lips have turned a bit blue and she holds out her hand and he goes and takes her hand and then sits down on the edge of the bed and he sits there holding Grandmother's hand and Father asks how she's doing and Grandmother tries to say something and Mother says that she seems happy, here at The Hospice she's probably getting the best care she could get anywhere, Mother says, and she says that she's bought a little fruit for Grandmother and a little chocolate, she says and she puts a white paper bag on Grandmother's bedside table and Father stands there and Asle sees that he doesn't know what to do or what to say, it's like he doesn't want to be taking up any space at all, Asle thinks, sitting there holding Grandmother's hand and Mother says that Asle is starting at The Academic High School in the morning and that they've rented a room for him, they put an ad in *The Hardanger Times* and got a phone call the day the ad was printed, there was a place for him in the attic of an old shoemaker's workshop, the husband of the woman who called had had a workshop, but he was dead, and whoever the shoemaker's apprentice at the time was used to live there but since he'd died no one had lived there, so the apartment had been empty for several years, but now she'd realised that maybe someone going to The Academic High School and who needed a rented room to live in could live there, she'd said, Mother says, and Father accepted right away, she says, so now both Grandmother and Asle will be living in Aga, Mother says and Grandmother nods and Asle feels her gently squeeze his hand

I'll come and visit you every day, Asle says

and he looks at Grandmother

I'll come every day when school gets out, he says

And if you want me to buy you anything I'll do it, he says

and Grandmother shakes her head

But maybe sometimes? he says

Yes well now that you're living in the same town you can go see Grandmother a lot, Father says

Yes, Mother says

and then they say take care

I'll come back tomorrow morning, Asle says

and Grandmother nods at him and Asle lets go of her hand and he sees that Mother and Father are already out in the hall and I look at the white road and I'm driving south and now it won't be long till I get to Bjørgvin, I think, and that's good, because then I'll drop off the paintings and then I'll go see Asle at The Hospital, I think and I look at the white road and I see Asle sitting in the car that's parked between the two green buildings, one big house and next to it is what must be The Shoemaker's Workshop, Asle thinks

I think this must be the place, Father says

and he gets out and stretches and then goes up the steps to the house and he stands there and looks at the nameplate and he knocks and then an old grey-haired woman comes out and she stands and talks to Father and then she goes back inside and then comes out and she's put on a coat and Asle can see that she's carrying a keyring and Mother says they should probably get out of the car and then she opens the car door and gets out and Asle opens his door and gets out and then he just stands there in his black velvet jacket with the brown leather shoulder bag on his shoulder and he's holding the easel in his hands and he doesn't really know what to do with himself and he hears Mother say hello and he looks down

Hello, yes, The Landlady says

Welcome, she says

Here he is, Mother says

Ah that's him, The Landlady says

and Asle stands there and he looks up and he sees The Landlady walking up to him taking little steps and Asle holds out his hand and she holds out her hand and they shake hands

Hello, Asle says

Hello, The Landlady says

Welcome, she says

and Asle sees Mother standing there squirming and he thinks that she's standing there embarrassed about him, about his long hair, his long brown hair, about him standing there holding an easel, that everything about him embarrasses her, Asle thinks

Yes so here he is, Mother says

and it's like she's saying it into thin air, without any connection to anything, Asle thinks

So, you're starting at The Academic High School, The Landlady says

Yes, Asle says

and they stand there silently

Are you looking forward to it? she says

Yes, Asle says

But it'll be a real change now, won't it, The Landlady says

Leaving home and living on your own, I mean, she says

Yes, Mother says

It's hard to believe he's already big enough to move out and live on his own, she says

That he's already so grown up, she says

Yes, it used to be that you were considered grown up once you'd gone to the minister and been confirmed, The Landlady says

Yes, Father says

And then you had to just take care of yourself, The Landlady says

and it's like she wants to tell them something, but she stops herself and doesn't and Asle thinks that she was almost certainly going to tell them something about how it was when she was a girl and about having been in service somewhere or another and then The Landlady says that for a few years before she was married she was in service for the minister in Barmen at his house and ever since she got married she's lived in this house, she says

Yes, Father says

I've lived all my adult life in this house here, The Landlady says

and she raises an arm slowly and she points at the green house they're standing next to

And my husband was a shoemaker, yes, she says

Yes, Father says

It was good steady work for many years, she says

Before the shops started selling shoes from foreign factories, she says

After that it was mostly patching and repairs, she says

Yes, that's how it goes, Father says

That's what happened, The Landlady says

and they stand there and no one says anything

There's a bed and everything else you need, a table and chair, both a toilet and a shower, The Landlady says and she points at The Shoemaker's Workshop

Let's go take a look, she says

Yes, Asle says

So, now you'll be living on your own, she says

That's how it is, Father says

And since you're from Barmen you need to rent a room since The Academic High School's in Aga, she says

and Father says that that's how it is, and it's not just people from Barmen, people from Stranda need to rent rooms here, he says and The Landlady nods

Yes there are lots of young people living in rented rooms in Aga, she says

and there's silence

Yes, she says

Thank you for answering the ad I put in *The Hardanger Times*, Father says

Well I'm a subscriber, The Landlady says

and she's started walking over to the door of The Shoemaker's Workshop and she's holding a key up to Asle and she says that this key, the biggest one, is for the front door, she says and then she unlocks the door and walks in and she turns on the light

There's the light switch, she says

and she looks back to see if Asle is there and he goes over to The Landlady and she points to the light switch and she says that when he's not at home it'd be nice if he turned out the light, to save a little on the electricity, she says and then she goes down a hall and there are whitewashed walls on both sides, and she points to a door

Here's the shower and the toilet, she says

Yes and let's keep looking, she says

and she points to a door farther down the hall

In there's the actual workshop, the shoemaker's workshop, where my husband made shoes, she says

And later just repaired shoes, she says

But through all those years he had a boy as an apprentice, she says

It was like he felt it was his duty, she says

and she looks at Mother and Father and she says he, the apprentice boy, always had lodgings up in the attic, and that's where Asle will have his rented room now, The Landlady says and she starts slowly climbing the stairs with Asle right behind her and when she gets to the top she unlocks a door and she goes in and she turns on the light and Asle goes in after her

Yes so here's your new home, The Landlady says

The room looks great, Asle says

It's nothing special, but it's a place to live anyway, she says

and Asle sees a bed and next to the bed there's a nightstand and there's a lamp mounted on the wall over the head of the bed

Yes you'll have light to read by too, as you can see, The Landlady says

And there's a table and chair in front of the window, she says

So you can do your reading there, she says

Yes, Asle says

Asle, that was your name, right? she says

Yes, my name's Asle, he says

and Asle sees that next to the table, in that corner, is a wardrobe and The Landlady says that he can keep his clothes in that wardrobe, or anything else, whatever he needs to keep there, she says and then she goes over to a door next to the hall door and she opens it and it's a little room with a bench and she says now this here's a little room but you can use it as a little kitchen, and Asle sees that there's a small window in the room and he says he's brought with him a studio stove with one burner

Yes, when you cook you can let the smoke go out through that window, The Landlady says and she says now it's nothing special, no, it's old and run-down and it hasn't been used in all these years, but lots of people have lived in this apartment before and no one ever complained, she says

Yes, Asle says

It all looks great, he says

So that's it, The Landlady says

and she stands there

You'll have to come over to the house and have a cup of coffee with me sometime, she says

and Asle says thank you thank you and then he puts the easel down on the floor, in front of the window, and then The Landlady takes out a pad of notepaper as though out of nowhere and Asle sees that it says Rent Book on top and The Landlady says that on the first of every month, if it's not a holiday and he's not back home at the time, he can come pay the rent and Asle nods and then they just stand there

Yes well there's probably not much more I need to show you, The Landlady says

and Father thanks her, thanks her very much for renting her home to Asle, it's not so easy to get a room in Aga so he really has to thank her, he says and The Landlady says it's nothing and then she goes over to the door and she leaves the room and goes downstairs and Father and then Mother and then Asle follow her and The Landlady stops outside The Shoemaker's Workshop and then she holds out the keyring to Asle and then she says to him welcome, and that she hopes he'll like it there and that everything goes well for him at The Academic High School, she says and Asle takes the keys

So I'll just go back inside then, it's a little chilly, The Landlady says

Yes, thank you again, and take care of yourself, Father says

Yes, take care of yourself, Mother says

and they see The Landlady go up to her house and up the steps to the front door and then Father says yes well they should probably just carry the things in now, he says

Yes, Asle says

and then Father goes and opens the boot of the car and picks up the studio stove with one burner and Asle takes the bag with the paintings and the sack of bed linens and Mother takes a box of plates and other kitchen things and they carry them inside and no one says anything and then Father goes and gets another two boxes and Asle and Mother go and get some shopping bags

We can help you unpack, Father says

No I'd rather do it myself, Asle says

But, Mother says

I want to unpack it myself, Asle says

and he goes and sits on the edge of the bed and Father and Mother stay standing there in the middle of the room and Asle rolls himself a cigarette and lights it and Mother says he probably doesn't have any ashtrays and then she takes a saucer out of one of the boxes and hands it to him and Asle says thanks and then he thinks that as soon as his parents leave he'll go to The Co-op Store in the centre of Aga and buy himself an ashtray and then Father says that they did bring some food with them but he'll need to buy himself some milk anyway, he says, and Asle says he'll go for a walk and go shopping, because it's not far to The Co-op Store, Asle says and he gets up and leaves the room

And then you'll go visit my mother in the morning? Father says

I'll visit her every day, Asle says

That's nice of you, Father says

And there's a phone booth next to The Co-op Store, and if anything comes up you should just call home, he says

and then it's silent and then Father says well he and Mother will just be driving back home then, he says

Okay, Asle says

But you really don't want us to help you unpack? Father says

No I'll do it myself, Asle says

and Father takes out his wallet and he says that now and every month until he's done at The Academic High School he'll get some money from him, for the rent, for food and clothes and whatever else he needs, schoolbooks and all that, it's not all that much money, nothing special, he's hardly a rich man, Father says, but he'll have the money he needs to get by, and today he needs a larger amount because the schoolbooks he needs will cost a good chunk of money, but books are so expensive, yes indeed, Father says and he hands Asle several notes and Asle takes them and says thank you

You have your wallet with you, right? Mother says

Yes, of course, Asle says

You can leave now, he says

Okay we will, Mother says

Yes, Father says

Now take good care of yourself, you hear, he says

Yes, Mother says

and Father holds out his hand to Asle and he says well good luck then Asle and Mother holds out her hand to him too and she says good luck and then Asle sees Mother go over to the door and she leaves and then Father is in the doorway and he stops and turns around and looks at Asle

Take care, he says

and then Father closes the door behind him and then Asle goes and sits down on the edge of the bed and then he lies down on the bed with his hands folded behind his neck and he puts the saucer he's using as an ashtray on his belly and Asle thinks that he'll be sixteen soon and finally, finally, he's being left in peace, he thinks, and the day he turns sixteen he's going to write to the minister in Barmen and withdraw from The National Church, he thinks and Asle smokes and he feels a lightness come over him and I'm sitting here in the car and I'm driving south and the main road is cleared and good to drive on, and I've seen some cars on the road but not many, and I think that the first thing I'll do when I get to Bjørgvin is park the car in front of The Beyer Gallery and then I'll give the pictures to Beyer and then I'll take a taxi to The Hospital to see Asle, and if I can't see him today either, yes, then I don't know, I think and I feel drowsy, yes, sleepy, because I didn't sleep much last night either, so that means both of the last two nights I didn't get much sleep, yes, maybe almost none, I think, and I think that before I go to The Beyer Gallery I need to drive past the block where Asle's apartment is, in Sailor's Cove, where I was the day before yesterday to get his dog, Bragi, and when I left Dylgja earlier today Bragi was still in my bed and I thought I didn't want to bring him to Bjørgvin, because it would just be a short trip, I think, I was just going to drop off my pictures, see Asle, and then drive back to Dylgja, I think, and I think that now I don't want to even look at the building where Asle's apartment is, I'll just look straight ahead and drive past it, I think and I drive steadily, confidently on south towards Bjørgvin and now I'll drive straight to The Beyer Gallery and then I'll drop off my paintings and put them in the side room, The Bank, as Beyer calls it, and I can do that whether Beyer is there in person or one of those young women he always has a new one of, the university girls, as Beyer says, he's gotten another new university girl to sit in The Gallery, he says, so it doesn't matter if I've arranged a fixed time with Beyer, there's always someone in the gallery, and that's what we've done for all these years now, I think and Beyer has called me on the phone, the same way he does every year, just for form's sake, as he says, we've arranged to have a Christmas exhibition this year too, and he says it with a little laugh, Christmas exhibition, because he knows I don't like to use that word, because the word Christmas, yes, Christmas itself, all the Christmas festivities, I don't like them, I think, but never mind that, because now I'm almost there and I'll be able to park my car in front of The Beyer Gallery, I think, because now, yes, now I'll drive straight to The Beyer Gallery and drop the paintings off and then take a taxi to The Hospital and visit Asle, I have to, I think, because, yes, maybe I should bring him something? or maybe he wants me to buy him something? anyway I'll take a taxi to The Hospital to see how Asle is doing and afterwards I'll take a taxi to St Paul's Church and sit there for a moment, because I'll be too late for morning mass and it'll be too long a wait until evening mass, and then I'll take a taxi to The Country Inn, even though it's not so far to walk and I know the way, I think and at The Country Inn I can get something warm to eat, yes, that's what I'll do, and then I'll go back to The Beyer Gallery and then I'll drive back home to Dylgja, because I don't need to do any shopping, I already bought everything I needed to buy yesterday, I think and there's not much traffic, it's been a while since I've seen another car, and I think that I like driving, it's like it calms me down, like I fall into a kind of daze, sort of, like I'm collected and focused just on driving, nothing else, yes, it's a little like when I paint, except then I basically always have to be listening for something new the whole time but when I'm driving I just listen without listening to the same thing the whole time, and while I'm listening it's like my whole life becomes calm and peaceful, everything that's happened, I think, and I think that it's not good to drive if you're too tired, if you're about to fall asleep, and I feel that I'm still tired so before I drive back home to Dylgja I should get a little sleep, or if nothing else I need a lot of coffee, I think and I've reached 1 High Street and there's a car in just one of the parking places in front of The Beyer Gallery, and it's Beyer's car, and I park my car next to his and I think so I'm here and I look at the whitewashed walls right in front of me and I think that if I just sit here a minute Beyer will probably come out, I think, and I stay sitting in the car, but no Beyer comes out, and I get out and go to the front door of

The Beyer Gallery and I see a scrap of paper hanging on the door and it says Be right back, and that's not really so surprising, it's happened plenty of times before when I've come to The Beyer Gallery without arranging a set time that there's been a scrap of paper like that on the door, and it's never when one of the university girls is in The Gallery but only when it's Beyer himself, I think, because Beyer sometimes puts up a sign like that when he has to run an errand or something, I think, and I think that in that case the first thing I'll do is take a taxi to The Hospital to visit Asle, but I'm so tired, so sleepy, so maybe I can just rest a little in the car, maybe even sleep a little too, I think and I get back into my car and I look at the white walls and I lean the front seat as far back as it can go, and I close my eyes, and now I'll just rest a little, I think, and then I want to pray, yes, I haven't prayed yet today, I think and I close my eyes and I breathe evenly in and out and then I make the sign of the cross and then I take out the brown rosary I have hanging around my neck under my black pullover, the rosary I got from Ales once, and I take the brown wooden cross between my thumb and index finger and I think now I need to get a little sleep and I think I need to pray and I see words before me and I say inside myself Pater noster Qui es in cælis Sanctificetur nomen tuum Adveniat regnum tuum Fiat voluntas tua sicut in cælo et in terra Panem nostrum quotidianum da nobis hodie et dimitte nobis debita nostra sicut et nos dimittimus debitoribus nostris Et ne nos inducas in tentationem sed libera nos a malo and I move my thumb and finger up to the first bead and I say Our Father Who art in heaven Hallowed be thy name Thy kingdom come Thy will be done on earth as it is in heaven Give us this day our daily bread and forgive us our trespasses as we forgive those who trespass against us And lead us not into temptation but deliver us from evil and I think over and over again Let thy kingdom come and then I think that maybe I'm getting tireder because I'm saying Salve Regina and I move my thumb and finger back down to the cross and then I see words and I start to say inside myself Salve Regina Mater misericordiæ Vita dulcedo et spes nostra salve Ad te clamamus Exsules filii Hevæ Ad te suspiramus Gementes et flentes in hac lacrimarum valle Eia ergo Advocata nostra Illos tuos misericordes oculos ad nos converte Et Iesum Benedictum fructum ventris tui Nobis post hoc exsilium ostende O clemens O pia O dulcis Virgo Maria and I repeat again and again Nobis post hoc exsilium ostende and I hold the brown wooden cross and then I say, over and over again inside myself while I breathe in deeply Lord and while I breathe out slowly Jesus and while I breathe in deeply Christ and while I breathe out slowly Have mercy and while I breathe in deeply On me

IV

And I see myself standing and looking at the picture with the two lines that cross near the middle, one brown and one purple, and I see that I've painted the lines slowly, with a lot of thick oil paint, and the paint has run, and where the brown line and the purple line cross the colours have blended nicely and dripped down and I think that I have to get rid of this picture, but I want to keep it? anyway I don't want Åsleik to get it, I think and I think I'll carry the picture upstairs to the attic and into the storeroom on the left and put it with the other pictures I keep in boxes there, the other paintings I don't want to sell, I think, and there's always one painting out leaning on a chair between the two small windows on the short wall in the same room, under the gable, in the middle, and the one I've had there for a long time now is the portrait I painted of Ales, I think and I look at the picture with the two lines that cross and I see myself sitting in my car in the parking space outside The Beyer Gallery and I look at the white walls in front of me and it's Wednesday today, I think, and it's already been such a long day, I think and won't Beyer come back to the gallery soon? I think and it's a little chilly and I put the seat back up the way it usually is when I'm driving and I wonder if I should start the engine and turn on the heat, but I decide not to and then I wrap my black coat around me better and I knot my scarf tighter around my neck and Beyer'll be back soon, I think and then I think that painting isn't something I've done for myself, it wasn't because I wanted to paint, but to serve something bigger, yes, maybe, I do sometimes dare to think things like that, that I want my paintings to do nothing less than serve the kingdom of God, I think, yes, and I thought that way before I was confirmed too, and that might have to do with the fact that I've always felt God's closeness, yes, whatever that is, I think, and call it whatever you want, but now, for one reason or another, it suddenly feels like I've said what I have to say, yes, like I don't have any desire to paint anymore, that there's no more to see, no more to add, but if I do stop painting then what'll I do with myself? maybe read more? because actually I like reading, and maybe I'll get a traditional Barmen pointed boat and start going sailing, when the weather's good, because I've always liked being out on the water, and I always thought I'd get a boat someday, yes, a boat and a dog, that's what everybody needs, I thought, but it didn't work out that way, I never got a boat or a dog either, I think, because I've always lived completely inside my painting, in a way, it was like there was no room for anything else, not a boat, not a dog, no matter how many times I thought that I'd like that, a boat or a dog, yes, that's something a person needs if they want a good life, I would think, and now I have a dog at my house, yes, Bragi, and I like that a lot, I think and I think that now I also feel like I want to get rid of all the paintings I still have, yes, the paintings I've kept all these years, including two of the first pictures I ever painted, yes, painted myself, not from photos of houses and buildings but from what I felt and saw, and those are two of the best pictures I ever painted, yes, I really think so, I think, and that's why, because they came right at the beginning, so to speak, I've usually had one of those two out leaning against the back of the chair, but now I've had the portrait I painted of Ales there for a long time, I think, and I have no desire to take it down, I don't want to take it down, yes, it's sort of found its permanent place there on the chair, but I do sometimes go into the storage space and take out a painting from there, and then I stand and look at it for a little while, I think and there are so many times I was sorry I'd sold my other earliest paintings, yes, I practically gave them away, they sold for so little or nothing, I think, and that was at an exhibition I put on myself at The Barmen Youth Centre, I think, yes, it's pathetic, and in the other room in the attic, the one I get to by taking the door on the right when I come up the stairs, I have my storeroom with tubes of oil paint, canvas, brushes, cans of turpentine, and wood for making stretchers, I think, and there's a storage space in that room too, but I rarely go into that one, and I don't really want to think about it because that's where I put Ales's clothes and other things, because when she died I couldn't bear to get rid of anything so I took it all, folded her clothes up as neatly as I could, her trousers, skirts, underwear, bras, all her clothes, and all the rest, her toiletries, her make-up, what little she used, no I don't want to think about that, not now, no, not now, I think and I think that Åsleik and I wrapped up the nine big paintings and the four small paintings in blankets today, thirteen paintings in all that I'd finished, and then we carried them out to my car and put them carefully in the back, because when I bought a new car, many years ago, when the one I'd bought with Ales and we'd used to move to the old house wasn't usable anymore, the most important thing for me was to make sure that my finished paintings could fit in the back, so I bought a large car, almost a small van, and it had to have a roof rack so I could tie lengths of wood for making stretchers to the roof, I think, and now I put the pictures nicely stacked in the back of the car, wrapped up well in blankets, and I'm happy to be getting rid of these pictures, yes, bringing them to Beyer, I think, but where is Beyer? where has he gone? I've been waiting a long time now, I think and I think that it'll be nice to get back home, it always is, whenever I'm away I'm constantly looking forward to getting back to our good old house there in Dylgja, because I always think of it as our house, even though I've been living there alone for so many years, I still think that it's our house, but soon it'll be time to learn to think about it as my house, not our house, yes, like that instead, my house, I think and I look at the white wall and now I see snowflakes falling one by one and landing on the windshield and I look straight ahead and I see Asle lying there in bed in The Hospital and a doctor opens the door and goes over to him and takes his pulse and his body is still shaking, still trembling

I hope it stops soon, The Doctor says

and the man sitting there keeping watch on him says that it keeps changing, sometimes he's almost not shaking at all but then he starts shaking again, he says and The Doctor says that's good to hear and then he goes over to the other bed and The Doctor puts his hand in front of the mouth and nose of the man lying there and takes his pulse and he says that he's gone and the man on the chair says he hadn't noticed anything unusual and The Doctor says he's dead and I see two people come in and then wheel the bed with the dead man out of the room and then Asle is lying there alone and the man sitting there gets up and goes over to the window and stays standing there looking out and then he looks at Asle and he sees that his body has started shaking again, up and down his body jerks, he sees, and I think that I don't understand why I suddenly decided I had to drive back into Bjørgvin to visit Asle and that was when I found him lying in the snow in The Lane, partly up on the stairs to a front door, lying there covered in snow, I think and I don't want to think about Asle anymore, I think and then I think that I'm a good driver, the only thing is I don't like driving in cities, because then I get flustered, yes, I get so confused that I could easily hit someone, I think and that would be pretty much the worse thing that could happen, I can't imagine anything worse than hitting someone with my car, being responsible for someone being killed or crippled because I hit them, no, even thinking about it is totally unbearable, I think and I sit in my car in the parking space in front of The Beyer Gallery and I look at the white wall in front of me and one snowflake after another lands on the windshield and I look at the white wall and I see Mother come running up and she calls Father and he comes and then they go to the room where Asle and Sister sleep and Asle is behind Father and he sees Father stand there and shake and shake his sister Alida and Asle hears Father say he doesn't know what's wrong, but Sister seems totally lifeless, yes, it's like she's dead, he says and Asle just stands there and then Father goes and calls The Doctor and Asle just stands there, and he thinks what happened? he doesn't understand a thing, he thinks and Mother and Father just stand there next to his sister Alida's bed, he thinks and then The Doctor comes and he goes in to Sister and he says he can only tell them the truth, he says, that she's dead, it doesn't happen often but sometimes children just die suddenly, and when is happens the reason is most often a congenital heart defect, The Doctor says, but the best thing would be if Sister had an autopsy, he says, because then they might find out the cause of death for certain, The Doctor says and then he leaves and I look at the white wall and so many snowflakes have landed on the windshield by now that the white wall is barely visible, and the snow is falling so thick that it's impossible to tell one snowflake from another, and I look at the white wall and I see Asle sitting in church, and everything is just horrible and awful, he thinks and he thinks that his sister Alida was carried away on a stretcher that was put into an ambulance, and that was the last he ever saw of Sister, he thinks, because she was put in a white coffin that was sealed up again and now it's at the front of the church and all the kids from school are there and some adults and everything's horrible and unbearable, Asle thinks and he hears The Minister say something about it being hard to find meaning in sister Alida dying so suddenly, it is hard to understand what the almighty God could have wanted to achieve with that, but still there is a meaning in it, even if we can't understand the meaning, The Minister says, and then he says that Christ died for our sins and because he rose from the dead we too will do the same one day, he says, someday Sister will rise up from the dead, but for now she's with God, now she is living in God's peace, so we shouldn't grieve, because Sister is happy now, she is in a good place, what Sister really was is there, what Sister is, her soul, her spirit, is gone now and only her body remains here, and that's not Sister, that is just a dead body, The Minister says and Asle thinks that he has to agree with The Minister about that, because his sister Alida's body lying there stiff and white and with no movement at all in it that isn't Sister, that is something else, something totally different from Sister, because sister Alida was a life in the body that's now lying there lifeless, up there in the white box, and when the life was gone Sister was gone too, that's how it was, none of sister Alida was there anymore because the corpse that lay there in the bed and that's lying here now in the white box isn't his sister Alida, just something stiff and cold, Asle thinks and he thinks that there's no meaning in the fact that his sister Alida died and it's not something that God could have possibly wanted, so it must be that something God didn't want to have happen happened, Asle thinks and I look at the white wall and the snow is now covering the whole windshield and I can't see the wall and I look at the windshield covered with snow and I think that it was to share in the human condition, our sorrows, that God became man and died and rose up again, because with him, with the resurrected Christ, all people were resurrected too, I think and I think that this is just a meaningless word, I think and I look at the windshield that's now totally covered with snow so that I can't see the white wall anymore and I think that since God is eternal and outside of space and time everything is simultaneous in God, yes, in God everything that has happened and is happening and will happen are all simultaneous, so that's why all the dead have already awoken, yes, they live, yes, they live the way they were and simultaneously as part of God, I think and I look at the snow covering the windshield and I see Asle sitting there in church and he's thinking that everything that idiot Minister up there is reeling off, about how there actually is meaning in the meaningless death of his sister Alida, is an insult, that's how he sees it, because Sister is dead and there's no meaning in it and so there's no meaning in life and you have to just live with that and that means you might as well be dead, Asle thinks, and if he wants to be able to live with meaningless suffering he needs to stop listening to the kind of meaningless talk that The

Minister is reeling off, Asle thinks, because the meaning The Minister is talking about is a kind of torment while meaninglessness gives you a kind of peace, you might say, Asle thinks and he thinks that he doesn't want to be confirmed and I sit in my car parked here in front of The Beyer Gallery and I look and look at the snow covering the windshield and I think that one of the most important things when it comes to painting is being able to stop at the right time, to know when a picture is saying what it can say, if you keep going too long then more often than not the picture'll be ruined, yes, I knew that even when I was painting my very first picture, I think, sure you can scrape it off and repaint it, or paint over it, but then the picture kind of no longer gives itself, and that's what a picture should do, it should come to you on its own, like something that just happens, like a gift, yes, a good picture is a gift, and a kind of prayer, it's both a gift and a prayer of gratitude, I think and I never could have painted a good picture through force of will, because art just happens, art occurs, that's how it is, and once I've gotten as far as I can with a picture I stand back and look at the picture in the dark, yes, look at it when it's as dark in the room as I can make it, I think, and in the summer it never gets really dark so that's why the autumn and winter are the best time to paint for me and the pictures I paint in spring and summer have to wait until autumn or winter before I can really see them, yes, in the darkness, yes, I need to see pictures in the dark to see if they shine, and to make them shine more, or better, or truer, or however it's possible to say it, anyway the picture has to have the shining darkness in it, I think and I think when I get home later today I should start painting again, because I have a bad feeling that something has stopped in a way, that I'm not going to be able to paint any more, that I don't have any desire to paint anymore, that I don't want to paint anymore, so I need to start painting something new today, I think, and I should get home as soon as I can so if only Beyer would show up now, I think, because what Beyer always wants is to open the show a little before Christmas, he thinks that's the best time to open a show if you want to sell as many pictures as you can, and then you can keep the show going until New Year's and then, at New Year's, is often when most of the pictures get sold, I think, and during Advent once I've driven down to Bjørgvin, like today, and delivered the paintings to Beyer it's like I'm finishing something so that I can start something new, I think and I think that I don't have any desire to start any new pictures, the desire I usually always have after I've delivered the paintings, yes, I usually feel a strong need to start painting again that same day, because it's like I'm starting a new picture after I've delivered the paintings because all the pictures in an exhibition go together in a way, yes, it's as if they're all one picture, I think, and this need to paint that I've had ever since I was a boy can't just suddenly disappear? yes, from the first time I painted I wanted to keep painting since I was so good at it, but after a while being good at it was totally unimportant, yes, it was a mistake, I didn't want to be good at it, I wanted to paint just so that I could say something that couldn't be said any other way, yes, paint from a faraway closeness, that's how I think about it, I think, yes, make the blackness shine, yes, paint away the shining darkness, I think, and how often I've thought these thoughts, I think, because I always think the same thoughts over and over again and I paint the same picture over and over again, yes, it's true, but at the same time every single picture is different, and then all the pictures go together in a kind of series, yes, every exhibition is its own series, and finally all the paintings I've ever painted go together and make up a single picture, I think, it's like there's a picture somewhere or other inside me that's my innermost picture, that I try again and again to paint away, and the closer I get to that picture the better the picture I've painted is, but the innermost picture isn't actually a picture of course, because the innermost picture doesn't exist, it just is in a way, without existing, it is but it doesn't exist, and somehow it's as if the picture that isn't a picture sort of leads all the other pictures and pulls them in, kind of, I think, but maybe I've now painted everything I can paint from this innermost picture of mine? I think, maybe I've now in a way entered into this innermost picture and thereby destroyed it? I think, but this going into your innermost picture, yes, seeing it, well that's probably the same thing as dying? I think, yes, maybe it's the same thing as seeing God? and whoever sees God has died, as is written, I think and I look at the snow that's covering the windshield and I see Asle standing there in the room and I see Mother standing there looking at him

You don't want to be confirmed? she says

and she plops down on the sofa

I've never heard of anyone not getting confirmed, she says

What kind of talk is that? she says

and she says that it's the old custom, confirmation is when you stop being a child and become a grown-up, she says

It's true what your mother is saying, Father says

and look he's said something for once, he hardly ever does, Asle thinks

You have to get confirmed, Father says

and he says that Asle'll get presents, and he and Mother will throw a party for him, and he'll get a dark suit and white shirt and tie, yes, the same as all the other boys his age, and all the girls will get a traditional dress for confirmation, Hardanger embroidery, that's just how it is, Father says and Asle thinks well then he'll get confirmed, that's easy enough, and he thinks that as soon as he's old enough, when he's sixteen, he'll write to The Minister and withdraw from The National Church, because Christianity the way it's preached is nothing but a way to torment people, and it's only getting worse, Asle thinks and I sit in the car and I shiver a little and I'm waiting for Beyer to come back to his gallery and I look at the snow that's covering the windshield and I see Asle sitting at the table in the rented room in Aga on the day he turned sixteen and he's writing a letter to The Minister in Stranda and he writes that he wants to withdraw from The National Church and I look at the snow that's covering the windshield and I think that it was only when I met Ales that I started thinking that only God was with sister Alida when she died, and that she was now with God in peace, in his peace, in God's light, I think, because God doesn't want us to die, he came down to Earth because people and God were separated and because God is love and free will is a prerequisite for love, and therefore also for sin, or death, yes, because that's what separates human beings from God, I think, and God and humanity were reunited in Christ, in and through and with his death on the cross, so now neither people nor God have to die, but does that mean anything? does it make sense to think things like that? I think, but that's how Ales used to think, I think and I think that Ales was born into The Catholic Church because her mother Judit was Catholic, she was from Austria and she'd fled to Norway, and Ales and I used to talk and talk together and eventually I understood that what she was saying was true, it was true in its way, because Ales and I went to mass together, and the Eucharist, as they say, means that both Christ and the people who take part in the ceremony together with him offer themselves up, in and through Christ's body in the transubstantiated host, as they say, and in that way they died together for dead they loved every time they went to mass, and in that way they rose up again with the dead they loved every time they went to mass, Ales said and it felt true, it felt real, I think and I think that it's obviously not the only truth but it's a truth, it too, I think, yes, it's almost like a language, because every language gives you access to its share of reality, and the different religions are different languages that can each have its truth, and its lack of truth, I think and it's foolish to think that God is anything defined, anything you can say something about, Ales said and of course she was right, I think and I think that people can't have free will if God is eternal and everything is in God, past, present, future, or actually of course it's possible, because God can know everything, can have everything in him, even if it isn't he who willed it, who set it in motion, I think, but thoughts like that don't mean much and really its only art, maybe, in the best case, that can say anything about the truth that belief contains, or not say anything about it but show it, I think and I think that Ales also said that God is not all-powerful, he is powerful in his powerlessness, it is God as Jesus Christ hanging powerless, nailed to the cross, who is powerful, it's his powerlessness that gives him power, that makes him all-powerful, for eternity, yes, God is powerless, not powerful, I think, anyway that's what Ales thought, I think and I think that maybe these are just empty thoughts but I think them anyway, that it's powerlessness that gives power, but whatever I think or don't think there's little or nothing to say, I think and I look at the snow covering the windshield and I think that I stopped at the turn-off near the brown house the day before yesterday and from there I could see two lovers together in a playground playing like children on the swings and seesaw and in the sandbox, and it was nice to see them, I think and I look at the snow covering the windshield and I think what ever happened to them all, well Sigve died many years ago, he dropped dead one morning while going to work, I know that, but what happened to Geir and Terje and to Olve who I played in the band with when I was going to middle school? and to Amund, who took over for me? I think and someone or other said that Olve went to prison after that, and that he'd been in various dance bands, I think, because after I moved to Aga I almost never went back to Barmen, I got anxious whenever I went, and I don't know why but it was like I was filled with unease and I would drive home the same day I went to visit, I never once spent the night in Barmen since the day I moved to Aga to go to The Academic High School, I think, and it's incredible that I started at The Academic High School because I was, well, to tell the truth I was really terrible in school, I was downright slow, and especially bad at maths, it was impossible for me to understand numbers, they just didn't mean anything to me, they gave me nothing, and honestly they still don't, I think, and that was why when I was going to primary school I used to sit and draw in my maths books and I drew so well that The Schoolmaster told my parents that I had a gift for drawing, and maybe for painting too, and so maybe they should buy me some painting supplies, and they did, but I was still just as bad when it came to maths, The Schoolmaster eventually managed to teach me the most basic things and after a lot of struggling I could do what I was asked to do, I learned that what mattered was not to try to think about it but just to do what I was told I should do, I had to keep every last thought out of my mind strictly in order do what The Schoolmaster said I needed to do, and that's how I got through maths problems, I think and I sit and look at the snow convering the windshield and I think that once I've dropped off the paintings I'll take a taxi straight to The Hospital, I have to go see Asle today, don't I? I think and if Asle wants me to run any errands for him I'll do it, and I still feel tired, sleepy, actually I'm exhausted now that I come to think of it, to tell the truth, because I'm not young anymore, no, to tell the truth I'm an old man, I think and I'm all alone in the world, yes, I'd have to say, there's almost no one besides Åsleik and Beyer that I'm in touch with, yes, really it's just the two of them, and then Asle, I think, because Ales and I lived pretty much entirely on our own, it was like we didn't need any other people besides each other, we shared our world, that was it, and naturally I also knew Åsleik and talked to him when Ales was alive but it was mostly after she died that we started seeing more of each other, and I've known Asle all these years, and I've known Beyer all these years, and Beyer and I are probably friends in our way, but we're probably mostly friends in art, to put it that way, or business partners, that's probably closer to the truth, Beyer would probably put it that way, I think and I look at the snow covering the windshield and I see Asle standing in front of Father listening to Father say that he thought Asle could try to put on an exhibition of the paintings he's painted, because that might make him a little money and that would come in handy in the autumn when he moved to Aga and started at The Academic High School, Father says, well it's not that he's sure someone would buy something, he's not, but it wouldn't hurt to try, Father says and then he says Asle could maybe show his paintings in The Barmen Youth Centre over the summer, since, well, people buy all sorts of things so who knows, maybe Asle can sell a picture or two, anyway it's worth trying, Father says, because there were so many people in town, both in Barmen and sometimes in Stranda too, who'd had him paint a picture of their house and farm and at least some of them would want to come see a show and now, over the summer, there were lots of city people too, especially from Bjørgvin, who drove through Barmen and maybe some of them would feel like stopping to take a look at the pictures, Father says and he says that he could ask the manager at The Co-op Store if Asle could put up a sign in the window saying that there's an art exhibition at The Barmen Youth Centre, no less, but in that case Asle would have to make a sign to hang in the window of The Co-op Store so that everyone in Barmen who went shopping at The Co-op Store would know about it, about there being an art exhibition at The Barmen Youth Centre, yes, Father says and of course people'll start to talk about it, yes, news of this art exhibition of Asle's will get around, so he's sure people will come look at the pictures at least, but as for whether anyone will want to buy one, no, he's not as sure about that, he has his doubts about that one, but, as they say, it's worth trying, Father says, and for all he knows maybe there are some folks who could see themselves buying one of these paintings of his even if they didn't look like anything, after all people are different, people like different things, he says, but if no one sees the paintings and they're just piled up in Asle's room then definitely no one will buy them, that's for sure, Father says, you need to show people the pictures if you want anyone to buy them, Father says and Asle can surely get permission to show his pictures in The Barmen Youth Centre, Father says and Asle thinks that's not such a bad idea, even if he doesn't sell a single painting well at least he'll have put on a show, so he should definitely go ask The Man in Charge of The Barmen Youth Group if he can put on an exhibition in The Barmen Youth Centre this summer, in July, and then he'll paint a sign that Father can hang up in one of the display windows at The Co-op Store, Asle thinks, and then people might come look at the pictures, people from Barmen who've already bought pictures from him and maybe some from Stranda, and maybe one or two people from Bjørgvin who happen to be driving through will stop in, who knows, Asle thinks, and then maybe he'll sell a painting, because these are so much better and truer than all the other pictures he's painted from photographs, he thinks, yes, he should definitely exhibit the art, yes, Asle thinks and I sit here in the car and I look at the snow covering the windshield and I think that for all I know it's still snowing and I think that now Beyer really needs to get back to his gallery soon and I look at the snow that's covering the windshield and I see Asle standing there in front of the sign hanging in the window of The Co-op Store and written on top is Art Exhibition and underneath Asle has painted a picture of The Barmen Youth Centre and under that he's written that there's an exhibition at The Barmen Youth Centre and it'll be open between two and five o'clock through the whole month of July, because the same day Father thought of the idea of this exhibition he's now looking at the sign for, Asle thinks, he, Asle, had gone to The Man in Charge of The Barmen Youth Group and asked if he could use The Youth Centre to put on a show of his paintings this summer and The Man in Charge had said yes of course, why not, he said and then Asle got the keys to The Barmen Youth Centre and I sit here in the car and it's cold and I think that now Beyer really needs to come soon so I can deliver the pictures and I look at the snow that's covering the windshield and I see Asle sitting there at a table in front of the stage in The Barmen Youth Centre and he's thinking he's chosen nine paintings for the show and then brought them over to The Barmen Youth Centre, it took several trips, but it wasn't more than a mile or so to walk so it was easy to do, and once he finally had all the paintings in The Barmen Youth Centre he took a hammer and nails and started hanging up the paintings, nine of them, he had more but there were two he didn't want to sell, that he wanted to keep for himself, and then there were some that he wasn't totally happy with, or else not totally done with, and he thought that these nine made a pretty good number to put up in the auditorium, and that these nine paintings made up a nice picture all together, but the painting at the back of the little stage, the scene of the village with the high cliff and the blue fjord and the blossoming birch trees kind of ruined things for the other pictures, they were kind of ashamed of it, Asle thought and then he went home to Mother, he thinks, sitting behind the table in The Barmen Youth Centre, and he asked if he could borrow four white sheets and he could and he took the sheets and went to The Barmen Youth Centre with them and by standing on a table that he found behind the set onstage he'd managed to drape the sheets over the stage set until finally it was entirely covered with white sheets and actually it looked a little like a ghost, Asle thinks, and that didn't matter, that didn't do anything to the paintings, he thinks and then the exhibition was ready and now he just has to wait to see if people will come look at it, Asle thinks and then he somehow got the table down off the stage into the room and found a chair behind the stage too and then he sat down behind the table, he put it right in front of the stage and now he's sitting there, he thinks, yes, he's sitting there looking at the paintings and now everything's ready, now people just need to come, he thinks and then he hears footsteps and the door opens and then The Man in Charge of The Barmen Youth Group comes in and he sees Asle sitting there behind the table and Asle stands up and goes over to The Man in Charge

I see you've hung up your paintings, he says

and The Man in Charge looks at a box of nails and a hammer that Asle has put down on the floor

Yes, Asle says

It went fine, I carried the pictures from home, it took a few trips but it went fine, it was easy, he says

And you hung them up today? The Man in Charge says

With nails, he says

Yes, Asle says

You didn't think about whether you'd be leaving marks on the walls? The Man in Charge says

And the auditorium's been painted pretty recently too you know, he says

But the pictures couldn't just sit on the floor, Asle says

No I suppose not, The Man in Charge says

But maybe you could've put them on chairs, each one on its own chair? he says

We take the chairs out whenever there's a dance, otherwise they're stacked up in the side room there, he says

and he points at a door

Well what's done is done, The Man in Charge says

and then he goes round and looks at the pictures and then stops and he looks at Asle and he says that these pictures were different from what he'd expected, Asle used to paint differently, he painted so that you could see what it was in the picture, sometimes you could even see that it was your own house he'd painted, but now, well, now it was impossible to tell what any of the pictures was supposed to be of, he'd just smeared paint around, no, why had he painted pictures like this?

he'd painted so many good pictures before, yes, they were hanging in practically every house in Barmen and some in Stranda too, pictures Asle had painted of houses, people's homes, of the barn, the farm, the fruit trees in bloom and the fjord and the cliff, but these paintings, no, they don't look like anything, if he'd known that Asle was wanting to show paintings like these at his exhibition he doesn't know if he'd have given him permission to show them at The Barmen Youth Centre, no indeed, The Man in Charge of The Barmen Youth Group says and he says he doesn't think any of the village folks are going to like these pictures at all, probably some'll come to look at the exhibition but once they start telling their friends how the pictures are painted probably not many more people will come to look, he says

No, no, I thought these pictures would look different, he says

That they'd look like something, the way your other pictures do, he says

and Asle thinks that The Man in Charge of The Barmen Youth Group doesn't understand pictures and art any better than a cow and maybe the other people in Barmen don't either, they probably don't understand pictures and art any better than a cow either, Asle thinks and I sit in my car that's parked next to Beyer's car in one of the parking spaces outside The Beyer Gallery and I think that now Beyer really has to come back to his gallery soon, I think, and I look at the snow covering the windshield and I see Asle sitting there behind a table in front of the stage in The Barmen Youth Centre and there's a sketchpad on the table in front of him and he's holding a pencil in his hand and Asle thinks that now there've been some people at the exhibition, people he's painted pictures for before, and they all say the same thing, he thinks, they say that this wasn't what they were expecting, they don't understand these pictures, and he, Asle, can paint so much better than this, because anyone can paint pictures like these, they say, you just smear some paint around, or however they put it, and then Asle sits there longer and no one comes and it doesn't really matter, he thinks, because he has his sketchpad and pencil and so he can sit there alone in the middle of all these paintings he's painted and sketch, he can sketch out new pictures he's thinking about painting, yes, he has nothing better to do anyway, does he? Asle thinks and every single sketch is something Asle thinks he'll paint in oil on canvas someday, because he's sketching out pictures he's seen and that are stored up in his head and that he wants to paint away, Asle thinks and then he thinks that Father, after he hadn't sold a single painting after several days, told him that maybe it'd be a good idea to thumbtack a slip of paper saying Sold under a couple of the pictures, because people are like that, once one person wants something other people want it, Father says

Yes that's how people are, he said

Once one person has something other people want it too, he said

and then Asle put up a slips of paper saying Sold, with thumbtacks, under five of the paintings and as soon as he'd done that, Asle thinks, someone comes in who'd been by to look at the exhibition before and he starts going from painting to painting and he looks at each painting for a long time and Asle stands up and goes over to him

Do you like the pictures? Asle says

and he thinks that this man had come and looked at the pictures once before already, there haven't been so many visitors to the exhibition that Asle can't remember every one of them, he thinks, and this man is especially easy to remember because he takes up so little space, he's so quiet, so short and slim

Are you from Stranda? Asle says

No, the man says

and Asle can hear right away that the man is from Bjørgvin and the man from Bjørgvin nods and then he says that he's from Bjørgvin, as Asle could probably hear, he says and he holds out his hand and Asle shakes it and the man says Beyer and Asle says Asle and then the man named Beyer says that he might like to buy a picture, he was here and he looked at the paintings a few days ago too and ever since then he couldn't forget them, he says

Yes, it's strange, Beyer says

There's something about these pictures that sticks in my mind, he says

and it was especially one of the pictures that stuck in his mind, and he really wanted to buy that picture, but now there's a slip of paper under it saying Sold so he guesses he'll just buy a different one, he says, but the question of course is how much Asle wants for the picture, he says and Asle thinks that he wants to make back what the picture cost him in any case and then he can maybe add a few kroner on top of that but not too much, because otherwise he probably won't sell a single picture, he thinks and then he says what he wants for the painting and Beyer says that he can certainly afford that much and so it's settled and then he walks around the room and looks at the pictures one after another and then he stops in front of one and looks at it for a long time and then he goes over to one of the picture with a Sold sign tacked up under it and then he goes over to Asle and says that he's found a painting he wants to buy, but he really regrets that not coming back out here sooner so that he could've bought the picture he saw so clearly in his mind, saw it again and again too, he says and Asle says that he can ask the person who bought that picture if he'd consider buying another one instead, so if Beyer could come back tomorrow maybe he'd be able to work things out so that he can buy the picture he'd rather have, Asle says

Thank you, Beyer says

Thanks very much, he says

Thank you, Asle says

and he says that not too many paintings have sold, he can see that for himself, and then Beyer leaves and now I'm tired of sitting and waiting, now Beyer really needs to come soon so I can drop off the paintings, I think, and I look at the snow that's covering the windshield and I see Asle sitting behind a table in The Barmen Youth Centre and he sees Beyer come walking up to him and Asle says that he got the other buyer to pick another picture instead so Beyer can have the picture he wants, Asle says and then Beyer says then he'll buy it and also the other one he liked, so two pictures, if they both cost the same, he says and Asle says that they do and then Beyer hands him the money and he says that since he has to drive back to Bjørgvin soon he'd appreciate it if he could take the pictures with him now and Asle says that's easy enough and then he writes Sold on two sheets of paper in the sketchpad and tears them out and then goes and takes down the two paintings Beyer's bought and puts them on the floor and then he hangs the sheets of paper saying Sold on the nails the paintings had been on and then Beyer takes the paintings and he says pleasure doing business with him and that he hopes they'll meet again, and that Asle needs to keep painting, he has a talent for painting, yes, he's very talented, he says, and then Beyer leaves and then Asle sits there and sketches some more and three more people come and say pretty much the same thing, that now that they'd thought about it there was something about these pictures after all and now they want to buy one, says each of the three people one after the other, they all say pretty much the same thing, and the strange thing is that Asle doesn't know any of them, but maybe that's not so strange, because they're all from Bjørgvin, and each of them chooses a painting and they ask how much he wants for it and Asle sticks to the same price for every painting, the price he'd told Beyer, and one after the other the people from Bjørgvin hand over the money and pay Asle and they ask if it's all right for them to take the painting with them right away and Asle says that's fine and after they've left he goes and takes down the signs saying Sold from under the pictures because there are signs under every one of the four pictures left, but none of them have really been sold, and he puts them up on the nails where the paintings that really did sell had been hanging, and now Asle has sold five pictures, so now it says Sold in five empty places on the wall and there are just four pictures left that haven't been sold, and now there's no sign saying Sold under any of them, Asle thinks, but it's not bad to have sold five paintings, he thinks and he sits down behind the table in front of the stage and then he sits there and sketches and he thinks that this is probably as good as it gets for him, he thinks, but he realises he misses the pictures that were sold, that are gone, Asle thinks and before long he's filled a sketchpad with designs for pictures that he has stuck in his head and he thinks that he'll paint all these sketches at some point, or maybe not all, but most of them anyway, yes, some of the sketches anyway will turn into oil on canvas, he thinks, will turn into paintings, Asle thinks and then he sees Beyer, the man who's already bought two paintings, come back in, and it's really about time someone came, Asle thinks, because there hasn't been anyone in to look at his exhibition for a while and he has only four paintings left to sell, so he thought what's the point of sitting here anymore, but he did write down an opening and closing date for the exhibition so he has to stick to it, Asle thinks and Beyer nods at Asle and says hello and then he goes and looks at the four paintings still hanging there, he goes from one painting to the other and he takes his time, he looks at painting after painting for a long time and Asle thinks it's strange that Beyer as he's called came back, and then Beyer comes walking up to Asle and he says that he likes Asle's pictures so much that he wants to buy all four that are still left, yes, if he can get them for the same price as before, he says

Yes your pictures really have something, Beyer says

Something all their own, he says

But of course I need to ask what you want for the pictures, he says

and Asle says that he can buy them for the same price as before and

Beyer says that in that case it's a deal and he takes out his wallet and he pays for the paintings and he says that the price is perfectly reasonable and Beyer says that he was on his way to Stranda where some friends of his have a cabin and he stopped at The Co-op Store and saw the sign for the art exhibition in the window there, yes, the sign was actually a painting, and even if the motif on the sign wasn't quite as interesting still The Barmen Youth Centre was painted well and that's why he thought he should go back to the art exhibition, he says

Yes you have a real future ahead of you, he says

I can see that, he says

And I really know about paintings, he says

and then he says again that his name is Beyer and then he asks again what Asle's name is and then he says that if he remembers correctly there were signs saying Sold under at least two of the pictures he just bought, he says and he looks at Asle who doesn't say anything and then Beyer says goodbye and he takes two of the paintings with him and Asle says that he can help him carry the other two out and then Beyer walks to his car and he puts the paintings in the back and lays a blanket between each painting and then Asle stands there and Beyer gets into his car and drives off and Asle goes back inside and he looks at the empty walls and he feels sad that all the painting are gone now, because actually he would've liked to keep all the paintings himself, Asle thinks, and he'd felt so calm and peaceful when he was sitting in The Youth Centre surrounded by his paintings and sketching out pictures that he was going to paint some time in the future, some of the sketches would turn into paintings anyway, and now, now there are no pictures left, so now it's become kind of empty and sad, Asle thinks and he thinks that the pictures he's painted of people's homes, yes, he's always been glad to get rid of those, the sooner the better really, but he likes these paintings more, and he feels sad and in a way heavy when he thinks about how they're gone now, he thinks and then Asle goes and rips all the signs saying Sold off the nails and throws them out in the litter basket outside The Youth Centre and he goes back in and pulls all the nails out of the walls and goes and throws them out in the litter basket too and then he takes down the sign saying Art Exhibition from the front door of The Barmen Youth Centre and throws it in the litter basket and Asle goes back in and puts the table and chair back behind the stage where he found them and then he takes down the sheets in front of the horrible set painting of Stranda in the blazing sun with a glittering blue fjord and a black cliff with white snow on top against the horizon and then he puts the sheets back in the shopping bag he'd brought them in, and he puts the hammer and the box of nails on top and then he puts his brown leather shoulder bag on and then Asle turns off the light and he leaves and he thinks he needs to put up a sign on the front door saying Sold Out and then he takes out the sketchpad and writes Sold Out on a page of it and then he takes out the thumbtacks that were holding up the earlier sign and uses them to put the sign saying Sold Out up on the front door of The Barmen Youth Centre and then he shuts the door and he goes to The Man in Charge of The Barmen Youth Group and gives him the keys

You're giving up? he says

Yes, Asle says

It's not so easy to sell paintings, is it, The Man in Charge says

No, Asle says

But thank you for letting me use The Youth Centre, he says

and then Asle walks home carrying the shopping bag and Mother asks why he's home already and Asle says that he's sold all the pictures, but actually he's sorry he sold them, because now he misses them and now he'll never get them back

No I don't believe it, Mother says

and she says no she just doesn't understand people, she can understand how he can sell his usual paintings, but that someone would pay good money for incomprehensible smears that don't look like anything, no, she can't understand that, Mother says and she says so the sign saying there's going to be an art exhibition hanging in the window of The Co-op Store, that'll have to be taken down

Yes, right, Asle says

and he takes the nails and the hammer out of the shopping bag and says that he'll just go put these back in the basement of The Old House and then he hands the bag with the white sheets to Mother and says thanks for the loan

I'll wash them now, she says

and then she says that Asle should go right now and take down the sign in the window of The Co-op Store

Yes I'll do that now, he says

No I never thought you'd sell those paintings, Mother says

Whoever bought them must have something wrong in the head, she says

and Asle says that there's one person who's sick in the head, who has something wrong with her mind, and that's her, Mother, and she says imagine saying something like that to your own mother and she says that he can't have gotten much money for his paintings did he and Asle says he sold them for the amount it cost him to make them plus a little extra

No, it's unbelievable, that you sold those pictures, I wouldn't have thought you'd sell a single one, Mother says

and she asks who bought the pictures and Asle says that a man named Beyer who lives in Bjørgvin bought most of them

Yes of course it had to be a Bjørgvinner who'd buy pictures like that, Mother says

No, well, Asle says

and then he goes into town to The Co-op Store and he takes the sign, or rather the painting that says Art Exhibition, out of the window and then he goes home with it under his arm and I sit here in the car and I look at the snow covering the windshield and then I turn on the windshield wipers and they sweep the snow away and I can see to the white wall and now raindrops are falling on the windshield, so now it's already started raining, I think, and I've been sitting in the car a long time now, and it's really cold and I'm shivering a little, I think, so now Beyer really needs to come back to his gallery soon so that we can carry the paintings in and put them in the gallery's side room, The Bank, as Beyer calls it, I think and actually I don't want to do that, I don't want to get rid of these paintings either, I think, it's like saying goodbye forever every time, and it's like I'm giving myself away bit by bit, I think, but I need something to live on too and I live on the sales of the pictures I paint, that's what I've lived on my whole life, I think, so it just has to be done, I have to just bring the paintings to Beyer's Bank, I think and I open the car door and I get out and the rain and cold hits me and I think anyway I can go check if the door to The Beyer Gallery is open, because maybe Beyer's come back to the gallery without my noticing it, that might very well have happened, I think and no sooner am I out of the car than I see Beyer standing in the gallery door holding the door open and he shouts that it's good my pictures are here, it's like it's not really Christmas without them, Beyer says and he says he has to admit he's been waiting for the pictures, he says and I jog over to the open door and Beyer holds out his hand to me and we shake hands and I see that the sign that was hanging on the door is gone and I think Beyer must have been in the gallery the whole time, he just didn't want to be disturbed, or else the sign on the door was a mistake, I think and Beyer says I should come in and Beyer is sort of beside himself with happiness at seeing me and he again says it's good to see me, because to tell the truth it's been almost a year since the last time we saw each other and I say it sure has

We're both getting old, you and me, he says

and I look at Beyer and I see that he has a cane in his left hand and I've never seen him with one before, but he has been a little unsteady on his feet for a few years, his walk has been kind of halting, but this is the first time I've seen him with a cane and then Beyer raises his cane into the air

Yes just look, he says

and he holds up his cane a little higher

I can get by without it but it's good to have it, he says

and I think that Beyer has aged a lot in just a year, I think and I see that you couldn't call his hair grey anymore, it's turned white, and Beyer has sort of gotten a little crooked and he lets go of my hand and then he says I look good

You haven't aged much since the last time I saw you, he says

and I don't know what I should say, and I just stand there

Yes you and I have been doing business together or whatever I should call it for many years now, Beyer says

Yes, I say

A generation at least, Beyer says

No much longer than that, he says

and he says that it must be getting on fifty years if you count the first time, when he bought six pictures from me when I was a boy putting on my first exhibition in The Barmen Youth Centre, Beyer says and then he stands there and doesn't say anything and then he looks right at me and then he asks if I remember the first time we met and I say of course I do, yes, I remember it like it was yesterday, and I was thinking about it just recently, I say and I think that Beyer has brought this up so many times, yes, this too has turned into something we do just to do it, something we talk about to kind of show how connected we are to each other

Yes, there in The Barmen Youth Centre, Beyer says

Yes, I bought five paintings from you then, he says

Six actually, I say

and it doesn't seem like Beyer hears what I'm saying

And I got my family and friends to buy the others you were selling, he says

and he says that he's heard that none of them regretted it, he says

And clever you had put up signs saying Sold under a few of the paintings even though they weren't sold, he says

and Beyer laughs and shakes his head

Yes I must admit I've used that trick lots of times myself, he says

And it works too, it works well, he says

and then there's silence

So I knew that not only could you paint, and that you had a great future as an artist ahead of you, but also that you understood how to sell things, Beyer says

Yes, good business sense, he says

It was my father who thought of it though, I say

Yes well then he has good business sense, Beyer says

You're descended from a real businessman, he says

and he says the word businessman in a way that clearly implies that this is really something I can be proud of

A businessman, yes, he says

My father built boats, traditional Barmen boats, and grew fruit, I say

Yes I know, Beyer says

and I don't say anything else and it's quiet for a moment and then I say that Father worked hard, both building his Barmen boats and then he kept working in his orchard, but no matter how much he worked he didn't make much money, we weren't rich in our house, so I wouldn't say Father was a real businessman exactly, I say

No, maybe not, Beyer says

But you, you have a sense for making money, he says

and I say that I need something to live on too, and for me it was living on painting these pictures, something you'd hardly believe was possible, at least where I grew up, there people lived so far apart that even if every last one bought a picture every now and then I wouldn't have sold many pictures, I say and Beyer chuckles and says very true, very true, yes, very true

I don't entirely understand it myself, how I managed it, I say

and then I say that it's thanks to him, thanks to Beyer, that I could do it, without his help it never would've worked, and that's precisely because I'm not a businessman at all, no, but it's also because I haven't thrown a lot of money around, I've scrimped and saved actually, I spend as little money as I can, I only have two pairs of shoes, one for winter and one for summer, and then one pair of dress shoes, and then a pair of big rubber boots that I cut down to shoes, for example these, I say, but when I do buy shoes I always buy expensive shoes, the best brands, I say, and those shoes last a long time, and sometimes I need to take them to the cobbler and eventually they're worn out and have to be thrown away but it's years between each time, I say and Beyer says now that I mention it he's noticed for a long time that I'm always wearing the same shoes, he says, just like I always wear black clothes, a black pullover of one kind or another and I'm always in black trousers and always in a black velvet jacket, and he's barely ever seen me without a brown leather shoulder bag on my shoulder, and then in the winter I wear the long black overcoat that I have on today, he's never seen me in a suit, but my shoes are always black, and then often, though not always, I have on some scarf or another

Yes I need my artist's scarf, I say

and I use those words because I know that if I don't Beyer will, if I don't say artist's scarf Beyer will, I think and I don't entirely like it when he says that because it's almost like he's looking down on me a little when he says those words, artist's scarf

Yes you allow yourself that much, Beyer says

and he says that even if I'm constantly wearing a new scarf, some of them are silk, he noticed that a long time ago, so I must have quite a big collection of scarves, he says and I think that I always asked Ales for a scarf as a present, and most of the time I got one too, either for my birthday or for Christmas, and that's why I have a lot of scarves, some of them nice scarves, and when I go out and see other people I usually like to wear a scarf, it's true, that's how it is, I think and it's quiet for a moment and then Beyer again says that it was very clever of me, sneaky even, to put up a sign saying Sold under pictures that weren't sold, yes, that means that I have a real business sense, he says, and that too is one of those terms I don't really like, but for Beyer like for most Bjørgvin people it's a compliment

A real business sense, yes, Beyer says

That was a good idea, he says

I never remember if it was me who thought of it, I say

It might have been my father, I don't exactly remember, I say

Yes, clever, I'd say sneaky even, whoever came up with it, Beyer says

and then I say, as I stand there, that I still think those nine pictures I sold back then are some of the best ones I ever painted and I say that I regret having sold them all, and that was a lesson for me, I say, because now I set aside pictures I don't want to sell in the attic of my house in Dylgja, in one of the crawlspaces, in a crate up there, and Beyer says that's interesting, hearing about the pictures up in the crate, and I say that I always have one of those paintings out on display, on a chair between two small windows in that same attic room, which painting it is changes but there's always one out, and I switch them sometimes but it's always a painting from the collection up there in the crates, I say and I say that it's probably to sort of remind myself that not everything I've done in life has been totally meaningless, I say

No, you've hardly done things that are meaningless, Beyer says

On the contrary, he says

and he says that he discovered me, it's surely fair to say that, and that his discovery of me is the most important thing he's done for Norwegian art, because now my pictures still aren't appreciated properly but that'll change, it just takes some time, the best artists aren't appreciated like they deserve until long after they're dead, Beyer says, yes it's almost always like that, he says

Quality, quality and truth always win out, he says

But it can take a while, he says

It takes a long time but in the end truth will out, as the Bard says, Beyer says

and he says that it might take a long time before my pictures are sold at the price they deserve, most likely neither he nor I will live to see it, in any case he won't, but I have to believe what he says even if neither of us will live long enough to confirm the truth of his words, he says, but I, my pictures, a day will come when they are recognised as the most important works of Norwegian painting, nothing less, he says

Oh now I don't know about that, I say

You know it perfectly well, he says

and Beyer's voice is firm

Yes, deep inside I probably do know something like that, I say

and then we're standing there in silence and Beyer says that I've already achieved a lot, I've had my work bought by the National Museum of Art in Oslo, I have several paintings there, and several public institutions have bought pictures, and I mustn't forget that The Bjørgvin Museum of Art has bought several paintings, still, most of my pictures, almost all, have been bought by ordinary people who really liked my pictures, and that's also because he didn't price them too high, a little high but not too high, since actually not a single one of my pictures has been sold for too high a price, he says, so you can't complain, he says, there's no reason to be dissatisfied, when I sometimes have even had shows at The Arts Festival in Bjørgvin, I've been an Arts

Festival Artist, which is maybe the greatest honour a Norwegian visual artist can be given, he says, admittedly there were some people who weren't happy about the show, there's always someone who feels the need to act all big and important, and the person who was, and still is, the art critic for *The Bjørgvin Times* wrote that choosing me as The Arts Festival Artist was extremely strange, there were lots of people who painted better than me, he wrote, that idiot, Beyer says, but the art critic for *The Bjørgvin Times* has never understood art and it's strange, Beyer says, that so often the people with the least feeling for what's good art and bad art are the ones who decide to study art and become art critics, so in a way it was just as well that *The Bjørgvin Times* doesn't even review my shows anymore, they did for the first few years, because back then Anne Sofie Grieg was the critic and she always wrote good, thorough reviews, but then the guy who thinks my pictures are too airy, too wispy, yes, too mystical, started writing for them and he only stopped recently and the newspaper started reviewing my shows again, and that's good too, really, maybe that's the best thing, despite everything, Beyer says and then he says that I probably won't come to the opening this year either, will I, no of course not, he says

No, I say

and he says that I've never been to a single one of my openings, and I don't agree to interviews anymore, he says, it was better when I did every now and then, and that was before I stopped drinking, no, I don't exactly make it easy for him to sell my pictures, I don't go to openings and I don't give interviews, Beyer says, and he says that even so, despite that, my pictures usually sell well, usually all my paintings sell, or almost all, and the ones that don't he keeps and when there are enough for a show of their own he sends them to The Kleinheinrich Gallery in Oslo, and they're sold there, yes, almost all of them, and the pictures that don't sell there he takes back, and sooner or later they'll be exhibited in Nidaros, he says, but my best paintings stay in Bjørgvin, Beyer says and he gives a good laugh and now, yes, now there'll soon be enough paintings that didn't sell either in Bjørgvin or in Oslo for a show in Nidaros, the exhibition planned for a long time at The Huysmann Gallery in Nidaros, yes, he and Huysmann have known each other for all these years, it's planned for this spring, so next year that'll be no fewer than three exhibitions, one in Oslo, one in Nidaros, and of course the yearly show at The Beyer Gallery, he says, next year I'll sell more paintings than ever before, Beyer says and he says that we can't just stay standing around like this chatting away, it's stopped raining so now we need to get the pictures inside, and then he puts a doorstop under the front door to hold it open and I go and open the door to the back of the car and then I say that I can carry the pictures inside on my own and Beyer says thanks thank you and he says that he's so eager to see the pictures that he can barely wait, he says and then I go and get two pictures and Beyer goes into the gallery and he opens the door to The Bank and I go in there and I carefully put the paintings down on the floor and then I go back out and get more paintings and carry them inside and then I get the last two and carry them in and put them down in The Bank and then I go back into the gallery and Beyer shuts the door to The Bank and he says that it's good to have the paintings safe and sound in The Bank, and he says that he's looking forward to taking what I call the blankets off the paintings like a child looks forward to Christmas presents, yes

That's how I like to do it, Beyer says

and I have to bring in the paintings wrapped in blankets, he says, and I say yes, right, and then we don't say anything

Yes, well, typical Bjørgvin weather today, Beyer says

As soon as we get some snow the rain starts, he says

Yes, I say

But it's good that it lets up every now and then between the showers, he says

And it feels good to have gotten the pictures in here, he says

and then Beyer says that he always waits to look at the pictures, to unwrap them and look at them, until he's about to hang the exhibition, and since that's what we always do he'll do it alone this year too? Beyer says and I nod and I've painted the pictures' titles on the back same as always, haven't I, on the top edge of the stretcher, and then signed the picture itself with a big A in the lower right corner? he says and I nod and then Beyer says so everything's as it should be and after he's unpacked the pictures and hung them the way they're going to be in the show he'll take a photograph of each picture and then he'll price the pictures and prepare a list of pictures with the title and price of each one, in the order they're hung in, he says

We'll do it the same way we've always done it, I say

Yes, this isn't our first time, is it, Beyer says

and he says it's my annual Christmas show, and I think I've never liked that expression, Christmas show, it's really a marketing term, but that's exactly what Beyer is like, in large part, he's a huckster, a businessman, and he likes words like that, and in a way it's good that he's like that because I need to make money and if Beyer wasn't a huckster I'd probably be in bad shape when it came to money, I think, and then I think that even though I like Beyer a lot there's something about him that makes me uncomfortable, so we've never truly become friends, we're too dissimilar for that, maybe it has to do with me being a country kid and he a city kid, maybe it's because his family are big city people and mine are more humble, just ordinary country people, I think, and I think Beyer's a good person, I like him, but I do get tired of him pretty quickly, he gets on my nerves, there's something about his eagerness that gets to me, so whenever we see each other it's always a pretty short meeting and a bit forced and I tell Beyer I have to leave, I have some errands I need to run, I say, and then I ask Beyer if he'd be so kind as to call me a cab and Beyer says of course of course and then he goes to the telephone and calls for a taxi and then he comes over to me and says that a taxi'll be here right away and then we stand there by the door to the gallery and look out at the rain and slush and neither of us says anything and then Beyer says just to say something that he's really looking forward to these pictures, he's as excited to take them out of their blankets as a little boy is to unwrap his Christmas presents, he says and he says that he has to wait, and not look, not peek, no, he'll wait until three days before the opening and only then will he take the blankets off the pictures, one by one, and then he'll look at each picture for a long time before carrying it into the gallery and putting it on the floor where he thinks it should be hung, and then he'll go and get a new picture, one by one, until all the pictures are standing against the wall on the floor of the gallery and then he'll stand and look at each picture for a long time one by one and think about how each picture goes with the next one and so on and then he'll move the pictures around until they're in the order he sees in his mind, and most of the time, when it comes to my paintings, he can feel sure of it pretty quickly but it doesn't always go so well with other artists, but it's important that the whole show is like a single picture, because as soon as someone comes into the room they should feel like they've kind of entered into a picture, the room itself should be like a picture, a picture you can enter into, Beyer says and I think that it's obvious that the picture all my pictures come from would in a way fill the room, I think and Beyer says that he doesn't know what exactly makes it that way, it's not something to put into words, because you can't put what a good picture says into words, and as for my pictures the closest he can get is to say that there's an approaching distance, something far away that gets closer, in my pictures, it's as if something imperceptible becomes perceptible and yet still stays imperceptible, it's still hidden, it is something staying hidden, if you can say it that way, my pictures kind of talk to the person looking and at the same time it's impossible to say what the picture says, because it's a silent kind of talking to you, yes, that's what it is for him, Beyer says and then he says that he's just blabbing away and I see a taxi pull into one of the parking places in front of The Beyer Gallery and stop next to my car and Beyer holds out his hand to me and says thank you thank you and we'll talk again soon and I say thank you too and then I go out to the taxi and I open the rear door and I get in and I say I want to go to The Hospital

I think I just drove you to The Hospital yesterday, or whatever day it was, The Taxi Driver says

It's possible, I say

and even though he recognises me I have no memory of him at all

Yes I do believe it must've been you, he says

May well be, I say

Are you going in for a checkup or something? The Taxi Driver says

and he turns his head a little to look at me

No I'm visiting a friend, I say

and The Taxi Driver drives and doesn't say anything and then he says that it's always like this in Bjørgvin, as soon as it snows it starts raining, he says, and that's all well and good as long as it doesn't get cold enough for the sludge to freeze to ice, yes, then you're risking life and limb to walk or drive in Bjørgvin, he says, but life must go on, even in icy conditions, The Taxi Driver says and then he sits there silent for a moment and then he signals and pulls over in front of The Hospital and stops by the entrance and he says how much it'll be and I pay and then I say thank you for the ride and then I go into The Hospital and I go over to the reception desk and the woman sitting there slides the window open and I say who I am and the person I'd like to see please and the woman sitting at the reception desk flips through some pages and then says that Asle has to rest, it's written here that no one can disturb him, no one can go see him, the doctors have decided that, he needs his rest, he needs to get his rest, he needs peace and quiet, she says and I ask when she thinks I'll be able to visit Asle and she says that she can't say and then she says that I can call The Hospital and ask when I can come

I guess you're saying he's seriously ill? I say

Yes that's what that means, she says

But is his life in danger? I say

It's possible, she says

and I stand without moving and without saying anything

I'm a close friend, it was me who brought him in, I say

and she nods

First we went to The Clinic and then they sent him here to The Hospital, I say

and she nods and says yes if someone is seriously ill then they're transferred at once from The Clinic to The Hospital

Yes, I say

But I just wonder if he needs anything? if there's anything I can bring him? or buy for him? I say

and the woman sitting at the reception says that I don't need to worry about that, he doesn't need anything besides what he has now, he's just lying in bed and sleeping most of the time to regain his strength, she says and I say thank you and I stare blankly straight ahead into empty space and nothingness and I see Asle lying there with lots of tubes connected to his body, and there's another bed in the room with someone lying in it, and then there's a man in a white coat sitting on a chair, and Asle's body is shaking and shaking, he's trembling the whole time, shuddering, and then he suddenly stops and is calm and the man sitting on the chair looks at Asle and then he gets up and goes over and shakes Asle by the shoulder

Asle, he says

Yes, Asle says

and it's as if he's saying it from far far away, but he says yes and then the man who shook him by the shoulder goes back and sits down on the chair again and then the woman sitting at the reception desk asks if everything's all right and I say yes and then I ask her if she can call me a taxi and she says that she can see a taxi sitting outside The Hospital, it's probably free, she says, so I could go ask if that one's free first, she says, and if it isn't free then of course she'll call a cab for me, she says and I say thank you thank you and then I say that I'll call tonight to ask if I can come in the morning and the woman sitting at the reception desk says that it's fine for me to wait until the morning, because they'll only decide in the morning if he's able to receive visitors or not, she says, and I say thanks very much, thank you for your help, I say and she says it was nothing and then I go out to the taxi that's stopped there and it's the same car that drove me to The Hospital still parked outside The Hospital and I look at The Taxi Driver and he nods and I open the rear door and I get in and The Taxi Driver says that was a short visit and I say that I couldn't see the person I wanted to see because The Doctor had said that he needed to rest, to sleep, and no one could visit him, I say, that was The Doctor's decision, I say

Yes that's how it is sometimes, The Taxi Driver says

Is that why you didn't drive away, because you thought that might happen? I say

No, The Taxi Driver says

and then he says that there's often someone in front of The Hospital who needs a taxi, so once he's driven here, if he's not called for another ride, then it's just as good to wait here, more often than not someone comes out before long who needs a taxi, he says, and now and then it's like what happened with me, that someone a person wants to visit isn't allowed to have visitors, for whatever reason, and then whoever took the taxi to The Hospital needs another taxi right away, he says

And where would you like to go now? he says

To The Country Inn, I say

Yes I thought so, he says

and then The Taxi Driver says that he's sure I've ridden with him before, he recognises me in any case, and he thinks that he's taken me to The Country Inn before, but he also thinks it was The Hospital, he doesn't exactly remember, but there's something familiar about me anyway, yes, now he remembers, his memory is so bad, he's driven me home to my apartment lots of times, yes, that's it, he's driven me lots of times from The Alehouse back to my apartment in Sailor's Cove, he says and I wasn't entirely sober then either, no, he says, far from it, he's driven me home from The Last Boat, that's it, The Taxi Driver says, yes, there's no doubt about it now, but no matter how drunk I was I've always behaved well, and I've always paid, given a good tip, yes, he remembers now, and then, many years ago, he also saw a picture of me in *The Bjørgvin Times*, I'm a painter and the article had something to do with an exhibition at The Beyer Gallery, so that was why he picked me up there, outside the gallery, he says, and my name is Asle or something like that, isn't it? The Taxi Driver says and I say yes, that's my name, yes, and I say I recognise him, The Taxi Driver, I recognise him too

So you're an artist? he says

Yes, at least I try, I say

But you make enough to live on from that? he says

More or less, I say

Well then, The Taxi Driver says

and then it's silent

Selling your pictures brings in enough for you to live on? he says

Yes, I say

Yes, aha, he says

and then he says that the kinds of pictures I paint must be really expensive, not for the likes of him, just for rich people, he says and I don't say anything

Or is that not true? he says

All kinds of people buy my pictures, I say

I don't believe it, The Taxi Driver says

and there's silence and then he asks if I'm going to have another show at The Beyer Gallery soon and I say yes, that a show of mine will be opening there soon

Then I think I'll go look at your pictures, he says

But they probably don't look like anything? he says

Anyway it probably costs a lot to get in, right, to your exhibition at The Beyer Gallery? he asks

and I say that it doesn't cost anything, anyone who wants to can go look at the paintings, I say and The Taxi Driver says well then he'll definitely go take a look since now it's like he knows me a little, the artist himself, yes, so he'll go look at my pictures because he likes paintings well enough, yes, even if they don't look like anything, the most important thing is for the picture to say something, kind of, that it's not just scribbles and smears but painted to really say something, yes, that's when he likes the painting, The Taxi Driver says and he turns around and looks straight at me before turning back forwards, he likes a painting if it has something to say, yes, he says, so he might really like my paintings, and since he's driven me home so many times he's now pretty interested in seeing how I paint, and now that he thinks about it he feels like he's driven me when I was sober too, yes indeed, he says and I see The Country Inn up ahead and The Taxi Driver pulls over and stops in front of The Coffeehouse

Yes well here we are, he says

and he turns his head to look at me and says how much it is and I hold out the money and he says yeah of course he remembers me, he's driven me home from The Alehouse, The Last Boat, so many times, how could he not have recognised me at once, no, he says, and Asle or something, that's my name, right? he says and I say yes and I pay and then The Taxi Driver says that this year he'll go look at my paintings, for sure, he says

Because they are paintings, right? he says

Yes, I say

Good, paintings are what I like, he says

and I say take care and he says thanks you too and then I open the door and get out and then I go right into The Coffeehouse and there, at the window table nearest the door, a woman with medium-length blonde hair is sitting, and her hair looks like the hair of the woman I met the day before yesterday, the one who showed me the way to The Country Inn when I somehow managed to get lost in the snowstorm here in Bjørgvin and who watched Asle's dog, who lived in The Lane, who was apparently named Guro, but then again there are so many women with medium-length blonde hair, and there's a suitcase and a couple of shopping bags next to her, so it can't be the woman I met the day before yesterday, but the woman sitting there does look like her, she really does, so it might be her, I think and I walk into The Coffeehouse and it's empty inside and I pick a window table as far back as possible and I take off my brown leather shoulder bag and put it down on a chair and then I take off my black coat and put it on top of the shoulder bag and I go over to the counter and I pour myself a coffee, and I take milk in my coffee, and then I go to the cash register and I see that they've hung up the lunch menu, so I can buy lunch now if I want, and I look over the menu and I see that there's nothing there I want, they sell homemade meatballs every day at The Coffeehouse but I don't feel like that today, or like any of the other dishes either, because I'm not that hungry, just a little hungry, it's like I have to eat just a little something, I think, so I'll probably get the usual then, I think and I say I'd like bacon and eggs please and the woman sitting at the register says that's fine, I can just find a table and sit down and she'll bring me my food, she says, I just need to get my own knife and fork, she says and then I get a knife and fork and napkin and I go put them on the table and then I go and get *The Northern Herald*, which is on a pole along with *The Bjørgvin Times*, and *The Northern Herald* is a good paper, every so often there's the rare good review of an art exhibition, sometimes of mine, not always just sarcastic criticism like in *The Bjørgvin Times*, I think and I cautiously peek over at the woman with the medium-length blonde hair and she looks exactly like the woman who helped me the day before yesterday, so it must be her, but surely it's just someone who looks like her because otherwise she'd surely have recognised me and said hello, or said something like wasn't I going right home yesterday? or had I driven back into Bjørgvin from Dylgja again today? she might have said, but she's just sitting there with a cup of coffee reading a newspaper, or looking at a newspaper anyway, and there's a suitcase on the floor next to her, and a couple of bags, so she's someone who's visiting town and is about to go home again, or maybe someone who's about to catch an express ferry either north or south, since the ferryboats are docked not far from The Coffeehouse, you just need to go a few hundred feet along The Pier and then there you are, and that's why there are often people who are about to take an express ferry sitting and waiting in The Coffeehouse, and if they need to spend the night in Bjørgvin they like spending the night at The Country Inn, I think and the woman's probably someone visiting town and most likely she's spent the night at The Country Inn and now she's sitting and waiting for an express ferry, you can say speedboat so why can't you say speedferry? and it'll go express, of course, to somewhere north or somewhere south, I think and then I realise that she's looking at me in a way that seems to mean she knows who I am and then she looks back down at her newspaper and then she looks up again and I think she definitely recognises me, or at least knows who I am, I think, but even if I can't see any difference between her and the woman from the day before yesterday, because I can't, it can't be the woman from the day before yesterday, so she must be recognising me from something else, maybe she's someone who saw a picture of me a long time ago in *The Bjørgvin Times*, when I was The Arts Festival Artist or something, and there were also some interviews in *The Northern Herald* before I totally stopped giving interviews, because if she was the woman from the day before yesterday she would absolutely for sure have said something to me, no, you again? hello, nice to see you again, something, she would have said something like that, but the woman sitting there now is just shyly looking down at a newspaper and sitting as if she's just thinking her thoughts, and I've found a window table all the way at the back of The Coffeehouse, and there's no one else here, just me and the woman with the medium-length blonde hair sitting at a table near the front door with a suitcase and a couple of bags next to her, and I'm sitting at a window table looking out, down at The Pier, at The Bay, and I think that even though there are two newspapers you can read for free at The Coffeehouse I always read only *The Northern Herald*, never *The Bjørgvin Times*, because *The Bjørgvin Times* is full of stupidity and foolishness and nothing else, I think and it looks like that's the paper the woman with the medium-length blonde hair is sitting there reading while I sit here paging through *The Northern Herald*, and it's really unbelievable how much she looks like the woman who helped me the day before yesterday, no, I don't want to think anymore about that, because it's eerie, almost uncanny, I think, and then there's the fact that I can't go see Asle, that must mean he's seriously ill, yes, maybe even dying, anyway it's possible that he'll die, and it was mostly to visit Asle that I came to Bjørgvin today, and also to deliver the pictures, but that could've waited a few days, and then I was thinking I'd go sit in St Paul's Church but that totally slipped my mind, yes, after I'd gone to The Hospital and hadn't been allowed in to see Asle I thought that all I wanted to do was go to The Coffeehouse and then drive back home to Dylgja, but there was no big hurry to take the pictures to Bjørgvin, actually I could've waited a few days before taking the paintings to The Beyer Gallery, I didn't need to drive to Bjørgvin until next week, so it was really only to look in on Asle that I drove to Bjørgvin again today, because maybe he needed something? maybe I could get him something from his apartment? something he wanted, maybe a sketchpad? a pencil? yes, everything's kind of run together a bit for me, I think, it's all a bit mixed up in my mind, but the day before yesterday I drove to and from Bjørgvin and then back to Bjørgvin again because I suddenly decided I needed to go see Asle, and I found him lying in the snow, he could have easily frozen to death, it was so cold, so it was certainly good that I came back, yes, no matter how much driving I'd just done, I think and then I see a woman come over and she has a plate with bread and eggs and bacon in her hands, the bacon is nice and crispy, the bacon at The Coffeehouse is always cut in thin slices and then almost charred, and then I feel how hungry I am and this'll be good, I think, because crispy bacon and eggs at The Coffeehouse, no, there's nothing better to eat than that, not in Bjørgvin anyway, unless it's the potato dumplings they serve at The Coffeehouse every Thursday, I think and I start eating right away, and I certainly was hungry, that's for sure, and it tastes good, and the reason I like bacon and eggs so much probably has something to do with always thinking it was so good when Grandmother made it for me when I was young, she fried the bacon and then fried the eggs with onions, and that might have been the very best thing in the world when I was little, I think and I eat and I take a sip of coffee and then I hear footsteps and I look over and I see the woman with the medium-length blonde hair, the woman named Guro, walking over to me and she says no, I'm back in Bjørgvin again? wasn't I going to drive straight home? she sure was surprised to see a man with a grey ponytail sitting there in the back of The Coffeehouse, and she thought it must be me, she was sure it was me, she says and I think that it must be the woman who was by the door who's come over, and that she seems to be the woman I talked to the day before yesterday, who took the dog to sleep at her place, and I look at the front door and the woman who was sitting by the door is still sitting there and looking down at her newspaper, and the suitcase and bags are still on the floor next to her, and the woman talking to me now, yes, this is Guro, and she looks exactly like the woman sitting by the door

What a surprise, she says

I thought you had to drive home, after you picked up the dog, she says

and I nod and chew and swallow the food in my mouth and then I say that I did drive home but then I thought it was time to bring the paintings for my next show to The Beyer Gallery, I say and the woman named Guro says that I usually have one exhibition a year at The Beyer Gallery, during Advent, it opens a little before Christmas, she says

Yes, I say

And I've seen, yes, well, I think I've seen every one of your exhibitions, she says

and I don't say anything

And I've bought two paintings, too, she says

and she says that she's probaby already told me but it's been many years since she could afford to buy pictures, now she can't, it was back when she lived with, yes, The Fiddler that she could afford paintings, but he'd cleared out to East Norway and moved in with some woman or another

And then I got some from you too, she says

and I look at her

You remember that much, don't you? she says

and I don't understand what she means

Since you've been in my place so many times, she says

and she smiles and winks at me

And spent the night lots of times too, she says

and I don't understand what she's saying, what she's talking about

But you probably don't remember that, you were probably drinking too much back then? she says

and she asks if she can sit down and I say of course she can, yes, please do, I say and she says that after she buys a cup of coffee she'll come and sit down and have a chat, she says and I see her go over to the counter and I eat the rest of my bacon and eggs and I think that now I'll again never get away from this Guro, I think, because, no, there's not something wrong with her, but I can't exactly say that I enjoy her company, I just wanted to sit by myself for a while, I think and I pick up my coffee cup and I drink up all the coffee and Guro comes back with her coffee cup and she puts it down on the other side of the table and she says she comes by The Coffeehouse almost every day

Yes, The Coffeehouse is like a second home for me, she says

and we don't say anything

And it's good that you can't buy beer or wine at The Coffeehouse, she says

and she says that otherwise she might all too easily do that, but in the morning, yes, during the day, it's better to avoid alcohol, she says, when he couldn't do that anymore was when it started to go wrong with The Fiddler and even then she didn't touch alcohol until late afternoon at the earliest, but sometimes she gets tired of sitting in the apartment with her Hardanger embroidery and then she likes walking over to The Coffeehouse, she says, yes, to see people, and run into people she knows sometimes too, sometimes there are people from back home there, people she knows from when she was growing up, visiting town on holiday, because nowadays almost everyone from the country comes for a visit at some point, well, no, not everyone, there are lots of people she knows who never leave where they're from, she says, it just never seems to happen, the same way they sort of never seem to do anything, yes, Hardanger was where they were born and Hardanger was where they stayed, and some of them have probably never seen anywhere else besides where in Hardanger they were born and raised, she says, it was like a rule in earlier times, for many of them, to stay where they were born, Guro says and I realise that I don't want to say anything and I think that I have to say that I have an appointment, something I need to do, that I have to go

Sorry, I have to go, I say

What? Guro says

Why? she says

I don't have much time, I say

You have to go? she says

Yes, I say

That wasn't much of a chat, she says

But you really should look me up next time you're in Bjørgvin, she says

and I say I will

You promise? she says

and then she smiles

You used to do it a lot, she says

and we don't say anything

But you don't really remember do you? she says

And I got a bunch of small pictures from you, she says

And then I bought two big ones, she says

Yes, my apartment's like a little gallery of your paintings, she says

I don't have much time, I say

Yes, I understand, she says

See you around, I say

Yes, see you soon, she says

and I get up and put on my long black coat and I drape the brown leather shoulder bag over my shoulder and I say bye and she says bye take care and then I go and now I should go straight to my car that's sitting parked outside The Beyer Gallery and then I should drive home to my good old house in Dylgja, and it'll be good to get home, it'll be so good to have a little peace and quiet, I think and now I shouldn't look at the woman sitting alone near the door, the woman who looks exactly like Guro, yes, there is no difference at all between them, I think, so now I just need to get outside and then I'll walk to my car that's sitting outside The Beyer Gallery, and then I'll drive home to Dylgja, and it'll be good to get home, I think, and I get outside and I go up the pavement and then I take a right and I walk for a bit and then I take a left and then I go up The Lane and it was 3, The Lane, where she lived, right? the woman who says her name is Guro and who says that I've been to her place so many times, and that I've given her paintings, but just small ones, and that she bought two paintings herself, and that her apartment there in The Lane is like a little gallery of my paintings, I think and it's grey nasty weather, it's been raining, and I walk through slush, the street's pretty slushy, but luckily it hasn't gotten cold enough for the slush to freeze into ice, otherwise it would be hard to walk on this steep Lane, but now it's fine, except just a little slippery, but if you have good shoes on it's fine and I do, I think, and I get to the top of The Lane and I turn right on High Street and I see my car parked in front of The Beyer Gallery next to Beyer's car and I go straight to my car and I get in and it starts on the first try and I turn the heat on full blast, because it's cold in the car, and I turn on the windshield wipers because the front windshield is totally covered with rain and sludge and then I pull out of the parking space and then I drive the roads I know, that I've driven on so many times, the way Beyer taught me to drive back in the day so that I could get out of Bjørgvin, and I realise that I'm not thinking about anything, it's like there's been too much for me, and it feels good to be driving, I notice, and the car just needs to warm up and then everything'll be good, and now I shouldn't think about anything, I think, and I realise that I don't have any desire to paint, and it's been a long time since I haven't wanted to paint, and then there's the picture with those two lines that cross, I don't want to see that picture again, I have to get rid of it, I have to paint over it, because it's a destructive picture, or maybe it's a good picture? but in any case I don't want to sell it, but maybe I can take it up to the attic and keep it with the other pictures I don't want to sell? I think and I reach the country road and the car is more or less warm now and I drive steadily and calmly, almost slowly, north and I feel something like happiness inside me, almost joy, because now I'll be home soon, now I'm going back home to my house in Dylgja, and if I don't want to paint anymore then I don't have to and it does me good to think that, to think that if I don't want to paint anymore I don't have to do it, I think and I drive north and I don't think about anything, I try not to think about anything and I don't look at the building where Asle's apartment is, in Sailor's Cove, and I won't look at the brown house where Ales and I used to live, or at the turn-off where I stopped the day before yesterday and saw the two young people in the playground there, I think and it's raining but the roads are clear and it's not slippery driving on them and I feel so tired and that's not so strange, because I drove to Bjørgvin today despite everything, and I brought my paintings to Beyer, and now I'm driving home again, and I went to The Hospital, and I wasn't allowed to see Asle, and I went to The Coffeehouse and got some food and talked with Guro there and also saw someone who looked exactly like her, a woman sitting near the front door with a suitcase and two bags next to her, so no wonder I'm tired, I think and I fall into a kind of daze, and it's nice driving a car when I don't think about anything and just pay attention to the driving, yes, there's something about it I really like, just driving along not thinking about anything, I think and now I'm at Instefjord and I take a left and I drive out along Sygne Fjord and now I won't look up at the grey house where Asle's sister lives, in Øygna, the woman who's also named Guro, I'll just keep driving, I think and I drive slowly and steadily along Sygne Fjord and I think that I don't want to look at Åsleik's house and farm when I get to them either, I think and I keep driving, and I drive past Åsleik's farm and I just keep driving, and I really like driving, because even if the roads are small and winding I really like it, I think and all the snow is gone now, the roads are clear, I haven't noticed any ice anywhere, and I see my house, my beautiful old house, and I'm filled with happiness and I turn into the driveway and I drive up and stop the car in front of the house and when I get out of the car I hear Bragi barking, poor Bragi, I wasn't thinking about you, I totally forgot about you, I think, poor you, you must be hungry and thirsty, and you must need to go out too, I think and it's so terrible, Bragi's barking, I think and I go into the house and I hear Bragi scratching at the door to the main room and I open the door and Bragi comes to me and he's jumping up at me and he's barking and wagging his tail and I pet his back

    Poor dog, Bragi, I say

    Poor doggy, you had to be alone for so long, Bragi, I say

    and I realise it's a little cold in the room, so I need to start a fire in the stove, I think, and then I'll lie down on the bench and rest a little, I think, but first Bragi needs to get some fresh air, I think and I go out into the hall and I open the front door and Bragi runs outside and over to the grass as quick as he can and as soon as he gets to the grass he lifts his leg and he stays there pissing for a long time and then he walks around sniffing a little and I call Bragi but he keeps on sniffing and I call Bragi lots of times but he doesn't listen and then I see that the dog is hunching up, with his rear end out, and his tail in the air, and he takes a good long shit and when he's done he comes running up towards me

    Good doggy, I say

    What a clever dog you are, Bragi, I say

and then I pet him on his back and we go in to the kitchen and I hear a clattering noise and I see Bragi bumping his empty water dish

No, you don't have any water, I say

and I pick up the bowl and I fill it with water and put it down for Bragi and he slurps and gulps his water

Oh you were really thirsty weren't you, I say

and Bragi gulps his water down until the bowl is totally empty and I refill it and put it down for him and he slurps just a little water and I see that the food bowl is empty too and I crumble a slice of bread into pieces and I put them in the bowl and Bragi goes over and eats some of the pieces of bread and then he looks up at me and I think that he must want something else to eat, and that's understandable, I think, and later, later I'll find something else for him, I think and with Bragi at my heels I go into the main room and I go hang my shoulder bag up on the hook and I go over to the stove and I put some kindling and a few wood chips in and put two good logs on top, good dry birchwood, and I light the kindling and the fire starts right away and I think that it's good Åsleik gave me all the wood I need for a fire, the chips, the kindling, the logs, I think and I stay standing there and I look at the logs and I don't think anything, I just feel empty and tired, and I feel a lightness, and I don't exactly know why, and then I think that it must be because I thought that there was no need for me to paint anymore, I think, because I don't feel the slightest desire to paint, I feel almost an aversion to it, and I can't ever remember feeling like that before, I think and then I shut the stove hatch and I go out into the hall and take off my coat and hang it in its place and I hang the scarf on its hook and then I go into the main room and put my velvet jacket on my chair next to the round table and I sit down in the chair and Bragi comes over and hops up and lies down in my lap and I stroke his back and I think that it's nice to have a dog, yes, I need to get myself a dog, that's what I actually want to do, and then I need to get a boat, a sailboat, I really want to do that too, I think, and I've been thinking about getting a dog and a boat for years and years but it never happened, I've been too busy painting, I think and I look at my fixed spot in the water, at my landmark, the tops of the pines in front of the house need to be in the middle of the middle right pane, because the window is divided in half, and can be opened from both sides, and each side of the window is divided into three panes, and the middle one on the right side is where the tops of the pines need to be, I think and then I look at my landmark, and at the waves out there in the Sygne Sea and I cross myself and then I take out the rosary I have around my neck under my pullover, the brown rosary with the wooden beads and a wooden cross, and I hold the cross tight and then I pray a silent prayer for Asle, that he'll get better, or if God wants to then he should take Asle back to himself and let him find rest in God's peace and I stay sitting there holding the cross at the bottom of the rosary with the brown wooden beads that I always have hanging around my neck and that I got from Ales once, I got lots of rosaries from her, and I've taken good care of all of them, and I got lots of scarves too, and I've also taken good care of those, because when Ales asked me what I wanted for Christmas or as a birthday present I always said I wanted either a rosary or a scarf and then she said didn't I have enough rosaries and scarves too and then I would answer yes, well, I did have a lot of rosaries and a lot of scarves but there's nothing wrong with that and then Ales would say that still I always used the same rosary, the brown one, yes, the one I still have on, and I said I have a collection of them and she said yes, yes, she knows, she can see that, because on the wall behind the head end of the bench in the main room I had put up a hook and I hung all the rosaries I had on it, and all of them were from Ales, I think and I look at the rosaries hanging there on the wall and I think that every so often I take them down and sit and look at one or more of them, especially at the ones Ales had, and she had only three, and I hung them up together with mine after she died, and when I sit with one of Ales's rosaries in my hands we kind of talk to each other for a long time, about anything and everything, before we say goodbye to each other and say that it won't be long before we meet again and then I hang the rosary back up on the hook, and I miss Ales so much, and why did she have to die and leave me, so young, so suddenly? I think and I hear Ales say that even though I always wear the same rosary I do change the scarf I wear, and I say that I'm absolutely sure I've worn all the scarves she's given me, and she says that I certainly have and then I hear Ales ask if I'm doing all right and then I see her sitting in her chair, there to my right, there next to the round table in front of the window, and I say I am, but I miss her so much, and also I'm so scared about Asle, I say and Ales says I shouldn't be, either he'll get better or God will take him back, so I shouldn't be scared for him, Ales says, and even though it's impossible to say anything about how she is, now that she's dead, because in a way she's not like anything, well yes she'd have to say that she's doing well, because there's kind of no other way to say how she's doing, and when we talk together we do have to use words, but words can say so little, almost nothing, and the less they say the more they say, in a way, Ales says and she says she's always near me and then I say that I can't always tell if it's God or her who's near me and Ales says that I don't need to think about that, and I sit there holding tight to the cross at the bottom of the rosary and I pray that things are good for Ales where she is now, that God is good to her and Ales says don't I understand that things are good for her and I say yes, yes, I can feel it inside, I say and then I say that I have the feeling that I don't want to paint anymore, and Ales says she can understand that, I've painted so many pictures, I've done my part, maybe I've painted my paintings, what I needed to paint, she says and even if I don't paint anymore I'll get by, I'll have enough to live on, Ales says and I say yes and then she says that maybe it won't be long now before I too come back to God, come back to where I come from, to where she is now, Ales says and I think that that's how it is, a person comes from God and goes back to God, I think, for the body is conceived and born, it grows and declines, it dies and vanishes, but the spirit is a unity of body and soul, the way form and content are an invisible unity in a good picture, yes, there's a spirit in the picture so to speak, yes, the same as in any work of art, in a good poem too, in a good piece of music, yes, there is a unity that's the spirit in the work and it's the spirit, the unity of body and soul, that rises up from the dead, yes, it's the resurrection of the flesh, and it happens all the time and it always happens when a person dies because then the person is washed clean of sin, what separates the person from God is gone, because then the person is back with God, yes, the innermost picture inside me that all the pictures I've tried to paint are attempting to look like, this innermost picture, that's a kind of soul and a kind of body in one, yes, that's my spirit, what I call spirit, it goes back to God and becomes part of God at the same time as it stays itself, I think and Ales says that it is like that, insofar as it can be thought and said in words that's what it's like, but it can't be said in words, she says and I say no of course not and I say that all religions and faith say, or try to say, something about that, and they all do say it but in different ways, they're like languages, I say, and actually they all say only the tiniest little bit about realities, yes, as I've so often said myself, just think if all the colours had names, yes, how infinitely many names that would be, I say and Ales says it wouldn't have been any better without language and it's because we have the same belief, the same language, yes, that we can talk together now, and it's our angels who let us do that, Ales says, because actually it's her angel and my angel that are talking to each other now, and for an angel to exist you have to believe it does, and you have to have a word for it, the word angel, and if you don't believe that God exists, well then God doesn't exist, neither in life nor when you're dead, so we need the word God, but deep down inside all people believe in God, they just don't know it, because God is so close that they don't notice him, and he's so far away that they don't notice him for that reason either, and it's just the same with the angel, with angels, but the dead are all still with God too, they've gone back to God, but they just don't know it, Ales says and I don't exactly know if I understand what she's saying and I don't exactly know what to say and then I say that I miss her and Ales says she misses me too, but even if we aren't together visibly on earth anymore we are still invisibly together and of course I can feel that, she says and I say I can, and she and I can talk sometimes together, I say and Ales says that we can but only because our angels are there and because I say or think her words, it's not she who's saying them, because now she is everything that exists in language, because God is the pure, the whole language, the language without division and separation, yes, something like that can be said too, Ales says and then she says that it won't be long before we're indivisibly together in God, the two of us together, like we were on earth, but in God, Ales says and she can't tell me what that's like, because people can't picture it, Ales says and I say that I'm tired and Ales says I can go lie down, yes, I need to, she says and I sit in my chair and I look at my landmark in the water, near the middle of the Sygne Sea, look out at the waves, and Ales's voice goes away and I hold the cross on the rosary tight and I see words before me and I say inside myself Pater noster Qui es in cælis Sanctificetur nomen tuum Adveniat regnum tuum Fiat voluntas tua sicut in cælo et in terra Panem nostrum quotidianum da nobis hodie et dimitte nobis debita nostra sicut et nos dimittimus debitoribus nostris Et ne nos inducas in tentationem sed libera nos a malo and I slide my thumb and finger up to the first bead between the cross and the group of three beads on the rosary and I say inside myself Our Father Who art in heaven Hallowed be thy name Thy kingdom come Thy will be done on earth as it is in heaven Give us this day our daily bread and forgive us our trespasses as we forgive those who trespass against us And lead us not into temptation but deliver us from evil and I slide my thumb and finger down to the brown wooden cross and I hold it and then I say, over and over again inside myself while I breathe in deeply Lord and while I breathe out slowly Jesus and while I breathe in deeply Christ and while I breathe out slowly Have mercy and while I breathe in deeply On me

V

And I see myself standing and looking at the picture with the two lines that cross near the middle and it's morning and today's Thursday and I've lit the stove and the room is starting to get warm, and yesterday I drove to Bjørgvin and delivered my paintings to Beyer, I think, and I feel exhausted and I stand in front of the easel and I look at those two lines that cross near the middle, one brown and one purple and I think that I don't like this picture, because I can't stand pictures that directly paint feelings even if I'm the only one who knows it, that isn't the kind of thing I paint, it's not the kind of thing I want to paint, because a painting can certainly be filled with feelings but you shouldn't paint feelings themselves, like screaming and weeping and wailing, I think, and I think that this is a truly bad painting, that's what it is, but at the same time it is what it needs to be, what it's going to be, it's done and there's no more to do on it and I hear Åsleik say St Andrew's Cross, emphasising the words, he says the words with pride, emphasising them, it's revolting, and it is a St Andrew's Cross, I think and I think that I need to put the picture away, or maybe I should just paint over it with white? I could do that, and once I've done it and the paint dries I can start painting a new picture on top of the St Andrew's Cross, but I don't want to do that, I don't have any desire to paint over this picture, in fact I have no desire whatsoever to paint anymore at all, I think, and the only thing I considered painting was painting over this picture in white, the same as I've done with so many other pictures, but I didn't do it, and maybe that's because there's something in this picture after all? maybe it's a good picture even though I don't like it? I think, because that often happens, that the pictures I dislike most are the best ones, and the ones I like best are the worst ones, strangely enough, that's the way it often is, how good or bad something is doesn't have anything to do with how much I like it or don't like it, only with how good or bad it is, whether it's good art or bad art, because art is about quality, not about liking or not liking it, not at all, and it's not about taste either, quality is something that just exists in the picture whether it's beautiful or ugly, and anyway for something to be beautiful it has to also be ugly, that's how it is, and of course good and evil exist in the same way, and right and wrong, and true and false, of course it can be hard to say whether something is good or evil, or right or wrong, or true or false, but most of the time it's clear enough, so it's usually easy to see if a painting is good or bad, if it's bad it's bad, and in that case it's just bad and there's nothing more to say about it, but if it's good it can be hard to say how good it is, and it's often the pictures I paint that I don't like, or don't entirely like, that are the best, that are my experience, they're a bit embarrassing for me in a way, it makes me feel a little queasy to look at them, I think and I don't want to look at this painting with the two lines crossing anymore and since I don't want to look at it I might as well put it aside with the other pictures leaning against the wall with the stretchers facing out, in the stack of pictures I'm not done with yet, there between the door to the side room and the hall door, I think, and my brown leather shoulder bag is hanging on the hook above them, because yesterday I drove all the paintings I was done with down to Beyer and dropped them off there, yes, after Åsleik had chosen the picture he wanted to give Sister for Christmas I drove the finished paintings down to Bjørgvin yesterday, so the place where the finished paintings usually go is empty now, I think, but I can't stand this picture with the two lines that cross, it makes me feel sick to look at it, I have to get rid of it, and maybe it's not even a picture at all? but at the same time I don't want to paint over it with white paint, and I don't want to set it aside in the stack of pictures I'm not totally satisfied with, and there are a lot of pictures there, and all of them are big paintings, or bigger, none are that big, and it's good they're big, I think, because I've realised I don't want to paint anymore at all, maybe I've painted enough, painted myself out, maybe I'm done, I'll give up painting, and the unfinished pictures actually are finished in their way, they're surely not that bad the way they are, I think and in that case I have, as I thought, enough pictures for three more shows aside from the ones I delivered yesterday, I think, so that's one exhibition at The Beyer Gallery, and then one in Oslo, which Beyer already has enough pictures for, and then finally the one in Nidaros, the exhibition at The Huysmann Gallery that's been planned for years, and that Beyer now thinks he has enough pictures for, out of the pictures that didn't sell either in Bjørgvin or in Oslo, so I can just bring all the pictures I have in my house to Dylgja, the unfinished ones over there plus the ones I have stored in crates, take them to Beyer and then he'll probably start in again talking about how I just never stop, I keep going like a roman-fleuve, he's said that over and over again, yes, it's just like with Åsleik, Åsleik feels proud of himself when he can use an unusual word and Beyer feels proud in the same way when he can use a French word or expression, roman-fleuve, Beyer says and he glows with pride and he says that every exhibition has a unity of its own, its own totality, or entirety, as if it's not completely ended or finished, as if there's something still fragmentary about it that as it were looks forward to the next one, that's also true, and so that's how one exhibition follows the other, like a river, yes, a picture-river, Beyer says and I think that with three exhibitions I'll probably make a decent amount of money, plus I have a little in the bank, and soon I'll be able to collect a pension and then I'll be set, I'll get money every month whether I do anything or not, I think, and it'll be good to get a fixed amount of money every month because to tell the truth that's never happened in my whole life, I've painted pictures to sell them and that's how I've made the money I need, I think, and if I stop painting and don't have to buy what I need for painting anymore then I'll hardly have any expenses, because I already have what I need, yes, my car is fine, I bought it just about five years ago, so I'll have that car for as long as I live, or as long as I'm able to drive, I think, but this painting here, the one with the two lines that cross, yes now what should I do with that? it was so wrong not to let Åsleik take it, he wanted it to give to Sister, but maybe I can put it up in the attic with the pictures I want to keep and not sell, and that I'm now kind of tempted to just get rid of, yes, that's probably what I'll do, but not right now, I think and I feel sure in my whole body that I have no desire to paint anymore, none at all, and I don't understand why this feeling has come over me so suddenly, I've always liked painting, ever since I was a boy, and I don't understand it, I think and I think that even if I don't like the picture of the two lines that cross each other it might still be a good picture, that may be, but I don't know if it's bad or good, I only know that I don't like it and that I don't want to paint over it with white paint and that anyway I probably need to put it away, I think and I think again that it was stupid not to let Åsleik have the painting to give to Sister for Christmas, but I didn't want to give it to him, still, that was the picture he wanted as a gift for Sister, and then he picked another one and took it instead, probably the best of the big paintings I'd finished for the show at The Beyer Gallery, the one called *Silent Boat*, yes, Åsleik knows whether a picture's good or bad, so now probably the best picture I've managed to paint since my last show at The Beyer Gallery hasn't gone to Bjørgvin, and there's a kind of floating boat in the picture Åsleik chose, and the picture is brown and purple, but what really makes the picture good and makes it shine is the thin layer of white paint white brushstrokes I added when I looked at the picture in the darkness, when I glazed it, as they say, and of course that's just the picture Åsleik wanted, the best picture I'd painted in a long time, and I couldn't say no, because he's always gotten his choice of paintings, he could choose freely, but only a small painting, this year was the first time I let him pick a big one and then of course he had to pick the best one, I think and I look at Bragi who's standing on the floor looking up at me and I say Bragi and he comes over to me and I rub his fur and I think I need to go get him a little food and see if he still has water, I think, and then do I need to walk him? since he is standing there looking at me? yes he's both hungry and thirsty and he needs to go, I think, but it's probably better if I let him outside first so that he can go, I think and I go out into the hall and I open the front door and I think that outside it's about as light as it's going to get this time of year, and I see Bragi run around in circles in the snow, because it snowed a lot again last night, snow one day and rain the next and then snow again the day after, I think and it's like Bragi is washing himself in the snow before he stops and raises one leg and his piss leaves a yellow hole in the snow, and he pisses for a long time, yes he sure needed to go, I think and then Bragi jumps around in the snow some more and spins and rolls around in the loose white snow and then I call him

   Bragi, Bragi, I call

and he comes running up to me and he stops in front of me and he shakes himself, shakes from side to side, so that most of the snow falls off him, and then I say let's go inside now and Bragi comes inside and I shut the door and we go back into the main room and I feel how tired I am, so tired, and I think I'll just sit down and I see my chair there next to the round table, the one on the left, and I go sit down in the chair and then Bragi comes and jumps up and lies down in my lap and I take my bearings, the tops of the pines outside my house need to be in the middle of the middle pane on the right of the divided window, and then I look at the sea, at the place in the water I always look at, near the middle of the Sygne Sea, at the waves and I see Asle sitting on his bed upstairs in The Shoemaker's Workshop and Mother and Father have just driven off and Asle lies down on the bed and he lies there and he stares straight ahead and he thinks that tomorrow he'll go to The Academic High School, and he thinks he knows the way there, and he'll leave for school nice and early, Asle thinks, and he'll be wearing his black velvet jacket and leather shoulder bag, the same as he always wears, he thinks, because he saw a black velvet jacket at a shop in Stranda and bought it on the spot, and in another shop he found the brown leather bag, and ever since then he's always had his black velvet jacket and brown leather shoulder bag on and Mother said that it looked so stupid, going around in a black velvet jacket, and then with his brown hair so long, down his back, and then with a shoulder bag too, Mother said and Asle told her she can say whatever she wants but he'll dress however he wants and have his hair how he wants it too, he says and then he walks away from Mother in his black velvet jacket and he has a sketchpad and a pencil in his brown leather shoulder bag, and now he'll have his schoolbooks in it too, Asle thinks and he sits up on the edge of the bed and he thinks he might as well take a walk outside and maybe go to The Co-op Store and buy himself something or other, because he's the one who has to go shopping for his own food now, he thinks, and then he needs to unpack the things he's brought with him and try to set them up as nicely and cosily as he can in this room he's rented in The Shoemaker's Workshop, Asle thinks and he gets up and then he stands there in his black velvet jacket and he feels his pockets to check if he has his tobacco pouch and matchbox, and if his wallet is in his inner pocket, and then he drapes the brown leather bag over his shoulder and he sees the keyring lying on the table and he picks it up and then Asle leaves and he locks the door to his room behind him and then he goes downstairs and goes outside and then he locks the front door and then he puts the keyring into the pocket of his velvet jacket and he takes the tobacco pouch out and rolls himself a cigarette and lights it and then he starts walking towards the centre of town, of Aga, and he thinks he'll go to The Co-op Store and buy himself an ashtray, that's the first thing he'll buy, he thinks and then he doesn't think anything else but he feels so light, yes, it's almost joy he feels, because now, now he doesn't live at home with Mother anymore, Mother who he's constantly getting into fights with, and he's done with seeing Father work and toil from dawn to dusk, either he's in The Woodshed building boats, he does that all winter, or else he's with the fruit trees in the orchard, constantly working there, and it doesn't bring in much, Asle thinks and he walks slowly down the road and then he hears someone calling Asle and he turns around and who should he see there walking behind him but Sigve, and Sigve is carrying a black bag in one hand and he raises his other hand and Asle raises his hand and he stops, because look at that, he hadn't thought of that, but Sigve, a few years older than Asle, yes, he recently moved to Aga too, to work at The Furniture Factory here, Asle thinks, Sigve's been working here for a few months now, he knew that, Asle thinks, because the day he went to Stranda and bought both the velvet jacket and the shoulder bag he'd taken the bus from Barmen with Sigve, Sigve had a couple of days off and was home visiting his parents, as he said, but then he had to go back to Aga, back to work at The Furniture Factory there, he said, and he liked it all right there, the days went by quickly, and Sigve had rented a little house, a little old house, almost right in the centre, Sigve had told him, and that was sure different than living in an attic in a boathouse, the way he'd had to live throughout his whole childhood, Sigve had said, and now Asle sees Sigve coming closer and closer and he stops and stands there and Asle looks down and he looks up and he hears Sigve say it's nice to see him, he's probably come to Aga now to go to The Academic High School and Asle says yes, he's just arrived

Your parents drove you, Sigve says

Yes, Asle says

Where are you living? Sigve says

There, Asle says

and he points at The Shoemaker's Workshop

In the green side building? Sigve asks

Yes, Asle says

and Sigve says that he walks past that house every day because The Furniture Factory, well, it's right there, he says and Sigve turns and points and there's a big long white building in a little dip on the other side of the road a few hundred yards behind them and now Asle sees that it says Furniture Factory on the front of the building

That's where I work, Sigve says

Aha, Asle says

So every single day I go past the building where you have a room now, and I've often wondered what kind of building it is, Sigve says

and he says that he can see it's now an outbuilding, but it doesn't exactly look like an normal house, he says and Asle says that there used to be a shoemaker's workshop there, and Asle even thinks of himself as living in The Shoemaker's Workshop and says he lives in The Shoemaker's Workshop, he says

So that's what it is, Sigve says

Yeah, Asle says

and then they stay standing there and neither one says anything and then Sigve says yes, well, so that's where he's living now, he says, and Asle says yes and he says that Father put an ad in *The Hardanger Times* and an old lady answered, it was the lady who lives in the green main house, she's really old, and she walks taking little bitty steps, Asle says, and Sigve says that he's noticed her, sometimes she'd be walking home after going shopping when he was going home from work, and she walks so slowly that almost as soon as he's seen her he's walked past her, he says and then he says that Asle was lucky to have found a whole house of his own and not to have to live in a room in someone's house where other people live, he says

Yeah, Asle says

It's much better to live by yourself, Sigve says

Of course, he says

I was lucky too, to get a little old house, and in the centre of town too, not far from The Co-op Store, he says

and Sigve says that The Boss at The Furniture Factory had told The Labour Office about the house so he was placed there, someone who'd worked at The Furniture Factory had quit and he'd been renting the house, so it was available

Aha, Asle says

and he and Sigve started walking towards The Co-op Store

The house is in a strange spot, Sigve says

Right between The Co-op Store and The Hospital, yes, all by itself kind of, he says

Yes, I've noticed that house, Asle says

It's hard not to, isn't it, Sigve says

Yes, it's in a strange spot for a house, Asle says

and Sigve says that that's probably why he was able to rent it, because with his history he wasn't really the first person someone would want to rent to, and definitely not if they knew he'd grown up in a boathouse

Is it a nice place? Asle says

Yeah, it is, Sigve says

and Asle says that he just got here, his parents just now drove him and his stuff to the room in the top floor of The Shoemaker's Workshop, and he said hello to The Landlady, and she looks really old, Asle says

and Sigve says he's really lucky he found somewhere he can live by himself, in his own house, most of the other people who come from Barmen or Stranda or wherever to go to The Academic High School have to live with housemates, there are young people from towns and farms across half of Vestland coming to The Academic High School, and some of them go home only for Christmas and summers, and over Easter, so the ones from Barmen or Stranda are lucky because they can go home every weekend if they want

I don't want to, Asle says

Go home every weekend? Sigve says

No, Asle says

Well then you don't have to, Sigve says

and he says that he doesn't go home to see his parents much either, but then again he's quite a bit older than Asle, he says

Yes, Asle says

and they get to The Co-op Store and Sigve points to The Hotel down by The Fjord, a nice old hotel, and Sigve says that he likes to go there every now and then for a beer and he says Asle should come with him sometime and Asle says that he's not old enough to buy beer and Sigve says that they're not so strict about that there at The Hotel, and if they do ask for proof of age well then it's easy enough to change his ID, yes, he did it at the post office when he got his red post-office savings-account book, Asle has one of those doesn't he? he says, and Asle says he does and Sigve says they can just change the ID card, the date of birth, he says and Asle says that he has one of those cards and a bankbook too and Sigve says everyone does, don't they, he says and you just need to make a little change to the last number, then he'll be eighteen just like that and be able to buy beer at The Co-op Store and The Hotel

But I can't just do that, can I? Asle says

Sure you can, Sigve says

It's not hard, he says

You just need to find a ballpoint pen that writes the same, because the date of birth is always written with a totally normal ballpoint pen, and then it's just about making sure the colours match, and then a one can be turned into a seven no problem, or a nine into a four, and other things are even easier, four to nine, you can change any number without it being noticeable, just take your time and be careful, because sometimes you need to carefully scrape away a little of the number that was there before, that happens sometimes, and it's easy enough with a needle, an ordinary pin, but usually you don't need to, Sigve says, and he says that Asle can come home with him and he'll change his birthdate on the ID right now, it doesn't take long, and then maybe they can go to The Hotel tonight and get a beer or two or three to celebrate that Asle's a free man now, Sigve says

Because you're a free man now, he says

You've left home and neither your mother nor your father can go chasing after you whatever you do anymore, he says

Yeah, it feels good, Asle says

I'm sure it does, Sigve says

and he asks if Asle wanted to buy something and he says he was thinking of buying an ashtray

An ashtray? Sigve says

Yes, Asle says

You're starting School tomorrow? Sigve says

Yes, Asle says

and Sigve asks if he's still painting and Asle says that he is, he paints and he draws, wherever he goes he has a sketchpad and pencil with him at all times in his shoulder bag, he says and then Sigve asks if he can hire him to paint a picture of the house he lives in and Asle thinks that he doesn't really want to, no, he really doesn't, but he can't really say no either, Asle thinks and he doesn't answer and Sigve says he'll pay for it of course and Asle nods, or maybe I can pay for it by buying you a few glasses of beer? Sigve says, does that sound good? he says and Asle nods and he says that if he's going to paint Sigve's house he needs a photograph to paint from and Sigve says he has one hanging on the wall, there was an old photo of the house hanging above the sofa when he moved in, and in that photo the house is in such a pretty location, because where The Co-op Store is now there used to be just a little shop, and The Hospital wasn't there yet either, so all you can see in the picture is the little shop that's been torn down, but he doesn't need to paint that, it's fine if he just paints the house and then a little bit of the hills around the house, he says

Grandma's in The Hospital, Asle says

Your grandma? Sigve says

Yes, Asle says

and Sigve asks if she's seriously sick and Asle says that she had a stroke, one day she didn't come outside like she usually did and the front door was locked so Mother couldn't get in and then she found Father and he broke down the door and went in and then he saw Grandmother lying in bed and she was just looking at Father, he'd said, and then she tried to say something but she couldn't, Asle says, and then Father called The Doctor and he came right away and he said that Grandmother had had a stroke, and Father tried to sit her up in bed, and she helped as much as she could, and then Grandmother was sitting there in bed and then Father and The Doctor tried to pick her up and Grandmother stood up, but she just stood, and she tried to walk and she did put one foot forward but it was like she couldn't move the other one

Were you at home? Sigve says

Yeah, Asle says

We were on winter break or whatever, he says

and he says that Grandmother couldn't really walk, so Father and The Doctor supported her and they walked slowly into the main room, because when Grandmother was holding Father with one arm and The Doctor with the other she could manage to move the other foot a little too without losing her balance, and they led Grandmother into the main room and sat her down on the bench there and then Grandmother managed to lie down herself on the bench and then she looked at Asle, he says

Yes, she's a good person, your Grandmother, Sigve says

Yes, Asle says

And I'm going to go see her every day, he says

You should, Sigve says

and he says that he and his parents drove to The Hospital to see her before they dropped his things off at the room he's renting, so he's already been to see her today, he says

Grandma and I have always been close, he says

Yes, Sigve says

While Mother and me argued pretty much all the time, he says

and Sigve doesn't say anything

And Father just kept his mouth shut, he says

No your father's never been much of a talker, Sigve says

He almost never says anything, Asle says

and he says that when Mother was arguing with him, which she did constantly, she used to say that Father needed to say something and then he'd mumble something about how Mother was right, something like that, Asle says and Sigve says that Father's a good man

I was thinking I'd buy a few beers, Sigve says

And some bread, he says

and then Sigve and Asle walk into The Co-op Store and Sigve goes and gets some bottles of beer and then a loaf of bread and he says they should look for an ashtray for Asle and then they go to the part of The Co-op Store where they sell various housewares and Asle sees an ashtray with a cover and a little bar sticking up on top and when you pull the lever the ashes and butts disappear, and there's something like a belt of brown fur around the ashtray, and he wants to buy it, Asle thinks and he tells Sigve

That one's not so cheap, he says

I'm buying it anyway, Asle says

and he takes the ashtray off the shelf and Asle says it's a pain they don't sell painting supplies at The Co-op Store and Sigve says yeah in that case he'll still have to take the bus to Stranda, to The Paint Store there, but there's a bus to Stranda about every hour, and there's a hotel there too, The Stranda Hotel, and now and then he sometimes takes the bus there to get a glass of beer or two at The Stranda Hotel, and sometimes he starts talking to someone there, yes, a painter lives there in Stranda, a picture painter, and he's usually at the hotel there, and Sigve's talked with him a lot, he's a smart guy, but dead broke, and he likes beer but he almost never has any money for more than a cup of coffee so he's always extremely happy when Sigve wants to buy him a pint, one day Sigve had asked him if he was hungry and he'd nodded and then Sigve had bought him an open-faced ground-beef sandwich and he'd thanked Sigve over and over and said he was really hungry, and he, the picture painter, yes, as a matter of fact his name is Asle too, and he can't be much older than you, Sigve says

And it's really strange, he says

Because he reminds me a lot of you, he says

Yes, Asle says

and Sigve says that the picture painter there, the one who's named Asle too and is about the same age as Asle, maybe a couple of years older, and who looks like Asle, yes, he gulped down that ground-beef sandwich practically in one bite, and then he'd said that that was the best meal he'd ever eaten in his life, yes, he was so hungry, so unbelievably hungry, Sigve says and then they walk to the cash registers and Sigve puts the bottles of beer down in front of the woman sitting at the register

Back again today, are you, she says

I don't come in that often, Sigve says

Yes you do, she says

and she rings up the price of the beer on the register and Sigve puts the bread down in front of her and she rings that up and says the total and Sigve takes out his wallet and pays and then he opens his bag and puts the bottles and the bread into the bag, and Asle had been wondering why Sigve was carrying that big black bag around and now he knows why, he thinks and Asle puts the ashtray down in front of the woman sitting at the register

So, you're buying yourself an ashtray, she says

I am, yes, Asle says

and she rings up the price and Asle takes out his wallet and pays and then he opens his shoulder bag and puts the ashtray in and he sees Sigve walk towards the door

Goodbye, the woman at the register says

Goodbye, thanks, Asle says

and he follows Sigve and when they're outside Sigve says that that he always carries his big bag with him when he goes to work in the morning and at The Furniture Factory they say that they can't understand why he brings such a big bag to work, all he has in it is lunch and coffee, they say and then they laugh, but let them laugh, because the reason he always has this bag with him is that it means he can buy a few bottles of beer on the way home, and a little something else, Sigve says and he asks if Asle wants to come over? then they can have a beer and maybe a sandwich, if he feels like it? and then Asle can take the photograph he's going to use to paint the house Sigve is renting, he says and Asle says he'd be glad to, it'd be nice to go over to his house, he says and Sigve says well then they should go straight there, it's not far, he says and they walk to Sigve's house and he unlocks the door and then asks Asle to come in and Asle goes into the hall and Sigve says that the door on the right is to the toilet, because they'd had a toilet and a shower put into the house, and the door to the left goes to the kitchen, Sigve says and then he opens that door and goes through it and he puts the bag down on the little kitchen table and then he opens another door and points and says that's the living room and Asle should go inside and Asle goes inside and there's a table there in the middle of the room with four chairs around it, one on each side, there's a chessboard on it, and then there's a big bookshelf and it's chock full of books all jumbled together, some standing up and some on their sides, some slanted to the side and others straight, and then there's a sofa along one wall and above it there's the old photograph of the house that Sigve was talking about, and there's one window on the short wall and in front of it's an old armchair, and then there's a door on the right and Sigve comes in with two glasses of beer and invites Asle to sit down and he nods at the table and Asle sits down and Sigve puts a glass down in front of Asle and then he puts the other glass down on the other side of the table, next to the chessboard, opposite Asle

Yes this is sure not like living up in the attic of a boathouse, Sigve says

and Asle doesn't say anything and then Sigve goes back out to the kitchen and he comes back in with the bottle of beer that's now a little less than half-full and he puts it down on the table between them and then he sits down and raises his glass and says cheers and Asle raises his glass and says cheers and then he drinks, and well he's never thought beer tastes all that good but even if it doesn't taste good it works, it calms him down, yes, when he drinks beer he feels that life is good, yes, better than it feels any other time, Asle thinks and he takes out his tobacco pouch and he rolls a cigarette and Sigve does the same and there's already an ashtray on the table and Asle lights his cigarette and then holds the match across for Sigve and lights his cigarette too and then they sit there and they're silent for a moment

So, today you left home, Sigve says

I was supposed to go to The Academic High School too, he says

and he points to the books and says that he reads a lot, all kinds of books, on every topic, now and then he reads poetry too, that may be what he likes to read best of all, he almost always gets something out of modern so-called incomprehensible poetry, not that he understands it either, in the usual way, but he does kind of understand it, in a different way, yes, it's like it's something you have to understand with something other than intelligence, or your mind, Sigve says and he takes a big sip

It's like those poems are incomprehensible the same way life is, he says

Yes, Asle says

and he says that he hasn't read that much, just what he's had to read for school and Sigve says that in that case he's missed out on a lot, but he can borrow a book or two and he should read them and then he'll understand what he means, he says, but he'll need them back, because the books he wants to lend me are two of his favourite books, Sigve says and he gets up and he starts rummaging around on the bookshelf

I can never find the book I'm looking for, he says

and Asle smokes and drinks his beer

Yes well here's one of them at least, it's stories, or something, by Samuel Beckett, he says

and Sigve hands Asle the book

Have you ever heard of him? Sigve says

No, Asle says

and Sigve keeps looking

Yes, these are good too, poems by Georg Trakl, he was from Austria so he wrote in German, but these are translations of course, he says

and you probably haven't heard of him either, Sigve says and Asle shakes his head and Sigve hands Asle that book too and he says that he should read both books and then he, Sigve, needs them back of course, he says, and Sigve says that he's bought all these books himself but he never buys books at the regular price, that would be too expensive, but every other year the bookshops have their big sale, The Aga Bookshop has the sale too, Asle does know that there's a bookshop in Aga, doesn't he? it's not far from here, when you're looking from The Co-op Store or from his house the bookshop's hidden behind The Church, and in fact Asle will have to go there tomorrow or one of these days to buy his schoolbooks, and there, at The Aga Bookshop, there's a book sale every so often and that's when Sigve buys books, he says and he falls silent and then he says that it was when he moved to Bjørgvin that things really went wrong for him, there was too much drinking, and he was friends with the wrong kind of people, as they say, but actually his friends were good people, not the wrong kind, no, but anyway it ended up with him getting fired from his job at a warehouse in Bjørgvin because he didn't go to work for several days, and because he'd never been totally sober when he was at work, at that was true enough, and then it led to more drinking and burglary and prison and the DT's, yes, if he didn't know what those were then he wasn't going to be the one to tell him, delirium tremems as they're called in Latin, the shakes, and he wouldn't wish them on his worst enemy, and then they had to transfer him from The Prison in Bjørgvin, the one by The Fishmarket, to The Hospital, and when he was better they sent him back to The Prison and when he'd served his sentence he went and bought himself a black bag of all things, yes, the one he still used, and the bag was black and plastic, with a zipper, and he bought himself three half-bottles of spirits and then a chessboard of all things, with pieces, and then he took the bus home to Barmen, yes, he and Asle saw each other the night he came home didn't they, and he'd probably told Asle all this then, yes, that was the same night that Asle had quit the band he was in, yes, Sigve had probably said more than he should have that time, that's for sure, he says, and he'd said that he had to go somewhere, hadn't he, and he showed up at his parents' house totally drunk, yes, it was shameful, and he'd probably said that he had to go back and see his parents sometime, Sigve says and he had to go home because he had nowhere else to go, nowhere to live, and in spite of everything it was better to spend the night in the attic of a boathouse than lying on the ground outside

I remember that, Asle says

I'm sure do you, Sigve says

I probably said way too much that night, he says

and Asle says that he remembers Sigve saying that he had to go see his parents again sometime, and then he'd handed Asle a bottle and Asle had taken a little sip of it and then Sigve had slapped himself on his cheeks and said again that he had to go see his parents again sometime and so he had better keep going, carrying his bag in one hand and the half-bottle of spirits in the other, Asle says and Sigve says that it's true what he's saying, because he remembers it all, well, most of it anyway, he thinks, Sigve says

But I wasn't wanting to talk about all that, he says

No, Asle says

That was a long time ago, Sigve says

I was on the skids, by the end I was drinking day and night, he says

and he says that now he has only one or two glasses a couple of nights a week and then on weekends, but he never drinks in the morning, never, he says, not even on his days off does he drink in the morning, because when you start doing that then look out, yes, he's learned that lesson all too well, he says, so even if Asle does it he can't start doing that, he can drink in the evening but never in the morning, Sigve says and Asle finishes his glass and Sigve pours him another one and then he says that it's strange how much Asle looks like the painter who lives in a rented room in Stranda and Asle thinks that he needs to go back to his own room now, he has to unpack and make things as comfortable as he can there, he has to set up his easel and painting things, the other things too, but it shouldn't take long, and then he wants to get some sleep and so Asle says that he should probably be getting home

Next time we'll have a beer at The Hotel, Sigve says

Yes, Asle says

And your ID card, the one you got from the post office, yeah, we can do something about that, like I said, Sigve says

Do you have it with you? he says

and Asle nods and he takes out his wallet and his ID card and he hands it to Sigve and he looks at it and he says that he'll be able to turn the nine at the end into a four easily, because it's written with a totally normal blue ballpoint pen, and he has several ballpoint pens, and one of them will have to look the same, and then maybe he'll just need to scrape a little at the top of the nine with a nail, carefully, yes, so carefully that no one will be able to tell and then, yes, with that Asle will be old enough to buy beer, both at The Co-op Store and at The Hotel, and if anything goes wrong, well then it's no big deal, they don't care if it's fake, Sigve says

Yeah, Asle says

and then Sigve gets a bunch of ballpoint pens and a piece of paper and an eraser and a nail and then he makes a little line on the paper with each of the pens and he picks one of them and then he starts scraping with the nail, gently, gently, scraping ink off the semicircle at the top of the nine and he is just barely touching the ID card with the point of the nail and then he carefully rubs it, he picks up the ID card and looks at it and then puts it back down and picks up a pen and then he kind of goes over the lines running up and down so that the number turns into a four and then Sigve picks up the ID card and says well that was easy enough, there's no way to see that that isn't a four, well maybe someone could tell if they looked at it with a magnifying glass but no one in a hotel or a shop will do that, so now Asle can buy as much beer as he wants, Sigve says

Thanks, Asle says

and then Asle says he's going home to his room

I have to unpack, and set up my easel at least, he says

Of course, Sigve says

But someday, sooner or later, we can maybe get a couple of beers at The Hotel, he says

and then Sigve says that Asle mustn't forget the photograph of the house and he goes and takes it down

Yes it sure looks like it's been hanging there a long time, Sigve says

and he says that Asle should just come by and knock whenever he wants, and then they'll go to The Hotel, at least if it's anytime in the afternoon or evening, he says and Asle says yes he will

Thanks for the beer, he says

No problem, Sigve says

and then Sigve says that he mustn't forget the books and then he dashes back into the living room and gets the two books and Asle takes them and opens his shoulder bag and puts them in

The Asle who lives in Stranda has a brown leather shoulder bag just like that, Sigve says

and Asle doesn't understand why Sigve keeps talking about that other Asle he's never met, but maybe it's just something that comes to mind? something to say? Asle thinks and he and Sigve say see you later and then Asle leaves and under his right arm he has the old photograph of the house Sigve's renting and Asle thinks that he should have gone to see Grandmother, but now he smells like beer, and she'd notice, and she wouldn't like that, so it would be just as well if he looked in on her tomorrow, and he's already been to see her once today, with his parents, and from now on he'll go and see Grandmother every day after he gets out of The Academic High School, he thinks, but that was good, the beer, so maybe he should go buy himself a bottle or two, Asle thinks and he walks into The Co-op Store and gets a bottle of beer and he goes over to the cash register and the woman sitting at the register asks if he can prove that he's eighteen and old enough to buy beer, yes, that's what she says, prove it, Asle thinks and he takes out his wallet and ID card and hands her the ID and she looks at it and hands it back to Asle and then she rings up the price on the cash register and Asle pays and he opens the shoulder bag and he puts the bottle in the shoulder bag, and then it's sitting there next to the sketchpad and the ashtray and the two books he's borrowed from Sigve, and then the woman sitting at the register says goodbye and Asle says goodbye and then he leaves and then he walks up the road, in his black velvet jacket, with his shoulder bag, with his long brown hair hanging down his back he walks up the road and I sit at the round table in front of the window and I look at the same spot in the water, at my landmark, at the waves there, and I might have dozed off a little, I think and the fire in the stove must have burned out and I realise I'm a little cold and it isn't dark outside yet but it's always a little dark all day at this time of year, and if I were doing what I usually did I would have long since been painting by now, but I realise that I just don't want to paint, I have no desire to paint, and I've always liked to paint, yes, I've liked it since I was a boy, and now, I think, I'll go light the stove again and get it a little warmer in the room, I think, and I then I probably should eat something? I think, so I'll just go make myself a sandwich, I think and I still feel so tired so tired and now maybe I want to get a little sleep? lie down on the bench? or maybe I'll read a little first? because I do feel like reading, I think, it's been a long time since I've felt like reading, because painting sort of took over, yes, took up all my time, but he, Sigve, used to read a lot, but then he died suddenly while walking to work at The Furniture Factory one morning, he just fell over, and he wasn't that old, I think, and Ales read a lot, she read everything, and in the last few years after she started painting icons she read mostly about icon painting of course but she also read a lot in the last few years she was alive from the Christian mystics from the Middle Ages, and she especially read a lot by Meister Eckhart, and I read him too, and so maybe I'll read some more Meister Eckhart now, I think and I think that Ales often used to say that there was something in Meister Eckhart's writings that I was also doing in my painting, not directly, of course, but in a way I was kind of doing the same thing, she said and she was definitely right about that and it's cold, I think, so I need to light a fire in the stove, I think and I think that Ales often said that it was these so-called Christians, Catholics and other kinds, who were always constantly misusing God's name, again and again, yes, the people who took God's name in vain the least were the ones who never took the word of God into their mouths at all, because, as Ales said, der Mensch kann nicht wissen, was Gott ist, that's what Meister Eckhart wrote, Ales said, and she said that Was Gott für sich selbst ist, das kann niemand begreifen, she said, yes, Gott ist keinem Dinge völlig nichts, Gott ist für sich selbst nicht völlig nichts, Gott ist nichts, was man in Worte fassen kann, Eckhart wrote, Ales said and she said that when she heard how many Christians misused God's name she thought that if God was the way they thought he was then she couldn't believe in him anyway, she said, I remember she said that one of the first days we were together, I think and I've read nowhere near enough but I have read a little now and then in The Bible, and there are passages there that have given me a lot, maybe most of all where it says that the kingdom of God is inside you, inside us, inside me, because I constantly feel something like God's nearness, I think, and Ales said that maybe what I felt was an angel passing over me? or maybe The Holy Spirit was nearby? she said, I think, but those are just words, because what's the difference really? I think, and I think that The Bible has to be interpreted, has to be read metaphorically, yes, like it's not the real thing but a picture, like a painting, with its own truth, because The Bible is literature, and when it comes right down to it literature and visual art are the same thing, I think, and to understand The Bible you have to start from its own spirit, for the letter kills but The Spirit gives life, as Paul wrote, I think, because even if The Bible is literature it's also more than literature, I think, and even I'm only a borderline member of The Catholic Church, I think, or really I'm outside it, because of how I think, still I've found my place in The Church, I think, and seeing oneself as Catholic isn't just a belief, it's a way of being alive and being in the world, one that's in a way like being an artist, since being a painter is also a way of living your life, a way of being in the world, and for me these two ways of being in the world go together well since they both create a kind of distance from the world, so to speak, and point towards something else, something that's both in the world, immanent, as they say, and that also points away from the world, something transcendent, as they say, and you can't entirely understand it, I think, and then I again think that the kingdom of God is within me, because a kingdom of God does exist, I think, and I can feel it when I make the sign of the cross, I think and I make the sign of the cross, and I do that all the time, but only when I'm alone, except in Church, and I sometimes do it many times a day, whenever the pain comes, and also when gratitude comes, yes, then too, yes I make the sign of the cross all the time and there's a power in doing it, yes, there definitely is, even if it's impossible to say what kind of power it is, because the power is outside of words, but it's there, the power, and that's a fact, and it's impossible to understand why it's like that since it's just not something you can understand, I think and I look at all the rosaries hanging on the wall on the short side of the room above the bench, because I do have a lot of rosaries, and I got all of them from Ales, and now the ones I got from Ales and Ales's too are there on a hook above the end of the bench, aside from the one I always wear, I think and I think that there is also a strange power in the Eucharist, yes, every time the priest holds up the bread in the consecration, as they call it, to change it into Christ's body a kind of light shines out from the host, yes, I see it, I see it with my own eyes, the host gives off a weak light in all directions, stronger or weaker, light comes from the host, or from something like a halo around it, sometimes you can only just make out the light, yes, it's like it's in a fog, but you can still make it out inside the fog, or else it's more like a halo around it, it's not something you can understand but I know what I know, I've seen what I've seen, and of course I might be imagining it but so what? I think and I think that words, yes, language, both connect us to God and separate us from Him, I think, and now it's gotten so cold that I need to light the stove, I think and I get up and Bragi falls onto the floor, because I'd forgotten he was lying asleep on my lap, that's too bad, again, I think and Bragi looks at me with his dog's eyes and then I go over to the stove and I put some wood chips and kindling and a log in and light it and it catches right away and I put another log in and I look at the logs and I think that I never would have become Catholic if Ales hadn't been Catholic, but I became one too, because I couldn't stop drinking so much, by the end I was drinking almost around the clock and I couldn't stop, and because to paint well I had to be sober, if I drank even a little I lost the concentration and precision you need for painting, so it was either alcohol or paintings, I think and when the alcohol was gone then the mass replaced it, because everyone needs something, in a way, I think and I think that near the end of when Ales and I were living in Bjørgvin I spent so much time in The Alehouse, I think, and Ales had to come get me more than a few times, I think, because sometimes I'd be drinking around the clock, and I never regretted converting, because becoming Catholic, not just feeling God's closeness all the time as I'd felt before I became Catholic too, was good for me, it's as simple as that, and Ales said everything so clearly, and I always think muddled thoughts, but now that I've realised I don't have any desire to paint any more should I maybe start reading more? because Ales read a lot, yes, she read and read, novels and plays and poetry, she read in all the Scandinavian languages and she read academic literature in English and German as well, so we were similar in that way, because even if I didn't graduate from The Academic High School I was on what they call the Modern Languages track but when I stopped going to The Academic High School and started at The Art

School I could barely read a book in either English or German, and not at all in French, but I learned English and German gradually, by reading, it was just French, yes, the only French that stuck were a few expressions that I'll probably always be able to rattle off, and as I stand there looking at the logs I think that I know so little, for example I don't even know something as simple as why I've always signed my paintings with a big A in the right-hand corner of the painting itself and painted the title on the top of the stretcher on the back, always in thick black paint, why did I do it in that particular way? I think and I think that all the titles were either in Norwegian, Nynorsk, or in Latin, and the ones in Latin were always quoted from somewhere in the Latin mass, because I prefer it when the mass is celebrated in Latin, I think and I can't just stay standing here looking at the logs through the open hatch of the stove, I think, and it's been a long time since I've eaten anything, so even if I don't feel hungry I should probably go make myself a sandwich, I think and I shut the hatch of the stove and I go out to the kitchen and I see the leg of lamb hanging there, and there's almost no meat left on it and I think that I am hungry and still I don't feel like eating, I think, but I will get myself a little something to drink, I think and I pour myself a glass of nice cold water and I drink it down in one gulp and I still feel tired, so maybe I'll just go lie down on the bench for a bit? I think and I go into the main room and lie down on the bench and spread the grey blanket over me, the one Grandmother handed to me when they came to take her to The Hospice and that I've had with me ever since, wherever I've lived, and Bragi hops up onto me and lies down curled up against my feet and I close my eyes and I see Asle sitting at the back desk of the classroom and The Teacher is standing up front at the lectern and he says that he'll be teaching us English, as a main subject, and French, which we'll all be starting together, he says, and to find out a little more about us he would like us to read a little English out loud for him, and he's taken a text that, if he may say so himself, he personally wrote for this very purpose, and divided it up into sections, he says and now each and every one of us will read our own section, and we might as well start on the right, yes, with you, The Teacher says and he looks at the girl sitting at the front desk to his right, and it would be nice if you all stayed sitting at the desks you're sitting at now, and if you would first say your name and then read, one section each, and while we're doing that he will make a name chart for the class to help him remember all our names, there are so many names to keep track of when you've been a teacher for as many years as he has, The Teacher says and then he gives a packet of sheets of paper stapled together to the girl sitting in the front desk of the row to the left of the row where Asle is sitting and she says her name and then she starts to read and as far as Asle can tell she reads English well, she pronounces the words nicely, and she reads with a nice flow to the sentences and then she's done and then she hands the packet of paper to the boy sitting at the desk behind her and he says his name and then he reads for a while and Asle can't hear if it's good or bad because he's suddenly filled with a kind of terror, the packet of paper is moving from desk to desk and getting closer and closer to him and soon it's going to reach him and then he'll have to say his name and then he'll have to read out loud and he's never felt terror like this before, and the terror gets stronger and stronger the closer the packet of paper gets and one person after another says their name and reads and never never in his life has Asle felt so scared, it's like his whole body has gone stiff and like the fear is a stake through his body, a stake paralyzing him, and he can't do this, he just has to get out, he can't do it, Asle thinks and he's breathing more heavily and he's afraid he'll fall off of his chair and his hands are all sweaty and he's clutching the desk and he bends forward over the desk and his hair hangs down in front of his face and his whole body is rigid and, and, he can't do this, he needs to run away, but he can't run away either, he thinks, because he can't, he can't move, he can't escape and the girl sitting at the desk in front of him turns around and looks at him and then she hands him the stapled packet of paper and Asle takes the packet and his hands are shaking so much that he's afraid the packet will fall to the floor but he manages to get it onto his desk and then he sits there and he starts reading, word by word, voice shaking, he stops, he skips over one word and then he hears The Teacher say thank you and Asle picks up the packet and his hands are shaking so much and then he turns and hands the quivering paper to the girl sitting at the desk next to him and she takes the paper from him and he turns back forwards and his whole body's shaking and the girl sitting next to him says her name and then she starts reading in a calm voice and it's nice hearing her read, her voice is so relaxed, and she reads in such a steady flow, Asle thinks and he realises that he's starting to calm down, and it's like the voice of the girl reading now is making him calmer, and what just happened? he thinks, and he thinks that having to read out loud has never made him scared before and he was always having to read out loud in school, he thinks, and he thinks that he can't go to school if he's like this, so he'll have to drop out of The Academic High School, he thinks or else he'll have to talk to The Teacher and tell him, say that he's scared to death of reading out loud and ask if he can get out of doing that, he thinks, or else he'll just have to drop out of The Academic High School, and he can do that, he doesn't need to go to The Academic High School, there's nothing forcing him to stay, he had to go to primary school and middle school but he doesn't have to go to The Academic High School, he thinks and The Teacher says that today's time is almost up, it's break-time, they got through about half the text this time and the rest of the class will say their names and read their sections next time, he says and Asle thinks that there's maths next period and even though he can't do maths and has never been able to do maths and will never learn how to do maths, and will never understand a thing in what they call mathematics, at least he won't have to read anything out loud, he thinks, and then the last period is history, and that's one subject Asle has always liked, and he won't have to read out loud then either, so he'll be spared today, but tomorrow there's French and then Norwegian, and he doesn't know a word of French so he won't have to read in that period, Asle thinks, but in Norwegian class he might have to read out loud and so he has to tell The Norwegian Teacher before then that he can't read out loud, that he's scared to death of that, yes, scared to death of hearing his own voice reading something out loud, so they'll have to let him get out of that or else he'll have to drop out of The Academic High School, that's what he has to say, Asle thinks and The Norwegian Teacher is also the instructor in history, and he was the one who wrote the weekly schedule up on the blackboard during the first period and told everyone what teachers they'd have, and what books they needed to buy, and he was dressed a little strangely, in grey trousers and a blue-grey velvet jacket, and he was wearing both a belt and suspenders, and both the belt and the suspenders were narrow, and both were clearly visible, and his trousers were wide, and his velvet jacket was too, and then he had a thin red tie on, while The Teacher they would have for English and French just wore trousers and a pullover, a grey pair of trousers and a white pullover with blue stripes and I lie here on the bench with the grey blanket tucked tight around me and I open my eyes and I scrunch my hands in Bragi's fur and I pull him closer to me and I close my eyes and Bragi moves a little and I pet him, I close my eyes and I see Asle standing there and he's telling Beyer that he doesn't want to go to the opening and Beyer says he's about to have his first show, doesn't he want to be there for the opening? and also, Beyer says, well, if the painter doesn't come then it's possible not a single painting will sell, he says, a totally unknown painter, making his debut, yes, and still a student at The Art School or at least until just recently, and now he doesn't want to come to the opening

No, unbelievable, Beyer says

You have to come to the opening, of course you do, all painters do that, Beyer says

I've never heard of anyone who doesn't, he says

and Beyer says no never before has that happened to him, of course Asle has to be at the opening, he says, all painters have to, that's just how it is, he says, because openings are when painters meet their audience, the people who might be spending all that money to buy a painting, and is it any surprise that they'd like to say hello to, or at any rate set eyes on, the artist who made the painting they're buying? Beyer says and Asle asks him to say hello to the people who come to the opening for him and say that he's afraid of crowds like that

It can't just be me, you have to be there to meet them yourself, Beyer says

But I can't do it, Asle says

and Beyer says Asle's done it before, both at The Academic High School, even if he didn't graduate, and at The Art School, even if he's dropped out of there too now, he says, so it's not like this'll be the first time he's been in a crowd like that, Beyer says and Asle says that he can manage to be in a crowd if he doesn't have to say anything, because he's scared to death of speaking in public, yes, even in a classroom, someday Asle'll tell Beyer about how it was at The Academic High School before he quit, he says and he hears Beyer say yes, well yes, artists are their own special kind of people, but in that case it was extra important that there be a debut-artist interview with Asle in *The Bjørgvin Times*, newspapers don't always want to print interviews with debut artists but it does happen, and since the pictures are so good, yes, anyone can see that, he thinks that they'll agree to set up an interview, Beyer says and Asle says well then he'll give an interview, he says and Beyer says at last, a good answer, he'll try to set up an appointment and it'll probably be at The Grand Café restaurant, he says, and Asle says that he's never been there before and doesn't know where it is, and Beyer says that if he gets an interview set up then Asle can just come to The Beyer Gallery beforehand, in time to get to the interview, and he'll take Asle to The Grand Café personally, he says and Asle thanks him and I lie here on the bench and I think that I can't just stay lying here like this, I think, but the room's nice and warm now and I close my eyes and I see Asle standing in the brown house looking out the window and he thinks that he was recently interviewed in *The Bjørgvin Times* and it was a real takedown under the title 'Fear of Crowds', Fear of, Fear of, Asle thought when he saw it, that's what he thought, Asle thinks and he sees a car drive by on the road down below, and the car, a small van, is one he's seen many times, Asle thinks and he thinks that the article in *The Bjørgvin Times* appeared with a large and bad photograph of him standing in his black velvet jacket with a scarf around his neck and with his brown leather shoulder bag in place and he was looking down so that his medium-length hair almost entirely covered his face and in the interview the journalist, he was from Bjørgvin, wrote that there was serious disagreement among the critics whether these were good paintings, and the question, he wrote, was being asked whether The Beyer Gallery, usually so dependable, had made a mistake this time, but that remained to be seen, and whether anyone would want to buy the paintings in the exhibition remained to be seen too, the critic wrote in *The Bjørgvin Times*, Asle thinks and he thinks that the interview was all obvious questions that Asle gave obvious answers to and he thinks that Beyer did say yes well about that interview, Asle thinks, there's not a single honest critic, they only became journalists because they couldn't do anything else, that's true, Beyer said, Asle thinks, and he thinks that the opening went fine without him being there and the review of the exhibition in *The Bjørgvin Times* could hardly have been worse, every picture shows a total and complete lack of talent, something like that is what the review said, Asle thinks and

Beyer said that the critic would be ashamed of his words someday, the newspapers' art critics were getting worse and worse over the years, it wasn't like it used to be back when Anne Sofie Grieg was the art critic for *The Bjørgvin Times*, she had never studied art history but she'd been to all the greatest art museums in Europe and she was a skilled pianist and she had a real eye for what was good art and bad art, but whether she'd gotten too old and didn't want to write anymore or for some other reason she didn't write about art in *The Bjørgvin Times* anymore anyway, now they had some whippersnapper as an art critic who'd gone to The University and who could only see concepts and theories instead of pictures, instead of art, Beyer said, but luckily, yes, luckily ordinary people could see better than him, because all of Asle's paintings had sold, and within two days, and that's even though Asle wasn't at the opening, and despite that terrible interview and photograph in *The Bjørgvin Times*, and despite the terrible review, if you can even call it a review, Beyer said, Asle thinks, and Beyer said to tell the truth he'd said beforehand to everyone who usually bought pictures or who even sometimes bought pictures that now they really had to step up and buy one because the pictures he was showing now were by the greatest talent he had ever come across in all his long years alive, he'd personally said that to anyone and everyone, Beyer said and, as he said, all the paintings sold in two days, he said, Asle thinks standing there looking out the window and I'm lying on the bench and now the room is nice and warm and then I say Bragi and he looks up at me with his dog's eyes and then I pet him on the back and I tuck the blanket a little tighter around him and I close my eyes and I see Asle standing in front of the door to the little house where Sigve lives, right between The Co-op Store and The Hospital, and he thinks that he was just in The Co-op Store buying two bottles of beer, and he has under his arm both the photograph he'd taken with him of the old house where Sigve used to live and the picture he's painted of the house, but it took him much too long to finish painting it, now he's finally finished it but he didn't paint it the way Sigve wanted him to paint it, Asle thinks, and he thinks that, today, like most school days, the first thing he did after his day at The Academic High School was over was to go to The Hospital, to the room when Grandmother was, but she was asleep, and he sat down on a chair in her room and he looked at Grandmother's face, especially her lips that had turned a little bluish, and her breathing was rapid and irregular and then Asle thought that he didn't want to wake Grandmother up, he would just come back later, Asle thinks and he knocks on Sigve's door and nothing happens and then he knocks again and a little harder this time and then he hears hurrying footsteps and Sigve opens the door and his eyes are half-closed and he says no, it's you, and he doesn't seem so happy to see Asle and then Sigve says that he just lay down for bit, and then he must have fallen asleep, but it's good that Asle dropped by and woke him up because if he'd slept any longer his sleep tonight would be ruined, that's happened more than a few times before, Sigve says and he says that Asle should come in and he goes in and Sigve shuts the front door behind him and locks the door and then they go into the living room

Yes so the school day's over too, he says

Yeah, Asle says

It went well today? Sigve says

Yes I'd say so, Asle says

That's good, Sigve says

and then it's silent and Asle thinks Sigve must not have noticed that he has both the photograph and the painting with him and he hands Sigve the painting and Sigve looks at it and it doesn't seem like he thinks there's anything special about it, anyway he doesn't say anything and then he goes and puts the painting down on the floor in front of the bookcase and Asle hands him the photograph and Sigve hangs it back up in its place over the sofa

It's nice to get that photograph back in its place, he says

I didn't like not having it, it was like something was missing when the photograph wasn't there, he says

I really missed it, he says

and then it's silent and then Sigve says that he'll treat Asle to a meal and some beer in exchange for the painting, and Asle, who was sure he'd get paid, that they'd agreed on that or had an unspoken agreement at least, feels a little disappointed but he doesn't say anything and then Sigve asks if Asle's eaten and he says that he ate a little something back at his room and Sigve says that he doesn't eat dinner every day, not at all, to tell the truth he comes home pretty rarely, maybe once or twice a week, yes sometimes he makes himself a meal, he can cook pretty well, getting better at least, he says and laughs, but today he wasn't that hungry, Sigve says and Asle says that he isn't either, but he has brought over two bottles of beer, so if Sigve's thirsty he could always have a glass, Asle says and Sigve says a glass of beer's always good, and Asle opens his shoulder bag

That's a nice bag you have there, Sigve says

and he says he's thought about that bag a lot, oddly enough, he says

Real leather, it looks like? he says

Yeah, Asle says

That can't have been cheap, Sigve says

I bought it when I sold my guitar, Asle says

Yes, that was something wasn't it, didn't one of you punch out another guy's tooth? Sigve says

Yeah, Asle says

You'll have to tell me about that sometime, Sigve says

and then he says that first they need a beer and Asle takes the two bottles out and puts them on the living-room table, next to the chessboard

Yes, one bottle each, he says

Sounds good, Sigve says

and he goes and gets an opener and two glasses and then Asle sits down and Sigve puts a glass down in front of him and another on the other side of the table, by his place, and then Sigve sits down, and then they each pour themselves some and then they sit there and they each roll a cigarette and light it and Sigve says it's good that the old photograph of the house is finally back where it belongs, he'd missed it, he'd been so used to seeing it there, Sigve says and Asle says that he's sorry it took so long to paint the picture and he thinks that Sigve's still not really happy with the picture he painted and it's quiet for a moment

I kind of thought the painting would be different, Sigve says

Yes, with colours, not just in black and white, he says

Yes it's almost all black and white, isn't it, he says

and Asle says that he's stopped painting houses and homes in beautiful spring weather with fruit trees in blossom and a smooth glassy fjord, and white snowcaps on the mountaintops, he doesn't want to paint any more sunny pictures like that, he says, but when Sigve asked him to paint a picture of the house he lived in he didn't want to say no, Asle says, and he thinks that now he's painted the house where Sigve lives but he truly did not want to paint it in colour, he thinks and Asle says that he painted the house in black and white just like the photograph

I'd been picturing more of a painting with colours, Sigve says

I thought all paintings had colours, actually, he says

But the house is white, and the roof is grey, there are big slate tiles on the roof that are grey, Asle says

But the hills are green, and the trees, you probably noticed the big tree next to the house? Sigve says

And the sky is blue, he says

and Asle says that, as he said, he's painted so many pictures of houses in colour and with a blue sky that he didn't want to paint any more of them and Sigve says he was thinking he'd hang the painting on the wall, it would kind of brighten things up a bit with a little colour, things are already kind of grey and black, he didn't need more of that, most of the year it's black and dark almost around the clock but the sun, the yellow sun, and the sky, the blue sky, he could use some more of that, he says and Asle says he knows all that but he's stopped painting pictures like that, he says

Yes well you need to paint the way you want, Sigve says

But let me take you out to a meal and a beer, you did paint it after all, he says

and Asle says that he'd rather be paid in money, and he says what he usually gets for painting a picture like that and Sigve says that that's not unreasonable so that's fine, he says and he raises his glass to Asle and says they should drink to their deal, their agreement, he says and they toast and drink and then Sigve says a little beer sure is good, that's for sure, yes, he says and he says he's glad he's finally living in his own place with a regular job, because that's what keeps a person from going crazy, yes, Asle knows what he's talking about now because he remembers the night Sigve arrived in Stranda on the bus from Bjørgvin to go home to his parents, because what else was he supposed to do? and then he ran into Asle, Sigve says and he was insanely worried about seeing his parents again, and that's why he'd been drinking himself blind drunk, to put it mildly, and then he'd gotten off the bus a long way before the closest stop and then he and Asle had run into each other and started talking and he'd probably told Asle more than he should have that night, but he probably knew it all already anyway, that his father had been a German soldier in Norway, that he was a so-called German baby, and how shameful that was, it was the worst shame possible, but to be honest no one in Barmen had ever teased him or bothered him about it, he had never heard anyone say a single insulting word about it, but still it was always there, in everything anyone said to him, it was there, in the ways people talked to him and looked at him, everything was kind of said in the way they talked to him and looked at him, or maybe he was just imagining it? that was possible, but a German baby was what he was and that was the truth and his father had most likely been taken out by some Barmen people and shot and tossed into The Fjord with a stone in a potato sack tied to his feet, yes, that's what people said at any rate, and his mother didn't want to talk about it, she wanted it all to be forgotten, but sometimes, and every time he was drunk, he'd question her and when she didn't want to say anything, the same as always, he'd sometimes grab her shoulders and shake her and then she'd say crying that his father had been shot and dumped in The Fjord and that the other Germans didn't know where he'd gone and they thought he'd just deserted, just snuck off like a traitor, that's what she said they'd said, something like that

But now we don't talk about it anymore, Sigve says

No, Asle says

and they drink and smoke and it doesn't take long before they've drunk all the beer since they've been smoking the whole time, as soon as one cigarette was done they rolled themselves a new one and Sigve says that they should either go to The Co-op Store and buy some more beer or go to The Hotel and get some beer there, Sigve says, no, actually, he says, they can take the bus to Stranda and go to The Stranda Hotel, they've talked about doing that so many times but they've never got around to it, and they'd definitely run into the other Asle there, his Namesake, the one who looks so much like Asle, even if he is a little older, or, damned if he knows, for all he knows they're the same age, yes, Asle must have almost met him before, Sigve says and if The Namesake isn't in The Stranda Hotel, because he usually goes there, and he never has money for beer so he drinks coffee, yes, if he's not already there at The Stranda Hotel then Sigve knows where he lives, he can tell him, it's in the basement of a house right up from The Stranda Hotel, yes, the other Asle, The Namesake yes, that's his name, he's found a house where he can live in the basement, Sigve says and he looks at the clock and he says that if they hurry they'll just catch the bus to Stranda in five minutes and Asle thinks why not, but he doesn't understand why Sigve isn't embarrassed to go to The Stranda Hotel since he'd robbed that exact place once, the first time Sigve had to go to prison, that's what he'd heard anyway, but he can't very well ask Sigve if it's true, and The Namesake, no, he probably doesn't look as much like him as Sigve likes to say, but if he's a painter too then it would be nice to meet him, Asle thinks and he gets up and Sigve picks up the glasses and empty bottles and carries them out to the kitchen and puts them down on the kitchen counter and says Ordnung muss sein in German and Asle drapes his shoulder bag over his shoulder and follows Sigve and then Sigve puts on some jacket or another, a kind of puffy jacket, and it has a zipper, it looks very strange, it's a weird blue colour that Asle could never have imagined painting, and Sigve pulls the zipper up and Asle goes out and Sigve follows him and he locks the front door and they walk over to the bus stop together and Sigve says that Asle won't believe it when he meets The Namesake, he says and a bus drives up and Sigve sticks out his hand and they get in the bus and Sigve pays and Asle pays and then they go to the back of the bus and sit down in the last row

I always like sitting in the back, Sigve says

Me too, Asle says

As far back as possible, he says

Yes, always, in the last row if it's free, Sigve says

and then they sit there next to each other in the last row and there are just one or two other passengers on the bus, an older married couple and an old woman, and they are sitting far away in the front of the bus and neither Asle nor Sigve says anything, they just sit there and Asle thinks that he still feels nervous and then Sigve says that Asle looks anxious, everything about him seems so anxious, he says, yes, like something really bad has just happened, he says and Asle doesn't answer and then Sigve says that Asle will feel a little more relaxed after he has a beer, yes, that'll do him good, Sigve says, after a few glasses he'll feel totally calm again, Sigve says and Asle asks how Sigve's day had been and he says that his day had been like every other day, his only bad days were the early days when he'd just started at The Furniture Factory, he says, because then he needed to say hello to The Boss and to this and that person working there and he really doesn't like having to talk to people he doesn't know, no, so that was really bad, Sigve says, and he didn't understand how to do the jobs he was told to do, they were actually super simple, just screwing the arms and legs onto a kind of chair they made there, but even that was something you had to learn, there's a knack to doing even that, and the guy who'd had that job before him and was leaving for a new and more challenging job taught Sigve what to do and he laughed and chuckled and showed Sigve where to place the chair leg before he attached it and where to place the armrests before screwing them on and where to put the finished chair down, and where to carry the chairs to, one in each hand, after he'd finished two chairs, and he had to avoid bumping into the doorframe of course, or whatever, yes, every job has things you have to do, Sigve says and in the early days he'd managed to make pretty much every mistake he could possibly make but after that everything went fine and the guy who'd told him what to do, and who was now off to do a bigger and more important task in the company, said that now he was up to speed, now he could do the job well on his own, but if he ever needed to ask about anything he should just ask, he said and then he left and then Sigve was there screwing legs and armrests onto chairs, and now he'd been there doing that for a couple of years, and it may not sound that nice but the truth is he likes that job, Sigve says, by this point what needs to get done happens by itself so to speak and while he's doing the job he can think about whatever he wants to think about, or can stop thinking and just space out, half go to sleep almost, yes, to tell the truth the lunch breaks had been the worst thing about the whole job, because obviously all the other people who worked at The Furniture Factory knew that he was a German baby, no one had said anything to him but he was sure they knew it, and he gradually stopped going to the cafeteria where the others ate, he just sat down on one of the finished chairs and ate the two sandwiches he brought with him every day, always brown cheese on bread, always, and drank the thermos of coffee he had with him, and that way he could avoid talking to anyone, except the guy who delivered the chair seats with the backs, and the guy who delivered the armrests, and the guy who delivered the chair legs, he exchanged a word or two with them, the first time anyway, but after a while the first guy would just come with the chair seats and backs and the second guy would just come with the arms and the third guy would just come with the legs and none of them would say anything, and that's how it was today, and he likes it like that, he's left alone, and every month he gets his pay, and the pay is pretty good, nothing you'll get exactly rich from but it's more than enough for him, Sigve says and Asle asks if it doesn't get boring and Sigve says it doesn't seem that way to him, and if it does get a little boring then he can always just think about the next chess move he's going to make

Chess move? Asle says

Yeah, I saw that you have a chessboard on your table, he says

Yeah, Sigve says

I taught myself chess when I was in prison, he says

and he says that when he got out the first thing he did was buy himself a black bag, black plastic, yes, the one he uses every day, and a chessboard with pieces, and since he didn't have anyone to play chess with he started playing something called postal chess, that means that every Friday he mails a letter with a chess move and every Wednesday he gets a letter from the guy he's playing against where the guy's written his move, and the correspondence continues until one of them wins or it's a draw, Sigve says and he has no idea who he's playing against, he just knows his name and address, yes well he doesn't even remember the guy's name, and definitely not his address, but as soon as he gets the letter with the other guy's chess move he starts thinking a lot about what his own next move should be, and before he gets the letter he thinks a lot about what move the guy he's playing against is going to make, Sigve says and then he's always reading a book, he says, and sometimes he thinks about what's written in the book, but then thoughts come to him about the times when he had the shakes, yes, as he'd said, and the times when he was in prison, but he was only in prison twice, people can say whatever they want, Sigve says, and then he says that the first time was when he and someone he used to drink with, yes, that was at The Stranda Hotel, where they're going now, they wanted something more to drink so badly when the bar was closed that they just broke down the door and went into The Stranda Hotel to find more to drink, yes, maybe even a bottle of spirits, and then The Policeman came of course and they were arrested and put in jail at The Police Station, but it was just a room with a bed and an ordinary door and by moving the bed so that they could press their backs against the end of the bed and their feet against the door they could put so much pressure on the door, because the guy he used to go drinking with was really strong, that they were able to push it out of the doorframe, yes, they broke down this door too and then they got as far as they could from The Police Station and they decided that the best thing to do would be go to Bjørgvin and then they started walking down the road that led to Bjørgvin, because sooner or later a bus would drive past, they thought, and then they tried to hitch a ride from every car that went by, but not many went by, since it was the middle of the night, and all the cars drove right past them and they walked and walked and they felt so tired, and then they sat down on a milk bench and they sat there and of course they nodded off every now and then too but every time a car drove by one of them stood up and walked out to the edge of the road and stuck out his hand with the thumb up and every single car kept driving and then they just had to wait until the next car, and a little eternity passed before the next car came by and none of the cars stopped so there was nothing to do but keep walking to the next bus stop, they'd get to it eventually, so they started walking down the road again and they were sobering up and they felt terrible all over and then, yes, finally a car stopped, and two men got out, and damn if it wasn't The Policeman and The Policeman's Partner and that was all right, he thought, that was fine too

So, here are our runaways, The Policeman said

They didn't get far, he said

and then The Policeman's Partner handcuffed them both and put them in the car and The Policeman said now he'd drive them straight to the prison in Bjørgvin, and then there'd be a trial and they wouldn't get out of there so easily, and if there was one thing he was sure of it was that this wasn't the only crime they had on their conscience, he said and then they were put in a real prison, this time, in separate cells, there was a bench and a writing desk with drawers and then somewhere to shit and piss, in the cell, and there were bars on the window, and then they were both found guilty and then they were sent to The Prison there in Bjørgvin, Sigve says, and then, yes, then you're sorry about all the stupid things you've done, he'll never be rid of these shameful marks, he says and he holds out his hands with the tattoos on them, three dots between thumb and index finger on his right hand, making a triangle, they call it a beggar's mark, he says, and in the same place on his left hand he has a heart, a cross, and an anchor, yes, a person does all sorts of crazy things when he's drunk, he says and the bus pulls over and stops in front of The Stranda Hotel and they get out and Asle says it'll be nice to get a glass of something now and Sigve says it sure will, that's the truth, and then the question is whether The Namesake will be there, he says, yes, he can go into The Stranda Hotel first and see if he's there and if not they can go up and knock on the basement door where he lives, because it has its own door, the basement, and he knows, as he said, where he lives, Sigve says, and now Asle should just stay there and wait and then he walks into The Stranda Hotel to see if The Namesake is sitting there and so Asle stands there, just standing around, in his black velvet jacket, and with the brown leather shoulder bag hanging over his shoulder, and with a scarf around his neck, and he rolls himself a cigarette and he lights it and then Sigve comes out and says yeah, his Namesake is in there, with *The Bjørgvin Times* and a cup of coffee, so they can just go on in, Sigve says and then Asle walks up the stairs and Sigve opens the door and Asle walks into the lobby, and next to the front desk there's a dining room, and Sigve goes inside and Asle follows him and there, at a table way at the back, with his back against the wall, by a window, there's a guy with long brown hair, and of course he's wearing a black velvet jacket, and a scarf around his neck, Asle sees and then Sigve says they need to go over and say hello to The Namesake and Asle walks towards The Namesake who looks up and Asle thinks that the guy sitting there looks like him, yes, Sigve was right, he thinks and Sigve and Asle go over to the table and Sigve says he thought the two of them should meet, because they're not all that different, he says and The Namesake gets up and holds out his hand to Asle and says Asle and Asle holds out his hand and says Asle and they shake hands

So we're both named Asle, Asle says

Yes, so we are, The Namesake says

and then he sits back down and Asle sits down in the chair opposite

The Namesake and he looks down and Sigve says well then they'll just get a beer, yes, he says and he looks at The Namesake

You probably don't have enough money for a beer? Sigve says

That's probably why you're drinking coffee? he says

Yeah, it's like you're psychic, The Namesake says

and Sigve says he doesn't need to be psychic to know that much and then he asks hasn't The Namesake sold any pictures recently and The Namesake says that he hasn't been painting the kinds of pictures people want to buy for a while now, he just paints the pictures he's going to paint and wants to paint and needs to paint, but he has started on two paintings of a sailboat in a storm, *Boat in a Storm* is the title, yes, the same title that he gives all his paintings like that, he says and he's planning to finish them both quickly, since he needs the money, and then he'll stand in front of The Stranda Hotel like usual, at the bottom of the stairs with the paintings leaning up along the ground-floor wall and see if anyone wants to buy a picture from him

You're still standing on the hotel steps selling pictures? Sigve says

Yes, The Namesake says

You said you'd stop doing that, Sigve says

I certainly did say that, The Namesake says

and then it's silence

But I need the money, he says

and then the woman who was sitting at reception comes walking towards to them and Sigve quietly tells Asle that her name is Gunvor and that she's the wife of the owner of The Stranda Hotel and she comes over to them and she asks what'll it be and Sigve says it'll be a glass of beer each, he says and she looks at Asle and she asks if he has proof of age and then Asle takes out his wallet and takes out his ID card and hands it to her and she looks at it and then she says three glasses of beer then and she gives Asle back his ID and she turns and walks away

I would never have thought you were eighteen years old, or well maybe I would, The Namesake says

and Sigve looks around and then says that Asle's not old enough, he's not eighteen, but they did a little something to his ID card and then suddenly he was eighteen and The Namesake says so that's how it is, he might have known, he did the same thing with his own ID, he says, and it was easy as can be, you'd almost think they made the IDs so that people could change the numbers on them, he says

Yeah, Sigve says

And if you work carefully no one can see that anything's been changed, he says

Anyway, you need to use a magnifying glass, he says

and then it's quiet and then Sigve sits down next to Asle and he looks at The Namesake and says that Asle is going to The Academic High School in Aga

So you're an advanced student then, The Namesake says

But he paints pictures, him too, Sigve says

Yes I thought so, The Namesake says

And he just painted a picture of the house I live in, well, you've been there, yes, from a photograph, the one hanging above the sofa in the living room, Sigve says

So you do that kind of thing, The Namesake says

I used to do it a lot, but I was so tired of painting houses and homes with a blue sky and a blue fjord and a white house and a birch tree just putting its leaves out and a black mountain with white snow on the top that I stopped that, so the picture of the house is in black and white, Asle says

and The Namesake says that he used to do that too

You painted pictured of people's homes for them too? Asle says

Let's not talk about that, The Namesake says

and Asle thinks that he doesn't want to ask The Namesake where he's from, but one thing's for sure, he's not from Barmen or Stranda, but he must be from some other town in Hardanger anyway, you can hear it in his voice, Asle thinks, and he thinks he'd rather not know exactly where The Namesake comes from, it's like he'd prefer not to know that

But lately I haven't wanted to paint any more happy little houses in happyland, it's just lies, The Namesake says

And then, he says

Yes, then I started thinking I'd rather make money painting pictures of boats in a storm at sea, and especially sailboats, but I've also painted steamships and you might say almost modern boats, wooden fishing smacks, that kind of thing, but those paintings are all just lies too, he says

Lies and fraud, he says

and again everyone stops talking

But you have to live on something, everyone needs a little money, he says

and he says, and he looks straight at Asle, that now he'll have two pictures like that done soon and then he'll set up outside The Stranda Hotel, in front of the stairs, with the pictures leaning against the ground-floor wall, he's already done that lots of times, and he always manages to sell the paintings, but it's no good to try to sell too many at once, he says, the best thing is to have just one or two to sell, because then you can get more money for each one, he says, and he says he hopes Asle's not getting any ideas into his head because this is his territory, he says, and he'd rather avoid any competition when it comes to selling paintings like this, he says and Asle hears what he's saying and he has suddenly started thinking about all the people who've sat in this hotel drinking beer, at one or another of these tables, and who are gone now, yes, the ones who are lying in their graves and the ones who've left nothing behind, and now he is sitting at a table in this old hotel, The Stranda Hotel, drinking beer, now it's his turn to be up on the earth, but not for long, and he doesn't know how long he has, no, and then he too will be in the ground, down in the dirt, and will there be anything of him left behind? yes well, aside from the remains lying down in the earth? no, nothing will be left, or maybe a few bones for a while, until they disappear too, so there's nothing left of all the many people who've sat in this old Stranda Hotel drinking beer, Asle thinks, but every single person is more than just bone and meat and fat, and hair and skin, there's a soul too, or a spirit, or both, or whatever you'd call it, whatever the difference is between soul and spirit, and the same way every single person looks different, yes well almost, yes, almost everyone but well it's basically impossible to see any difference between him and The Namesake, he and every other person also has a soul, or maybe a spirit, that's totally unlike other people's, so if he and The Namesake look exactly the same then their souls, their spirits, can't be as similar as their appearance, he thinks

Well you're off in dreamland, The Namesake says

What are you thinking about? he says

I was thinking about all the people who've sat and drank beer at one of the tables in this old hotel and are gone now, Asle says

Yes, The Namesake says

What I'm trying to paint has something to do with them, he says

Same with me, Asle says

But what we're talking about now isn't something that can be said, it can just be painted, maybe, yes, it can be shown in a way, The Namesake says

Yes, Asle says

and it gets quiet and then Gunvor comes over with a tray that has three bottles of beer and three glasses on it and she puts a glass and a bottle down in front of each of them and then she pours a little beer into each glass and she says enjoy and Sigve says thank you and that he'll be paying, but they might be having a couple more rounds probably so maybe he can wait until later to pay, he says and Gunvor says that's fine and she leaves and then Sigve says can't they talk about something else, because this is starting to sound like prayers at a meeting house or a sermon in church or something

Let's drink and be merry, he says

While we still can, he says

and he raises his glass

Yes, The Namesake says

and he raises his glass and then Asle raises his glass and they toast and they drink and then they bang their glasses back down on the table and then they each start rolling a cigarette and they light them and then Sigve says that it's good to be alive, just a glass or two of something and life is good, he says

Yes, Asle says

Yes, it feels good, he says

It calms me down, he says

and The Namesake nods and then none of them says anything

Well that was quite a silence, The Namesake says

Nothing wrong with a little silence, Sigve says

and then The Namesake says someone he knew has moved in with him, now the two of them are living together in one room there in The Basement, she'd started working as a maid at The Stranda Hotel and at first she lived in one of the ordinary hotel rooms herself, but she didn't like that, so she moved in with him, they agreed that she should move in one night when he was sitting here having a beer and she came and sat down at his table, he says and she's there at home in The Basement right now, he says and then he says that he's going to try to get into The Art School in Bjørgvin, one of these days he's going to bring some of his paintings and take the bus to Bjørgvin and then he'll go up to The Art School and show them his paintings and if he starts there, yes, then he too will get an artist's stipend, The Namesake says, so now if he just finishes the two paintings he's working on and gets them sold and gets the money for the bus he'll go to Bjørgvin and try to get a spot at The Art School, he says, and Asle says that he thought you needed to have gone to an academic high school to get into The Art School, that's why he was going to The Academic High School, not because he wanted to but because he wanted to get into The Art School, he says and The Namesake says that that is how it is but it's possible to make an exception to the rule, if a painter's good enough he can get in even if he hasn't gone to The Academic High School, he says and he wasn't clear about that either, he says, but then he wrote to The Art School and asked if that ever happened and got an answer and it said in the letter that it was possible to get into The Art School without having gone to an academic high school if you painted good enough pictures, he says, and Asle thinks how about that, yes, so maybe he doesn't need to slog through all of The Academic High School, because the pictures he paints are good enough, he's sure of that, or maybe that's just something he's imagining and they aren't as good as he thinks they are and it'll be easier for him to get into The Art School if he has his examen artium, so it's probably better if he finishes The Academic High School after all, he thinks, and he feels calmer now, the beer has taken his fear away and The Namesake says that the woman who's moved in with him is a few years older than him, her name is Liv and now she's going to have a baby too, yes, they're going to have a baby together, he's already about to become a father, young as he is, The Namesake says and Sigve says well he's going to be a young father and The Namesake says that it isn't something he wanted, so of course that's what happened, but what will be will be, and if he gets a spot at The Art School and gets an artist's stipend and they find a place to live in Bjørgvin it'll probably all work out, he says, because there must be cheap apartments to rent at what they call The Student's Home, maybe they can get a place there, he says and then he finishes his drink and Sigve says live and let live and both Sigve and Asle have a lot of beer left in their glass and The Namesake says that he should probably get home to Liv, she must be waiting for him, because he said he would just go out for a little walk, he says and he gets up and he says that he needs to finish painting those two sailboats, and he signs all these pictures of boats in a rough sea in the lower right corner, he writes Helle Halle there, and so unclearly that it's illegible and whenever the buyers ask him what his name is he says Helle Halle, The Namesake says and he puts his shoulder bag on and then he says see you and he leaves and then Sigve and Asle are sitting there and Sigve moves over to the other side of the table where The Namesake had been sitting and he moves the empty coffee cup and the empty beer glass that The Namesake left behind over to the side of the table and then he takes his own beer glass and puts it in front of him and Asle takes a sip of his beer and then he looks out the window at The Fjord and it's almost totally still, it's not entirely calm but almost, because there's a light wind making small waves on The Fjord, and every single wave is different, if you look closely you can see that there isn't a single wave that's exactly like another, the same way there's not a single cloud that's exactly like another cloud, all the waves are different, and all the clouds are different, Asle thinks and that's how they are in a good painting too, no wave is just a wave and no cloud is just a cloud, they're like that only in pictures of a sailboat in a storm, as The Namesake puts it, and that's probably why he thinks these paintings are so bad, and that he paints them quickly and badly just to make money, since those are the kinds of painting that people want to buy, Asle thinks, and then he thinks that it's strange that people like so much to buy bad paintings but no one wants to buy the good ones, no, it's impossible to understand, Asle thinks and then he hears Sigve say that he needs to drink, too, not just think or dream or whatever it is

he's doing and Asle sees that Sigve has finished his glass and Asle sees
that his is only half-drunk so he takes a good sip and Sigve says that as
soon as Gunvor shows up, because she's always checking to see if the
customers want anything, they'll order another drink, Sigve says, yes,
he's been to The Stranda Hotel so many times that he even knows that
the woman who was sitting at the reception desk and who's serving
them now is named Gunvor and that her husband, who owns the
hotel, is named Stein, they're both named Stein, The Stranda Hotel
has been in the same family for generations, Sigve says and no sooner
has he said it than Asle sees Gunvor appear and Sigve raises his hand
and she comes over right away and Sigve says that he'd like to order
two more beers and Gunvor says that'll be fine and then she takes
away the empty glass and empty bottle and empty coffee cup that The
Namesake left and then she walks away and Sigve says yes, her name
is Gunvor, and she married into the family, and then there's silence
and then Asle thinks so it was The Stranda Hotel that Sigve broke into
back in the day and Sigve says that it was The Stranda Hotel that he
and the other crook broke into to get more to drink, but he'd accepted
his punishment and settled things with Gunvor and her husband,
he says and then he says that he assumed Asle wanted another beer
too, yes, at least one and I'm lying on the bench with the grey blanket
wrapped around me, the one Grandmother had on her when she was
lying on the bench in The Old House after she'd had her stroke and
that I took with me when I moved to Aga to live in a rented room and
that's followed me everywhere I've lived since then, I think and I see
that now there's just embers lit in the stove, and it's a little cold in
the room now, so I should put a couple more logs in, I think but I stay
lying down because sometimes it takes a real effort just to get to my
feet, I think and then I suddenly hear footsteps and I see the door to
the hallway open and there, yes, right there in the middle of the hall
is Åsleik and he's downright brandishing a cured leg of lamb waving it

back and forth over his shoulder like he's about to throw it at me and I think I must have dozed off a bit yes

You're too old to be driving to Bjørgvin constantly, Åsleik says

It tires you out too much, he says

You're wearing yourself out, he says

Your hair's gone greyer in just a few days, I can see it, he says

and Åsleik says was there really any rush to drive those paintings down to Bjørgvin? and anyway why didn't I take them with me on Monday when I drove down to Bjørgvin not once but twice? he says, why did I have to drive them down separately yesterday? what am I doing? Åsleik says and he says now I need to relax a bit, and get some food in me, because even if I am a bit on the heavy side, and you'd have to say I am, I have to admit, at least I'm not a liar, then I've gotten thinner in the last couple of days and the last time he stopped by he saw that there wasn't much meat left on the leg of lamb hanging in the kitchen so he thought he'd bring over a new one, but it's not, it's not without an ulterior motive, as I've probably guessed, because it's about the time I'll be cutting up the rest of the cured lamb bones into parts and cooking them with potato dumplings and once they've been cooking long enough I'll add a little smoked sausage and carrots and turnips to the water, Åsleik says and then I'll fry up some bacon and that'll be dinner, he says, the way I've always done it, I usually ask him to come over a couple of times a year for potato dumplings cooked in stock from what's left of the leg of lamb, Åsleik says, and he can see that it won't be long until the next time, because there's not much meat left on the mutton leg, as city folks call it, that's hanging in the kitchen, Åsleik says, but first they should probably have their Advent dinners at each other's houses, and even though he felt like having the Christmas lamb ribs that he's been soaking since yesterday and today he took The Boat to Vik to shop on both days, the water was calm and beautiful today, and he bought a lot of turnips, potatoes he has from his own garden of course, and he's told me again and again that I could have some of his potatoes but I've always said no thank you and he can't understand why, but I just don't want potatoes, only Christmas lamb ribs and lutefisk and dry-cured mutton and a little salt cod, and it's true that that's the best he has to offer, but he doesn't grow turnips himself so he had to buy them, but what with the price of turnips these days he should just grow the turnips himself next year, Åsleik says and he says that it's cold in my room and I sit up on the bench and I see that the fire's gone out in the stove and Åsleik goes over to the stove and now I can feel how cold it is in the room, but of course I didn't feel it that much when I was lying there sleeping, and I must have been asleep since I didn't hear Åsleik's tractor, I think and Åsleik says he walked on over today because it's important to keep active, and it's not that far anyway, but it is a ways, he says and what was it Åsleik was saying, that we should eat Christmas lamb ribs today? yes well we usually have Christmas lamb and lutefisk at each other's house during Advent, along with always doing that on New Year's Eve we usually have some during Advent and every other year I go to Åsleik's for lamb ribs and he comes over to my house for lutefisk, and in the other years it's reversed, that's how it's been for years, and this year it's Åsleik's turn to make the lamb ribs, but anyway we usually invite each other to these Advent meals well in advance, so this is rather sudden, isn't it, yes, Åsleik just decided that we should have lamb ribs today and so that's that, today already, and it's just because Åsleik felt like having lamb ribs, but I don't feel like lamb ribs, not right when I've just woken up in any case, I think, and the truth is I don't feel like having any food at all, I think, so I think I'll say thank you but no to Åsleik's invitation and he can just have his lamb ribs alone, I think, but that would probably be wrong? and lamb ribs certainly are good, because Åsleik's lamb ribs always taste unbelievably delicious, and I've already eaten up, by myself, one of the two sides of lamb that I get from Åsleik every year, yes, sometimes I make a few potato dumplings to go with it, and two carrots, and then I melt some margarine to put on the dumplings, and that tastes at least as good as lamb ribs with mashed turnips, maybe even better, I think and I then think that Åsleik and I always talk about food, it seems like that anyway, I think, and now is that anything for two older guys to talk about, one of them, Åsleik, almost totally bald with just a little long thin white hair around his bald spot, and then he has a big grey beard, and he trims both of them himself, hair and beard, with scissors, and that's why it's always cut so unevenly, and he can't be trimming his hair and beard too often either, I think, but it's not like I look any better with this long grey hair of mine always tied back with a black hair tie, I think, but it doesn't help much, because my hair is so thin up top that a bald spot shows through, so even if I tie my hair back with a black hair tie the bald spot is still visible through the strands of hair, and I have a grey beard too, at first I trimmed my beard with scissors too, that was when I had a really long beard, but then I got an electric trimmer and I started keeping my beard short, really short, so almost as soon as I wake up I trim my beard, but that doesn't make me look all that much better, no, neither of us looks too good, Åsleik or me, I think and then Åsleik stands there by the stove and he looks at me and he says I need to come over to his house tonight and have dinner, Christmas is getting closer, in spite of everything, and we usually always have dinner at each other's house during Advent, these Advent meals of ours, he says, so if the invitation's a little sudden for me maybe I'll want to come have dinner with him once I collect my thoughts a little, he says and I say yes I guess I will

And it's a good thing you woke me up, otherwise I wouldn't have been able to get to sleep tonight, I say

It's not good to sleep too much during the day, no, Åsleik says

and I say no, I can't just sleep the days away, and Åsleik says that the whole time he's known me, and it's getting on many years now, he has never seen me drive back and forth to Bjørgvin on the same day and then drive back to Bjørgvin again that same day and drive home the next day and then drive back to Bjørgvin yet again the day after that, no, he doesn't understand what's going on with me? he says, what's come over me? and I don't need to tell him, of course, yes well the last time was because I had to take in the paintings for the regular Christmas exhibition, which always opens right before Christmas, that makes sense, and a couple of days before that, yes, on Monday, I had shopping to do in Bjørgvin, both for myself and for him, he says, but why did I drive back a second time that same day? and why didn't I bring the paintings with me on one of those two times I drove down? no, he doesn't understand, and it doesn't seem like I'm doing too well, yes, he can't say I'm looking too healthy, Åsleik says, or actually I'm still healthy but it's like something's happened that's worrying me, and to tell the truth that was really why he decided I could use a little hearty food, Åsleik says, yes, he thought a lamb-rib dinner would do me good, and a little juicy mutton, he says and again he holds the mutton leg out to me and I say thank you and I just sit there on the bench and Åsleik says so we'll talk more tonight then? at seven o'clock? he says and I say yes, yes, thank you, it's a little sudden for me but I'm sure it'll be delicious, I say and I just sit there on the bench and Åsleik says that I'm clearly not in the mood to talk much right now and he probably should be getting home anyway, maybe he shouldn't have bothered me, and even woken me up? he says and I say again that no, it was good, if I'd slept any longer I wouldn't have been able to get to sleep tonight and I don't like lying awake in bed, so many thoughts come into my head, I say and then I don't say anything else and Åsleik says he'll go home to check on the lamb ribs in the steam cooker, he's never overcooked the lamb ribs before but still you need to pay attention, he remembers that his mother used to stand there the whole time and check to see that there was still water in the pan, yes, actually she was most likely really doing it to enjoy the good smell of the lamb ribs, that was the main reason, Åsleik says, but anyway he shouldn't stand here chit-chatting, he'll just leave me alone now

We'll talk tonight then, I say

And I'm looking forward to the meal, Åsleik says

Yes, we'll talk later, I say

Around seven o'clock, he says

and then Åsleik says that he'll leave the mutton leg on the kitchen table and I can hang it up myself and he stays standing there and I'm sitting on the bench and I look at the round table with the two chairs, there was one for Ales and one for me, and Ales's chair is still there and I look at her empty chair, and now surely Ales will come soon? I think, yes, I always think that, and then with her chair standing there empty like always, and I couldn't bring myself to get rid of it either, it was like I would be desecrating Ales's memory in a way if I did that, and that was something I didn't want, yes, that's what I would have been doing if I did that, but constantly thinking that Ales had to be back soon now, seeing the empty chair and thinking that Ales was still alive and about to come home, no, being like that was no good either, I think, but the chair is still there, and one day when Åsleik was over and I was sitting in my chair he sat down in the empty chair next to me and I was suddenly shocked and afraid, yes, it was like I was suddenly jealous and I told Åsleik he had to get up

Get up, I said

and he stood up right away and he looked at me taken aback

I didn't know, he said

and I felt ashamed of myself

Sorry, I said

I didn't know, he said again

No of course, I say

But that's Ales's chair, I say

and then it was quiet for a long time and then Åsleik asked if maybe it was a bad idea to have the chair always there, the chair where Ales used to sit, he said and I said no, no, it's not bad, but I didn't want anyone else to sit there, because it was like desecrating Ales's memory, I said and Åsleik said that when Ales was alive he used to sit in that chair all the time and I sat in the other chair and we'd sit there and look out at the water and I said that's how it was but that was when Ales was alive and was either in the room with us or was somewhere else in the house, but now, now that she's gone, yes, now it's only her chair, even I never sit in it, I said and then Åsleik asked didn't I want to get rid of the chair, maybe move it into The Parlour? he said and I said I wanted the empty chair to stay where it is now and Åsleik again said sorry

I didn't know that's how it was, he said

No, how could you, I said

No, he said

and I stand up from the bench and I go and sit down in my chair next to the round table and I look at Åsleik and I say that I often sit and look out at the water, yes, either I'm standing and painting or I'm lying on the bench or I'm sitting in my chair looking out at the water, the sea, out across the Sygne Sea, yes, I say, and I've probably told him that I have a fixed landmark, I say and Åsleik shakes his head and I say that I always look at the same spot in the water, at my landmark, I say and Åsleik says he needs to get home and then he says we'll talk later and then he says that he'll leave the mutton leg on the kitchen table and I see Åsleik go out to the kitchen and shut the kitchen door behind him and I think that the sea is always there to be seen, yes, I can see all the way out to the mouth of The Fjord and the open sea, yes, I see the Sygne Sea and the islets and reefs out there, the holms and skerries, and the islands protecting the mouth of The Fjord, and then I see the spaces between the islands where it opens out and you can see the ocean itself, yes, even if it's dark or snowing hard or a heavy rain or there's a fog I can see the water, the waves, the ocean, and it's impossible to understand, actually, I think as I sit there in the chair at the round table and I take my bearings and I look at the spot I always look at in the water and I see Asle standing in the hall outside the classroom waiting for The Teacher who teaches English and French and he sees The Teacher come walking up to him and he's wearing his grey trousers and white pullover with blue stripes again today and he's carrying some books and when he gets to Asle he says why aren't you going into class?

But, Asle says

Yes, The Teacher says

I, you know, Asle says

Yes, The Teacher says

Yes I, Asle says

Yes I, I, I'm too scared to read aloud, he says

Scared to read aloud? The Teacher says

and it's like he can't believe what he's hearing

Yes, Asle says

and The Teacher looks at him and Asle can tell that he doesn't believe what he's saying and Asle says he wants to ask him if he could not read out loud in class and The Teacher looks at him and then he says that he often has some student or a row of students recite something, as he's noticed already, so it would be a bit strange if he didn't read too, he says and Asle can tell that The Teacher doesn't believe him and then The Teacher says that he'll try to take this into consideration so Asle won't have to read so much, maybe just one or two sentences, but it is important that he practise his pronunciation, The Teacher says and then he asks if Asle would prefer that he ask him questions? to hear whether or not he's done his homework, his reading? and Asle says that would be great and there's something like mockery in The Teacher's voice and then Asle says that that was all he wanted to say and The Teacher says they should go in then, today in any case he won't have to read anything out loud, because he'd heard him stumbling and skipping words last time, but his pronunciation is good, yes, his English is good, so he'll be able to learn to speak English well, and they'll see how it goes with French but anyway they need to go into the classroom now, The Teacher says and Asle goes in and he has his brown leather shoulder bag on and he goes over to his desk in the very back of the classroom near the middle and I look at the water, there at my landmark, at the waves, and I get up from the chair and I go out to the kitchen and there on the kitchen table I see a big leg of mutton, yes, Åsleik is generous, I think, he likes to give people things, and plus he's so proud of the food he's prepared, the Christmas lamb ribs, the lutefisk, I think, but it is rather sudden being invited over for a lamb-rib dinner tonight, because strictly speaking I don't feel like eating any food, I have absolutely no appetite for anything, but it'll still taste good anyway, I think and then I take the new leg of lamb and it's heavy in my hand and I put it back down on the kitchen table and then I take the lamb bone off the hook on the wall where it's hanging, and it's almost just bone now, and I put it on the kitchen table and then hang the new leg up and I look at the old leg of lamb on the table and I think that I am hungry, but I'm not in the mood for any food today and I think that later I'll cut it up into pieces and then boil it with potato dumplings, but I won't do that for a while, so I should just stick this leg of lamb in the freezer I have in the hall, I think, and then I'll cut it up into pieces later, I think and I go out into the hall and I see the telephone sitting there and it doesn't ring very often, it sometimes happens that Asle calls, and now I need to call The Hospital and ask how he's doing, and whether I can see him, I think, but that can wait a little, I think, and it sometimes happens every now and then that Beyer calls me, and then there's Åsleik sometimes, usually to ask me if I can buy him something he needs the next time I'm in Bjørgvin, and that's why I keep a notepad and pencil next to the phone on its table there in the hall, that's where I write down what Åsleik's asking me to buy, or when the appointment is if Beyer and I are arranging to see each other, and sometimes every now and then I call Asle too, and then we usually set a time to meet at The Alehouse and then I always call The Country Inn to book my regular room, Room 407, and then Asle and I meet at The Alehouse and have a big dinner, and he has a lot of beer and stronger stuff with it, I used to drink with him before and quite a lot too but that was before Ales and I moved to the brown house, yes, you'd have to say that strictly speaking we moved out of Bjørgvin to the brown house to get away because I was drinking too much, to tell the truth, for a while it was almost nothing but drinking and no painting, and Ales thought I had to stop drinking, and she was completely right, and strangely enough I was able to totally stop drinking, I think, but I don't want to think about that anymore, I think, and first I stopped smoking, because I smoked all the time, lighting each cigarette with the end of the other so to speak, and then one day it felt like I had smoked as much as I was meant to smoke, and I stopped, first smoking, then drinking, and after a while I hardly ever went to restaurants or bars, just to cafés, aside from meeting Asle at The Alehouse every now and then, at The Last Boat, that's how it was, I think and when we met there Asle's always had a little to drink beforehand, and when I see that I start getting a little anxious and I say that it's night for me, I go to bed early, I always turn in at around nine o'clock, I would say and then Asle says he'll stay for a while at The Alehouse, because someone needs to man The Last Boat, he says and he laughs and I say yes we've drunk a lot together over the years you and me and Asle says yes we sure have but that was before I moved out of Bjørgvin and before Ales got me to stop drinking, because it was she who got me to stop, wasn't it? yes, he was sure it was, just as I'd said, because after Ales and I left Bjørgvin it wasn't like we never drank together again, we still met at The Alehouse sometimes, but then I would only drink coffee or water, or else we'd sometimes meet at The Coffeehouse instead, that was usually in the mornings before I went to mass at St Paul's Church, I think, and I think that I need to call The Hospital to hear how Asle is doing, and check if I can come and see him? or if I can bring him something from his apartment anyway, if I can maybe buy him something he might need? I think and no sooner did I think that than Bragi is standing there next to me looking up at me with his dog's eyes and I ask if he wants to go outside and I go and open the front door and Bragi runs out as fast as he can and I leave the door open and I think I need to call The Hospital, because even if I can't see Asle maybe I can bring him something from his apartment? books, maybe? because he was always reading some book or another, and I can give the books or whatever to the woman at the reception desk and then she or someone else can pass them along to Asle, I think, because while I don't read much and am only now thinking seriously about starting to read, Asle has read constantly, yes, it's almost impossible to truly believe how much he's read, or how much he's drunk, for that matter, yes I need to call The Hospital, I think, but not just now, I'm too tired, and anyway I can't drive back to Bjørgvin today so I can call in the morning, because then I can maybe drive back to Bjørgvin to see Asle, that's certainly possible, I think and I feel tired and I step into the cut-off boots I keep by the front door and I go outside and I see snowflakes coming gently down one after another, so now it's already started snowing again, snow one day and rain the next, like always, I think and I see Bragi standing there and doing his business and then running around in circles while the snowflakes come gently down over him and stick to his fur and then I call for Bragi and he comes running over right away and he runs into the hall and I shut the door and I think that I should have painted a little, and right away something like a darkness falls down over and inside me and I think that I don't have the strength to paint anymore, I've done my part, I've done all the painting I'm going to do, I'm done with painting, I don't want to paint anymore, I think, enough is enough, I think and I go into the main room and over there on the easel I see the bad painting with the two lines that cross in the middle, no, I can't look at it, I can't even take the picture down from the easel and put it in the pile with the other paintings I'm not totally done with yet, that I'm not totally satisfied with, I just can't, I think and I look at the easel and I think that when I look at the easel now, isn't it like, the thought comes into my head, isn't it like God is there too, in the easel? like, yes, like God is looking out at me from the easel? I think, and now I just have to not go crazy, I think, because it's like God is looking at me from every single thing, I think and I look around and it's like God is in everything around me, I think, and like he's looking at me from every single thing, I think and I think isn't the round table clearly saying with its silence that God is nearby? and the two chairs? and the one Ales always sat in, especially clearly, God is so clearly looking at me from that chair, I think, and I think that it's when I'm most alone, in my darkness, my loneliness, because it really is lonely, to tell the truth, and when I'm as quiet as I can be, that God is closest, in his distance, and I really have, almost like a monk, I think, and then I start laughing because you can hardly imagine anyone less like a monk than me, I think, or maybe well maybe there is a similarity, because maybe I've withdrawn from life too, a little like a monk, I think, into this wordless painting, yes, into loneliness, I could probably put it that way except it sounds so wrong, I think, but I really have withdrawn into the wordless prayer of painting, maybe it's all right to put it that way, and it does sound wrong, I think, and it's also the peace painting gives, I've also withdrawn into that, I think, but this is the wrong word, it's too big a word, the truth is just that I stood there and painted, day in and day out, all these years, with all the humility I have in me I stood there and painted, and I probably need to keep standing there painting because what else can I do, really? but I don't want to paint anymore, I think, and if I don't want to paint anymore I don't have to, I think and then I think that God has been staying hidden this whole time, yes, it's like he shows himself by concealing himself, in life, in things, in what is, yes, in paintings too of course, and maybe it's like the more God conceals himself the more he shows himself, and vice versa, yes, the more he shows himself, or is shown, you can say it either way, the more he conceals himself, I think, yes, God reveals himself by hiding, and it is in the hiddenness of God, God's hiddenness, that I can forget myself and hide myself, and only there, I think, and this is not something I can understand, there's nothing comprehensible about it, but it's when you understand that you can't understand God that you understand him, and isn't that so obvious that it doesn't even need to be said? doesn't need to be thought? yes, it's just as obvious as the fact that God's words are silent, I think, because they are, but that's completely obvious too, because God's language speaks silently from everything that exists, and this silence was first broken when The Word came into the world, when Christ came down to earth, only then could God's word be heard, yes, and be thought, too, but do I really believe this? I think, does it mean anything? I think, no, maybe not, but maybe a person can be hidden in Christ, in his word, and that's because there's hope in God's great silence? but do I believe that? no, maybe not, not literally, but God's nearness isn't something I need to believe in, because the darker I am the closer God is, I think, that's a fact, I think and it's something I'll always think even if I don't get any farther with my thoughts than that, it's only with painting that I get any farther, but, farther? what do I mean by that? I think, I've just now thought that I don't want to, that I can't, paint anymore, I think and I look at the chair where Ales used to sit and I think that this silent language from the chair is real, it's true, it's ridiculous but that's what I seriously think, yes, that God's silent language comes from the chair, yes, that God is looking at me from Ales's chair and silently speaking to me, I think, because there's a silence hidden in everything that is, and it's this stillness that is the innermost part of everything real, I think, and it's this stillness that is God's creative silence, as Ales used to say, because God is an uncreated light, she said and I've experienced myself that the black darkness is God's light, this darkness that can be both in me and around me, yes, this darkness I now feel that I am, because in the darkness is a stillness where God's voice sounds in silence, I think and I see the chair where I always sit next to the round table and I go over to the chair and I sit down and I find my bearings and then I look at my landmark, at the waves, and I think that often when I sit like this and look at the water I pray a silent prayer and then Ales is near me too, and my parents, and my sister Alida, and Grandmother, and Sigve, and I get very still inside, and I think that everyone has a deep longing inside them, we always always long for something and we believe that what we long for is this or that, this person or that person, this thing or that thing, but actually we're longing for God, because the human being is a continuous prayer, a person is a prayer through his or her longing, I think and then I look at the chair next to me and I see Ales sitting there and then she starts singing softly, almost inaudibly, she sings Amazing grace How sweet the song That saved a wretch like me I once was lost But now am found Was blind but now I see and then I see Ales stand up and disappear and as she disappears I hear her singing again in an almost inaudible voice Amazing grace How sweet the song That saved a wretch like me I once was lost But now am found Was blind but now I see and I grip the edge of the table tight and then I look at Bragi standing there and looking at me with his dog's eyes and I think that dogs understand so much but they can't say anything about it, or else they can say it with their dog's eyes, and in that way they're like good art, because art can't say anything either, not really, it can only say something else while keeping silent about what it actually wants to say, that's what art is like and faith and dogs' silent understanding too, it's like they're all the same, no now I'm getting in over my head with these thoughts, I think, because I've never been a thinker, and the only language I've so to speak mastered is the language of pictures, I think, and all my thoughts are sort of jumbled together, it's like they don't exist in any order but sort of all at the same time, I think and I look at Bragi and I think maybe he's hungry or thirsty, and it's good to think about that, I think, because I'm trying to comprehend the incomprehensible but it doesn't work, I think and I get up and go out to the kitchen and Bragi follows me and I see that there's no water in his bowl and I fill the bowl with water and he laps and laps at his water and then I cut a slice of bread and break it apart into pieces and put the pieces into the other dish I've set out for Bragi, but he just sniffs at the bread and then he slinks back off into the main room and I think that I really need to find something else for Bragi to eat soon, I think and I think that now I'll go sit in my chair again and then I'll pray for Asle to get better, I think and I go into the main room and I see my black velvet jacket hanging over the back of the chair where I always sit and it's always like that, I always hang my velvet jacket over the back of the chair, I think and I think that I never got rid of Ales's clothes, I put them in boxes nice and neatly and put the boxes up in crates in the attic room, the room where I keep my paintings, so that if Ales one day decides to rise from the dead and come walking into her old house she won't be missing a single article of clothing or anything else of hers, because I've taken care of everything, yes, it really is complete madness, I think, but I couldn't manage to give Ales's clothes or anything else she owned to The Second-Hand Shop, it was too much, and so everything just stayed how it was when she died, it stayed that way for a long time but eventually I gathered her clothes up and put them in boxes and stored them up in the attic and one of these days I need to get hold of myself and come to my senses and drive the boxes of clothes to Bjørgvin and give them to The Second-Hand Shop so someone else can use them, because now they're no good to anyone, I think and I think that in one attic room there's now the portrait I painted of Ales out, leaned against the back of a chair, because that's one of the pictures I didn't want to sell, and that I'll never sell, that is the only picture I will never sell, all the other pictures I'd be happy to sell, as I'm now thinking I'm going to do, but I want to keep the portrait of Ales, and that's so obvious it doesn't even need to be said, I think and when I thought I'd sell all the pictures it was so unthinkable that I'd sell the portrait of Ales that I didn't even think that I wouldn't sell it, I think, and her portrait has been leaning against the back of a chair between the two small windows for such a long time now, I think, several years at least, I think and I stand in the main room and I look at the empty chair where Ales always sat and I think that either I need to get rid of the empty chair or else let Åsleik sit in it, or anyone else who comes over for a visit, but who would that be? I can't remember having anyone else come visit except Åsleik in all these years, just him, no one else, I think, but I just don't want Åsleik to sit in that chair, or anyone else for that matter, so that means the chair is going to just stay there empty, I think, so maybe I should ask Åsleik if he wants to carry the chair into The Parlour? where all of Ales's paintings still are the way they were, where everything is still the way she left it the day she went to The Hospital never to return, I think, and so should I ask Åsleik to put the chair in front of the window there, I think, but no, how can I even think that, of course Ales's chair has to stay where it's always been, how can I even think otherwise, I think and I go and sit down in my chair and I look at the spot out there in the Sygne Sea that I always look at and I look at the waves and I see Asle sitting on the bus from Aga to Stranda and he's thinking that actually it's going pretty well at The Academic High School, because even if he put it off much longer than he should have he did eventually talk to The Teacher who taught Norwegian and History, the homeroom teacher, and to The Teacher who taught German, and they'd understood right away what reading out loud was like for him and they'd both said that they wouldn't ask him to read out loud, but, they'd both said, if he did feel able to read something should raise his hand or give a sign in some other way that he felt able to do it and then they could ask him to read, but if he didn't they wouldn't, they'd said and Asle was so grateful to them for understanding him, and they'd both said that they'd had no problem understanding it, and then Asle thought that people sure were different, because these two teachers had understood how he felt while The Teacher he had in English and French hadn't believed him, he'd thought Asle was trying to trick him, that Asle wanted to get out of doing work or something, that he didn't want to do what he was supposed to, while these two other teachers had understood at once the fear that was torturing him, so there was a big difference between people, he'd learned that then and there, Asle thinks, and then he thinks that every day after he finished at The Academic High School he went to see Grandmother at The Hospital, and even if she couldn't talk anymore, even if the only words she'd been able to say for a long time were gone now, they were still together in a way, he and Grandmother, and there was life in her eyes, and she could laugh if he said something funny, he thinks, but these last few days she'd changed, she'd turned kind of bluish over her whole face but especially on her lips, her lips had been a bit blue for a long time but now the blue was stronger, whiter and stronger, Grandmother had turned so white, and when he went to see her today her face was almost grey, Asle thinks, sitting there in the bus going to Stranda because he's out of white oil paint and he needs some, because he can't paint without white, he thinks, even if painting if you look at it in a certain way is the art of colour there's no way he can paint without also using a lot of white, and that's obvious enough, it's pretty straightforward, but he also needs to use a lot of black since you often need black to get a picture into harmony, and everything needs to be right in a painting, everything needs to go together, there needs to be a very precise balance in the picture, and to get that balance black can be really useful, Asle thinks and I sit at the round table and now I can feel so clearly that Ales is sitting in the chair next to mine, and she puts her hand over my hand and then we hold each other's hand and stay sitting like that, holding each other's hand, and neither of us says anything and I see Asle sitting on the bus to Stranda and he's thinking that when he gets there he'll go straight to The Paint Shop and buy a big tube of white oil paint and then he'll take the same bus back to Aga that he came on, because the bus goes back to Aga fifteen minutes after it arrives in Stranda, Asle thinks and the bus stops in Stranda and Asle gets out of the bus and then he goes straight to The Paint Shop, because he has hardly any time, since the bus is heading back to Aga in fifteen minutes and he wanted to catch the bus, Asle thinks, because he's in the middle of a picture, and if he wants to do more on it he needs to get hold of some white oil paint, Asle thinks and he goes into The Paint Shop and who should he see standing in front of the tubes of oil paint but The Namesake, his long brown hair, the black velvet jacket, the brown leather shoulder bag, the scarf around his neck, and Asle thinks that of course they're dressed the same today too, and of course he should go up to The Namesake and of course now he'll have to talk to him, and wasn't once enough? Asle thinks, but he needs his white oil paint and he's going to get it so he doesn't leave The Paint Shop, he doesn't have time to leave and come back to The Paint Shop after The Namesake has left, Asle thinks, he needs to just pick up a big tube of white oil paint right now and then go back home to his rented room so that he can keep working on the painting he's in the middle of, Asle thinks and he walks straight to the shelf where the tubes of oil paint are and The Namesake looks at him

No, it's you, he says

Nice to see you again, he says

and he holds out his hand and The Namesake and Asle shake hands

Yes, a lot has happened since we last saw each other, The Namesake says

and Asle thinks he needs to say he doesn't have time and then he sees the tubes of white paint and he picks up two big tubes and The Namesake says yes you can't do anything without white

Yes, a lot's happened, The Namesake says

I, he says

Yes, you need to hear this, he says

I've been accepted at The Art School, The Namesake says

Yeah I took the bus to Bjørgvin and went to The Art School and showed my paintings to the first person I saw, I showed him the best paintings I'd done and he said I had talent, it was a long time since he'd seen pictures that showed such talent, so even if I didn't have an examen artium, yes well what did that really have to do with being able to paint? yes, he was completely sure that The Principal would let me start at The Art School, The Namesake says

and he says that then they went to The Principal and The Principal said that since his paintings showed such clear talent of course he could start at The Art School without an examen artium and The Namesake asked, The Namesake says, if he couldn't maybe start right away and The Principal said that there was always a place for a talent like his, so it would be fine, he said and The Namesake said that he lived in Stranda but that he was going to try to find a place to live either in Bjørgvin or near Bjørgvin as soon as possible so that he could start at The Art School as soon as he could and The Principal asked if he had money, and he'd said hardly any and The Principal said that now that he was a student at The Art School he could apply for an artist's stipend and then he asked for his name and address and birthdate and he asked to see his ID card, because he had to see that if The Namesake was going to start at The Art School and when The Principal saw his birthdate he'd said that his age was also a factor in letting him start right away at The Art School and then The Principal wrote out a letter stating that he had been accepted to The Art School because his paintings showed clear talent and he gave Asle a form and said he had to fill out the form and include it with the letter and apply for an artist's stipend, yes, the students who went to The Art School got a higher stipend than other students, which was reasonable enough, The Principal said and then he shook hands with The Namesake and it was really great that he got into The Art School, he says, because Liv, yes, Asle probably remembered he'd told him about her, she was very pregnant now, her belly had grown so big that it looked like it was about to burst, and she wanted to give birth in The Hospital and she said that she wanted to go to Sartor where her parents lived as soon as she could, because the childbirth was getting close, she might be giving birth any day now, and he could come along to Sartor and they could stay for a while at her parents' house until they got a place of their own to live, preferably in Bjørgvin, she said, and now, yes, he was actually just standing there looking at the tubes of oil paint without planning to buy anything because he had to pack up everything he owned, all of it, and Liv had to pack up everything she owned, and she found room for everything in her one suitcase but it was harder for him since he had to bring all his paintings with him, and of course the easel and brushes and all the other painting things, but he didn't have many clothes to pack, so if The Bus Driver wasn't too difficult there'd be enough room for everything in the baggage compartment, he says

Congratulations on getting into The Art School, Asle says

And you'll be next, The Namesake says

I hope I get in, Asle says

You will, I'm sure of it, The Namesake says

and then Asle says that he doesn't have much time, he just got off the bus from Aga and he's in the middle of a painting and he ran out of white paint again so he was planning to take the same bus back, he says and The Namesake says he won't hold him up and keep him from catching the bus and he says he's never spoken to Liv's parents, who live in Sartor, and she hasn't asked them either if it's okay that she, or they, come there, or if she, well, they, can live there for a while, she hasn't even told her parents that she's pregnant, she doesn't talk to her parents much, but she did tell her mother over the phone that she'd be taking a trip home soon, she went down to the phone booth in the centre of Stranda and called her mother, and her mother had said of course she was welcome to come, she was so happy she'd be seeing Liv again, it had been so long since the last time, and she was sure that her father felt the same way, of her three sisters who used to live in the house the youngest sister had moved out too in the autumn, she too had gone away, the same way the three other sisters had done before her, so now there was plenty of room in the house, and it would be so nice to see her again, her mother had said and then she'd chattered on about this and that, about the difficult neighbour lady, about Liv's uncle, her father's brother who'd ended up homeless in Bjørgvin and so on and so forth and Liv didn't say a word about being pregnant and that he as the father was going to be with her, he says and Asle has already gone over to the cash register and The Namesake has walked next to him and the man at the register says so you're still painting are you, it's a good thing we have customers like you, he says and Asle says that he doesn't have much time since he needs to catch the bus to Aga and then Asle pays and he leaves and The Namesake leaves with him and The Namesake says that the one thing he's dreading is going home to Liv's parents in Sartor, because what if they don't want him there? maybe Liv's father won't want him to paint because he might get the floor dirty or something? he thinks, he says, and also he was about to be a father, and he was so young, and he didn't own anything, an easel and a few brushes and some pictures and that was it, and he who had thought he would never get married or have children because he'd never be able to, he, yes, he was about to be a father soon, he says and the bus is luckily still there, Asle thinks, so now he can finally get rid of The Namesake, he thinks

The bus is there already, The Namesake says

It's lucky I made it, Asle says

And you were also lucky because they don't always have tubes of white oil paint at The Paint Shop, at least not big ones, The Namesake says

and he says that there've been a few times he's had to wait almost two weeks to get white oil paint, yes, it was unbelievable, it was almost like The Paint Shop was intentionally trying to not carry white oil paint, he says and Asle says that the bus door is open so he better get on right away and The Namesake says yes he should, and so he hopes they meet again at The Art School, he says and Asle says he hopes so too and The Namesake holds out his hand and they shake hands and then The Namesake says that they'll see each other at The Art School in Bjørgvin then, sooner or later, and Asle says that the only question now is whether they'll take him and The Namesake says he's sure they will and Asle thinks now how can The Namesake be so sure that he'll get into The Art School too, he has never even seen one of his paintings, so it's just something he's saying, Asle thinks and he gets on the bus and he tells The Bus Driver that he's going to Aga and The Bus Driver says so he wants to go back home right away and Asle doesn't answer and he pays the fare and he goes to the back of the bus and he sits down in the back seat and then he looks out the window and he sees The Namesake standing there and the bus starts up and pulls away and The Namesake raises his hand and waves at him and Asle waves back and he thinks well now The Namesake has already gotten a spot at The Art

School while he's still slogging away at The Academic High School and is afraid to go to school, he's constantly thinking that he might have to read out loud, because The Teacher in English and French who clearly owns only a grey pair of trousers and a white pullover with blue stripes, or else he has several of the same kind of trousers and pullovers, now rarely asks students down a row one after the other to read out loud but he does constantly ask this or that individual person to read aloud and Asle has noticed that he looks at him and that he kind of threatens to ask him to read, so now he'll just have to start skipping school on the days he has English, because French classes are just words and Asle thinks that the pronunciation is impossible, he will never be able to make those sounds, and there's not one of the other students in the class who can do it either and The Teacher in the grey trousers and white pullover with blue stripes moans and groans and beats his breast and says that this is hopeless, it's patently clear that the situation is hopeless, and he uses those two words all the time, hopeless and patently, and it'll be a long time before they can read any text out loud in French so he doesn't have much to worry about there, but two days a week, Tuesday and Thursday, he has two hours of English each day and now he'll just have to cut school on those days, he's thought many times that he should but he's gone to school anyway, but now he'll miss two days of school every single week, and whatever happens will happen, Asle thinks sitting there on the bus and he thinks that every Monday and every Wednesday he's scared all afternoon and all evening, frightened of the next day, that he might have to read out loud, and so that's when he usually goes to see Sigve and Sigve answers whenever he knocks on the door, even if he's not always so glad to see him, but he always invites him in, and usually Asle has a couple of beers with him or else they go to The Hotel and buy a glass or two there, and that helps, but first he goes to see Grandmother at The Hospital, but she's just getting worse and worse, it's like she's disappearing into her own world more and more and her face is getting kind of greyer and greyer and she's asleep more and more often when he comes by and when she is he leaves right away and just lets her keep sleeping since if he does wake her up he's often not sure if she knows he's there, only sometimes does she look at him clearly and recognise him, and she's entirely stopped talking, now she just nods or shakes her head, Asle thinks, but he always holds Grandmother's hand, and her hand is always cold, he thinks sitting there on the bus and then he thinks that The Namesake got into The Art School without going to The Academic High School, without an examen artium, he could do that too, so one of these days he'll take some of his paintings and get on a bus to Bjørgvin and show the people there the pictures and try to get a spot at The Art School, because exceptions are made for people like them, people who haven't gone to The Academic High School but who get in by reason of talent alone, and if he gets a spot at The Art School he'll stop going to The Academic High School that same day, Asle thinks and he sees that the bus is getting close to The Shoemaker's Workshop where he lives and he pulls the cord and the bus stops and Asle gets out and he goes straight home and he knows exactly where the painting needs a little white paint, there are three places, one place that needs a light thin stroke with movement in it and two others that need a thin overpainting, he thinks and he thinks that tomorrow he has English again so he won't go to school, he's decided that, and before long he'll take the bus to Bjørgvin and then he'll bring the two books that Sigve lent him a long time ago, that he still hasn't read, and he'll read them on the bus, because he hasn't even opened the books, Asle thinks, and then he'll go to The Art School and show them some paintings and try to get a spot even though he doesn't have an examen artium and if he gets a spot he'll stop going to The Academic High School, and this is already a huge relief, he thinks and I sit there and I look at my fixed spot in the water, my bearings, the tops of the pine trees in front of the house need to be in the middle of the middle pane on the right, because the window is divided in two and can be opened from either side and each half of the window is divided into three panes and it's the middle of the right-hand pane that the treetops have to be in, I think and then I look at my landmark and at the waves and I see Asle get out the old suitcase he brought with him from the attic in The Old House when he moved to his rented room and he chooses several pictures and wraps them as well as he can in the grey blanket he got from Grandmother and puts them in the suitcase and he thinks that he should have gone and seen Grandmother at The Hospital but he'd rather go see Sigve and maybe they'll have a beer or two at The Hotel, he thinks and then he puts on his black velvet jacket and brown leather shoulder bag and a scarf and then he'll goes straight to Sigve's, Asle thinks, because now he's finally taken the big decision that he's been thinking about for such a long time, he put it off for too long, he thinks, but now he wants to try to get into The Art School without finishing at The Academic High School, and The Namesake could do it so he should be able to do it too, Asle thinks as he's walking from the old house to Sigve's and he knocks on the door and no one answers so he waits a little bit and he hears someone walking around inside so he knocks again and he hears footsteps coming towards the door and it opens and there's Sigve and he is definitely not so happy to see Asle

No, it's you, Sigve says

and Asle says that he has to tell Sigve something and Sigve invites him in and then Asle says that he's going to try to get into The Art School in Bjørgvin without having graduated from The Academic High School, because if The Namesake could get into The Art School in Bjørgvin without having gone to The Academic High School, just on the strength of his pictures, he should be able to as well, so tomorrow he's going to cut school and take some paintings and go to Bjørgvin and go to The Art School and ask if he can go to The Art School without having finished The Academic High School and taken an examen artium, Asle says and it seems like Sigve isn't entirely following him and Asle sees that the picture he painted of Sigve's house, which had been standing on the floor in front of the bookcase for such a long time now, isn't there anymore, so Sigve must have moved it somewhere else even though it really isn't such a bad painting, Asle thinks and he thinks that it looks like Sigve has been lying down, asleep, and that Asle woke him up, and Sigve says that's very nice and then Sigve says that he was asleep, he was drinking really late last night but he did make it to work, and he got those damn armrests and chair legs attached but it wasn't exactly a great day, no, he says and then Asle says that maybe they could go get a glass or two at The Hotel and Sigve says that after yesterday he really shouldn't, but it sure feels like he could use a glass or two, he says and Asle says that they can go to The Hotel and Sigve says yes, okay, they'll do that and then Sigve says that it was like something snapped in him yesterday a little, no, he doesn't know exactly what came over him but anyway he got angry, and it was mostly himself that he was angry at, because he's never been the type to blame other people, no, he says and then Asle says, saying he doesn't really want to say it, that he wants to apologise for giving Sigve a painting of his house that wasn't the way Sigve wanted it, but actually he'd stopped painting pictures like that, he had painted enough pictures like that, because they weren't real pictures, they were just pointless, really, anyway they weren't art, Asle says and he says that he said he wanted to paint a picture of Sigve's house to be nice, since Sigve had asked him to, and Sigve says that he'd only asked Asle to paint a picture to be nice to him, and then they both laugh a little, and then Sigve says that Asle can just go to The Hotel and have a drink and he'll come a little later, he needs a little time to get ready

In that case I'll go see Grandmother at The Hospital first, Asle says

Yes you go see her every day, Sigve says

She'll miss you if you move to Bjørgvin, he says

I hadn't thought of that, Asle says

and then Asle goes to The Hospital to see Grandmother and he sees her lying in bed and she's asleep and her face is almost totally grey, with a little blue on her whole face, and he sits down on the edge of the bed and he takes her hand and it's so cold and stiff and then he says something but Grandmother doesn't answer and he hears her breathing but there's a long time between each time she breathes in and breathes out and Asle thinks that since he and Mother never got along too well it was Grandmother he was closest to when he was growing up, always, if it wasn't for her he doesn't know what would have happened to him, Asle thinks and he thinks that he's seen her anyway even if she didn't know it, and he thinks that now it's decided and there's no doubt about it, tomorrow he's going to skip school and take the bus to Bjørgvin, he thinks and now it'll be good to have a couple of glasses of beer, Asle thinks and he goes to The Hotel and he sits down and he orders a glass of beer and then he thinks that Grandmother is going to die tonight, and that's another reason to quit at The Academic High School, so tomorrow he'll skip school and go to Bjørgvin and The Art School and then whatever's going to happen will happen, he thinks and I sit on my chair and look out at the fixed point out on the Sygne Sea, like I'm in the habit of doing, and I notice that Ales is sitting here next to me and she's holding my hand and I think that yes, really, it was the night before I went to Bjørgvin with my pictures to try to get into The Art School that my Grandmother died, I think and then I hear Ales say your Grandmother's in a good place now and I feel that Ales is so close so close, she's sitting in the chair next to me and I can feel her hand in mine so clearly and I look at the chair and of course I don't see anything and I let go of Ales's hand and then I put my arm around her shoulders and I look at the waves and I see Asle and Liv, and she has a big belly, they're sitting on the bus to

Bjørgvin and they look so strange sitting there, she with her jacket open because she can't close it since her belly is so big and he with the brown leather shoulder bag on his lap and he thinks that now he's given up the room he was renting in the basement and Liv has given up her job at The Stranda Hotel, so now there's nothing keeping them in Stranda anymore and all their earthly goods, as they say, are packed up and sitting in the bus's baggage compartment now, and The Bus Driver wasn't a problem, he was helpful and put their vanload of stuff into the baggage compartment in the best way, Asle had his things in two empty boxes he'd gotten from The Co-op Store in Stranda and his pictures put away in an old suitcase, and he'd packed his clothes and the other things he had, painting supplies, some books, not much more than that, in two boxes and Liv had her big suitcase and now they're sitting there in the bus and Asle thinks that he's worried about going home to Liv's parents, because what will they say? she hasn't told them she was pregnant, and hasn't told them anything about him, and hasn't told her parents that they'd be arriving today, and what will Liv's father and mother say? Asle thinks and it seems like Liv is thinking the same thing because she says she wishes she'd called her mother and said they were coming and that she's expecting a baby, and that Asle is coming with her, but she was so worried about doing it, she says, and now, now that it is the way it is, her parents can't very well do anything but let them stay in the house, in her childhood home out on Sartor, there's nothing there but some rocky hills and heather and they can see the ocean if they walk just ten or twenty feet up the hill sheltering the house where she grew up, she says and Asle says that he's thinking about the same thing and he says that when they get to Bjørgvin they'll have to get everything they have out of the bus and then hope that the bus to Sartor leaves from the terminal not too long after their bus arrives, and so he'll carry all their stuff over to the terminal, he says and Liv says that she can carry her suitcase herself and Asle says that in that case he'll only need to make two trips, there's the two boxes with the clothes and painting supplies and then the easel and the paintings in the suitcase, and he can't carry all of that in one trip, but he can do it in two, he says and Liv says that if she remembers correctly it's not very far from the gate where the bus from Stranda stops to the gate that the bus to Sartor leaves from, so that'll be fine, but it'll be harder when they get to Sartor, because it's a good long way from the bus stop there up to the house where she grew up, she says, so maybe she should go up first? and she can take her suitcase with her, and then Asle can stay and wait and she'll come back down for him, because then her parents will see the condition she's in, and at the same time she'll tell them that he, Asle, is with her and is standing and waiting down at the bus stop with their things and then maybe her father, since he'll already be home from work, he works at a fishery, will come with her and help carry their things up to the house? she says and Asle says that that sounds good and he says that she needs to tell them at the same time that they're going to be staying there just a short time, until they've found a place to live in Bjørgvin, and that he's about to start at The Art School there, and that they'll probably be able to rent an apartment at The Student Home, he says and Liv says she will tell them that, she says and I sit in the chair here next to the round table and I look and look at the same spot in the water, in the Sygne Sea, and I have my arm around Ales's shoulders and I think that I should have said a prayer for Asle, and then I collect myself and then I pray for God to let Asle get better, and if he can't get better then for God to take him into himself and give him peace, take him into his kingdom, God's kingdom, God's peace, God's light, I pray and I look at the waves and I see Asle sitting there at the table in The Hotel and he's finished his beer and now he's sitting and looking at the woman who's standing behind the reception desk and she's not that much older than him, and it must be the daughter of the owners of the hotel, that's what Sigve has said, so he can order another glass and Sigve'll be here soon too, Asle thinks and I take my arm off Ales's shoulders and I say to Ales now I'm going to drop by Åsleik's and then Ales says that she is always with me, she is always near me, wherever I am, she says and I think now I should probably drive to Åsleik's, shouldn't I, and even if I'm not that hungry it'll be nice to have some good tasty lamb ribs, it's been a long time since I've eaten that, and Åsleik is a good cook, I think and I get up from the chair and Bragi falls down onto the floor and I never seem to remember that he always comes and sits in my lap when I sit in that chair, I think and I put on my black velvet jacket and my shoulder bag and a scarf and I go outside and it's mild, it's stopped snowing, and it's only snowed a little, and I wipe the snow off the windshield with my hand and anyway it's not cold, I think and I get into my car and then I drive slowly over to Åsleik's, it's not very far, but it is a certain distance away and the road is winding and covered in snow and I think it'll still be good to have some of his lamb ribs, even if I don't really feel like eating I can still tell I'm hungry now and that it'll be good to eat something, I think and I drive carefully over to Åsleik's house and I look at the white road and I see Asle standing at The Art School stammering and stuttering and he's taken the paintings wrapped in the grey blanket he got from Grandmother out of the old suitcase and he shows them to the painting teacher he met who's said his name is Eiliv Pedersen and he says that in his opinion Asle can get in without having graduated from The Academic High School and taken the examen artium, but it's The Principal who decides, he says, but he can follow him and they'll see The Principal, he says and they go to The Principal and he says to Asle hasn't he just recently come and showed him his pictures already? and Asle says no he hasn't and Eiliv Pedersen says he'd been wondering exactly the same thing too, yes, Asle and someone else who had recently come and asked for a spot looked so much like each other, and their pictures were similar too, Eiliv

Pedersen says and The Principal asks Asle if he can see his ID card and he says that if he's old enough and paints that well then yes he can come, that's clear, The Principal says and he congratulates Asle and says that he can now say he is, or is about to be, a student at The Art School in Bjørgvin, but he's so sure that Asle has already come and been given a spot, he says, but it must just be someone who looks like Asle, he says, or maybe he's gotten so old now that his memory is going? yes, well, be that as it may he's certain that Asle paints well enough that it would be a big mistake not to give him a spot at The Art School even without an examen artium, it's precisely to let in people like him that this rule exists, The Principal says and Eiliv Pedersen says that he's in complete agreement and Asle feels so relieved that he could almost faint, because now, now he can stop going to The Academic High School right away, he thinks and he thinks that now that he's about to get an artist's stipend to go to The Art School Father can stop giving him money every month, because Father works and toils and is not paid well for his fruit and even if he does sell the boats he builds, Barmen boats they're called, he used to mostly build traditional pointed rowboats but in recent years he's built them mostly with glass sterns so that it's easy to attach an outboard motor to the boat, because that's the kind of boat people want now, Father says, and he doesn't make all that much money for his boats since most people want to buy plastic boats now, they're easier to maintain, so there's less and less demand for the boats Father builds, on the other hand there are fewer and fewer people who build wooden boats so Father can still sell his boats, and from the money Father makes he then has to give him, Asle, money every month, Asle thinks, but now, now that he's about to start getting an artist's stipend Father can stop needing to part with the little money he makes even though Father works day and night, and Asle will get by with the money Father's already given him until he gets his first artist's stipend, because he has a little money set aside, since he's always been careful with his money, Asle thinks and he thinks that it's hard to believe he can now get away from the grey trousers and the white pullover with blue stripes, now he'll just leave The Academic High School that terrified him so much that he was never entirely free from the anxiety, or whatever you call it, he thinks, now he'll put an ad in *The Bjørgvin Times* looking for an apartment and then as soon as he's found an apartment he'll move from Aga to Bjørgvin, Asle thinks and I drive slowly and I look at the white road and then, all of a sudden, I see a deer leaping across the road and I stop the car, there are constantly deer here, because there are a lot of deer in Dylgja, and especially when it's dark they like to leap out into the road, and right across the road, and right in front of cars too, I think, and it's pure dumb luck that I've never hit a deer, I think and I've stopped the car but the engine's still running and the lights are still on and I look at the white road and I see Asle walking towards the room he's rented at The Shoemaker's Workshop and he's thinking that everything went great, he put an ad in *The Bjørgvin Times* and got a letter and few days later, it was an older woman who wrote to him, she lived alone, she wrote, and she was a teacher, or rather a retired teacher, but she still taught classes every now and then if a teacher was sick or something, she wrote and she had always had renters and a student from Hardanger had lived with her for several years, lived there the whole time he'd been a student, and now she was hoping to get a new renter to live there like the one from Hardanger, someone who was going to study in Bjørgvin, so if he wanted he could come and look at the room she had to rent out, it was on the sixth floor in a townhouse, and she's sure they can work out the rent, the only requirement she had was that he take out the rubbish for her once a week and lend a hand if there was something that needed lifting and she couldn't lift it alone, and change the lightbulbs when one of them went out, she wrote and she gave him her phone number and that same day Asle takes the letter and walks to the phone booth next to The Co-op Store and calls her and they agree that he'll come by the next day, and Asle says that he'll take the bus from Aga to Bjørgvin early in the morning and then go back that afternoon or evening, and the woman, who is from Bjørgvin and speaks like a Bjørgvinner, says that it's best if he comes by around three o'clock, and Asle says that's fine, and then she says that she lives at 7 University Street and it says Herdis Åsen on the door, she says and University Street runs from the city centre up to The University and the apartment is on the sixth floor, with no lift, so there're a lot of stairs to walk up, she says, so it's settled, she says and if Asle can't come then he has her phone number and he can just call her and they'll figure out something else, she says, and then she says that if Asle does live there then he can use her phone as long as he doesn't make too many calls, and as long as other people don't call him too often, she says and I think that I can't just stay sitting like this in my car and I look at the white road and I see Asle sitting on the bus to Bjørgvin, he is sitting in his black velvet jacket and he's put his brown leather shoulder bag down on the seat next to him and he's thinking that he doesn't know his way around Bjørgvin at all, yes, he's probably been there only a few times, he thinks and he remembers nothing or hardly anything about it, he thinks and I sit in my car and I look at the white road and I see Asle standing there and he asks The Bus Driver if he knows where University Street is and he says he doesn't but that it must not be far from The University, as the name says, so he'll just have to go out the door of The Bus Station and turn right and go straight until he gets to a big square, and from there, from The Fishmarket as it's called, take a left and go straight for a while towards a church and The University is behind the church and University Street must be around there somewhere, he says and Asle thanks him and then he walks just the way The Bus Driver told him he should and he gets to the big square and he sees a church up on a hill and then he walks towards the church and then he sees a sign that says University Street and then he walks to a door that says 7 on it and he looks at his watch and it's only twelve, and he wasn't supposed to come look at the room until three, so he has plenty of time, and what should he do now? he thinks, because he can't just stay standing outside the door for three hours, he thinks, and so he goes back the same way he came, because he'd seen that there was a café at The Bus Station itself, he'd seen a sign saying Bus Café over a door, Asle thinks, and then there was a kiosk next to the café selling newspapers so he might as well go to the kiosk and buy a newspaper and then go to The Bus Café and buy a cup of coffee, or maybe a glass of beer, Asle thinks and he walks back the same way, and that goes fine, and at The Kiosk he buys *The Bjørgvin Times* and then he walks through the door with Bus Café over it and he goes over to the counter and he says he'd like a glass of beer and the woman standing behind the counter says there's no way he's old enough to buy beer, if he wants a beer he needs to show an ID, she says and Asle takes out his wallet and takes out the ID card and the woman standing behind the counter looks at it and then she hands it back to him and then she pours a pint from the tap and puts it down in front of Asle and he pays and goes and sits down at a window table, and there's nobody else in The Bus Café, but someone will come in soon, Asle thinks and he looks out the window and people are constantly walking by outside The Bus Station, young and old, and there's a street right in front of The Bus Station and it has two lanes and cars are driving by the whole time, life was going by at breakneck speed out there, Asle feels, and then he opens *The Bjørgvin Times* and starts flipping through the paper and he turns to the pages called Arts and there are a lot of book reviews in there, and a review of an exhibition that the painter Eiliv Pedersen is having now in The Beyer Gallery, and that must be the man Asle talked to when he went to The Art School to show them his pictures, the one who'd recommended that he be given a spot at The

Art School, the one who'd taken him and his paintings with him to talk to The Principal, Asle thinks and the woman who wrote the review was named Anne Sofie Grieg and she wrote that this may be the best show Eiliv Pedersen has ever had, it says, and it's been too long since Eiliv Pedersen has shown his work and that must have something to do with the fact that he works as a teacher at The Art School, where he is almost solely responsible for all the courses in the Painting track, which is taking up too much of his time, and really it's too bad that such an eminent painter, with such clear and obvious gifts, because no one with eyes can be in any possible doubt about that, has to spend so much of his time teaching instead of painting, and since it's so rare that Eiliv Pedersen has a show everyone needs to take advantage of this chance to go see the show at The Beyer Gallery, the critic apparently named Anne Sofie Grieg writes and Asle looks up and he sees that a few tables away from where he's sitting there's a girl alone at a table, and she wasn't sitting there when he came in, when he sat down, but now she's sitting there facing him, and their eyes meet, and it's like right away their eyes rested in each other's and neither her eyes nor his eyes looked away, she has dark eyes and they're so clear and then she has long dark hair, and he didn't really know why they were sitting there and looking into each other's eyes, it kind of felt right that they do that, but eventually Asle decides that they've sat looking into each other's eyes long enough and he drinks a little beer and sees her drink a little of her coffee and he looks down at the newspaper, and he takes another sip of beer, and it's still cold and good, and he rereads the review Anne Sofie Grieg wrote about the exhibition of Eiliv Pedersen's paintings and it says there that The Beyer Gallery is open every day between ten and seven, on weekends too, and people now need to take the opportunity to see these paintings by Eiliv Pedersen, one of Norway's foremost artists, even though he's never been given anything like the recognition he deserves, yes, even The Bjørgvin Museum of Art owns just one painting by Eiliv Pedersen, and what a shame that is, and what about The National Museum of Art? isn't it time that they buy one, or better yet, several of his paintings? she writes, and anyone who has wanted to buy a single painting ever in their lives has to take the chance they have now, she writes and the whole time Asle feels the eyes of the girl sitting across from him looking at him and it's good, it feels good that she's looking at him, Asle thinks, but he'd still rather not look up, even if it was good when their eyes met, good to look her in the eye, he thinks and the exhibition, in The Beyer Gallery it's called, he would like to go see it, he thinks, but does he even know where The Beyer Gallery is? it says that it's at 1 High Street, but of course he doesn't know where that is, Asle thinks, so he'll probably never get to see an exhibition of paintings by Eiliv Pedersen, who paints so much in grey and white, and who likes to paint a woman sitting by a window, as it says in the review by Anne Sofie Grieg, and who paints pictures that have such great stillness in them, as Anne Sofie Grieg also writes, Asle thinks and he drinks his beer and he thinks that it's always so good to have a glass of beer, yes, several glasses, it makes him calm, and life begins to feel livable, he thinks and he looks up and again he looks into the dark eyes of the girl sitting a few tables away from him, facing him, the girl with the long dark hair, and he looks down at the newspaper again and then he looks at the watch that he got from Grandmother as a confirmation present and he sees that's it's now one o'clock, so it won't be long now before he can go to 7 University Street to look at the room he might rent, and he doesn't remember the landlady's name, but her apartment was on the sixth floor, and he has the letter from her with him, and her name is in the letter if he can't remember it, but he thinks it was Herdis Åsen, Asle thinks and he takes the letter out of the pocket of his black velvet jacket and yes, yes, it says Herdis Åsen at the bottom of the letter and he sees that it says 7 University Street and he puts the letter back in his pocket and he drinks a little beer and he sees that the glass is about half-empty, there's a little more than half the glass left and he sees the girl a few tables away from him get up and Asle looks down at his newspaper and then she stops next to his table

Nice to meet you, she says

and she laughs and Asle stands up

You too, he says

and they hold out their hands to each other and then they stay standing and holding each other's hand

My name's Asle, he says

And my name's Ales, she says

No, are you joking? he says

No, no, my name's Ales, she says

We have almost the same name, Asle says

Yes, strange, she says

Yes, Asle says

and she says well isn't that strange and then she asks what Asle is doing here in Bjørgvin and he says that he's going to go look at a room, because he's about to start at The Art School, he says and they're still standing there holding each other's hand and Ales says that she is too, if she gets in, because last year she went to The Academic High School, The Cathedral School, she says, but as Asle can understand she doesn't go every day, sometimes she skips school, yes, she really and truly doesn't want to go there, because she's unhappy whenever she's there, but her mother, yes, her mother Judit, that's her name, thinks that she needs to graduate from The Academic High School, she says and Asle nods and he says that he stopped going, or is about to stop going, to The Academic High School so that he can start at The Art School and then he says that he took his paintings to The Art School and asked if he could start at The Art School even though he didn't have an examen artium, just based on the pictures he's painted, and that a teacher looked at them, he says, and then the teacher took the pictures to The

Principal who said there was a spot for him, it's been a long time since he'd seen such a clear talent, The Principal said, Asle says and he feels a little embarrassed and Ales says that the teacher must have been Eiliv Pedersen, because he's the one who teaches oil painting, in the track called Painting, and then there's another track called Drawing, and she thought she would like either track just as well so she's going to apply for both, she says and Asle says that he's moving to Bjørgvin soon, yes, as soon as he finds a room to rent, he says and Ales says she understands exactly how he doesn't want to stay at The Academic High School any longer, she doesn't either, but now she'll be done in the spring, and even if she has bad marks in almost every subject she thinks that maybe her drawings and paintings aren't the worst in the world, or anyway they might be good enough for her to get into The Art School as long as she's finished at The Academic High School and taken her examen artium, she says, but it probably won't be as easy as it was for him, she'll still have to go through the usual admissions process, and maybe she'll get accepted and maybe she won't, she says and Asle asks how the process works and Ales says that first you have to spend two days drawing from a live model, and he probably knows the difference between a nude and a sketch? she asks, and Asle shakes his head and says he hasn't heard of that and Ales says that when you draw a nude you draw a whole body and the model has to sit in the same position for a long time, taking breaks every once in a while, but when you make a sketch the model holds their pose for a very short time, maybe ten or twenty seconds, and you have to make a drawing in that amount of time, yes, that's kind of the most important thing, finishing, Ales says, and you draw with pencil or charcoal, yes, that's the admissions test, but she isn't so good at drawing, she just thinks it'll go better if she draws in charcoal, and erases with a kneaded eraser, because that doesn't just erase the charcoal it kind of spreads it around a little too, and she thinks that that can make a more or less bad drawing at least a little better

Kneaded eraser, Asle says

Yes it's a kind of ball of putty that you erase with when you're drawing in charcoal, she says

You don't know that? she says

No, Asle says

I've always just drawn with a pencil and I've never used a ball of putty, for whatever reason, so I just keep the mistakes and let them be wrong, because it's often the mistakes that eventually lead to something right, he says

and Ales says yes and that the sheets of paper for drawings in the admissions tests are twenty inches wide by sixty inches high and you're supposed to draw a whole person on that, a man or a woman who's sitting there, and you're supposed to draw him or her from head to foot, and that'll be hard for her, well, she isn't so good at drawing, she'd asked her mother to sit for her as a model, but it ended up with the two of them laughing and joking, and then, when she applies for a place at The Art School, she'll have to turn in between three and five of her own pictures, drawings, paintings, watercolours, whatever she wants, yes, but there needs to be at least one painting, and then one of the pictures has to be a still life, she says and she does have two watercolours she's happy with anyway, and then, yes, you have to go off and wait a few days until they decide who's going to get a spot and who isn't, and the names of the people who get into The Art School are written up on a sheet of paper that's hung up on the bulletin board by the entrance, and the worst thing is that you don't know how long it'll take for the admissions to be decided, she thinks it usually takes a week but the decisions can also be made sooner, so people go and check the bulletin board constantly, yes, of course, that's how it is, Ales says and since she can't get into The Art School like him without going through the normal admissions, it's only the exceptions who get in that way, and people who clearly have talent but who haven't taken an examen artium for whatever reason, and age is also a factor, Ales says and Asle thinks so it's because he, or Sigve, faked his ID card that he got into The Art School and not, as he thought, because his pictures were so good, he thinks and they let got of each other's hand and then Ales puts her arm around Asle and pulls him towards her and then lets go of him

You have such nice long hair, she says

You too, Asle says

You have brown hair and I have dark hair, Ales says

and she says she usually has her hair in a ponytail or a braid, and she was wearing it like that when she got to The Bus Café too, but when she saw him she untied her hair and let it fall loose, she says, and Asle says that her hair is dark, and it's almost as long as his hair, and while his eyes are blue hers are dark

Can I sit with you? Ales says

Yes of course, Asle says

and then Ales sits down and Asle says that he's just read a review of an exhibition that a painter named Eiliv Pedersen has up at The Beyer Gallery and he says that he thought it was maybe Eiliv Pedersen that he showed his paintings to and Ales says that it definitely was, and that it's a good exhibition, actually she doesn't know how much she likes Pedersen's paintings but she has to give him one thing, that he always uses such muffled colours, there are a lot of different greys and almost-whites in everything he paints, you almost can't call what's in his paintings colours in the usual sense, and then they all run together, there are no clear and definite edges or transitions in his pictures, everything kind of runs together, Ales says and Asle says that he'd really like to see the exhibition but he doesn't know his way around Bjørgvin at all and he has to go to the house of the woman who might rent him a room at three o'clock and she asks where that is and he says it's on University Street and then she says that in that case it's no problem to go to The Beyer Gallery to see the Eiliv Pedersen exhibition and then she can go with him to University Street after that, she says and Asle says yes, yes, he'd really like that, if she doesn't mind, and she says no of course not, there's no harm in seeing the exhibition a second time, she says, because she already saw the exhibition the day after the opening, with her mother Judit, she says

Because both you and I are going to have Eiliv Pedersen as a painting teacher, she says

Yes well you will anyway, and I will if I get into The Art School, she says

His show got a very good review in *The Bjørgvin Times* anyway, Asle says

and he hands her the newspaper and she reads it and she says that was really a good review, and Anne Sofie Grieg knows what she's talking about, she doesn't have a degree, she used to be a housewife, but she and her husband, a lawyer, travelled a lot to lots of European cities and they visited most of the great art museums, plus she's read a lot, yes, her mother and Anne Sofie Grieg are friends and they see each other now and then, Ales says and she says that it's unbelievable how many art books Anne Sofie Grieg has at home, she's been to her house a few times with her mother Judit, she says and then they stand up and Asle puts his brown leather shoulder bag on and Ales says that it's a nice bag and then she takes his hand

Because now we're a couple, at least sort of, she says

and then they leave The Bus Café and they go straight up the road, the way Asle had already gone, and then Ales takes a right and they walk down a few little alleys and Asle has no idea where they are

Now we're boyfriend and girlfriend, Ales says

Yes, Asle says

Have you ever had a girlfriend before? she asks

No, Asle says

I've never had a boyfriend either, Ales says

But I do now, she says

and I sit in my car, and I'm sure that a deer is about to come leaping across the road or that I'll be able to see one or more deer in the light from my car, I think, but I can't just stay sitting here like this because Åsleik is waiting for me, I think and then I see a deer standing by the side of the road and then the deer stands there and looks at me and I look into the deer's eyes and he looks me in the eye and I just sit in my car and the deer just stands there by the side of the road and we look into each other's eyes and then the deer turns slowly away and vanishes into the darkness and I start driving and I look at the white road and I see Asle sitting in a living room and Liv sitting next to him and Liv's mother comes in with a plate of open-faced sandwiches and puts it down on the coffee table in front of them and she says that Liv's father should sit down too and Asle thinks that they can't stay here at Liv's parents' house, because even if it is all right with Liv's mother it isn't all right with her father, he hasn't said a single word to Asle since they arrived, not even Come in or Welcome, and hasn't greeted him, and now her father is saying he's not hungry and that he thinks he'll go lie down, it's been a long hard day at work and he's tired, he says and then he says good night and Asle thinks they need to leave, but where will they go? yes well there's got to be someplace to live for them too? he thinks, but if he doesn't have money, well, then what do they have? he thinks, so they'll probably have to stay for free at Liv's parents' house for a while, but then, and it won't be long, then he'll get an artist's stipend and maybe they'll also get assigned an apartment at The Student Home, since they'll have a child, that would be good, anyway Asle has applied for a place there but surely there's a waiting list for the places like that, so he doesn't know, but anyway he'll find some other place to live, plus maybe Liv would rather live with her parents until they're ready to get their own place to live, Asle thinks and I sit in my car and I look at the white road and

I drive slowly and now I see the turn-off to Åsleik's farm and I drive up the driveway and the light from my car is now shining on Åsleik's house and damned if I don't see Åsleik standing out there in front of his house, next to his tractor, yes, Åsleik is standing there waiting for me, I think, even though it's pretty cold out, and at least those lamb ribs are sure going to taste good, I think, because it was good that I slept for a couple of hours today, yes, that did me a lot of good, so now it feels like I'm back on my feet, I think and I pull up in front of Åsleik's house

Finally you're here, he says

Am I late? I say

Yes well I'm hungry in any case, he says

and Åsleik says that the lamb has been sitting and steaming for hours but that's not a problem, it only makes the lamb better, since it's from a ewe and not a lamb, he says, but it's been hours since the mashed turnips were done, and they're good, and the secret to making good mashed turnips is easy enough, you just cut the turnips up into small pieces and boil them for a long time in their own juice, yes, much longer than you'd actually need for the pieces to get soft, and it's fine to mash them, and then you have to pour out all the cooking water, of course, and then the rest of the water steams from the cut-up turnips and then you add a lot of butter, really a lot, and then of course you mash it and finally add a little salt to taste, and maybe a little pepper, Åsleik says and I say well I know that much, I say and I notice that Åsleik seems a little offended and then he says let's get inside, it's too cold to be standing outside, and I say that I was surprised to see Åsleik standing outside the house and he says he was waiting for me, hunger was gnawing at his stomach, and when the gnawing got worse he had to come outside to see if I was driving up, and finally I did, and the potatoes were done a long time ago too, but they've been covered and with lots of dishtowels on the lid of the pot so he hopes they're still fairly hot, and if they're not totally hot that doesn't really matter, Åsleik says and I say I'm sure it'll all be delicious and Åsleik says that Sister called him today and she said she'd seen me at The Coffeehouse yesterday but she hadn't had the courage to talk to me, even though she wanted to, she'd just gone into Bjørgvin to do some Christmas shopping, and when she was waiting for the ferry to take her back home, first she took the ferry to Instefjord and then the bus to Øygna, yes well I knew how it was, when she was sitting there waiting she saw me come into The Coffeehouse and she'd thought about telling me that her house was full of my paintings but she hadn't dared, she'd said, and then she'd asked him again if maybe I'd think about coming to celebrate Christmas with them

Yes, maybe, I say

Seriously, you think you will? Åsleik says

You're not just fooling around? he says

You've always said no before, he says

Yes, I say

and Åsleik says it would be so nice if I came with him on The Boat and the two of us took it to Øygna, there's a bay there, and it's a good harbour, he says, and it would be so nice for both him and Sister if I would honour them with his company, he says

Yes, yes, I think I will come this year, like I said, I say

I hear you saying it but now I'm having a hard time believing my own ears, Åsleik says

and he says he doesn't know how many times he's asked me to come, and I never wanted to, and I think that I don't really understand it myself, yes, why I want to go with Åsleik to celebrate Christmas at Sister's house this year, and so it was her I saw sitting in The Coffeehouse yesterday, all the way at the front, by the door, the woman with a suitcase and some shopping bags on the floor next to her and who looked exactly like the Guro who lived in The Lane, I think and so this year I've said that I want to go with Åsleik and celebrate Christmas at Sister's house in Øygna, I think, and I think that I have no desire to paint any more pictures, I've painted enough, I think, and now I want to try to sell all the paintings I have and then I'll have done my part, said what I have to say, I think, and Åsleik asks me to come in and I take off my shoes in the hall, they're just the cut-off boots, and then I go into the main room and everything there is the same as before, I don't think Åsleik has changed anything since his parents died, the cushions, the pictures, everything, everything is the way it's always been, I think and I realise that it makes me feel comfortable that everything's the way it's always been and Åsleik probably feels that way too, so that must be why he hasn't changed anything, I think, and Åsleik has set the big table in the middle of the room nicely, with his nice silverware, and there's the tablecloth, and there's a pitcher of water on it and a bottle of beer and a bottle of stronger stuff and in front of where Åsleik usually sits, facing the hall door, there are two glasses, a beer glass and a shot glass, and then opposite Åsleik there's just a big regular glass, and the pitcher of water is next to it and Åsleik says that I should sit down at the table and then he'll just warm up the mashed turnips a little but it won't take long, he says and Åsleik goes out to the kitchen and he comes back in and he says that it's so nice that I'm thinking about spending Christmas with him and Sister in Øygna, not least because it'll be much nicer taking The Boat to Øygna together, because to tell the truth he's never liked being alone in a boat, and he always is, yes, it's only because he doesn't have anyone to come with him, because it's much nicer, and safer too, if there're two people, Åsleik says and then it was also quite a coincidence that Sister and I ran into each other yesterday, because we've never set eyes on each other before, no, well, not that he knows of, Åsleik says

No I've never met your sister, I say

and I say that I noticed someone sitting at the first table at The

Coffeehouse, right by the front door, next to the window, she had medium-length blonde hair and she had a suitcase and some shopping bags on the floor next to her, I say and Åsleik says that must have been Sister, anyway she does have medium-length blonde hair, and her name is Guro, yes, he says, and in those shopping bags, in one of them, was both wine and spirits, because Sister, yes well Guro, she likes the stronger stuff, yes, maybe a little too much even, no, it's not that she drinks all that often, no, she doesn't have the occasion to, seeing how she lives, and then she also doesn't have that much money, he says, but when she does get the chance she likes to toss 'em down, yes, Åsleik says and he goes out to the kitchen and then he comes back with a dish of potatoes in one hand and a dish of mashed turnips in the other and then he goes out again and comes back with a huge plate with a heap of lamb ribs, yes, they're really long ribs and the smell of the smoked Christmas lamb is incredible and Åsleik puts the plate down on the table

And here we go, he says

and he gestures to the plate of lamb ribs with both hands to sort of present it and I take a generous helping right away, three good-sized ribs, and then Åsleik opens the bottle of beer and he pours himself some and then he opens the bottle of spirits, it's only about half-full, and he says he hasn't tasted spirits since the Christmas ribs last year, and he pours himself a little shot and I pick up the pitcher of water and fill my glass

Yes well you're sure missing out, Åsleik says

and he raises his shot glass to me

I've had my share, more than my share, I say

and Åsleik says well then that's the way it is, he says and then he serves himself, he also takes three large ribs and then he passes me the dish of potatoes and I serve myself and I pass it back to him and while Åsleik serves himself some potatoes I serve myself mashed turnips and I pass the plate on to Åsleik and he looks at me and he raises his beer glass

Cheers, Åsleik says

Yes, cheers, I say

and I raise my glass of water and then we toast and drink, he drinks his beer and I drink my water and then he takes a little nip of his stronger stuff and I cut off a bite of the perfectly tender lamb rib and damn if it doesn't taste incredibly good, I think and I say that Åsleik, yes, when it comes to food he's a real genius, I say and Åsleik says that Sister's lamb ribs are even better, he has to admit it, and I'll soon see for myself, Åsleik says and then we eat slowly and in silence and then Åsleik says now isn't that strange, that I've lived in Dylgja for so many years and never once set eyes on Sister before today, and that was only because we both happened to be in The Coffeehouse

No, it's odd, there aren't that many people who live around here, I say

You're right it is, Åsleik says

Yes, and Sister's name is Guro even if I always just call her Sister, he says

Guro, yes, I say

So it's agreed, this year we'll take The Boat together and celebrate Christmas at Sister's house? Åsleik says

Yes, I say

Let's drink to that, he says

and Åsleik raises his shot glass and I raise my water glass and we toast and then something comes over me suddenly, something like terror, yes, I'm almost overwhelmed with the same fear, the same anxiety, that came over me when I had to read out loud at The Academic High School and I say I need to get back home, I say and Åsleik looks at me not understanding

Well that was a rush job, he says

Yes, well, I say

and I've stood up and I say thank you for the wonderful meal, it tasted unbelievably good, I say

But why do you have to leave so soon all of a sudden? Åsleik says

and I don't know what to say and just say that I remembered something and I say we'll talk soon and I go out to my car and I feel that some of my fear has gone away and I start the car and I think that I need to say an Ave Maria to myself, that usually helps when the fear comes, which does happen, even if not too often, and never without some specific reason, and then I say Ave Maria and that usually helps, I think and sitting there in my car I take my rosary out from under my pullover and I think now do I really believe in this, no, not really, I think and I hold the cross between my thumb and finger and I say inside myself Ave Maria Gratia plena Dominus tecum Benedicta tu in mulieribus et benedictus fructus ventris tui Iesus Sancta Maria Mater Dei Ora pro nobis peccatoribus nunc et in hora mortis nostræ and I move my thumb and finger up to the first bead and I say inside myself Pater noster Qui es in cælis Sanctificetur nomen tuum Adveniat regnum tuum Fiat voluntas tua sicut in cælo et in terra Panem nostrum quotidianum da nobis hodie et dimitte nobis debita nostra sicut et nos dimittimus debitoribus nostris Et ne nos inducas in tentationem sed libera nos a malo and I move my thumb and finger down to the cross and I say Our Father Who art in heaven Hallowed be thy name Thy kingdom come Thy will be done on earth as it is in heaven Give us this day our daily bread and forgive us our trespasses as we forgive those who trespass against us And lead us not into temptation but deliver us from evil and I hold the brown wooden cross between my thumb and finger and then I say, over and over again inside myself while I breathe in deeply Lord and while I breathe out slowly Jesus and while I breathe in deeply Christ and while I breathe out slowly Have mercy and while I breathe in deeply On me

A New Name

'Just a fool! Just a poet!'
Friedrich Nietzsche

VI

And I see myself standing there looking at the two lines that cross in the middle, one brown and one purple, and I see that I've painted the lines slowly, with a lot of thick oil paint, and the paint has run, and where the brown and purple lines cross the colours have blended beautifully and I think that I can't look at this picture anymore, it's been sitting on the easel for a long time now, a couple of weeks maybe, so now I have to either paint over it in white or else put it up in the attic, in the crates where I keep the pictures I don't want to sell, but I've already thought that thought day after day, I think and then I take hold of the stretcher and let go of it again and I realise that I, who have spent my whole life painting, oil paint on canvas, yes, ever since I was a boy, I don't want to paint anymore, ever, all the pleasure I used to take in painting is gone, I think and for a couple of weeks now I haven't painted anything, and I haven't once taken my sketchpad out of the brown leather shoulder bag hanging above the stack of paintings I've set aside, over there between the hall door and the bedroom door, and I think that I want to get rid of this painting and get rid of the easel, the tubes of oil paint, yes, everything, yes, I want to get rid of everything on the table in the main room, everything that has to do with painting in this room that's been both a living room and a painting studio, and that's how it's been since Ales and I moved in here so long ago, so long ago, because it's all just disturbing me now and I need to get rid of it, get it out of here, and I don't understand what's happened to me but something has, something's happened, and what it is doesn't really matter, I think and I hear Åsleik say *St Andrew's Cross*, emphasising the words, saying it with that revolting stress on the words, he's proving he knows something too so he says it like that, with pride, yes, he's simple, Åsleik is, that's the right word for it, simple, I think and I think that I told him I'd go to Øygna with him to celebrate Christmas with Sister, as he calls her, this woman whose name is Guro, at her house, and that's really the best thing for me since if I stay home alone all I'll do is lie in bed, I won't even get up, yes well maybe get up to get myself some water if I'm thirsty and food if I'm hungry, other than that I'll just lie in bed in the bedroom without even turning the light on and I'll keep it as dark as I can, and then I'll try to get some sleep, and I'll try not to think about anything, because I want to let everything be empty, yes, empty and silent, yes silent, yes, silent and dark, because the only thing I long for is silence, yes, I want everything to stay perfectly silent, I want a silence to come down over me like snow and cover me, yes, I want a silence to come falling down over everything that exists, and also me, yes, over me, yes, let a silence snow down and cover me, make me invisible, make everything invisible, make everything go away, I think and all these thoughts will go away, all the pictures I have, all the pictures gathered up in my memory tormenting me will go away and I will be empty, just empty, I will become a silent nothing, a silent darkness, and maybe what I'm thinking about now is God's peace, or maybe it isn't? maybe it has nothing to do with what people call God? I think, if it's even possible to talk about God, if that even means anything, because isn't God just something that is, not something you can say anything about? I think and I think that still, praying is good for me, yes, praying with a rosary the way I do, and going to mass is too, but it's a long drive to Bjørgvin, anyway driving there and back the same day is a lot of driving, I don't like doing that, I think, and I've spent the night at The Country Inn so many times too, I think, but every year I've gone to mass on Christmas Day, and I would have done that this year too if I wasn't going to go celebrate Christmas Eve at Sister's house with Åsleik, so there's not going to be any Christmas Mass for me this year, I think and I stand there in front of the easel and then I go and sit down by the window and I look out the window and even though it's dark I see the driveway that I had built running down to the country road and I see snow, just snow and the islets and reefs, the holms and skerries, yes, the Sygne Sea, and I can see all the way out to the mouth of The Fjord and the open sea, even when it's dark I can see it all well and I think that I need to get rid of that picture, I need to put it away, I don't want to look at it anymore, I don't want it in the main room anymore, I need to get rid of it, I think and then I go over to the easel and I take the stretcher and I lift the picture off the easel and I put it in the stack of unfinished pictures under the peg where my brown leather shoulder bag is hanging, between the bedroom door and the hall door and above the stack of paintings I'm still not satisfied with, and I look at the wall next to the kitchen door and there aren't any pictures there since I drove them down to Bjørgvin a couple of weeks ago, down to The Beyer Gallery, I think and I see Bragi standing there by the kitchen door looking at me, and it's like he's feeling sorry for me, I think, yes, it's like Bragi wants to comfort me but he doesn't know how to do it, and I see his dog eyes, and it's like they understand everything, yes, like nothing is hidden from them, I think, and Bragi is always near me, when I'm lying on the bench he comes and lies down next to me and as soon as I lie down in bed in the bedroom at night he follows me and jumps up into bed, no, life was never so good without a dog, without Bragi, I think, but Asle will get better soon and I'll have to give Bragi back, I think and then I'll get myself a dog of my own, that's for sure, I think, because I've never had a dog before, even though I've thought so many times that I wanted one, I kept thinking I should get a dog, and a boat too, a Barmen boat, but up until now all I did was think about it

Yes, good boy Bragi, I say

and right away he starts wagging his tail and I think he needs to go outside

You can go outside for a bit now, Bragi, yes, I say

and I go and open the front door and Bragi runs out into the snow, but it's not snowing now, and it's colder, yes, it's really a cold clear night and I see the stars shining clearly up in space, and I see the moon, it's big and round and yellow, I think and I think that it's God shining from the moon, and from the stars, yes, in a way, even if he isn't anything, and doesn't have any how, and doesn't have any why, yes, because God doesn't have a why any more than, yes, than the moon does, or the stars, the moon is just there, the stars are just there, yes, a flower is just there, and a deer, because both the moon and the stars and flowers and deer just are what they are, but they have their how in opposition to God, I think and I'm cold, and it's Friday today and it's night-time and tomorrow is Little Christmas Eve, the day before Christmas Eve, and this year on Christmas Eve day I'm going to go with Åsleik to Øygna to celebrate Christmas with his sister Guro, and every year, since The Fiddler left Sister, Åsleik has asked me if I'd come with him, because when Sister and The Fiddler lived together Åsleik didn't spend Christmas at Sister's, and for at least ten years I've said that I'd rather spend Christmas alone but this year I don't want to be alone, I don't want anything, to tell the truth, and in any case I really don't want to paint anymore, and that's very strange, I think and I call for Bragi and he comes padding over and we go inside and he shakes himself off, shakes the snow off, and I shut the front door and I go into what's now the living room and the studio and what'll soon be just the living room and then I realise I'm tired, I should have lain down, I think and then I go and sit down in my chair next to the round table and I look out into the darkness, look at my landmark, my spot out there in the Sygne Sea and I look at the waves and I see Asle leave the apartment at 7 University Street where there's the room he's renting from Herdis Åsen and walk to The Art School and he thinks that he draws from a model every day, for three hours, sketching it's called, and then there's art history class two hours a week, and that may be what he gets the most out of, yes, the professor who gives the lectures, Professor Christie, is an Art History professor at the University of Bjørgvin, and what sticks with him is less what Professor Christie says than the slides of artworks he shows, Asle thinks, and Professor Christie says that it's obvious that the greatest artists do something different, they bring something new into the world with their own unique quality, their entirely unique art, yes, they create a new way of seeing that no one had ever known before, and after an artist like that has finished his work the world looks different, Professor Christie said, but it was the pictures he showed that made the biggest impression on Asle, and the books he referred to, which you could borrow from The Art School, because there was a big library there, but there was a long waiting list, for example he'd put himself on the list for a book of paintings by Lars Hertervig and it had taken three months before he could borrow the book, and then he could keep it for just a month, Asle thinks, but then he ran across a smaller book of paintings by Lars Hertervig in a bookshop in Bjørgvin and he bought the book and it was small enough to fit in the inside pocket of his black velvet jacket and then he started going around with it in his pocket all the time, he took it with him everywhere and looked at the pictures whenever he could, when he was sitting on a bench in a park, or when he was sitting alone in The Coffeehouse or The Alehouse, and then there was The Bjørgvin Museum of Art, yes, that may have been what Asle got the most of all out of, because the truth is he had never seen any real paintings before he moved to Bjørgvin, and students always learned that in their first few days at The Art School, yes, it was Eiliv Pedersen who said that, that they had to go to The Bjørgvin Museum of Art as much as they could, and they should really stay there for an hour, yes, or several hours, looking at one single picture, but if they'd never been there before they might as well get a general impression of the whole collection sooner rather than later, he said, and then they should pick one picture and really get to know it, and it was good to sketch it, or for that matter make a sketch in dialogue with the picture, Eiliv Pedersen had said, Asle thinks and if they were good enough painters maybe The Bjørgvin Museum of Art would end up buying one of their own paintings someday, or more than one, and that was a great honour, he'd said, yes, the greatest honour aside from being The Festival Artist in Bjørgvin and aside from The National Museum of Art in Oslo buying one or more of your paintings, he'd said, Asle thinks and he thinks that anyway he'll be satisfied if he can just paint pictures and if he can make enough money to live on just by painting, he thinks and I sit there at the round table and I look out into the darkness and even though it's dark I can see the water, see the waves out there at my spot in the middle of the Sygne Sea, yes, I can see the water, see the waves, as clearly as if it were daylight, and tonight the water is pretty calm, I think sitting there and taking my bearings from that same spot in the water, yes, there's a spot near the middle of the Sygne Sea that's my place, I think and I think that tonight Åsleik's going to come over and have lutefisk at my house, and I'm not in much of a mood to have a visitor, because it's like I can't manage to do anything, no, not even sit here in my chair, I think, but I have to be somewhere, and I have to be doing something, and tomorrow it'll be Little Christmas Eve and then it'll be Christmas Eve itself, and I told Åsleik I'll go with him to celebrate Christmas at Sister's house, and on Christmas Eve morning or maybe early afternoon we're going to go in his Boat to Øygna, that's what we've arranged, I think and I look at my landmark, I look at the waves there, and then I see Ales and Asle walking there, hand in hand

I can't believe we met, Ales says

Yes, Asle says

It's incredible, she says

Yes, he says

and they keep walking, hand in hand

And that we became a couple the moment we saw each other, Ales says

Yes, right in The Bus Café, she says

Yes, Asle says

It just happened, she says

and Ales laughs and Asle feels how good it is to be holding Ales's hand in his hand and he doesn't entirely understand what's happening and what happened, he thinks, because he was just sitting there in The Bus Café and then suddenly Ales was there, yes, she showed up as if out of nowhere and then sat down and then their eyes met, he thinks and Ales says that it's very strange, she never goes to that café usually, The Bus Café, because it doesn't have the best reputation, she says, so she was there for the very first time today, to tell the truth, she says, and why would she have gone to The Bus Café today of all days, and why was Asle sitting there today of all days, no, she can't understand it, or rather she can understand it, because it was God's will, she says and Asle hears what she's saying but he is entirely in the good warmth from her hand and they walk out onto a wide street and Ales says this is High Street, and there, at 1 High Street, and she points, in the big white building there, that's The Beyer Gallery, yes, there's no question it's the biggest and most important gallery in Bjørgvin, and she's gone to all the exhibitions there since she was a little girl, because her mother Judit likes to go to exhibitions, she's from Austria, she comes from a small town outside of Vienna, a town with the big name Hainburg an der Donau, while Ales's father was Norwegian, from West Norway, he was like people from there are, he came from a place called Dylgja where almost no one lives, but his sister, old Alise, still lives there in a nice old white house, she says and Asle says that he's heard the name Dylgja but he doesn't know quite where it is and Ales says that it's nice there, it's in a good location on the Sygne Sea, yes, the sea that Sygnefjord opens out into, before it goes out to the ocean, she says and then she says that her father was a good man, and he, a country boy as he always liked to call himself, especially after he'd had a little something to drink, yes, he, the country boy, became a doctor, and it was while he was in

Austria studying to become a doctor that he and her mother Judit met, and when he was done with medical school they moved to Norway and to Bjørgvin and then they both started working at The Hospital in Bjørgvin, and her mother Judit still works there, yes, she's a nurse, Ales says, and, as her father liked to say, that wasn't the worst thing in the world for a boy from Dylgja to be, a doctor, but, Ales says, last year he died suddenly, and he wasn't that old, and it was definitely because he drank so much, he drank so much that he died of it, Ales says, but she doesn't want to talk about that or think about that now, not today when she and Asle have just met, she says and Asle looks at his watch and he asks if they can go to 1 University Street right away, he's worried about getting there too late, he says, the woman who wants to rent him the room and he have agreed to meet there at three o'clock, he says and Ales says of course they can, but they have plenty of time, she says and they walk down the street called High Street and then Ales practically drags him down into a little alleyway called The Lane and Asle sees The Lane written on a street sign and wow is it narrow

This is one of the narrowest alleyways in Bjørgvin, she says

and Asle doesn't say anything and they walk hand in hand down The Lane and then Ales suddenly stops and then she puts her arms around Asle and presses her mouth to his and then they stand there and they have their tongues in each other's mouths and then they suddenly let go of each other and they hold hands again and then they walk down The Lane and Ales says that if they take a right and go down that street they'll be able to see The Country Inn, the hotel where people visiting Bjørgvin from the nearby countryside often stay, and on the ground floor there's The Coffeehouse, one of the cosiest cafés in Bjørgvin, she often goes there herself, she sits there and sketches, she says, and what she actually likes to do there is sit at a table and secretly look up at this or that person and then she tries to do a drawing of him or her, Ales says, and then she says that Asle is really lucky to have a place at The

Art School already, and then she says that today they won't turn right and go to The Coffeehouse, they can do that another day, they'll go left and when they get to the end of the street they'll see The Fishmarket, and once they've reached the end of that street they can just take a right and go straight and then they'll be at University Street, Ales says and she says that his name is Asle and her name is Ales but that's all they know about each other, or almost all anyway, he says, so maybe they can sit down somewhere and just sort of be together, Ales says and they've reached The Fishmarket and she points to a bench near the water's edge, with a view of The Bay, and they go sit down on the bench and Asle puts his shoulder bag in his lap and he opens it and he takes out his sketchpad and then he writes down his address in Aga, and then he writes 7 University Street, and he says that they need to go to 7 University Street soon and Ales says that if she remembers correctly he'd said 1 not 7 and Asle says that he has the letter from the woman who wants to rent him the room in his jacket pocket so he can always check, he says and then he takes out the letter and it says 7 University Street, he says and he says that the woman he'll be renting a room from is named Herdis Åsen and Ales says that she feels a little jealous just hearing him say her name and Asle says that she's an old woman and Ales asks how he knows that and Asle says that he knows because he's talked to her on the phone and he could hear from her voice that she was an old woman from Bjørgvin and he says that this Herdis Åsen had said she'd rented a room to a student from Hardanger for years but now he was done with his studies, she'd said, and so she'd be glad to have someone else from Hardanger as her next renter, Asle says and then he tears the page he's written the addresses on out of his sketchpad and hands the page to Ales and then he hands her the sketchpad and the pencil and she writes down her name and her address and a telephone number and she says that this is where she lives with her mother Judit, the two of them live alone in an apartment not far from The Coffeehouse, that's why she goes there a lot to sit in peace and quiet and do her sketching, like she'd been planning to do today for instance, but then she decided to take a walk first and she walked by The Bus Station and she saw the sign saying The Bus Café and then she thought she'd never been there, it might be nice to go see how it is in there, she'd thought, because she'd heard different things about that café, she says and luckily she went in so that the two of them could meet and now they'll have to write letters to each other, yes, until Asle moves to Bjørgvin, and he says that that won't be long, as soon as he rents the room from that woman Herdis Åsen he'll quit The Academic High School right away and give notice at his room in Aga and he'll put everything he owns in the luggage area in the back of the bus, and then he'll just take a taxi from The Bus Station over to his room on University Street, he says, and Ales says she can certainly help him move in, when the time comes, she says, and Asle takes back the sketchpad and pencil that Ales is holding out to him

Yes, that's my mother's phone number, but of course you can call me there, she says

and Asle says that he doesn't have his own phone number, but the woman he's probably renting the room from had said that she has a phone and Asle could use it, as long as he didn't make too many calls, or receive too many calls, that's what she'd said, and he thought he'd never use the phone at all but now that Ales has given him her phone number she can have his, he'll give it to her, Asle says and Ales says that's great, it's good that they'll be able to reach each other by phone, she says and then she hands the torn-out page to Asle and he copies the phone number from the letter Herdis Åsen sent him onto it and gives it to Ales and she says that now they probably should get going soon if he wants to keep his appointment with this Herdis Åsen, up on 7 University Street, she says and Asle puts the sketchpad and pencil back in the shoulder bag and then Ales and Asle walk hand in hand across The Fishmarket and then up a street Asle doesn't recognise

It's really unbelievable that we met each other today, Ales says

I feel so happy, so lucky, she says

It was an act of God, she says

and Asle doesn't say anything but he feels how good it is to feel the warmth from Ales's hand, and how well their hands fit together, in a way, everything feels right somehow, and everything is so simple, and nothing is embarrassing or wrong or difficult, everything is clear and obvious, Asle thinks walking along with Ales and not saying anything and then Ales points and says there it is, in that courtyard, that's where this Herdis Åsen woman lives, and Asle says it's on the sixth floor and Ales says she can go up with him and then Asle puts his hand on the handle of the front door and it's unlocked and Ales says that Herdis Åsen must have left the door open because he was coming, she says and I sit in the chair by the window and I look at my spot out in the Sygne Sea, the spot I always look at, my landmark, I look at the waves there and I think that it's like time has just stopped, something I've never experienced before, and I look at the empty chair where Ales used to sit, the one that was her chair, and it's empty, and yet Ales is sitting there, I think, because now I can clearly feel that Ales is sitting there, the way I can so often see her, I think and I look out at the water again, at the Sygne Sea, at my spot there and I can feel so clearly that Ales is sitting there in the chair next to me and I think that it's already been many years since Ales died, she died and I lost her much too soon, we didn't get to spend that many years together, and children, no, we didn't have children, so now I'm alone, and it's already been many years since my parents died, first Mother, and not long after that Father died, and my sister Alida died all the way back when I was just a boy, I think, and she died so suddenly, she was just lying there dead in her bed, I think and I don't want to think about that, and I think that I should have called The Hospital and asked how Asle is doing, but now it's too late, now it's night and I've called so many times, and I always get the same answer, that he needs his rest and can't have visitors, I think, so I'll just call tomorrow, on Little Christmas Eve, I think, because almost every single day in the past couple of weeks I've called and asked if I can come see Asle and the woman I talk to at reception at The Hospital always says that the best thing for him would be not to get visitors, she says and when I ask how he's doing she always says that there's no news, she says everything's about the same, I think, but Asle has children, I think, there's The Boy who's grown up and lives in Oslo, yes, the son he had with Liv is all grown up, and then there's The Son and The Daughter, the children from his second marriage, with Siv, but their mother took them with her when she moved to be with a man in Trøndelag, and those children aren't grown up yet, I think and I think that Åsleik's coming over tonight to have lutefisk at my house, since this year it's my turn to host the lutefisk dinner, because we have lutefisk together once every Advent and lamb ribs together too, one year I serve lutefisk and Åsleik serves lamb ribs and the next year it's the other way around, and every year we have lamb ribs together again on New Year's Eve, one year at Åsleik's house and the next year at mine, and this year it's me who's going to be hosting the lamb ribs dinner on New Year's Eve, I think, and I usually look forward to these meals, but this year the lamb ribs I ate at Åsleik's didn't taste so special, and now it feels like a bit of a chore to have to prepare the meal, it's like I don't know how to peel potatoes and carrots anymore, how to dice bacon, but I just need to do it, I think and I look at my watch and when I do I think about Ales, because I got the watch as a Christmas present from her once, I think, yes, for years before that I used to wear a watch I got from Grandmother as a confirmation present, and then I got this watch from Ales and that's the one I've had ever since, I think and I see that Åsleik will be here any minute so I need to set the table and put the potatoes on to boil, I think, and I get up and I go away from the window and I look at the empty easel and I'm sort of filled with happiness and then I go out to the kitchen and I get out plates and knives and forks and I set the kitchen table like I always do, and next to Åsleik's plate I put a beer glass and a shot glass and next to my plate I put just an ordinary water glass and I think that I can probably put the potatoes on right away, I think and I peel the potatoes and carrots and I put the potatoes in a pot of water with salt and then I turn on the stove, and it's a good quick stove so it won't take long for the water to boil and then I turn the stove down to the lowest heat, and even then the water is boiling more than it really needs to, but that's how it is now, yes, it probably doesn't matter, I think, and I put the carrots in the pot and now I can fry up some bacon at once, I think and I dice the bacon and I put it in the frying pan and I turn on that burner and it doesn't take long for it to start to crackle and sizzle in the pan, it's a good old cast-iron pan that was there when Ales and I moved into the house, yes, it was here like so many other things, and like so many other things that were in the house it also stayed, I think and I've been feeling kind of rough today, I think, but the good smell of frying bacon kind of brings me back to life, and I suddenly realise I'm hungry, because I haven't eaten anything all day, have I, I think, and despite everything lutefisk is one of the best foods I know of, maybe the very best, I think and I see the big pieces of fish lying there and I put a big pot on the stove, with lots of salt in the water, and I turn up the stove full strength, but I'll put the pieces of fish in the boiling water only when Åsleik gets here, because you have to be really precise when you're cooking lutefisk, you have to pay close attention the whole time so that the fish gets cooked just right, not too much, so that it falls apart, and not too little, so that it's hard and inedible, I think, and obviously you have to make sure at all costs that the bacon doesn't get burnt, so it's important to keep an eye on that, I think and I turn off the burner that the frying pan is on and then I stir the bacon and I stand there and look at it and I stir it several times and then I move the frying pan onto a cold burner and then I hear the screeching and grinding of Åsleik's tractor and I go out into the hall and I stand in the front doorway and Bragi comes and stands next to me and I see Åsleik's tractor come around the corner and stop and then I see Åsleik get out of the driver's cab and he comes walking towards me

Dinner'll be ready soon, I say

It'll be good to eat something, Åsleik says

I'm really hungry, he says

and we go inside into the hall and Åsleik takes off his boots and his snowsuit and his fur hat with earflaps and then he goes into the main room and I follow him and then he says that it sure is a bit cold in the room and he goes over to the stove and he says that the embers are still glowing and he puts a log on and I go out to the kitchen and I look at the water boiling and I put the lutefisk in the boiling water piece by piece and Åsleik comes into the kitchen and he says he forgot the beer and spirits in the tractor so he'll just go get the bottles

Because there's nothing like that in your house, he says

I've had my allotted portion, I say

Yes yes, Åsleik says

and he goes out and I've put all the pieces of lutefisk into the boiling water and I stand there looking at them and Åsleik comes into the kitchen and he says Sister sure was happy when she heard that I'm going to come celebrate Christmas with them this year, really strangely happy, he says and I say that he should just pour his own glass

Yes I've already set the table as you can see, I say

And the food's almost ready, I say

and Åsleik asks for an opener and I find one for him and then he opens his bottle of beer and he goes and sits down on the bench along the side of the kitchen table, by the wall, and he pours himself some beer and spirits and he takes a little sip of the spirits and then he says again that yes, Sister sure was happy I was going to come for Christmas this year, no, he can't believe how happy she was, he says and then I go get the food and I put it on the table and then I sit down at the head of the table and we serve ourselves and eat and neither of us says anything

You're a bit out of it today, Åsleik says

Yes I feel a bit tired, maybe, I say

But that's how it should be on Little Little Christmas Eve, as we used to say when we were kids, he says

Maybe you said that too, he says

and I say that we did

That was part of the rush to get everything ready for Christmas, he says

and then we sit there and eat without saying anything and Åsleik drinks beer and sips his spirits and I think maybe Åsleik can help me carry my paintings and painting supplies up to the attic, because now I can't paint anymore, not that either, and as for why I should have suddenly just felt that I didn't want to paint anymore, that's something else I can't say anything about, and I think that I can ask Åsleik if he'll help me carry the pile of paintings leaning there between the bedroom door and the door to the main room up to the attic, to the storage space where I keep the paintings I didn't want to sell

Yes, that was good food, Åsleik says

and I don't say anything and we eat and the food doesn't taste especially good to me and I see Åsleik drink down the rest of his beer

That sure tasted good, he says

and then he finishes his spirits in one gulp and I don't say anything

Thanks for dinner, Åsleik says

It really tasted great, he says

and then we sit there and we don't say anything

Not too chatty today are you, Åsleik says

and I don't say anything and then we sit there in silence and then Åsleik says well he'll probably just head home so I can lie down if I'm tired and then he says thanks for the meal and we'll see each other on Christmas Eve, in the morning or early afternoon, it would be best if we set out as soon as it's light, so if I could come over to his house at around nine that would be good, Åsleik says, but actually the best thing would be if he called me when he thought it was almost time to head out, he says and then he again says thanks for dinner, it really tasted great and then he takes his bottle of spirits with him and he leaves the empty beer bottle behind and I say we'll talk soon and I see Åsleik go out into the hall and I get up and I start to clear the table and I think that Åsleik left almost as soon as he came, I think and then I hear the sound of his tractor motor and I go and sit down in my chair by the round table and I look at the sea, at the Sygne Sea, at my spot there and I think why do I sit here all the time looking and looking at my fixed spot, at the waves there, even though it's dark now, and it's night, and I should have gone and lain down, I think and I think that I don't understand this, no more than I understand how when I wake up in the middle of the night it's always like Ales is lying in bed next to me, always, I wake up and then it takes some time before I understand that she's not there, but that's not true, because she is there actually, we're lying next to each other like we did when she was alive, I think and then I think that I don't know anything, but nothing means anything, yes, the only thing that gives meaning is what doesn't mean anything in the normal sense, that Jesus Christ was nailed to the cross, died, and was resurrected, and when that happened death, that came into the world when the world became the world as we know it with its endless cycle of life and death, was banished from human reality, of course a person dies in this visible world, in the world as it's been ever since the incomprehensible thing that we now call The Fall, and the body disappears, either it crumbles away in the earth or gets burnt up in an oven, it disappears one way or another, the visible disappears, but the soul is raised up by the spirit, it is reborn in and with God because Jesus Christ invalidated the old world, Jesus Christ, God's son, and people think that literally, as if God were a kind of human father and Jesus Christ a kind of human son of a human father and it's no wonder that people then think that that's foolish nonsense, because obviously it's just an image to say that God is a father and Jesus Christ is a son and The Holy Spirit is the creative power that mediates between the two, that's just a way of trying to put something into words, and it doesn't really matter whether or not it really happened like that, as long as it happens in the heart, in the soul, because the spirit, The Spirit, is real, and so is The Fall, whatever that might be, that's also just a way of saying that there was a break between God and humankind when death came into the world, and what the cause of that was, no, we can't know, certum est quia impossibile est, but, yes well I think and think and I don't understand what I'm thinking, and I don't know what I believe or don't believe, but for me God is near, and at the same time far, completely near and completely far, and somehow you get closer to God in Jesus Christ than you do by thinking about God entirely without human characteristics, yes, in thinking about God as a person who at one point in time you could talk to and be with like any other person, yes, the way I can be with Åsleik now, I think, because after I met Ales and she took me to St Paul's Church, yes, yes, then, I think and I think that I don't want to think more about Ales and I think that it's obvious that you can't come to faith through reason, belief is grace, a gift of grace as it's called, and if someone has faith then they also know what grace is but if they don't have faith then they don't know either what grace is or what a gift of grace is, they don't know that everything is a gift, I think, but anyway those are just words, and words always lie, I never believe in words, and I also don't believe in what I think in words, I think and I think that it's only in my pictures, when I've painted well, that something can be said, yes, a little something, about what I've experienced and what I know, and then it's said not by the picture itself, not by the colours, the shapes, yes, well, everything that's in the picture, and also not by what the picture represents somehow or another, but only by the picture's own distinct unity of form and content in one, like the spirit, and this unity, this spirit is as invisible as the picture, the painting, is visible, and what the picture is in reality is this spirit, that's what a picture really is, neither matter nor soul but both parts at the same time and together they make up what I think of as spirit, and maybe that's why my good paintings, yes, all good paintings, have something to do with what I, what Christians, call The Holy Spirit, because all good art has this spirit, good pictures, good poems, good music, and what makes it good is not the material, not matter, and it's not the content, the idea, the thought, no, what makes it good is just this unity of matter and form and soul that becomes spirit, I think, no I'm not thinking clearly now, I think and I've thought thoughts like this so many times, I think, that because pictures have a spirit painting can be compared to praying, that a picture is a prayer, I think, that the pictures I paint are prayer and confession and penance all at once, the way good poems are too, yes, you could say all good art is like that in the end because all good art finds its way to the same place, I think and I think that these thoughts are probably just as stupid as all the other thoughts I think, I think, sitting there looking out the window, out into the darkness, at my landmark there in the Sygne Sea, at the waves and I see Asle sitting in The Alehouse and he raises his pint and says cheers and Siv raises her glass and they toast and then Asle says that there are a bunch of cafés and restaurants and bars in Bjørgvin but he likes it better at The Alehouse than for example at The Artist Café, because there are real people at The Alehouse while there's nothing but climbers at The Artist Café, it's like everyone's always chasing after something, all the regulars there seem to want something, without it being a real longing, it's just something artificial, something rigid, just willed, something worldly with nothing of heaven in it, Asle says and also it's like everyone's supposed to be friends and like each other, and they act like they do, but actually they're all competing with each other, in a way that sort of doesn't look like competing, and everyone is supposed to somehow be their own person, be original or whatever, and that's why everyone is actually like everyone else and none of them is their own person, they're all imitators, because everybody trying to be original just makes everybody an imitator, and that's what culture is, probably, he says, it's probably just one person being like another person that creates a culture, for example wearing a suit and tie, while what art is, yes, art is everyone just being like themselves, and totally themselves, Asle says and there's not a single person in The Alehouse who's like any other person here, except for the fact that they're drinking beer and smoking and the fact that most of them are or have been sailors, but it's like life itself has forced them to be what they've become, life made them become themselves, Asle says and Siv says now don't exaggerate and then she holds his hand and then they sit there holding hands

And you're married and everything, she says

A father even, she says

and Asle doesn't know what to answer and Siv says she won't keep this up much longer now, either he has to leave Liv or else it needs to be over between them, she says and something in Asle rips and breaks and he doesn't know what to say or what to do and then he says that he'll try to rent a room for himself and Siv says that they can live together, the two of them, she's rented an apartment and they can live there together and his son could come visit them, it's probably too expensive for her to pay for the whole apartment alone but if there were two of them to pay the rent it would probably work, because artist stipends aren't that much to live on, she says and Asle feels such love for Siv it almost drives him crazy and he just can't go home to Liv and their son and try to act normal and then Siv says that she doesn't like it very much at The Alehouse and Asle says that it's probably just a place for old sea dogs and not for young women and Siv says that they can go home to the apartment she's rented and she says she can make dinner for them and she has wine at home and beer too, Siv says and Asle says that he'll just finish his pint and then they can go, and Siv says he can finish her pint too, and then she asks what Liv is up to and Asle says that she's working shifts at a hospice now but that she's talked about getting the high-school certificate she needs to enrol in The Nursing School

She could do that, she's smart, Siv says

Yes, Asle says

and he finishes his pint and Siv takes a little sip of hers and then puts it down in front of Asle and they each roll a cigarette and then they sit there smoking and Siv says that she's starting to wonder if she should drop out of The Art School, now that she's seen what the other students can do, yes, it's like what she can do is so little, and Asle asks what she'll do then and she says that she's interested in literature, and she's always been good at languages, so maybe she'd be better off going to The University, she says, and she can study literature there, or languages, she says, but then she'll probably become a teacher, and if there's anything she has no desire to be it's a teacher, so she doesn't know, Siv says and she stubs out her cigarette and then she says that it's time for them to go, now they'll go home to the apartment she's rented, she says, and she was lucky to find it, she says, but it was too expensive for her even though her parents were nice and gave her some money every month, she says and Asle finishes Siv's pint and then they get up and leave and they're walking next to each other

Don't you want to hold my hand? Siv says

Yeah, Asle says

and I sit here in my chair and I look at my spot out there in the Sygne

Sea, and even though it's dark I see the water so clearly, I see the waves, and at night they're not so high, I think and then I get up and I see the empty easel and then I go over to it and I stand there and look at the easel and now there's no picture there, and I can't remember the last time there wasn't a canvas on a stretcher there and I look at the empty easel and I see Asle walk down the street away from The Alehouse, in his black velvet jacket, with his brown shoulder bag, and he's holding Siv's hand and he thinks that he and Liv are officially married now, they got married at The Courthouse, Liv was there with him and their best man and maid of honour, and Liv had picked her sister to be maid of honour and so Asle thought he could ask a childhood friend of his, his best friend from childhood, Tor, if he'd be his best man, and he'd agree to even though he and Asle hadn't spoken since middle school, yes, since Asle dropped out early in tenth grade and moved to Stranda, but Asle didn't really have anyone else he could ask and so he called Tor and it was an easy conversation, everything was like it was before, and Tor told him that after middle school he'd gone to The Agricultural School in Utvik for a year and now he'd taken over the family farm since his father wasn't in such good health anymore, he didn't exactly know what was wrong with him but it was one thing and another and so now he was a farmer with three cows and over a hundred sheep, so really he was a sheep farmer, and he liked being a farmer, Tor had said, yes, it was much better being a farmer than going to school, and he'd probably never be rich but he made enough to live on, maybe a little more, he said and then Asle said that it was going to be a very simple wedding, a so-called civil ceremony, because while other people were getting confirmed he had left The National Church, so it wasn't going to be any kind of church wedding, Asle said and Tor said Asle had probably been the first person ever in their village not to be confirmed, and there was no one in the village who had longer hair than he'd had, Tor said and Asle said that that was something he was proud of, yes, that he'd done it, yes, refused to get confirmed and left The National Church, and he wasn't sorry that he'd dropped out of school in tenth grade either, at first it had been hard, he just got yelled at at home, not by Father, but Mother scolded him nonstop, and then he rented himself a basement room in Stranda, and then everything came together, and to make some money for a little food and his painting supplies he'd started painting pictures called *Boat in a Storm* and he'd propped them up by the stairs of The Stranda Hotel to sell them, and they were mostly pictures of sailboats in storms and damn if he didn't sell them, and that's how he made enough money to get by and then he met a girl named Liv who worked as a chambermaid in The Stranda Hotel and then she got pregnant and they had a son and now they were going to get married, it was Mother who'd nagged them to get married and eventually they thought it might be nice since Mother had said that she and Father would pay for the wedding, and, yes well, now he'd started at The Art School in Bjørgvin, because he got in, just from his pictures, and then he and Liv had rented an apartment at The Student Home, yes, it was because they had a child that they were able to get a place there, yes, well, so now they were going to get married at The Courthouse and he needed a best man and he was happy and grateful that Tor was thinking he might be willing to do it, he was worried about calling up out of the blue and asking him and Tor said of course he would be his best man but that he hadn't been to Bjørgvin since he was a kid so he'd never be able to find his way around there, he said and Asle said he should just take the bus to The Bus Station and then he'd fetch him there and when it was time to go back home Asle would bring him to The Bus Station so he didn't need to worry about that, he said, and Asle said they'd found a neighbour in The Student Home who would look after their son while they got married at The Courthouse, he said and afterwards they'd have the reception at The Grand Café, in a separate room, just the four of them, they'd have a big meal there with everything and then they'd head home to the apartment in The Student Home and Tor could spend the night there, and Liv had asked one of her sisters if she'd be the maid of honour, and she'd said yes, so that's four, Asle said on the phone and he told Tor what day the wedding would be and Tor came to Bjørgvin in his best suit and Asle had bought himself a suit at The Second-Hand Shop in Sailor's Cove, that was where he'd bought all his clothes since he'd moved to Bjørgvin, and Liv had borrowed a wedding dress from her sister that fit her almost perfectly, and then Asle had bought a bridal bouquet for her and the wedding party took a taxi to a photographer first, because they wanted a real wedding photo, and he didn't really know why but that's how it was, Asle thinks, and then they took another taxi to The Courthouse and they were married and then they took a taxi to The Grand Café and got their private room, and they ordered a full menu and drank a lot of wine and then Liv started saying that Asle had only married her because he kind of had to, since his parents wanted him to, and because they had a child together and he said well they were married now anyway and she kept going and kept going and then they drank cognac with their coffee and Asle's father had given him money to pay with, and he paid for the private room and the good food and the good drinks, and then the wedding party took a taxi to The Student Home, it was him and Liv and Tor and Liv's sister, and when they got out of the taxi Liv screamed loud in the darkness and then she threw the bridal bouquet right into Asle's face and he managed to catch it before it hit the ground and they hurried through the rain to the apartment in The Student Home and Asle was carrying the bridal bouquet and Liv was almost howling as she walked and her sister was trying to comfort her and Tor and Asle walked next to each other after Liv and her sister and they stayed outside until Liv and her sister had taken the lift and then they went inside and took the lift upstairs and when they entered the apartment

Liv was lying on the sofa and her sister looked at them and she shook her head and Asle put the bouquet down on the kitchen table and he said so now they were married, he and Liv, and Liv's sister told her now she was married and Liv said goddammit if this was what it was like to be married then she wasn't interested, because Asle didn't care about her at all, she'd never realised it, not as clearly as she did today, on her own wedding day of all days, she said and her sister said she didn't know what she was talking about, everything had gone so well, and the wedding picture will definitely be beautiful and then Liv got up and she picked the bouquet up from the kitchen table and threw it on the floor and her sister went and picked it up and she said now she needed to rest, probably the best thing to do would be to go and lie down, she said, and she'd help her take off her wedding dress and they went into the bedroom and Asle heard Liv crying and her sister comforting her and then he said that he'd bought a bottle of whisky and then he poured a big glass for Tor and a big glass for himself and then he said that they needed a little water so that it would be the right strength but Tor had to decide for himself how strong he wanted his to be, Asle said and he turned the tap on and put a little water in his glass, had a taste, and then put a little more water in the glass and Tor did the same thing and then they went into the living room and sat down and Tor said that this was a nice apartment and Asle said they'd really been lucky to get an apartment in The Student Home, and it wasn't too expensive, it was expensive enough, but he was getting something called an artist stipend and Liv was working a few shifts at a hospice so they were managing fine, and his parents had paid for the wedding, because Mother had nagged and nagged them to get married, so finally he'd said yes, they'd just do it and then Tor asked if he'd proposed to her and Asle said he never proposed and he said it just happened, they would get married because everything would be the same as it was before, he said and Tor said that he wasn't exactly looking forward to getting married himself after having been to this wedding and then they both started laughing and they laughed and laughed until finally Asle managed to stop laughing and he said that probably not all weddings were necessarily like this and Tor said he certainly hoped not, but obviously they couldn't be, he said and then they sat in silence for a bit and then Asle asked if Tor wanted to go to sleep, there was a blanket and pillow under the sofa they were sitting on, it was what they call a sofa-bed, he said and Tor said he was actually extremely tired, and he could feel that he'd certainly drunk enough, he said and then they got up and Alse opened up the sofa and Tor said yes that sure is a sofa-bed and while Tor stood there holding his glass and taking a cautious little sip of his drink every now and then Asle made up the bed and now there was only the sound of sobbing from the bedroom and then Liv's sister came out and said that her husband was still outside waiting for her and she said that it was too bad Liv had gotten so drunk, and so out of control, she said, but she'd come back tomorrow, she said, or in any case the day after tomorrow, she said and laughed and Asle thanked her very much for having agreed to be Liv's maid of honour and Liv's sister said there was no reason to thank her and she congratulated him on becoming a married man and then she said that she'd kept her husband waiting long enough, and besides it was a long drive back to Sartor, she said, so they said goodbye and then Asle walked Liv's sister out to the entryway and they said goodbye and he went back into the apartment and when he walked into the living room Tor was there in just his underpants and he'd put his clothes on the armchair and Tor said he was tired and he emptied his glass and went and put it on the kitchen counter and Asle said that he'd take him to The Bus Station tomorrow morning or early afternoon of course and Tor said thanks and then Asle said that he was the one who should be thanking him for helping, for agreeing to be his best man, and Tor said there was no reason to thank him, but it had been quite a wedding, Tor said and then Asle drank the rest of the drink in his glass and then they said good night to each other and then Asle went quietly into the bedroom and he saw Liv lying outstretched on the bed, on top of the covers, in her wedding dress, and he left the door open and got undressed in the light from the hall and put his clothes on a chair and then gingerly closed the door and then he lay down on the bed as quietly and carefully as he could and he lay on his side and he thought that it was really stupid getting married, he and Liv, but anyway it'd been nice to see Tor again and get to talk with him a little, Asle thought and he thought how was this all going to end? no, he didn't know, he thought, Asle thinks walking down the street in his black velvet jacket, with his brown shoulder bag, holding Siv's hand, and he thinks that he lay there on his wedding night and saw pictures before his eyes and he saw six different pictures that he had to paint away, pictures that had lodged in his mind and that he now saw before his eyes one after the other, there was one picture of Tor's hands and then one of just one of Tor's hands, both from when he'd picked Tor up at The Bus Station, and then one of Liv bending forward to straighten her wedding dress, and then one of the photographer's face when he told them he was about to take a picture and one of the waiter's face as he looked at the table right before he served the first course and then one of Liv's sister holding Liv in her arms after she'd thrown the bridal bouquet at him, these pictures were painted inside his skull as it were, it was like his skull was a canvas, Asle thinks and he's tried to paint them all away, but he hasn't been able to, he thinks walking down the street there in his black velvet jacket, and with his brown shoulder bag, and holding Siv's hand and neither of them says anything and I sit in my chair and I look out into the darkness at my landmark there in the Sygne Sea, and I see the water so clearly, I see the waves, and I don't understand how I can see the water, the waves, yes, even though it's totally dark, I think and tomorrow is Little Christmas Eve and then it'll be Christmas Eve and I'll go with Åsleik to celebrate Christmas with him and Sister in Øygna, I think and I really have no desire to do that but I did say yes, yes well I said yes, I think and I think that it's like all my strength has been taken away from me and I need to go lie down, I feel so exhausted, it's like I don't even have the strength to get up and go lie down, I think sitting there in the chair looking at my spot out there in the middle of the Sygne Sea and I look at the waves and I see Asle and Siv walking hand in hand down a street in Bjørgvin and then they go up some stairs and Siv unlocks the door to the apartment she's renting and Asle goes inside and he shuts the door after him and then Siv throws her arms around him and she holds him close and they kiss each other, a long kiss, and then Siv says that it's nothing special but it's somewhere to live, she says and then they go into a room that's both a studio and a living room, and the floor is almost covered with drawings and paintings

I like painting on the floor, Siv says

Looks that way, Asle says

I should try that too, he says

You've never tried it? Siv says

No, never, Asle says

and Siv says he really needs to try it, it's almost like a totally different surface, plus you can use thick paint without the colours running together, and the surface of the picture can be much more built up too, she says and Asle says yes of course and then Asle lies down on the sofa and then Siv comes over and lies next to him

Now it's you and me, Siv says

Yes, Asle says

and then they lie there and hold each other and Siv says that it's a little cold and she still hasn't shown him the bedroom and then they get up and they go into the bedroom and there's a mattress on the floor and Asle lies down on it and Siv says that it's a little cold in there and she gets a blanket and spreads it over Asle and he lies there and he thinks that he needs to leave Liv, and leave The Boy, and move out, and it hurts so much to think that he's going to leave him, but they'll have to still see each other, at least once a week they'll have to still be able to see each other, Asle thinks and then he says that he has to go home and Siv says she can't bear to think about him going home to her and that his home is here now and he can, yes, he has to move in with her whenever he wants, because there's more than enough room for them both, she says, and she'll straighten up, since she's spread her stuff out everywhere, but he can paint in the main room and she can paint in the bedroom and then they'll have the kitchen as a kind of common room, she says, and she says that sounds so stupid, she can hear how dumb she sounds, she says and Asle gets up and goes and gets dressed and he says that he needs to go now and Siv says well then talk to you tomorrow and she says that she'll miss him and that she thinks about him all the time, she doesn't do anything else, just thinks about him, she can't get herself to think about anything else, she says and the thought that he's going home to another woman drives her completely crazy, Siv says and Asle says that he'll come here, he'll move in with her and Siv says that he and Liv are married and he says he'll have to get a divorce and she says that'll take a long time, first he'll have to separate and then it takes a year or so and only then will he be able to get divorced, Siv says and Asle says he'll tell Liv everything tonight, that he's found another woman, and that sounds so stupid, found another woman, yes that does sound stupid, Siv says and they really don't need to talk about it too much, because it'll go badly no matter what they say, everything just has to happen, she says and then she asks when they'll see each other again and Asle says probably tomorrow at The Art School and she says no, she wants to see him tonight, can't he come over tonight so that everything's over and done with, Siv says and Asle says he needs to go and Siv asks can't she make him a little dinner and Asle gets embarrassed and then Siv says that she bought enough food for dinner for them both

That sounds great, he says

Well it's not all that, Siv says

It's just normal food, she says

That's what I like best, normal food, Asle says

and Siv says she knows, that's why she bought pork chops, since she knows he likes that, because lots of times when they've eaten together at the café he's ordered pork chops, she says and Asle says that that was nice of her and then she says she'll start cooking then and Asle can just sketch or whatever he wants to do and then Asle goes and takes his sketchpad out of the brown leather shoulder bag in the hall and he goes and lies back down on the sofa and then he just lies there and looks at the pencil and at the blank white page in the sketchpad and then he draws the face of a screaming baby, and then he draws it seen from various angles, and he wants it just to be a rough sketch, just practice, but it sort of doesn't turn out that way, it turns into real drawings that are really saying something, and he doesn't like it, and now he wants to draw something else and he starts to draw a boat and he gives it nice lines and three strakes and an old-fashioned pointed bow, it's a traditional Barmen boat he's drawn, just the boat, and with a couple of oars lying on the seats, and it's a nice boat, and now there's the good smell of cooking meat from the kitchen and then Siv is standing in the doorway and she asks him if he wants a bottle of beer

See, I planned everything, she says

Yes, thanks, Asle says

and Siv goes back out to the kitchen and then she comes back in with a half-bottle of beer and a glass and Asle puts the sketchpad down

You don't want me to see what you've been drawing? Siv says

and Asle doesn't answer and he picks up the bottle and the glass and he pours the beer into the glass and he tastes it and then he puts it down on the coffee table and Siv says that the table is ugly as hell but she got it for next to nothing at The Second-Hand Shop, the sofa too, she says

And now I've got it all dirty with paint on it too, she says

and tubes of oil paint and brushes are sitting on the table and Asle takes a sip of beer and Siv says she has to check on the food so the chops don't burn and then she goes back out to the kitchen and Asle thinks that he's never been there, in the kitchen, and he drinks more beer and then he sketches a big empty open boat in a rough sea and he thinks that it's almost a bit like the paintings he painted and sold to make money when he was living in Stranda and then Siv is standing in the doorway and she says dinner's ready and they pretty much have to eat in the living room, she says, because the kitchen's so small that there's no room to eat in there, she says and Asle gets up and then he's standing in the kitchen doorway and he sees a short kitchen counter with two cupboard doors under it and a stove and a cupboard hanging over the stove and then there's a window and Siv takes a plate out of the cupboard and then she puts a pork chop on the plate and then a kind of mashed red vegetables he's never seen before and he asks what it is and Siv says does he really not know what it is? it's red-carrot mash, yes, it was totally normal at her house when she was growing up, she says and then she puts a couple of potatoes on the plate and then she asks if he wants melted butter on his potatoes and he says yes and then Siv takes a spoon and scoops some up and pours it over the potatoes and then she gives him a knife and fork and Asle goes out to the living room and he clears a space in front of him on the coffee table for his and Siv's plates and then Siv comes in with her plate and she says enjoy and Asle takes a bite of the food and it tastes great, and the carrot mash is sweet and goes perfectly with the fried pork chops, and they eat in silence

That was really good, Asle says

Just normal food, nothing special, Siv says

and they eat and don't say anything and Asle thinks damn he was hungry, but now, now he has to go home to Liv, she's maybe waiting for him

I hope it was good, Siv says

It was definitely good, Asle says

and then he says thank you for dinner and that he has to go now and Siv asks him if he's coming back tonight and he says maybe, and she says just maybe and then Asle leaves and I sit in my chair here and look at the sea, at my landmark, I'm looking straight ahead the whole time, just at the water, at the waves there at one spot in the middle of the Sygne Sea and I think I should have called to find out how Asle is doing, but I probably wouldn't have found out anything, every time I call they just say that he's pretty much the same and that he needs his rest and that it's better for him if he doesn't have any visitors now, the woman who answers the phone always says that, because it's always a woman who answers the phone, but the voices are always different, I think, and one of them said that his three children had come to see him but he'd had hardly any contact with his children after his two divorces, a little with The Boy, as he called him, the one who lives in Oslo, his son from his first marriage, but he'd had almost no contact with The Daughter and The Son, at first after the divorce The Daughter and The Son had stayed with him every other weekend, but then Siv, their mother, found another man and moved to Trøndelag or some other city with The Daughter and The Son, and then the two women he'd once been married to had come to see him, she said and she said that he was doing much worse after one of the women he'd once been married to had visited, and she probably shouldn't have said that, she said, but since she knew that he and I were close friends she sort of decided she could tell me, she said, but I mustn't tell anyone that she'd said that, she said and I think that still I should call The Hospital and I get up and go out into the hall and I pick up the phone and I dial The Hospital's number and I say, like I always do, every time, that I'm a good friend of Asle's and I'd like to come see him, because maybe there's something he needs? I say, and yes, I've already gone and picked up his dog, someone from The Hospital came with me and unlocked the door to his apartment, so maybe I can bring him something? I say and I say that it was me who got Asle admitted, and who has his dog now, I say and I look down and I see Bragi sitting on his haunches right in front of me and looking at me with his dog's eyes and she says that she'll ask and I just stand there with the telephone in my hand and then after a while the voice comes back and she says that Asle isn't well enough to have visitors yet, so, unfortunately, she says and I ask if I can call again tomorrow and she says of course I can and I say thank you and she says it was nothing and I hang up the phone and I go into the main room and I look at the empty easel and then I go over to the round table and I put on my black velvet jacket, because it's so cold in the room, I think, but I can't bring myself to light the stove, and I haven't even turned on the electric heater, I think and I go back out into the hall and I put on my long black coat, and I put on a scarf, and then I go get the grey blanket that's on the bench and I drape it over my shoulders, the blanket Grandma had around her when she lay on the bench back in The Old House and couldn't talk or walk, the one she handed to me when they put her on a stretcher to carry her out to the ambulance, I think, that blanket has stayed with me, wherever I lived I had that blanket with me, I think and I sit down again in my chair by the round table and I tuck the blanket tight around me and I take my bearings and then I sit there and look at the waves and I see Asle standing there and he's holding The Boy in his arms and he's rocking him back and forth and Liv is sitting there on the sofa and she's crying and crying and then Asle goes into the bedroom carrying The Boy and he puts him down on the bed and then he gets the sketchpad and pencil from the leather shoulder bag in the hall and then he sits down on the edge of the bed and he starts drawing a girl about twenty years old lying outstretched on the floor and it's hard to tell if she's alive or dead and he draws a girl who's sitting on a sofa and crying and crying and the whole time he hears Liv crying and crying and Asle shuts his eyes and he looks straight ahead into the nothingness and then he sees three new pictures lodge themselves forever in his mind, there's one of a young woman lying on the floor who looks more dead than alive, and then there's one of a young woman who's sitting on a sofa crying and crying and then there's a picture of a boy not even one year old lying with his hands and feet spread out on a double bed and crying and crying and Asle thinks that he needs to paint these pictures away, but maybe he can't, because there are some pictures that just stay there, he thinks and then he sees Grandfather's black boots in the rain, always that picture comes to him, he'll never be rid of it, no matter how many times he's tried to paint a boot in the rain he has never been able to get rid of that picture, Asle thinks and he'll probably never really be able to get rid of a picture, that's just something he wants to do, or imagines he can do, because once a picture has lodged inside him it's stuck there, but when one of the painful pictures turns up it's less painful if he's tried to paint it away, it becomes fainter then somehow, he thinks and he thinks that he's tired, because he doesn't think he's slept at all tonight, or maybe a little, he thinks and he thinks that it was good he got home in time, if he'd come home any later Liv might be dead now, because he got her to The Hospital and there they pumped her stomach, got all the pills she'd taken out of her, he thinks, but The Boy had slept well and heavily all night, he thinks and he hears Liv crying and crying and he picks up The Boy and goes into the living room and then he stands there and rocks The Boy back and forth and he looks at Liv who's sitting there on the sofa and crying and crying and Asle asks if she wants anything, because someone has to say something, he thinks and Liv just shakes her head and Asle sits down next to her and he puts his arm around her shoulders and she lets it just stay there and then she twists away a little so that his arm falls down off her shoulders and Asle takes his arm back and he asks where Liv got the pills from and she doesn't answer, she just cries and cries and Asle gets up and he stands there and rocks The Boy back and forth and he thinks that he didn't take off his black velvet jacket when he got home last night or since, he sleeps in it sometimes, he thinks and Liv just cries and cries and Asle rocks The Boy back and forth and he asks if Liv feels like holding The Boy and she doesn't answer, she just keeps crying and Asle asks where Liv got the pills from and she doesn't answer and Asle rocks The Boy back and forth and Liv cries and cries and now she really needs to stop this crying soon, he thinks, she hasn't said a word since she got back from The Hospital she's just sat there on the sofa crying and crying and Asle asks again where she got the pills from

My mother, Liv says

From your mother? Asle says

You took them from your mother? he says

and Liv doesn't answer

I took the pills from Mother, she says

and Liv cries and cries and Asle can tell that she's trying to stop but the tears just keep flowing and flowing

Gradually, over a long time, she says

and Asle rocks The Boy back and forth and he thinks that Liv stole medicine from her mother over a long time, every time she went to visit her on Sartor, maybe all the way back to the first time they went there she did that and he'd never noticed anything, he'd noticed nothing, nothing, he thinks, because he's just been caught up with drawing and painting, and with these pictures he has in his head, Asle thinks and he thinks that when The Boy was born he had just started at The Art

School and they were living with Liv's parents out on Sartor before they were told they could move into the apartment at The Student Home, he thinks and he looks at the easel there in the living room, and his painting supplies are on the coffee table, and hanging on the walls in the living room and in the hall and in the bedroom are the paintings he's finished or is still working on and Liv is sitting on the sofa crying and crying and Asle rocks The Boy back and forth and he thinks that Liv can't just keep crying and crying, he has to do something, he thinks and I sit and look at my landmark out there in the Sygne Sea, I look at the waves there and I think that Åsleik came over and had lutefisk at my house today, and I usually always look forward to that meal, but today I was so exhausted, or whatever it was, but Åsleik took it well and I think he liked the food even if not that much was said during the meal, I think and look at the water, at my landmark, at the waves there, and I think that today it felt like nothing had any meaning for me anymore, and painting, no, I can't paint anymore, so I'll just have to live with these pictures in my head as best I can, I think and I look at my landmark, at the waves and I see Asle standing and holding The Boy in his arms and he's rocking him back and forth and I look at my landmark out there in the middle of the Sygne Sea and I close my eyes and I feel that Ales is near me now, and then I feel her take my hand and then we sit there holding hands, and it's so good to feel Ales's hand, I think and I think that sometimes it's hard to know if what's there is God's nearness or Ales, and maybe there's no difference? I think and I think that I read in a poem once that God is my dead friend, that's what it said, and there's something true in that, I think and I look at my landmark, at the waves and I see Asle standing in front of the open front door at 7 University Street and Ales is standing next to him and suddenly it's like something comes over her, Asle sees, and Ales says that she has to go soon, so if it takes a long time, yes, at Herdis Åsen's house, then, yes, she might not be able to wait for him, but they'll absolutely see each other again soon, because starting today they are a pair, they're Asle and Ales, she says, and she'll write a letter to him every night, she promises, Ales says and Asle just looks at her and then Ales jumps into his arms and she hugs him tight and Asle hugs her tight and then they pull away from each other and then Ales says anyway, she has to go now, she says, and so Asle can settle into the apartment in peace and quiet and then they'll see each other again soon, she says, yes, now he just needs to go rent that room from that Herdis Åsen or whatever her name is, she says and Ales says she sincerely hopes she's an ugly old hag, she says and Asle says well she's definitely old, judging from her voice on the phone, and judging from her handwriting in the letter he got she's no spring chicken, no, he says and then Ales throws her arms around him and gives him a quick kiss on the mouth and then she says she's just kidding

I can't believe we found each other today, she says

And it'll be for our whole lives, she says

And maybe it was decided by providence, she says

Or maybe it just happened by chance, she says

and she says that it seems like some things are decided by providence while others aren't, yes, they just happen by chance, but even if it was just by chance then it happened anyway and now it's up to them, to her, to him, to make what's happened, that they met, as beautiful as possible, Ales says and Asle says that he can't show up late to his appointment with Herdis Åsen and Ales says that he better go and look at the apartment then and get that out of the way, she says, and it's probably best if he goes alone, she says, or else he probably won't get the room since this Herdis Åsen woman will probably think he's going to have women over all the time and she probably won't like that, that's probably what this Herdis Åsen is like, Ales says

Women over, right, Asle says

Now I need to go, Ales says

and she says she has something she needs to do, she says, so she needs to go, and she says that she wonders if he's going to live in that room there at all, at Herdis Åsen's, anyway it won't be for long, Ales says and Asle doesn't understand what she means and then he sees Ales stand there and Asle opens the front door and he goes inside and he goes up all those stairs changing direction at every landing, and at every landing there are two doors, one on the left, one on the right, and all in all there are twelve apartments in the building, and Herdis Åsen lives in one of the apartments on the top floor, Herdis Åsen who will rent him a room if she thinks he deserves it and if she wants him living in her apartment, Asle thinks and he rings the doorbell under the nameplate that says Herdis Åsen and after a moment he hears light footsteps coming and then the door opens and a little old woman, probably around seventy, opens the door and looks at him, and she's wearing glasses, and her hair is pretty short, and she has lots of wrinkles in her face, and a heavy smell of cigarette smoke comes out of the apartment

No I don't believe my eyes, Herdis Åsen says

and she says Asle should come in and he walks into the entryway and she holds out her hand to him, and her fingers are long and thin, and she's wearing lots of rings, and her nails are painted a dark red colour and Asle holds out his hand and they shake hands and he feels that her hand is cold and she stays standing there holding his hand for a long time, and then she lets go of his hand and Asle thinks that it's no doubt already decided that he'll rent a room at Herdis Åsen's because she goes over to a door next to the front door and she opens it and invites him into the room and there's a bed and a desk and a bookshelf and a wardrobe and then a dresser, and on the dresser is a hotplate with one burner, a breadbox, a cutting board, and then a kind of basin to wash the dishes in, and there's a dishtowel hanging on the wall and all the furniture is nice old furniture, well-made city furniture, Asle thinks, and he sees that the bed is made, everything's tucked in tight and Herdis Åsen says that this is what she has to offer, she says, and then she goes out into the hall and Asle follows her and she shows him a room with a toilet and another with a shower, and she says that since she showers in the morning it would be nice if he could shower at night, and in the room with the shower there's also a washing machine and she'll explain how to use it later, she usually washes her clothes every Friday and then hangs them up to dry on the lines there, she says and she points at a few cords hung from one wall to the other under the ceiling, more or less over their heads, so it would be nice if for example he could wash his clothes on Mondays, she says, yes yes, she says and then she opens a door and Herdis Åsen says he should come right in and then she walks into a living room, and there is good well-made old city furniture in that room too, a sofa and coffee table, a big table with chairs, a secretaire, and there are paintings on the walls, hung right next to each other, and Asle sees at once that they're good paintings, but he can't tell who painted them, and she says that she's interested in art so she's had enough money to buy a few pictures over the years, or really she didn't have enough money but she bought them anyway, and to be honest she's bought a lot of pictures over the years, she has a lot more than are hanging on the walls, there are stacks of them in the wardrobe in her bedroom, Herdis Åsen says and Asle sees that there's a big heavy bookshelf in the living room, and Herdis Åsen says that she used to be a high-school teacher, her subjects were Norwegian and German, but now she's retired, of course every now and then she still teaches, if someone needs a substitute, she says, and her father was a professor of Nynorsk at The University in Bjørgvin, and even though she grew up in Bjørgvin she's always had a good feel for Nynorsk, and for the dialects related to Nynorsk, yes, that's why she's always taken in renters from Hardanger, and the most recent one lived there for the whole time he was a student, and now, like the other people who'd rented a room from her, he'd become a teacher at a rural high school, Herdis Åsen says and she says that all her previous renters have been male students at The University, humanities students one and all, and now they're scattered around the country at various high schools, and one of them has meanwhile become a professor of Nordic Literature at The University in Oslo, Herdis Åsen says and she goes into the kitchen and she says that she'd rather keep this room for herself, but there are cafés at The Art School and he can probably buy his food there? and he can keep bread and cold cuts and milk and things like that in his room, she doesn't know if he noticed, she says, but there was a breadbox on the dresser and a cutting board and a basin for washing dishes, and in the bottom drawer there are a couple of pots and a frying pan and some dishes and cups and mugs, everything a person might need to make a little food, but all her earlier renters bought food at the cafeteria at The University and he probably can too, maybe? if not then there's a cafeteria at The Art School? because even if he's going to The Art School he'll be allowed to go to The Cafeteria at The University, she says, or else there are more than enough reasonable cafés in Bjørgvin, and the people who've stayed in her rented room before usually went to The Coffeehouse, in any case you used to be able to get a reasonably priced dinner there, but they've probably raised the prices in recent years, she says, and she herself never goes there, when she eats out she always goes to The Grand Café, the prices there are affordable enough for her and the food is good, and besides she can get nice wine there that isn't too expensive, she says, and she has to have wine with her food, every day she has wine with her food, yes, and even if she skips the food sometimes she doesn't skip the wine, she takes a glass every day, at least one, Herdis Åsen says and she goes back into the living room and she says that she has a little collection of books and she points at the bookshelf, she'd inherited thousands of books from her father, she says, but she sold most of them to The

Holberg Antiquariat down by The Fishmarket, and if he was interested in books at all he had to stop by there someday, she says, but, as he can see, yes, she kept some books, yes, it was mostly the Nynorsk and German literature she was interested in, even when she was young, she says, so both the Nynorsk classics and some of the contemporary Nynorsk writers are there on her shelf, and then the German classics, she's less familiar with contemporary German literature, but she has some of the most well-known contemporary German writers on her shelves too, and she's probably read most of the books there, she says, because she reads constantly, but now it's one book in one book out, and either she gives the book that needs to go out to someone as a gift or else she sets it aside and when she has enough books set aside she takes them to The Holberg Antiquariat down by The Fishmarket and she gets paid next to nothing for them, but that doesn't matter, she has her pension so she gets by, and then she makes a little money from these hours she's substitute teaching, she says, and then she'll also get a little rental money from the room, she says and she looks at Asle, but, yes, he should know it's not for the money that she rents out a room, not at all, she says and then Herdis Åsen opens another door and she invites Asle to step inside and Asle sees in front of him a rosemaling canopy bed, it's high and quite wide and there's a high-backed chair by the side of the bed, and it has carved dragons on the ends of the arms

I inherited the bed and the chair from my parents, Herdis Åsen says

and she's lit a cigarette and she holds out a pack of cigarettes to Asle and she asks if he smokes and he says he does, and Asle takes a cigarette and says thank you and then Herdis Åsen takes her lighter and holds out a light for Asle and he takes a good drag on his cigarette and she says he probably hand-rolls his cigarettes, doesn't he, and Asle says he does and then Herdis Åsen picks up an ashtray from the nightstand next to the other side of the bed, there's a high-backed chair next to one side of the bed and a nightstand next to the other, and the nightstand too is rosemaling, and first she taps the ash off her cigarette then she holds out the ashtray to Asle who taps his ash off, and then she asks when he can move in and Asle says that he's not entirely sure but as soon as possible, actually, he says and Herdis Åsen asks if he's starting at The Art School right away and Asle says yes and she asks isn't he going to high school, and Asle says that he went to The Academic High School, in Aga, yes, but that he didn't like it there and that's why he tried to get into The Art School before he was done with The Academic High School and he got a spot thanks to the paintings he showed them

Then you must have real talent, Herdis Åsen says

Well I don't know, Asle says

Yes you do, she says

Yes I guess I do, he says

and she says wouldn't it have been better for him if he'd finished high school with an examen artium, something he'd have for later in life? because being able to live as an artist, to live off his art, live off selling paintings, well, that's not so easy, she says, even if there are galleries in all the big cities in Norway now, and even if The Beyer Gallery in Bjørgvin has no problem selling pictures, she says, but Beyer is very particular about which artists he takes on at his gallery, yes, it's much harder to get an exhibition at The Beyer Gallery than to get into The Art School, she says and they go into the living room and Herdis Åsen says that all the pictures, except the old ones, in the thick frames, yes he can see which ones are old and which are new, she bought all the new pictures from Beyer, and anyway they were family, he used to be married to her sister, so he was technically her brother-in-law, but, yes well, it's been many years since her sister died, so Beyer was a widower now, Herdis Åsen says and because she was single she'd often, when her dear departed sister was alive, gone on holiday with them, yes, to the big cities of Europe, so she'd been inside a lot of art museums, but most of the time they'd travelled to Italy, to Rome, because Rome was the place Beyer liked best, but if Asle had talent and painted good pictures she'd be happy to introduce him to Beyer one evening, she could invite him over for dinner and then he could have a look at Asle's paintings and if he showed at The Beyer Gallery then that would really be something, to tell the truth, because lots of graduating classes from The Art School can go by before Beyer finally thinks anyone's paintings are good enough for their own exhibition, Herdis Åsen says and she stubs out her cigarette and Asle stubs out his and he says that if she wants to have him in her apartment he'd be happy to rent the room from her, as long as it's all right for him to paint pictures in the room, he says and Herdis Åsen says that that's fine, but he should call her before he comes with his things and moves in, she says and Asle says of course he'll do that and I sit there in my chair and I look at the sea, at the waves, instead of standing by the easel looking at the picture I now just sit and look at the sea, I think and I feel no need to paint anymore, none at all, and again I think that I need to call The Hospital to find out how Asle is doing, and if I can come visit him soon, because now he's been in The Hospital for weeks and he surely has to get better soon, better enough for me to visit him anyway, but I just called, so I can't call again right away, I think, something must be wrong with me for me to even think of it, I think and even if I did call I'd only hear that it was best for Asle if I don't come and see him, so I should drive to Bjørgvin instead on Christmas Day, but no, I can't, because this year I'm going with Åsleik to celebrate Christmas at Sister's house, I forgot about that, I think, and that'll make it a long time since I've been to mass, I think and I feel a strong need to take part in the mass again, and be forgiven, and take communion, and usually I always drive to Bjørgvin on Christmas Day to go to mass, even though I like the simple mass on normal weekdays better, I go to high mass on Christmas Day but there's a completely different spirit in the simple everyday masses, almost no one goes to those masses as opposed to high masses on Sunday mornings, then it's almost full in St Paul's Church, and there's singing, yes, a choir, and full organ music, yes, all things considered it was very nice but for me it was the quiet moments with just the words from the priest and the answers from the people that were the best masses, and when the people there, five or six or seven of us, stood up to take communion there was a wonderful sense of atonement, yes, of peace that came over everything, I think, and maybe I'll want to paint pictures again if I just go to mass and sit peacefully and pray a silent prayer as the host, Christ's transfigured body, dissolves in my mouth and I become part of Christ's mystical body, become part of the communion of saints, and when as a part of it I turn towards God, in silence, and then I always pray for people I've known who are dead now, and especially for Ales, and then I pray for the living people who I feel might need someone to pray for them, and it would be so good, as the host dissolves in my mouth, to pray for Asle, pray that he'll get better, or pray that God takes him back if that's what would be best and lets Asle find peace in God, in God's peace and God's light, because Asle never really fit in in this world, and something bigger than life spoke from his pictures with such a clear and silent voice, but that's how it is with all good pictures, I think and I look at my landmark, at the waves and I see Asle lying in a bed and he's shaking, his body is trembling, and The Doctor says that he doesn't understand why it's not stopping, and it's strange too, that the spasms haven't stopped, they've been going on for a long time now, yes, days, weeks, The Doctor says and they've given him as much medicine as they can, and that's helped, and most of the time he's asleep, The Doctor says and I see that Asle is getting fed intravenously, as they say, and he's peeing through a catheter, as they call it, I see and Asle's just lying there and when he wakes up he just thinks confusedly that he might as well die and finally be done with it, so that he's done, Asle thinks and then he disappears into a doze again and the shaking takes hold of his body and he thinks that she's standing there saying she can't do it anymore and The Doctor says and she says she wants a divorce and a little room of painting supplies and he thinks that really he didn't need any more room yes even after their son was born yes the apartment in The Student Home yes before he was born Liv's father and it was good to move in and she lies there and she's just barely breathing and Siv and to be at The Student Home and paint and The Boy and Liv lay on the floor a glass of alcohol diluted with water drink the whole glass and Siv comes into the living room and she can't stand looking at him standing there painting anymore become a teacher have children paint and then drink and she is so exhausted she might collapse at any time painting and she just can't imagine and Bjørgviner Bjørgvin Bjørgviner and she lets go of his arm and never been in love before no never and the paintbrush the kitchen vodka and she went to get The Son from nursery school bought toilet paper dinner that meat a glass of vodka no she can't stand it anymore and bread milk The Son and The Daughter sleep in that morning a two-room apartment forcing her he just taking and doesn't know and never come back and never been in love quiet in love that was gone and never should have moved in together and she walks down the street and her long black hair flows her long black raincoat flutters on her back vodka and her long black hair flows down her back her long black raincoat flutters out to either side teacher and that big apartment and The Son and The Daughter and a door slams shut boiled carrots and then good mashed potatoes there's nothing like she makes good mashed potatoes and he never does anything around the house and Mama wants a little food and one day Papa and plates and knives and forks and I want a divorce and looking down at the floor and lying there thinking it over for a long time probably have to him too and then he has to learn to pick up a child from nursery school he and people he and a half-bottle of vodka go to a shop an advance on mother's inheritance gives her economic and moral support and love he's always known and never cared he just stands there and then a black raincoat and the door opens and going over to the window just like that flowing hair the black raincoat open and fluttering to each side the sofa her body moving the fluttering black raincoat vodka and he's not worth much of anything not worth living be alone die and he can decide to go out to sea the waves and The Son and The Daughter vodka and there's a little left in the bottle take a walk divide up the things lie down and now it's finally decided not saying anything and going to The Alehouse and going to bed her flowing black raincoat hair and The Doctor says won't this shaking ever stop and The Nurse says yes it's so strange, yes, he's just lying there shaking and shaking and The Doctor says won't these spasms stop and I get up and I think I need to call The Hospital and hear how Asle is doing and I go out into the hall and pick up the phone and I hold it to my ear and I see the phone number for The Hospital written on a slip of paper that's on the telephone stand and I think now I've called there every day for a long time, and I called just now, what's wrong with me? I think and I always get the same answer, and I can't call The Hospital again already, I think and I'd rather drive to Bjørgvin on Christmas Day and go to Christmas mass in the morning, the way I usually do, but no, I can't this year, because I'll be in Øygna with Åsleik celebrating Christmas at Sister's, I think, but maybe I can drive down to Bjørgvin after Åsleik and I get home on The Boat? because the plan is to go to Øygna in The Boat as soon as it's light in the morning on Christmas Eve day, probably around noon, and come back home from Øygna to Dylgja the next day, yes, as early as we can, and then after we get home I can drive to The Hospital and check on Asle, and when I say how long a drive it was to come see him they'll probably have to let me in, I think, and maybe there's an evening mass too that I can go to on Christmas Day? I think and I go and sit back down in my chair by the round table and I look out the window at my spot there in the Sygne Sea and I think that it's my own darkness I'm sitting and looking into and that's why I can see the water, the waves, in spite of the darkness and I look at my landmark, at the waves and I see Asle running down the stairs in 7 University Street and he's happy and carefree, because now he not only has a place at The Art School, he's rented a room too, right in the middle of Bjørgvin, just a short walk from The Art School, yes, Herdis Åsen said so when he was leaving and she thanked him for wanting to rent a room from her and then Herdis Åsen said she was looking forward to him moving in, the only thing, yes, the only thing she asked was that he take the trash out for her, well, for her and for himself, it had to be done every Wednesday night, she said and Asle had said of course he could do that, and then they said so long until next time and Asle ran off down the stairs and he thinks that he'll be living at Herdis Åsen's for a long time, she sort of won't want to let him go, he thinks, and Ales had said that she had to leave, she had to do something, but she never said what, he thinks, and he never got to ask her either, and he runs down the stairs because now he'll maybe see Ales again, he thinks, but maybe she left when he went up to look at the room, she said she had something to do, that's all she said, and that she'd write to him, Asle thinks and he thinks that since he spent so long at Herdis Åsen's she definitely must have left, he thinks and he runs down the stairs and he opens the front door of 7 University Street and he goes out and he can't see Ales anywhere, and she did say she had something to do, and said something about how she couldn't wait for him if he was going to be too long, or did she say that? and what did she have to do? why is she gone? why did she leave? Asle thinks, because there's no Ales to be seen, nowhere, and why didn't he hurry up? why did he spend such a long time up at Herdis Åsen's? but he couldn't just leave, could he? she wanted to just show him the apartment and the room and as soon as she did that he left, Asle thinks, and is it really true in reality that he and Ales met today?

that they met at The Bus Café? and that they became boyfriend and girlfriend? or is that just something he imagined? because it can't be possible, things like that aren't possible, Asle thinks and he thinks that Ales gave him her address and he reaches into the pocket of his black velvet jacket and he takes out a slip of paper where Ales wrote her name and address and phone number, and she lives with her mother, so that's where he can reach her, but had they said goodbye to each other? and didn't Ales say that she'd wait for him? and now there's no Ales here, Asle thinks, and he looks at his watch and it's two hours before the bus to Aga leaves from The Bus Station, and, no, he doesn't understand why there's no Ales here, did she regret what she'd said and just leave him? what's happened? he thinks and I look at my landmark there in the Sygne Sea, I look at the waves and I see Asle walk into The Newsstand at The Bus Station and he thinks that now he'll buy a *Northern Herald* and then he'll go to The Bus Café and buy a pint and then he'll sit there, because it's a long time, yes, almost two hours that he has to wait for the bus to leave for Aga, but he'll drink a pint, slowly, and he can read the newspaper, and if he feels like it he can draw a sketch or two, because there are lots of pictures that lodged in him today, yes, so many that he feels almost overwhelmed and desperate when he thinks about all the pictures that got into his head today and it's like every one of them weighs so much, Asle thinks and now he's at The Newsstand and he buys a copy of *The Northern Herald* and then he goes into The Bus Café and he sees that there's almost no one there, but sitting at a window in the back of the café with her back to the wall is a woman with medium-length blonde hair, and she looks like she's a few years older than Asle and she sits there looking out the window, and there's a glass of wine in front of her, and then, at the other end of the café, there's the man with long dark hair who looks just like Asle, who's always wearing a black velvet jacket and carrying a brown leather shoulder bag, and who hangs around and paints, just like Asle, the guy Asle met at The Stranda Hotel when he and Sigve went there, and ran into at The Paint Shop, and he too is sitting by a window, and he's sitting with his back to the woman with the medium-length blonde hair and there's a pint of beer in front of him and Asle thinks that it's really strange that he's sitting there, because he's the one who made Asle think about applying for a spot at The Art School just with the pictures he'd painted, without an examen artium, Asle thinks and it's sort of like he doesn't like seeing him sitting there, and he doesn't know why he doesn't like it, and Asle thinks that he hopes this Namesake, because his name is Asle too, hasn't noticed him, but of course he will, Asle thinks and then he goes to the counter and says he'd like to buy a pint please and the man standing behind the counter who can't be much older than Asle looks suspiciously at him and then he pours a pint from the tap and Asle pays and he notices that the woman with the medium-length blonde hair is looking at him and he doesn't look at her, he looks straight ahead and then he looks at The Namesake and he sees that he's sitting with a sketchpad in front of him and he's lost in the drawing he's working on and Asle goes and sits down by a window a few tables away from the woman with the medium-length blonde hair with his back to her and so that The Namesake has his back to him, and then he takes a sip of beer and he looks out the window and he sees people arriving at and leaving The Bus Station, some are carrying suitcases and shopping bags, some are empty-handed, some are walking with a spring in their step, some are limping, now and then there's someone walking with a cane, and then he sees a man with long grey hair tied back in a hairtie, and he's dressed in a black velvet jacket, just like Asle, and he's wearing a brown leather shoulder bag, and he's walking with a cane, and Asle doesn't know why a picture of this man gets lodged inside him but now he has a picture of him lodged in his mind, yes, it's like he has a camera in his head, Asle thinks, no, he mustn't think things like that, but still that's kind of how it is, in a way, yes, and every so often this camera takes a picture entirely by itself and the picture gets stored in his head, or it's like it gets glued into a photo album in there, and then it pops up every now and then, and then he sees it perfectly clearly before his eyes, and when a picture like that pops up it's like everything that's happening around him, in the real world, goes away and it's like he sees nothing but that picture, and why do pictures get stuck in his head like that? no, he doesn't know, and he doesn't know why they suddenly pop up in his head either, he doesn't understand, why would he be like that? and it's to get rid of these pictures that he paints, actually that's the only reason why, because it's always one of these pictures that he, no, not paints, but he tries to get rid of one of these pictures by painting a picture that's like it, Asle thinks, and the reason a picture gets stuck inside him must be that it says something to him, and it's what the picture says that he tries to paint, yes, to make it go away, and in a way the picture kind of turns into part of himself, something he in a way understands and that anyway doesn't bother him anymore, or bothers him less anyway, Asle thinks and he raises his glass and he takes a good sip of beer and he thinks that at least two maybe three pictures have lodged in his head since he got to The Bus Café and he looks at The Namesake's back and he sees the door of The Bus Café open and a woman with long black hair walks in and she goes straight to The Namesake and he gets up and then they give each other a hug and then they kiss each other and Asle hears The Namesake say it's nice to see you Siv and she says it's nice to see you too Asle, because, no, this can't go on, she says, I miss you all the time, she says and she sits down across from The Namesake and he says he's missed her too and it's so good to see you again Siv, he says

It can't go on like this anymore, Siv says

and The Namesake says that soon now, yes, he'll tell Liv about them soon, but she must know about it already, and it probably wasn't because of the two of them that she wanted to kill herself, because she'd been stealing pills from her mother for a long time, she'd said, and storing them up, he says and trying to kill yourself while there's a baby not even a year old lying there crying all alone is just wrong, he says

No it's unbelievable, he says

And of course I think it's my fault, he says

and the woman named Siv says it's not his fault, he's tried to take care of Liv as best he could, that's all, they just met and then she lived with him in his room there in Stranda and then she got pregnant, she says, but he must have liked her? have been in love with her? been attracted to her anyway?, and fuck, fuck, fuck, Siv says and it almost looks like she's about to leave and The Namesake says she needs to calm down, because it's just her now, but he does have to think about The Boy too, he says, yes, Liv's better now, and now she can take care of the baby, so soon, very soon, he'll tell her about the two of them, The Namesake says and Asle thinks why are The Namesake and the woman named Siv sitting in The Bus Café talking loud enough for other people to hear them about things that are none of anybody else's business? things that are only for the two of them? things that it only disturbs other people to have to listen to? Asle thinks and he looks up and he turns around and his eyes meet the eyes of the woman with the medium-length blonde hair, she is sitting and looking at him, and Asle turns back around right away and he looks down at the table and he starts to flip through the newspaper and he pages through the whole newspaper and there's nothing in there he especially pays attention to, and he flips back to the death notices and he reads through them, and it's strange how many people have died, both young and old, people from all the cities in West Norway, Asle thinks and he doesn't understand it, people are born, people die, just a few years of struggle and toil to get through their life one way or another and then they die, they come from nothing, they're just born, and they go back to nothing, they're just gone, and then there're these years they call life, a life, a human life, Asle thinks and he sees The Namesake get up and the woman who'd sat down across from him gets up too, and then The Namesake puts the sketchpad and pencil into the brown leather shoulder bag and puts it on and Asle looks down at the newspaper, at the page with the death notices and then he hears a voice say no it's you and Asle looks up and he sees The Namesake standing there looking at him

It's been a while, Asle says

Yeah, remember those days at The Stranda Hotel? The Namesake says

Yeah, Asle says

And the last time we talked was probably at The Paint Shop back in Stranda, The Namesake says

and there's silence and Asle sees that the woman named Siv has walked to the door of The Bus Café and stopped

And all sorts of things have happened to me since then, The Namesake says

Yes, Asle says

and to him it's unbearable how much the two of them look alike but The Namesake doesn't seem to notice or care, for him it's just like they're two people the same age and that they wear similar clothes and look a little like each other, Asle thinks and The Namesake tells him that maybe he remembers him telling him that he was going to be a father and Asle nods and he says he's become a father, yes, the father of a baby boy not even one year old, he says and he's started at The Art School and he and Liv, yes, that's the name of the woman he lives with, he probably told him about her back at The Stranda Hotel? The Namesake says, yes, first they moved to Sartor, yes, to her parents' place, and then they moved to Bjørgvin, when they got an apartment at The Student Home, and now they live there, he says and the woman named Siv comes walking back to The Namesake

Let's go, she says

and she takes The Namesake's arm and Asle looks at her and he sees that she looks like she's totally mixed up, she's sad and she's angry and everything you can imagine, he thinks

Take care, The Namesake says

And give my regards to The Stranda Hotel, he says

and The Namesake laughs and he says Asle should say hi to his friend too, the guy with the tattoos, his name was Sigve right, The Namesake says and he looks at Siv and points with his left hand to the spot between the thumb and index finger of his right hand and he says that the guy he's talking about had a heart, an anchor, and a cross tattooed between the thumb and index finger of one hand and on the other, he says, and he points with his other hand to the same spot on the other hand, he had a tattoo of three dots in a triangle

A beggar's mark, he says

Bet you didn't know that, he says

and Siv shakes her head and she tugs at The Namesake's arm

We need to go now, she says

Yes well take care, The Namesake says

Take care, Asle says

and he sees Siv almost drag The Namesake to the door with her and Asle hears her say something about how he doesn't need to tell people about things like that and then she says something about it scaring people and Asle turns around and looks behind him and he sees the woman with the medium-length blonde hair still sitting and looking at him and then he turns to face forwards again and looks down at the page with the death notices and he thinks why is she sitting there looking at him, he thinks and he takes out his tobacco pouch and he rolls himself a cigarette, lights it, and takes a good drag of it and he feels a kind of wellbeing spread through his body, he thinks and he puts down the paper and he drinks his beer and he looks at his watch and he sees that there's only about an hour now until the bus is supposed to leave, and he thinks he'll just go to the gate the buses to Aga leave from and there was nothing worth reading in *The Northern Herald*, so he'll just leave the newspaper here, Asle thinks and then he gets up and he puts on his brown leather shoulder bag and he thinks he won't look at the woman with the medium-length blonde hair and he walks out the door and I sit there in my chair by the round table and now I've closed my eyes, and I just sit there, and I think that nothing has any point, any meaning, but what kind of empty weightless words are these? point? meaning? nothing like that exists because credibile est quia ineptum est, that's how it is, or certum est quia impossibile est, so it was said and that's how it is, and it's so cold that I can't even get undressed to go lie down, I just sit there in my chair, next to the round table, in my black coat and with the grey blanket wrapped around me, I sit there and Bragi is lying in my lap and I think that God is so far away that no one can say anything about him and that's why all ideas about God are wrong, and at the same time he is so close that we almost can't notice him, because he is the foundation in a person, or the abyss, you can call it whatever you want, I think and I often think about the picture that's kind of innermost inside me, and it's good and bad equally, it doesn't matter what you call it, or I think about God's shining darkness inside me, a darkness that's also a light, and that's also a nothing, that is not a thing, I think and we come from God and we go back to God, I think and I think that now I need to stop with these thoughts of mine, they don't go anywhere, I think and I think that I want to lie down on the bench and I get up and Bragi falls to the floor, yes, every time, I think and I think that I'm so tired so tired and I lie down on the bench and I spread the grey blanket over me and Bragi jumps up and lies down next to my feet and I feel how good it is to have him lying here next to me and I take out the rosary I always have hanging around my neck, that I got from Ales a long time ago, it's brown, with wooden beads and a wooden cross, and now I'll pray with my rosary the way I often do, not for any reason except that it gives me calm, gives me peace, I think and I always pray with my eyes closed, and with silence inside me, first I make the sign of the cross and then I pray the Apostles' Creed while holding the cross, and then an Our Father while holding the first bead, then an Ave Maria three times while holding the next three beads one by one, then the shorter Gloria, as it's called, in the space before the next bead where I pray the Our Father again and then I pray the doxology, as it's called, in the Our Father at the first bead above the cross and then finally I recite Salve Regina while I hold the cross, and I switch back and forth between using Nynorsk and using Latin but I always recite Salve Regina in Latin, because it's impossible to translate it, all you can do is make a version of it, I think and then I usually make a sign of the cross at the end and I make a sign of the cross and I start to say The Apostles' Creed silently inside me and I say I believe in God the Father almighty and I think that actually I don't believe in what I'm saying, or else I believe in it in a certain sense, so I can't exactly say that I don't believe in it, but it's good to think about the fact that the apostles said these words too, yes, the first Christians, the ones who were called the humble, I think, and if God isn't almighty, but is more likely powerless, still he's there in everything that is and everything that happens, because that's how it has to be if God put limits on himself by giving human beings free will, since God is love and love is inconceivable without free will, so he can't be all-powerful, and the same thing is true of nature, if God created the laws that nature follows then the laws are what's in control, I think and if God hadn't given himself limits, for whatever reason, then he wouldn't be all-powerful either, not in any thinkable way, I think, because that can't be thought, but there's one thing I'm sure of and that's that the greater the despair and suffering is, the closer God is, I think and I say Who created the heavens and the earth and the words are simple, they're words everyone can understand, and that's why the meaning too of these words is something for everyone, but if you get hung up on the literal meaning, to the extent you can, then the words become meaningless, and I used to do that myself, because it's almost like the people who spoke these words when I was growing up believed it, believed in the literal meaning of what they said, in God a father who lived up in the sky somewhere, who was all-powerful and who used that power to even exterminate millions of Jews, I think, but those who think of God like that are truly sinning, misusing God's name, or maybe they're not, they don't know any better, and I shouldn't judge them, because judge not lest ye be judged, as is written, but I can't help it, I think it's blasphemous to think like that, and the people who believe in the God they told us about when I was growing up in Barmen believe in a false idol, they're misusing God's name, pure and simple, and may God forgive them, and he does, for God's grace is so all-encompassing that it's wrong to distinguish the grace as something particular, as grace, I think, and now how can I know that? I think, and it's equally wrong to say that God is almighty, yes, all-powerful, because then how does it make sense that God became human and shared our powerless condition? for such is the foolishness we preach, as Paul wrote, I think and I say to myself inside myself And in Jesus Christ His only son Our Lord He was conceived by the power of The Holy Spirit and born of the Virgin Mary He suffered under Pontius Pilate, Was crucified, died, and was buried He descended to the dead On the third day he rose again He ascended to heaven Is seated at the right hand of God the Father He will come again to judge the living and the dead and I think that when Jesus Christ in the utmost powerlessness died on the cross it was God himself who died, because The Father and I are one, it says in scripture, yes, then it was the old God, the vengeful God as described in The Old Testament who died, the God of vengeance died with Jesus Christ dead on the cross, and rose up again with Jesus Christ, the resurrection of God, and with his disappearing from the created world a new connection between God and humanity was formed, but not in this world, or rather it was like an annihilation of this world, it was like in opposition to this world that the good Lord now existed in humanity, yes, like a shining darkness deep inside people, yes, maybe you can think of it as like The Holy Spirit, I think and I say to myself I believe in the Holy Spirit The Holy Catholic Church The communion of saints The forgiveness of sins The resurrection of the body And the life everlasting and I think that the humble Christians have thought about and pondered all this, all these things, for more than two thousand years, how God can be all-powerful, be all-knowing, and be love at the same time, and I think that it's wrong to think like this, because in a certain sense God isn't anything, he is a dark shining nothingness, a nothing, a not, and at the same time he is also in everything that is, he is being, a distance that is also closeness, because God is both in and gone from the created world, which is outside the creator, outside of God, I think, all of space with our little planet where human beings exist is in a certain sense there so that God can exist, because without human beings God would not have become God but something else instead, I think, and when what we know as our earth, and the space we're in, is gone, then nothing will be there, the nothingness will be there, the nothingness that God is, because God is eternal, and eternity can't be any thing, anything finite, anything in space, so God is the whole past, the whole present, the whole future outside time and space, and that is why God reaches from eternity to eternity, and he knows everything, he is all-knowing, and that's why everything that happens is in a way predetermined because it already exists in God's eternity, in God's mind, even the freely willed actions are all in God's everything and nothing, because even after all of creation is gone there will be nothing there, nothingness, that's how it is with everything that is, with each individual person, after the individual, the person is gone from creation they will be in God's eternity, as nothing, there in God's shining darkness, in his nothingness, because everything comes from nothing and to nothing it will return, it comes from God, who is therefore so close, so close, since he is inside every single person, yes, he is the foundation, the abyss, yes, the innermost picture in everyone, like a full void, like a shining darkness, I think, and this was why everything came into existence, so that God could exist, because he is in every human being, because God becomes God in the soul and the soul becomes the soul in God, as Meister Eckhart wrote, and no one else has made belief more understandable, more comprehensibly incomprehensible, no one else has opened up the kingdom of God to me like Meister Eckhart, and if it wasn't for him I would never have found words for the closeness of God, for the closeness that God in his silence gives me, yes, gives to all people, whether they realise it or not, and of course Meister Eckhart is right about how many of the people who don't believe in God are people who really do, while the ones who are doing all kinds of things to show that they believe in God actually believe in something other than God, they believe in an idol, because they believe in good works, in repentance and fasting, in sacraments, in the liturgy, in this or that conduct bringing them closer to God, yes, most of those who are inside are outside, and most who are outside are inside, the first shall be last, as is written, but even so both prayer and mass, and most of all the eucharist, can lead us closer to God, closer to eternity and nothingness, closer to the shining darkness inside us, because I experience that every time I go to mass or see the halo around the host, or the glimmer coming from it, the light, in the transfiguration happening, in the consecration, I think and I think and think and there's probably nothing especially smart about what I'm thinking, I think and I think why does The Fjord exist? and the ocean? and the sky? and why do I exist? why is there anything rather than nothing? I think and everything exists at some point and stops existing at some point, not just me, because obviously both my paintings and I myself will cease to be, how ridiculous is it to think that anything in creation won't disappear and turn into nothing, even the most beautiful painting, the most worthwhile painting in the world will be gone someday, the same way whoever painted it will be long gone, and the greatest poem will disappear, because everything disappears, and eventually there'll be nothing left, and then the kingdom of God will have come, yes, Let thy kingdom come, I think, but right now, yes, right now the kingdom of God is in everyone, and God's being, his uncreated darkness and light, his nothingness, speaks and is silent from what exists, from the water, from the sky, from the good paintings, yes, from the round table right here next to me God silently speaks, and from the two chairs next to the table, yes, God is looking at me from the table, from the chairs, I think, because, yes, Nah ist und schwer zu fassen der Gott Wo aber Gefahr ist wächst das Rettende auch, I think and I think that to think like I'm doing now doesn't go anywhere, because my thinking is so muddled, I'm so tired that the thoughts just keep going and going and turn what is utterly simple and clear into something incomprensible and unclear, I think, but no, I always think like this, whether I'm tired or not, and I think as clearly as I can, but I'm not up to it, so it just turns into meaningless irrational words, maybe, I think, and really I'm just trying to say in words what I know, know for sure and for certain, I think and I think that Jesus Christ will come again to pass judgement on the living and the dead, and then I think that those are just words, words, because Jesus Christ is always coming back, in every single moment, in every single instant and he is judging, both in life and in death, and turning everything evil into nothingness while everything good, all love, everything from God and with God, continues to exist,

I think and then I say to myself I believe in the communion of saints, and I think that yes I do believe in a communion of all people who have been freed from their evil, who have become their own nothingness, who have become the part of God that is inside them, everyone who has ever lived and who is now dead make up a community, a communion of the saints, because the evil has been taken from them and turned into nothing, yes, I like to think that that's what burns up in hell, evil is what disappears there, not people! because a person is so much more than evil, a person is created in God's image! I think, and insofar as evil becomes nothing, becomes not, it, yes, in a way it falls out of time and space, the evil and the good together, and they become one in the kingdom of God, I think and here again are these clumsy words, these words that separate a person from God, and at the same time in some incomprehensible way connect a person to God and then I say to myself The resurrection of the body and the life everlasting and I think that what I'm saying is that a person is not just body and soul, there is spirit that connects the body and the soul, the same connection, the same undifferentiating connection, between what we like to call form and what we like to call content that makes a painting good, or makes a good poem good, and that makes good music good, yes, that exists when one thing can't be separated from the other, when form can't be separated from content, it's precisely when they meet that the spirit in a work of art becomes something particular, that at the same time is totally universal, I think and it is this unity that's resurrected when the flesh is resurrected, as a transfigured body, as a spiritualised body, as Paul wrote, and this happens as soon as a person dies and leaves time and space, not at some point somewhere or other in the future, because time, with its before and now and after, is a part of this evil, fallen world, the same way space is too, with its proximities and distances, but when a person dies and leaves time, leaves space, goes to God, as something completely particular and completely universal at the same time, not mixed, not divided up, that's what I think and I think how can I know that? I can't know whether or not things are like what I say they're like, maybe they're totally different, but that's how I'm able to think about it, or keep trying to at least, it's probably impossible for anyone else to understand what I think and the truth exists in the unspoken, since it disappears and goes away when someone tries to say it, because thou shalt not make any image of God, as stands written, and that's probably exactly what I'm doing now, and precisely what I'm not doing when I'm painting and manage to paint well, then I make an image of something totally different and in that way maybe an image of God, but I can't think such things, I think and then I close my eyes and am so tired so tired and I pray God forgive me my sins, because God is near whether a person prays or not, and in a way praying brings a person farther from God, as Meister Eckhart wrote, and that's because a human being is a prayer in himself or herself, in his or her yearning, I think and I think that's enough now and then I call Bragi and he jumps up from where he's lying next to my feet and he looks at me and his eyes sparkle in the darkness

I don't understand anything, I don't, I say

and Bragi looks at me with those sparkling eyes, his dog's eyes, and then I close my eyes

Good boy, Bragi, I say

and I think that I think thoughts but they were all thought better by Meister Eckhart, He From Whom God Hid Nothing, that's what they called him, and if it wasn't for his writings, and for Ales, I would never have converted and become Catholic, that's for sure, I think, but maybe in that case I would have been closer to God than I am now? maybe I was closer to God before I converted and became Catholic? I think

You're a nice dog, Bragi, yes, I say

and I think that I'm tired but I still can't get to sleep and I think that

I'm in bad shape, I feel so tired and weak that I'm not sure how much more I'll be able to do, and I don't want to paint more paintings in any case, what's done is good, I think, but what am I supposed to do if I don't paint? I think, because aside from Åsleik, well, who is there to talk to? yes well I talk to Beyer a couple times a year, but other than that I have no contact with anyone, and there aren't so many people in Dylgja, and I can't even imagine moving away and leaving Dylgja, it's in Dylgja that I've lived my life, and my life is the life I lived with Ales, the time before that and the time after that don't count somehow, they're somehow not my life, I think and I make another sign of the cross, how many times a day do I do that? no, I don't know, but every time I feel a kind of pain, yes, I make the sign of the cross and I think that without really understanding why I've now lost all my desire to paint, it's like I've finished the painting I'm supposed to do, ever since Asle was admitted to The Hospital and they didn't let me see him I've had no more desire to paint, and the bad picture, the one with the two lines that cross, luckily it's not on the easel anymore, I've put it away, put it at the front of the stack of the unfinished paintings, with the stretcher facing out, I think and I think that it's probably going to be morning soon, I think and I close my eyes and I see Asle sitting on the bus to Bjørgvin and he's thinking that everything he owns is packed in two boxes he got at The Co-op Store, and he put his sheets and blankets in the burlap sack Mother put them in when he moved to Aga, and he has his painting supplies in the old suitcase that used to be in the attic of The Old House and then there's the easel and everything fit in the luggage compartment in the back of the bus going to Bjørgvin and Asle thinks that when he was there to rent his room he met Ales, they met entirely by chance at The Bus Café there, and as soon as they met they were boyfriend and girlfriend, and since then they'd written letters to each other every day, as soon as he got a letter from Ales he wrote one to her, and as soon as she got a letter from him she wrote one to him, Asle thinks and now when he gets to The Bus Station in Bjørgvin Ales will be there waiting for him at the gate, that's what she wrote, and then they'll take a taxi to 7 University Street, because even though it's expensive there's no way they can carry all the things, and anyway it wasn't that far from The Bus Station to 7 University Street, was what Ales wrote, and now Asle is sitting on the bus and everything he owns is in the luggage area and he thinks how lucky he's been, not only did he get a spot at The Art School without his examen artium, without having to finish all three years of The Academic High School, but he found and rented a room in Bjørgvin not too far from The Art School, and so he could quit The Academic High School, and the day he did that was a great day for him, Asle thinks, yes, there've been several great days in his life recently, but the greatest was the day he met Ales, and next was the day he got into The Art School, and in third place was the day a few days ago when he went to The Principal of The Academic High School and told him he was leaving, Asle thinks and I lie there on the bench with my black coat on, with the blanket tucked tight around me, and it's so cold in the room, but I don't have the strength to get up and light the stove, and I'm so tired but I can't get to sleep, I think and Åsleik came over and had lutefisk here last night, and now it's probably already midnight, maybe, I think, it's probably Little Christmas Eve already, maybe, I think, and the lutefisk was as it should be but somehow it didn't taste good to me, I think and I lie there with my eyes closed and I see Asle walking from The Shoemaker's Workshop and he stops at the door to The Landlady's house and he rings the doorbell and she comes and opens the door and she says no, is it you, and Asle says he has to tell her that he's going to move to Bjørgvin to start at The Art School there, and that he's already found a room in Bjørgvin, so he's come to give up his room, he says and The Landlady says that it's too bad Asle's leaving, she'd liked having him living there at The Shoemaker's Workshop, it felt safer, to be honest, she says, but if he's moving to Bjørgvin then that's the way it is of course, yes, she says and then she asks him if she can offer him a little coffee or a roll and Asle has no choice but to say yes, he thinks and The Landlady says he should come in and Asle takes off his shoes in the hall and goes into the living room and The Landlady says he should sit down on the sofa and then she walks on her slightly stiff feet out to the kitchen and she comes back in with a flower-pattern tablecloth and carefully puts it down on the coffee table and spreads it, and then she goes out to the kitchen again and then comes back with some rolls on a flower-pattern dish, and the tablecloth and dish have the same kind of flowers on them, and then she goes out to the kitchen and gets a coffeepot and she pours coffee, first Asle's then her own, and then she says enjoy and Asle takes a roll, since really he has no choice, even though he doesn't like rolls, and he takes a bite and he chews and chews and then he raises his coffee cup to his mouth and takes a sip

Milk and sugar? The Landlady says

I forgot to ask you, didn't I, she says

Maybe a little milk, Asle says

Since I don't take any myself I forgot to offer any, she says

I like it black, she says

and then The Landlady goes out to the kitchen and she comes back with a little pitcher of milk that she puts down in front of Asle and he pours a little milk into his cup and then there's silence for a bit and then The Landlady says it's strange isn't it, how some people like milk in their coffee, and some people like sugar, and some both, and some neither, she says

Yes, Asle says

People are different, he says

and after that there's silence again and then The Landlady says that she doesn't entirely understand why she never rented out the room upstairs in The Shoemaker's Workshop before, it just never happened, she sort of never realised she could, because The Shoemaker's Workshop sort of belonged totally and completely to her husband, her good husband, now long since passed, so she sort of had nothing to do with the house, that's how it was when her dear husband was alive and then that's how it stayed afterwards too, when he was gone, but now, yes, now that she's had a renter for the first time she'll keep doing it in future too, that's for sure, because in a strange way it was like having a little company in her life having a young man living up there in The Shoemaker's Workshop, it made her feel safe, and it's hard to believe but in a strange way it gave her a feeling like her husband was still alive, even though he's been dead all these years, she says, and she tends to his grave as best she can, for as long as she lives he'll have a well-tended grave, The Landlady says and when her own time comes she will lie in the same grave as him, and, yes, that'll feel safe too, yes, death loses a bit of its sting when she thinks that she'll be sleeping in the same grave as her husband for all eternity, she says, because everything else, well, the stuff about the resurrection of the flesh and all that, no, she can't quite picture that or bring herself to believe in it, but lying in the same grave as her husband, that feels right and safe, The Landlady says and Asle has managed to eat almost the whole roll and he drinks his coffee

Are you taking the bus to Bjørgvin tomorrow already? The Landlady says then

and Asle nods and says that yes he's going to Bjørgvin tomorrow

Then you probably have a lot to do, The Landlady says

Packing and tidying up and cleaning, because you do need to make sure you clean up after yourself, you know, she says

and then The Landlady says that she used to be able to do things like that herself but she's now so stiff and sore that it's more than she can manage to keep her own house clean, isn't it, she says, and having things spick and span in her house had always been especially important for her, not being slovenly in any way, because she was never slovenly, no indeed, she says and it's like there's a kind of anger flaring up in her voice

I'm no slob, no, she says

and Asle doesn't know what to say, because he sort of can't say you're right you're not slovenly because then it's kind of like she is in a way, he thinks, and so he doesn't say anything and he chews at the rest of his roll and then The Landlady holds up the dish to him and says he should take another roll and Asle says no thank you, thank you so much

This is plenty, he says

You'll have a little more coffee, though, won't you? she says

and Asle shakes his head and says that now he has to get busy packing and getting everything ready so he can take the bus to Bjørgvin tomorrow, he says

I suppose you do, The Landlady says

and Asle hears that there's something hurt in her voice and then she says that he can take a few rolls, for the road, yes, The Landlady says and isn't it strange that today when she went shopping at The Co-op Store she bought herself a bag of rolls, now why would she have done that? yes, it's as if she knew someone would be paying her a visit today, but she didn't know, now did she, she says and then she gets up and she takes the flower-patterned dish of rolls and goes out to the kitchen and then she comes back in with a paper bag and she hands it to Asle and he says thanks thanks and The Landlady says that it's too bad he couldn't live here longer, but since he got a spot at The Art School over in Bjørgvin well what has to be must be, she says and Asle holds out his hand to her and he and The Landlady shake hands and then he says thank you so much for everything, and for the coffee and rolls, he says and The Landlady says it was nothing and then Asle leaves and he turns around in the doorway and he sees that The Landlady has raised her hand and is waving to him and he raises his hand and waves back and then he's out of the house and he thinks it was good to get that over with, but what in the world is he going to do with these rolls? he doesn't like rolls, and it would be too bad just to throw them away, he thinks and he's almost done with his packing already, he's already packed everything he owns in two boxes he got from The Co-op Store, and then he packed his painting supplies in the old suitcase that used to belong to his grandparents that he'd brought with him from the attic in The Old House when he moved into his room, and he'd layered the grey blanket he got from Grandma between the paintings as best he could, he thinks and now he needs to go over to Sigve's and give him back the two books he'd borrowed from him such a long time ago, he mustn't forget that, and truth be told he's barely opened them, and he doesn't even remember who wrote them, but he did read a couple of pages of each of them, and the rolls, yes, maybe Sigve likes rolls and so he can give them to him? Asle thinks and he puts the two books and the bag with the rolls in his shoulder bag and he goes out and he thinks that he has to go see Grandma today, he thinks, he has to do that today even if she doesn't even notice when he comes in the room anymore, so that's why he's been going to see her less and less often, Asle thinks and he goes over to Sigve's place and he knocks on the door, he is knocking on Sigve's door for maybe the last time, Asle thinks and Sigve opens the door and Asle asks if Sigve likes rolls and Sigve answers what kind of question is that, but, sure yeah and Asle says he doesn't like rolls so if Sigve wants these rolls he can have them, he says and Asle takes the bag of rolls out of his shoulder bag, he got these rolls from The Landlady, he says and he hands Sigve the bag and Sigve says thanks, thank you, he says

But come in, Sigve says

and Asle goes inside and shuts the door behind him

And tomorrow you're off, Sigve says

Yes, Asle says

616 Jon Fosse

and then no one says anything and Sigve puts the bag of rolls down on the kitchen counter and then he says that he's going to still be living in this little old house the rest of his days, but he didn't pay Asle enough for the painting, he says and he takes out a few banknotes and hands them to Asle and he says thank you for painting a picture of my house and there's a kind of embarrassing silence, and it's as if Sigve is sorry he took the picture, because it's nowhere to be seen since Sigve never hung it up, but what did he do with it? Asle thinks, maybe it's under the sofa? he thinks, because he can't just have thrown it away can he? he thinks, but Sigve thought it was too dark and too sad, that painting, because it was a sad painting, to tell the truth, but it was a good painting, maybe one of the best he's painted, and then in black and white, yes, in just black and white and grey and with the tiniest bit of blue in one or two places, Asle thinks and he doesn't really think Sigve threw out the painting

Thanks a lot, Asle says

Don't mention it, Sigve says

and he says that since Asle is moving to Bjørgvin tomorrow they probably don't have time to head over to The Hotel and have a farewell glass together, but he does have a couple of bottles of beer here, he says and then Sigve goes and gets two glasses and one bottle of beer and he opens the bottle and hands it to Asle who pours some for both Sigve and himself and then he puts the bottle down on the table and they drink and Asle looks at the chessboard, there at the end of the table, with the pieces in various positions on it and Asle thinks he doesn't understand how Sigve can spend so much of his time thinking about how he's going to move one of his pieces on his next turn, but he probably needs something like that to think about so as not to think about something else, Asle thinks, and he himself doesn't even know how to play chess, he thinks

I'll miss you, Sigve says

And it's not an easy career you've chosen, if you want to make a living painting pictures, he says

and Asle says all he wants to do is paint, everything else will happen however it happens, he says

It's probably more of a calling than a normal job that puts food on the table, Sigve says

and there's a silence and then Sigve says that maybe they can meet up in Bjørgvin sometime, because when he has time off he sometimes takes a trip there, and when he gets out of the bus at The Bus Station there the first thing he always does is go to a place called The Bus Café to get a pint or two or three and then he walks over to The Fishmarket and on the way there he buys himself a bottle of something stronger and then he sits down at The Fishmarket and secretly takes a sip every so often, and he looks at the people, at the boats, and then he glances up at The Prison and feels how good it is not to be locked up in there anymore, and sometimes he drops by The Alehouse, because they have good beer and good food there at a reasonable price, so Asle should go there, Sigve says and Asle says that he has to look in on Grandma and Sigve says he understands, that he has to say goodbye to her, and that'll probably be another loss for her, not to have Asle come see her, because he goes to see her so often, he says, but after he's seen his Grandmother they could probably meet up afterwards and have a farewell glass of something at The Hotel, he says, because he's going over to The Hotel right now, he says and then Asle says he can't forget, he has the two books he borrowed with him, he says and he says that he read a little of them, and he liked what he read, but he didn't read enough to get that much out of them, Asle says and he takes the books out of the shoulder bag and hands them to Sigve and says thanks for loaning them to him and Sigve says it was nice to hear that Asle read a little of them anyway and then Sigve says it sure will be lonely for his Grandmother now once Asle stops going by to say hello to her and

Asle says that he can't talk with Grandma anymore, she just lies there, she doesn't even notice that he's there, that he's come, but even so he still likes to say a few words and then hold her hand, he says and Sigve says well all right then and then Asle says bye and that he'll see him at The Hotel after he's gone and seen Grandma and Sigve says good and then Asle goes to The Hospice and to the room where Grandma is lying and he knocks on the door and as usual no one answers and he opens the door and he sees that the bed is empty, and he thinks now that's strange, he thinks and he stays standing there for a moment looking at the empty bed and then someone who works at The Hospice comes and she says she's so sorry but his Grandmother died today, earlier today, around eight o'clock, she says and Asle just nods and then he quietly leaves and he thinks now Grandma is gone, now the best friend he ever had in his life is gone forever, he thinks and he thinks that he has no desire to go to The Hotel to drink beer with Sigve, but he probably has to go anyway, because a promise is a promise, he thinks and then he walks into The Hotel and he sees Sigve sitting there with his glass of beer and Asle says Grandma died and he'd rather just go back to his room now and Sigve says it's really sad to hear that, his Grandmother was old and sick but she was his Grandmother, and it's always terrible when someone is gone forever, Sigve says and Asle says that he doesn't know what to say but he wants to go back home to his room, he says and Sigve says he understands, Asle would rather be alone since his Grandmother just died, he says and then Sigve says that he'll miss Asle, it was a lot nicer for him since Asle moved to Aga, he says, because before Asle came he had no one to talk to or have a beer with, he says, and now things'll go back to how they were before, he says, yes, he'll drink his beers and smoke his cigarettes alone, Sigve says and Asle says again that he's going back to his room and Sigve says well then he'll just stay here alone at his table with his glass of beer and have a good long think about what his next move should be in the chess game, because he needs to send the card tonight, he says and then Sigve says they'll see each other again, wherever it might be, but maybe in Bjørgvin sometime, he says

I'm going home now, Asle says

It's sad about your Grandmother, Sigve says

and he stands up and then Sigve and Asle shake hands and he says bye and then Asle goes home to his room and he notices that he's tired and sad and he thinks again and again that his Grandma is dead now, she is gone forever, he thinks and he thinks that he wants to go lie down right now, and he lies down, but he doesn't fall asleep, because he's thinking the whole time about Grandma who's lying there cold and dead in The Hospice and he thinks that in a week he'll have to go to Barmen and go to her funeral, because she'll be laid to rest in the grave next to Grandpa's, Asle thinks, and he thinks that he needs to get up early tomorrow, he thinks, because the bus leaves at eight o'clock, he thinks and he'll have to make two trips to bring everything to the bus stop, he thinks, so he needs to set the alarm clock for seven, he thinks, and he still has his clothes on, Asle thinks and then he stands up and gets undressed and he sets the alarm clock for seven and then he thinks that he should get the grey blanket Grandma gave him when she was being sent to The Hospice and wrap it tight around him and then he realises that he can't, he's already packed it in the suitcase, wrapped it around the paintings in the suitcase, Asle thinks and I lie there on the bench, and Bragi is lying up next to me, and now it'll be morning soon, and I should have stood up and gone and lit a fire in the stove, I think, but I'm so tired I just can't, I think and I shut my eyes and I see Asle sit up in bed and the alarm clock is ringing and he turns the alarm off and he gets up right away and he puts his clothes on, and he thinks that he has everything packed and ready, he's carried it bit by bit down to the ground floor, now there's nothing left but the sheets, and obviously he has to just roll them up and put them in the burlap sack, he thinks, and the sack is already lying there folded up on the table, and if The Landlady doesn't answer when he rings the bell to drop off the keys he'll just leave them in her mailbox, Asle thinks, but he doesn't have all that much time, he thinks and he rolls up the duvet and the sheet and he pushes the roll down into the sack and then he puts the alarm clock in the sack and he looks at the hotplate he got from Father and he thinks that he'll just leave that behind, he can't drag it along with him and he can't really use it in the room he's renting from Herdis Åsen anyway, Asle thinks and then he turns off the light and he locks the door and he thinks that Grandma died yesterday, that suddenly comes to him, and he feels a surge of loss inside him and he goes down the stairs and he goes and puts the bag outside The Shoemaker's Workshop's door and then he gets his other things and puts them there too, and then he locks the door and he thinks he just has to do everything as he'd planned even if Grandma is dead and he goes and rings The Landlady's doorbell and he stands there waiting and then he hears footsteps and then the door opens

Yes I just wanted to, Asle says

and he holds out the keys

I wanted to drop these off, he says

Yes thank you, The Landlady says

and then there's silence

Good luck in Bjørgvin, she says

I've been to Bjørgvin too, you know, but that was many years ago, she says

Back when I was young, yes, just a girl, she says

and Asle just stands there

Yes, thank you, he says

It was a pleasure to have you living there in The Shoemaker's Workshop, The Landlady says

and Asle holds out his hand and they shake hands and then Asle walks away and he hears The Landlady turn the key in the door and now he takes the boxes first, both of them, and they're pretty heavy, and it's quite a chore to carry them to the bus stop, and then he goes back and gets his easel and burlap sack and it's much easier to carry those and finally he gets the suitcase and then he stands there at the bus stop with everything he owns and he's also a bit worried about whether there'll be room for everything in the luggage area of the bus and he's thinking the whole time that Grandma is dead, she died yesterday and now she's lying there in The Hospice cold and dead, he thinks and the bus comes and Asle holds out his hand and the bus stops and The Bus Driver gets out and he says well now that's quite a load he has with him there, this is a bus, you know, not a truck, a moving truck, he says, but we can always try, he says, and then hope that there aren't too many other people today with so many things, he says and then they put the boxes and the burlap sack and the suitcase and the easel up into the empty baggage area in the back of the bus and The Bus Driver gets into the bus and Asle goes in after him and he says he's going to Bjørgvin and The Bus Driver says so he's moving to Bjørgvin too, almost every single young person from the country is moving to Bjørgvin nowadays, and he doesn't see what's so much better about living there than in some place or another in the country, The Bus Driver says and Asle doesn't say anything and he goes and sits down at the back of the bus like he usually does, in the back seat, and there's just one other passenger, an old woman, and she's sitting all the way in the front, and she looks a little like his Grandma, he thinks, and now Grandma is dead, she's gone forever, he thinks and the bus starts and he looks at The Shoemaker's Workshop and Asle thinks that he forgot to wash up in the room the way The Landlady asked him to, and that's terrible, he thinks, because now it's too late, he thinks and then he looks at The Fjord, and at Gallows Holm out there in The Fjord and he looks across The Fjord, at the mountains on the other side, one mountain behind another in a line reaching back, and all the way at the top of the highest mountain he sees the big white snowdrifts, and above that the sky and it's deep blue today and there are almost no clouds, he thinks, and it's like the sky is his Grandmother, he thinks, but no it's Ales who's the sky, he thinks, because Ales is the sky too above his dead Grandmother, Asle thinks and he feels deep inside that this is his country, his landscape, and it always will be, because he has so so many pictures of this landscape fixed in his mind, some are of the landscape itself but most are of a face, or of people where something or another can somehow be seen in a face, in a movement, in a look, whatever it is, those black boots of Grandfather's in the rain, a dark rowboat on a beach at low tide, a heavy slate slab on a boathouse roof, he thinks and all the pictures are so clear, and he can get rid of them one by one, and all the pictures say something more than themselves, it's impossible to understand, Asle thinks, and they're disturbing, these pictures, he thinks, but it helps to paint, because he always paints one of the pictures he has in his mind, but he never paints it the way it is in his mind, he starts off from it, he makes the silent voice in the picture he has in his head become clearer, he gets what he's seen to say what it wants to say, just clearer, because a painting is a silent voice that speaks, and the voice says that there is a silence that at the same time brings something close, no, now he's thinking beyond his abilities, Asle thinks and he closes his eyes and he hears the engine rumbling and The Bus Driver shifts gears up and down and he notices how the bus moves down the winding roads in short bursts, and every so often the bus stops, or has to move to the side to let another vehicle pass, either a car behind him or a car coming towards him, Asle thinks and he thinks again and again that Grandma's dead now, she's lying there alone now, cold and dead in The Hospice, he thinks and then he thinks about Ales, because now it's she who is the sky over everything in the world, he thinks, yes, Ales is even the sky over his dead Grandmother now, Asle thinks and he doesn't really know what's going to happen, how life will be, but he knows that he wants to paint pictures, and he knows that he wants to get the silence, yes, the silent mute language into the pictures, to make them talk in their silent way, he thinks, and he has to, because that's the only way he can live with all the pictures he has lodged in his mind, he thinks and just today there are at least five, maybe ten, that have lodged there, he can't count them, but his things sitting next to the ground-floor wall of The Shoemaker's Workshop, the arms coming into view when The Landlady opened the door, her face with something moving over it, something came, was there, was gone, all at once, and then the other pictures, how The Bus Driver's body moved when he put the suitcase up into the bus, no he can't tell how many of these pictures have joined the collection he has in his head today, Asle thinks and he closes his eyes and he sees Grandma lying there in bed at The Hospice and her face is grey and light blue, her lips are a different blue, and he's holding her hand and he feels how sleepy he is and yesterday Grandma died, he thinks and he feels grief, you'd have to call it, but maybe he felt more grief when Grandma was driven away from the house, from The Old House, where she'd lived her whole life, to The Hospice, when she handed him the grey blanket, Asle thinks, and he thinks that he doesn't want to tell Ales that his Grandma died yesterday, or he wants to tell her but not today, he thinks and he stretches out on the back seat and half lies down there, and then he must have fallen asleep, because he jolts and sits up and he sees that the bus is pulling into a gate at The Bus Station in Bjørgvin and Asle looks out the window and he sees Ales is there, but she doesn't see him, she's standing on the opposite side of the bus from where he's sitting and Asle gets out of the bus and he goes over to Ales and then she sees him and they go up to each other and they give each other a hug and it feels like they've never been apart, that's how it feels in a way, and it feels safer somehow that they'll be in the same city from now on, Asle thinks and then their mouths find each other, right there at the gate, and then they stand there and kiss and it feels entirely right, and it's like they never want to stop, they let the kiss just go on and on and it's like time doesn't exist, Asle thinks and then he thinks that they can't really just stand here like this kissing in broad daylight and at The Bus Station too, he thinks and I lie there and now the sun must be coming up soon, I think, and it's Little Christmas Eve today and I really have to get up soon, but it's so dark, and it's so cold in the room, I think and I close my eyes and I see Ales and Asle standing in front of 7 University Street and Ales goes and opens the front door and she stands there with the suitcase in one hand and holds the door open with the other and she says she knew the door wouldn't be locked and Asle carries the easel and the two boxes and the burlap sack inside and puts them on the floor under the mailboxes and Ales says it was good they took a taxi, it would have been too much to carry, even though it's not exactly a huge amount to move, and even though it's not that far a walk from The Bus Station, and even though the taxi ride wasn't exactly cheap, she says and she says that it's probably better to carry it upstairs in two trips and then Asle starts walking up the stairs with the two boxes and Ales walks behind him with the suitcase and they don't say anything and then an older man in a hat and coat and with a cane comes walking stiffly down the stairs and he says good day and both Ales and Asle say good day and then they keep going and Ales says that that was a fine example of an older Bjørgviner, a real Bjørgvin man, you don't see many like him around anymore, but when she was a girl there were lots of them, older men always went out in either a hat or a sailor's cap with a visor, she says and they carry the things up from one landing to the next and then they put the things down outside the door with the nameplate saying Herdis Åsen and then they take each other's hands and they go downstairs and Asle lets go of Ales and picks up the easel in one empty hand and the burlap sack in the other and Ales says that she can carry the easel or the sack and Asle says no, he'll carry them himself, he says and then they go back up all the stairs to the sixth floor and Asle puts the easel and sack down and then Ales says that maybe she should leave and wait for him outside and Asle gets almost scared

No you can't leave, Asle says

I can wait outside, Ales says

No, Asle says

and he thinks about the last time, yes, when Ales was gone when he got outside, and doesn't want that to happen again today, he thinks and he thinks that he doesn't want to ask Ales why she left so suddenly last time and wasn't there, it feels wrong to ask, he thinks and he thinks about Grandma, about how she's gone forever now, and he'll tell Ales about that, but not today, he thinks and Asle rings the doorbell and they hear footsteps and the door opens and Asle and Herdis Åsen look straight at each other and she says welcome and she holds out her hand and she and Asle shake hands and he thinks that it's strange that Herdis Åsen sort of doesn't notice Ales, or at least she's acting like she doesn't, and it's like Ales shrinks in on herself and tries to be as small and invisible as she can, she really turns almost invisible, Asle thinks and he feels that Ales doesn't want him to point her out to Herdis Åsen, she wants to be as invisible as she can manage to be and then he sees Herdis Åsen look at Ales and a dislike comes over her face, as though what she was seeing was somehow disgusting, but Herdis Åsen doesn't say a single word, she just looks away from Ales towards Asle and says he should bring his things inside, this wasn't a huge amount for someone moving, she says and she opens the door wider and Asle picks up the two boxes and then he goes inside and Herdis Åsen opens the door next to the front door and she says that this is his room, here it is, his room, his home, so to speak, now the two of them will be sharing house and home, in a way, Herdis Åsen says and she laughs and Asle goes out and gets the easel and burlap sack and Ales says that she'll go downstairs and wait outside, she doesn't feel exactly welcome here, she says and Asle feels anxiety, yes, fear grip him and he says she can't leave and Ales says no, really, she'll wait outside, she absolutely will, she says and then Herdis Åsen is standing in the doorway and she says that she doesn't like rules, not too many rules, but there's one rule that has applied to all the renters she's ever had, and she's had quite a few over the years, and that is that they can't bring girls to the room, she says and then Herdis Åsen looks straight at Ales standing there and Ales looks down and then Asle says this is Ales, his girlfriend and Herdis Åsen doesn't say anything and already she is heading back inside and Ales says she's going to go wait outside now and Asle says that he'll come as soon as he can and Ales nods and then she starts to walk down the stairs and Asle watches her go and he's filled with an unbelievable love like nothing he's ever felt and he hears Herdis Åsen say that he should come inside now and then Asle goes into the entryway and Herdis Åsen says that she already took him through the apartment when he was here before and she'd said what he could and couldn't do, and she doesn't want to go through it again, but anyway he needs to remember to take out the garbage every Wednesday afternoon or evening, that was the most important thing, aside from not having girls in the room, and, well, maybe she forgot to tell him that when he was here, but she takes for granted that people know the rules of proper behaviour, she would have thought they'd go without saying, actually, because otherwise what would her apartment turn into? Herdis Åsen says, there'd be some, she says and she stops short and Asle doesn't say anything and so, yes, so he mustn't lose the keys of course, Herdis Åsen says and she holds up a keyring and she holds up one key on the ring and she says this is for the apartment door, and she holds up another key and she says this is for the street door, and then she holds up a third key and she says this is to his room, but none of her previous renters have ever used it, they left the door to the room unlocked, and in any case there was one thing that was absolutely certain, she would never rummage around in there, in his room, she says and Asle nods and then he walks into the room, into his own rented room, and he says he has his sheets in the burlap sack and Herdis Åsen laughs and says yes yes, yes, you have to carry them in something, why not a burlap sack? she says and then she says that he should just get settled in and then she says that she's baked a cake and would love to offer him cake and coffee and then a glass of wine afterwards would be nice to celebrate his moving in, she says, yes, once he's relaxed a bit, made himself at home a bit, they'd have a little celebration, Herdis Åsen says and Asle says thank you, thanks so much, but his girlfriend is standing outside waiting for him, he says

So, you have a girlfriend? Herdis Åsen says

Yes, Asle says

and Herdis Åsen shakes her head and she says that she's stayed away from that sort of thing her whole life, she'd managed to get through life unmarried and if there was one thing she was proud of it was probably that, she says, but the cake will keep, so later, tonight, if he doesn't spend too long mooning around with that girlfriend of his, he's welcome to have a little welcome party, she says, and in the worst case, if he can't get rid of that female of his, yes, she hopes he forgives her for talking like this, they can just have their welcome party tomorrow, because the cake will keep until tomorrow, Herdis Åsen says and she turns around and Asle sees her cross the hall and go into the living room and then he leaves the apartment and he finds his key and he locks the door behind him and then he runs as fast as he can down the stairs, he jumps down the stairs and he thinks as long as Ales is there now, and she's not gone like last time, he'd thought so many times about why she didn't wait for him that time, but he didn't, and doesn't, want to ask Ales why she didn't wait for him, Asle thinks and he thinks that the thing about not being allowed to have girls in the room was definitely just something Herdis Åsen came up with on the spot when she saw Ales, because it didn't exactly seem like the two of them liked each other very much, no, Herdis Åsen didn't like Ales and Ales didn't like Herdis Åsen, and it must have been because she didn't like Ales for whatever reason that Herdis Åsen brought up this rule, this rule of proper behaviour as she put it, that he wasn't allowed to have girls in the room, Asle thinks, and Herdis Åsen wasn't exactly insulted when he said that Ales was waiting for him outside but she was a little sorry, somehow, he'd noticed that, Asle thinks, and of course it was stupid that she'd baked a cake and everything, and bought wine, and then he just left without letting them have the moving-in party she'd planned, Asle thinks, but he's going to eat cake and drink coffee and wine with Herdis Åsen tomorrow instead, because now he wants to see Ales again, Asle thinks as he jumps down the stairs and goes out the front door and then he sees Ales standing there on the pavement and a lightness comes over him like pure happiness and Ales looks straight at him and Ales says that he can't stay living there at Herdis Åsen's for long if she can't come see him and Asle says that Herdis Åsen hadn't said anything about that before when he came and looked at the room, when it was being decided if he'd rent the room or not, he says and I lie there on the bench, and it's dark in the room, but I'm sure that it's morning now, and today is Saturday and it's Little Christmas Eve, I think and now I need to get up, and I can't remember ever having put on my long black coat and gone and lain down on the bench without getting undressed, just spreading the grey blanket over me, I think and I think that I'm so tired so tired, it's like I can only just stand up, because I didn't get to sleep at all, I think, and it's so cold in the room and I can't bear to light the stove, but I have my coat on and it's good against the cold and Bragi's lying here next to me, curled tight against me and I've spread the grey blanket over us both and I think that I'm so tired so tired and I close my eyes and I see Asle walking down the hall in The Student Home and he's thinking he told Siv they'd talk tomorrow and he said goodbye and Siv didn't answer and then he went to the bus stop as fast as he could without running and then he took the bus to The Student Home, Asle thinks and he walks down the hall to the apartment he and Liv are renting at The Student Home and he hears a baby crying and crying and he walks down the hall and the crying gets louder and he unlocks the door to the apartment he and Liv are renting at The Student Home and it's The Boy who's crying and he goes into the bedroom and he sees The Boy lying there alone in the middle of the double bed with his arms and legs stretched out to the sides and Asle picks him up and holds him close and he rubs The Boy's back and the crying gets softer and then he starts to walk with The Boy around the bedroom and he goes into the living room and he can't see Liv anywhere, maybe she just went out and left The Boy lying all alone? Asle thinks, but she can't have done that, can she? he thinks and he doesn't understand why Liv isn't home and The Boy cries and cries and Asle goes into the bathroom and Liv is lying there on the floor and Asle bends down and he shakes her and she doesn't wake up and Asle puts his hand up to her mouth and he checks if she's breathing and she's breathing but just barely and The Boy is screaming like never before and Asle is like a pole of fear and what should he do? and he shakes Liv's shoulder again, and she doesn't wake up, and he tries to open her eyelids and they fall back closed and he takes a glass of cold water and he throws water in her face and she just lies there like nothing happened and then he sees there's an empty pillbox on the washstand and he thinks Liv took all the pills that were in the box and he thinks he has to call for an ambulance, now, right away, and The Boy cries and cries and Asle strokes his back and he says shh, calm down, Papa's home now, quiet down now like a good boy just quiet down now, Asle says and he says to himself that he has to take everything calmly and I lie there on the bench and I think that it's morning now, yes, definitely, and it's Little Christmas Eve today, I think, so I'll just get up now, but before I get up I want to pray and I cross myself and then I take out the rosary I have hanging around my neck, under my sweater, the rosary I got from Ales once and I hold the brown wooden cross between my thumb and index finger and I say inside myself Pater noster Qui es in cælis Sanctificetur nomen tuum Adveniat regnum tuum Fiat voluntas tua sicut in cælo et in terra Panem nostrum cotidianum da nobis hodie et dimitte nobis debita nostra sicut et nos dimittimus debitoribus nostris Et ne nos inducas in tentationem sed libera nos a malo and I move my thumb and index finger up to the first bead and I say Our Father Who art in heaven Hallowed be thy name Thy kingdom come Thy will be done on earth as it is in heaven Give us this day our daily bread and forgive us our trespasses as we forgive those who trespass against us And lead us not into temptation but deliver us from evil and I move my thumb and index finger back down and I hold onto the brown wooden cross and then I say, again and again inside myself, while I breathe in deeply Lord and while I breathe out slowly Jesus and while I breathe in deeply Christ and while I breathe out slowly Have mercy and while I breathe in deeply On me

VII

And I see myself standing there looking at the painting in the pile with the stretcher facing out, it's morning and I got up and turned on the light in the room, but I still have my black coat on, and Bragi is next to me, and I think that today is Saturday and it's Little Christmas Eve and I look at the stretcher of the outermost painting in the stack and *St Andrew's Cross* is painted on the stretcher in thick black oil paint, impasto, they call it, and I think again that I don't want to keep these paintings that I don't think are totally finished here in the main room anymore, because strictly speaking they are finished, or as finished as they'll ever be, they're as finished as I can make them, I think and I think that I don't have any desire to paint anymore, yes, I have a real aversion to even the thought of painting anymore and I don't understand what changed so suddenly inside me, because it used to be that I had to paint, not just to support myself but to get rid of all these pictures lodged in my head, I think and I realise that there are still pictures in my head but I also realise that they are about to fade away on their own, they are about to come together into one slow picture that doesn't need to be painted and won't be and can't be, yes, the pictures are about to come together into a stillness, a calm silence, I think and I feel filled with something like peace, it's strange how suddenly something can change, I think and I think that I want to carry the stack of paintings that I thought I wasn't done with but that actually I am done with up to the attic and put them with the paintings I've set aside in the storage space in one of the attic rooms, and that I go up to the attic to look at now and then when I get stuck and can't paint, and then I've always had one of those pictures out, leaning against the back of a chair between the two little windows, in the middle, under the peak of the gable, I think and I see that there are five paintings I thought I wasn't finished with, and all of them are big, or among the bigger ones, because usually I have two stacks there, one with bigger paintings and one with smaller paintings, with my leather shoulder bag hanging between the two stacks, on its peg, but now there's just one stack in the middle, under the shoulder bag, and then I take the pictures under my arms and go up to the attic and I look at the portrait of Ales that's leaning against the back of the chair there between the two little windows in the gable, and then I go into the storage space and I put the pictures down, leaning them against the other pictures that are stacked there, and now there are nine pictures there in all, all with their stretchers facing out, so there were only four pictures along with the portrait of Ales that I kept and didn't want to sell, I think and two of them are some of the first pictures I painted, I think, so now I have nine paintings I can sell, that's enough for one more exhibition, but only one, I think, and the portrait of Ales is the only picture I want to keep, I think and I think that I committed to one exhibition in six months at The Kleinheinrich Gallery in Oslo, but Beyer has all the pictures they need for that, paintings that weren't sold in Bjørgvin, and strangely enough several of them are some of the best pictures I've painted, in my opinion, and in Beyer's opinion too, and then there's an exhibition planned in Nidaros, at The Huysmann Gallery, and they've been talking about that forever, yes, almost as long as I've known Beyer, I think, and Beyer's been keeping for that show the paintings that didn't sell in Bjørgvin or in Oslo, and truth be told they are all some of the best I've ever painted, so the pictures I have up in the storage space will be for my next and last exhibition at The Beyer Gallery, I think, and then it's over, my exhibition next year will be the last one I have at The Beyer Gallery, and the pictures I've painted that Beyer will have to sell off after the exhibition will be the ones that weren't sold in Oslo or in Nidaros or that won't have sold in next year's exhibition at The Beyer Gallery, I think, and, I think, yes, I can just take all the pictures I have stored now and bring them to Beyer's right away, he called me a few days ago and told me that we were selling well this year, and that there were just three pictures that hadn't sold, he said, and he thought they'd get sold before he closed the gallery for Christmas Eve day, or in any case on one of the days between Christmas and New Year's, so I'd made a nice sum of money, he said, and then I'll probably make some more money from the three exhibitions I still have planned, I think and I've always lived modestly and set aside part of my money, so I won't starve even if I stop painting, I think and I think that I paid membership dues to the Norway Artists Association every year, and they give out stipends, but I've never applied for one, because I never needed to, but maybe I can apply for one too and even get one, since I've never applied for one before, that's why I never got one, aside from the artist's stipend I got when I went to The Art School, I think, because there are various stipends you can apply for, and I believe there's a stipend for deserving older artists too, and I guess that's what I am now, I'm older anyway, however deserving I might be, yes, well, opinions vary on that, but now do the members, or some of the members, of the Norway Artists Association think I deserve their support, well, no, I don't think so, they probably think I don't, they probably think I've been a hack my whole life who's just smeared up paintings for money, yes, I'm afraid that's how they see me as a painter, but anyway I can apply for a stipend from the Norway Artists Association, it's worth a try, and then I'm also a member of something called West Norway Artists, and I think they also have a little money in stipends to give out, and in that case I can apply for a stipend from them too, I think and it won't be that many years before I can collect a pension, and I'm really looking forward to that, getting money every month whether I do anything or not, anyway I'll probably be one of the people who gets the lowest amount but that'll be more than enough for me, I think, because if I stop painting and I don't need to buy painting supplies anymore then I won't have big expenses at all, and it'll be good to get a little money regularly every month, because to tell the truth I've never had that happen to me in my whole life, I've painted pictures to sell them and that's how I made the money I needed, I think, and I have everything I need, the house is mine, and I have a good car, a car I bought only around five years ago, so I'll have it as long as I live, or as long as I'm still allowed to drive, I think and it feels good to think that I'm not going to paint anymore, that it's over, that I've done my part, what I wanted to do was paint and I painted, year after year, and all those years I was actually painting away at the same picture, and the closer I got to my own picture deep inside me the better I painted, and these unfinished pictures are really most likely finished too, in their way, yes, in fact precisely because they're not finished, because it doesn't feel right to stop when something's finished since my inner pictures in their own picture are always pointing towards something beyond themselves, there is a kind of longing for afar in all the pictures, and at the same time what the pictures are yearning for is always in them already, I think and I stay there looking at the picture of Ales, I haven't painted many portraits, just this one of Ales plus one more, I think, because back when I lived in Herdis Åsen's apartment I painted a portrait of her and was paid well for it, we agreed that I could not pay rent for six months as payment for the picture, and since I moved out after just a couple of weeks I was paid in cash instead, and the picture of Herdis Åsen wasn't so terrible either, it was a bit forced, a bit fake in a way, but the portrait I painted of Ales is just how she was, how she was with her light, I think and it's also the only picture I'm going to keep, not because it's a picture I painted but because it's a picture of Ales, I think, because I only painted that one portrait of Ales and I did that after I'd painted the portrait of Herdis Åsen and Ales didn't like that I'd painted a portrait of Herdis Åsen and not of her, I think and I stand there and look at the portrait of Ales and I go and sit down in the chair I have up there a few steps away from the chair where I have the picture leaning against the back, and I look at the portrait of Ales and I see Asle running down the stairs from the room he's renting now at 7 University Street and he thinks that it was kind of too bad that Herdis Åsen had baked a cake and sort of prepared a moving-in party and then he just left, but Ales is on the street outside waiting for him, isn't she, and the only thing Asle wants is to see Ales again, to be with her, he thinks and he goes out the front door and he doesn't see Ales anywhere, no matter where he looks, and a feeling of despair starts to come over him and he thinks no, she can't have just left, no, not again, no, not this time too, no, not that, Asle thinks and then he hears Ales shout Asle and then he sees her sitting on a bench a little way up University Street, there's something like a little park there, and Asle runs over to Ales and he sits down next to her and she puts her arm around his shoulders and she says no, he can't live there, in that room there, the landlady there is totally impossible, and it was pretty obvious that she couldn't stand her, Ales says, it was like she'd done something terrible to her even though they'd never seen each other before, not that she can remember anyway, Ales says, no, she's never seen her before, she says, and then she looked rather slovenly, like a drunk, yes, like an old tart, to be honest, Ales says and that comes as a surprise to Asle, he'd never thought anything like that about Herdis Åsen, he saw her more like an educated older lady, maybe she did drink rather a lot, she certainly smoked too much, that's for sure, he practically never saw her without a cigarette in one hand and an ashtray in the other, and she always took very deep drags of her cigarette, he thinks and Ales says the smell, yes, it stank of old alcohol, and perfume, and smoke pouring out into the main stairwell of the building, she says, no, he can't live there, but she, yes, she might be able to find him another place to live, Ales says and she puts her other hand on Asle's belly and then he puts his arm around her shoulders and then they sit there with their arms around each other and then Ales brings her mouth over to his ear and then she whispers to him

Asle and Ales, she whispers

and he whispers into her ear

Ales and Asle, he whispers

and she says that it's strange that they have such similar names, the letters are the same, you just have to move them around a little

And neither name's all that common either, she says

Ales isn't anyway, Asle says

and she says that Asle may be more common than Ales, but she doesn't know anyone else named either Asle or Ales, so both names are pretty unusual, she says and Asle says that he doesn't think he knows anyone else named either Ales or Asle either and I sit and look at the portrait I painted of Ales and I think that I can drive all the pictures I have here that are done to The Beyer Gallery as soon as today, because even the ones I thought of as unfinished are actually finished, but I won't sell the portrait of Ales, I think and I look at the portrait of Ales and I see Ales and Asle cross a street and Ales says that the street is called Canon Street and she points and says there's St Paul's Church, and she's been there a lot, because her mother Judit was and is a believing baptised Christian, yes, Catholic, and she's Catholic too, Ales says, yes, so now he knows, she says and later they'll need to go into the church, maybe even today, she says and then she gives Asle a sudden kiss on the cheek and then she says look, The Bus Station's over there, and there's the sign for The Bus Café, she says and she points to it and she says that surely he remembers and she laughs and Asle says that if there's one thing in the world he remembers it's that, he says, yes, that's for sure, he says and Ales says that they should go back there together sometime, but now she wants them to go to Ridge Street, because that's where she lives, with her mother Judit, at 29 Ridge Street, she's lived there her whole life, Ales says and it's not far from here, she says and Asle feels afraid, feels a kind of terror and Ales asks doesn't he want them to go to Ridge Street

Don't you want to see where I live? Ales says

Yeah, Asle says

But, he says

But what? she says

I'm kind of afraid to meet your mother Judit, he says

and Asle says that he doesn't know why but he doesn't feel like meeting her mother Judit, not today, there has already been so much today, he says and Ales says that they don't need to go into the house if he doesn't want to, they can do that later, some other day, and he can meet her mother Judit then, and then Ales can show him her pictures, she says and she is so looking forward to seeing his pictures, she says

They're in the old suitcase, Asle says

And if it weren't for that Herdis Åsen woman I could see your pictures today, Ales says

Yes, Asle says

and he and Ales keep walking and Ales says he can't stay in that room in Herdis Åsen's apartment and Asle thinks that he could have taken the suitcase with him and shown Ales his paintings outside, but he didn't think of it, he thinks

I can bring my suitcase of paintings outside, he says

That would be too ridiculous, Ales says

and then she says that there, over there, where Ridge Street starts, and she points and then they start to cross Ridge Street and Asle lets go of Ales's hand and she says he doesn't need to worry about her mother seeing them, she's at work, so he can feel free to hold her hand, she says and Asle takes her hand and then she holds his hand tight and they cross Ridge Street hand in hand and Ales points to a nice white old wooden house, the kind there are so many of in Bjørgvin, yes, Bjørgvin houses they call them, and she says that that's where she lives, and he remembers the address right? she says

29 Ridge Street, Asle says

Not bad, Ales says

and Asle says no not bad at all and Ales says that he doesn't need to come home with her today, even if her mother Judit isn't home, but before long he'll have to come look at her pictures and meet her mother, her mother Judit, she says

But not today, Asle says

We can wait a little, he says

Yes, Ales says

and they keep walking and Ales says that now they can go to The Bjørgvin Museum of Art, because there are lots of good pictures to see there, she says, but actually they could maybe do that another day, because now they're pretty near The Beyer Gallery, they just need to go up the next street, with the fitting name, Steep Street, and then they'll be up on High Street and that's where The Beyer Gallery is, which is without question the most important gallery in Bjørgvin, and there's a show there now of paintings by Eiliv Pedersen, yes, he was reading the review by Anne Sofie Grieg of that show in *The Bjørgvin Times* at The Bus Café, yes, the first time they met, and the only time they met before today, Ales says and she says that it was a tremendous review and Asle says that he really wants to see Eiliv Pedersen's pictures so nothing would be better than going to The Beyer Gallery, he says and Ales says that most of the reviews have been positive, almost too much in her opinion, there was something hollow about them, but he, Eiliv Pedersen, is the one that Asle is going to have as his painting teacher at The Art School, she says, and he's a very good painter in her opinion, Asle mustn't misunderstand what she's saying, he is without question the best painter living and working in Bjørgvin, a leading light, and The Beyer Gallery is without a doubt the best gallery in Bjørgvin, she says, it's one of the most important galleries in all of Norway even, yes, aside from being made Arts Festival Artist at The Arts Festival in Bjørgvin and having an Arts Festival Exhibition, having a show at

The Beyer Gallery might be the most prestigious place you can have a show in the whole country, Ales says and she doesn't believe that she herself will ever have an exhibition there but maybe Asle will have an exhibition there someday, she believes that, actually she's sure of it, she just knows it, Ales says, and Beyer himself is often there in his gallery, so if they're lucky he'll have a chance to meet Beyer today, she says, and she and her parents have gone to The Beyer Gallery ever since she was a girl because her parents were friends with Beyer, he's a widower and lives alone so it sometimes happened that he came over to their house for Christmas Eve, and when Ales and her mother Judit went to celebrate Midnight Mass in St Paul's Church Beyer and Father stayed home with their drinks, yes, that's how it was, Ales says, and only when she and her mother Judit came back home did Beyer go back to his own place and to his art, as he would say, because he had no other faith, no other religion besides art, Beyer liked to say, Ales says and she says that she must have seen every exhibition they've had at The Beyer Gallery since she was seven years old or somewhere around there, she says, and at home they have several paintings by Eiliv Pedersen, Ales says as she and Asle walk hand in hand and then she says that now it's not far to walk before they get to The Beyer Gallery, they can even see the building now, and she points to a big white wooden building up ahead, with a big parking lot in front of it, and big windows facing the street

Beyer lives upstairs, Ales says

And the gallery's downstairs, she says

He lives alone, he has ever since his wife died, she says

and then Ales and Asle walk hand in hand towards The Beyer Gallery and Ales opens the door and they go inside and then they stand there holding each other's hands and Asle sees that a man is sitting at a heavy old brownish desk at the back of the room and Ales whispers that that's Beyer and Asle thinks no, it can't be him! he can't believe the man sitting there is the one who bought so many of his pictures when he was a boy with a show at The Barmen Youth Centre, Asle thinks and he's barely changed at all in the years since, he thinks and Beyer looks at them and he stands up and he goes over to Ales and he says it's nice that she wants to see the Eiliv Pedersen exhibition again, and it's nice that you've got a boyfriend, he says and Ales says yes and then Beyer looks at Asle and he says he has a feeling that, yes, yes, he's seen him before, yes, now he remembers, Beyer says, you're the boy who had an exhibition at The Barmen Youth Centre several years ago and I bought five of your paintings, yes, now he remembers! no, is it really you! Beyer says and he holds out his hand to Asle and he shakes Asle's hand and Beyer asks if Asle has started at The Art School now and Asle says well he's about to and Beyer says that he's sure he'll do well because there was a lot of talent in the five pictures he bought that time and to tell the truth he has them hanging in his own apartment, every one of them, Beyer says and he says that they'll be talking again many times in the future, you can be sure of that, he says and then he holds out his hand to Asle again and they shake hands and Beyer holds Asle's hand for a long time and then he says that now they should look at all the paintings and neither Ales nor Asle says anything and Beyer goes and sits back down behind his desk and Ales and Asle go from picture to picture and Asle thinks that Eiliv Pedersen is really getting at something in his pictures, something he's never seen in the work of other painters, and he can't quite understand what it is he's getting at, and he does it almost without using colours, just a little blue or green maybe, or pink, otherwise it's all grey and white and black, yes, there's a muffled black colour in most of the paintings, Asle thinks and Ales asks him if he likes the pictures and he says yes, yes, they're really good, he says and Ales says yeah, yes, she likes them too, but there's something like a distance in the pictures, and she can't quite get on board with that, she says and they walk towards the door and then Beyer calls out we'll talk soon, we'll talk soon, no, wait a second, he

642 Jon Fosse

calls out and he comes walking over to them and he tells Ales that it was nice of her to come in for another look at the Eiliv Pedersen show, yes, Pedersen rarely exhibits but one of the first exhibitions he ever held in his gallery, Beyer says, was of paintings by Eiliv Pedersen, he says and he looks at Asle and he says that he remembers it well, he says, it was hard to sell even a single picture, the people who bought art in Bjørgvin back then were extremely tied to traditional ways of judging what was a good picture or a bad picture, but eventually their eyes were opened to Eiliv Pedersen so after a few years all the pictures from the first exhibition had sold, and this time the paintings all sold the first day, but like always he'd given some buyers the right of first refusal, because the best customers and art collectors get their pictures in advance, you need to take good care of your good customers, Beyer says, and they, these select good customers, and friends, he might add, had seen the exhibition the night before the opening and by the end of that night more than half the pictures had been sold already and the rest sold before the first day they officially went on sale, damn if they didn't, he's never seen anything like it, Beyer says and Ales says that since Asle's going to start at The Art School, in Painting, she thought she'd show him the exhibition by the painter who's going to be his teacher, she says

You'll have the best teacher you can have in Eiliv Pedersen, Beyer says

No, it was so nice to see you again, he says

and then Beyer says that he'd really like to see Asle's paintings when the time comes and Asle says thank you, and that he has some finished paintings in an old suitcase he brought with him to Bjørgvin and Beyer starts to laugh and Ales says that Asle got into The Art School without an examen artium, she says, he got in because of those pictures, she says and Asle nods and Beyer remembers it well, he says, he hated high school too, so he can certainly understand why Asle would have dropped out of high school, and in that case the pictures Asle has already painted must really be good, otherwise he wouldn't have been admitted into The Art School with just them, Beyer says and he says that it must have been Eiliv Pedersen who thought that Asle should start at The Art School, but Asle probably doesn't remember the name of the person he showed his pictures to, Beyer says and Asle says yes he doesn't remember

No, it was really great seeing you again, Beyer says

But now I shouldn't keep you any longer, he says

and then Beyer says that he'll always be more than happy to look at Asle's pictures and Asle says he really appreciates that, thank you, and he says that he can bring the suitcase to the gallery sometime and Beyer laughs and says he should definitely do that and Ales says yes, really, she and Asle will come by one of these days with the suitcase and Beyer says that he means it they should

It was really unbelievable seeing you again, Beyer says

Time just flies by, he says

The last time I saw you you were just a boy, and now here you are as a grown man, he says

and then Beyer says goodbye and that they need to come show him Asle's paintings as soon as they can and then Beyer goes and sits back down behind his desk and Asle stays standing there looking at a picture

Should we go, Ales says

I just want to look at the pictures a little more, Asle says

and then Ales and Asle go over to one painting again and then the door opens and a woman with medium-length blonde hair comes in and it's like something comes over Ales and she tugs a little on Asle's hand and then they go to the front door and then they leave and Ales says that there's something she doesn't like about that woman, with the medium-length blonde hair, she runs into her so often, and the way she looked at Asle, looked at him like she'd fallen in love with him, to be honest, she saw that too, Ales says and Asle says he didn't notice and Ales says that was probably because he was so busy looking at the pictures and he says that he really liked Eiliv Pedersen's paintings, he's never seen anything like them, the pictures were really well painted, he says, and it's hard to believe there are so many greys, he says, because all the pictures were done in all grey, and then a little black in some places, and a little pink, and then the brushstrokes, they looked accidental in their absolutely precise movements, they were incredibly good paintings and almost all of them were of a woman sitting by a window, and all were entirely their own thing in a way, they were their own world, they all had this invisible thing that became visible in them, but in a different way in each different picture

I wonder who that woman is, Ales says

Unbelievably good pictures, Asle says

I run into her all the time, Ales says

I don't understand, she says

And I've never liked her, and then the way she looked at you, she says

I'm lucky I'm going to have Eiliv Pedersen as my teacher, Asle says

and Ales and Asle cross High Street and Asle says that the paintings were awfully expensive and still they all sold, he says and Ales says he'd already met Beyer before and Asle says it's a stupid story, but when he was a boy he put on an exhibition in The Barmen Youth Centre, yes, he grew up in Barmen before he moved to Aga to go to The Academic High School, and Beyer was passing through and he stopped and came in and looked at the paintings and then he bought five of them, and then it was Beyer's relatives or friends who bought the rest, he says, but he had no idea that the man buying the pictures, whose name he didn't even remember, ran a gallery in Bjørgvin, or maybe he hadn't even said his name at the time, the thought hadn't ever crossed his mind and he almost couldn't believe his eyes when he saw the man he'd sold five paintings to sitting there behind the desk, he says and Ales says that Beyer would never have done that, bought his paintings, yes, if he hadn't thought very highly of them, she says, and didn't he also say that he had the pictures hanging in his apartment, she says, and that's saying something, she says and she says that every single one of Eiliv Pedersen's paintings has already sold, and that's how it almost always is at The Beyer Gallery, Beyer almost always manages to sell all the pictures in an exhibition, yes, he could probably sell anything, she says, but they say, and it's true, she knows it's true, she says, that a picture with a slip of paper underneath it saying Sold may not actually be sold, it's so that the people in the gallery will believe that there's a lot of interest in the pictures, because the next day there won't be a slip of paper there and there'll often be a slip of paper saying Sold under a different picture, yes, she's seen that herself, many times, because she often went to see the same exhibition several times, Ales says, but now why is she telling him about that, Ales says and then she says that she doesn't understand why she always feels uncomfortable when she runs into that woman with the medium-length blonde hair, the one who came into the gallery, she says and they turn left and Asle sees a sign that says The Lane and Ales says that he probably remembers that they went down this little alley the last time he was in Bjørgvin, when they met for the first time, she says and she says that Asle will definitely like going to The Coffeehouse, lots of artists go there during the day, but never in the evening, because they don't sell beer or wine at The Coffeehouse, and there are lots of people from the countryside there too, people waiting to take the express ferry either north or south and Asle says that he'd love to go to The Coffeehouse, and he says wow this is a narrow lane and Ales says yes it's not called The Lane for nothing, she says, and when they get to the bottom of The Lane Ales points to the intersection to the right and says that over there, a little way down the side street, is The Country Inn, and on the ground floor, with a view of The Wharf, is The Coffeehouse, so they're almost there, she says and Ales and Asle walk hand in hand over to The Coffeehouse and it's totally empty and Ales goes to a table all the way in the back, in a nook by a window, and with a view of The Wharf, and Asle puts his brown leather shoulder bag down on a chair at the table and then they go over to the counter and Ales says she'll have a cup of black coffee and Asle pours coffee for both of them and then puts a little milk in his cup and then he says that he's kind of hungry, so he'd be happy to get something to eat, maybe an open-faced ground-beef sandwich, he says and Ales says that she's not hungry and Asle tells the woman sitting at the cash register that he'd like an open-faced ground-beef sandwich

Then that's what you'll get, she says

I'll bring it over in a minute and the silverware's over there, she says and Asle pays and Ales is already on her way back to the table they'd picked and Asle gets a knife and fork and a napkin and follows her and Ales sits down with her back to the room so that she's looking straight out at the street or diagonally out at The Wharf and she says that this is her favourite place to sit, at this table, and with her back turned to the other customers, if there are any, and even if there aren't, but there'll be plenty of customers here soon, because it's getting close to the time when people come to The Coffeehouse to get lunch, and there are some customers who eat lunch at The Coffeehouse practically every day, Ales says and Asle says that he'll probably start coming to The Coffeehouse a lot

Yes, Ales says

I thought so, she says

and she says that she thought she wanted to live outside of Bjørgvin, and that, if they have children, she says and she stops and she blushes and she says yes so if she ever becomes a mother and she gives a little laugh and then they sit there and Ales puts her arms on the table and reaches out towards Asle and he takes her hands and then they sit there like that for a moment before taking a little sip of their coffees and Ales says that she so likes sitting in The Coffeehouse and looking out at The Wharf, at the fishing boats being moored and unmoored, at the people walking past, at the express ferries docked there, just sitting like this and looking, and it often rains, but not today, and that's probably because Asle moved to Bjørgvin today, Ales says and she says that today is one of the great days, one of the days when something happens, yes, an event, because it's so strange, day after day goes by and it's like time is just passing, but then something happens, and when it happens the time passes slowly, and the time that passes slowly doesn't disappear, it becomes, yes, a kind of event, so actually there are two kinds of time, the time that just passes and that really matters only so that daily life can move along its course and then the other time, the actual time, which is made up of events, and that time can last, can become lasting, Ales says and she says that that's how her mother Judit talks about it, how she divides up time, she says, because she and her mother Judit talk about all kinds of things together, Ales says and Asle thinks that his Grandmother died yesterday, but he doesn't want to tell Ales that, not now, he thinks and Ales says here she is babbling away and Asle says that he thinks he understands what she means and then Ales makes the sign of the cross sitting there and Asle has never seen anyone make the sign of the cross before and Ales says that now they're boyfriend and girlfriend

Yes, says Asle

Ales and Asle, he says

Asle and Ales, she says

and Asle looks up and he sees the woman who was sitting at the register come over to their table with an open-faced ground-beef sandwich and she hands it to him and he starts eating right away and he says that it tastes really good, and that he's very hungry, he says and Ales says that the ground-beef sandwiches and the meatballs are both good at The Coffeehouse, they sure know how to make them, she says and Asle asks if she wants some and she says no thanks and then he silently keeps eating and then he looks up and he sees the woman with the medium-length blonde hair, the one who came into The Beyer Gallery, walk in the door of The Coffeehouse and she takes off her scarf and drapes it over the back of a chair at a table by a window a few tables away from them and Ales asks what is it and she says he doesn't need to say it, she knows already, and then Ales turns around and she tells Asle she knew it, and now she's standing there staring at him, fuck, that woman, Ales says and Asle quickly eats up the rest of his open-faced sandwich and drinks up the rest of his coffee and he says he can tell Ales wants to leave and she says yes and they get up and Asle puts his leather shoulder bag back on and then they head straight for the door and Asle can tell that the woman with the medium-length blonde hair is looking at him but he doesn't look back and when they get outside Ales says of course, of course she had to show up and had to look at him with eyes full of admiration like she was in love, she says and Asle says that he didn't look at her and Ales says no why would he and then they stand there outside The Country Inn and Ales asks if he wants her to walk him back to his rented room and Asle says that if he's going to go back to his room she basically has to come with him because otherwise he'll never find it, he says and then Ales throws her arms around him and then Ales and Asle stand there in front of The Country Inn hugging each other and I sit there in the chair and I look at the portrait of Ales that's leaning against the back of the other chair and I think that I can't drive the pictures down to Beyer today, because it's Little Christmas Eve today and tomorrow on Christmas Eve Åsleik and I are taking The Boat to Øygna, up by Instefjord, so I probably need to pack soon and get ready, and the dog, yes, what about the dog? what should I do with Bragi? yes, I hadn't thought of him, but obviously he has to come with me, because he can't just stay home alone here, no, impossible, I think and I stand up and I go downstairs and I go into the main room and I see Bragi lying there on the bench and I call him and then he comes shuffling over to me and I think that he's showing his age, the dog too, he has lots of grey hairs around his snout, in the fur on his body too in some places, yes, he's so old now that he can barely manage to stand totally steady on his feet after he's been sleeping, I think and then I stroke his back and I think that now I need to light the stove soon, warm up the room, and even the electric heater is off, even though it's so cold, I think and so I have to take off my black coat and hang it where it goes in the hall, and just think, I slept on the bench last night, in my coat, no, that's just not right, and I can't remember ever having done that before, I think and so I need to pack, I think and there's probably not much I need to bring, but I do need to dress up a bit for Christmas Eve, put on a suit and tie, I think and I go into the bedroom and I take down my old suitcase, the same one I brought with me when I moved to the rented room, and that belonged to my grandparents, the one that carried my paintings that I brought with me when I was trying to get admitted to The Art School, and when I moved to Bjørgvin, and I carried them in this same suitcase when I went to show my paintings to Beyer, I think and I take the suitcase down from the top shelf and lay it on the bed and I open it and then I put a suit and white shirt and tie in the suitcase, then I put my nice shoes that are in a black bag into the suitcase, and there's probably not much more that I need to take, I think, yes well the book I'm in the middle of, I need to bring that, and once again I'm reading Meister Eckhart and the book I'm reading now is called *Unity with God*, I just started it, but it really is worth reading even though I hardly understand anything, neither of Meister Eckhart, whom I've read again and again over all these years, nor of life, or maybe I should read Meister Eckhart's *From Whom God Hid Nothing* again, I think, but I can just take both, and aside from those two books I'll only take a toothbrush and toothpaste, but I need to pack that in the morning, I haven't brushed my teeth yet today, I think and I shut the suitcase and then I carry the suitcase into the main room and I put it down between the hall door and the kitchen door, where the stack of unfinished paintings used to be, and under the peg where my brown leather shoulder bag is hanging, and I stand and look at my chair on the left by the round table and I look at Ales's chair and I see her sitting there, I think and I go sit down in my chair and I look at the fixed spot I always like to look at in the water, my landmark, the tops of the fir trees in front of my house go in the middle of the middle windowpane in the right-hand part, because the window is divided in half, and it can be opened from either side, and each half of the window is divided into three panes, and it's the middle third in the right-hand half that needs to line up with the tops of the fir trees, that's how I take my bearings, and I look and look at my spot in the Sygne Sea and I notice that Ales is sitting in her chair next to me and she's holding her hand out to me and I take her hand and I look at my spot out there in the water, I look at the waves and I see Ales and Asle walking, hand in hand, over to St Paul's Church, because Ales has said that they should go into the church, they have to do that, she said, because for her there is so much of life bound up with the church and nothing but the church, and it's not an especially big and grand church, it's definitely not a cathedral, it's just a small and rather dark church, but there are so few Catholics in Bjørgvin, actually in all of Norway, that they didn't need to build a big church and didn't have the money to either, Ales says and she says that she was baptised in this church and went to first communion here

That means when you go to the altar for the first time, she says

Yes, first communion, she says

I've never been to a first communion, Asle says

and Ales says that right over there, he can see it, yes, there's The Bus Café, she says, and the day they met was the first time she'd been in there, like she said, she'd walked past it lots of times and then she decided she wanted to see what it was like inside, because The Bus Café doesn't exactly have a great reputation, the rumours are that women sell their bodies in there and stuff like that, but that's at night, Ales says, and the fact that she would go into The Bus Café on just that day, at just the time Asle was there too, so that they could meet, no, it couldn't be an accident, there was providence in it, God's providence, it was predestined, Ales says and Asle hears what she's saying and he can sort of understand what she means, maybe, but he can't follow all of it, even if, strangely, ever since he met Ales he's noticed that he's been thinking about something like God's nearness, but that doesn't need any church, any first communion, it doesn't need any God who became man and was crucified and died and rose up from the dead and was taken up to Heaven by the God he in a way also was, because he was God, yes, part of God, he didn't really need any other God to take him up to Heaven, Asle thinks and he says that he'll have to go to mass with her sometime and Ales says yes, they should, but there's no mass happening now at St Paul's Church, but she'd still like to go inside the church with him, because the church is always open, she says and they go up the steps to St Paul's Church and Ales lets go of Asle's hand and she opens the door to the church and Asle walks in and it's totally dark in the church, and all the way in the back left corner, under a statue of the Virgin Mary with the child Jesus in her arms, there are a lot of little candles burning and at the front of The Church there is a little red light, behind the altar, above a cupboard there, and to the right of the door there's a basin of water and a similar one on the left and Ales says softly that it's holy water in the basins and Ales goes over to the basin on the right and she dips two fingers of her right hand into the water and then she slowly puts her fingers first on her forehead and then on her chest and then to her left shoulder and then to her right shoulder and then she looks at the red light and then Ales kneels and then she gets up and then she stands looking at the red light up ahead above the altar

There's something there, she says

and then she bows her head and then she takes Asle's hand and brings him with her into the half-darkness under a staircase that must go up to a gallery or something, Asle thinks and then she kneels and Asle just stands there and he feels filled with something, yes, something takes him and lifts him up in a way and then he rests in this lifting up, and everything is completely silent, and it's like the silence is filled with something, and it's like what fills the silence is filling him now, Asle thinks and then he kind of doesn't think anymore and he is just there in the silence until it's finally something he doesn't even feel, he's just there, in the silence, he is the silence, he thinks and then Ales gets up and she looks at him and then she goes and lights two candles under the statue of the Virgin Mary with the child Jesus and then she goes and dips two fingers into the basin of holy water on the right and crosses herself and Asle also dips two fingers of his right hand into the basin of holy water and then Ales takes his hand and she moves it to his forehead, to his chest, to his left shoulder, to his right shoulder and then she walks towards the door and again she makes the sign of the cross and Asle does too but he's a little unsure if he's doing it right and even so he feels the power of the sign of the cross fill him and then Ales takes his hand and then they go outside and Ales shuts the door behind them

Now we're married, Ales says

and Asle nods

In reality we're married, she says

and Asle nods and Ales says that now she can take him back to his rented room on University Street, it's not far to walk, just a little way on Canon Street, where St Paul's Church is, and then University Street is the first street on the right, Ales says and then Ales and Asle walk away from St Paul's Church hand in hand and Ales says that they'll see each other again tomorrow, but she has to go to school tomorrow, she can't cut school every day, she has to finish at the academic high school and take her examen artium if she's going to have any chance of getting into The Art School, but then, after she's done with school tomorrow, then they can meet outside where she lives, Ales says and Asle says that he'd rather they meet at The Coffeehouse and Ales says that he'll never find the way there alone, but he can always just ask people, and if he gets totally lost he can always take a taxi, but he's going to have to learn to find his way around on his own, at least to The Art School and to The Coffeehouse, Ales says and she laughs a little

I'll do my best, Asle says

So we'll meet at The Coffeehouse at three tomorrow? Asle says

and Ales and Asle stand in front of the door at 7 University Street and then they hug each other and Ales finds his mouth and his tongue and they kiss for a long time and then they let each other go and Ales says that she's not too happy that he's going up to that Herdis Åsen woman or whatever her name is, but that's what he has to do, he has his room and his things there, but they should find another room for him soon, or, yes, maybe they can move in together? she says, she isn't too Catholic for that, she says, and she laughs a little, and in reality they're married now, they're married before God now, she says and then she kind of tears herself away and Asle stays standing there and watches her go and when she's very far away from him she stops and turns around and she raises her hand and waves and he raises his hand and waves and then she blows him a kiss and he blows her a kiss and then he sees her disappear around the streetcorner they'd just come around and then he stands there in front of the door to 7 University Street and he unlocks the door and goes inside and he locks the door behind him, because he thinks Herdis Åsen told him he should do that, or maybe she didn't say it, he doesn't totally remember, Asle thinks and he goes up step after step until finally he gets to the sixth floor and he sees that the nameplate says Borch on the door facing the one that says Herdis Åsen and he unlocks the door where it says Herdis Åsen on the nameplate and he goes inside and he locks the door again and then there's the sound of footsteps and he sees Herdis Åsen come walking towards him, she is wearing a white house coat, and she has pink slippers on, and she has her cigarette in one hand and her ashtray in the other hand and she says that it was nice of him to come back, yes, he sure took his time with that female, she says

And remember, no girls in the room, Herdis Åsen says

No, Asle says

But I thought you'd come home later, she says

and Asle hasn't thought about the time at all and Herdis Åsen says so then, it's not too late to have a coffee and some cake maybe, after all she'd baked the cake for his arrival, because he was moving into her apartment, it was to mark that, yes, to put together a little moving-in party, that's why she had baked a cake, and so it was too bad that none of the cake had been eaten, and for no other reason besides that female, Herdis Åsen says and then she says that the cake could wait until tomorrow but it'd taste better today, it's best to have cake freshly baked of course, she says and Asle takes his shoes off and puts his brown leather shoulderbag down on the floor and Herdis Åsen says that it's fine that he's taking his shoes and bag off in the hall this time but in general she'd like him to keep both his shoes and his bag in his room, but now he should come with her, Herdis Åsen says and she goes and opens the door to the living room and Asle walks in after her and the round table in the living room is set for two people, plate and knife and coffee mug and wine-glass, and he sees that the wine bottle on the table is almost empty, and that there's just a little wine left in one of the glasses, and he sees Herdis Åsen stub out her cigarette and put the ashtray down on the table and then take her glass and drink a little of it

I prefer white wine, Herdis Åsen says

And this is a good white wine, she says

And it wasn't cheap, she says

and then Herdis Åsen says that she thought she should have a little since they were supposed to celebrate his moving into her apartment, but because of that female it didn't go how she'd imagined it, Herdis Åsen says and she asks if he'd like to have a little wine and Asle says yes thank you and then Herdis Åsen pours wine into the empty glass and he raises his glass and takes a little sip and the wine tastes good and has a long aftertaste

Isn't that a nice wine? Herdis Åsen says

Yeah, Asle says

and then she says they should toast, yes, toast to his moving into her apartment, she says and they bring their glasses together and clink them and say cheers and then Herdis Åsen says that it's nicer if he doesn't hold his hand around the glass itself but holds the stem like she's doing and then Asle puts the glass down on the table and picks it up again by the stem and then they toast again and then Herdis Åsen says that he should have a seat

Go ahead and sit on the sofa, she says

and Asle goes over to the sofa and sits down and then Herdis Åsen goes out to her kitchen and she comes back in with a cake on a dish and Asle has never liked cake, and damned if he knows what kind of cake it is, but it's big in any case

The coffee's almost done, and then we can eat, Herdis Åsen says

and she asks if he usually takes milk and sugar in his coffee and Asle says he likes a little milk in his coffee and Herdis Åsen says she does too and then she goes out to the kitchen and she comes back with a little pitcher and puts it on the table

So you can just have a seat at the table, she says

and Asle goes and sits down on the chair at the place setting he took the glass from and Herdis Åsen pours his coffee and pours herself coffee and she puts the pot she has the coffee in down on the table and then she hands him the little pitcher of milk and then he pours a little milk into his coffee and hands the pitcher to Herdis Åsen and she pours milk into her coffee and then she says that now he should help himself to some cake and Asle sits there a little confused and then she asks him to pass her his plate and then she cuts a big piece of cake and puts it on the plate and hands it to Asle

I hope you like it, she says

and Asle takes the plate and since there's a fork on the table he realises he's supposed to eat the cake with a fork, something he's not used to, because he's always eaten cake with a spoon to the extent he's eaten cake at all, and he takes a bite and it tastes like cake, yes, nothing more and nothing less, so it doesn't taste good, and he chews and chews and then he has a sip of coffee and washes the cake down with it and with the coffee the cake tastes better

So you're going to get married too, Herdis Åsen says

and Asle knows that when you put a piece of cake on a plate then if it's standing on its side the person whose plate it is will get married, and he sees that his piece of cake is standing on its side, he thinks

Just as long as it's not to that girl I met today, Herdis Åsen says

That was no kind of girl for you, she says

I could see right away that the two of you don't belong together, she says

and she picks up her plate and her piece of cake is lying on the plate

No, I'll never get married, she says

And that's probably for the best, she says

and then Herdis Åsen eats her cake and she asks Asle if he likes the cake and he says yes, yes the cake is really good and he chews and chews and washes it down with coffee

Now you need to eat up, as you can see there's lots of cake, Herdis Åsen says

and Asle doesn't say anything and Herdis Åsen has finished her piece of cake and she says cake's not the worst thing now is it, so he mustn't be shy, he should eat up, she says and then she raises her glass and she says in her opinion both white wine and coffee go well with cake, and especially both together, she says and Asle sees that he's barely managed to get half his piece of cake down and he takes another bite and chews and chews and then washes it down with wine, yes, he empties the glass and Herdis Åsen says she needs to open up another bottle of wine and then she takes the empty bottle and goes out to the kitchen and Asle hears a cork being pulled out and then Herdis Åsen comes back in with a bottle of wine and she says that this is a reasonably priced wine, but definitely drinkable, she says and she pours him a glass and she says he's eating so little and Asle says that he wasn't very hungry

Or maybe you don't like cake? Herdis Åsen says

Not usually, but this cake is very good, Asle says

Well you're polite at least, Herdis Åsen says

and then she pours wine into her own glass and then she raises her glass to Asle and he raises his and she says that she's glad to have a man in the house again, she likes it better when she doesn't have to live alone in this big apartment, she says, and so what if he doesn't like cake, real men usually don't, Herdis Åsen says and she says that tomorrow she has some substitute hours at the school, and cake will certainly go over well in the break room, she says, and besides it was mostly to celebrate him moving in that she'd baked a cake, of course, and plus she likes baking, especially cakes, there aren't many feminine chores she bothers with much, she can't even knit, and she's never even tried to crochet, but baking, and especially cake, yes, she's always liked doing that, Herdis Åsen says and now Asle can just take his glass and have a seat on the sofa again and then she'll just take the cake away, yes, the failed cake, she says with a laugh, and the plates and all the rest of it, Herdis Åsen says and Asle goes and sits down on the sofa and he drinks wine and he feels that he's already getting a little tipsy and he looks around the room, it's packed with pictures, big paintings, small paintings, and he sees at least two that must have been painted by Eiliv Pedersen, and there are also several Norwegian Romantic paintings, and a portrait of Herdis Åsen as a young woman, and then there's the big heavy built-in bookshelves, brown, and then there's another book cabinet in the same style as the bookshelves, and he hadn't noticed that that one was there before, and both the book cabinet and the bookshelves seem to be what they call Jugendstil, Asle thinks and he finishes his glass and damn that was good wine, the first wine was clearly the better of the two but the second wine was good too, yes, he hasn't drunk too much wine in his life, but now he's drunk wine, and he can choose, he's always picked red wine before, yes, red wine is better than white wine, no doubt about that, he thinks and Herdis Åsen comes in and she takes her glass and she drinks up the wine in it and then she refills her glass

Oh I didn't notice you'd finished yours, yes, what a hostess I am, she says

and then she refills Asle's glass and puts the bottle down on the coffee table and then she sits down on the sofa next to Asle

I see you have pictures by Eiliv Pedersen, Asle says

Ah, you know his work, Herdis Åsen says

Of course you would, she says

Yes, now that I think about it, she says

and then Herdis Åsen says that when she was young she knew Eiliv Pedersen well, very well indeed she might say, so she got those paintings from him personally, as a present, but even if the pictures were painted by the young Eiliv Pedersen they're still his, he's still him, she's recently been to see his latest exhibition, yes, the one at The Beyer Gallery now, and Asle should go too, Herdis Åsen says and then she points to the portrait of herself as a young woman

Yes, I was pretty back then, she says

and no one says anything and Herdis Åsen lights a cigarette and she asks if Asle could bring her the ashtray, it's on the living-room table, she says and he does and then he stands and looks at the portrait of Herdis Åsen as a young woman, and it is of a beautiful woman, and the picture is painted well, he thinks and Herdis Åsen says that it was a young man who painted that, and no one says anything, and Herdis Åsen says that when she sat as a model it took forever, at least that's how it felt, she says and she gives a short laugh and Asle takes out his packet of tobacco and he rolls himself a cigarette

I didn't know you were a smoker too, Herdis Åsen says

and Asle says that he's smoked almost since elementary school, and he'd liked it from the first time he ever smoked, it was a friend who stole a pack of cigarettes from his Grandfather and then they went out to a boathouse and that's where he smoked for the first time and he liked it from the first puff, but his friend got sick and threw up and kept on vomiting and said that he'd never be a smoker and so he gave Asle both the pack of cigarettes and the box of matches, yes, that nice tingling in his body, and how after he's smoked a kind of calm spreads all through him, Asle says and Herdis Åsen says it wasn't like that for her, she can remember her first smoke very well, she remembers it like her first kiss, she says and laughs, but they probably shouldn't talk about things like that, about kissing and things like that, she says and gives a short laugh and then she says that they were still kids in the street, and one of them had managed to get a packet of tobacco, he must have stolen it somehow or another, she doesn't know, but all the kids rolled themselves something resembling a cigarette, it wasn't easy, it took a lot of cigarette paper to do it, and if she remembers right they eventually ran out of cigarette paper, but they all got something to smoke anyway and to tell the truth she threw up, yes, embarrassing isn't it, she couldn't keep going, she threw up, and it was a long time until the next time she smoked, and then it was a cigarette, not rolling tobacco, and that went great, that was when she was a student in Berlin, she was studying German, because she's taught German and Norwegian all these years, as she'd said, yes, Herdis Åsen says and she has a sip of wine and then smokes more of her cigarette, and she says that she's smoked since her time in Berlin, but never rolling tobacco, just cigarettes, she says, and she smokes too much, she tries to keep herself to a pack a day but it often happens that she starts a second and that's too much, she says and then she stubs out her cigarette and then they both drink wine

And then it's not hard to have too much wine too, she says

and no one says anything

I live alone, she says

and again no one says anything

That's how it is, she says

and then she says no, she shouldn't complain, she has it good, as good as she can have it probably, she says and besides, yes, she just thought of something, yes, maybe Asle can paint a portrait of her? and Asle thinks that he doesn't want to but that he probably has to say yes now that she's asked

I could do that, he says

Of course I'd pay you, she says

and she says maybe they can start it tomorrow, if Asle wants to and if he has time, and he asks her how big she wants the portrait to be and she says it doesn't need to be that big, but maybe Asle could paint her while she's lying in the high rosemaling canopy bed, because that bed is really her favourite place to be, Herdis Åsen says and she gets up and she takes her wine-glass with her and goes into her bedroom and she says that Asle should come and he stubs out his cigarette and gets up and follows her and then Herdis Åsen lies down, in her white house dress, and with her pink slippers on, and with her glass in her hand, on the bed, a rosemaling canopy bed, and with lots of pillows, and she half sits half lies in bed and she asks Asle to sit down on the chair next to the bed, the one with the high back, and Herdis Åsen finishes her glass of wine and she asks if Asle can go get the bottle and pour her a little wine and Asle says yes and then he puts his glass down on the floor and he goes and gets the bottle and it's almost empty and then he pours what's left into Herdis Åsen's glass

So we finished that bottle too, she says

I'll have to go buy some wine tomorrow, she says

and Asle picks his glass up from the floor and he finishes it and then he says thank you very much for the cake

It was nothing, Herdis Åsen says

And for the coffee, he says

And the wine, he says

and Asle says that it's probably time for him to go lie down, it's been a long day, he says and then Herdis Åsen says it has, but he should remember what she said, that he doesn't have permission to have girls in the room, she says and Asle says that he understands, yes, and Herdis Åsen says it must sound like she's just nagging and griping and Asle doesn't says anything and she says maybe she's had a little too much to drink, she says and she hands the empty wine-glass to Asle and he takes it and then she says it would be nice if he'd put the bottle and glasses in the kitchen and Asle says he'll do that and then he stands there with the empty bottle in one hand and the two wine-glasses in the other and he says good night and Herdis Åsen says that it would be good for her if they could start on the portrait tomorrow, and maybe it would work better if she sat for it in his room, but she'd really rather he paint her lying in bed, because it's less tiring to lie down than sit, she says and Asle says that should be fine and then Herdis Åsen says that she wants to make herself look nice and put on make-up, she doesn't want to look slovenly in the portrait, she says

I'll do my best, Asle says

And I'll make myself look as good as I can, Herdis Åsen says

But it's not so easy to look good when you're as old as I am now, she says

And as wrinkled, she says

They say that women who smoke get more wrinkles than women who don't, she says

I got mine anyway, she says

and Asle says good night and Herdis Åsen says good night and then Asle goes and puts the empty bottle and the two glasses in the kitchen and then he goes out into the hallway and he picks up his shoes and shoulder bag and then he goes into his room and he puts his shoes and shoulder bag down on the floor and then he stands there and looks at the bed and then he makes the sign of the cross, but he doesn't remember exactly how he's supposed to do it, and he tries several times, and then he does it right, he thinks, and again he brings one hand slowly to his forehead, to his chest, to his left shoulder, and to his right shoulder and he feels something happen to him, he feels filled with a strength, or something, or whatever you'd call it, but he is filled with something, something that wasn't there before he made the sign of the cross, Asle thinks and he gets undressed and he puts the clothes on the chair by the desk and then he lies right down in bed and he can feel the good strong rush the wine gave him and he closes his eyes and he breathes slowly and regularly and he thinks that tomorrow he and Ales will meet at The Coffeehouse at three o'clock, he thinks and I sit here in my chair and I look at my fixed spot in the water, at my landmark, at the waves, and I'm still in my black coat, and I still haven't lit the stove, and Bragi is lying in my lap, and now I need to light the stove soon and take off this black coat of mine, I think and I look at the waves and I see Asle walk into The Coffeehouse and at first he doesn't see anyone there and then he sees the woman with the medium-length blonde hair sitting just inside the door and she's sitting and looking out at The Wharf and The Bay and Asle thinks that she always has to be here and that Ales is not going to like that she's sitting there, Asle thinks and he pours himself a cup of coffee and puts a little milk in the cup and then he goes over to the register to pay and then he goes and puts the cup down on the table all the way in the back and he puts his shoulder bag on a chair and then he sits down with his back to the woman with the medium-length blonde hair, and he can feel very clearly that she's looking at him, and there was a suitcase next to her, and some shopping bags, so maybe she's sitting there waiting for the express ferry, and so she lives either north or south of Bjørgvin, because one boat goes south and one goes north, Asle thinks and he takes out his tobacco pouch and he rolls himself a cigarette and he lights it and it tastes good and feels good, coffee and a cigarette, he hasn't eaten anything yet today but he's not hungry, he doesn't like food in the morning, it's only much later in the day that he likes to eat, often not until evening, he thinks, so he can't understand people who eat breakfast, he has never done that, all right maybe when he was a little kid but he can't ever remember having eaten breakfast later, the first thing he has in the morning is a cigarette, and then another cigarette, and then maybe a cup of coffee, Asle thinks and he looks at his watch and it's only two-thirty, so he's early, he is always early when there's somewhere he has to be, yes, usually, but when he was in elementary school he was never early, he was always a little late, always, Asle thinks and he drinks his coffee and smokes and then he hears footsteps and he turns around and he sees Ales coming over to him and he gets up and he walks towards her and they meet and they hug each other and they kiss each other and he can feel both the woman at the register and the woman with the medium-length blonde hair looking at them and Ales says that he's here early and Asle says he always is, and he's bought himself a coffee, and does she want anything, he asks and Ales says that she'd like a cup of coffee, she says and Asle goes to pour another coffee and then Ales hurries over to him and says quietly no, she doesn't want anything, because they need to leave, because, yes, she, the woman who's always looking at him, who's always there, yes, they'll never get away from her, Ales says, so they should just leave, and she can't follow them, probably, Ales says and Asle puts the cup back and then he goes and gets his tobacco pouch and Ales says he should just finish smoking the cigarette in the ashtray and drinking his coffee, of course, and Asle puts out his cigarette and puts it in his tobacco pouch and then he gulps down the rest of his coffee in one sip standing up and Ales says he should take his time, she didn't mean it like that, she says, they don't have to leave right this second, but still, that woman, with the medium-length blonde hair, she's here again, she says and Asle puts his brown leather shoulder bag on and then Ales takes his hand and then they walk to the front door and Asle doesn't look at the woman sitting there in the corner, the woman with the medium-length blonde hair, he opens the front door with his free hand and Ales leaves and then he leaves and the door shuts behind them and Ales says that it's a nice day so they can just go down The Wharf, because there are benches where they can sit, she says, and she has so much to tell him, she says and they go and find a bench to sit on and they sit down and sit there and look at The Bay, the water is dead calm and the houses on the other side of The Bay are mirrored in the water

It's not often the water's so still, Asle says

No, no, almost never, Ales says

And the houses on the other side are mirrored in the water, she says and then she says that it's probably for them that the water's so still today and Asle doesn't say anything and then they hear a motor start growling and Asle sees that one of the express ferries is leaving the quay and then the wake from the boat makes the dead-calm water move and the mirror image of the houses turns into fragments and disappears and Ales says now he needs to listen and Asle takes out his tobacco pouch and takes the half-smoked cigarette out, yes, now you need to listen, Ales says

You have to meet my mother Judit today, she says

Your mother Judit? Asle says

and he's both surprised and startled, because that was sudden, everything's happening so fast now, kind of, and he feels like he's not entirely ready to go along with her

We're going to go to my house in an hour and then you'll meet my mother Judit, Ales says

But do we really need to be in such a hurry? Asle says

Yes, Ales says

and no one says anything, and then Asle says that the express ferry that just left is going south so the one that's still there must be going north, he says and he hears how meaningless what he's saying is, it's as if he's just saying something to say something and Ales says yes and then she says that he has to meet her mother Judit since they're married now, because they are, yes, in a way, she says

Yes, Asle says

Yes, exactly, Ales says

and then she says that they were married yesterday in St Paul's Church, so they are married before God and Asle thinks that maybe they did that, yes, got married yesterday in the church and he thinks that it's not always so easy to understand what Ales means, and he can probably think that way too, but he does feel that this is all very strange, taken together, sitting like this on a bench and looking at the water, at The Bay, and hearing Ales say that they are married before God and that he has to meet her mother Judit today

And you remember we live on Ridge Street, Ales says

and she says that Asle has to meet her mother Judit before the two of them move in together, and Asle hears what Ales is saying but he doesn't understand it, they're going to move in together? cohabitate? and he's just moved into the room at Herdis Åsen's, he thinks

Because you can't keep living there with that Herdis Åsen, Ales says

It's fine, Asle says

No, Ales says

No it's not fine, she says

and that's why she's rented a little apartment for the two of them, yes, actually it was her mother Judit who helped her, because a friend of Judit's has a house in The Hills and there's a basement apartment in the house and at first her mother Judit thought she was too young to move out and live by herself, and then she'd thought that she certainly couldn't move in with a man she'd just met, no, impossible, you can't do something like that, her mother Judit had said and then Ales said that she was completely certain that this was the right thing to do, she just knew it deep inside, and her mother Judit had looked at her and then she'd fallen into her silence, because mother Judit could kind of just fall into herself and become silent, it seemed very strange to other people, but she was so used to her mother Judit going into her silence that she almost didn't even notice it, and she herself had also started to go into a wordless silence sometimes, or maybe a better way to put it is fall into it, yes, she says

I understand, Asle says

and after her mother Judit had been in that silence, and maybe she herself too, her mother Judit had said that it was probably right, what Ales was saying, and then her mother Judit had said that she knew a friend who had a house in The Hills with a basement apartment that was empty now, her daughter had lived there while she was studying in Bjørgvin, but now she was married and they'd moved to Oslo, it was just a couple of years ago, but the friend hadn't been able to bring herself to rent out the apartment, it was just standing empty, but she'd often spoken about how she had to hurry up and rent out that basement apartment already, but it had never gone beyond just talk, she dreaded putting an ad in the paper, having people who might consider renting the apartment come by to look at it, having to talk to them, that was one thing, and the other thing was that she hated having people she didn't know living so close to her, but for whatever reason her friend had never managed to rent out that basement apartment, and it's in a nice location, with a view over the whole centre of Bjørgvin, and you can see a lot of The City Fjord from there, it was a nice little two-room apartment, with a very big main room and a very small kitchen, her mother Judit had said and then she'd said that maybe Ales could rent it, it might be good for her to live alone, but she wasn't entirely sure if it was right for Ales to live there with a man, with a man she'd just met and she didn't really know, she had just fallen so much in love that she didn't know what was best for her, she'd said and Ales had said that she'd decided, and so her mother Judit said that she'd call up her friend and ask if Ales, yes, if they could rent the apartment in the basement

Do you know what the friend does, Asle says

She works with my mother, Ales says

She's a nurse too, she says

And a widow too, she says

And she has a daughter, like I said, who lives in Oslo now, but the daughter's a lot older than me, she says

and she says that her parents were old when she was born, but she's probably already said that, Ales says and she says that now Asle needs to listen and then she says that her mother Judit had called this friend, whose name is Hjørdis

That's almost like Herdis, Asle says

Yes, right, Ales says

Yes and so my mother Judit's friend said that it was great for her if I wanted to rent her apartment, that was a better arrangement for her too, because it wasn't so nice living alone in a big house, she'd said, she says

And then my mother Judit said that I, yes, that you and I would move there together and then the friend, Hjørdis, yes, gave a big laugh and said that that was wonderful, because they could use a man in the house, there was always something in an old house, she had often thought about selling the house for just that reason, she'd said, Ales says

But I, Asle says

You won't need to do anything, Ales says

It's just, I'm really clumsy, Asle says

That doesn't matter, Ales says

and she says that maybe they can shovel the snow for her mother Judit's friend in the winter, if there's any snow, because there's often no snow in Bjørgvin, so it probably wouldn't be that often, but she, the friend, yes, Hjørdis, had mentioned shovelling snow, it was because she said it, Ales says and she says so now she's found and rented an apartment for them, and they can move in whenever they want, she says and Asle hears footsteps and he turns around and he sees the woman with the medium-length blonde hair come walking along The Wharf and she has a suitcase in one hand and shopping bags in the other and Ales turns around too and she says she's always there, she doesn't understand it, why would she always be wherever we are? she says and they look at her and they see her go on board the express ferry that's docked at the quay

At least she doesn't live in Bjørgvin, Asle says

That's good, Ales says

But I don't understand why I see her so often, she says

Yeah, Asle says

Well so let's go and you can meet my mother Judit, Ales says

And after that we'll go look at the apartment, and if the friend isn't home we can see it from the outside at least, she says

Yeah, Asle says

So let's go, Ales says

and they stand up and walk hand in hand along The Wharf and I sit and look at my spot out there in the water, I look at the waves and as I see Ales and Asle walk along The Wharf I think that Ales and I weren't given that many years together but I'm grateful for the years we did have, I think and Ales is sitting next to me and we're holding hands and I feel her so close so close, I think, and I still haven't taken off my black coat, and I still haven't lit the stove, it's crazy, I think and I look at my landmark in the water, at the waves there, and I sit and hold Ales's hand and we stay sitting like that for a long time just holding hands and then Ales lets go of my hand and I look at the waves and I see Asle standing there, he is wearing a black suit, a white shirt, and a purple tie, and Ales is in a white dress, and her mother Judit is in a purple dress, and Ales and her mother Judit are sitting to one side of the altar, each in their own chair, and sitting on the other side of the altar is the woman Ales and Asle are renting the basement apartment from, Ales's mother Judit's friend, and Father Brochmann is standing in front of Asle dressed in a priest's white robe, and a friend of mother Judit's is standing behind Asle, Asle doesn't know him, but he's the same age as mother Judit and he's a doctor at The Hospital, and he's Catholic, he converted to The Catholic Church, and he has his hand on Asle's right shoulder, and Asle thinks that he didn't know who he could ask to be his witness when he decided to convert and be confirmed, he didn't know any Catholic he could ask, and so mother Judit said she could ask someone she knew and he'd said he'd be glad to be a witness and now he's standing behind Asle with his hand on Asle's right shoulder and Father Brochmann is standing in front of Asle and Asle thinks that it was mother Judit who suggested that Asle go to Father Brochmann once he'd decided that he wanted to convert to The Catholic Church if possible, and it was mother Judit who first got in touch with Father Brochmann, he is actually German but he's worked in Norway pretty much his whole life, Asle thinks and he and Father Brochmann met a few times, Asle thinks and he'd said that it was Ales who really wanted him to convert, but it wasn't like he didn't want it himself too, and he'd said that it was Ales who'd brought him to mass, and also they'd often gone into the church just to sit there and one time there was a woman there and she was kneeling, deep in prayer, and this picture, of the kneeling woman completely lost in prayer, and her collectedness and the power, or whatever you'd call it, coming from her lodged inside him, Asle had told Father Brochmann, and Asle thinks that this picture is sometimes sitting on the top of his collection of all the pictures he has in his head, he thinks, and there it sits speaking silently to him, Asle thinks standing there in front of Father Brochmann, and Asle thinks that he'd told Father Brochmann that this kneeling woman, alone in St Paul's Church, one Monday morning, around ten-thirty, had meant so much to him and actually it was then and there that it was decided for him that he might convert, he'd told Father Brochmann and then he told Father Brochmann, Asle thinks, that everything else about the mass, the sign of the cross when you go into the church, and when you leave the church, the sign of the cross when the priest starts the mass and when he ends it, and then, right at the end, when the priest says Go in peace, yes, all of that spoke to him, and filled him with peace in a way, Asle had said, he thinks standing there in front of Father Brochmann, and then the silence when the bread and wine were held up and then seeing Ales and the other people, and usually there weren't that many, falling silent one after the other and walking in silence up to the altar to take the body of Christ and the blood of Christ and then walking with head bent back down the centre aisle in the nave of the church after having received the host, with hands folded, and then sitting back down where they'd been sitting before with their hands together in prayer, some kneeling, some sitting with heads bent, but everyone deep in prayer, and then the grand silence that filled the church, yes, Asle wanted, if possible, to become a part of that history, that community, he'd said, he thinks standing there in front of Father Brochmann, so if it was possible he would really like to be accepted into The Catholic Church, yes, become part of the Catholic community, Asle had said, he thinks, and then he and Father Brochmann had met a few times and talked about faith, about what it meant to become Catholic, and then Father Brochmann wrote to The Bishop in Oslo and recommended that he accept Asle into The Catholic Church, Asle thinks and now here he is standing in front of Father Brochmann and now, right now, Father Brochmann is drawing a cross on Asle's forehead with the consecrated oil, and the cross sticks to him, it sticks to his forehead, it sticks inside him, in all of him, Asle thinks, and from now on he will feel that cross wherever he is, he thinks, a cross drawn with consecrated oil, Asle thinks and then he goes and sits down next to Ales and the man who had put his hand on Asle's right shoulder goes and sits down next to mother Judit and then Father Brochmann says This is my body and he raises up the host and he raises up the chalice and says This is my blood and then Father Brochmann walks over to them and then Asle holds out his hands placed like a cross, left hand over right, like a throne, the way both Ales and Father Brochmann had told him to do it, and Father Brochmann places the host in his hand and Asle says Amen and then he puts the host in his mouth and he folds his hands and bows his head and shuts his eyes and in a silent prayer without words he sits there and he feels peace spreading through his whole body, Asle thinks, and then, finally, after a long silence, Father Brochmann begins to speak and says a prayer and then at the end he says Go in peace and everyone answers Thanks be to God and then they get up and everyone's happy and then they take a taxi home to mother Judit's where she's left a lamb roast in the oven to keep it warm and she's also invited Beyer to the celebratory meal, and he comes, and then they eat and drink red wine and then Father Brochmann has to go since he has to hold mass that evening, he says and Beyer says to Asle that maybe it's time to start thinking about an exhibition now and Asle doesn't say anything and then Ales says that Asle has had a picture accepted for the West Norway Art Exhibition and one for the Autumn Exhibition and Beyer says he'd like to see Asle's new pictures as soon as possible, today even, yes, that's how impatient he is, Beyer says and I sit in my chair by the round table and I look at the waves out there in the Sygne Sea and I see Ales and Asle walking with Beyer up in The Hills

It's a small apartment, Ales says

And it's all messy right now, she says

That doesn't matter, Beyer says

and they go into the apartment and Ales apologises again for all the mess, because there are canvases and easels and tubes of oil paint and a worn-out sofa and it's like nothing goes together and Ales asks Beyer if he'd like a cup of coffee and he says no, no, he's already been fed enough today but he'd really like to see the pictures, both hers and Asle's, he says and Ales says that she doesn't want to show him any of hers, because when you're busy working on something, yes, something just for yourself, it can kind of destroy it, or the painting can sort of get stuck, if you show it to anyone and Beyer says that he understands, but he does need to see Asle's paintings, after all that's why he, an old man, dragged himself up into The Hills, to see the pictures, he says and they go into the living room and then Asle shows him one painting after another, he has nine finished paintings in the room, and then he has quite a few more in a storeroom down in the cellar, he says and Beyer says that there is not the slightest doubt in his soul, yes, Asle simply must have his debut exhibition and it has to be in the spring, and then, Beyer says, he can use the fact that Asle has had pictures accepted in both the West Norway Art Exhibition and the Autumn Exhibition, but if he had room in his schedule, yes, he would show Asle's pictures right away, because talent shines from these pictures, he can see it, and he can always see right away if an artist has talent, and it all depends on talent, it's a gift, yes, a gift of grace the Catholics would probably say, and he has to admit that if there's anything that could make him believe, believe in something big, something bigger than life, yes, it's when he sees talent in a picture, and in Asle's pictures there is such obvious talent that he's never seen anything like it, he says, yes, Asle's talent is so self-evident that he will definitely encounter a lot of resistance, because it's like great talent awakens opposition, yes, it scares people, and irritates them, and it gets bad reviews, but for whatever reason it's different with the people who buy pictures, they buy what they like and what they think is worth the money, and what they buy, with few exceptions, are pictures that show talent, Beyer says, anyway that's how it is in his gallery, he says, and Beyer asks if he can also see the paintings that are down in the cellar storeroom right now and so Asle and Beyer, both wearing a black suit and tie, go down the steep old steps to the cellar and in the light that there is down there Asle shows Beyer the paintings he's keeping there and Beyer says that Asle already has enough pictures for two shows, so there'll be two, but there has to be a year between them, and now that he's seen these paintings too he's changed his opinion somewhat, he wants Asle to exhibit them in the weeks before Christmas, he should be able to squeeze in an exhibition during Advent, Beyer says, because that's when pictures sell the best, he says and he says that he feels strongly that Asle's pictures will sell well and Asle doesn't know what to say and doesn't say anything

If that works for you, of course, Beyer says

Yes, Asle says

and he thinks that he'd realised he would have to exhibit his pictures sooner or later, have his debut exhibition, but he'd imagined his first show would be after he'd graduated from The Art School, because that was how it was usually done, but Asle's painting teacher, Eiliv Pedersen, had also told Asle that he already painted well enough to have his first show, he thinks and just then Beyer says that Eiliv Pedersen had mentioned a student of his who was good enough to have a show already and that must have been Asle, even though he didn't say the student's name, and Beyer hadn't thought anything more about it, he says, but now, yes, today, now it was decided, Asle would have a Christmas exhibition this year and another one next year, Beyer says and he looks at Asle who stands there and looks down at the floor and then Beyer says that there sure are a lot of empty bottles of spirits here in the cellar and Asle doesn't know what he should say and then Beyer says that Asle mustn't drink too much, he has seen alcohol destroy all too many great talents, and it was often the greatest that alcohol took, and if it didn't destroy the talent it still eventually destroyed the person, so he needs to be careful about alcohol, Beyer says and Asle doesn't know what he should say, because he probably does drink too much, yes, Ales says so too, because it's now up to a half-bottle of spirits a day, but he doesn't start drinking before five o'clock, and he never paints after he's had something to drink, he thinks, but Beyer's probably right, and Ales too, because once it hits five o'clock, yes, well, it's time for a glass, kind of, it's turned into a habit, and there aren't many days he doesn't drink, and then he really craves a glass, Asle thinks and then Beyer starts to go up the stairs and Asle follows him and when they're upstairs Beyer says yes he has certainly seen enough pictures today for two exhibitions, and he will have two exhibitions, the first one before Christmas this year and the second before Christmas next year, he says and I sit here and I look at the water, at my spot out there in the Sygne Sea, at the waves out there and I think that today is Saturday and it's Little Christmas Eve and Åsleik came over yesterday to have lutefisk, and the food was good, yes, but I wasn't really feeling my best, I think, and it's ridiculous that even now, so late in the day, I haven't even lit the stove and that I'm still sitting in my black coat, yes, I even spent the night on the bench in my coat, what is wrong with me? I think, and tomorrow I'll go with Åsleik and celebrate Christmas at Sister's house, and I really don't feel like doing that, but now that I've said I'd go with him to Sister's house to celebrate Christmas I have to do it, I think, and then I need to quickly call The Hospital and ask if I can visit Asle, I think and I look at my landmark out there in the Sygne Sea, always, I'm always sitting and looking at my landmark and I look at the waves and I see Asle standing and looking at a picture that's on an easel, and he thinks that no sooner has he moved into Herdis Åsen's apartment than Ales found a basement apartment for them in The Hills, or else her mother Judit arranged for them to rent a basement apartment from a friend of hers, Asle thinks and he thinks that he really isn't looking forward to telling Herdis Åsen that he's going to move out, he thinks and I sit and look at my landmark, and now I almost can't stand looking at it anymore, because I'm just sitting here looking and looking, I think and I look at the waves and I see Asle standing in the hall in front of Herdis Åsen

That's too bad, you're moving out already, so soon, you only just moved in, she says

and Asle says that he's sorry about that, but he and his girlfriend, yes, the woman she'd met, were going to move in together into a basement apartment in The Hills, he says

It was quite a short stay, if you can put it like that, Herdis Åsen says

and then she says that she thought it was too bad that Asle was moving out, they got along well together, she says and so what'll happen with the portrait of her he was going to paint? she says

Yes, I need to paint it, Asle says

As soon as I saw that girl I knew that it'd end up like this, Herdis Åsen says and she says it's that female who made him move out and Asle stands there in front of Herdis Åsen and looks down

I'm right, aren't I, Herdis Åsen says

and Asle doesn't answer

There's nothing wrong with you, it's just that girl, she says

and Herdis Åsen says that Asle probably wanted to be able to bring her to his room, naturally he wanted that, she thought so, and that was why she said that the only rule was that he couldn't have girls in his room, but she wasn't generally prudish and she'd made up that rule on the spot, because of course it had sometimes happened that previous renters had had girls in the room with them, it was a normal thing, but she just couldn't tolerate that from the girl who was standing there in the doorway before he even moved in and that was why she'd said that, Herdis Åsen says and Asle says that since he was moving out so soon, well, if she really wanted him to paint her portrait he would probably have to do it now, he says

Now? Herdis Åsen says

Yes, before I move out, he says

And when will that be? she says

Soon, Asle says

and Herdis Åsen says that in that case they should probably get started right away, he can go get his things ready, and she wants to be painted sitting in her bed, and with a glass of wine in her hand, she says and Asle goes into his room and takes the canvas he thought he'd use, that he'd already stretched on a stretcher, and he puts the painting supplies he'll need in one of the boxes he had with him when he moved in and that he'd kept, in the wardrobe where he kept his clothes, and he picks up the easel too and then he goes out into the hall and he thinks that he'll stand and wait there, because he obviously can't just walk into Herdis Åsen's living room, and certainly not into her bedroom, of course not, he thinks and so he stands there and waits with the stretched canvas in one hand, the easel in the other, and the box of painting things on the floor at his feet and he thinks that now she really needs to come soon, he thinks and then Herdis Åsen comes out into the hall, and her lips are bright red, and her eyebrows totally black, and somehow or another she has managed to cover up almost all the wrinkles on her face, and she's wearing a red dress, and it's as low-cut as a dress can possibly be, and it clings to her body, and it's very short and Asle thinks that she doesn't look right at all, he thinks

So now we can start, Herdis Åsen says

and she goes into the living room, and into her bedroom, and Asle follows her and she goes over to the nightstand and raises a glass with a long stem that she's filled with wine and then she lies down on the bed, outstretched, she lies on her side with one foot over the other and she's propped up on one arm and with her other hand she sort of holds the long narrow wine-glass out in front of her, like she's about to hand it to someone, and Asle asks if she wants him to paint her whole body or just her face and she says he should do it however he wants and Asle thinks that he wants to paint her head and upper body, her face and the long wine-glass create a balance in the picture and he starts painting and then Herdis Åsen starts telling him about all the men who've pursued her, and it still hasn't stopped, don't think it has, there are still some men who send her flowers or invite her out to dinner at the finest restaurants, she says and Asle doesn't say anything and she tells him about one after another of these men and he hears her say this and a picture of her face has lodged in his head, of her upper body with her small breasts held firmly in her bra, and that low-cut red dress showing just about everything, and then the bent arm sort of offering the long narrow wine-glass, and Asle thinks that there is something so helpless, so human, about what he's seeing, yes, something so beautifully ugly that it kind of lifts up the picture he's painting, yes, it'll be beautiful, because the picture of Herdis Åsen as he just saw her in the hall has entered him and lodged there, he thinks, so he is painting so to speak both the inner picture lodged inside him and the one he sees in front of him and Asle looks at Herdis Åsen every now and then but it's mostly to be nice to her, he thinks and then he paints her younger than she is, she almost looks like a woman who's younger than forty anyway, yes, younger, Asle thinks and it's quick and easy to paint the portrait, and Asle himself feels that it's turning out to be a good painting, and then he paints an A in the bottom right corner in black, and it blends together with the still-wet oil paint, the way he likes it to do, and then he says that she can come look at it now, if she wants

You're done already, Herdis Åsen says

I think so, Asle says

You can really do a good job that fast, I don't know, Herdis Åsen says and she gets up and comes over and stands and looks at the painting and Asle can tell that she is more than satisfied, she is really and truly happy, yes, delighted to see the picture, and that makes Asle glad too and Herdis Åsen says that since Asle has painted such a beautiful portrait of her he won't have to pay any rent, since he hardly lived in the room anyway, and of course she'll pay him too for the picture and she asks him what he wants for it and Asle says an amount and Herdis Åsen says that's way too little and then she goes and gets her purse and she pays him double what he'd asked for and she says that the picture probably needs a while to dry and Asle says it does and Herdis Åsen says that she wants to hang the picture up on the wall across from the bed, that's where it'll hang, and she asks if Asle can help her hang it up and then the picture can hang there and dry, because it smells so good, the oil paint, she says and Asle says he can do that, she must have a hammer and nail lying around somewhere, he says and Herdis Åsen says she does, yes, and then Asle says that he'll move out tomorrow

You're in that much of a hurry, Herdis Åsen says

We arranged it like that, me and Ales, that's her name, yes, who I'm moving in with, he says

and then he turns the picture over and then he paints *Herdis Åsen* in thick black oil paint on the top of the stretcher and then he puts the painting down leaning against the wall where Herdis Åsen said she wanted the picture hung and then he puts his painting things in the box and folds up the easel and Herdis Åsen stands and looks at the portrait and she says that he was so nice, really, because she's not as beautiful as she is in the picture, and then there's such a remarkable feeling of elevation in the picture, of being lifted up, she says and Asle says that if she gets the hammer and a nail they can figure out where she wants the picture and Herdis Åsen leaves the room and Asle stands and looks at the portrait, and he's happy with what he sees, it turned out to be not just a good portrait but a good picture too, he thinks and then Herdis Åsen comes back with a hammer and a nail and Asle holds the picture up and asks if it's good like that, and Herdis Åsen says yes the picture should hang just like that, she says and then Asle picks up the hammer and nail and he hammers in the nail and then Asle lifts up the picture and hangs it there on the nail and Herdis Åsen says that she's very happy with the picture and thanks him very much, she says and I sit here and look and look at the water, at the waves, at my spot out there in the Sygne Sea and I close my eyes and I open them and I think that my not having lit the stove, and not even turning on the electric heater, and not taking off my coat, yes, sleeping in it even, there on the bench, this is falling apart, nothing less, I think and I think that I should have called The Hospital and asked if I could go visit Asle, asked how he's doing, but I've already done that, and not that long ago, or maybe I haven't just called? I think and I'm not sure if I did or not, and that must be because I've already done it so many times, and every time I get the same answer, that Asle needs rest, and that it would be best if I didn't come see him, I think and I think that in that case Asle will have to be in The

Hospital over Christmas and maybe it's better that way, because otherwise he'd probably have been alone in his apartment, the way he usually spends Christmas, and he didn't think that was so bad, he'd said, he spent it like a normal day, he thought almost nothing about it being Christmas, but it was hard to completely not think about it, he'd said, because it was like everything around him was saying it was Christmas, he'd said, and a person shouldn't be alone at Christmas, that's somehow been decided once and for all, he'd said and I pet Bragi's back and then I fold my hands so that the thumbs make a cross, yes, a St Andrew's Cross as Åsleik says, *St Andrew's Cross, St Andrew's Cross,* but now I want to just be silent, I think and I breathe calmly in and out and then I say Our Father who art in Heaven Pater noster qui es in cælis and I think what do I mean? why am I saying these words? who am I turning towards? I think and it's just words, yes, images, metaphorical language, they call it, that means something other than it says, because God is obviously not a father, I think, but when I say these words I feel clearly, yes, even more clearly, this nearness, yes, the nearness of God, and of Ales, I think and I think that it's this wordless nearness I'm talking to now, that of God, who is near me and who is in me, I think and I think about Meister Eckhart who said that without human beings God would not exist, and without God human beings would not exist, because I, and everyone, and everything come from God, and if God withdraws back into himself then I and everything else will disappear, Meister Eckhart wrote, I think, and God is nowhere, because he is outside of everything that is, and at the same time he is in everything that is, and people say that the place where he is is up in the sky, because human beings look up and if humanity can find any word for where God, who isn't anywhere, must be, yes, then it's up in the sky, in the heavens, Our Father who art in Heaven Pater noster qui es in cælis and yes, there, outside time and space, outside creation, and in all of creation, and inside me, right in the middle, and in other people, yes, in everyone, is the uncreated, that which has never been born and so it can never die or else it is born again and again all the time, I think, yes, Meister Eckhart wrote that it's Jesus Christ who is born again and again inside the soul, down at the bottom, in the soil, the foundation, the abyss, and we rise up from the dead all the time in the same way, I think and I try to stay perfectly still and silent, and I listen to the silence, and I say Hallowed be thy name Sanctificetur nomen tuum and a blessing settles over everything all at once, everything is hallowed, everything becomes whole, everything becomes sacred and I say Thy kingdom come Adveniat regnum tuum and may it be so, and it's going to happen, and it's happening right now, because the kingdom of God is already between us, and inside us, and just as there once was the kingdom of God so too there will be the kingdom of God again, and then creation will no longer be separate from the creator, but united with him in uncreated love, but then won't God disappear? won't everything disappear? turn to nothing? I think and I think that it's not like that, but it can be thought of like that, and interpreting, yes, saying something about God, and about the kingdom of God, yes, is always very close to misusing God's name, so God forgive me, because only silence can say anything about God, about the kingdom of God, because God hides in silence, I think, and also in love, I think and I feel that Ales is near me and then she puts her arm around my shoulders Thy will be done Fiat voluntas tua and God's will is love, peace and love, and I try to get rid of words, get rid of pictures, and I feel how right it is to pray that God's will be done, yes, on earth as it is in Heaven, Sicut in cælo et in terra and I feel that that's enough, what it means becomes clear and I understand what it means, and still I can't manage to say it, I think, yes Fiat voluntas tua sicut in cælo et in terra and I think that that's how Jesus Christ taught his apostles to pray, and in so doing also taught me how I should pray, and The Son of Man was someone you can talk to, he was God who became man and who died, to share our suffering, our death, and who rose up from the dead, and vanished into the kingdom of God, and with him all people, all, yes, all, everyone who ever lived, everyone who's alive now, everyone who's going to live, yes, everyone is of God and comes from God and will go back to God, to the kingdom of God, and it doesn't make sense, it's total foolishness, but it is foolishness we preach, as Paul wrote, I think, and maybe God is closest of all to those who are poor in spirit, those who never think about God, yes, because they shall inherit the kingdom of God, as is written, I think and it's always these words, yes, these words that only have meaning when they contradict each other, and Meister Eckhart has thought almost everything I think before I did, I think, but isn't every human being a unity of opposites, yes, a paradox, they call it, coincidentia oppositorum, they call it, with a body and a soul, like how Christ was both human and God, yes, Jesus Christ is himself the paradox that contains the paradox that all people are, I think, so that the cross is the symbol of the paradox, I think and I think that since faith is paradoxical, self-contradictory, they call it, it can never be understood with reason, because reason has to follow the usual logic where A and not-A, as they put it, can never be true at the same time, while in faith they are both true, three is the same as one, the way it is in the Three-in-One God, in the trinity, they call it, I think, and always these thoughts, these thoughts that never go anywhere, I think and I say Give us this day our daily bread Panem nostrum cotidianum da nobis hodie And forgive us our trespasses as we forgive those who trespass against us Et dimitte nobis debita nostra sicut et nos dimittimus debitoribus nostris And lead us not into temptation Et ne nos inducas in tentationem but deliver us from evil Sed libera nos a malo I think and I say Amen and then Ales lets go of my shoulder and she takes my hand and I think that today is Saturday and that it's Little Christmas Eve and tomorrow Åsleik and I are going to take The Boat to Øygna and Åsleik's going to call me tomorrow when he thinks it's the right time to set out, I think and I think that now it's Christmas again, now it's Christmas again, and the years go by faster and faster, I think, Christmas again, Christmas again, I think and I think that for the first time I'm going to be with Åsleik celebrating Christmas at Sister's house, at the house of the woman named Guro, I don't even know how many times Åsleik has asked me if I wanted to come with him and celebrate Christmas at Sister's, and this year I said yes, and I don't totally understand why, I think, but anyway tomorrow Åsleik and I are going to go on his Boat to see Sister who lives in Øygna, way up in Sygnefjord, on a bay, not far from Instefjord, I think and I need to bring a Christmas present for Sister, I think, but what should it be? I think, I'm so old that I could forget something as obvious as the fact that I need to bring a Christmas present for Sister, the woman named Guro, since I'm going to spend Christmas with her and Åsleik, I think but I didn't buy anything I can give her for Christmas so I'll just have to give her a painting too, and I have a painting, they're all packed up in the storage room, but I need those for the exhibition, and so what else can I give her? I think and I think at the same time how little I want to give her anything else so I guess I'll just paint a picture now and give it to her, paint it quickly, because a picture can be painted fast, or I can keep working on it forever until either I finally feel happy with it or paint over it in white, that's how it is, but now I need to quickly paint a picture I can give Sister as a Christmas present, I think, and it should be small, and I have to paint it not too thickly so that the paint will be dry by tomorrow morning when we get on board Åsleik's Boat to go up Sygnefjord to Øygna, no, the paint won't be dry by then but it has to be dry by Christmas Eve itself, and I have no desire at all to paint another picture, I feel such distaste at the thought of it that I almost can't stand up, I think and I let go of Ales's hand and I stand up and Bragi tumbles onto the floor and again I forgot he was lying asleep in my lap, I am never going to learn to remember that, I think and then I go up to the attic and I find the smallest canvas I've already stretched and I go downstairs and put it on the easel, but what should I paint? it should probably be a kind of portrait of a woman's face, I'll paint the face of the woman named Guro who watched the dog that night, I think and then I call Bragi and he comes over to me and I pet his back, I grip and tug at his fur, and I have several pictures of the face of the woman named Guro lodged in my mind, one of them that's lodged there was when she raised her wine-glass to her mouth back at Food and Drink and I'll paint that picture, I think and I pick up the palette and I think that I'll paint the picture in different grey colours and then with a little pink and maybe just the slightest bit of blue, I think and I paint as fast as I can and I see that it's turning out to be a good painting, of a twisted face, a face with pain and suffering in it, but with a clear longing in it, I think, and I see that I've painted it thicker than I thought, that's not good, because it's Little Christmas Eve today and the paint won't be dry by tomorrow morning, but anyway it'll be dry enough to bring on The Boat, I think, and then it'll dry more in The Boat and then I'll wrap it before we get back on land, I think, and it feels good to paint a picture, but now I don't want to paint anymore, not for a long time in any case, maybe never again, I think and I think that I might as well carry all the tubes of oil paint, yes, all the painting supplies into The Parlor, where Ales used to be with her painting things, and where the books are, but no, no I don't want to do that, because that room should stay the way it was when Ales left it, I think, but today's the day to carry things out, get rid of things, now's the time to make decisions and changes, I think and I go out to the kitchen and get some shopping bags that are in the cupboard under the sink and I put the tubes of oil paint and brushes and all of the painting things I have in the main room into the shopping bags and I go up to the attic and I put the bags into the storage room where I have painting things stored, boards, tubes of oil paint, brushes, palette knives, turpentine, rags, scrapers, I have all of that stored up there and I go back down to the living room and then I take the picture I just painted off the easel and put it down over there next to the kitchen door and then I fold up the easel and I carry it up to the attic and put it down in the storage room and I think so that's over and done with, I think and I think that I've already packed my suitcase and so I'm ready for my trip, and the suitcase is standing where the unfinished paintings used to be, between the door to the bedroom and the door to the main room, under the peg where my brown leather shoulder bag is hanging, and the painting I'm going to give Sister, the woman called Guro, for Christmas is standing there to dry next to the kitchen door, and it'll probably have to lie out drying in The Boat too, because I used a lot of oil paint and painted in thick strokes, so I'll bring a little paper and string in the suitcase and then I'll wrap the painting on The Boat just before Åsleik and I tie up The Boat to walk up to Sister's, I think and I go out to the hall cupboard, the one under the stairs, because I have a roll of brown packing paper there, and I unroll it and tear off a length of it and then I get a length of string and a black marker and I go into the main room and open the suitcase and lay it flat on the floor and then I put the brown packing paper, the string, and the marker into the suitcase, on top of the suit, and then I shut the suitcase again and put it back against the wall, in the middle, under the peg where my leather shoulder bag is hanging, and it's the good old suitcase that has come with me through all these years, I think and I go and sit down in my chair over by the round table and after a while I look at the empty chair there next to me and I see Ales sitting there and I take her hand and I look at my landmark and I look at the waves and I see Asle standing by the window in an old brown house and he's looking out and he sees that it's just starting to get dark and I sit there and look at the waves and I see Ales and Asle stand and look at the brown house, it's tall and narrow and it's on a beautifully built foundation wall

It really needs a paint job, Asle says

Yes, Ales says

and then she says that it's pretty now too, but it's true, the house should have been repainted a long time ago, she says

It's almost falling apart, she says

But it might be nice inside, Asle says

and he says that he doesn't understand how anyone could let such a nice old house just fall apart and not rent it out, not do anything to maintain it, he says and I sit and look at my landmark out there in the middle of the Sygne Sea and I think that I'm always just sitting and looking at the water, and that it's so good to feel Ales's hand, I think and I still haven't lit the stove, I think and I look at the waves and I see Asle standing and looking out the window in the brown house, and he sees that it's slowly started to get dark and he thinks that again it was Beyer who came to his aid, he'd told Beyer that both he and Ales were thinking they needed a bigger place to live, it was a bit cramped in the little two-room basement apartment since they both wanted to both live and work there, and then Beyer helped them find this house to rent, Asle thinks standing there looking out the window at the trees on the other side of the road, and now the leaves have turned such beautiful colours, and he doesn't want to think about colours, he wants to just look at the colours and see them get darker the more the day darkens, Asle thinks and he thinks that it's hard to believe but all the pictures in his debut exhibition had sold, unbelievable, Beyer had said and then he'd said that since Asle had told him that they'd like to live outside of Bjørgvin he'd spoken to a friend who had a house that Ales and Asle could rent, it was this friend's childhood home, ten or fifteen miles, drive north of Bjørgvin, the friend's mother had lived there until a few years ago but ever since she died the house has stood empty, and the friend who's lived all these years in Bjørgvin, he was a doctor at The Hospital, yes, Sande was his name, was also one of his best clients, Beyer had said and then Ales and Asle had rented the house, and then they'd moved to the old house, ten or fifteen miles north of Bjørgvin,

Asle thinks standing there looking out the window and he sees a car drive past on the road, a small van, and he's seen this car or van several times, Asle thinks and he thinks that Sande, the doctor who'd rented them this house, had said that they should arrange things however they wanted, Asle thinks, and he thinks that he and Ales got the keys to the brown house and they drove to the house and let themselves in and it smelled stuffy in the hall and they opened the door to the right and there was a little kitchen, with an oven and refrigerator, and old cupboards, and an old table with old chairs, he thinks and then there was a door to the living room and the living room was empty, only a sofa, a coffee table, and an armchair were still there, and then a dining table with six chairs, and through the living room there was a big bedroom and there was a double bed in there with a duvet and a pillow with no sheets or pillowcase and there was a door from the bedroom out to the hall and there were stairs from the hall up to the attic and there was a little hallway with a door to the left and a door to the right and there was a bed in each of the two rooms and then Ales and Asle went back downstairs and then they sat right down on the sofa and sat there and looked at all their stuff on the floor in the middle of the room, they'd left some in the hall but brought most of it into the living room, and now there was a whole heap of it standing there, and both he and Ales were tired, Asle thinks, and so they lay down on the sofa and they lay there with their arms around each other, he thinks and then Ales said that she wanted to stop going to The Art School and Asle asked why and she said that she didn't think she was ever going to paint well enough and Asle said that he thought she was a good painter and Ales said that's just it, she was good, just good, no matter what she painted it turned out just good, somehow, dutiful and good and totally without anything that made it stand out, she said, because what was necessary, what it needed, wasn't there, yes, what made art art was missing, what went beyond the picture and made it something other than just a picture, Ales said and Asle asked if she was completely sure that she wanted to stop and he said that if she stopped going to The Art School then he would too, he said, because he didn't feel that he was learning anything new anymore, and then it was so distracting to have to stand there in The Painting Hall with the other students and paint there, he said and then Ales said that in that case they would both stop, because she was also sure that Asle already had what he needed to be able to paint the way he wanted and should, because actually there was just one thing he needed, and whatever it was, yes, he had it, she said, but she didn't have that one thing, Ales said and Asle didn't say anything, and Ales said that he could just keep painting but she on the other hand thought she should start as a student at The University, she wanted to study art history, and especially icons, and then she wanted to start painting icons, because as long as she could understand what an icon was and how it was painted she was sure that painting icons was the right thing for her to do, she felt something almost like a calling to do it, if she could use such a big word, she said and Asle said that she should think it over and Ales said that she didn't know if he'd noticed, he often spent so much time in his own world, but she'd recently been reading lots of books about icons, both histories and books about how icons are made, and there was no one in Norway as far as she knew who painted icons, no one from Norway anyway, and you had to order from abroad what you need to paint them, she said and Asle said that he'd always liked icons and Ales said that she knew that icons were what she should paint, not paintings, she'd be an icon painter, not an art painter, she was just as sure of that as she was of the fact that he and she belonged together, she said and Asle said that he'd support her as well as he could whatever she wanted to do, he said and Ales said that she'd been a little worried about telling him, but now she'd said it at last, and she wasn't worried about telling The Principal at The Art School that she was going to stop going there, and Art History was an open major at The University so she could start going to lectures there right away, and one of the professors there was also an expert on icons, she said, he wrote his dissertation about something to do with icons, and he often came to mass, so Asle must have seen him, he has long grey hair and a long grey beard, she said, and Asle said that he'd certainly noticed the man with the long grey hair and the long grey beard, he said and he said that in that case it was decided, then, yes, they'd both stop going to The Art School and then she'd start as a student at The University and learn how to make icons, that was probably best, and he would keep painting his pictures, Asle said and then he said that they could go see The Principal at The Art School as soon as Monday and tell him they were quitting, he said, Asle thinks as he stands there in front of the window watching it slowly get darker and darker outside and he thinks that then Ales and he were standing outside the door to The Principal's office at The Art School and they knocked and he came and opened the door and Ales said first that she'd decided to stop going to The Art School, she didn't want to paint pictures, but icons, she said and as a first step she wanted to study art history at The University, she'd said and The Principal had nodded and said that she knew best, and of course he would accept her decision, he said and Ales thanked him and then Asle had said that he was going to stop going too, he wanted to be a full-time painter and The Principal said he could understand why Asle would want that, and he just had to accept it, he said and then Ales and Asle shook hands with The Principal and they thanked him and The Principal wished them the best and they left The Principal's office and Asle said that he wanted to go see Eiliv Pedersen and thank him for all his teaching and Ales said that she would go straight up the hill to The University and register as an Art History student and then they each went their way, Ales left The Art School and walked up the hill to The University and Asle walked into The Painting Hall where everyone taking Painting was standing and painting, and actually that was what bothered him the most, that he had to stand there with all the others and paint together, it distracted him so much, it was downright destructive for his pictures, Asle thought and he saw Eiliv Pedersen standing there saying something to one of the other students in Painting and Asle waited until he was finished and then went over to Eiliv Pedersen and said that he'd decided to stop coming to The Art School and Eiliv Pedersen said that he could understand that, because Asle was such a good painter that he at least didn't have much he could teach him, he said, yes, probably the other way around would be more accurate, he said and Asle didn't know what to say and he thought that it was all wrong but he couldn't say anything to contradict him and then Asle said that he just wanted to thank him for all the lessons, he had learned a lot from Eiliv Pedersen, and not least from his paintings, seeing them had been very important for him, Asle said and Eiliv Pedersen said again that he's known for a long time that Asle has reached where he's going, yes, or in any case gone as far as The Art School can take him, and now there's just the enormous, lifelong work of painting picture after picture, now he needs to just keep doing it and doing it and not care about what art critics or other people who supposedly understand art have to say, but Asle probably learned all that after the exhibition he'd had at The Beyer Gallery, because he must never care about reviews, or else he should just listen to criticism from people who can paint, yes, who have painted excellent pictures themselves, because actually it was only the people who've done something who can judge whether something is good or bad, and then there weren't more than a few so-called normal people who had a kind of access to the understanding of art that let them say something about the quality of a picture, and quality, that's what it's all about, Eiliv Pedersen said and then he said that Asle had chosen a hard life by choosing art, but in his case it was the right choice, Eiliv Pedersen said and then he held out his hand to

Asle and Asle held out his hand to Eiliv Pedersen and then they shook hands and then Eiliv Pedersen said that he wished Asle the best, Asle thinks standing at the window in the brown house looking out and he thinks that it's getting darker, but slowly, and it's beautiful watching the leaves, in all their colours, yes, autumn is his time of year, Asle thinks and then he sees the old big car or small van drive past on the road again and I sit here in my chair by the round table and I look at my landmark out there in the middle of the Sygne Sea, at the waves out there, I hold Ales's hand and I look at the empty chair where Ales liked to sit, because we sat like this a lot, just sat without saying anything, I think, and it's good holding Ales's hand, I think and I look at the waves and I see Asle standing there in front of the window

You've been standing there long enough now, Ales says

and she goes over to the window and she takes Asle's hand and then they stand there hand in hand and they look out the window and then Ales asks why don't they go for a walk, before it gets totally dark, she says and Asle says yes they must do that, he says and then they go out into the hall and Asle puts on his long black coat and Ales takes a scarf out of a box and she hands it to him and she says he needs a scarf and then Asle puts on his brown leather shoulder bag and Ales says you can't go anywhere without that bag, she says and they go out and then, hand in hand, they start walking down the country road

Look over there, there's a playground, Ales says

There sure is, Asle says

That's strange, you can't see a single other house, she says

But there are swings and seesaws and a sandbox, she says

and Ales asks why don't they go down to the playground and Asle says they should, and there's a path down to the playground and it runs over a hill and ends at a hilltop

There must be houses with children on the other side of the hill, Asle says

Yes, there must be, Ales says

and she and Asle walk down the path and they go into the playground

Now it's almost dark, even if it's only afternoon, but soon it'll be evening, Asle says

Yes, Ales says

and then she goes over to the swing and she sits on it and then she asks Asle to give her a push and he goes and grabs the ropes holding the greying wooden seat that Ales is sitting on and he pulls her slowly back, and then he lets go and he pulls her back again and he lets her go

More, harder, Ales says

and Asle pulls and gives a stronger push

Even harder, Ales says

and Asle pushes even harder

More, harder, Ales says

and it's like she's screaming and Asle pulls as hard as he can and Ales flies as high as the swing can go and then Ales shrieks and he lets go of the swing and then Asle steps back and then he sees a man come walking down the path, and he's in a long black coat, and he has long grey hair tied back in a hair tie and Ales says that was really great, she says, it was like being a child again, she says

And there's a seesaw, she says

And there's the sandbox, she says

and the path of the swing gets shorter and shorter and then Ales stops the swing entirely with her feet and Asle goes over to her and he puts his hands on her shoulders

I'm just like a child again, Ales says

and Asle says nothing and I sit there in my chair by the round table and I look at my landmark out in the water, I look at the waves, at the eternal waves, I think and I think that I want to go to mass, and I should have driven into Bjørgvin so I could go to mass on Christmas Day, the way I usually do, but there'll be none of that this year, since for some strange reason I said yes to celebrating Christmas with Åsleik and Sister, whose name is Guro, and what's said is said, a promise is a promise, I think and then I think that yes, now that I've decided that I'm going to stop painting I can drive to Bjørgvin today and drop off these nine pictures too, the ones I kept, to be sold at the next exhibition at The Beyer Gallery, I think, and then I can go to mass in the evening and then, yes, I don't know how many times I've called to try to get permission to see Asle, but they always say the same thing, that he can't have visitors, but maybe if I just show up in person at The Hospital and say that I want to see him they'll let me, I think, so then I have three things to do in Bjørgvin, deliver my paintings, go to mass, and go to The Hospital and ask if I can see Asle, I think, and then I can spend the night at The Country Inn and then drive back home early tomorrow, yes, at the crack of dawn, so that tomorrow morning, yes, when it gets light, Åsleik and I can go in his Boat to Sister's to celebrate Christmas, and I think that Beyer will probably be surprised if I show up with new paintings already, so maybe it's best if I call him, but if he isn't in his gallery I can probably just bring the pictures into The Beyer Gallery myself, and if the side room, yes, The Bank, is locked I'll just put the pictures in some other place, maybe behind the desk, but I have to talk to Beyer in any case, I think and Ales lets go of my hand and I get up and I go out into the hall and I look up Beyer's phone number in the phone book, and the truth is I haven't called him that many times, I think, and I pick up the receiver and I dial the number and I hear Beyer's voice say Beyer here and I say

It's me, I say

Well, it's you, Beyer says

Yes now this is unexpected, he says

The guy doesn't call all that often, he says

and he says that if I'm wondering how it went with the sale he is happy to report that it couldn't have gone better, because all the pictures are now sold, so as far as that goes he could have shut The Beyer Gallery and taken Christmas off, but he'd said that he'd be open both today, on Little Christmas Eve, and tomorrow, Christmas Eve, because there are always people who are late buying Christmas presents, and it's often people who are flush with money and bad with time, Beyer says and he laughs and he is getting on a roll with his chatting away like Bjørgvin people do and I say he needs to listen to something

Yes, Beyer says

I'd like to bring by nine paintings for you today, I say

and there's silence on the telephone

I have nine paintings here, four of them are pictures I didn't want to sell, for various reasons, maybe they're strange, but I've probably told you about them, I say

and Beyer says that he doesn't recall that I have, but it sounds very interesting, he says, and I then say that there are four pictures I set aside to work on more but now I think they're done

But is it really so urgent, Beyer says

Yes, I say

and I think that I'm not planning to say that I'm not going to paint any more pictures, because then Beyer will only say that it's just an idea, I'll definitely paint more, of course I will, I'm just tired and feeling a bit rundown, he'll say and Beyer says that even if this is unexpected he is obviously, when it comes to me, always happy to see me and my pictures, and then, he says, yes, then maybe he can take down some of the ones that have already sold and hang up some of the ones I'm bringing, because the ones he has stored in The Bank he's already promised that Kleinheinrich could show in Oslo, or Huysmann in Nidaros, but damn if he wasn't tempted to get two or three of the pictures and hang them, he must admit, Beyer says, but now we'll just see if we can get a few more pictures sold before Christmas, he says and Beyer's all eager now and he says the best thing would be if I could come as quick as I can, and I said that I'd thought these pictures could be for next year's show, and Beyer says that there'll be more pictures for next year's show, so everything'll be great, and I say that in that case I'll just wrap my paintings in blankets and carry them out to the car and then drive down to Bjørgvin right now, I say and Beyer says that in that case he'll be waiting for me in the gallery even if I get there after closing time, because he needs to keep the gallery open tomorrow, even though it's Christmas Eve tomorrow, even if it's a Sunday this year, because that's the day of the year when he usually sells the most pictures, he says and I say thank you so much and then we say we'll see each other soon and I hang up the phone and I think that the best thing to do would be to call The Country Inn and see if they have a room free tonight and I find the phone number in the phone book and I dial it and I ask if they have a room free and I say that 407 is my usual room at The Country Inn and The Bjørgvin Man says that they do have room for me, as always, and Room 407 is free, he says, so then I can have my usual room, he says and I say that in that case I'll reserve the room and The Bjørgvin Man says certainly and I hang up the phone and I go up to the attic and get blankets from the attic room I use as a kind of storeroom and I go into the other attic room where I keep paintings in crates and I wrap each and every one of them in its own blanket and then I carry them downstairs and I step into my shoes and I go outside and put them in the back of the car and I feel how good it is to be getting all the paintings out of the house, so now the only picture I still have is the portrait of Ales, which is still leaning against the back of the chair up in the attic room, and then the picture of Guro that's drying next to the kitchen door, but that'll be out of the house first thing tomorrow, I think and I go inside and I call Bragi and he wakes up and looks at me with his dog's eyes and then I say come and he comes and he stops next to me and then I put my brown leather shoulder bag on and I think now what's wrong with me, sleeping all night on the bench in my coat, and I haven't taken it off yet today, and now I'm going to drive back to Bjørgvin again, I think, and under my coat I'm wearing my black velvet jacket, so I slept in that too, I think and I go out to the kitchen and Bragi follows me and then he drinks up all the water that's in the bowl and I give him fresh water from the tap and he drinks a little of that too

You were thirsty, weren't you Bragi, I say

and I think that he needs a little something to eat too, and I cut a slice of bread and crumble it into pieces and put the pieces in the bowl and Bragi goes and sniffs a little at the bread, but he doesn't eat any and I think that he probably isn't hungry then, and I go to the hall door and I say come on Bragi and he reluctantly follows me and I turn off the kitchen light and the hall light and I go outside and Bragi goes a little ways out onto the hill and first he raises his right back leg and he takes a good long piss and then he squats and then stays like that to shit and he clearly doesn't really need to because he squats and pushes several times but then it works and then I open the back door of the car and Bragi hops in and lies right down on the back seat and I shut the door and I get into the car and I start it and it hasn't snowed for several days and the roads are well cleared, with firm dry snow, so they're good to drive on and I think that it'll be good to get rid of the paintings, finally, finally get rid of them, and then it'll be good to go to mass tonight, I think, and not least to go check on Asle, I think and I drive and I don't think about anything, that's maybe what I like best about driving, that the thoughts sort of go away and I get absorbed in just driving, that I fall into a kind of stupor and get a kind of break or rest or whatever it is, I think and then I see snowflakes start to land on the windshield one by one and I'm getting close to the playground and I see two people walking hand in hand towards me along the road and I think that those are the people I saw down in the playground when I was driving back from Bjørgvin not so long ago, and he has medium-length brown hair, and she has long dark hair and Asle thinks here comes that car again, a small van, yes, he's seen it several times, there aren't that many cars he notices but he remembers seeing this particular one before

I've seen that car a bunch of times, Asle says

I don't remember seeing it before, Ales says

and I think that it's not so far to the playground, and to the turn-off, but I don't feel tired, and the young couple step off onto the side of the road and stop and stand there, and I see that he's wrapped his arms around her back and snowflakes are slowly coming down over them and now it's not far to drive to the old house Ales and I rented, first there's the playground and then the turn-off and then I drive by the old brown house, I think, and no one has lived there since we moved out and moved to the old white house in Dylgja, I think, and the house has become more and more rundown and I don't like looking at that good old house just falling apart and that's probably why I don't want to look at it, I think and I look at the two people standing on the side of the road and snowflakes are landing in his medium-length brown hair and in her long dark hair and I drive past them and I get closer to the playground and I don't want to look down at it or at the turn-off and I get to the brown house and I do look at the house after all and it is a lot more rundown than it was when we lived there, now the little house is about to collapse, yes, some shingles have already fallen off the roof, and I don't like looking at the house, and yet I almost always do it, I think and I see a young man with medium-length brown hair standing in the window looking out and I look straight ahead and I try not to think about anything, or to just think that now I'm going to drive to The Beyer Gallery, drop off the paintings with Beyer, and then take a taxi to The Hospital to see Asle, and if they don't let me in now then yes well I don't know, I think, and after I've seen Asle I'll take a taxi to St Paul's Church and it'll be fine if I get there early, then I can sit in the church and listen to the silence, because it's in the silence that God is nearest, I think and then I'll be there for mass, and it's been a long time now since I've taken communion, I think and then I'll walk to The Country Inn, and I know how to get from St Paul's Church to The Country Inn very well, I've done it so many times, I think, it's very easy, I should be able manage that, anyway it'll be fine, I think and I drive and I fall into a stupor and I'm absorbed in just driving and before I know it I've reached The Beyer Gallery and as soon as I stop the car Beyer is standing in the door and he waves to me and he comes walking over to me and he holds out his hand and we shake hands and he says no, this is a surprise, but actually it'll work out splendidly, as they say, because, like he said, yes, he's sold all of the pictures in the Christmas exhibition, he says, and he can most likely get a few of the ones I'm bringing him now sold tomorrow, on Christmas Eve day itself, he says and I open the door to the back of the van and Bragi starts barking and I say hush, quiet now, I say and Beyer asks if I have a dog now and I say it's just a dog I'm taking care of and Beyer says that I've said so many times that I thought I should get a dog, especially after I became a widower, he says, but I never did, Beyer says and he asks if I like looking after dogs and I say it's fine, and he asks if I've thought about getting a dog of my own now and I say I may do that and then Beyer says that the door to The Bank is already open

And Doctor Sande, yes, you remember him, Beyer says

Yes, you rented a house from him, he says

Yes, he bought three pictures this year, he says

Three pictures, he says

and I don't say anything

But what made you decide all of a sudden that you wanted to drive down and deliver some pictures to me, Beyer says

and I don't answer

No, well, if you don't want to tell me then don't tell me, he says

You've never been a big talker, he says

and I don't say anything and then Beyer and I start to carry the pictures inside and he says we'll put them right in The Bank and that he'll look at them tonight, after the gallery has closed for the day, he says and it doesn't take long to carry all the pictures inside and I stand there with blankets in my hands and Beyer asks what I'm going to do now and I say that first I'll go to The Coffeehouse and get a little food and Beyer says I should do that, yes, like usual, and I can tell he wants to ask me more questions about why I came so soon with new pictures, and why I drove down to Bjørgvin today at all, and he tries to let it go, but he can't contain himself

Is it something about a woman? he says

and Beyer is sort of whispering to me

Since you've lived alone all these years it's about time, he says

and I shake my head and then I think that maybe Beyer's kind of right about it, because that woman Guro, who lives in The Lane, no, it's not exactly a thing about a woman like Beyer says but it is kind of like that a little, I think, but I promised to be eternally faithful to Ales so I can at least keep that promise for the length of a human life

But it's none of my business, Beyer says

and then I say Merry Christmas and Beyer says Merry Christmas and then he says he can't remember my pictures ever having sold so quickly any other year, he says, and he says that when pictures sell so well it's fun to be a gallerist, he says, and he was already going to be open tomorrow too, on Christmas Eve itself, even though it's Sunday, maybe it's not exactly legal, for all he knows, but never mind about that, he says, since Christmas Eve, he says, is the day when he sells the most pictures all year, because there are always some of the wealthier Bjørgvin men who wait till the last minute to buy something for the lady of the house, he says and I don't say anything

No, I won't hold you up, Beyer says

and then he opens the door for me and I go outside and I think that now all I have to do, as I've done so many times before, is cross High

Street and then take a left down The Lane and then I'll pass by the house where Guro has an apartment on the ground floor and I think that it'd be really bad if it's like Beyer says and I'm involved in something to do with a woman, but if I am then it'd have to be with Guro, I think and in my long black coat, and with my brown leather shoulder bag, I cross High Street, and then I take a left and start to walk down The Lane and right away I realise that there's a smell of something burnt and I see that the windows are broken and the woodwork is burnt in an apartment there, on the ground floor, and I think that can't be Guro's apartment where there was a fire, can it? yes, it looks like it, and I stop and I stand there looking at the broken windows and the burnt-up wood panelling and I see how the grey and black burn marks are almost screaming at the white, it's almost like most of the places are grey, and there's a strong burnt smell and I think that that really is Guro's apartment that caught fire, and then this strong smell of smoke, it smells burnt, nothing else, and it must be Guro's apartment where there was the fire, I think, and Guro smoked so much, she would roll a cigarette, smoke it, stub it out, roll a new cigarette, smoke it, stub it out, roll a new cigarette, she smoked constantly, I think, so she was probably smoking in bed and that's probably how the fire started, I think, and now that too is just too horrible, I think and I see an older Bjørgvin man come walking up The Lane and I say excuse me but I see there's been a fire

It's just too horrible, he says

and he shakes his head

Yes, I say

And someone died in the fire too, he says

Someone died? I say

A woman, middle-aged, he says

She'd lived in that apartment for years, he says

And then, yes, it must have been the smoke that killed her, he says

Was her name Guro? I say

Yes, he says

and we stay standing there looking at the burnt-out apartment

These things happen, he says

Yes, I say

and then he wishes me Merry Christmas and I thank him and wish him the same and then he keeps walking and I stay standing there looking at the burnt-out apartment and then I think now Guro's dead, yes, it's sad, it's always sad when someone is taken away forever, but now Guro is with God, now she's resting in God, in God's peace, in God's light, I think, I'm sure of it, so when I look at it more clearly it's not so sad, not that Guro went to church or was a Christian or anything, no, far from it, she probably wasn't a believer at all, but she had a lot of God in her, and now that part of her is back with God again, like she is, like what was deepest inside her is, it's impossible to understand it but that's how it is, I think, now Guro is part of God and at the same time herself, I think and then I make the sign of the cross right there in front of the burnt-out apartment and then I walk farther down The Lane and I think that not many of the people who believe they're inside really are, but many of the people who are outside, those are the ones who are inside, the first shall be last, as is written, I think and then I walk over to The Country Inn and I think that now I'll go check in and then I'll have The Bjørgvin Man, it'll of course be him sitting there at the reception desk now, call me a taxi, and I walk into the lobby and of course it's The Bjørgvin Man sitting there at reception

So, here you are again, he says

It hasn't been so long, he says

And you want Room 407, he says

That's what you said on the phone anyway, he says

and I nod and The Bjørgvin Man stands up and takes a key off the hook on the wall behind him and he hands me the key and I thank him and then I ask if The Bjørgvin Man can call me a taxi and he says of course and he calls and then he says the taxi will be here right away and I hand the key back to The Bjørgvin Man and he hangs it on the hook behind him and then I go outside and I stand there and I'm not thinking anything, I just feel empty, and the smell of something burnt reaches all the way to The Country Inn, and then I see the taxi coming and I get in the back and I say I'd like to go to The Hospital and The Taxi Driver asks if I'm visiting someone there and I just answer yes and he says that that must be rough to be in The Hospital over Christmas and I say yes and then he keeps quiet and he stops in front of The Hospital and I pay and I go into The Hospital and straight to the reception desk and I ask if there's any way I can get to see Asle, he's a good friend, and the woman sitting there says she is so sorry, he died last night, he passed away quietly and peacefully, she says and I turn around and I go outside and the taxi is still standing there and I ask The Taxi Driver to take me to St Paul's Church and he says that'll be fine and I realise that I can't think clearly, I'm not sad, I'm nothing, just empty, just an empty blackness, I think and The Taxi Driver stops by St Paul's Church and I pay and I go into the church, dip my fingertips into the basin with the holy water, make the sign of the cross, and go to the third pew from the back on the left, I kneel and then sit down at the end of the pew and I think that I always sit there, because that was where Ales always sat, and where we always sat together, I think and then I bow my head and I fold my hands and then one by one people come into St Paul's Church, all of them silently, and they all kneel or bow their head before they sit down and I try to be as silent as I can and I sit there on the outer edge of the third pew from the back on the left in St Paul's Church and I realise that Ales, even though she's been dead for so long, is sitting next to me, the way she used to, and I take her hand and I hold her hand and I shut my eyes and now I just want to be silent and I breathe calmly in and out and then I fall into myself and I think that Asle is dead, and Guro is dead, and I sink into the usual course of the mass, and tonight it's a Latin mass and it's Father Brochmann who is celebrating mass and the familiar words feel comforting, drained as they are of meaning in the usual sense, instead they have a kind of silence inside them and they fill the silence with meaning, with God's closeness, and the close human community is a shining unity when the people there in the church, about ten people, stand up and pronounce the beautiful words Kyrie eleison Christe eleison, first Father Brochmann, then the congregation, it's said three times, and then the congregation says the Pater noster together and when I and the others kneel for the consecration, when Father Brochmann in persona Christi says Accipite et manducate ex hoc omnes Hoc est enim corpus meum quod pro vobis tradetur and then lifts up the host that has now become Christ's body, become all of him, gathered into his transfigured spiritual body, become Christ's mystical body, and the moment of transformation happens I see a halo appear around the host, and Father Brochmann says Accipite et bibite ex eo omnes Hic est enim calix sanguinis mei novi et æterni testamenti qui pro vobis et pro multis effundetur in remissionem peccatorum Hoc facite in meam commemorationem and lifts up the chalice and the wine is transformed into Christ's blood, into everything Christ is, gathered into his spiritual transfigured body, it is one with God, I see a flash of light come from the chalice in the moment of the consecration, and then the deep feeling of truth when the Mysterium fidei is recited, and faith, hope, and charity fill the congregation sitting there and Father Brochmann says the Peace Prayer with Christ's words Pacem relinquo vobis Pacem meam do vobis and Father Brochmann says Pax Domini sit semper vobiscum and I feel how good it is to hear Father Brochmann pray to let me, me, Asle, receive God's peace and I know that before long I will go up to the altar and then Father Brochmann will put the host in my left hand that's crossed over my right hand as he says Corpus Christi and I will say Amen and put the host in my mouth and then with my hands together in front of me I will go back down to my place, there on the outside of the third pew from the back on the left, and then I will fold my hands and bow my head and close my eyes and as the host, Christ's body, dissolves in my mouth I will gather everything I have into a prayer for God to take both Guro and Asle into himself and for them to find peace in God, find rest in God's light, that they might become part of the kingdom of God, again and again I think that and then I give thanks for my life and for letting me meet Asle and I give thanks for having met Guro and then I just say thank you and then I pray that the pictures I've painted might be a help to others, and I fall silent inside myself and then Father Brochmann starts to pray a prayer and everyone stands up and then finally he says in Norwegian Go in peace and I sit down and I close my eyes and one by one people leave the church and again I pray for Guro and Asle to find peace in God, that they might become part of God's kingdom, God's light, and then I stand up, bend my knee, and then I go and dip my fingertips into the basin of holy water and I make the sign of the cross and then I leave St Paul's Church and I start to walk straight to The Country Inn and I think that as soon as I get there I will lie down and go to sleep, and I feel so tired that it won't be hard to get to sleep at all, I think and then tomorrow at the crack of dawn I will drive to Dylgja, because tomorrow Åsleik and I are going to take The Boat to Øygna, way up in Sygnefjord, not far from Instefjord, almost all the way up Sygnefjord, to celebrate Christmas at Sister's, as Åsleik always says, but her name is Guro, I think and then I remember that Bragi is alone in the car, and he needs to be walked, needs something to drink, but he'll probably manage all right alone for a few more hours, a short night, because right now I so don't want to go up The Lane and see the broken windows and the burnt-up walls of the apartment that used to be Guro's, and then that burnt smell, I think and I go straight to The Country Inn and once I get to The Country Inn I just nod to the woman who's sitting at reception now, because now The Bjørgvin Man is off for the night, and the woman sitting there now is someone I've never seen before as far as I can remember and I say 407 thanks and she stands up and takes the key off the hook and hands it to me and I say thanks and I go take the lift up to the fourth floor and I walk to Room 407 and I turn on the light and it's nice and warm in the room, and it feels good to walk into a warm room after having sat in the cold church, and having walked from St Paul's Church to The Country Inn through the cold night, I think and I take off my shoulder bag and put it on the floor and then I take off my black coat, and now I've definitely been wearing it for more than a full day, because last night I slept in my coat on the bench in the main room back home in Dylgja, and then I take off my black velvet jacket, and I've been wearing that even longer, I think and I drape it over the back of the chair next to the desk and then I pick up the brown leather shoulder bag and put it down on the chair and then I take off my scarf and pullover and trousers and put them on the chair and I lie down on the bed and oh it is so good to lie down in a bed with fresh clean sheets, I think, no, how can something so normal feel so good, I think and then I turn off the light and then I hold the cross at the bottom of the rosary I have hanging around my neck, that I got from Ales once, with brown wooden beads and a brown wooden cross, and while I hold the cross in my hand I say out loud Ave Maria and I say to myself Ave Maria Gratia plena Dominus tecum Benedicta tu in mulieribus et benedictus fructus ventris tui Jesus Sancta Maria Mater Dei Ora pro nobis peccatoribus nunc et in hora mortis nostræ and then I breathe slowly in and out and then I slip into sleep and I sleep, I wake up, and I think that I was so tired last night that I fell asleep right away, and I slept heavily and peacefully, I think, and today it's Sunday and it's Christmas Eve day itself, I think and I think that now it'll be good to take a shower, because I really feel dirty all over, and I get up and I take a shower and then I dry my long grey hair with a hair dryer and I tie my hair back in a ponytail and then I get dressed and I think I should have brought fresh clean clothes with me, but later today I'll dress up in my best suit, because today is Christmas Eve, I think and then I put on the black velvet jacket and I drape the shoulder bag over my shoulder and I drape the coat over one arm and then I take the lift downstairs and I walk into the place that's The Coffeehouse during the day but in the morning it's the breakfast room for guests at The Country Inn and I get myself a little coffee with milk, but I don't feel like eating and then I go and drop the key off with the woman who's sitting at reception and I pay for my room and then the woman sitting at reception and I wish each other Merry Christmas and then I put on my black coat and I go outside and I don't look at Guro's burnt-out apartment, I just walk straight ahead and then I cross High Street and there in front of The Beyer Gallery is my car and I unlock it and right away Bragi wakes up and jumps up and down and wags his tail and then I open the back door and pull him out and Bragi runs like crazy around the parking lot and I call Bragi and he comes right away and hops in the back door that I'm holding open and he lies down on the back seat and I get in and sit down in the driver's seat and I start the car and I drive out of the centre of Bjørgvin, the difficult way that Beyer taught me a long time ago, and I drive north and I approach Sailor's Cove and I don't want to look at the building where Asle used to have his apartment and I drive past the building and I drive north and I look at the white roads and it's a cold, clear morning with shining stars and a practically full moon and I think that I don't want to look at the house Ales and I rented and lived in, I think and I drive north to Dylgja and I think that now, now I want to just drive and be empty, and not think about anything, not about Asle, not about Guro, I think and I don't want to look at the turn-off, not at the playground either, I think and I think that it wouldn't surprise me if Åsleik had already called to say I should get ready and we should set out soon, because it's light so few hours a day in this time of year and we have to use those hours, I think and then I just drive and I don't think anything and I look up at the brown house and I see a young man with medium-length brown hair standing and looking out the window and then a young woman with long dark hair comes and stands right next to him and then they stand there and look out and Asle thinks there's that car again, that small van, he thinks and I think that now I mustn't look at the two of them in the window, I think and I look at the white roads in front of me and I keep driving and then I get to Instefjord and then to Øygna, and now it's almost totally light out, I think and I think that I don't want to look up at Sister's house, where the woman named Guro lives, and I look at the white roads and I drive slowly onwards and then I'm at Dylgja and I drive past Åsleik's house and then up the driveway to my own house and I park the car in front and I open the back door and pull Bragi out and as usual he can't wait to jump out into the snow and lift his leg and there's an ugly yellow spot in the snow behind him and then he bends his back and shits, and I stand there looking at him and then I open the door and I call Bragi and he comes leaping over and I go into the kitchen and then I hear the phone ring and I go out into the hall and pick up the receiver and it's Åsleik and he says where was I? or was I sleeping that heavily? did I forget that today is Christmas Eve and that we're supposed to take The Boat to Øygna to celebrate Christmas at Sister's? he says and I say no I didn't forget and Åsleik says that he's called several times, because we should set out soon, we agreed that we'd set out as soon as it was light, he says, and it's a long trip to Sygnefjord, and it'll get dark early, we need to go while it's still light, yes, like we agreed, so now I need to come right over to his place at once, because sailing in the dark is no fun at all, not to mention tying up to the dock, Åsleik says and I say I'll come right over

Yes, right away, Åsleik says

Yes, I say

But why didn't you answer the phone? he says

and I don't say anything, but anyway it's good I finally answered, Åsleik says, because didn't he say that we had to leave early, we had to set sail as soon as it was light out, he'd said and I say yes, yes, I know, I remember he said that, I say and of course we need to, it is much better to take The Boat when it's light out than when it's dark, of course, I say

Yes, Åsleik says

So you need to come over now, he says

and I hear in his voice that he's a little annoyed, and I say again that I'll come right over and Åsleik says that he's ready and that it would be best to set out as soon as we can, he says and I say I'm going to hang up the phone and then drive right over and then Åsleik says that in that case he'll go down to The Boat and wait there for me to come and then we'll set out, he says, because there aren't that many hours of daylight at this time of year, yes, as he's said, and as I know perfectly well, he says and I say I'm coming right over and then I say I'll see him soon and I hang up the phone and then I go into the main room and I touch the picture I painted for Sister and it's almost dry and I pick it up and then I pick up the suitcase that's standing there between the bedroom door and the hall door and then I call Bragi and he comes running and I go outside and Bragi follows me and I shut the front door behind me and I think that no one in Dylgja locks their door, it's the custom in Dylgja to leave your door unlocked, I think and I go over to my car and then I put the suitcase in the back and then I lay the painting that's still not totally dry on top of the suitcase and then I open the back door and Bragi hops in and I get into the car and then I drive off to Åsleik's farm, and there's a short narrow path running down to the boathouse and his dock, and I drive down it and then I park next to the boathouse and I see Åsleik standing on the deck of his Boat, of course it had to be a boat like that, with a wheelhouse in front and a deck in back, and I pick up my shoulder bag and go out and I hear thumping from the engine of The Boat and I drape the leather shoulder bag over my shoulder and I open the back of the car and I take out the painting and the suitcase

Don't you ever take off that black coat, Åsleik says

Or that shoulder bag, he says

and I shut the hatch of the car and Åsleik again shouts that he knew it, he knew I was going to show up with that brown leather shoulder bag and wearing that black coat and with a scarf around my neck and I'm probably wearing that black velvet jacket under my coat too, he says, and now here I am, he was right, but a suitcase in The Boat, no, a suitcase on a boat is bad luck no matter how old and nice a suitcase it is, don't I even know that, Åsleik says, suitcases and women are bad luck on boats, he thought I knew that much, only sailor bags belong on a boat, and in the old days sailor trunks on big boats, Åsleik says, and his sailor bag is already stowed in its place on the part of the deck closest to the bow in the cabin, he says and I walk towards The Boat and Åsleik, and the motor says thump thump and I see a black cloud of exhaust rise up from the stern and then I hand the suitcase to Åsleik and he says that since I didn't know any better, or couldn't help it, we'll just have to hope for the best, better a little luck than a lot of brains, he says, and then I hand him the painting and I say that he needs to be careful because the picture isn't totally dry yet so he has to lay it paint side up and he takes the painting and he says that this is a nice portrait I painted of Sister and that Guro will be very happy to get it, and it's unbelievable that it can look so much like her when I've only seen her once, in The Coffeehouse recently, Åsleik says and I say I was thinking I needed to bring a Christmas present for Sister and I couldn't find anything to buy her so I thought I might as well paint a picture for her, I say and I say that I don't know if it's good or bad, and I say that I think the face I painted both does and doesn't look like Sister, I say, because I've never met her, strangely enough, or not before I saw her in The Coffeehouse recently, I say, because that probably was Sister I saw then, I say and Åsleik says that anyway it's a picture of Sister I painted, so it definitely must have been her that I saw sitting at The Coffeehouse, with her suitcase and shopping bags, he says and I say that I don't know if she'll like the picture but the important thing is that I've brought her a Christmas present, I say and Åsleik says that Sister will be very happy to get the picture, he says and I say that I have wrapping paper for the picture in my suitcase and then Åsleik says that the picture I've painted looks exactly like Sister down to the last detail, it's absolutely unbelievable that I was able to paint her so accurately having only seen her once in The Coffeehouse, he says and then he puts the painting up on the square box covering the engine and I see that the picture is shaking a little up and down with the thumping of the engine and then Åsleik says again that the picture looks just like Sister down to the last detail, so if I really saw her just that one time then yes he doesn't understand how I could have painted it, that I was able to do that, because he's never showed me a photograph of Sister anyway, he doesn't even have one, he says then I hear Bragi bark

Mustn't forget the dog, Åsleik says

Yes, Bragi, he says

That would have been bad, I say

and I go open the back door of the car and Bragi hops out and I slam the door shut and then I go over to The Boat and Bragi follows me and he looks scared of The Boat and then I pick him up and hand him to Åsleik and Bragi whines and whimpers and whines and Åsleik takes him and puts him down on the deck and Bragi lies right down and then he's lying there shivering and looking up at me with his scared dog's eyes

Doesn't look like much of a ship dog, Åsleik says

He's lying there shivering and whimpering so low you almost can't hear him, he says and I untie the front mooring and I throw the rope to Åsleik and he coils it up nicely and then he lifts up the front fender and right away the bow starts to drift away from the dock and Åsleik says we're lucky, we have the current with us, the trip up Sygnefjord goes much quicker with the current than against it, it can take almost twice as long if it's running against you, Åsleik says and I untie the rear mooring and I coil the rope as I walk towards The Boat and I hold tight to the rope so that the stern of The Boat is right up next to the dock and Åsleik holds The Boat close to the dock too with a boathook and then I step down onto the gunwale and then down onto the deck and Åsleik shoves off with the boathook and right away The Boat moves out into the water and already we're a few feet from land and Åsleik brings the stern fender on board and then he goes into the wheelhouse and turns the wheel so that the bow is pointing straight up Sygnefjord and I take the suitcase and painting and go into the wheelhouse and Åsleik says again a suitcase on a boat, like I'm on a cruise, yes, like this was some kind of luxury yacht I was vacationing on, one of those ships that's constantly sailing up into Sygnefjord and back down out of Sygnefjord on summer days, he says and he says that he's often thought about what it would be like on board a ship like that, and what it would be like on the bridge steering a ship like that, pulling into shore must be really hard, you'd have to steer it very precisely, because there are lots of skerries in the water, so it'd be a real tricky business, Åsleik says, yes, he who has spent his whole life sailing in these waters knows them well, but there were not a few skerries he's passed over that weren't on any charts and that he hadn't known about before, he says, but the skippers used well-known routes that had been taken many times, because cruise ships have been sailing up into and back down out of Sygnefjord all these years, so they had their fixed routes, and that's why it always went well, he's never heard about a single cruise ship running aground on any skerry, Åsleik says and I go into the cabin and Bragi comes slinking after me and he is moving as little as he can and once he's in the cabin he lies right down in the corner on the port side next to the door to the wheelhouse and I put my suitcase up in the bow, behind Åsleik's sailor bag, and then I lay the painting on top of the suitcase and then I put my shoulder bag down on the deck and then I go out of the cabin and I stand next to Åsleik there in the wheelhouse and he says that the weather is good, couldn't be better, almost, there are always some little billows but once we get some water astern it'll give The Boat a little extra speed, and with the current the trip'll be fine, Åsleik says and he says that yes, yes, it'll be all right, he says

Are you scared, Åsleik says

Are you scared of the water? he says

No, I say

You seem a little scared, he says

No I wouldn't say I'm scared, I say

Just a little nervous, Åsleik says

Yes, I say

and then it's silent and Åsleik sits down at the wheel and he holds the wheel in one hand and he says that it's not often I'm on board a boat, is it, and I say that I practically grew up in a boat and Åsleik says that he knows that perfectly well, he was just thinking, because I grew up in Hardanger, by Hardanger Fjord, he says and I say I was in a boat the whole time I was growing up, in a pointed boat, a so-called Barmen boat, I say and Åsleik says that he must be getting old because I've told him that many times, he says and I've often said that I wanted to get a boat of my own, but I never did get a boat, he says and I think that now that I've stopped painting I need to get a boat, because I need something to do and something to keep me busy, so I need to get a boat, a Barmen boat with a pointed bow and a flat stern and with a little outboard motor

I think I should get a boat, I say

You've said that before, Åsleik says

and he says that as long as he's known me I've talked about how I should get a boat and a dog, I've even said that a person needs them for a good life, yes, a boat and a dog, he says and it's silent again and then I sit down, because in the wheelhouse there's a chair at the wheel on the starboard side and another chair on the port side, and in between there's the door that leads into the cabin and that can be shut with a hook on the starboard side, and behind Åsleik there's a little hotplate and I look at it and Åsleik says that it's good to have a primus stove, you can boil yourself some coffee, and fry up bacon and eggs, get something warm in you, and that can be good, because it can get cold on the water, but he has a little stove and when it gets too badly cold he turns the stove on, and he says that the stove is firmly attached to the deck behind me and I turn around and I see the stove and Åsleik says maybe he'll warm it up a little? he says and he asks me if I can take The Boat and I go over and take the wheel and it's a small wheel, with pegs around the rim, and Åsleik points at a little holm near the middle of The Fjord way up ahead and he says I should steer towards that, he says and I sit down at the wheel and I let go of the wheel and right away The Boat starts to head towards land and I straighten the wheel up again and steer towards the holm in the middle of The Fjord way up ahead

Now it should get a little warmer soon, Åsleik says

and I see him go into the cabin and then he comes out and he has a bottle of beer with him and he goes and opens a drawer under the primus and he takes out a bottle opener and he opens the bottle and then he sits down in the chair on the port side and he sits there for a long time and then he raises the bottle to his mouth and drinks

It's not often that I'm not at the wheel myself, I can't even remember the last time, it must have been when my father was still alive, Åsleik says

and I say that's not true, because he and I have been on the water together lots of times, we've gone to Vik to go shopping lots of times, I say and Åsleik says yes that's true, he's so forgetful nowadays, he says

But it's been a long time in any case, he says

Yes, I say

Maybe ten years, at least, he says

Something like that, I say

and Åsleik says that since he's always been at the wheel himself, for at least ten years in any case, it's really nice now to be able to just sit and be a passenger, because he could probably say that that's what he was now even if it was he who owned The Boat, Åsleik says and I say that it's been a long time since I've been at the wheel, but everything's fine, it's good, I say and Åsleik takes a sip

It's nice with beer, he says

I almost never drink beer at home, but I do a lot in The Boat, he says

and it's silent

I think it has to do with my always having been a little scared of being in a boat, I've always been a little scared of the water, Åsleik says

and I don't say anything

Yes, it's true, Åsleik says

It's not because I like being in a boat that I've spent so much time in one, it's because I had to, he says

To make a living, he says

and it's silent for a moment

And that's probably about my father having been lost at sea, he says

Yes, I say

and it's silent for a moment

They never found him, Åsleik says

No, I say

and it's silent again

No you've got it better, just painting pictures, but you need talent for that, it's like you need a gift of grace, Åsleik says

But gifts of grace come from God and I never believed in that, he says

and I don't say anything

No, never, Åsleik says

Believed in God, I mean, he says

and it's silent and Åsleik says that no one can say anything for certain about the big things, the biggest things, sea and sky, life and death, he says and he drinks his beer and he says that all of that is like an unknown darkness, we come from an unknown darkness and we return to an unknown darkness, that's how it is, there's nothing more to say about that, and as for whether a person was something in the darkness before being born, and whether they turn into something there after they die, no one can say anything or know anything about that, so for him all that's possible is wonder, he doesn't have any answers, Åsleik says and he finishes his bottle of beer and then he gets up and goes out on deck and I turn around and I see out the porthole at the back of the wheelhouse Åsleik throwing the empty bottle into the water and then he stands on his sea legs in a wide stance and he opens his fly and takes out his penis and pisses into the water in a nice arc and then I suddenly think about the boy who drowned when I was little, his name was Bård, and he was from the neighbouring farm, and then he fell out of their Barmen boat, a two-oar boat, and into The Fjord and he couldn't swim and he clearly couldn't get back on board the boat, so he never got to be very old, I think and I start to think about my sister Alida, she also died so long ago, both Ales and Sister are dead, and my sister Alida died so suddenly, I think, and the night before last Asle died and I can't think about that, I really just can't, and then the woman Guro, who lived in The Lane and who died in a fire, I think and it's horrible to think about, I think and I see Åsleik come back in and he goes into the cabin and gets a new bottle of beer and he opens it and he says you need to drink on Christmas, it's an old custom, back in the old days people said you should drink on Christmas, when the sun turns you should celebrate it, celebrate that the light was going to come back, that the grass would be green again, yes, that spring would come, would have to come, that winter would have to be over soon, people thought, and that's why they drank and went on a bender and travelled to be together, often from far away, to be together, to drink on Christmas, that's how it was, and the same thing in summer, when the sun turns, you should drink your way through Midsummer's Eve and a long way into the next morning, Midsummer's Day, that was the custom in these parts, it was still like that in his youth, and there was a bonfire on Midsummer's Eve and you could see a bonfire burning from every corner of Sygnefjord, he says, yes, it was like people were greeting each other with the bonfires they lit on Midsummer's Eve, and then there was dancing and drinking, and then you needed a fiddler, and even if there wasn't a fiddler in every village you didn't have to go too far to find one, they used to say that every real village needed a shoemaker, a blacksmith, and a fiddler, Åsleik says, that's how it was, he says and I sit there and keep a straight course for the holm in the middle of The Fjord and Åsleik says it's nice to have company, man is man's delight, as the saying goes, Åsleik says and I sit there and look at the holm out there in the middle of The Fjord and then Åsleik says that the holm I'm steering towards used to be where they had executions, and that's why it's called Gallows Holm, the same as another small island near Aga, a lot of Satan's witches were burnt there, and a lot of Satan's henchmen, he says, it was a long time ago, but he can remember Grandfather telling him about it, Åsleik says and it's silent and I think and I look at the waves and I see Ales standing there in her white dress, because she wanted a white wedding dress, Asle thinks and he bought himself a black suit and black dress shoes at The Second-Hand Shop in Sailor's Cove, where Ales and he bought most of what they needed during all their years together, dishes, clothes, almost everything they needed they bought there

You look good in a suit, Ales says

Yes how could we have managed without The Second-Hand Shop, Asle says

and he gives a little laugh

You can say that again, Ales says

and I look at the holm, at Gallows Holm, there in the middle of The Fjord, that apparently used to be a place of execution, and I think damn it's good that The Second-Hand Shop is there in Sailor's Cove, because often when I'm in Bjørgvin I look in there, there in Sailor's Cove, a little north of the centre of the city of Bjørgvin itself, I think and I think that I bought my black suit and white shirt and tie and dress shoes there when we were going to get married, and it's exactly the same suit, the same shirt, the same tie, and the same shoes that are now in the old suitcase up in the bow, I think, and Ales bought her beautiful white wedding dress there, and it's still in her clothes closet in the house up in Dylgja, I think and I look at the waves and I see Ales standing there in her white wedding dress and she is carrying a white wedding bouquet, because she so wanted one, so even though it was expensive we had to buy one, Ales had said, Asle thinks, and now Ales is standing there in her white wedding dress and with her white wedding bouquet and they took a taxi to St Paul's Church, where the wedding was to take place, and it was Father Brochmann, who would later confirm Asle, and who had earlier confirmed Ales, who would marry them, and the maid of honour and best man would be mother Judit, as Ales's maid of honour, and then Beyer, as Asle's best man, Asle thinks and he thought that they didn't need to get married, that cohabitating, as it was called, wasn't a deadly sin because they were married before each other, and they were married before God, and he said that really they had been married for a long time, ever since that day in St Paul's

Church, there in the half-darkness under the steps and Ales said that it was her mother Judit who so wanted them to get married, yes, visibly married, they should at least get married, mother Judit had said so many times, Ales said, but Ales herself didn't think it was important that they get married, yes, visibly, as it were, she said, since they had been invisibly married for a long time, before each other and before God, she said and Asle had said that they could just get married visibly then, since it was so important to her mother Judit, he thinks and now Ales and Asle are standing there in St Paul's Church, he, Asle, in his black suit and she, Ales, in her white wedding dress and Asle has cut his hair and it's medium-length and brushed behind his ears now, and Ales has put her hair up and I hear Åsleik say that it's been a long time since I stopped drinking

Yes, it was too much drinking, way too much, I say

It was when you moved to Dylgja, Åsleik says

No before then, I say

But you probably don't want to talk about that, he says

and I think, well, I can talk about anything, I think

I was drinking way too much, I say

And it could have turned out badly if I hadn't stopped, I say

By the end all I was doing was drinking, I wasn't painting, I didn't do anything but drink, I say

and I say that Ales, my love, had a father who drank himself to death, and Ales got me to stop drinking, and we rented a house north of Bjørgvin so that I would stop drinking, yes, that was another reason for it, yes, before we took over the house from Ales's aunt, old Alise, I say and Åsleik says that he remembers old Alise very well, it was always nice to have a little chat with her, he says and he drinks his beer and he says that beer, yes, beer and stronger stuff too, are among the good things in life, and even if he's never had any kind of drinking problem, yes, well, he had to admit that he did drink too much now and then, but then he never drank the next day, even the thought of beer or stronger drinks the next day just made him sick, he says

For a while before I stopped I was drinking round the clock, in the morning, during the day, in the evening, yes, even in the middle of the night, I say

No that's no good, Åsleik says

No it wasn't, I say

and I say that I even had what they call delirium tremens, the shakes, yes, he's probably heard about those, I say

Yes, Åsleik says

And I shook and shook and saw the most powerful visions, and the sharpest colours, and the strangest shapes, and I wasn't sure where I was, I say

You can die from something like that, Åsleik says

And I shook and shook, I say

and it falls silent and Åsleik says that he can understand very well why I totally stopped drinking, he says

But why did you drink so much? Åsleik says

It's like it wasn't me who drank, in the end it was the alcohol that was doing the drinking, not me, I say

and I say that I have nothing against other people drinking, it's not like when they drink I feel like I want a beer or glass of wine or something stronger, not at all, on the contrary, I'm happy that other people are drinking and I can see that it's good for them in a way, I'm never going to be for temperance or anything, I say

You were drinking yourself to death, Åsleik says

Yes I believe I was, I say

and it falls silent and I say that after lying with the shakes for a few days and seeing all the colours in the world I saw something white inside me and I held tight to it and then and there, in the middle of the shakes, in my delirium, my delirium tremens, I decided, while holding tight to that white colour, I made an agreement with myself that I wasn't going to drink anymore, and I didn't either, I say and Åsleik says that he still has a little spirits left in a bottle and he wants to have it, he says and then Åsleik goes into the cabin and he comes out again with a bottle that has just a little in it, down at the bottom, and he says that every Christmas he gets a bottle of spirits as a Christmas present from Sister, from Guro, yes, whom I'm finally about to meet soon, and it's about time, and some of it gets drunk on Christmas Eve afternoon, because they usually hand out their presents before the meal, to tell the truth there are only two presents, the picture Sister gets from him and then the bottle of spirits he gets from Sister, and whatever doesn't get drunk on Christmas Eve he takes home with him, but you couldn't call him a heavy drinker, no, because there's still, after a year, a little left in the bottle, and that's how it usually is every year, he usually brings the rest of last year's bottle with him when he comes to eat dinner at my house and when he sails to Sister's to celebrate Christmas, and he usually drinks up the last of it on the trip there, Åsleik says and he twists out the cork and he takes a swig

That tasted good, he says

And it feels good, he says

and then Åsleik drinks a little beer and then he says that now that we're near Gallows Holm I should take my bearings from the headland over there, he says and he points, and I turn the wheel and we glide slowly on towards the headland

This isn't exactly an express ferry here, Åsleik says

But it'll get there, he says

and Åsleik says that the trip to Sister's isn't all that long but we've hit a bit of cross-current now, he says, I can feel The Boat starting to rock back and forth a little, he says

Yes, I say

So we'll get there a little later, I say

Yes, Åsleik says

and then it's silent

You used to smoke too? Åsleik says

Yes, I say

But you quit that too, Åsleik says

Yes when we moved to Dylgja, I say

Why'd you quit? Åsleik says

and I say that Ales didn't smoke, and even though she never said she didn't like my smoking I had a feeling she didn't, I say, and then I also smoked way too much, it turned into a problem for myself as well as Ales, sometimes I'd even get up in the middle of the night to smoke, I say

Yes you were a real smoker then, Åsleik says

Yes, I say

Wasn't it hard to quit smoking? Åsleik says

Actually it wasn't, I say

When I quit smoking I started taking snuff, I say

and then it's silent

I never smoked, Åsleik says

I've never even tasted a cigarette, he says and I say that really it was Ales who got me to both quit drinking and quit smoking and Åsleik says yes and then it's silent and I look at the waves and I see Ales and Asle standing there outside St Paul's Church, and now they are married, so now what God has joined together no man can put asunder, Father Brochmann said, Asle thinks and now Beyer has gone to find two taxis, now they'll go home to 29 Ridge Street, and there's food there, a festive meal, it's almost ready, because there's mother Judit's lamb roast keeping warm in the oven and they've bought the best red wine, and it wasn't cheap, mother Judit said, Asle thinks and mother Judit says well it's not every day that your only daughter gets married is it, she says

This is a great day, Father Brochmann says

and Ales and Asle stand there holding each other's hands, and they're both shivering a little

It'll be nice to get back inside, Asle says

Yes, really nice, Ales says

and Asle holds Ales tighter and he rubs her back and she says that feels good, really good and I see Åsleik raise the bottle of spirits and he takes a big swig and then he goes out on deck and he throws the empty bottle into the water and I hear him say farewell and then he comes back in with beer bottles in one hand and says that he can take The Boat now for a bit, so I can take a little rest in the cabin if I want, he says

And so you can wrap the picture you want to give Sister, if it's dry enough, he says

and I get up and Åsleik sits down at the wheel with one hand on the wheel and the beer bottles in the other and I stay standing next to him and I tell him that when I was young there was a neighbour boy, his name was Bård, and he drowned, he pulled the family boat in towards land, got on board and then pulled the boat out into The Fjord with him in it and then somehow he fell into the water and he couldn't swim and he couldn't get back on board the boat again, I say, and he hadn't even started school, I say

Lots of lives have been lost at sea, Åsleik says

I just suddenly thought about that, I say

It's the kind of thing you never forget, Åsleik says

No, I say

and there's silence and then I go into the cabin and I see Bragi lying there in the corner where he went and lay down when we set out, and now he gets up and goes and lies down on the deck up at the very front of the ship, at the bow, and he curls up and damn, it looks like he's shaking a little too, I think and I touch the picture and it's almost totally dry, anyway dry enough to wrap if I don't press the paper against the paint and if I use a good amount of paper and wrap it loosely, I think and I pick up the picture and put it on the berth and I open the suitcase and I take out the brown packing paper, the length of string, and the black marker and I carefully wrap the picture in the paper and then I write To Guro and under that Merry Christmas and under both From Asle and then I tie the string around the package and I put the rest of the packing paper and string and the black marker back in the suitcase and shut it and then I put the wrapped picture on top of the suitcase, behind Åsleik's sailor bag and I think that I'd imagined putting the picture in the suitcase but the best thing to do would be to carry it under one arm, since the paint isn't entirely dry and, worst case, the paper might stick to the picture, I think, but if I walk in with a picture under my arm then Sister, Guro, will know what she's going to get for Christmas from me as soon as she sees me, so maybe I will put the picture in the suitcase, I think, but in spite of everything it's probably better if she knows what she's getting than if she gets a ruined picture, I think and I leave the picture lying on the suitcase and I lie down on the berth in the cabin and I shut my eyes and I see Ales standing in front of Asle and she's saying she wants to move to the old white house in Dylgja, where her father's sister lives, old Alise, and that it's already been decided that she'll inherit the house, because there aren't any other heirs, she says and she says that they might as well move there now, because old Alise would be happy to have someone else living in the house, she's old now, and frail, she's many many years older than Father, and she can use help with so many things, and they can live in two rooms up in the attic, that both have storage spaces, and then old Alise can live downstairs the same as she does now and then they'll share the kitchen, and the toilet and the shower that Father had put into the house, because when he was growing up they had an outhouse, and when they needed to wash up Mother heated up water and they bathed in a zinc tub, Father had always said, Ales says and then Asle says that he doesn't want to live with anybody else, it's not nice, and it's so distracting, he says and I hear Åsleik shouting and asking if everything's all right and I answer with my eyes closed that everything's fine, I just lay down for a bit, I say and I lie there with my eyes closed and I see Ales and Asle sitting in mother Judit's car, Ales sitting in front next to her mother Judit and Asle sitting in the back and he's thinking that now they're going to drive out to Dylgja to go to old Alise's funeral and then they're going to go look at the house where old Alise had lived and Ales wants them to move into and I hear Åsleik say as long as I don't fall asleep now and I say I'm just resting a little and I see Asle looking at the house where old Alise had lived, it's a nice old house, painted white, up on a rocky hill and with a view of the Sygne Sea and I see Ales come and take Asle's hand and then they walk into the house together with mother Judit and Ales says that everything in the house is the way it was when old Alise lived there, because she lived at home until the end, but then she had a stroke and she couldn't manage at home alone anymore and then she was moved to The Hospice in Vik, and after that it wasn't long before she died, Ales says, and how many bodices for the national folk costume had old Alise sewed, and how many tablecloths and table runners in Hardanger embroidery, no, nobody knew, because that's how she made a living as best she could, Ales says and Asle says that it's a beautiful old house, and no damage like there is to the house they're living in now, he says

So you can imagine living in this house, Ales says

Yes, Asle says

I can hardly think of any place better to work and to live, he says

and then mother Judit says that in that case it's decided, yes, they would move into the old white house and Ales says that it won't be long before she finally takes her art history exams, about the place of icons in the Norwegian Christian tradition or rather their lack of place there, and after that they can move to Dylgja, she says and I hear Åsleik shout to ask if I can steer for a minute and I get up and go out the door from the cabin and go into the wheelhouse and Åsleik is already standing in the middle of the wheelhouse with one hand on the wheel

I really need to piss, he says

And besides the bottle's empty, he says

and Åsleik holds up the empty beer bottle and then he lets go of the wheel and I take it and I see that it's still a good long way to the headland we're steering towards and Åsleik says that when he takes The Boat alone he usually lets it drift when he goes out on deck to piss and I sit on the chair at the wheel and I notice that Ales is standing next to me and I say to her that we had it good then, in that time, in those years, when we lived together in the house there in Dylgja, it's just it was so few years, too few, I say and Ales doesn't say anything and I look at the headland and I steer towards it and Ales stands close to me and she says it won't be long before we're together again and I say that I've lived alone in the house long enough now, yes, for many years, I say and she says I moved in right after old Alise's funeral was over while she was preparing to take her art history exams, about icons in Norway, and in addition to the usual required reading she had also read everything she could find about icon painting, and right after she quit The Art School she'd sent away to Sweden for the things that she needed to paint icons and then she started painting icons too, yes, as she's sure I remember, Ales says, and it didn't take long before she'd painted her first icon, she says and I hear Åsleik say damn if I'm not sitting here talking to myself and he can take the wheel again now, he says

I was talking to myself? I say

Yes, Åsleik says

and he says we're getting close

It took its time, this trip, I say

The more times you take it, the shorter it feels, Åsleik says

It's like that with everything, probably, I say

The first time you walk some path, it feels the longest, Åsleik says

And it's like that in a boat too, he says

and I go back into the cabin and I lie back down on the berth and I close my eyes and I see Ales sitting there in The Parlour in the white house in Dylgja and she's working on an icon and Asle thinks that now it'll soon be a year that they've been living in Dylgja and he thinks that no one taught Ales anything about painting icons, she learned it all herself from books, he thinks and Ales looks up at him

How's it going, Asle says

Not bad, she says

The icon I'm working on is of John in the cave on Patmos, and I think it'll turn out beautiful, yes, as it should be, Ales says

Yes, Asle says

But you don't feel like painting again, he says

No, Ales says

Now I paint icons, just icons, she says

and then she says that it's good he paints pictures that they can sell, because how will she ever sell these icons of hers, no, she has no idea, Ales says and Asle says that she can sell them eventually, no need to worry about that, he says

You think so, Ales says

I am absolutely sure of it, he says

For example, we could put up a sign on the bulletin board outside St Paul's Church saying that you have icons for sale, he says

and Ales says that she never thought these icons of hers were good enough that she could sell them, she says and I hear Åsleik shout and say he needs to piss again, his bladder's not that big, so it'd be nice if I could take over The Boat now, he says and I go back into the wheelhouse and I take the wheel and Åsleik goes out and I hear him almost shout that yes, you know how when you start pissing you piss in one go, almost, he shouts and then he comes back in and sits down on the chair on the port side

I've drunk enough now, he says

Now I won't drink any more, no, not till the lamb ribs, he says

and he says that he feels hunger gnawing at him at the very thought, because Sister's lamb ribs taste unbelievably good, I should really be looking forward to them, he says, yes, so there's something good about Christmas too, he says and then he falls silent sitting there

Did you hear any more about that friend of yours, your Namesake, the one in The Hospital, Åsleik says

and I think that I can't remember having told Åsleik anything about Asle being in The Hospital, but I must have, because my memory's not so good, I think

He died, I say

and it's silent

So, he's dead, Åsleik says

Yes, I say

He died the night before Little Christmas Eve, I say

and then I say that I drove back into Bjørgvin

Yes, Åsleik says

To see your friend, your Namesake there, in The Hospital, he says

Yes, I say

And when you got to The Hospital they told you he was dead, Åsleik says

and I nod and Åsleik says that must have been very hard for me, because the two of us, me and him, my Namesake, had been good friends all these years, he knows that, he says

Yes, I say

So it's really good that you're not home alone on Christmas, Åsleik says

and I don't answer, and it's silent for a long time

So you drove to and from Bjørgvin today too, Åsleik says

No, I spent the night at The Country Inn, I say

You drove to Bjørgvin yesterday and then drove back home early today, Åsleik says

Yes, I say

So that's why you didn't pick up the phone, he says

I heard it ringing as soon as I walked in the door and that's when I picked up, I say

and it's silent and then Åsleik sighs and says that he'd already called lots of times by then and he has to admit he was a little worried about me, he thought maybe something had happened to me, because I usually always answer the phone when he calls, he says and he says he thought for a minute about maybe taking the tractor and coming over to my house and it's silent and then Åsleik says yes, it must be very hard for me that my Namesake is dead, because my Namesake and I knew each other for so long, he knows that much, he says, but I'm not really someone who lets many things slip, and he doesn't even know if my parents are alive or dead, he says

They're dead, I say

and Åsleik doesn't say anything and it's silent and then he says that when we're past the headland he'll take over The Boat, since from there it's just a short way into a bay, and all the way up in the bay there's a dock, because even if Sister's house isn't on the water, it's up on a steep hill, as I've seen myself lots of times of course, her property still includes both a boathouse and a dock, but hardly anyone's been to the boathouse in a generation, yes, he's taken a look inside, and there were two old Barmen boats in there, and the boats looked nice and undamaged, so if someone just waxed them and took a little care of them, and let the wood swell for a few days, they'd be truly shipshape, but no one ever took them out onto the water anymore, because The Fiddler, the one who skipped out, the one from East Norway, he had no interest in the sea or in boats, but then again he was an East Norway man from inland, from far to the east in Telemark somewhere, Åsleik says and then it's silent and I think that maybe I can buy one of those Barmen boats from Sister, and then one day I can go over there and wax it and fix it up

I should get a boat, I say

I'm sure you can have one of Sister's Barmen boats, Åsleik says

But I want an outboard motor on the boat, I say

and Åsleik says that even if it has a pointed bow and stern there's always some way to find a solution so that I can have a little outboard motor on the boat, he says

Yes, I say

and Åsleik says that he can come with me and wax and fix up the boat, and then he can tow it to Dylgja with The Boat, he says and I say we'll see and Åsleik says I've been talking about getting a boat all these years but it never actually happened, I never got a boat, yes, I talked about wanting a boat and a dog and now that my Namesake is dead his dog is probably mine now, Åsleik says and I say yes and Åsleik says that in that case at least I have a dog of my own now, now all that's missing is a boat, he says and then there's silence

That's sad, about your Namesake, Åsleik says

And now there'll probably be a funeral in the week after Christmas, he says

and again there's silence

Was he Catholic too? Åsleik says

No, I say

and again there's silence and I say he wasn't part of any religious community, and he'll probably be buried without a ceremony, I say

Did he have family, Åsleik says

One daughter and one son, The Daughter and The Son, as he used to say, and then The Boy, as he used to say, even though he's grown up now, I say

He was married, Åsleik says

Twice, I say

And he lived alone, Åsleik says

Yes, I say

And then he drank himself to death, I guess, Åsleik says

I guess he did, I say

and I think that I never met any of Asle's children, and I don't have an address or a phone number for any of them, I think and I look at the headland and how am I supposed to know when he's going to be buried? and where? I think, because I definitely want to be there, but then I have to find out The Boy's phone number, I think and then we've rounded the headland and Åsleik says he can take The Boat now, and when we get to where we're going to tie up at the dock I'll need to help him a little, it's much easier to tie up with two people, he says and I see a boathouse and a dock there in front of us and Åsleik takes the wheel and I sit down in the chair on the port side and I look at the little waves there by the shore and I see Asle sitting outside a door in a corridor in The Hospital and he's waiting for Ales

We're almost there now, Åsleik says

and I see Asle sitting and holding Ales's hand and she's lying there in a bed in The Hospital, and she's unbelievably thin now, he thinks, and she's sleeping, and Asle feels that he's about to start crying and then he places her hands carefully on the covers and then he goes over to the window and stands there and looks out, it's a cold autumn day, with a clear blue sky, and then he feels like a warm light is coming at him from behind and the light goes through him and he sees the light spread out like a beam, like a kind of column of shining golden dust the light spreads out across the blue sky and he doesn't understand what he's seeing and he sees that the light is dissolving and vanishing into the blue sky as infinitely many twinkles and Asle turns around and he goes over to Ales and he takes her hand and it's lifeless and he puts it back down and then he puts his hand in front of her mouth and he can't feel any breath and he kisses her cheek and then he pulls the cord you're supposed to pull if you need help and then he takes Ales's lifeless hand again and a nurse comes and takes Ales's pulse and she can't feel any pulse and then she says now she's finally at peace, now the pain has stopped, she says and she says that she needs to get a doctor and a doctor comes and he confirms that Ales is dead, I think and I dry my wet eyes with the back of my hand and Åsleik notices that something's wrong and he says we'll be docking soon now and I feel that Ales is so close so close, she is sitting right here in my lap with her arms around my back and then we give each other a kiss and then she leans into me and rests there and I know that she is resting in God now, yes, the way I am resting in God too, and that we are resting there together, and I never could imagine being with any other woman after Ales was gone, I think and Ales says that there was the two of us, that's just how it was, yes, as she knew, as she said the first time we met in The Bus Café, she says and then Åsleik says that a boat's what I need, he says, and now it's time for me to go out on deck and I have to just do what he says, yes, first put the fender out on the starboard side, and if there's a current it can be hard to get right up next to The Dock so it'd be nice if I took the boathook and stood ready to pull The Boat in towards The Dock if needed and then I need to take the stern rope with me and climb up onto The Dock and tie it to the bollard farthest out on The Dock, Åsleik says and then he'll go up into the bow and throw me the other rope and then I'll tie that to the bollard farthest in on The Dock, Åsleik says, when there are two people it's easy, it's worse when you have to do everything alone, he says and I put my shoulder bag on and I go out on deck and pick up the boathook and I pick up the rope sitting there nicely coiled on the deck and Åsleik shouts that first I have to put the fender out and I put the rope down and first I put out the fender that's on the rear deck and then I climb out on the gunwale while I hold on tight to the railing on the wheelhouse's roof and then I put out the fender that's on the forward deck and I go back and pick the boathook and rope back up and Åsleik shouts that he should be able to manoeuvre The Boat pretty close to The Dock, but the current is pushing us away from The Dock, so I'll need to be quick and pull The Boat all the way in to The Dock with the boathook when I can and then get up onto The Dock, and it won't be that slippery, because there's still just dry snow on The Dock, Åsleik says and he backs up The Boat, steers it in toward The Dock, backs up again, then steers it in towards The Dock and when we're a few yards from The Dock Åsleik backs up hard and then The Boat gives a little jolt forwards and he puts the motor into neutral and I grab the edge of the dock with the boathook and I pull The Boat in towards The Dock and I take the rope and climb up onto The Dock and I see the bollard sticking up from the snow and I tie the line to it with two half hitches, they're called, and then I hurry in on The Dock and Åsleik is already standing on the deck by the bow and he throws me the rope and I pull The Boat in towards The Dock and tie the line to the bollard with another two half hitches and then I see Åsleik stand on the deck in the bow and he says that that couldn't have gone better, he says and now he just has to idle the motor and let it cool down for a bit, he says and he walks carefully aft on the gunwale while holding the railing on the wheelhouse roof

No, couldn't've gone better, he says again

Because it can be hard to bring her in, he says

If you're alone anyway, he says

But the worst is gusts and rain, he says

and then Åsleik disappears into the wheelhouse and then he comes back out with his sailor bag and he hands it to me and I take it and then he goes back into the wheelhouse and he comes back out with the picture I painted that he's going to give Sister and it's wrapped in Christmas paper with angels and fairies and whatever, and there's a red ribbon around the package holding a slip of paper that says To my dear sister Guro Merry Christmas From your brother Åsleik and he hands me the picture and I take it and put it down next to the sailor bag and then Åsleik goes into the wheelhouse and turns off the motor and it makes a few last thump thumps and Åsleik comes out of the wheelhouse and it's like he wants to climb up onto The Dock

My suitcase, I say

And the picture, my present, I say

And Bragi, I say

The suitcase, right, Åsleik says

and it sounds like scorn in his voice and he goes and gets the picture I'm going to give Sister as a Christmas present and he holds it up towards me

Didn't exactly go all out with the wrapping did you, he says

and I take the picture and I don't say anything and I put it down in front of Åsleik's picture and he holds up my old suitcase and puts it on the fender and I take the suitcase and put it down on The Dock and then Bragi comes running out on deck and Åsleik says yes you too, we mustn't forget you, no, he says and then he holds up the dog and hands him to me and I take Bragi, and oh how he's shaking, I think and I put him down on The Dock and he stands there with his tail between his legs and then I take my suitcase and my painting and I walk in on The Dock with Bragi at my heels and I hear Åsleik say that I'm quite a sight there in my long black coat, and with that brown leather shoulder bag, and with my grey hair tied in a little hair tie, and the hair just partly covers my bald patch, and then with that dog padding behind me, he says and I've reached land and I stop and I turn around and then I see Åsleik putting one foot over the gunwale and onto The Dock and then he holds onto the gunwale and he puts his other foot on shore too

My body's so stiff nowadays, he says

and Åsleik picks up his sailor bag and his picture and walks slowly

in on The Dock a bit stiffly and with his feet splayed and then he stops
and looks up at Sister's house, it's a little grey house, and there's light
in all the windows

Yes well it's Christmas again, Åsleik says

So it is, I say

You don't like Christmas, he says

No, I haven't liked Christmas since I was a little boy, I say

Me neither, Åsleik says

and then we start to walk on a snow-covered path up to the country
road and on the other side of the road a path has been beaten to the grey
house where Sister lives, and the house looks so rundown, it should
have been painted years and years ago, I think and then Sister comes
into view around the corner and she's wearing a Christmas pullover
and she waves at us and Åsleik lifts up the picture he's carrying and I
lift up mine

Welcome to my home, Sister calls

Yes now it's Christmas again Guro, Åsleik calls

and she doesn't answer and I see her medium-length blonde hair
and I see that she's holding a lit cigarette and then she takes a deep drag
at the cigarette and to me she looks so much like the Guro who lived
in The Lane that I couldn't have told them apart if I didn't know they
weren't the same person, this Guro and the one who just died in a fire,
I think, and Asle is dead, I think, and I can't think about that anymore,
I think and then we get to the house and Guro shakes my hand and
I say well we've never met and she says maybe not but she has seen
me before, she's seen photographs of me in *The Bjørgvin Times* lots of
times and then she saw me at The Coffeehouse in Bjørgvin

I always like to go there when I'm in Bjørgvin, I say

Me too, she says

I never go to Bjørgvin without stopping in at The Coffeehouse,
she says

And it hasn't been long since the last time I saw you there, she says

No, I say

and she says that she tries to make a living by sewing tablecloths, big and small, and table runners, short and long, in Hardanger embroidery, and then bodices for folk costumes, the decorative bodices, she says, and it's all right, she makes just enough for what she needs, just enough to keep poverty at bay, she says, and when she's finished sewing a bunch of tablecloths, table runners, and bodices, she takes the bus to Bjørgvin and brings them to The Craft Centre, and then she always buys there what she can't find at The Country Store in Instefjord, where she usually buys whatever she needs, and that's easy enough, because it's just a half a mile away or so, she says, and she doesn't eat much, so it's mostly tobacco and cigarette paper she needs to buy, and that doesn't add up to all that much, she says and she laughs

Yes, Merry Christmas, Åsleik says

Merry Christmas, yes, Guro says

Merry Christmas, I say

and then she says we should come in, and it's a roomy house, she says, she usually sleeps in the bedroom off the living room but there are two bedrooms up in the attic, and she's made up one for Åsleik, she says

You'll sleep in the attic room you always sleep in, she says

and Åsleik nods

And then I made up the bed in the other room for you, she says

and she looks at me and then she says with a laugh that her house is filled with pictures I've painted, no, she doesn't even know how many years it's been that Åsleik's given her a picture I painted for Christmas, and she understands that my paintings sell for good prices, so she's probably strictly speaking quite rich thanks to my paintings, and if she's not mistaken her collection of my paintings is going to increase by two this year, one of them bigger than any she has so far, and she likes my paintings so much, they give her a kind of peace, she says, so she'll never sell a single one if she doesn't have to, she says and I say I thought about how she has so many smaller paintings of mine, she must have more of them than anyone, and to tell the truth they are the very best small or smaller pictures I've painted, because she should know that her brother Åsleik has an eye for art, he chose the pictures himself and he always chose the one that I myself thought was the best, I say and I'm looking forward to seeing the pictures again, I say and then she says that she can show me every single picture, if I want, but now we need to come inside, she says and she goes and opens the front door and I go into the hall with my suitcase and the painting wrapped in brown packing paper and Bragi comes padding along at my heels

You have a dog too, she says

That's how it worked out, I say

and I see that several paintings of mine are hanging in the hall, and I feel them all again, there is a mix of newer and older pictures, and thought went into where they're hung and then I see a steep set of stairs going up to the attic and on the wall alongside the stairs there are more pictures I painted

Yes, you can see for yourself, Guro says

I have paintings of yours everywhere, she says

and she has a Christmas tree so she can put the present I brought under the tree, she says and I nod and I hand her the package and then she opens the door to the kitchen and goes away and there's a wonderful smell of smoked lamb ribs and I turn around and I see Åsleik coming into the hall with his sailor bag and with his painting wrapped in Christmas paper with angels and fairies and whatever and he says my goodness, he can't think of any food that smells better, Åsleik says and Guro comes back out and Åsleik hands her the wrapped picture

And here's a little present, or maybe a little bigger, he says

Because she probably wants to put the presents under the Christmas tree like usual, he says

and Guro takes it and disappears back into the kitchen

No food in the world smells better, Åsleik says

and Guro comes out into the hall and she says maybe before anything else she should show me the room where I'll be sleeping, she says

Hey, Guro, Åsleik says

Yes, she says

You have two boats sitting in your boathouse, well, in case you didn't know, two Barmen boats, and Asle has been saying for as long as I've known him that he wants a boat, so I was wondering if he could have one of yours, he says

and Guro says that if I want one of the boats then yes, I'd be welcome to take it, yes, take both for all she cares, but they'll sink as soon as they touch the water, she says

I, I don't know, I say

If you want a boat? Åsleik asks

Yes, I say

No, no, he says

You've been talking about it all these years anyway, he says

Yes, I say

and then there's silence

But if you want one of the boats, or both, you can have them, Guro says

and I say I don't know really and Åsleik says no well if I don't want a boat I don't want a boat, that's how it is, he says and I ask if Guro has pictures hanging in the living room, and she says yes, she has pictures hanging in both the living room and the bedroom where she sleeps, just through the living room, and I ask if I can see the paintings right now and she says of course and then Åsleik says that he'll take his sailor bag up to the attic room he'll be sleeping in and then he starts going up the stairs and I put the suitcase down and I follow Guro into her kitchen, and it's small, and there's smoke from a huge pan, and two more big pans are standing ready, in one there are peeled potatoes and in the other rutabaga cut into pieces, I think and then Guro picks up a glass of red wine that's standing on the kitchen table and then we go into the main room and there's a stove in one corner and it's warm and the room feels good and Bragi goes over and lies down in front of the stove and Guro says she didn't know I had a dog, Åsleik had never told her, but she likes dogs so it's great, she says and I see that there is brown panelling on the walls in the room and pictures I've painted are hanging on all the walls and in the middle of the room there's a scraggly little pine tree and the four gifts are under it and I go from wall to wall and I take a look at every picture as quickly as I can while Guro sips her wine and then Guro opens the door to the bedroom

Please come in, she says

and she laughs and I go into her bedroom and there's barely room for a bed and a nightstand and a wardrobe in there, and there too paintings of mine fill the walls, and I feel almost like it's too much and I go back out

It's gotten to be a lot of pictures over the years, Guro says

Yes, I say

and she asks if she can take me upstairs to the room where I'll be sleeping and I say yes thank you and then she starts up the stairs with her wine-glass and I pick up the suitcase and follow her and along the stairs too there are paintings, with maybe a foot and a half between them, and they're all good paintings, I think and up in the attic I see that there's not a single picture hanging in the upstairs hall and Guro points at a door and she says I'll sleep there and she opens the door and I go into a little white-painted room and I don't see a single picture in there either

I hung all the pictures either downstairs or along the stairs, Guro says

and then she says that she didn't put a single picture upstairs, not in this room and not in the room Åsleik is going to sleep in or in the hall either, yes, as I saw, she says and she says that she doesn't know why, but well that's how it's always been, she says and she drinks a little wine and I see that there's a bed with a nightstand in a corner, and next to the nightstand is a chair, and I put the suitcase down on the floor and I take my shoulder bag off and put it on the chair and I take my coat off and drape it on the chair and Guro says I could have hung up my coat down in the hall and I say it's fine to keep it on the chair and then I stand there in my black velvet jacket and Guro says that the food's cooking, so there'll be lamb ribs to eat soon, she says and she says that she's already had a couple of glasses of wine, she indulges in more than one glass every now and then, she says, anyway when it's Christmas, but I probably don't want any wine, because according to Åsleik I don't drink, she says and I say that I haven't had a taste of beer, wine, or anything stronger in many years

You used to drink too much, she says

Yes, I say

and she says I should make myself at home and arrange things however I want and then she leaves and she shuts the door behind her and I realise that I'm tired, and that the floor is kind of rocking a little, yes, like The Boat was, and I lie down on the bed, with my shoes and my black velvet jacket on, and I stretch out my legs and I put my folded hands behind my neck and rest my hands and head on the pillow and I feel how close Ales is, and Asle, and also how close the Guro who lived in The Lane is and I hear a knock on the door and I say come in and I see Guro come in and she is carrying a full wine-glass

When I have such fine folk in the house I have to talk to them a little, don't I, she says and she laughs and she sits down on the edge of the bed and then she says that she lived with a man for many years, he was from East Norway, and it didn't exactly cost nothing to have him in the house, but he always brought in a little something, he was a fiddler, and he was handy, he did a good job taking care of the house, he painted the house, managed things, mowed the lawn, yes, as long as he was living at her place everything was in order, as they say, but ever since he skipped out things have begun to fall apart more and more, Guro says and she drinks a little wine and she puts her free hand on my belly

And you're a widower, she says

and I nod

And you've been one for a long time, she says

and I nod again and then it's silent and she slowly moves her hand farther down towards my fly

Yes, I say

But my wife and I are still married, I say

You can't be married to someone who's dead, Guro says

and she rubs my fly up and down and she opens it and I take her hand away and I see her blush and then she says she really should go downstairs and check on the food and she wants a cigarette too, she smokes almost constantly, she smokes way too much, she says and I see the woman named Guro leave the room and she shuts the door behind her and I think that she talks and walks and is in every way like the Guro who just died in the fire in The Lane, and I should go to her funeral, but I won't do it, because I don't know when and where it will be, and I don't know who I can ask about it, I think and I lie on my side and I take out my rosary, the one I got from Ales once, with the brown wooden beads and a cross, and I think that now I need to sleep a little, rest a little, I think and I shut my eyes and I see Asle sitting in an attic in an outbuilding and he's paging through a book, and he's sitting in a boat with Father, and he's sitting on a bus and he's thinking about how a friend of his is dead, he just found out about it and I see Asle lying in a bed and reading around in a book, he draws, he paints, he drinks beer, he smokes, and then I see The Boy toddling around on the floor and Asle walks up and down the street, he drinks beer, she is naked and she is lying there in bed and he doesn't know what he should do he touches her and he feels he wants to lie on her and he does and he doesn't dare push into her something holds him back he doesn't dare because as soon as he gets close a fear comes over him and he pulls back and she just lies there and her name is Liv and he lies on her and then he's sitting at a desk and he stands there and smokes rolls a cigarette books a teacher is talking he asks the classroom tubes of oil paint and Åsleik who says *St Andrew's Cross* and who comes with dried fish her face all lit up so that you could see her angel roman-fleuve the other schoolchildren students and The Painting Hall girls boys coincidentia oppositorum cigarettes beer drinking beer talking and then just going there and waiting and then, finally, finally he's born, finally he comes out into the world, out into the light, and then Asle is a father, he is young, very young, but he has become a father and long brown hair and everyone else who is so much better than him he's worth nothing and she just wants to be with the others with all of them with all the others and it's over and he wants to lie down and go to sleep in the snow because it's so far to walk rubs and rubs Bragi's fur and he is so tired so drunk he sees the stars and then he and Father are in a boat they're fishing and books The Boat drawings paintings books and I want to get a dog and a boat, a Barmen boat, I think and painting just painting just that and beer alcohol that good rush Ales's face her eyes and her hand in mine Painting and the best first nothing special then Liv better and better and sister Alida who died Ales and him Drawing the neighbour boy who drowned Liv and Bård Painting and he hadn't even started school and I drink and she says I mustn't drink every single night a little rush every night and he trembles and shakes and it's like he's held tight by fear visions that there can be colours that happen inside him and he doesn't drink more painting money no money sells pictures makes money doesn't have money exhibition exhibitions shopping for painting things tubes of oil paint canvas always oil paint and canvas always canvas stretchers boards stretchers tacks canvas her and the woman who comes and sits down at the table and they start talking and she's seen his exhibitions home with her lying next to each other kissing her only son kissing her they take off their clothes he pushes inside her they lie next to each other they talk go home she's lying there the son is sleeping go home she's lying there she's lying on the floor she's barely breathing ambulance boy crying The Boy cries howls ambulance he and the son she writes him letters and he thinks he should get a dog and then a boat a Barmen boat cries and cries they meet kiss eat together he sits and drinks boat and dog that's what a person needs and she comes and sits down exhibitions oil painting canvas stretchers need to find a place to live and Åsleik says he can have one of the Barmen boats that's sitting in the boathouse and the boats boards nowhere to go pictures the others alcohol feeling warm beer and Ales her warmth the mark of the cross on my forehead consecrated oil there for all time always and another glass of beer her hand on my fly talk about something alcohol laugh she comes in and it's Christmas lamb ribs summer her parents the house the white house silence and drinking smoking and then neither drinking nor smoking and Father who never spoke painting never gave up kept at it people can say whatever they want he just kept at it dark eyes child several children painting look there the house he sits and drinks children painting their house should have been painted pictures dog eyes tubes of oil paint days nights not getting to sleep and he lies there and he shakes up and down jerking trembling shaking and the man sitting there gets up and I sit there and then I lie on the floor I lie there in the snow and my body jerks up and down and I look at the picture no children had no children those two lines that cross each other one brown and one purple Åsleik your angel Ales your hand and there's nothing more to do on the picture so I'll just put it away a good picture maybe disappear into the picture if he can change into something way back there and I get up and I go over to the picture the halo around the host clouds grey clouds the sparkling of the chalice and then I lift the picture off the easel and I put it back on the easel these pictures I'm working on and that I'm still not done with transformations brown leather shoulder bag draped over if not always then often and he presses his fingers against the shoulder of the man lying in the bed and he just lies there and he holds his hand in front of the man's mouth and he doesn't feel any breath and he feels for his pulse and he goes out and now I need to get a little sleep soon and I don't want to know what time it is, I think, but I'm so restless, I don't know what's wrong and I see Ales's face, and it's the whole sky and in the sky is Grandmother's face and she is so close so close and I can't get to sleep I hold the brown cross on my rosary between thumb and index finger and I think that I, what's I in me, can never die because it was never born, because ich bin ungeboren, Meister Eckhart wrote and I see the words before me nach der Weise meiner Ungeborenheit kann ich niemals sterben, nach der Weise meiner Ungeborenheit bin ich ewig gewesen und bin ich jetzt und werde ich ewig bleiben, I think, because in jenem Sein Gottes nämlich wo Gott über allem Sein und über aller Unterschiedenheit ist, dort war ich selber and I breathe evenly in and evenly out and I say inside myself kyrie and I breathe out and eleison and I breathe in and christe and I breathe out and eleison and I breathe in and I move my thumb up to the first bead and I say inside myself Our Father Who art in heaven Hallowed be thy name Thy kingdom come Thy will be done on earth as it is in heaven Give us this day our daily bread and forgive us our trespasses as we forgive those who trespass against us And lead us not into temptation but deliver us from evil and I think that I never should have come with Åsleik to celebrate Christmas at Sister's house, the woman named Guro, the other Guro, I think and then I feel Ales lying next to me and she lies there holding me and I move my thumb and finger back to the cross and I say inside myself Pater noster qui es in cælis Sanctificetur nomen tuum Adveniat regnum tuum Fiat voluntas tua sicut in cælo et in terra Panem nostrum cotidianum da nobis hodie Et dimitte nobis debita nostra sicut et nos dimittimus debitoribus nostris Et ne nos inducas in tentationem sed libera nos a malo and I hold the cross and I grip the first bead between the cross and the three beads in a row and I say inside myself Our Father Who art in heaven Hallowed be thy name Thy kingdom come Thy will be done on earth as it is in heaven Give us this day our daily bread and forgive us our trespasses as we forgive those who trespass against us And lead us not into temptation but deliver us from evil and I move my thumb and finger up to the first of the three beads in a row and I say inside myself Ave Maria Gratia plena Dominus tecum Benedicta tu in mulieribus et benedictus fructus ventris tui Jesus Sancta Maria Mater Dei Ora pro nobis peccatoribus nunc et in hora mortis nostræ and I breathe slowly in and out and in and I move my thumb and finger up to the second bead and I say inside myself Hail Mary Full of grace The Lord is with thee Blessed art thou among women and blessed is the fruit of thy womb Jesus Holy Mary Mother of God Pray for us sinners now and in the hour of our death and I breathe evenly and I think yes like this nothing else nothing more because I didn't care about the others and I breathe slowly in and out and I move my thumb and finger up to the third bead and I say to myself Ave Maria Gratia plena Dominus tecum Benedicta tu in mulieribus et benedictus fructus ventris tui Iesus Sancta Maria Mater Dei and I a ball of blue light shoots into my forehead and bursts and I say reeling inside myself Ora pro nobis peccatoribus nunc et in hora

About the author and translator

Jon Fosse was born in 1959 on the west coast of Norway and is the recipient of countless prestigious prizes, both in his native Norway and abroad. Since his 1983 fiction debut, *Raudt, svart* (Red, Black), Fosse has written prose, poetry, essays, short stories, children's books, and over forty plays, with more than a thousand productions performed and translations into fifty languages.

Damion Searls is a translator from German, Norwegian, French, and Dutch and a writer in English. He has translated seven books and a libretto by Jon Fosse – *Melancholy* (co-translated with Grethe Kvernes), *Aliss at the Fire, Morning and Evening* (novel and libretto), *Scenes from a Childhood, The Other Name: Septology I–II, I is Another: Septology III–V* and *A New Name: Septology VI–VII* – and books by many other classic modern writers.